GLIMMER

ALSO BY MARJORIE B. KELLOGG
AVAILABLE FROM DAW BOOKS

LEAR'S DAUGHTERS

The Dragon Quartet

THE BOOK OF EARTH

THE BOOK OF WATER

THE BOOK OF FIRE

THE BOOK OF AIR

GLIMMER

MARJORIE B. KELLOGG

DAW BOOKS, INC.
DONALD A. WOLLHEIM FOUNDER

1745 Broadway, New York, NY 10019
ELIZABETH R. WOLLHEIM
SHEILA E. GILBERY
PUBLISHERS
www.dawbooks.com

First Printing, October 2021
1 2 3 4 5 6 7 8 9

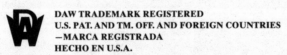

DAW TRADEMARK REGISTERED
U.S. PAT. AND TM. OFF. AND FOREIGN COUNTRIES
—MARCA REGISTRADA
HECHO EN U.S.A.

PRINTED IN THE U.S.A.

To my brothers John and Jarvis,
and in memory of our sister Nancy, triplet number three

W hen the fog clears, even for a moment, it can really turn your head around. I'm talking brain fog here: suddenly it was like, hello, it's Glim, finally having a thought about something other than survival.

A brief thought, but a beginning. Here's how it went.

Heading out on my usual shift. Been soloing less than a week, foraging through the steamy, dark, flooded city. Hated it. Most of us did, 'cept the adrenaline freaks. Each time the job posts went up, I'd mention other tasks I'd score better at, but hey, we were the young and able-bodied, so night was our beat. Beefing only got you a stern reminder that picking kept the den clothed and fed.

"Oughta call it what it is," my buddy Rubio groused, scrubbing his black scrawl of hair like it was the culprit. "Call it trash collecting. Junk mongering. Scavenging."

"Recycling?"

"Theft."

"Not anymore." Like most newbies, I took den practice at face value: we went to bed with our bellies full. What else could matter? "Like, no evac's coming back for his stuff any time soon. Or ever."

Rubio could dismiss entire arguments with a twitch of one shoulder.

"C'mon, Rube. Maybe tonight you get lucky."

"Ran outa that a long time ago."

Every night was hard, but out on the walkway that night, getting up our nerve seemed harder than usual. The overcast hung so thick and low, even the heat had weight, like stew on a slow boil. The dark uptown skyline wore a moonglow of cloud along its peaks. The water below us, what we called the Lagoon, was opaque and still as glass. Slack water.

I scowled at the looming sky. "Smells like rain."

"A thousand toxins drifting from the sky . . ." he sang softly.

"Rain's cleaner now, with the factories mostly down."

"Good thing, since we're drinking it. When's high tide?"

"Do you *ever* check the tables?"

"Why? When I have you to tell me." Rubio slouched on the railing for

a long cough, scrawny legs rattling in his boot cuffs. His lungs sounded full
of liquid.

No use me trying to help. "Maybe you shouldn't . . ."

"I'm fine," he croaked.

The scarred-up dude with one arm was on front door watch. He brandished his torch like it was us he was guarding the den from. "Yo! Gitcher
selfs upright! Git out there an' show sum pride! Doncha be scurryin' roun'
lika buncha marks!"

Rubio roused, sharp as an angry bird, stoking a snarl I knew he'd regret.
I nudged him quiet. The watch dude was old and half-cracked, but he was
usually cool, so you had to wonder what'd got into him. Likely, weather on
the way. I felt it, too, an itch I couldn't scratch, ever since my tumble in
Abel's Wave. That night, I could barely sit still.

"Don't jump!" Plastic soles clomped on the boards behind us as Big Grace
and Rivera pulled up laughing beside us at the rail.

"Might be for the best," Rubio muttered hoarsely.

Grace was tall as Rubio, muscular and often loud. When he called her
the Amazon, she'd grin like it was a compliment, though he swore she
didn't get the reference. I only did 'cause he'd told me.

Rivera, Grace's opposite, flared delicate nostrils at the heavy air. "A real
shit night."

Grace elbowed in next to Rubio. "There's talk of another coup uptown."

This perked him up. "What sector?"

"Inwood."

He frowned. "That's one of the stable co-ops."

"Only thing permanent is change." Grace's blond matched my own pale
chop, but her long braid dropped out the back of her street cap like a tow
rope. She and Rivera were rarely seen apart, spawning rumors they were an
item. But Grace had a clear eye for the guys, so who knew? "The intel's not
clear. Something going on."

"Just let it stay up there," murmured Rivera. "Where you all headed?"

Rubio coughed and spat, watched it drop into the water. "West Forties."

Gracie showed well-nourished teeth. "I got Broadway and 15th."

"Dog! So close!"

"And dry all the way."

"Mine's the lamest," I said. "West Teens."

"Why bother? Picked over long ago!" Rivera wound her dark braid up under her cap—out of grab range, like we were taught. She was careful—well, we all were, but Rivera always played it by the book.

I sighed. "They say new stuff's washing in since the last blow."

"Then let them go find it," Gracie snorted. "The river's as freaky as a cut snake over there. Never know where it'll be next."

I nodded, like snakes were my lot in life. Not all dens picked at night. A few didn't pick at all. But ours ran day and night, so there we were, four sorry pickers in dirt-colored street gear, staring down at the water's dark mirror as if waiting for a sign.

The watch dude rattled his torch again. Sparks flew past our noses.

Gracie hauled her boots up tight and shoved away from the rail. "Might as well."

Rubio nodded. "Might as."

"Watch yourselves."

"Always do."

We adjusted our headlamps, our pale third eyes. The walkways kept us dry till pavement showed at Third and 15th. From there, we went our separate ways.

By 2 a.m., I was nosing slowly along West 18th. My lamp was funky, not fully charged, so I was more than usually paranoid about flooded cellar holes or drowned subway stairs. Dropping into one of those could rouse the old nightmare of being sucked into an underwater vortex, and then . . . well, panic on the streets was never a good idea.

Still hard for me to be out there with confidence. First, step quiet, like my street coach called it. Ears and eyes sharp. And trust your nose. That night, I was keeping downwind of the recent collapse of a six-story on 17th. Maybe some good pick in the rubble—two families had been squatting there—but also toxics and dust. Bodies, too, from the stink of it, and I'm no fan of stealing from the dead. Plenty of pickers will, but no way I'm grabbing for anything a corpse still has a grip on.

Corner of 18th and Seventh, my ears turned me uptown. With the tide coming in, the black river lapped greedily along the avenues to the west, the debris mats shifting in the current, groaning like drowning souls. Rubio says if God had known what we'd do to his lovely planet, he'd have made us keep our gills, but who swims anymore? Even with the ocean washing in and out each day, a dip in its oily sludge could burn you raw. Night pickers learned to listen up and hear the water's messages.

And wear boots. We all had boots of some sort, though I still hadn't cadged a pair that really fit me.

I asked Rubio, "Hey, did all the size eights make it into people's luggage and off Island before the Wave?"

He rolled his eyes. "Which one?"

For once, I got a chuckle out of him, so I wasn't about to argue that Superstorm Abel had been the biggest and baddest. Rubio didn't see much cause for humor in this life, 'cept the darker sort. Or the sort where I was the butt, mocking my naïveté and ignorance.

But he never said: *doncha remember?* Not once he got that everything before Abel's Wave was a blank for me—my name, my history, everything that tells you who you are. What I mean by brain fog. The den shrink called it 'dissociative fugue' and 'loss of access to autobiography.' In short, I was compensating. Plenty of memory-related trauma in the den: too little, too much, too vague, way too vivid. If you lived through Abel's Wave—or any Wave—you likely didn't want to remember. Just moving on took all your concentration.

As for the boots, good ones were something bright to hope for, every time I went out. Always a chance those my-size hip-waders would float right into my hands on the outgoing tide. But not that night. My pick sack hung limp at my back and the dark streets seemed scoured of anything worth taking.

But you can't just give up. Show up empty before the end of shift and you'll find yourself begging a friend for a meal chit. So I kept on. I was prodding my pry-bar into the trunk of a burnt-out taxi when I spotted a glow up ahead. That made me go still and quiet—and douse my headlamp. 'Cept for the collapsed squat, this was a famously deserted sector, and I'd bypassed the nearest known den back on 16th.

I recalled Grace's news about trouble uptown. Or . . . oh crap, if there *was* weather coming, it could be Storm Worshippers! The latest wacko sect, pledged to a hurricane goddess and reputedly into human sacrifice. Rubio scoffed at the rumors, and I'd yet to run into any, but out there alone, the prospect scared me silly.

But I was improving at panic control. I managed to keep my head. Like, Stormies meant bonfires. That cool, steady glow was no bonfire. And Stormies supposedly did this ferocious chanting you could hear blocks away.

I listened till my earlobes ached. Nothing.

Smart move was a quick retreat. But here's where things changed. First time in my short memory, I did not turn tail. Sure, my body coiled to run, but my brain held back. Like the tender inside-out skin I'd worn since the Wave had finally turned right-side-in. Like I'd grown a bit of shell. I felt . . . not whole, not strong, not even confident, but . . . ready to let curiosity lead me. You'll think, no big deal, but it was, because I moved toward the glow instead of away from it.

You didn't have to go uptown to know artificial light still reigned in the drier heights of the Island. Lots of solar and wind, biofuel generators, tidal turbines, even a few working power lines. But down here in the flooded Dark, anyone making power should be rationing it this time of night. If the light had been moving, like uptown joyriders out to crack some downtown heads, I'd have split for sure, but . . . if there was news to take home, it could be worth as much as a good night's picking.

Knowledge is power, Rubio was fond of saying, and I had so little of both. So I hauled my new nerve up around me and crept ahead, shadow to shadow, rubble pile to rubble pile.

Southwest corner of 23rd, a sturdy ten-story leaked bright stripes through third-floor storm shutters. A generator rumbled from a lower floor, the quiet, expensive kind. Out front, a single ancient streetlamp leaned over the broken sidewalk like a drunk, pulsing to the generator's rhythm. I stared at the barricaded glow from a doorway across the avenue. I'd been here on a training run hardly a month ago: the whole sector had been dark and desolate. Was this some new den, staking claim to a bit of neutral turf?

The dens kept their distance from each other, but basic cooperation was the norm. Word would get out if a new one started up, rich enough to run a nighttime generator, never mind power a personal streetlight. And den homes had a beehive hum to them, never mind sentries 24/7. Like, my sneak wasn't all that great yet. Any watch dude worth his sign would have spotted me long ago.

Which meant some other kind of newcomers, who could afford to live uptown but chose not to, for reasons of their own—like, stealthy ones. All those grills and grates and shutters would require some serious rebuild, and they'd sure been quiet about it. I prowled a bit more, but the place kept its secrets. Pretty slim, as news goes, but a thin mist was gathering. Rain would be next. I voted for home.

And then that girl showed up.

A soft patter coming around the corner of 23rd. I streak to the nearest door shadow, then lean my nose out for a peek.

It's a girl on tippy-toe, like a dancer late for an entrance, splashing through the shallows where the crossing dips and holds water. A girl. Alone. She's moving right along, but not like she's running from something.

She was my middling height, maybe a little older. Hair my color but straighter, and cut too short for her blunt jaw, like easy care meant more than looks. But her clothes said the opposite, pale and clean even in the steamy heat, uptown clean and uptown simple, floating around her in layers like bird feathers. She was as bright and shiny as the silver dollar my den boss kept tucked in his old leather vest. Could she have just left the lit-up building by some back door? That would explain her being this far downtown and still so clean. And wearing a plump backpack, right out in plain sight.

Really, what was she thinking?

I wrapped my oversized street tee around me and made like a statue in my dark doorway. If some silly uptowner wanted to get herself napped or worse, that was her biz and none of mine. She loped right by me. Could've reached out and grabbed her. Others would've, even in my den. Fair game, after all. But I'm a picker. Mugger is a different line of training.

Anyhow, it was like watching a piece of art fly by. She practically glowed.

I flattened into my recess, but not soon enough. Quick reflexes, for an uptowner . . . if that's really what she was. She slowed and glanced back, scanning the shadows, like she sensed more than saw me. But spill from the streetlamp must've put a shine on my eyeballs, and she focused right on me. Her eyes tensed with interest, and something else I couldn't read. I snarled and puffed myself up, to show I wouldn't come easy. But then, more splashing and thudding, and her gaze slid back uptown. Since she'd already tagged me, I eased out for a look and wished I hadn't.

Serious trouble pounding around the corner: two big thugs in slick, black body armor. Where'd *they* come from? Maybe it was *their* mystery building, and they'd seen her pass by? Didn't matter. I'd lingered too long.

The girl spiked a look at me and cocked an eyebrow. A question more than a plea, but like I said, I'm not a fighter. I shook my head, jerked a thumb for her to take a hike. She didn't look half played out. Probably hadn't planned on a random streetlamp picking her up like a damn searchlight, but she could lose them in a few blocks where it got dark again. Meanwhile, if she didn't move along, she'd bring the thugs down on me. I scouted my exit down a next-door alley, praying she wouldn't follow.

The damn girl just shrugged, adjusted her grip on the pack strap, and turned to face the incoming. I pressed a fist to my jaw to keep from howling out loud. Trying to get us both killed? A rich girl could be armed—might explain her stupid bravado—but I was stuck with my pry-bar and a pocketknife.

I jiggled the door behind me. Jammed, fused, swelled up from too many floods. Kick it in? Might as well send up a flare. Options zero, I ducked out of my niche and into the alley, clear of the lamplight. With luck, they'd be too intent on the girl to notice. The narrow passage vanished into junk piles and deep night. I listened for moving water, heard only the clomp of boots on pavement. A blocky shape loomed at the edge of the dark, maybe an overturned dumpster. Cover. I could be there in seconds.

Instead, plastered against the rough brick, stomach somewhere up in my throat, I stayed to watch. Call me crazy, but I just *had* to see what happened next.

And then things got really strange. The girl wheeled around, her hair brighter than the streetlamp. As she turned, she cocked an arm and let the backpack roll off her shoulder in a powered arc. It hit the wet pavement with a muffled thump and skated hissing into the darkness. Right to my feet.

What the hell?

I stared at her, at the pack, and back again. Her breath came fast but even, and she held her ground as she eyeballed the approaching threat. After that first messaging glance, she never looked my way again. Not giving me up to the thugs? Radical. But she'd want something in return for such generosity. Time to play my part and be quick about it, if only I knew what it was.

She shifted back and forth on the balls of her feet. Impatient. Not with the thugs, surely. With me? Finally, I got it. I snatched up the pack and light-footed down the alley, hurdling puddles and brick heaps and broken glass, my pry-bar ready to hammer whatever might be lurking in the dumpster shadow.

The rusted bin was half crushed, but enough to hide me. A brief skittering as I poked my bar around. Whatever it was left. Couldn't use my head-lamp till I was well out of there. I hugged the pack like a shield and hunkered down to reconnoiter. The girl had planted her feet. Her face was in profile, but I was pretty sure she was grinning.

Was it the girl they were after, or her pack? Pressed to my chest, it felt soft but bulgy, obviously full. Snug, reinforced corners. Heavy-duty straps. Probably waterproof. My picker's grab bag was a grad gift from my street coach, but it was stained, patched, and smelly by comparison. This high-quality item wouldn't have been ditched my way unless it held something of interest, something the girl didn't want the thugs to have, or something she didn't want to be caught with.

So probably I didn't want to be caught with it either, maybe shouldn't bring it home to my den. I'd forgot to feel for wires like we were taught, but if she was tossing it around, likely it wouldn't explode on me. Maybe I was meant to get on out of there and ditch it for her on the way.

I listened for clues in the sounds whispering along the alley walls. Snarled commands, the girl's taunting replies, all in growls and murmurs, like they were trying to keep the volume down. More like a family argument than a mugging.

Okay. One more peek around the dumpster's edge. What could it hurt?

The three of them circled in the misted gleam of the streetlamp. The guys' voices rasped and broke, like teenagers. Rubio said uptown biz men recruited disposable young muscle from the squatter camps, offering food, shelter, and the latest jazz weaponry. New to the game, these boys?

I tried to put it all together. Like, the boys hadn't hauled out fancy hardware and zapped her, so someone wanted this girl alive and conscious. And she wasn't screaming bloody murder because, in this neighborhood, the rare passerby might be meaner than the thug-boys. She was putting up a fight and a damn good one, for all her uptown flounce and glow. Basic martial arts training at least, like we had at the den. All the smooth moves. A real bundle of surprises.

The mist had thickened into rain, curtains of filth drifting through the lamplight. The girl feinted backward, hit a puddle, went down hard but bounded right up, dripping oily muck. I couldn't figure why she didn't cut and run. Maybe for the pack, that I was meant to guard till she'd put the boys down?

Which was looking not so far off.

My street nerves twitched to be out of there, but curiosity still ruled me and she was a wonder to watch. Sheened with sweat, her face lit with a predator's grin, she had one thug face down on the broken street and the other limping and swearing, favoring his right arm.

This girl was a freakin' ninja!

I blinked away rain and recalculated. Once she finished, she'd come looking for her pack. Not twigging me to the thugs had likely saved my life, so I'd be honor-bound to give it to her. Street rules.

But only if she asked.

That broke the holding spell. Why give her the chance? My duty was to my den. Whatever hid in this overstuffed bag, some of it had to be good pick. The pack alone could earn me a whole stack of meal chits.

This time my body won before my brain had time to argue. I wished her victory, stuffed the pack into my grab bag and deserted out the back. Sorry, ninja girl, but that's life downtown. Where you're from, you can just order up a new one.

could've shot right home to the den. Should have. Coming in early is just fine if your pack is full. And I set off with honest intent, racing through risky turf in the pitch black until it was safe to use my headlamp, glad for the now furious downpour covering the racket of my flight. Already savoring a rare triumph at the tellers' counter and my street coach's surprised approval. Even Rubio would boast of such a haul.

At 14th and Sixth, I took a doorway breather. Without the rain battering my ears, a new thought swam up, guilty as a conspirator's whisper: maybe check out the contents *before* you take it home?

Not necessarily a bad idea.

Just taking the appropriate precaution, right? What if the pack was stuffed with dead rats or toxic junk?

Sure.

Guarding my interests? Like, good to assess what I had, in case the tellers tried to stiff me at the counter?

All of the above, but mostly, curiosity waylaid me. Not claiming any special intuition, and yet . . . something about the pack, the girl, the whole bizarre event, stirred up an info junkie's need to know. Before anyone else did.

But I'd need a dry retreat before the homeward leg, to do a quick inventory. There was a spot I'd sheltered my first night out when a gale blew up. Not too far out of my way. I plotted a route.

Fourteenth was still choked with the ruins of the flood wall built after the first superstorm cluster, long before Abel. Abel was my Wave, and called the worst yet, but there'd been plenty bad ones before it. The old debris had been dozed into a flattened central mound running between Eighth and Third Avenues. No good as a wall but useful higher ground that stayed dry during most high tides. My usual route home. Often there was traffic: tonight, it was two pickers struggling with handcarts and a runner speeding by on den biz so urgent, she nearly knocked me off the edge. Sporting a bulging grab bag, I was prime meat for anyone stronger, faster, negligent of the rules. In daylight, enforcers from the closest den kept things smooth. At night, their coverage was less reliable. You were pretty much on your own.

At Sixth, I let the handcarts pass, then clambered down to the wet, cratered street. A light flared a few doors down from the corner. I dropped like a stone behind the rusted skeleton of a bus just as a guy stepped out with a lantern, hooded against the rain. He scanned the darkness and hurried east. I waited till his misted halo crossed Fifth. When nothing more stirred, I moved onward. Where I was headed, I wanted to be my secret.

At West 12th, I slipped into an air shaft between two stone five-stories, set on a brief neck of higher ground. As newer-built blocks all around crumbled and went under, this two-hundred-year-old pair had stood up to most everything sea and storm could throw at them. The next big surge might claim them, with the river already knocking at their back doors, but for now, their opposite L-shapes embraced a puddled courtyard and the small, once-lovely building hidden within.

I'd cased it up and down. Spookily empty. Not like picked over, but as if its formers had the sense to get out early, when evacs were voluntary, maybe back in the 50s after Olav. Took everything with them but a scattering of crumbling paper and some unwanted tables and chairs. You could do that then. Lock your doors and pretend you'd be back.

I described it to Rubio so I could learn about it—no problem with his memory, and he knew about buildings from his life before, in an architect's office. It was a stack of three rooms, one per floor, with high ceilings and fireplaces, a curving staircase and all this carved wood. Rube called it a mews house, said I was lucky to find one still standing. He quizzed me about the condition of the woodwork, asked would I take him there? I'm sure he caught my wince. Though it was share and share alike in the dens, especially with friends, there were limits. Sure, someday, I said, but in case the old place still had treasures to reveal, I always had a ready excuse why I couldn't.

Dreaming of concealed hatches, hidden dry attics, and unbuckling the girl's fine pack, I splashed across the dark courtyard and was halfway up the worn stone steps before my headlamp picked out the fancy front door askew on its hinges, its paneling splintered by vicious, repeated blows. Slime water cascaded noisily from a broken gutter and across the polished floor of the entry. Muddy footprints sprawled across the perfect tiles.

I stood in the rain and stared, for way too long. A crash of glass brought

me to. I doused my lamp and backed into darkness to peer up at the weathered façade. Sure enough, light flickered at a second-floor window. A torch,
or an old chair set ablaze. The light flared, more glass breaking, and a ricochet of male laughter rose like heat from the shattered windows.

I shuddered and got ready to run.

Pickers tend to move fast and quiet. Our deal is to collect the merchandise, not destroy it. This had to be gang members, or even rogues, not
joined up at all. Burnouts who lucked into a booze cache and were wasted
enough to drink it up instead of holding it for sale or barter. Worse, it could
be a posse from BlackAdder, ranging out of their territory. I wouldn't be
sheltering there tonight, or anywhere near.

I brushed water from my cheeks—tears, rain, maybe both. The assholes
might not burn the place down, but probably they would, like so many
others, each with a history, and all that good picking gone to waste. I loved
this little building, for the story it told of a vanished age of peace and plenty.
Or so I imagined, despite Rubio's irked denials.

"How do you think things got this bad in the first place?" he'd growl.

"*Somebody* had the time and money to build it."

"Well, it wouldn't have been you!"

"That's not the point!"

But maybe it was. Why was I so drawn to the mews house? What if it
held a clue to my past? Rubio wouldn't hear of it, and I'd stalk off, furious
that he'd made me weep.

Later, he'd swear it was for my own good. "Got to nip those delusions in
the bud."

I got it soon enough. This house, old way before I was born, could only
have belonged to the seriously rich. Whatever my status before Abel, Rube
would point out, it was dicey enough to get me, and likely my family, left
behind.

"Only the rich got evac'd?"

"Not early on, but later, you had to have . . . means."

'Means' meant more than cash. It meant connections to power. Uptown
connections.

I didn't care. The house was mine in my heart. I'd walked its rooms,
filling them with expectation. But these days, all you could really expect
was loss. No special find stayed secret, everything was vulnerable. If it wasn't

the weather destroying things, it was stupid human nature. I was lucky to have a den to go home to and a dry bed to sleep in.

But I wasn't counting my blessings then. As I lingered in the narrow air shaft, gritty runoff sluicing down my neck and my feet ankle-deep in mud, I felt a hole in my hopes where the mews house had been. Wouldn't you know, the lure of the girl's pack was right there to fill in? I resisted, but not for long. A simmer of misdirected outrage nudged it along—like, if this is how life's going to treat me, fuck 'em all! Soon I was headed for the next dry hide-hole on my list.

You see, by my den's rules, a picker could claim one object from each night's take, so long as there was more than one and it wasn't a firearm. But this pack was full. Had to be lots of stuff in there. What if I wanted more than one?

Yes, that would be grabby. A betrayal of share and share alike. "In Unity is Survival," went the den motto. You heard it all the time. If one person starts putting their own needs first, then everyone's going to want to.

Scary. Hadn't even opened the pack and here I was, plotting to keep more of its contents. Best see what was in there before getting too carried away.

My second-choice pop-in was on the way home and a lot less luxurious: the back half of a truck trailer crushed against a collapsed wall on 13th, accessible by teetering along the debris piles. Only one of the double doors worked, and I had to shut it against the downpour. Inside, it was lightless and close, and had sprung a few leaks since I was last there, so the tilted floor was slippery and wet. But it was shelter of a sort. I found a perch and did some slow breathing to quiet my claustrophobia while the rain hammered the metal sheeting inches above my head. Got calm enough to hoist my grab bag to my lap, wipe my hands extra hard on my T-shirt, and pull out the pack. I clicked on my headlamp. It sputtered, oozed out a ghost of light, and died.

So I'd be trusting my fingers to give me some idea of what I had.

I felt around the outer pockets. Maybe the girl had a live phone, not that it would work down here. And who would I call? My den boss decreed them junk, wouldn't let them in the den. Pockets empty anyway, like she knew those were easily picked. I parted the main flap's Velcro and reached in oh-so-carefully. Stupid to soil the merchandise, never mind trip a fuse.

Quick count: a stack of clothing, top-quality, clean, dry, and neatly folded—the girl had to be near my size, and I could really use a new pair of jeans. Under that, three foil-wrapped blocks stopped me short, but nothing suspicious was attached to them. Might be protein bars, which would make the tellers very happy. Then, ah! Two ziplocks stuffed with pills in blister packs. Maybe drugs for Rubio?

Finally, hidden in the folds, a plastic sheath bound with a flat, springy band. A gentle squeeze got a crinkle of paper. Paper. Huh. Biz letters, or maybe a map of the waterways?

Except, when stuff is tied up so neat and tidy, it's usually for a major reason. Like, what's so important, you'd carry it around in hard copy? Ink, paper, a working printer—tough stuff to come by. So, what? Love letters? A pretty girl would have lovers.

My arm deep in the pack, I squeezed again, wishing sound alone would tell.

It could be nothing. Or . . . and here's where the hole in my hopes sent me way out on a limb, but why not? What if? It could be . . . pickers looked for them all the time . . . *documents*. The sort uptowners still went to the trouble of printing out: identification papers, ration cards, boat licenses, housing and travel permissions—the proof of your official existence as a citizen . . . that is, if you had one. Which, as a den rat, I did not.

I knew the drill from Rubio's endless history lessons—for my own good, of course. The checkpoints went up when martial law was declared again, after Superstorm Ruby and the epidemic that followed. (This was three clusters before Abel, before either of us was born—Rubio was named for her.) Islanders had to register within two weeks or be listed as deceased. A lot of downtowners, avoiding contagion or still digging out from the surge, never got the chance. Even if you did, you had to have all the right papers to begin with. If my parents had them, I might have had them, too, before Abel. But when you're hauled half-drowned and bare-assed from the rubble, small chance you'll be able to produce your ID.

So . . . might be documents. Oh my. Wasn't just the close space making my chest heave. But . . . the girl's personal ID? Would she toss it away so easy?

Maybe, if that's what the thug boys were after. Or if it wasn't really hers. Documents. What if? What if!

I dug the sheath and ziplocks out of the pack. The pills rattled in their little plastic domes. In the dark, no way to ID them. Might find a light between here and the den, but most likely I'd have to wait for my bunk to read labels. Even then . . . well, I was no medic.

Shaking off second thoughts, I stuffed packet and pills into my belly wallet, the one thing denfolk wore day and night, to protect the few precious things any of us possessed. Our one place of privacy.

Just keeping them dry. Making sure they stay safe. Sure.

Meanwhile, I'd missed the silence outside my stuffy hide. I cracked open the trailer door. Dripping everywhere and the gutters awash, but the sky had shut off its spigots at last. Maybe my luck was in for a change.

Back on the street, heading home, I did my usual due diligence: watching, listening, walking soft. But the packet kept claiming my attention. Like, if it was papers, maybe they were forged or stolen, so the girl was looking to dump them, making me the random street snatch who'd clear the evidence. Well, a fair trade: I disappear her hot papers, I get her fully stuffed pack. But had she meant me to keep it? I'd left without finding out.

Getting to know someone in the den, pretty quick things got around to what's your story? Everyone had one, even long-time denfolk, mostly about how they meant to get off the Island but hadn't managed yet. Oh, you could leave, if you had a boat or wanted to risk a swim. But without papers, there was nowhere you'd be allowed to land. So it was, well, I'm just waiting till I feel stronger. Or, can't seem to contact my Mainland relatives. Or, not enough cash, not enough clout, but mostly . . . lost all my ID.

To ward off despair, table talk in the den was often about when life got back to normal—when the bridges reopened, when the water went down— what Rubio called Den Myth #1. Abel had wrecked the last of the cell towers, and no one was coming to fix them anytime soon, not downtown at least. So, with services down, news of the Mainland was scant and unreliable. Still, it had to be better there, right? It was the only normal we could imagine.

A way off the Island? Right there in my belly pack? What if? *What if!*

Even if the papers weren't legit, good use could be made of them till they tripped some official wire uptown.

Or . . . I could use them, on my own.

That whisper again, tugging at my ear with needle teeth.

Den conditioning is strong. It works its way in deep, especially if it's all you know . . . or can remember. Right there on the sluicing pavement, I got the shakes so bad I had to drop my head between my knees.

Was I really thinking of stealing from my den?

A tearing noise from uptown brought me upright. A drawn-out ripping, then a pop, followed by a muted cheering. The sound of wood being scavenged from some scaffold or walkway. Fuel for a Storm Worshipper bonfire?

Time to hustle. The night streets weren't the smartest place to work out a dilemma. Especially one based on a mere crinkle of paper in the dark.

But I had to wonder: when I finally held the contents of my belly pack up to the light, would I know what to do?

THREE

Y ou might ask, in a world defined by scavenging and thievery, what's so bad about helping yourself now and then? A den loyalist would say: when daily life's this sketchy, it pays to play by the rules. Den rules, that is. *In unity is survival.*

But on the trudge home, my brain was doing somersaults. Do it, don't do it. Betray the den I owed my life to or give in to dreams of freedom and the Mainland. Tough choice.

My den was called Unca Joe, for reasons best known to Cline Rousseau, its leader and founder, and a handful of older residents. Something to do with a favorite former den home, a few blocks away on Lafayette. The older dens cultivated their histories—Rubio would say, embroidered them—so I learned it well, if only secondhand. Encouraged a sense of stability, however illusory.

Next, you'll ask: why? Like, as the seas rose and the storms pounded in one after the other, as life in the city got less and less manageable, why did anyone stay behind?

Us younger denfolk mostly didn't get the choice. But early on, when the Melt was starting and evacs were merely recommended, there was always a core of diehards who refused to leave. Like Rubio's parents, and later, Rubio, who swore it never occurred to him. My family too, had to be. Why else was I still here when Abel roared upriver? I didn't feel this fixated loyalty to the Island, but I kind of did to my den. After all, it was all I knew.

On the street, Joe was said to be one of the good dens: well-organized, less infighting, better food and medical care, fewer casualties and less attrition, due to our rigorous training program, and reasonable rather than hardline discipline. Even Rubio agreed its success was largely due to Rousseau, who'd been into community organizing since the Twins, a double-header of super-storms back in the 2080s. Now at the far end of fifty, he'd had time to work things out.

"We don't take in just anybody. Useful skills, a must." The boss man would bend a stern eye at me or maybe Rivera, both recent newbies. "Of course, I made an exception in your case." Then he'd toss a rueful shrug, like doubting the wisdom of his generosity. Always keeping us on edge, y'know?

The official version of the Joe creation myth begins with those first evacuations, while Greenland was still frozen and anyone who could moved uptown. With each successive superstorm, another sector went under water, and more services were lost. Going it alone downtown got tricky, so the die-hards who couldn't afford to move gathered in groups, gangs, extended family units. As Rubio put it, things got tribal real fast.

Was Unca Joe the first official den? Many Joes would claim it. Midway through the Melt, Rousseau and some pals got washed out of a flood zone B community center and were squatting in a chunky building at the top of Lafayette Street. It was old and deserted, its ground floor flooded, so no one noticed, and they settled in. Even the law had moved uptown, with zones A, B, and now C awash from sea-level rise. Several years later, Hurricane Misha's stunning high tides brought a massive surge which never fully receded. Lucky for Rousseau and friends, the Lafayette squat stayed dry above the second floor, but their numbers swelled with rescues and refugees. Had to move to larger quarters. Soon after came Abel. And my new life began.

I asked Rubio one time, "If the dens have been going so long, how come people still talk like it's a short-term thing, like, till the climate gets fixed and the water goes down?"

"You mean, people like Rousseau?"

"Well . . . among others." Rube and I had differing views about Rousseau.

"I don't."

"You don't think anything good can happen."

Rubio sniffed and glanced away. "Rousseau just can't face the music."

"What music?"

His laugh wasn't always nice.

I sighed. "Do you hang out with me hoping I'll say something stupid?"

"Doesn't happen as often as it used to."

"Sorry to ruin your fun."

He was like that when he wasn't feeling good.

Right after Abel, the Joes could've moved further uptown. Along with one more zone of services drowned—power, sewage, water—the midtown barriers and checkpoints lay shattered. Underground, the Hudson and East rivers had merged into a grand estuary. But Midtown was tidal—alternately wet and dry, a problem for feet or boats—and soon uptown was being gated off into walled districts, what Rubio called 'city states.' Downtown was left to the dens. They'd evolved there, knew how to deal with it, and at that point, nobody else wanted it. Unca Joe's new den filled an entire block, offering space to expand, and the flooded streets around it formed a protective moat, just when BlackAdder formed up and den security was becoming a concern. The Joes stayed put.

The building had tall, airy rooms, a few still holding on to the elaborate plaster work of three centuries earlier. Even its newer sections were built to last. The thick foundations stood up to the storms and raging river currents while steel and glass thrown up two hundred years later went under from corrosion, undermining, and crap construction.

Often, in my bunk after a shift, I'd wrack my brain for the slightest memory of Superstorm Abel, even a single image that wasn't borrowed from someone else's tale. It was painful work and it got me down, so I hadn't tried it in a while. But that night, the girl and the pack and my raging dilemma stirred it all up again.

The streets were quiet. Dawn was soon and the rain had eased. In a few more blocks, I'd run out of dry land and take to the Second Avenue walkway. Almost home, and I'm deep in my thoughts.

Suddenly, a clatter of voices offside.

"She said I was making it up?"

"Yeah. What'd you tell her?"

So loud! And I'm a scared rabbit, scooting behind a jumble of tree roots, barely enough to hide me from this pair of fools strolling along like I'd just been, paying attention to nothing but their own brain farts. Like my street coach says, any time's a bad time to get careless. It's a wonder any of us survive in this city.

"I told her the truth," complains one. "After Abel wiped out my family's squat and them with it, I was hiding out with this older dude, an' one day, he didn't come home."

"Always the risk. So what happened?"

"Well, I don't know, do I?"

They sounded so young, shambling along, one voice hoarser than the other, probably heading for the walkway. The walkways are neutral territory, so semi-safe at least and often there's a spill of light from upper-story squatters' digs to guide your way. But this pair were carrying lanterns, tossing a bobbing glow at their feet. Had to be brand-newbies.

"She thinks I'm not legit."

"What, like a . . . spy or something? From some other den?"

"I guess. I told her the squat was stocked up, so I did okay . . . for a while."

"It's no fun on your own."

Well, that was sure an understatement.

First-time pickers always want a buddy to work with. Sounds like a smart idea. But Rousseau says company's distracting and I saw how right he was. These two were just blah, blah, blah. Anyone could've jumped them, right there at the water's edge.

Lucky for them, no one did, and I was too beat for even a fun little scare. Well, c'mon—it's tempting when someone's even greener than you are. But I could hear them getting to be friends. You needed friends in a den.

"But mostly, I was running out of food and water."

"Right," drawled his pal, like he'd been there, too.

Just voices in the dark, till I got a better look as they paused at the walkway stair to adjust their packs, hooking the lanterns to the rail. Two teener Black kids, preppy, with soft faces, wearing gloves. Lanterns and gloves. Newbies for sure. Like, refugees from one of the districts Abel had washed out of Midtown. That could be my story, too, if I could only remember it.

I didn't blame them for the luxuries. It's safer to work in the dark, but the walkways are tricky if you don't know them by heart. Lashed and bolted to the building fronts a story or two above flood level, they're narrow and rough-built, mostly from storm debris. They take unexpected turns, stepups or down. Don't always have railings. Plenty near-pitches of my own into the oily drink to keep me humble. I peered hard to make out the boys' den sign, but likely they hadn't earned it yet. I'd embroidered the red 'J' on my own cap just before my first solo. Ladysmith's was the nearest den, if the boys were headed home. A good den, word was, but really, these two deserved better prep before being turned out to pick their keep. Maybe best they were paired up.

I let them mount the long gangway and clump along for a block or so, then followed, slow and silent. Pretty sure they never tagged me. And I spotted Rubio long before they did. Only a ragged silhouette against a gray hint of dawn, lounging in the middle of the bridge at Second and 12th, but I'd recognize that stoop anywhere. The boys slowed like they meant to cross at the bridge, then saw him and scuttled away to the smaller crossover four blocks down.

"Rube!" I trotted up noisily, not sure he'd heard me, or even seen the boys slink by. Or he heard but wasn't letting on. You couldn't always tell. "Yo, Rube!"

I get distracted on occasion, had been just moments ago. But Rubio was plain absent-minded. A cause for concern, along with his weak health, his habitual gloom, never mind his heretical notions. Been an only child, he said. Never played well with others. But in a den, you had to at least make the effort.

I looked him over, tall and sick-skinny, alone in the open and gone somewhere inside his head. Somewhere in the past, bet on it. Not paying a lick of attention. What's a pal to do?

First, hide my fat grab bag behind my back. His bag was a flat puddle by his feet. Then I sidled up beside him. Elbows on the rail, shoulders hunched up around his ears, he stared out at the Stuy Square marina as if it wasn't there.

"Hey."

"Hey." He was hoarser than he'd been at the start of shift.

"I love this view."

"Why?"

"Why not? All the lights and everything? Like life's still going on somewhere?"

"Who made you Little Mary Sunshine? Don't know a waste of power when you see it?"

"The marina dudes can afford it."

"None of us can afford it! Waste not, want not!"

I couldn't disagree, not even to rouse him.

The 12th Street Bridge was a patchwork of rusted metal and warped boards arching two full stories above the water, to allow the bigger boats to pass beneath. It offered a sweeping panorama of the Stuyvesant marina a couple blocks uptown, with its solar arrays powering lighted guard towers and twinkling boat lamps, masquerading as a place of safety and good fortune when, really, it was a haven for pirates and rich uptown biz men. The Mainland net, when the signal wasn't down, referred to Stuy Marina as Pirate Cove.

Leaning into the dented steel railing, as big around as my thigh, I breathed in the rank, salty damp and watched the occasional boat glide by on the outgoing tide, oars stroking, a fleet shadow trailing a blur of running lanterns, or the on-duty light of a pedal-powered water-taxi on call to the island towers down at the Battery, a far outpost of the more adventurous money. Other shapes slipped by in darkness, leaving only a wake to slap against eroding brick and stone, going about errands they preferred to keep private.

"I like it anyway, all lit up at night." I wasn't going to say something lame like, it might be nice living on a boat in Pirate Cove, or how a boat at mooring with its portholes lit filled me with longing. Not till I knew why I felt that way. "Makes things look almost normal."

"Only if boats on Broadway is your idea of normal."

Bad idea to point out that, riding on a ridge, Broadway was dry from Washington Square all the way uptown. Rube liked the sound of it his way.

Smarter, better educated than most in the den and prickly as a porcupine, Rubio didn't have a lot of friends. He had so much to say, so much information and opinions to spread about and all of it important, at least to him. His tendency to lecture sent most denfolk fleeing for their bunks. I often wondered why I put up with him, but his encyclopedic knowledge was a bridge to my past, and in a pinch, no friend was more reliable. I trusted him like no other, except maybe Rousseau. Rube recognized how tender I was. He never made a move on me and he repaid patience with loyalty. But when his illness peaked, he was at his prickliest. Then, even simple conversation was an effort.

I moved on. "Feels like a storm coming."

"What else is new?"

"I mean a big one."

"You got the same weather report I did before we went out. Nothing about a storm."

"I'm only saying . . ."

"Your interior barometer again?"

"Forget it." Wasn't going to let him start in on what he called my magical thinking. I nodded at the lowering cloud cover, touched by yet another wet dawn. "Least we can see our way home."

"Home," he muttered, like it was the last place he wanted to be.

Blinking lights against the metallic sky announced early-morning drone deliveries to the marina. Food, clean water, medications . . . all the necessities, straight from the Mainland. At least, so we assumed.

I gave up on the good news. "River's come up another foot along Eighth. The 14th Street crossing is puddling."

"This thing's not done yet." He coughed and spat into the water sliding by below, his hawk dropping among the scatter of debris washed downstream by the tide. "Time to look for higher ground. Too bad the boss man won't listen."

No one like Rubio for twisting casual chat into a complaint session. "He's looking."

"How hard is he looking?"

"Tough to find a place as good as Unca Joe."

"Bullshit. A whole island of higher and drier. Rousseau's stuck in an obsolete model. What worked for a den in the first years ain't going to work after Abel and onward."

"We eat. We sleep safe and dry. Why make it a crisis? Besides, it's only half an island, most of which we got edged out of."

"A little muscle could change that."

"Oh, yeah? You ready to get into fighting trim?" I stared at him. "C'mon, Rube. Where would either of us be without Rousseau and Unca Joe?"

This only made Rubio hunch deeper into his shoulders, so his wiry man-bun hiked up behind his ears. He flicked his head to settle it. He only wore it to annoy Rousseau, who preached short hair and shaven cheeks as practical and hygienic. "Just 'cause he saved your life doesn't mean he's God."

A guy in our bunk tier told me Rubio had issues with authority. No kidding.

I said, "Let's not do this now, okay? It's been a long night."

"Sure. No problem." But it clearly was. He turned back to stare out at the marina, where the boat lanterns were now winking out to save power.

"Hope those boys made it home to their den," I mused.

"What boys?"

"Two baby Smiths, I'm guessing. Walked right by your nose, but never mind."

Dawn was far enough along to show up the intricate structure of the walkways, always a puzzle. Like, what was attached to what? How could battered, sea-soaked wood hold up charred lengths of steel? How could something so fragile-looking stay so strong, through storm after storm?

"So, why?" Rubio murmured after a while.

"Why what?"

"Why do you like it here?"

"Forget it. You'll just make fun."

He shook his head. "Promise."

I turned to him: high, bony cheeks, a thick brush of shorter hair wild as a scrawl of charcoal against his too-pale forehead. Not a handsome face, but certainly distinctive. "Okay. I like it because it seems, y'know . . . familiar. Not a lot does, as you know, but here . . . well, it's like I know it, like maybe I lived around here, before."

"In the East Village? Mostly flooded before you were born."

I nodded at the marina. "I mean, up there."

"Further fantasies of a privileged past? Even if, after Abel, you'd hardly recognize it."

Abel had hit Manhattan broadside from the east. Rubio could list every building that went down or under, but it was a previous superstorm, Misha, that had brought him to Unca Joe. Born and raised in Brooklyn, he lost his parents in one of the epidemics, but found a new family at a forward-looking design and construction firm that had moved *into* Manhattan after sea-level rise became undeniable. They were determined to reconfigure the bottom of the island along the lines of Venice—a place Rubio could describe in infinite detail though he'd never been there. They would bring life and culture back to downtown. Misha's Wave took out the company headquarters along with the chief architect and most of the staff. Rubio's optimism died with them.

"It's not recognizing, it's . . . sensing." Now and then, I'd be gripped by some urge, maybe an action I'd be halfway into before I'd thought it out, and I'd be left stranded, wondering what I'd meant to do. "Like my body knows where it belongs, even if I don't. Maybe why Unca Joe is right for me. Like, some westside den wouldn't feel so much like home."

How much of who you are is memory and experience? How much is hard-wired?

"Home?" Rubio straightened, circled his long arms to take in the derelict buildings, the black water, the floating debris. "This feels like home? This wreck, this rat's nest, this . . . garbage dump? This feels like home?"

So many different shades of loss in this broken city, so many sorts of cripple.

"You could support me in this, y'know! Sometimes it's like you don't want me to remember."

"Really? Who spends half his days bringing you up to date?"

"With your life, not mine!"

But Rubio had no room for sympathy that day. "Thing is, Glim, you might have to be satisfied learning about before, and never knowing your personal part in it."

He watched my face crumple, like he'd been waiting to see how long it took, then glanced away, letting a coughing fit seize him. Maybe real, maybe a distraction, maybe both. He caught every bug, new and old. Compromised immune system, he said. Too many antibiotics as a boy, and now the very thing he needed, no longer in reliable supply. So, he was feeling like shit and I was the first target to come along.

"You wouldn't have to be out here hating it so much if you'd make more of an effort in the den. You know, play politics a little?" I got this advice often enough myself. "Earn a post inside with the clerks or tellers. It's bad for you, out here in the damp. And you got more brain than all of 'em combined. You're wasted out on the streets."

The coughing passed. Rube drew in a rough breath, reaching for a laugh. "Oh, I'm wasted all right." But since his health was the only dark subject he refused to dwell on, bringing it up finally got him off his rant. "So, you showed up all grins and giggles. Had a good night?"

My turn to shrug and avoid. "Moderate."

I didn't have a lot of secrets, least not that I could remember, and Rube knew most of them. But tonight's encounter I wouldn't, couldn't share with him. Maybe once I had a better handle on it myself. My fingers had strayed to my gut wallet, where the waterproof corners of the plastic folder and the blister packs poked into my skin, pre-punishment for the crime I was contemplating. Did guilt show on my face, in my eyes?

I swung my heavy grab bag up onto the rail. "Need a lift?"

He reached for his own empty bag and shook it dismally.

Going home light was never good, and Rube did it more often than most. Said he didn't have the picking 'knack,' but I thought it was more his distraction. Gaunt as he was, he shouldn't be missing meals for not earning his chits. Worse, the medics might decide there were better uses for the malaria pills the den scrounged for him. Every dry, unlooted apartment broken into, the medicine cabinet was the first point of search. I could give him the blister packs, but who knew what was in them? Instead, I fished around in my bag and hauled out the two shrink-wrapped blocks. The labels were unreadable in the faint dawn light: Chinese or something. "Here. Turn these in. I got enough to keep the tellers happy."

His mouth tightened, but he weighed them on his palm. "Protein?"

"Maybe."

"My birthday's next week. Twenty-seven and counting."

"Lucky you." He knew the date and everything. Made me jealous.

He shoved the bricks in his bag. He'd thank me later, when he was feeling better.

The rain went from gentle to mean again as we stood high above the flooded street. I spotted a shadowy unknown climbing the gangway up at 13th. Bulky and broad-shouldered, moved like he knew his way around.

"Ready to head in?" I pointed out the intruder.

Rubio shrugged. "No profit here but the riches of solitude."

"Who're you quoting now?"

"Me."

I laughed and nudged him ahead of me onto the walkway.

We tramped through the rain in silence for a few blocks, eyes fixed on the dim and unreliable path, each wrestling with our own demons, but with a sharp ear for the guy behind. At least he was pacing us, not trying to catch up—proper protocol among denfolk on the walkways. About where the first line of Unca Joe sentries should have demanded the night's password, Rubio slowed.

"Action up ahead."

We stopped between 9th and 10th, listening hard. Shouts and cries from downtown. The walkway kinked around a couple of tall rubble mounds blocking the view toward Unca Joe.

"Engine," Rube noted.

The rising whine of a boat motor. Not a sound you heard that often, least not downtown. Unca Joe kept a motor dinghy at our dock. It ran on bio-diesel from the kitchen, but we rarely had enough to start it.

"Is it ours?"

"Not unless it's had a major tune-up. Listen to that purr!" He crossed eagerly to the rail.

A long, sleek dart with a hooded cockpit and headlights slewed round the corner at Second and 9th, tossing up a plume of spray. As it gunned by, heading north, the big guy behind us caught up.

"Passing!" he bellowed.

A Joe enforcer. Rube and I shrank against the building to let him by.

"What's up?" I called as he barreled past.

"Gonna find out!"

Down at 8th, a mob of Joes racing uptown along the walkway pulled up at the corner, leaning over the rail to watch the speedster vanish behind the spume of its own wake. Amid a jumble of shouts and curses, they whirled and ran back the way they came, the big guy racing to catch up. The planking shivered beneath us.

Rubio stared after the boat like an envious kid. "Definitely uptown."

"Not the law?" The police amphibians were usually old and cumbersome, but who knew? They still had some access to fuel supplies.

"Why would the law waste their time down here? No, that'll be private money."

That seemed even less likely, until I recalled the girl's thuglets in their shiny black armor, helmets, and face masks, new equipment a lot flashier than they were.

Rubio leaned toward downtown. "Better check it out."

Like me, not a fighter. We went in slow. The sentries were AWOL at the second checkpoint, too—downtown of the two rubble piles, where the walkway snaked east of the wide harbor of Astor Place and split, one leg turning west past Unca Joe toward the dry ridge of Broadway, the other continuing downtown. Around the turn, bright tongues of flame obscured the dark lower floors of our den, gilding its double-arched window casings and sturdy cornice lines, flaring on the scarred glass towers looming on either side of the Lagoon.

I panicked. "We're on fire!"

"It's just torches."

But a lot of them, and people ganged up along the walkway crossing Unca Joe's stone and brick façade.

Two of our war canoes were in the water, lanterns flickering in the bows, fully manned but paddling in indecisive circles in front of the building. The walkway by the main entry swayed faintly on its legs, packed with denfolk yelling down to the canoe crews, waving and shaking their fists like in an old video of a sports arena.

I surged forward, but Rubio grabbed my arm.

"Simmer down, Glim. That boat's halfway to Inwood by now."

I was sorry to have missed the excitement, now that it was over. "We scared them off!"

Rubio rolled his eyes. "Yeah, with our Jedi high-tech paddlers. Nah, more likely the fifty screaming-mimis at the top of the water gate got 'em laughing so hard, they had to leave or piss their pants."

"It could've been Adders!"

He shook his head. "That boat was on a joyride. Show off, stir up green envy in the broken heart of Downtown."

But I thought it was his own envy he meant. I was proud to see the canoe crews on duty, circling the Lagoon. "Have some respect, Rube! After the sentries and the enforcers, the crews are our next level of defense!" Which is how Rousseau always put it.

"Okay, I'm grateful."

"No, you're disgusting!"

The smell and flicker of the torches, their hiss in the slackening rain . . . it stirred up your adrenaline. I picked up speed. Sometimes Rubio just deserved to be left behind.

The outliers of the crowd raised a raucous welcome as we came along the walkway.

I spotted a girl I knew. "Louka! Qué tal?"

A wild grin lit the shadow beneath Louka's cap brim. Pumped up, but I could see her fright was genuine. "Uptown bastards tryin' ta sneak in through the water gate!"

"Sneak in?" I leaned over the rail for a look. The river lapped halfway up the tall first story. A small boat could slip in under the blown-out window arches, to tie up at the float moored at the base of the old elevator shaft, but hard to believe that speedster would've fit. Still, it was the easiest way in. From there, a ladder climbed to the core of the den. A kayaker bobbed just outside one of the windows, paddle akimbo, peering anxiously into the darkness. Heated voices echoed off the stonework. "Who's down at the dock?"

"Rousseau. In seconds." Louka's small fists punched the air. "He sent 'em packin'!"

"How many?"

"Lots!"

"Two," corrected the next guy over, the enforcer who'd passed us on the walkway. "The max load on a boat like that. They really thought they had a chance with two?"

"A chance at what?" Rubio arrived like he'd been running hard, though I knew he hadn't. "They were just yanking our chain, man."

The guy dry-eyed him. "Who says?"

"The mother went right past me. A dude and a dudess in a sweet little boat. Speedy fucker." Rubio liked to talk tough with other guys around. "Just a joyride."

"Maybe one of their treasure hunts," a deeper voice put in.

"Treasure?" Louka was petite and pretty, even in picker duds, if you ignored the scars beneath her oversized cap brim. Also, still young enough to believe shrill girly astonishment was alluring. Which apparently it was, as all the guys turned her way, even Rubio.

"Not real treasure," Deep Voice supplied. "More like, y'know, go find an old dog collar with the license still on. Or a readable MetroCard."

The enforcer grinned. "Or a den girl's damp panties."

"Euww!" squealed Louka.

I swung away, adrenaline draining. Panties? As if. Most of us wore anything we could get clean enough: cut-off sweats, men's old jockey shorts, whatever. Meanwhile, the rain was coming down hard again, and I'd had it. At the narrow main entrance from the walkway, the only sentry still on the job was the one-armed watch dude. Did he ever sleep? He took my password, frisked me soberly for weapons, and sent me on through.

Another pumped-up crowd jammed the mudroom, where the entry ramp dropped through a third-story window into the old elevator lobby. The chatter was deafening. Clearly the most excitement we'd had in weeks. The dim space smelled of sweat, mold, wet work clothes, and used-up oxygen. The water-stained walls were lined with hooks and cubbies to stash dirty boots and rain ponchos before invading the cleaner areas of the den.

Pale dawn seeped through the tall windows in the stairwell across the hall, hardly enough to see by but enough to shut down the sensor-driven LED cluster overhead. I nosed through the mob gathered around the empty elevator shaft where the ladder rose from the dock. Spotting a half-empty cubby and a free hook, I shouldered my way to it, listening to the news grow more dramatic with each retelling. Half-listening, actually. More like, thinking hard and fast. I'd reached the point of no return.

Any picker coming off duty was required first thing to report their take to the tellers in the main hall, so I had to be sure in my mind before I walked in there. But I knew already what I would do. And in case I wasn't feeling guilty enough, as I stripped down to my damp undershirt and hung my sodden work clothes on the hook, a gust of cheers blew up and Rousseau climbed like a hero out of the elevator shaft, shaking his head, waving off questions and concerns. He halted on the top rung, waiting for the din to ease. Rousseau never liked shouting over other people's noise.

"It's all over, folks, nothing much to it. Go on back to what you were doing."

Instead, he got a chorus of FAQs: *Boss, what about this? What about that? What if they come back, what if they bring their friends?* Didn't want to let him off easy.

"Boss, was it Adders?" a final voice shrilled.

"No, no, not Adders."

Rousseau was a big man, ebony-skinned and well-muscled, solid rather than tall. He moved with grace and an old-fashioned formality totally at odds with his casual garb: an old leather vest over a bare chest, well-worn jeans and bare callused feet. The formality enforced a halo of private space around him, even in a crowd. You never saw anyone hug Rousseau, or pat him on the back, even the guys in his cadre from before. He was never just folks. A handshake was as close as you got.

Insistent now, he raised both palms, pale against his dark, scarred arms. His voice was deep and practiced. "Listen up! There's nothing to worry about, so let's settle on down. It's dawn time. Night shift's coming in. They need their tallies done so they can hit the Mess or their bunks. Let's be on about it!"

The mob parted obediently to let him through to the big central hall, dubbed Main, then piled in after him to mill about and bring their racket inside.

Rubio caught up at the cubbies. "Always sounds like he's at a press conference."

Whatever that was.

"You could learn from him." I flashed him a sour grin. Really didn't want him around right then, with my decision to be sure of. "I gotta go tally."

"What's the rush?"

"I'm starving. Aren't you?" Too late to change my mind now. I tightened the strap on my gut wallet, shouldered my grab bag, and headed inside. Man, sometimes Rubio was a real pain in the ass.

FOUR

I n Main, a raucous party was heating up.

Someone raised a victory chant. "Joes, one! Invaders, zero!"

We had parties now and then, when Rousseau figured the worker bees needed a reward, but this one got going on its own. People I hardly knew kept slapping me on the back as I shouldered through the press. I nodded and grinned till my jaw hurt, but right then, partying was the last thing on my mind.

I met Big Gracie struggling back from the cram of scouts turning in reports, pickers toting up their take at the tellers' counter, plus the clueless just getting in the way. Her scowl lightened when she saw me.

"Took for friggin' ever!" Shed of her thick-soled boots, Grace didn't loom so tall. Her cheeks wore an irritated flush under smears of mud and sweat. She swigged from her water bottle. "A few shots fired, and the place goes apeshit."

"Shots were fired?"

"Well, maybe. Someone said. That's new, huh, them comin' right to our door?"

"Nervy," I agreed. "I heard it was rich kids joyriding."

"Yeah? Who said that?" Her battle stance eased off a bit.

"Some of the guys." I knew Grace wouldn't credit Rubio, not without backup. 'Blowhard' and 'limp-dick' were the least of what I'd heard her call him.

"Well, better than Adders. Could've been, right?" A tetchy wave at my grab bag. "Hope yours goes smoother than mine."

Always a chance. "What, higher mathematics?"

"Wouldn'ta thought so. Ain't that why they call it a *counter*, meaning they're supposed to be able to?"

A favorite den sport, arguing with the tellers, least till the guy behind you got pissed 'cause you're holding up his dinner, or his breakfast.

Grace shoved back her worn-soft ball cap, its entwined 'NY' near invisible but the over-sewn red 'J' glowing bright. "Shit. What a night! Seen Rivera?"

"Not yet. Message, if I do?"

"Nah. Meet up at breakfast, most like. Damn, I miss my fuckin' phone!"

"Someday."

"Someone'd have to be thinking about us down here for that to happen."

Did I miss my phone? Rubio said there'd been no service downtown after Hasan, about the time a teenaged Grace came to Unca Joe, and no attempts at repairs in the ten years since. Possible I never had one. "The boss'd let us have 'em if they worked."

"Maybe."

Grace normally oozed confidence. Now I wondered how deep that really ran. Had the raid shaken her more than she'd care to admit?

"You worried about Rivera?"

She caught herself gnawing her lip. "Nah. Di can take care of herself."

Because Rivera was only small next to Gracie, with a rep for being ferocious on the judo mat, I just nodded. Neither of us was looking for real conversation, not in the middle of a melee. Grace tossed me a smirk and headed for the showers.

Main was a smelly, echoing, two-story box with a balcony wrapping 360 and traces of ancient blue paint still clinging to its moldy walls. A mismatched row of bars scavenged from derelict saloons ran along one side, where it was business as usual for the clerks and tellers laboring to tally the night's finds while the rest of the den jazzed all around them.

Scanning the line-up, I chose the old Korean woman because she was the most burned out and asked the fewest questions—too busy nattering at the tellers to either side of her. I queued up, trying not to look as ragged as I felt. Good that things were moving slow. Each picker turning in their stuff and getting their chits took me one step closer to now or never.

Easy enough to say: one is the rule, make your choice and be done with it. Till then, I'd never questioned it. But then, I'd never picked a haul that truly tempted me. Rubio would call it a moral crossroads, and I wasn't dealing with it well. I'd let it tangle up with my issues of identity. Like, if I knew who I was, would I know better what to do?

Playing at casual but twitching inside, I let my gaze drift overhead. With the heavy cloud layer, the solars were struggling, so most of the hall's lamps were offline to save juice, and the weak dawn hadn't begun its daily ooze down the tall well from the central skylight up on the roof. This huge, ribbed circle of milky glass must have been a wonder in the glory days. We kept it leak-free and as clean as we could in a dirty climate, so it still let in some natural light.

To edge aside last-second qualms, I pondered Rousseau's cell phone ban, which I'd also taken for granted. Like, how do we know they won't work if we never give 'em a try? And, could we fix the towers ourselves? Had we even tried? My mind drifted, until a hand clamped hard on my shoulder, nails digging in.

"Hava good night, Glimmagirl?"

"Ow-oo!" I squawked, once I got my breath.

My street coach beamed at me with jovial savagery. Even he was high on the raid.

"Jeez, Spunk!" I pried his fingers off my abused collarbone.

He two-slapped my fat grab bag like it was a drum. "Looks lika winna!"

"Did okay, for once."

"Doan git greedy nah!" He eased off and regarded me, deepening my sense of teetering on a precipice.

Spunk had a drinker's red-rimmed eyes without ever taking a drop, and wild red hair to match. Adrenaline was his drug of choice. He walked with a lazy limp that vanished out on the streets, which he ruled like a feral cat. You could take him for dumb or deranged, so newbies often underestimated him. I learned pretty quick that he read most of us loud and clear. The thought made me glance away from his scrutiny.

"So, what izzit?" Still wet from the rain, he leaned in close to talk without bellowing over the din. He smelled like the river. "Trouble out dere?"

"Nah, just . . . you know. Bad draw. Seems I get a lot of them."

He shrugged cheerfully, his bony arms flopping up and down as if aiming for flight. "But yer buildin' good rep. Life'll improve. Shur dat's all yer worried about?"

Spunk claimed to be fifty, looked older. He'd lived on and off the streets all his life, until Rousseau showed him what his mission was. Even so, the den hemmed him in. He came and went, and his bunk was a tent on the roof. Maybe why he was always so windblown. He had no time for slackers or fibbers, and he'd saved my life more than once during training runs. I adored him.

"It's just the usual. Stuff gets to me." I made a show of nothing-serious, but in case he saw through that, I told him about the ransacked mews house. At least that was the truth.

"Yah, good call. Dint wanna be goin' in dere on yer lonesome. Mebbe we check it out two-some one night."

"You're on." I bent my head. "If they haven't torched it already."

"Yah. So it go."

Time to change the subject. "Big excitement, huh? Uptowner raid?"

He cackled darkly. "Dress rehearsal."

"How do you mean?"

"Fer da real t'ing."

That gave me a chill. "What would that be?"

"When dey come fer us full-tilt."

"The uptowners?"

"Whoevah!"

Was he winding me up? Sometimes he liked to spook us. "I heard shots were fired."

"Shots?" His pale eyes narrowed, like, had he missed something? He seemed to decide he'd pushed this game too far. "Nah, dis was jus' rich kids. But dey're somet'ing ta watch out fer, too, y'know."

"Really? Since when?"

"I call 'em Abel's Orphans. Parents long las' gave up an' lef' town. Mebbe dead. Kids stayin' on cuz dey can, up dere in Dryland. No one ta say no, so dey're usin' da town like dere playgroun'." Spunk's face twisted as he leaned into his rant. "Racin' around, harassin' da honest workin' folk! Kin come an' go as dey like, an' a course da Law doan touch 'em!"

A long speech for Spunk. The raid—or rich kids—had him really riled. 'Rich kids' was sort of a construct to me. Like Adders or Storm Worshippers, I'd never actually met one. Or maybe I just had. Was that my ninja girl's crowd? Had to wonder at the coincidence.

"What about our crew? Everyone get back okay tonight?"

Spunk glanced away, his high draining off to a slight frown. He tracked another young picker elbowing across the crowded hall with a rusted metal box hiked up under one arm. "I guess. Coupla dust-ups, accident or two. Ain't what it use'ta be out dere. But nobody hurt too bad."

Spunk's 'used-to-be' was less than four months ago, after Abel slammed through and its higher-than-ever surge retreated the little it was going to. Picking was at a high point. Lots to be had out there, long as you didn't mind trolling through collapsed buildings, smashed-up boats, or rotting layers of drowned citizens and their pets. What Rubio called 'your usual post-hurricane holocaust.' But there was enough to go around, so the streets were quiet. At least according to the old hands. To us newbies, it was your-life-on-the-line, every minute.

"Nobody hurt too bad?" I prompted, since that usually meant *somebody'd* ended up at the medics. But Spunk didn't advertise mistakes or failures. Like it might break our spirit or something. He taught us how the city was one vast booby trap, getting worse as tides strengthened, bolts corroded, foundations weakened. He trained us how to avoid the random rapist, rogue, or mugger. He did his best to prepare us. But as pickings got slim again, as at some point they must, pickers might start turning on each other. A scary thought we only shared behind Spunk's back.

"Not ta worry." He grinned, baring receding gums. "So. See ya in da Mess?"

"Maybe. I'm pretty beat."

"Doan be starvin' yerself, nah."

Palms up, I made the weighing gesture. "Food? Sleep." I let the sleep hand sink low.

"Gotcha. Next time, den. Keep doin' whatcher doin'."

I nodded. If only he knew. A hot jolt of guilt convinced me he might, he did. But his eagle gaze had shifted to the swinging doors of the mess hall. None of us was immune to the lure of food.

A sharp crack made us both jump and turn. The room stilled. But it was just clumsy hands at the tellers' counter, the metal box shedding rust on the floor, the young picker apologizing. Relieved faces all around.

Spunk gave his signature cackle and slapped my arm. "Okay, kiddo. Step quiet!"

"You got it."

When he moved off, my hands shook. First time I'd lied to him. Ever.

By the time I faced the skanky teller, the choice had already been made, somewhere in the back of my head. I cashed in the pile of clothing, almost-new jeans and pretty, patterned T-shirts, then declared the turned-out, empty backpack as my picker's choice for the night. I noted more than one glance sliding enviously over my good fortune. One item I'd missed was a pair of stiff leather wrist cuffs stuffed in an inside pocket. Didn't exactly fit the girl's image as I'd seen it, but who knew what she might be into? I handed them over with the rest. Even when the old crab shorted me a chit, I didn't fuss. Sucking in my gut to hide the swell of my belly wallet, I just wanted out of there.

Now, if I could just act normal, not look rushed or too eager, stick to routine. Like getting something to eat. I considered my eight-chit handful. A fortune. Just one would buy a meal in the Mess but I'd have to sit down and chat.

Meanwhile, here's Rubio chumming up beside me. He'd changed out of his wet streeties. His loose denim shirt hung like a sack on him, long sleeves rolled down to his wrists. Even in the daytime heat, he'd get chilled. He waved six chits like a trophy.

"You got that much?" Being pissed at him never lasted me long.

Even a half-smile on him was a rare sight. "Organic protein. Right up to date. Teller nearly creamed herself. Sorry you gave 'em up?" He nodded toward the mess hall as the red doors swung open, spitting out a clatter of voices and dishware. "C'mon, I'll treat you."

People were singing in there, boisterous, off-key. I wrinkled my nose. "Don't think so."

"What? Smells good to me."

"Eat my share. I'm beat." I *had* to get out of there. "I'll grab take-out at the counter."

He sighed and glanced away over the mob. For all his prickliness, he didn't much like eating, or even being, alone.

I nudged him. "I heard there's an extra beer ration."

"So? You like beer."

"Only when I'm awake."

"It'd help you sleep."

"I sleep fine. Hey, isn't that Louka in there, on the harmony line? Buy her one."

That did it. Rube was as dumb as the next guy when it came to girls, so we weren't on each other's sex radar. That left us free to be good pals, which was just as well, since my radar was in hiatus and touching still roused me to panic. So off he went. I felt bad for abandoning him, but I had business with my belly pack. Past time to see if the contents were worth the risk I was taking.

But still, we all gotta eat.

Next over from the tellers, the picked goods were swapped, bartered, or shelved for later. Canned or packaged food went straight to the Mess, but for the dawn-yawners like me, there was Café Remains, a stack of pass-through shelves from the kitchen where the menu was whatever could be spared: small packs, individual servings, fruit or veggies best eaten raw, half-stale baked goods, and of course, mess hall leftovers, when there were any.

Another long line there, with the noise and heat still punched to max, and me like to jump out of my skin with keeping cool. Tight around me, denfolk milled and postured, trading puffed-up tales of the raid, thronging toward the Mess for that extra ration, rigged out in flashy down-time wear: rags and flood debris repurposed as den finery, feathers and sparkle-beads, small found objects tinkling on every seam. Fashion pandemonium.

I got my food at last—six rice cakes, one wrinkled apple, and a cooked bird leg cost me three chits. At least filling my water bottle was free. I turned and ran into a wall.

"Hey, I like eatin' in bed, too. Wanna join me?"

A wall of muscle. It was the panties dude from the walkway.

We were pressed so close, I had to look up at him. "Excuse me?"

"You. Me. We could get away from it all."

"I don't even know your name."

"No problemo. I'm Ace."

Sure you are.

Easy enough to lean up, whisper how I had the clap, did he mind? Send him off soon enough. But he was big, looming over me with a beery grin, and there was no place to run. My tongue went numb. The chatter around me morphed into an echoing rush of water. Waves? Then someone jostled, shoving me sideways so I had to dance and twist to hold on to my food, and the surge of bodies carried him away from me . . . it was over.

I weaseled my way into the stair hall and slumped against a wall, dry-mouthed and gasping. I wasn't worried about pursuit. He'd find someone else to hit on. But one more for the list next time I saw the shrink. I knew the conditions that set me off and tried to avoid them. So unfair that the terror revisited, but not the root memory.

Next, to the media loft for a weather check before bed. We all did it. Look strange if I didn't. I pushed off the wall and trudged up the stairs.

Overlooking Main, two big screens dominated the far end of the balcony. One usually played an old video from our vast library plucked from the waters. The other showed whatever the Mainland net had up and running, if anything. This depended on the weather and energy supplies, both ours and theirs, what satellites still functioned, and who controlled any of that at the time. Mainland politics had most to do with it, but figuring out who was in charge over there at any given moment was the unsolved mystery. If you're confused, join the crowd. But it was the best we could do with scavenged equipment and a wrecked downtown infrastructure. Of course, following over-there politics didn't put dinner on the table or tell you the next day's weather, but it was crucial if you aimed to go there.

The CB sets took up a far corner, reliable but short range, so mostly for emergency inter-den contact. A bank of desks and tables straggled along the next long wall, holding a ragtag assortment of computers, each with quirks and bugs and trauma-related issues, just like the rest of us. Our oldest and youngest were best at repairs, the oldest 'cause they'd been engineers and had the skills, the youngest—our Wiz kids or Wizzers—'cause they'd never had a machine that didn't need fixing.

"When I joined," Rube told me once, "the den still had an uptown bank account. We could pay for cable and internet. Online shopping with drone delivery was reasonable. When Misha took everything down as usual, most of it never came up again. The bank went bust, and now, even if we had the credit, we're too few down here for any provider to risk going up against the cease-and-desist by offering downtown service. The Feds want us out of here! We're a pain in their ass!"

"Ready anytime," I grinned. "Mainland or Bust!"

"No. Don't you see? Being here, unruly independents, we mess up their scheme."

Scheme? Sure. Rubio and his issues with authority. But I should've listened.

The loft wasn't crowded, not on an extra-beer night. A screen or two glowed as I came out of the window-bright stair hall and let my eyes adjust. Patient faces intent on searching up distant relatives or scrolling through casualty lists, still being updated even months after Abel. The sort of data free government internet was willing to provide, when it could.

A junkyard of old chairs and sofas ate up the rest of the space. On my way to the weather desk, I stumbled over a dude sacked out in the aisle, apologized, and two steps later wrecked my shin on the leg of a chair.

And wouldn't you know, a beer-oiled gang of Rousseau's 'young lads,' the enforcer crowd, had hijacked the news screen, hooting and hollering and spraying foam at each other. Sometimes, when it got plain lethal outside, Rousseau cleared the main hall and staged unruly basketball tournaments to let 'the lads' run off steam, instead of harassing us girls. The den's first line of defense, maybe, but in a group, they could be mean, and I meant to stay clear of them. The net's weather feed would have to do me.

I was too night-blind to see till I was right on top of my favorite computer—already taken. Damn! Could take longer if I had to jigger a new machine!

Slipping past, I saw it was Ellie Mae had my spot, otherwise known as Crazy Ellie. A real old-timer, she claimed to have been a scientist before, a PhD in Astrophysics. Rubio went on about what that meant, but ran out of details pretty quick. The gossip was that Ellie Mae had come to Unca Joe spouting a lot of grim views about the future of the planet and the impossibility of a short-term climate fix, even though everyone (but Rubio) would tell you the whole world's resources were focused on finding one. After a chat with Rousseau, she toned down her act. The boss didn't hold with wild ideas or daunting pessimism.

So now, if you sat next to Ellie Mae in the Mess, she smiled and asked after your night's picking, like any other nice elderkin. Meanwhile, there she was, slamming away at my keypad, so intent she didn't see me go by, keeping her unpopular obsessions to herself.

Three machines along, I found an old keyboard model that could limp up tomorrow's stats. Weather was Topic Numero Uno, after all. No one bothered to lie about it. If something big was coming, you might find an actual human reporting it, from some safely inland site. But that morning, only the robo-crawl below a slide show of nature porn from before. Today would be unseasonably warm, possible t-storms, periods of heavy rain. What else is new? But I'd been right about the river creeping up the avenues.

"Sea level still rising," I muttered. When were they gonna get things under control?

"S'up, kiddo?"

"Hah?"

"Wow! Jumpy, aren't we?" A chair scraped. My friend Jenn plopped down beside me, mug in hand. Was it a nudge from fate that kept putting bunk delays in my way?

I made my shoulders relax. "Hair-trigger Glim, they call me."

"Sorry! Whacha lookin' at?"

"The usual. S'up wit you? You gave up on the brew riot?"

She offered the mug. "Swill. That crowd could get drunk on air."

I sipped, handed it back. "Watering it again. A shame to poison good beer."

"Or even not so good." Jenn shrugged and took a long pull. "When in Rome . . ."

We laughed. She'd had the cot next to me in the Ward, post-Wave recovery and rehab. She'd suffered worse physical injuries, only brief memory loss. We'd helped each other through it, so we'd bonded, but were still unsure if each could move past the other being a reminder of all that pain and confusion. Like, was that same ember of terror banked in my eyes that I saw in hers? Plus, Jenn was nutty as granola, though you'd never know it to look at her right then.

Anyhow, we behaved like real friends. She'd shared her birth name with me—Myra, which she hated. Her den name honored a friend lost in Dara. I was sorry I couldn't offer mine in return. S'okay, kiddo, she'd say. It'll come to you someday. Still, I always felt she was testing me, to see if I was trustworthy. Not sure about what. Not sure if I was. Especially now.

I nodded at the screen. "Just the basics, I'm afraid."

She squinted at the crawl. "Any chance for a dry one?"

A picker's nightly wish. "Might have to wait a few days."

Jenn was tall, thirtyish, and rail-thin like most of us—any den rat who could stay heavy had a glandular disorder. Her straight hair was cropped like a bowl, and you could feel her big, musical voice hum in your chest. Her wry smile was mostly for show, of course. She could make nice with anyone, but it had nothing to do with being happy. Like me, she'd lost everything, her entire before, the difference being that she could tell you about it. The family and friends dead or fled over the years, the budding career in web design cut short, the lover who convinced her to stay and stay, first after Hasan, then Felix, then left on his own in a panic just before Abel. While my issues were trauma related, hers were likely genetic. Bipolar, the shrink suggested. She'd learned to cope pretty well, and he helped with meds when he could get them.

"You mind?"

I sat back, slid the keyboard over. "All yours."

But she wasn't after a better weather report. Her arm's-length mix of salvaged bangles sparkled and clinked as she tapped out a long, complicated run, murmuring about the way cooler tech she'd always had before.

"Still looking for those cousins in Minnesota?"

"Pretty sure I've found them. I just can't get them to find me back." She waited, fingers twitching, then went at it again. "Hard to know for sure. Connections are so round-about now."

"Maybe they're worried about having another mouth to feed."

Her hands flattened on the keyboard. I might as well have punched her.

"I didn't . . . I mean, I'm sure they'll . . ." Would I ever think before I spoke?

Her lips were pressed tight. "I suppose their equipment could be down. Maybe they've moved further into the mountains. I hope nothing's happened to them. I'm sure they'd answer if they . . ."

As far as I knew, Jenn had never met these relatives. I tugged the edge of her vermilion sleeve. "This is new, yeah?" I could usually suss out her mood by how much color she had on. If bright, she was working hard to keep it up. "I really love it!"

"Never say 'new'!" She'd showered and changed into her personal version of den chic—scraps of cloth pieced together in a crazy quilt, an explosion of color against the faded tints of the media loft. Jenn favored loose, what she called 'organic' shapes, stitched with more formal, repeating patterns in contrasting yarns. "Don't tell, okay? I've been keeping back the occasional choice bit of fabric."

So! I wasn't the only one. Probably everyone stole a little now and then, and I was just late to the game. Whew! "How do you know all the bits will go together?"

"That's the fun challenge." To Jenn, color coordination was a native language. She focused on the computer. "Oh, this is so slow, and I get so friggin' frustrated! But wait . . . you do stumble across some weird shit when you're deep searching. Check this out."

New images filled the screen.

"What's that?" I asked mostly to buy a moment, so I wouldn't gawk too hard—at a half dozen naked people dancing around a pile of burning wood rubble. "Is that . . . ?"

"Storm Worshippers. Got to be."

"They really do that?" I leaned in closer but there wasn't that much to see. At bottom right, a timing record ticked along. "Dated last week?"

Jenn nodded. "Like the old CCTV surveillance system, 'cept I think it's handheld. Maybe a cell phone."

"Stormies taking video of themselves?"

"Don't think so. There's more." Tapping away, Jenn made a noise in her throat, somewhere between a grunt and a growl. "I had it just last night . . . ah, here we go."

Now we saw what looked like an uptown checkpoint—barbed wire and concrete barriers. A well-dressed couple was arguing fiercely with a trio of armed guards, waving some kind of documents in their stony faces. Before we knew it, the guards were aiming weapons at them, not just stunners or Tasers, but serious military gear. The couple retreated, the man scowling, the woman in tears.

"Wish there was audio," Jenn murmured.

"Where is that?" The buildings were too generic for an ID. "Is it real?"

"Hard to say. Every so often, these vignettes pop up. Could be uptown, could be just over the river. It's like someone's doing their own local bad-news briefing."

"But why?" I didn't ask how, 'cause that would be beyond me. "What's the point?"

Jenn gave me a patient look. "Truth is the point. Someone's trying to share real-world data with us."

"You don't think we get enough reality out picking every night?"

"Only our limited version." She jabbed a finger at the screen. "When was the last time you tried to walk through a checkpoint?"

Well, never, at least not in present memory. "If it's real. I mean, if they have all the right papers, why would there be a problem?"

Jenn shrugged and hit a key. We watched the couple get turned away again.

"Asshole!" Across the loft, the enforcer gang whooped and jeered at whatever they had up on the big screen.

"Morons! Shoulda thoughta that before ya left the Island!"

I turned to peer through the forest of waving, muscled arms at a video of a crowd pushing and shoving in front of a tall metal gate. "What are they on about?"

"Oh, old footage, I think, from after Felix. Food riots at some processing center. The Mainland put stuff like that on auto-loop to discourage refu-gees. I'm surprised it's still up and running."

It made sense that the Mainland feed was intended less for a small popu-lation of den rats than it was to calm panic uptown and along the coasts, to convince people to stay where Abel had left them until order was restored. But would it ever be?

I turned back to our screen. "You're taking this so calmly."

"How should I take it?"

"Well, you're as keen as anyone to get off the Island." I recalled Grace's earlier rumor report, about the Inwood coup. Was that what the video was telling us, that the rules were changing . . . again?

"I am! We are! But to do it, we need to know how things really stand, right? It's fab that someone's out there trying to tell us." She patted the keyboard fondly. "My news gal."

I started. I'd just been thinking of my own ninja girl. "How do you know it's a woman?"

"Just a feeling I have."

Burned into my brain: an image of the couple's fists clutching papers. I hiked up my belly pack and rose. "I gotta crash."

"Yeah, me too."

"See ya." I reached for my grab bag.

Jenn followed it with her eyes. "Hear you had good picking tonight."

"Damn, word sure gets around!"

"Rubio, bragging in the Mess."

"Shoulda known. You do a guy a favor and look what happens."

"So? Show!"

Wary of the wallet swell rounding my gut, I pulled out the girl's backpack to be admired.

Jenn petted it and slung it over her shoulder, preening like a media model. "Nice, with your new outfit."

She tossed her head. "I'll borrow it for my next date at the Plaza." Envy must have bloomed in my eyes, or admiration, something that made her self-conscious. She unslung the pack and handed it back. "I'll make you something to go with it. You cadge the fabric."

"I'll see what I can do."

"No, seriously. You're always in work duds, Glim. You need something to show off in."

I wasn't sure about that. Not yet. "Hey, thanks for the offer."

Jenn let the pack strap slide through her clever fingers, sorry to see it go. "Gonna make it your night bag?"

"No way!" I grinned recklessly. "Gonna make it my *luggage*."

"So right!" She laughed, we slapped palms and chorused: "Mainland or Bust!"

Because all denfolk, even the worst skeptics, assumed there'd be an end to den life, even if it wasn't on the Mainland. Rousseau called it an article of faith: the situation would improve, even return to some version of business as usual. I believed it. Needed to. It helped get me up in the morning.

I slid the folded pack into my grab bag and creaked to my feet. "Heading in?"

Jenn shifted over to my chair. "In a bit. Some stuff I want to look at."

Me, too. Only it's not on any computer. "Don't work too long." She'd be there till noon, on the trail of those elusive relatives. "By the way, you see Rivera on your way in?"

Jenn was already deep in her links and connections. "Mmm, no, but hard to find anyone in that crowd . . . why?"

"Grace was looking for her."

"Ah, they'll find each other."

"Right."

On my way to the bunk hall, I passed by Ellie Mae again, still bent over her computer. All sorts of graphs and figures on her screen, too, but the images caught my eye: vast red plains, dry wind-scoured hills of barren rock under a cloudless, greenish sky.

"Wow!" I hadn't meant to stop, or even slow down, but I saw she had a thumb drive plugged into the laptop's side. Mining her own personal data. Rude to interrupt, but I wondered: what gets an old woman out of bed so early? "Where is that?"

"Oh," she replied, eyes dreamy, like we'd been chatting all along. "That's just Mars. Isn't it lovely?"

Mars? That's where Ellie Mae went in her dreams?

I rolled my eyes in best Rubio fashion and made for my bunk.

FIVE

When Unca Joe's shrink declared me stable enough to leave the Ward, I took a lousy bunk assignment without a murmur: top-level, third floor corner. A lucky break, it turned out. I was still real tender in close company, and a far bunk got me up and out of the constant mob scene in the tiers. With no one above or to the left, and hard plaster wall on two sides, even the regulation four by eight felt reasonably spacious and secure. And the climb would help me get back in shape.

But the real payback was the tall, arched window overlooking the Lagoon. A source of light and air, fresh as it ever got. Of course, half the glass was blown out and replaced with water-stained plywood. Might be glad of it if it ever got cold again.

As if. Standard picker joke when we turned up some evac's old parka or woolens, stashed in a forgotten storage closet or trunk: *gettin' ready for winter?*

But one lower pane still had all its glass. Plus, I'd chipped off a bottom corner of the ply to let in the breeze, then tacked on a scavenged scrap of screen to keep out the vermin. Plenty of glass lying around on the streets to fix up a few more, but wrangling big pieces home would be tricky. Anyway, too much open glass was a security risk.

Best of all, a massive chunk of cornice clung to the ceiling corner, tall as my arm span. Its plaster curves and curlicues were soot-stained and chalky with damp, its broken ends raw. Rubio had put his architect's eye on it, said he wouldn't want to be sleeping under it.

"Friggin' sword of Damocles." Rube's bunk was second below mine.

But I liked the look of it. No one else had one, and midway down its elaborate profile, a secondary dado gave me a handy storage shelf.

Dado. Fancy word for s-curve. Rubio's, of course. When I'd first showed it to him, he'd gone on for twenty minutes about the use of the cornice in building design.

I was more interested in why this big lump of plaster appealed to me. "Maybe there was stuff like that where I lived before."

"Maybe. If you were old money. That kind of detail was spendy even two centuries ago when those buildings were built."

"So maybe I was!"

Once again, the Rubio eye roll. "Oh, you're not gonna start claiming celebrity dad or lost Russian royalty . . ."

"Course not!" I knew that was uncool. We had a few who didn't. When all records are lost along with family and friends, you can become what you want. Or you can try. Takes style, Jenn would add, noting how little of that was found in a den. I figured her contempt for such fantasies was meant to prove her Minnesota relatives were humble but real. I hoped they were. "If we were rich, we'd have got out in time."

"Probably." When Rube sucked in his cheeks like that, his face got all cadaverous. "Maybe you were long-term squatters in an older luxury building. Plenty did after the first cycles of superstorms, with all those big apartments empty and the best available shelter."

"You mean, like us now?"

"You call this luxury?" He gave his usual sour grin, but I knew he was thinking there'd been plenty of chance to get out if you had foresight and a place to go. If my family was rich, they must have left without me. And that was too sad to consider.

"So, we were poor. That's okay, too."

"I'm guessing more middle class. 'Cause of how you talk."

"What's wrong with it?"

"Nothing. But it's different when you're not trying to talk den."

"I don't try to talk any special way . . ."

"You want to hear this or not?"

"I guess."

I always listened to Rubio, even when I didn't like what he had to say. He could shake me out of my survivor's tight self-focus, open up a broader perspective on things.

Wondering how many beers he was tossing back down in the Mess, I crossed the upper hallway to the bunk tiers. The wooden sleeping racks rose the full height of the room, a sturdy four-layered jungle-gym of salvaged beams and planking. The cheers and jeers from the media loft faded behind the snores of tired pickers who'd already hit the sack, and the constant creaking and shuddering of old wood under their weight. One of the old-timers called it like being aboard ship, the kind with sails instead of engines, like those I'd watch from the roof gardens, stirred with longing. Big-bellied white curves, gliding up the East River over Brooklyn. Silent with distance, just wind-driven grace and speed. As free as birds.

It was never really quiet in the tiers, but tonight it was noisier than usual. Both shifts had been roused by the raid alarm, turned out for the excitement and stayed up for extra beer rations. At the turn into F-tier, a bunch of carousers clogged the aisle, beer mugs and pick sacks scattered about to trip up the unwary. Mostly older teens I knew by name but who still felt it their manly duty to hustle me and grab my butt. Like, wouldn't I be hurt if they didn't? Usually, I'd just give a friendly snarl and shove past. But I was still touchy from my Ace-scare down in Main.

"Glimmy, Glimmy, how do you shine?" one of them burped in my ear.

My limbs jerked into a clinch. "Hands to yourself, asshole!"

"Aww, it's us. Be nice . . ."

An arm slid around my waist. "How 'bout a little drink?"

My hiss spiraled toward a screech.

"Leave her!"

My tier-mate Jake Reilly—early joiners often went by their own names in the den—stood at the corner, deploying his best what-the-fuck scowl. He wasn't a big guy. Several of the boys easily outweighed him. But he had the advantage of age, rank, and a shabby sort of charisma. The crush broke up. Half of it monkeyed up the bunk racks to their beds, whooping and cackling. The remains put on beery grins and started up a shoving match that shuffled them away along the tier.

"And keep it down, will ya?" Jake spat after them. "People are trying to sleep!"

More raucous laughter. I slid off toward safer ground.

"Idiots!" He came back around the corner. "A little watered hooch, and they forsake all reason. You cool, Glim?"

Backed up against our own tier, I nodded. "I'm good."

"No, you're not. You're shaking."

"I'm fine."

"Listen, I don't think they'd actually . . ."

"I know that." Which, of course, I didn't. Not for sure. I scaled the racks to toss my grab bag onto my bunk, hang my pry-bar on its hook, and give myself a moment to recover.

"A laugh and a knee to the nuts would dampen their fun," Jake called up to me.

Spunk taught us the move, to fight off a street attack. In practice, I was good. But when the threat felt real, the laughter deserted me and I froze every time. "It's reflex. I can't seem to . . ."

"I know. Give it time."

Back on mission, I turned my back to stow the blister packs in my grab bag, slimming down my gut wallet. Not the best hiding place, but lockups weren't allowed in our den. Few of us had a lot that was precious, but after losing so much to whichever Wave, you wanted to keep what little you had. We wore wallets 24/7, even to sleep. Best was a waterproof one—I'd traded hard for mine—you could wear it in the showers.

I changed into a dry T-shirt and cut-off sweats, grabbed my food, then pulled my bunk curtains, even the mosquito netting, tight before climbing down to be neighborly and eat my chow. "You heading out?"

"Where else?" Jake settled on his floor-level bunk so he could squint into the slice of mirror he'd hung on a tier leg and finish combing his long black hair into artful shape.

"Well, maybe you're shining up for a date."

He sighed. "Not this morning. Duty calls."

"Lo siento mucho, amigo."

"Me, too."

Jake was one of Rousseau's original cadre, which gave him special status in the den. He never abused it, but he sure was flirty. He couldn't pass a woman by without a come-hither glance. Nothing rude or grabby. Pure force of habit, he'd say. His idea of flattery, like the boys next tier, 'cept Jake had way more finesse. We'd had it out early on, and he knew where I stood. Not like we were pals—he was too top-brass for that—but we got along. As a junior tier-mate, I was his responsibility. He'd offered free flirting lessons as protective coloring, so my denmates wouldn't see me as antisocial and thus fair prey. But I was a reluctant learner, so he made it a game between us, which felt okay. Almost. After Rubio, I trusted Jake as much as any guy in the den—as long as he stayed at arm's length.

I leaned against the opposite tier and unwrapped my scrawny chicken leg. "Big night."

"Not like some are claiming."

"I got in at the end. So, no shots?"

"No shots, no injuries, no water-gate landing! You'd think they wanted it to happen!"

"They're bored."

"I had better things to do last night." Jake stood to tidy his blankets, managing to convey that sleep had had nothing to do with it. A middling build but black-Irish handsome, he had a blue-gazed, haunted look that all the women fell for . . . well, except me. Even Jenn had an eye for Jake, though I warned her off him often enough, figuring she needed something stable. Tried steering her Rubio's way, since she could match him for brain power, but she'd said, oh no, she wasn't hooking up with a guy who might go and die on her.

"Plenty of chores to keep people busy." Jake patted his neatly cornered blanket. "Sit down and eat. Better for your digestion."

I perched at the far end of his bunk. "Thanks."

He sent me his patented bedtime glance, forcing a giggle out of me. "That's better. Good pickings?"

I let my shoulders sag. "Did you see my draw?"

His smile was alluring, no question—intimate, needy, a subtle hint at tragedy. Jenn said it made her want to take care of him. He claimed to be an actor, back when the theatres were open, and I could believe it. He had a quote for everything. When Rubio went on about people talking a certain way, I thought of Jake's voice—modulated, faintly self-conscious, like he was always listening to himself. "Who'd you piss off this time?"

"Jeez, if I knew, I wouldn't do it."

"You're not taking advantage of your natural assets." He lifted his mirror shard off its hook and held it up for me. "When was the last time you took a look? Hair growing out all blond and curly, getting some curves back. 'When unexpected beauty burns / Like sudden sunlight on the sea.' Right? Time to use what you got."

Beauty? Hardly. A compliment from Jake was always a means to an end. But I knew it was my means he was looking after. Like what Jenn had said about me always living in street clothes.

"Thanks, but . . ."

"I know. Still working things out, and you know I got your back. But you shouldn't let it go too long, y'know?"

Was there something less playful in his advice this time, some hidden message? Was it time to start listening harder?

"I got nothing but time." The medics guessed I wasn't much over twenty.

"Maybe. If any of us do." His shrug expressed vast regret for all of life's injustices. "And, you know . . . fruit can spoil on the vine." He grinned.

I grinned back. "I'll keep it in mind. So where're you headed?"

He accepted my left turn and got sly. "Classified."

"C'mon. You oughta share the adventure. Wish I had your job. You get to stay clean and dry and all."

"Depends on the weather." Jake worked the day shift, on assignment to the Souk, the wildcat public market taken root in the bedrock high ground of Central Park, west of the farm plots. He'd trade the best of our pickings for necessities the den couldn't supply—flour, drugs, electronics, depending on what was available. I coveted his unpatched jeans and canvas vest made entirely of zippered pockets, never mind his daytime work schedule.

"If you're looking to promotion, remember what I said, okay?" He re-hung his mirror, then pressed palms to temples, smoothing back his hair just so. Some would call it preening, but to me it was about getting himself ready to face the city for another day. "And when the time comes, you know where to find a little friendly coaching."

"Yeah. If you can fit me into your busy schedule."

His blue eyes were as innocent as a rain-washed sky, but he was pleased I'd noticed. Hard not to, the way he went at it. Not much privacy in a den.

Meanwhile, not like I was a virgin or anything. The docs had surveyed me inside and out after Rousseau hauled me in from the debris. But what-ever my sex life was before, lost now in the memory gap, there was a shadow on it, expressed in unruly dreams, in my sudden panics, in the way I flinched when even friends laid a hand on me. The door to that recall was locked and bolted. Fine with me. I wasn't ready to open it yet.

"Home, sweet home, an' the gang's all here!" Peeto, our cross-the-aisle neighbor and a night-shifter like me, slouched around the edge of the tier still in wet streeties and dropped heavily on his bunk to haul off sodden, cracked-sole high-tops. "Rainin' like a bastard out there."

Jake's nose crinkled. "Man, don't bring those stinkers in here! What's the mudroom for, huh?"

"I leave 'em there, someone'll steal 'em!"

"Who the hell'd want them?"

"So where's the Rubester? He didn't get back?"

"He got back." Did Peeto really think the three of us were his 'gang'?

Rubio had the bunk just above Jake, which put him opposite Peeto and gave him and Jake common cause. When not bitching together about Peeto, they talked about women and Manhattan in the old days—pre-Abel, pre-Felix, still some theatres, clubs, restaurants around. You'd think it was Eden. Not much else to share, certainly not their den politics, but enough to keep them friendly. A girl we rarely saw had the third between me and Rubio. Her lover in B-Tier wouldn't set foot in our side after Peeto spread a nasty rumor about her.

Peter Sweeney was small and soft-bodied, not with fat but like his muscles had all gone slack from lack of conviction. He had a narrow face and a pointy little rat nose. My evil brain always drew on whiskers. Jake and Peeto were not friends, though they'd both been with Unca Joe since the beginning. Rubio was sure Peeto had something serious on Rousseau or some other senior member. Why keep him around otherwise?

Jake stood braced against the tier, glaring at Peeto's shoes.

Time to play referee. "Things quiet down out there yet?"

"Nah, still millin' and shoutin', like they won the war." Peeto's let's-be-pals grin said he'd had a slow night on the street, and was looking to share someone's grub, maybe in trade for last-second gossip. "Grace got herself called up to the office, and Rivera came in all cut up."

"Cut up? Rivera?"

"Ever the bearer of bad news," Jake muttered.

"What happened?" I slid my food behind my back before Peeto could ask for some.

"Back-talked a teller." Peeto rubbed his palms cheerfully. "Such a mouth on her!"

No wonder Grace was so jacked up when I'd seen her.

Jake smirked despite himself. "Gracie can hold her own all right."

"I meant what about Rivera?"

"Up to the medics with a bad slice down one . . ."

"Hold the gore. I'm eating."

"You asked . . ."

"I mean, is she okay?"

"She'll do. Might leave a scar. Shame, on such a pretty little . . ."

"Will you get those friggin' clodhoppers out of here?" Jake insisted.

"Jeez! You guys want the latest or don't ya?"

"Not at your price."

Exit time. I rewrapped my half-eaten meal and slipped it into my waist-band, making to head up to my bunk. "Listen, Peeto, an okay pair of hikers came in tonight, while I was tallying up. Might fit you. Oughta go check 'em out, before someone else scoops 'em."

"Got nothing to trade." Peeto spread empty, filth-darkened palms.

Jake looked away, disgusted. "Just claim a need."

"Got a bigger need for dinner. One need a night, that's the rule."

Jake fished in a pocket, flipped him a single chit. "Go down to the Mess, for crissakes. But wash up first!"

"Hope there's something good left . . ."

I hated when Peeto whined, which was most of the time. And no way was I mentioning Rubio, happily chowing down on his own pocketful of chits. Peeto'd be down there in seconds asking for a handout. When he started in again on Grace and her mouth, Jake turned on his heel and left.

"You could thank the man, at least!" I said.

He saluted Jake's receding back. "Sure, okay. Thanks."

"Check out those boots." I yawned like fit to drop and climbed up to my bunk. When I slid the curtains aside, it took me a moment to register.

Wait. Empty. *Empty?*

I shook the folds of the drape, then the netting. Nothing fell out. Tossed back my thin blanket. Rolled back the edges of my sleeping pad. Nothing. I searched the corners, up and down, but in a four-by-eight space, how many places can you lose a biggish object? My pry-bar and my damp under-shirt hung proper on their hooks, but my grab bag and all its contents were . . . gone.

I clung to the edge of my bunk. Any second, the top of my head might blow off.

Think. Think. Think!

"Peeto!" I peered over the edge, then up and down the tier. "Peeto? You see anyone up here while we talked?"

But he'd already split, his stinky shoes leaving mud puddles on the scuffed linoleum. The aisle was as empty as my bunk.

Shit.

I'd had stuff stolen before. A fact of life in the dens. I recalled those envious glances down at the tellers. But . . . but . . . but . . . this was my best take ever. I couldn't quite make it real. My grab bag, the girl's fancy pack, the two blister packs of . . . whatever. Gone.

Had it got all quiet in the tiers of a sudden? And Peeto whispered off so fast?

Peeto was no pal, but I'd pegged him as a whiner and a mooch, not a thief. He could've gone down to cadge those boots . . . but what if that food-and-need spiel was just a distraction, while some confederate spidered across the upper bunks and stole my stuff?

What to do?

Think, think, think.

I felt like I'd spent the whole night telling myself to get a grip. Normally I'd charge down to the swap manager and yell theft—the squeaky wheel and all. I'd claimed the girl's pack legally, after all, and in a tight community, someone's sure to notice if you show up with stuff known to belong to someone else. Jenn could swear to the pack being mine, even if the skanky teller would not.

The blister packs were problematic. Should've left them in my gut wallet. But a den thief wasn't likely to rat out his victim for illegal possession and have to explain how he got the goods in the first place. I was thinking 'he,' but it could've been anyone.

Either way, I was probably safe. Just a lot poorer than I'd been a few minutes ago.

Wait. My brain was so fried, I'd forgot. I rolled into my bunk and lay flat with relief.

Not *all* gone.

I sat up and drew the curtains again. A shard of gray light edged past the smudges on my window. I shoved my food aside and unzipped my waist pack. Just slipping my fingers around the mystery packet eased the ache of loss.

This could be the worst or the best of my haul.

I loosed the binding and slid the contents out of their plastic sheath.

A chunk of it dropped into my lap: a thin, hard rectangle swaddled in what, even in the dim light, I knew for a worn cloth napkin. Picker training taught us about fabrics. Occasionally, you'd turn up a lode of fine clothing or old linens that the water hadn't ruined, miracle survivors like us. Decent sheets and towels tallied high at the tellers, for the unused-to comfort they supplied.

I unfolded the wrapping. Inside was a small book.

A book. About the size of my two cupped palms. Old, by the look of it, same vintage as the napkin. I turned it curiously this way and that, looking for a power tab. But no, this was the real thing, bound in leather, stained and sueded with use. The dim daylight picked out traces of gold bordering the front cover.

I balanced it on one knee. A book. What a weird thing to carry around, hidden away like you couldn't bear to be without it. Especially weird for a ninja girl with private heat on her tail. You'd think she wouldn't want the extra weight.

I slid a finger along the worn spine, the girl's glow still bright in my mind. I hoped she'd put the thug boys down hard and made a good escape. Careful not to crack the spine, I let the book yawn open at random. The pages were thick and yellowed, both sides covered with a faded handwritten scrawl. A tricky read. Hard to make out with each letter sliding into the next. But I could read it well enough to see it was a personal story. Stuff about waves and wind. Someone's storm diary fished out of the flood? I didn't think so. Not enough water damage. And the things it mentioned—a harbor, a crew, a ship and passengers, the open ocean—it had to be from way long ago, before the sea crawled up the streets of Manhattan and swallowed the Mississippi Delta.

A hardback book was rare in the den. One in good shape, rarer still. But I liked to think there'd been books, even real books, in my hidden past. A book felt right in my hand. Up on my dado shelf lived a pair of water-buckled paperbacks I'd got for free, since no one else wanted them. I read them over and over. I'd been called a suck-up for reading through the dozen or so on Rousseau's library shelf. As if anyone could suck up to Rousseau.

I closed the book, rewrapped it gently, and set it aside for when I had better light. A book like this had to be worth something, more than Unca Joe's tellers would offer. They'd see it as a stack of old paper, good for starting fires. As Rubio often mourned, no place for art in a survival economy. But someone would want it, right?

I'd need a source who knew books to tell me its real value, which likely meant someone outside the den, maybe someone at the Souk. Where I'd never been.

Crap! I'm doing it again!

I buried my head in my hands. What was going on with me? Sneak off to the Souk? Behind Rousseau's back, behind the den's? Try as I might, the thought wouldn't leave.

The book could wait. There was still the stack of paper and plastic to explore.

I lifted the top layer, unfolded it, laid it out on the blanket. Then the next and the next. When the space was filled, I sat back, unable to do more than gawk.

It was everything. ID, food and water ration cards, even a current med card for an uptown clinic and pharmacy. Uptown, past the checkpoints.

Unbelievable.

I held the ID closer to the window. Maybe the ninja girl's, maybe some borrowed identity. Hard to tell from the fuzzy holo—longer hair, a goofy innocent grin—but nothing was obviously altered. Could still be a good forgery, but that would require electronic scrutiny I had no access to. Could that be done at the Souk as well?

Papers. The whole nine yards. A treasure trove. Maybe.

I flicked the stiff plastic with a fingernail. Wide awake now, I set the ID card down alongside the rest and stared at it all for a while.

One item remained: a sealed blue envelope from the bottom of the stack. I pried up the flap, eased out its contents. More paper, more rectangles of plastic. I laid this new set out on top of the rest. And truly could not believe my eyes.

Bright against the mud-colored blanket were exit and travel permissions, ferry vouchers, tickets, boarding passes, transit visas, immunity certificates, baggage stamps. As best I could tell, everything you'd need to score a trip off the Island and far inland, away from the encroaching seas, from the refugee camps, from everything.

I squinted at the top sheet of printed itinerary. Day of departure: April 5th.

What was today? Sometime in March? The tellers kept track. I could check at the desk come evening.

I flopped on my back, reminding myself to breathe.

Rubio told me once about lotteries from before, when ordinary folks won unimaginable sums of money and hadn't a clue what to do with it. I was sure I'd know . . . until now. My options? One, turn it all in, take my cut and let Rousseau deal with it. I'd get serious credit, doled out over time in food chits and medical care. Two, try to sell it myself. Fortunes were paid for legit documents, supposedly.

What would I do with a fortune?

Like, how to explain that new set of rain gear or clean sheets on my bunk? Even if I could wend a safe path through the black market, where to hide my sudden wealth while I spent it? Nowhere in the den, if stuff could vanish the minute I turned my back.

Okay. Third, final, and scariest option: use the stuff myself, at least some of it. The girl's ID might do for *me*, maybe good enough to get me through some checkpoints, score some proper clothing, maybe other uptown stuff. I'd have to clean up a lot, but we were a good match in age and stature. Okay, she looked a lot better fed, but was it our resemblance she'd noted when her gaze caught mine? She wouldn't have seen, with it shoved under my street cap, that my hair was the same blond as hers. I could grow mine out and practice looking naïve. Rube would say I already had that down pat.

About those lottery winners. Rube emphasized how no good had come of their sudden unearned luck. But after all I'd been through, didn't I deserve a little extra? And given the horrors going on in this town, this country, this whole wrecked world, how could taking a bit more than my share, just this once, rank high on the scale of evils?

My gut churned. Easy up, Glim. You don't want to toss all over your bunk.

Who was this person who'd taken over? Didn't I owe Rousseau and the den my life?

Go slow. Step by step.

Say I did use the tickets—where would I end up? Blinded by the glare of all the stamps and visas, I hadn't registered the final destination. I paged through the itinerary: Jersey Archipelago, Scranton International, Denver International, then four places I'd never heard of, each leg involving a smaller and more primitive mode of transportation. The last one said simply "Arkadia" and named a road intersection to stand at until "a friend came by."

Arkadia? A friend?

Sounded like code to me. Or bullshit. My street skepticism kicked in, but then I pictured the girl again, taking on two built-up young toughs and holding her own. Like, if the documents were worthless, why would she have gone to all that trouble?

Just had to figure it out.

SIX

V oices along the tier yanked me out of my wild pondering. The victory celebrants, turning in at last. I scurried to gather up the papers and stuff them into my gut wallet.

". . . an' there's no friggin' water!"

"Why it says just three showers at a time . . ."

"Hahaha! The las' one went all down his front!"

No bothering to keep the racket down. The whole tier shuddered as they clambered up to their bunks. If I'd been asleep, I'd sure be awake now.

Some of the muttering and banging stopped down below me. Rubio kicking at the dried mud from Peeto's shoes and complaining louder than usual.

I nosed through my drapes and leaned over the edge. "Had a few?"

Rubio flopped a hand back and forth. "Eh."

"Didya buy Louka one?"

"Did. More than." He was struggling to set his feet on the ladder. "But she took off with some ape named Ace. What kind of idiot calls himself Ace?"

I guffawed. Sure, now I could laugh about it.

"Why's that so funny?"

"Not you, dude, don't worry." I watched his upward progress. "You gonna make it okay?"

"I'm fine." When he said it so huffily, he usually wasn't, but he managed to hoist himself the last few rungs and tumble flat onto his bunk. "Ahh-hhh . . ." After a moment, he said, "There's all this talk of the shots fired at the raid. You hear any shots fired?"

"Fake news, according to Jake."

"Mmmm. Well, the lads are pissed. Calling for reprisal."

"Just what we need." I squinted at the wall clock down at the end of the tier. "Got four hours till reveille. You want a wake-up?"

But he was already asleep. Like I wanted to be. But I was too wired, too confused, and way too pissed at Peeto, even with no proof it was him who'd ripped me off.

Times I laid awake, I'd grab one of my two books off the dado shelf. Didn't matter which one. I knew them both by heart. If pages were missing, I made up the in-between, a new story each time. Reading soothed me, the dance of word and narrative.

But wait, I had a new one, with both its covers and the pages not all smudged or stuck together. Why not give it a try? I retrieved the old book, unwrapped it, and lay back, to begin at the beginning.

First thing up was the date: 22nd February, 1849.

Yes, this book was old, all right. I turned it into the brightening daylight, working to decipher the writer's scrawl and old-fashioned language:

> *"The following record made from time to time is not designed as an accurate or definite log showing the Latitude & Longitude of every day, but to merely give a few of the incidents which took place in the voyage to California around Cape Horn."*

That whole long trip by boat? No air travel in 1849, I knew that much. I called up a mental map to imagine the route, then realized I didn't know where it had started.

> *"After the usual trifling hindrances always consequent upon a start on such a long voyage, we came at last to the parting with friends and acquaintances, a time long to be remembered by me & by every other in our little band of adventurers. It was a singular feeling mixed up with joy, sorrow, hope & fear. It certainly is a consolation to know we have those friends that take so much trouble to be with us in the last hours of our stay in the land of our childhood. God bless them."*

Huh. Good luck with that. Rubio claimed to believe in God, though how anyone could these days was a mystery to me. He'd love this relic of another age, but to share it, I'd need a story of where it came from. Maybe say I found it in the mews house? He'd buy that, and see reason to keep it secret.

> *"We left the wharf at precisely 25 m. of Two O.C., on the 22nd day of Feb. 1849, the birthday of the father of our glorious union. I felt a*

little anxious at starting for sea, the weather looking as it did, winds S.E., and every indication of a storm. We sailed down the harbor while our friends cheered us and we answering heartily back now and then with a shot from our little cannonade, which made the echoes fly."

But what wharf? What harbor? I thought of evacuees leaving Manhattan. Were they seen off with such ceremony by their less frightened friends, who fully expected everyone to return, once the hysteria died down?

"And though our spirits were saddened and gloomy, yet we all were looking anxiously ahead, hoping to reap a golden reward for the risks we were to run."

Waves and water. Storms. A long and difficult voyage. Like an old romance. Facing terrible risks for the sake of a 'golden reward.' Say, like the risk I was taking, keeping valuables back from my den. This guy was whispering to me down the years. 'Cept I had no travel plans, not any time soon. If I kept the papers, I might use the local documents but surely sell the tickets. Wherever this Arkadia was, what would I do there, with no friends or relatives to take me in? Couldn't just throw yourself on the mercy of strangers, not in this world.

"We had duplicates of everything likely to be carried away, together with canvas and rigging sufficient for five years. We also had a very bountiful provision list: enough in store for at least eighteen months if we should get no fresh or put in even in that time; also about 300 gals. of water, liquors, wines, medicines, arms & ammunition, etc. I felt confident and had no fear of the result if a storm did occur."

I tried to imagine not being able to go outside the den for eighteen months. A long time to be self-sufficient. Or to be cooped up with the same people, whose company you hadn't chosen.

"Our Capt. thought it prudent to come to anchor off Fort Diamond and wait to see what the morning would show. After that, we piped all

hands forward to the cabin and cast lots for the berths, after which each one commenced arranging his sleeping apartment. I drew one of the worst, but by paying one dollar in hand, took the 2nd best in the cabin."

Could you pay someone off at Unca Joe for a better bunk? Certainly not Rousseau. No matter, I liked my top-corner bunk. Going to sea sounded a lot like den life: close quarters, competition for resources, a world of storms and deep water outside.

Where was Fort Diamond . . . if it still existed? The yawns were catching up with me. The antique sentences were as good as a lullaby. Tomorrow was soon enough for the showers, especially with the water used up. Barely remembered to hide the book away in my wallet. One fleeting thought about what I'd do to Peeto, and I tumbled into sleep.

SEVEN

"Rise and shine, dudes!"

The call rang down the tier. Night shift wake-up, 4 p.m. by the wind-up clock in the hallway, and a lot of us dragging hard out of our bunks that afternoon. I heard Rubio coughing, and knocked at his bunk on the way by.

"Already?" He stuck his head around his drape, yawning.

"Don't you just look like hell."

He groaned. "Does watered beer make you piss more?"

"Not a clue. Listen, you hear Peeto go by?"

Best to catch the little creep before he went down to the Mess. Wasn't sure how to come at him. A straight-out accusation would only net a denial—but I'd figure something out once I clamped hands on him.

"Why would I want to?" Rubio considered vaguely. "Why would you?"

"Never mind. See you down."

I washed every day, almost a compulsion. I hated feeling the way Peeto's hands always looked, so I knew it was a habit laid down long ago, a shard of my past. I honored it. But not everyone did. Direct orders were not Rousseau's style, but on shut-in days, the den got so ripe, he'd send someone around to make pointed suggestions.

Pausing outside the women's showers, I weighed my options. It was a mob scene inside. Big Gracie was holding court under the center LED cluster, her blow-by-blow of her teller-tussle ricocheting off the concrete and repurposed subway tile at high volume. A few of the younger girls cheered her on, pulling on work clothes, crowding around the single mirror to braid up their hair for the shift. Didn't know any of them too well—they bunked in Grace's tier. I could get in and out pretty quick. I went in and grabbed my scrap of towel off its hook.

"Any word on Rivera?" I called over the gurgle of water and the slap of wet feet.

Gracie paused mid-story. "Yeah, she got cut up bad, but she'll make it okay."

"Good news." So Peeto hadn't ramped up the incident to suit his purpose. Getting chased on the streets or even busted up some was one thing.
But getting sliced and diced? That made me shiver.

A corner spigot came free, so I ducked in and soaped up fast. The water
was outdoor temperature, warm enough to cut the grease and dirt. If it went
below sixty, heaters would supposedly kick in. Had yet to see that happen.

The woman next spigot over wasn't cheering. Ash-brown skin drawn
tight over raised veins, gray dusting her stiff curls. Rosemary or Thyme,
some herb name I couldn't bring to mind.

I nodded toward Gracie and her audience. "She say how it went down?"

"Ummm. Likely a guy from Tall Tommy."

A solid, older den over west. "Not them!"

She shrugged.

"But we have a deal with them."

"Well, it was dark. But she saw a lot of tattoos."

Tall Tommy, for whatever reason, was into full-body decoration. They
were also—or at least, their leader was—famously hot-tempered, and dens
tended to clump like to like. But we'd never been warned against them.
"Why would they go after her?"

"Why would anyone?"

"I mean, it could've been anyone . . . some rogue, even an Adder. Adders
like tattoos."

"An Adder would've finished her off, just for the fun of it."

Then dragged her home for the cook pot, if rumors were actual.

My neighbor lifted her face to her spigot, lips tight. This water you did
not want to swallow. "Word is the deals aren't being enforced like they
used to."

The trickle down my back was turning colder. "Why not?"

"Hard to say." Her look said: yet another thing I can do nothing about.

"But that means . . ."

"Yep. The streets will get a whole lot nastier." She chortled bleakly. "Don't
know why anyone's surprised. The calm after the storm never lasts long."

I sucked in my lip. "That's what Rubio says."

"Old Mr. Doom and Gloom?"

"He's not so old." Just looks it, I allowed. She had to be near senior
herself.

"Figure of speech." She reached to shut the water off. She was missing part of two fingers and had ridged burn scars from wrist to elbow. "He a friend of yours?"

"Tier-mate." Didn't want her thinking I was dating him or anything. "He means well."

"Could've fooled me. But in that case . . ." She leaned in to whisper. "Tell him maybe lighten up a bit. Give his cred a boost, y'know?"

"His cred?"

"Yeah. People take it bad, his talking against the den." She glanced away to check who might be listening.

"He doesn't!" Well, of course he did, but . . . "I mean, only that he thinks it's important to share ideas, work out the kinks in the system. Improve things. For the future of the den."

"Well, maybe he shouldn't share so loudly." She floated a grin, like this was all just casual gossip. "Look, it's nice you're loyal. Why not hint that toning it down might win him better luck with the ladies. As it is, they're afraid to be seen with him."

I returned a rueful nod. Rubio was desperate to snag a girlfriend. She'd hit on the one thing that might convince him to play politics, and it was kindly meant. But there was a warning there, too: tell your friend the walls have ears, and they're not liking what they hear. As a senior, she might be close to Rousseau. "Thanks. I'll pass that on."

Minutes later, I was dried, dressed, and on my way downstairs.

Returning day-shifters crowded the teller lines as I pushed through Main toward the din of voices, dish rattle, and the scrape of chairs on concrete inside the Mess. I paused outside the doors. My guilt, the bag's theft, now Rubio in trouble—my brain was buzzing.

The Mess, windowless and starkly lit by solar LEDs, was not a room you wanted to spend time in if you cared about looking your best or preserving your hearing. The ceiling was low, amping the constant clatter. The cinderblock walls were painted whatever color we could scavenge enough of to cover all of one. The mismatched tables were always jammed at mealtime, like now, breakfast for us, dinner for day shifters, and no one thought about keeping their voice down.

A roar erupted by the Blue Wall as I came in—Rousseau's lads clustered at a big table, fists pounding wood and metal, one guy up on a bench, bellowing and gesturing, and a crowd gathering to egg him on. Wouldn't you know, it was my old pal Ace.

"That raid was a call to action! If we let 'em get away with it, they'll be back tomorrow and the next day and the next!"

I fast-stepped past, surprised he could muster up such a complete sentence. But he was clearly their epicenter: blondly handsome, cheeks flushed with bloodlust, voice pitched to carry. Hard to come by matching duds in storm-wracked Manhattan, but this crowd was sure working on a uniform: their tees were all some shade of red. A disturbingly ruddy swath against the wall's peeling aquamarine.

I grabbed toast and a precious slice of our roof-grown ham at the service hatch, greeted the cooks inside, paid my chit, signed for my milk ration. Not just the powder and water glop today, so the roof goats must be milking again. No sign of Peeto anywhere.

Jake and Spunk had claimed one of the small tables over by Green, as far away from Blue as they could get. I was halfway to join them before I saw they were doubling down on Rubio about something. Not so you'd notice unless you were looking, but I always was. Rubio hated being scolded, but these were the two guys in the den he most liked hanging with, so he just slumped in his chair, spooning eggs into his mouth and scowling. Then a white-aproned figure glided up to Jake's side, half-filled tray balanced on his hip, and the lecture abruptly ended.

Jake, his black hair more mussed than usual, smoothed his growl and produced a weary smile. "Hey, there, Sam. Looking to clear up?"

Times I was feeling most confused and sorry for myself, I sat at one of Sam's tables, for a stiff reminder that things could be worse. Seemed just the day for it. Sam would find this ruckus deeply unsettling.

Say-it-Again Sam was the surest sign of a good heart behind Rousseau's stern façade. He didn't go out. Ever. He'd never find his way back to the den. Rousseau gave him in-house chores: feeding the chickens in the roof coops, busing tables in the Mess, and he had that down pretty well. He was neat as a pin, wore button shirts with rolled-down sleeves, and was always clean-shaved. New razors were scarce, so Sam used a battered straight razor that some picker had brought in as a curiosity, plus soap we made in the kitchen. He never cut himself. Given Rousseau's disapproval of facial hair, lots of the guys traded food or goods for Sam's careful barbering. Several times during his Mess shift, he'd retreat to the men's to comb his few gray hairs into more precise order.

He'd worked in restaurants before, so the Mess fit his comfort level.

Sometimes he forgot what slot the forks or spoons went in, or he'd throw perfectly good leftovers into the compost pails, but he always did up his collar and tucked in his shirt. Rubio said he should have 'OCD' tattooed on his forehead.

About once a meal, every meal, Sam cornered some willing—or not so willing—sucker who'd just settled in to savor a ration of home brew.

"Say it again," Sam would beg quietly. "I forgot what you told me."

And whoever sat nearest would begin the story of Abel's Wave or some other Wave, then pass the turn around. I always begged off. No way stuff I'd only heard secondhand could satisfy the stark urgency in Sam's eyes. Yep, my deal could've been a lot worse.

Just as I was pulling out a stool, I spotted Peeto sidling back into the food line, bowl in hand. Likely gonna claim his first dropped on the floor. No way I could call him out here in the Mess. Besides, I wanted to hear what was up with these guys. Peeto had to wait.

"Little snake!" I slid into the space between Spunk and Rubio, hoping to diffuse the tension a little.

Rube's arm jerked. "Who, me?"

Did I say it out loud? "No! Sorry!" Get a grip, Glim! "What's with those guys at Blue?"

"Pissant heroics." Rubio shoveled more scrambled egg into his mouth. He had a stretched-out sweatshirt layered over his street tee, so probably his chills were back. "They can't believe someone out there's daring to diss them."

"Louka's beery boyfriend."

He snorted. "Breeding will tell . . ."

"Listen." I leaned in close. "I had a chat in the showers you need to hear about, but not here." The noise swelled over at Blue. "Are they serious about a reprisal raid?"

Rube grimaced across the litter of mugs and porridge bowls. "They seem to think so."

"Against who?"

"Ain't figured that out yet, have they."

"And Rousseau's cool with it?"

"Hmmm. An interesting question. Rather an overt challenge to his non-aggression policy, wouldn't you say?"

That irked me. "So you support this mayhem because it makes trouble for Rousseau?"

"Of course I don't support it. But I am curious about how it will play out."

"Careful whacha wish fer," muttered Spunk, scraping the last bit of rice from his bowl.

Across the table, Jake was running an old storm story for Sam, a dramatic and personal version with himself as the star. As he got into it, his posture lightened and the moody angles of his face lost years. I loved watching Jake perform. Easy then to imagine him framed on screen, sculpted by sidelight, romancing some starlet.

". . . the rain was pounding way up in the grid. We really had to project. Maybe forty people in the house. The stage manager wanted to call the show, but the second act had just gone up and we all said, no, no, no, we can . . ."

I tuned in with one ear, having heard it before.

Spunk screeched his chair closer and jutted his whiskery horse-chin. He was bare-armed in a tank top. He never felt cold. "Someone steal yer lunch?"

"What?" Steal? My shoulders slid into lockdown. "What d'you mean?"

"Yer frownin' fit ta beat."

"Me? Oh. Just listening to Jake."

He grinned. "Dat'll do it, alright."

I didn't really believe Spunk could read my mind, but sometimes, 'specially when he fixed those sleepless eyes on me, he came way too close. I straightened up and waved my fork toward Blue. "Hard to eat with all that going on!"

He threw a hard stare down the hall. "S'like dey jess learned dey got balls."

"Couldn't you stop them?"

"Me? Nah. Dat's Cline's how-dya-do." Spunk alone used Rousseau's first name. Always gave me a start—was it true familiarity or an affectation?

"Well, somebody ought to. How come they can say whatever they want, and Rubio can't? He's not screaming at the top of his lungs!"

Rubio ticked me a glance and shook his head once.

Spunk said, "If ya doan git dat, ya bettah learn."

This wasn't one I was going to win. I let it pass and dug into my food.

Jake uncorked his water bottle, took a swig. He was always gentle with Sam, but he'd run out of steam. "Hold on, Sam, okay? Let me get some chow in." Being just off shift, this was dinner for him. His performance glow faded, leaving him irritable, too tired even to flirt.

"Rough day at the Souk?" I was sympathetic, but also curious. If the Souk was to be a goal, I'd need to know more about it than I did.

"No more than usual," he mumbled into his stew bowl.

Sam set down his tray and dropped into the last empty chair, smoothing wrinkles from his cook's apron. He folded his clean, pale hands precisely in front of him, but his eyes followed Jake's every spoonful.

"Sam, Sam, let the man eat. My turn." Rube shoved his half-eaten food aside and cleared his throat to compete with the racket from Blue. Worried me how hoarse he was. "So, ten years after Jake was treading water on West 46th, I was . . ."

Rubio's storm story was dark and chaotic, heavy with gory detail and the gross failure of "the authorities" to manage the situation. At some point, he'd always exclaim, "And the politicians ran for their lives!" Sam grinned and clapped his soft palms, even though by his storm, most of them were long gone from the Island. If the center of power moves to high ground, the politicians are bound to follow.

Thing was, he'd forget it all by the next day, maybe the next hour. My past was hidden in shock and trauma. Sam's past was intact, but brain injuries had wiped his ability to remember anything since. So it never mattered what storm you were talking about. It was all one big storm to Sam, and he was always riveted.

Any doubt which of us was the most tragic?

Sam was in his sixties, so there was plenty he did remember. The early years of the Big Melt, the seas rising and the storms' increasing frequency and ferocity. He could tell you how denial and corrupt leadership congealed into global paralysis. He could detail the belated efforts to prepare: the flood walls and dykes, the tunnel plugs and pump stations, the solar panels sprouting on every rooftop among gardens and windmills. It made me shiver when he described his building in the Village, how after a while, only a few apartments on each floor were occupied, and then, only his. Then came Superstorm Hasan, and Sam's memory went out with the tide.

We all got into telling our own storm story. Each time a tale was told, its trauma seemed farther away. Maybe why mine still held me in its grip. No story yet to tell.

Rube had just started in on Misha's giant surge, how he'd watched it roll in and engulf the bottom floors of his office building, where he and his few diehard colleagues were living and working, how the foundations shook.

His hands swiveled in the air and his brush of hair seemed to stand up as if in a gale. Abruptly, Sam noticed the clutter on the table as if for the first time. He stood, crammed his tray with empty bowls and mugs, rearranged them twice, then hustled off for the kitchen, chasing some distant alarm only he could hear.

"Overload." Rubio dropped his arms to his thighs, spent.

"Or maybe it was them . . ."

The rabble-rousers were on the move. They'd fanned out from their corner, bulling around among the tables, goading everyone to high-five their bellows for revenge. A total violation of the mess hall code of conduct.

Spunk said, "Heah dey come . . ."

Jake and Spunk were huddled over mugs of herbal, having moved on to discussing the other dens. A favorite topic, based mostly on hearsay, but as Rousseau's right hands, these two had visited the dens we had deals with, so had some clue what they were talking about. I listened in.

"Ladysmith's wort' keepin' an eye on." The tense curl of Spunk's bony back said he and Jake were ignoring the approaching racket on purpose.

Jake brushed crumbs off his vest of many pockets. "Greenhorns."

"Mebbe. But growin'. Der gittin' da idea. Maxine takes in more newbies den mos'. Even some we olda dens t'row out."

"Which keeps the skill level minimal. Between us, Tom, and Empire, we've pretty much siphoned off the best. What's left, you might not want to let in the door."

The human surge crested loudly behind us and suddenly, Rube and me were getting nudged on the shoulders. Ace and two identical, red-shirted buddies.

"All rise for Unca Joe!" Nudge, nudge. "Stand up for your den!" Nudge, nudge.

"Ow!" I saw Ace was pummeling Rubio extra hard. "Leave him alone, you creeps!"

"Only the strong survive!"

Rubio buried his head in his arms. I started pummeling back, but it was like pounding stone. Spunk reached sideways, grabbed my wrists, and pressed them into my lap. Then he rose, nice and easy, and put his nose right up in Ace's face. One hand rested on the big Kevlar sheath on his belt. "Das enough. Bugga fuckin' off."

Ace tensed and got snarly, but his buddies plucked at his T-shirt.

"Not him," one advised.

Real quiet now at our table. Pretty quick, Ace saw the light. He clapped Spunk on the bicep, then grabbed his arm, hoisting it into the air. "Thank you, brother, for your support!"

Spunk jerked free. "Get lost."

And after a few grumbles, they did, taking their noise elsewhere. We settled back to our meal. Or un-settled. Rubio's jaw was tight, his thin neck flushed with humiliation.

"Now dat can't go on," Spunk said, as the normal mess hall buzz surrounded us again.

"Rousseau's been too soft with them," Jake agreed. "Best have a word with him."

Trying to lighten things up, I said, "We should send them over to Ladysmith's."

"Serve 'em right," nodded Spunk.

From the depths of his turmoil, Rubio said, "Maxine's all right."

That did it. Sides were chosen, the lads forgotten. For the time being, at least.

Jake shook his head. "Yes and no. All her best people get fed up and go looking for another den. Some place more . . . managed."

"Or micromanaged," retorted Rubio. "Nothing wrong with a little less restriction. You just don't like that women run the place."

"Me?" Jake's dark brows arched in amusement. "Who you talkin' to?"

Spunk's elbow dug sharp into my side. "He's pissed dey ain' invited him for da night."

"I'm working on that." Jake shied a grin at me like a ball I was meant to field. "Besides, plenty of fine ladies right here at home."

But Rubio wasn't letting levity take hold. "Over there, everyone's got a vote."

"Indeed they do," Jake said. "And then Maxine does whatever she wants."

"That's not what I hear . . ."

Time for another redirect. "You think it's true a Tommy cut up Rivera?"

Jake stared at me. "What?"

Spunk sucked his teeth. "Wouldn't be spreadin' dat rumah aroun'."

"Tom would never go for that," Jake insisted. "He's the one pushing for a cooperative police force."

"Jess wha' we need," muttered Spunk.

Jake looked at him. "Wouldn't be the worst idea."

Rubio crossed his arms, readying his bomb. "At least Tommy lets them carry. And Maxine allows edged weapons."

Oh, Rubio. Just the sort of remark the shower woman warned about. Rousseau's weapons ban limited us to the barely lethal, like the little jack-knife I carried in my gut wallet.

Spunk straightened. "Yeah, an' Tom's always havin' ta break up stand-offs in da Mess! Moah dan one firefight right in da den!" He eyed Rubio sideways. "Dat whachu want?"

"The Souk makes the Tommys check their weapons at the gate," Jake added. "They're a rough lot over there."

"Rousseau's got da right ideah."

Rubio's chin jutted. "Easy for you to say, with that big old blade on your belt."

Spunk's hunting knife was an object of envy, with its ten-inch blade and wicked edge.

He shrugged. "Priv'lege of rank."

"And a deterrent," Jake noted. "Imagine a moment ago if all those revved-up boyos could pull a weapon."

Rube's mouth thinned. "BlackAdder wouldn't have done Vanya if he had a gun."

I kicked Rubio under the table to warn him off where he was going.

"You don' know dat." Spunk started stacking his dishes.

"And we don't know it was BlackAdder," said Jake.

Vanya was Rubio's best buddy before me, till he staggered home one night and bled to death on the floor of Main before the medics could save him. BlackAdder was the rogue den of our nightmares. They got blamed for anything truly horrible that went down.

"So, you'd know what to do with a gun if you had one?" Jake scoffed.

"Yeah, I would. I had one before. Didn't you?"

"What? Hell, no. Why would I?"

Rubio let the tiniest curl of satisfaction ease his glower. "I thought every-one did."

Spunk nodded thoughtfully. "Mos' did, once t'ings started goin' sideways."

"Fuck you both," Jake growled. "I'm an actor, not a vigilante!"

I played a compromise card. "I heard Revelations lets you check out a weapon when you leave the den."

"See? Someone's got some sense," Rubio seconded.

I nodded, ready to move on.

Not Rubio. He had a rat by the tail. "At least Maxine picked a building taller than the next wave. Ladysmith's won't be needing to move anytime soon."

Jake shoved his chair back with a screech. "Give it a damn rest, will you? You'll friggin' fight about anything!"

Nearby tables glanced our way, sure that trouble was starting up again.

And there was Sam, his brow wrinkled in confusion, easing in between Jake and Rubio, his tray held up like a shield. "So, tell me again. Are they all gone? Everyone but us?"

I smiled him relief and gratitude. He couldn't tell you any of our names, but he had a true instinct for diplomacy.

Jake exhaled noisily, white-knuckled on the table edge. "No, Sam, not all. Plenty still living uptown, in the high and dry. And the rest'll be back, soon as the water goes down." He rose, replaced his chair deliberately, picked up his dishes, and stalked off toward the return hatch.

"Nah look whachu did," scolded Spunk.

"Not my fault if he's deep in avoidance," Rubio returned.

Sam's laser gaze focused on Rubio. "Uptown?"

"Sure, Sam. Inwood. Washington Heights, Fort Tryon. West Harlem and the upper West Side. All that."

"But who?" Sam would unspool a list of lost neighbors and friends if you even hinted you were willing to listen. I'd sat through it once, in case some name rang a bell. None did.

"Nobody ya'd know, Sammy." Spunk got up. He never saw the point of the Sam ordeal, plus he had a girlfriend in C Tier. Maybe hoping for a quickie before heading out.

"You don't know," Rubio countered. "He might've."

"He lived downtown."

"Even so, he could've. I knew uptowners. Clients, mostly, but I knew them."

"La-de-dah!" Spunk poked Rube in the shoulder, grinned and sauntered off.

Rubio scowled after him. "Uptowner staff, then! Who stayed on. Or casino workers, hotel staff, waiters in restaurants he worked in, maybe the owners!"

But Spunk was through the doors.

I said, "Gotta go check my draw."

Rube threw me a look. Like, how could I leave when he hadn't won a single argument?

"Which restaurants?" I heard Sam ask as the doors closed behind me.

And Rube would dutifully list the few left uptown, along with their much-reduced menus. He might even add the hardy handful of hotels, casinos, and clubs still open for business in the uptown towers, serving tourists from the Mainland who boated in between storms for a day or a week of urban rustic and nostalgia.

Life, it seems—and commerce—will always fill an empty niche.

After all, as Rubio would insist, this is still America.

EIGHT

S o, it's not quite right my claiming that *everything* before Abel was a blank. Or, not quite *accurate*, Jenn would say, correcting my grammar.

When I came to in the Ward so vague and silent, the medics were sure I had brain damage. But they'd put paper and pencil by my cot in case it was just my voice I'd lost. A few days later, I started writing down the days of the week. Numbers came next, then the fifty-two states. Weird, huh? I mean, how the brain works? The shrink said it could be my language center just firing at random. That's until I put the numbers to work in basic math and finally croaked out the obvious: "Where am I?"

Or something like that. Anyhow, the physical world and the words to describe it came back to me in fits and starts. The door would open, spit out a bunch of words and concepts, then slam shut again. Memory quakes, I called them, 'cause they were seismic and left me wiped to the core. After a big one, I'd sleep the whole day. Like the kid two beds over with his seizures.

And still missing in action was how all those words and their real-time objects fit together as a history of events, and what my connection was to any of it. As if I'd walked through my pre-Abel life touching nothing, leaving no trace. A ghost. The invisible girl.

Might explain why I liked books. They had a beginning and a middle, not just an end, and it all tied together somehow. Lot of comfort in that.

But as the real-life Mess doors swung behind me, I knew that between Sam and me, I had the better deal. Starting from scratch wasn't so bad as long as you could hold on to each day's revelations and apply them to the next. That's what a baby does, right? That's how you build a life.

Out in Main, the evening hustle was in full swing, plus a lot of extra buzz due to the attack on Rivera. More than one dark-shifter—women, mostly—muttering, "Maybe not the best idea, going out the first night after?"

On the other hand: "One bad dude ain't makin' me run tail!"

Or: "Just let him try me! He'll be friggin' sorry!"

And so on.

Gracie was ready to go hunting. I could've stayed in, since I'd brought so much home the night before. But that could be seen as boasting. Or bring an eye on me I didn't want. So I lined up at the duty counter to get my night's assignment like usual.

I was only five from the front when I saw Peeto slink away from the Swap Desk with those old boots I'd mentioned clutched in his grimy rat paws. I ducked out of line and pushed after him through the crowd. I caught him at the door and hooked an arm around his shoulders, making it look friendly 'case anyone was watching.

"Yo, Peeto, gotta talk to you, dude."

"Huh? What?" He knew something was off. I'd never laid a finger on him, never mind let him touch me. He tried to move past, but I body-checked him sideways, pressed his back against the wall. I said I'm not a fighter, but Peeto didn't scare me. He hugged the boots to his chest, like maybe it was them I was after.

"Who tossed my bunk?"

"Yer what?" He clutched the boots tighter. "When?"

"This morning." Didn't want too big a scene, so I shook him only a little. "Who was your friend while you were distracting me?"

"I wasn't . . . wait, whachu nailin' me fer?"

"Well, funny thing happened. My grab bag was on my bunk, then you came in yammering, and later my bag was gone."

He narrowed his eyes at me, like, was I having him on? "You forgot where ya left it?"

"Not a chance!" I shook him again. "Where is it?"

"It's out in the mudroom!"

"What?" That slowed me down some. "Don't bullshit me!"

"I'm not! You go look!"

"How'd it get there?"

"How am I supposta know! It's yer bag!"

"But maybe you put it there!"

"No way!" Peeto rolled his whole head, like he was dealing with an id-iot. "I just *seen* it, gettin' my old sneaks to turn in fer these." He put the boots up to my face. They were dank with mildew. "Like you said I should."

I wasn't winning this bout either. "How'd you know which one's mine?"

"I got eyes, don't I? See it every night ya leave the tier."

Couldn't deny that, and now we were attracting attention. I eased off my grip, dusted his rucked-up tee into place. "Okay. You show me. I ain't lettin' go till I see it."

We nosed through the throng and into the mudroom. Sure enough, my old grab bag hung in a cubby alongside yesterday's dried-out street shirt. Too weird.

Peeto did a spread-hands shrug, like he was sorry to be proved right.

"Empty!" I knew, even before I hefted it.

"End of shift, right? What'd ya expect?"

"I had my night's claim in there and now it's gone." Never mind the blister packs I'd kept back but hadn't claimed.

He got all droopy-eyed sympathetic. "Oh, yeah, that's bad, alright. Like what I tole Jake about my sneaks. Ya can't leave nothing around if ya wanna hang onto it."

So somehow, it ended up my fault for not being vigilant. But who . . . ?

The perfect crime. Steal the bag, take the contents, return the bag, no proof of theft. Too clever for Peeto? I'd been so sure it was him, but now I wondered. While I swore at the tightened ties, needing to check inside, Peeto slipped away into the rush heading out for the night. Mission not accomplished. I hoped Rivera's knifer went after him this time.

And now I'd be late for the work call, which we shouldn't be having anyway. Fuming, I went back to the duty desk, elbowing against the outbound tide. The line was shortening, so my turn came quick.

"Glimmer 56: East Side, Madison and 60th."

That sucked the rage right out of me. I almost asked if he had it wrong, but the duty officer barked me away. "Next!"

I side-stepped out of line, taking it in. Whooh! Fate or coincidence? You got an intersection, and your duty was to work a five-block square around it. So, not only my first chance at the Midtown East Side, but well within range of the Souk, just when I'd turned my thoughts to it. I got out fast, before he changed his mind.

Up on the walkway, Rubio and Jenn stood along the rail, chatting like old buddies, which I'd been sure they weren't. Maybe a show of unity in honor of Rivera? The yellowish dusk polished Jenn's hair to a cap of gold, bright against Rubio's darkness. Hot as an oven out there, but he was bundled up and shivering. No question his malaria was acting up again.

"S'up, dudes?" I called.

They looked up and waved but put their chat away. I didn't take it personally. Likely just gossip, which they both loved, even though Rube'd tell you not to listen to such crap.

As I came up, he drawled, "That a shit-eating grin or a grimace of pain?"

"Shock of the draw."

"Why?" Jenn looked worried. "Where'd you get?"

"Madison and 60th." I did a little goal dance. "Best post ever?"

"All right!" We thumb-bumped.

I leaned against the railing. Maybe their chat been . . . well, personal? So great if Jenn would be Rube's girlfriend! But their views of the future were polar opposites: she so desperate to leave the Island, he eager to make a better life right here. That alone would keep them apart. "I've never done the East Side."

"Not all that different." Rubio waved an arm uptown like he could see it all. "Still got to climb a shitload of stairs. And there's more chance of running into surprise residents."

"Of a classier sort," Jenn put in.

"A classier mugger?"

"No, really!" Jenn was happy for me. "No shaky walkways, more dry land, less flood damage, even the occasional police patrol."

I frowned. "And that's a good thing?"

"Sure. They keep the rogue factor down. Don't worry. They're easy enough to avoid. Meanwhile, if you find a stash, the goods are high-quality."

"A big if, since it's also the most picked-over sector." Rubio's gaze was drawn aside as a chorus of shouts rose from below. A burst of torchlight on water, cascading rings of reflection. "Well, look at that."

The canoe crews were launched and circling the Lagoon. Rubio lifted his hands to start up mocking applause.

I yanked them down. "Are you insane?"

In the flaring light, I'd seen faces who'd been pounding on us in the Mess.

He sighed. "Might just be."

I peered across the oily water. "Are they really going on a raid?"

"Maybe just a drill," said Jenn.

"Who will they go after?"

Rubio yawned hugely. "Who's on the hate list this week?"

"We don't hate anyone," Jenn returned.

"Speak for yourself." The bow flares threw Rube's thin face into harsh relief.

So right, I thought. They'll think of someone.

"They'll go stir up the ants' nest," Jenn fretted, then turned her back on the wannabe warriors as if they weren't there. "Yes, the East Side was always different. I grew up on the West Side, and going east was like visiting another planet. They were much more proactive when the weather got really bad."

"West Side is blessed with higher ground. Bedrock." Rubio watched the canoes as their circles widened, in and out of the darker corners where the side streets crossed and taller buildings threw an opaque shade. The crews were stoking up their courage. "But the East Side had the resources. They'd lived through the failure of the Big U, so they started earlier, got the pass-thrus legislated and built before the water was too high. My firm designed a few of them."

"Cool!" I'd never seen a pass-thru, but knew them from picker training. Whole floors cleared in neighboring high-rises, creating a public footpath above the high-water mark on a north/south diagonal up the East Side.

"We did some of the footbridges across the streets and avenues, too. Not always in the most logical place, thanks to various deniers who refused to give up their gazillion-dollar digs for the public good. It helps to know your way around them."

On a roll again: New-York-born-and-bred, can't imagine living anywhere else. But the details of how Rube got left behind aren't so upbeat. His malaria acted up during Superstorm Misha's approach. His firm's Mainland office sent a 'copter to evacuate the diehard remaining staff. But Rube was so sick, the pilot decided he was contagious and took off without him. After the storm, no one came looking for him. He called it 'culling,' like it was a rational thing to do. Even when his city dumped him like garbage, he stayed loyal. Manhattan was Rubio's true den.

"I'll manage," I said. "I have a map."

"They're handing out maps now?"

I grinned and tapped my temple.

Jenn said, "Least you'll be under cover if it rains."

We looked to the sky in unison. Another heavy moist night like the last one, just as hot and even stiller. Ominously still.

"Make that a 'when,'" Rubio said.

Our roof station only gave us local conditions. We looked to AM radio for long-range data, though broadcasts were irregular, so home-site prediction was a matter of instinct and experience.

"Where're you headed?" I asked Jenn.

"45th and Broadway. Jake's old-time beat."

I'd worked that area on occasion. "Those old theatres give me the creeps. So big and dark, and there's nothing much in 'em."

"There's ghosts. Jake swears they're haunted. Hey, we're scaring me! Good picking! See you at downtime." She gave a mock salute and strode off along the walkway, heading uptown.

Maybe there was a new outfit in my future. When Jenn went off with such bravado, she'd usually recalled a wholesale fabric store or garment studio within her night's draw. Not the street-level variety—to the trade only. Up a few stories, safe from the Wave. IT was her livelihood before, but as she would say, fashion was her passion.

I was all set to follow when Rubio pinned my arm to the rail.

"Don't want to miss this, do you?"

Rousseau had fired up our biofuel outboard and hauled up inside the ring of canoes. He cut the sputtering engine and stood, his bare chest sheened, his favorite vest dark with sweat. Balancing easily, he stepped to the center of the boat. "Okay, lads. Listen up!"

The paddlers hushed and slewed their bows inward, stroking gentle figure-eights to keep the canoes in place.

"Such reverence," muttered Rubio.

I dug an elbow into his ribs. "You want them after you twice in one night?"

Rousseau's resonant baritone carried over the water. He didn't have to shout. "It's a hot night and I know you're eager to go out and kick some butt."

A round of cheers and manly roaring. Paddles slapping the water.

"You think Jake writes his dialogue? Any moment it'll be, 'We few, we happy few, we band of . . . '"

"Will you shut up?" I hissed.

Rousseau signaled for quiet. "I get it. I do. You want someone to pay for hurting our little girl! But hear me! We do things differently, here at Unca Joe."

Murmurs only this time. Paddles dripped. Concentric ripples chased each other toward the edges of the flooded square.

"We do not provoke. We do not attack. We don't even know who we're after."

Total silence. The water gone still as a mirror, reflecting the deepening sky.

"So, instead? We defend."

"Uh-oh," Rubio breathed in my ear. "Daddy's taking their toys away."

But in the circle of torchlight, Rousseau's grin showed pale in his dark face, fervent and rousing. He stretched both arms toward the leaden sky and clenched his fists. Rubio might question his sincerity, but I could not. "And to defend, we must be able. We must be ready. We must be strong!"

Hopeful murmurs again.

"So, tonight's mission will be a drill. You will not engage. You will . . ."

"Like Jenn said." I was relieved.

"Ah well." Rubio seemed as disappointed as the crews, maybe because Rousseau had done something he actually agreed with. Smart, not to shut their anger down completely. Even a drill would blow off some steam.

"No point in a fleet of canoes going up against a speedboat," I said.

"Or whatever else they might run into." Rubio coughed, spat over the rail. We pushed off and moved along uptown. "I heard he was a priest before."

"He. You mean, Rousseau? C'mon!"

"Yep. A Catholic priest. Some say a monk. In some radical urban order. Dedicated to vows of poverty and serving the poor and homeless."

"Then I guess he still is."

Rubio shook his head. "I can't quite see it."

"Why?" This could be treacherous ground. "What, he's not, like, y'know, holy enough?"

He coughed longer this time and paused to spit again, then wiped his mouth with a scrap of cloth. "I'm guessing you weren't Catholic. No, I'm sure you weren't. But I was. And I knew embezzling priests, pill-popping priests, fornicating and pedophile priests, priests who were abusive or drunks. Think of a sin, they committed it. But even so, even the worst of them, they all had this . . . I don't know . . . basic fear of God. With Rousseau, it's like he's doing the work God *ought* to be doing, if only he believed in Him."

I wasn't getting into matters of belief with Rubio. "What does it matter, as long as the work gets done? Not a lot of other people bothering."

He shrugged. "Maybe it doesn't matter."

But I knew he thought it did. "Maybe you should stay in tonight, Rube."

"Why?"

"You don't sound too good."

"Que sera. I drew the Flatiron. Don't get that chance too often."

"Sick and sweaty, and you're still obsessing about architecture?"

"Architecture is my life," he replied loftily. And then, "At least it was."

You couldn't ever tell Rubio what was good for him, so I nodded and linked elbows. "C'mon. I'll walk you partway."

NINE

W e hiked uptown as night fell in earnest, taking the Second Avenue walkway just to 11th, where pavement poked above water for a single block. We dropped to street level and crossed over to Third, pocked and puddled but mostly above the tide.

"Plenty dry ground for us tonight." Rubio was actually smiling.

"And new territory. I get to see real trees!"

Downtown, the trees had all drowned or been swept away in one surge or another. Or cut up for firewood. Even uptown trees struggled, with too-wet feet, whipped by coastal winds, unsure of what climate they were living in.

"Don't let the novelty put you off guard."

"Why would I?"

Now it was just us, maybe I'd tell him about the drugs I'd tried to cadge for him. The ninja girl didn't have to figure in. But first, I downloaded my chat in the shower.

Rubio tossed his head. "Boss can't take a little constructive criticism?"

"It's not just Rousseau. Why else all that special treatment at breakfast?"

"I don't care what those assholes think, if they ever do."

"Rube, it's not what they think. It's what they'll do to you."

"Might does not make right," he muttered.

"I'll carve that on your memorial plaque."

Maybe I wouldn't share my other news. Rube would never rat on me, but what if he decided reporting the theft might push his agenda with Rousseau, like, see what your rules and regulations make people do? Anyhow, better know my own mind about the papers before I asked anyone else what to do with them.

At 20th, we neared the old mansions of Gramercy Park, with their kitchen basements awash with the swelling river and a faint, airy glow from the unusual number of still-inhabited upper floors.

Rubio gazed up at a high row of lit windows. "Really old money is set in its ways. A lot of them supported the Venice plan."

"The way you tell it, the Venice idea was seen as too radical."

"Too romantic." He nudged my arm. "You're going up by the Causeway? Walk west to the park and we'll say hi to Mr. Booth."

"Causeway's the quickest route, right?"

He nodded. "But kind of exposed. All civilians up there."

He meant, not denfolk. "Time I learned to deal with that."

A block over, we stopped to peer through tall iron fencing at the sodden paths inside Gramercy Park proper, where the statue of Edwin Booth surveyed dead formal gardens and bare ranks of trees drowning in the rising water table.

"What Jenn said about security patrols? Try to look like you belong, or they'll nab you. The Causeway is uptowner turf."

"What're they gonna do, arrest me? No more jails."

"No, but they might have some fun with you, before tossing you over the edge."

To contain my shudder, I studied the sturdy bronze man who'd weathered so many storms up there on his pedestal. One hand pressed reverently to his chest, the other raised as if about to speak. Actor cliché, Jake called it. When he gave us lessons in walking and talking like someone we weren't, he was big on looking natural.

"Spunk says there's rich kids going feral, like in that speedster, and maybe one of them got Rivera."

Rubio leaned back against the fence, tilting his chin toward the luminous cloud cover. His mind was elsewhere. "If anyone asks, say you're a friend of the Murrays."

"Who's that?"

"The Murrays of Murray Hill." His gaze had softened. "Long ago, they built on an actual glacial hill, now the east 30s. Later, it became fashionable. With all the storms the years have thrown at them, those grand old brownstones have barely got their feet wet."

I grabbed his arm. "Engine!"

We backed into deeper darkness as a robo-taxi bumped along the ruts of Lexington and dropped a fare at the top of the square. Two people hurried up steep iron stairs. Steel gates squealed on corroded hinges, then slammed as the couple vanished inside. The cab locked up, blacked its windows, and scooted back north.

"Dinner uptown." Rubio was caught in his reverie. "Lucky bastards.

Holding out to the end. Like Murray Hill, where the remaining wealthy families diked up a private compound, betting their deep pockets that good walls will hold back the tide until things get better."

"The old-money version of a den," I said. "Seems crazy. With their means, they could go anywhere."

He shrugged. "The stranglehold of tradition? Once-priceless real estate might be priceless once again? People get stuck in a way of living."

"You'd like to be them." Hadn't meant it as an accusation, but it must've come out that way, 'cause Rubio got huffy.

"Why not? Wouldn't you?"

"No! I mean, you know . . ." I wriggled my shoulders. "Just doesn't feel like me."

"What do you know about it? You don't even know who you are!"

"Hey!"

He glanced away, ashamed. "I didn't . . ."

"Yeah, you did, and by the way, it's not true. There's a me inside that doesn't need memories to know who she is! Sort of."

He peered down at me like I'd grown another ear. "This is new."

"Maybe. Well, yes. And that me thinks it's not so great to wall up and keep all the good stuff for yourself!"

"Like we do in the dens?"

Well, he had me there.

"You see? Everything's relative." Rube leaned in to press his point. "Like the Causeway. Murray Hill built it as a *public* facility, following the old-style mandate of fulfilling civic duty. They preserved vintage buildings. They planted hardy trees and salt-tolerant shrubs. They drone in food and merchandise. They're trying to keep the city alive!"

"Alive for anyone who can afford it!" We learned about the Causeway in our training: an elevated boulevard above Lexington, from 31st all the way to 45th, the full width of the avenue. A sort of mall, only still functioning, with stores and restaurants, thirty feet in the air. "They just needed somewhere close by to shop!"

"Listen to you!" Rubio eased back, like my words had nudged him. "That old you must've been a Democrat."

"Is that bad?" My outburst surprised me, too. Where'd that all come from?

"It was a political stance. Brilliant in theory. Inefficient in practice." He looked me over. "Maybe you should've got some real clothes from Jenn, to blend in better."

I glared at him. "These are my besties!"

"At least they're clean." He pushed off from the fence. I thought the lecture was over, but he pointed to the weathered stone façades ringing Gramercy Park. "In buildings of a certain vintage, the second story was often the more formal story. Columns, tall windows, elaborate casings, heavy cornices, you see? On the Causeway, they turned the grandest ones into second-floor entrances from the raised street."

The sky had gone dead black.

"Night's marching on." I wanted to be back on task. "After the Causeway, I'll take the pass-thrus. Over past Saint Pat's."

"Give him my love."

"I'll just be passing by."

He was wishing I'd go in and light a candle for him. Did it once, at a downtown church kept open by Revelations, the God den. Its roof was half gone, but they held daily service there, rain or shine. I went in to see if church felt like something I might have done before. But, no, not a tingle. I don't do religion now and I didn't do it then. Pretty sure of that.

Another burst of night noise made me jump. A banging and clattering this time, too close and nearing.

We ducked instinctively, then crab-walked along the fence to where the dead shrubbery made a screen. Four or five dim figures moved east along the far side of the park.

"Not pickers," murmured Rubio. "Way too loud."

"And too many of them."

"What are they dragging?"

"It's got wheels." I caught the rhythmic squeak of an axle. "A cart of some kind?"

As we squinted through the brush and tree trunks, one pair stopped to yank on the battered planks barricading a front stoop. The gate resisted with a tortured screech, then collapsed in a heap. They tossed the pieces on top of their load. Clatter, thud, clang, repeat. People who make that much noise in the night city are either insane or figure they can take on whatever comes along. Or both.

"All anyone ever does in this city is destroy things!" I hated the waste. "Friggin' random violence!"

"Shhh!" Rubio shifted sideways for a better view. "Wooden wheels. Handmade. They're like something out of a Bruegel painting." Then he laid a hand on my arm and hissed so low I could barely hear him. "Maybe not so random. Don't freak out, okay? I'm thinking Storm Worshippers, harvesting fuel for their next bonfire."

"What! Stormies?" I shrank into myself, ready to run. "The real thing?"

"It's a guess. Sit tight. They're too busy to notice us."

They did seem engrossed in their vandalism, plus heading away from our planned routes. Once my heart slowed some, I made a closer study: three men, two women. Thin, dirty, and bedraggled, like the rest of us downtowners. No horns on their heads, no hooves on their crusty bare feet.

I told Rubio about the video Jenn had found. "But these all have clothes."

"Yeah, the bare-ass thing is only for their bonfires."

"How do you know?"

He shrugged like he had a secret source, likely just the usual gossip and den lore. If he'd seen Stormies before, he'd have boasted about it.

"Don't look like much, do they."

"Not now, when they're just a bunch of squatters. But when the storms come, they gather in herds, and once they get into their trance state, it's all hive mind and no mercy."

Or so it was said.

"The lunatic fringe," Rubio mused. "The city's always had one, but now they've found a god that appears to them on a regular basis." He sounded envious.

"Told you there was weather coming. Can we leave now?"

As the Stormies rattled and banged their way east toward Second, we slipped west along the fencing until their noise receded.

Rubio was grinning, mostly with relief. "Nothing like a bit of excitement . . ."

"The kind I don't need." At Lex, I turned north. "I'm out of here."

"Yep. Keep an eye out. If there's real weather coming, the Stormies will be stirring."

"Maybe you should pay the Gimme herbalists a visit. You'll be right there."

"Maybe I will."

But I knew he wouldn't. Those earthy women seemed to intimidate him. I watched him slink west along 21st Street. He coughed a long string as he vanished into the night. No question his health was worsening. Maybe it wasn't just malaria. Maybe it was TB. Rousseau's medics said a lot of the old diseases were showing up again, along with all the new ones. People lacked immunity and it was so hard to find drugs, never mind current vaccines. Maybe at the Souk I could trade the old book for the up-to-date meds Rubio needed. First, I'd better learn what they were.

Tucking that idea away, I went along up Lex. Even two long blocks to the east, I could smell the damp green of Madison Square, the home of Gimme Shelter. More of a farm than a den, and vulnerable, living in scattered commercial buildings around the square. But as long as enough grass grew to feed their livestock and their vegetable gardens stayed dry enough to plant, they swore to stick it out. Gimme Shelter took in only women, mostly who'd been abused or terrorized by men, but also pregnant den ladies about to deliver. Unca Joe's shrink had once asked if I'd feel more comfortable there. I'd said I wasn't scared of men in general, just the ones who hit on me. After all, a man had saved my life and I was grateful. I had none of the Gimmes' special skills for herbal healing or midwifery. They were strong and independent but, y'know . . . not denned up. I worried for their safety.

The moist night air diffused light, so I could see the Causeway's glow from blocks away. Day-shift pickers avoided it, with its patrols of Murray Hill's private police watching out for Mainland tourists who stopped by for lunch on their way to gawk at the Empire State Building and other landmarks of Manhattan's glorious past.

When the weather cooperated, they sat outside the cafés, sipping tea droned in from the mountains of small countries otherwise swallowed up by oceans. They took pictures with their cell phones—unreliable for anything else even this far uptown—selfies and each other carefree in front of the view down the cross-streets to the ever-widening East River Estuary. Back in their high-ground, gated burbs, they'd boast of seeing the *real* Manhattan-Under-Water.

Or so it was said. As a night-shifter, tourists felt as distant to me as Adders or Storm Worshippers. Recent den word was that the tourist trade was slacking off. Good riddance, then. They weren't adding to the den economy.

And at night, the Causeway was a different story.

After the tour boats pulled away and the cops retreated to the lighted protection of the shops, a tougher, livelier crowd showed up—in town with a bodyguard, taking a break from the clubs and casinos, doing biz over late night suppers droned in from afar. Often the artists and musicians brought in to entertain the tourists by day stayed to drink up their pay by night. Some brave souls came by from neighborhood buildings where squatters and stay-behinds piggy-backed on the relative security of living next door to Murray Hill. A more local crowd, but a crowd none the less. Strangers, of a sort I wasn't used to.

Which had me on super-alert, climbing the wide stair at the downtown end of the Causeway. No picking planned here. Just passing through, quick and quiet. They'd never notice.

Up top, electronic music beat a quick tempo. The spruced-up but mostly empty storefronts flashed neon and fake candlelight. The sad, stunted trees were strung with twinkle lights and had a few real leaves on them. If not for the heat and the odors of harbor and garbage wafting up from below, you could almost believe all was well with the world—the very myth its merchants were desperate to promote. No barter system in these cafés, and I had none of their sort of credit. Still, I slowed for a bit of eyes-wide window-shopping. This brief stretch of artificial civilization felt like a dose of hope. A vision of my future life on the Mainland. And there was always a chance, in a new neighborhood, that something might stir up a memory, some familiarity, like sensing what was around the next corner.

But nothing about the Causeway felt like home, so I veered back to the midline and strode along purposefully, like it was what I did every day and night.

Halfway along, the tables outside a lit-up café overflowed with loud young people carousing. A uniformed guard watched from the door. Inside, bartenders waited stiffly at their posts. A metal chair scraped, a glass smashed the pavement, laughter erupted. The guard stayed where he was.

I picked up my pace.

Further on, a smaller group, mostly girls, compared the design and prices of their new shoes in the gilded glow from a shop window. Silvery phone cuffs encircled their wrists, useless here except as a fashion basic. Their short, filmy dresses and bangled ankles glittered as they danced about, gripping each other's shoulders for balance, flirting with the few boys among them by ignoring them entirely. Real uptowner kids, surely too young and soft to be Spunk's ferals. Kids whose parents never left, never had to leave. The Power Elite.

I made sure not to stare as I passed, but I did swallow a sigh. How did that feel, being so at home amid all this glamor? What was life really like uptown? What did they do all day, other than shop and flirt? Could I have been one of them, before Abel?

No, that didn't feel right. I moved on.

At the north end of the Causeway, a stair led down to the 44th Street Marina. Several brightly colored motorboats were tied up nose-in along the main dock, awaiting the return of the revelers.

Farther along the dock, a gangway led up to the pass-thru that would take me west and uptown. Close by, a large covered launch was pulled in broadside, surprising as the water was shallow here and tidal. This boat could take you a long way and at high speed. Upriver past the Palisades, or all the way Down East to the rumored safe ports, if they'd let you in. Now, its polished foredeck was decorated with lounging young men. A light glowed through the canvas canopy. Girlish chatter drifted on the humid air. Topside, two of the boys passed a bottle, bored and languorous. The third slept or was passed out entirely.

Right off, I wished for the crowd again. Other than the boys, the dock was deserted. I'd have to walk by them to get to the gangway. Turn back? My night would be a total loss. Besides, the boys seemed deeply focused on their drinking. Probably all too drunk to move. And it was a public dock. I had as much right to it as . . .

"Hey, girl," one of them called. "So late and out all alone?"

Shit. Here we go.

Light from the shops up above glinted in his eyes. He had dark, mussed-up hair and the wild, beautiful face of a predator. A twinge at the back of my brain. Something about him. Did I know this boy? No way I could.

He set the bottle down and sat up. His eyes said: At last! Entertainment.

Too late for retreat. A dozen steps to the gangway, and damn them all, anyway.

The second one, slack-jawed and pudgy, rose up on one elbow. "Well, hello! Lookin' for c'mpany?"

Really, how could they bear being so predictable? But now there were two of them, and more possibly Spunk's ferals. Not much chance of help around here, not for someone like me. Time to fall back on Jake's acting lessons, and bull through it. As I neared the step-up to the gangway, the dark-haired one stretched gracefully and draped his leg across both railings. Not too drunk to move at all. I stopped, sighing as if his idea of fun was just massively uncool.

He leaned in, silky hair flowing across his brow. "Really shouldn't be wandering about at night, y'know. Not without protection."

"Prote'tion, yeah!" his drunker pal crowed, making a move to shift upright, and failing. "We'll giv' ya prote'tion! C'mon up here an' lemme prote't ya, nice 'n hard!"

Could I flirt my way out of this? Jake would be proud, but no, I'd never manage it.

I looked Dark Boy in the eye. "I'm fine, thank you. I'm almost home."

Briefly, he believed me. He nodded, then bent his knee to lift his leg out of my way. Then the subtext in my gaze sank in, the bitterness I couldn't bury deep enough. For his clean, stylish clothes, his artfully messed hair, but mostly for his unscarred skin, his healthy shine, his unbroken body. And meanwhile, my clothes, my ragged hair, my skinny limbs, everything about me gave me away. Rube was right. Should've borrowed from Jenn.

"No." Dark Boy dropped his leg again. "I don't think you are."

He wasn't much bigger than me, and his friend showed no sign of making it to his feet. Still, like with Ace, a need was rising to scream and flail about. I had stay calm, maybe let resentment override panic.

"Yes, I am. It's right up there." I pointed to a high, lighted window a block to the west, and jiggled my pack. "My mom ran out of hooch."

I knew it was off the instant I said it.

"*Hooch*?" Dark Boy laughed. "Nice try, den rat. You'll have to do better than that if you want to pass up here."

"I don't need to pass."

"No?" He lifted the barrier of his leg suggestively. "I thought you wanted to go home."

"Yes, I . . . uh . . ." Getting flustered now, too fritzed to play word games. Alarms starting up in my head. Something almost remembered. I couldn't keep my eyes from flicking around like a trapped squirrel.

"She wans sompin' else." The drunk struggled again, aiming to slide off the boat onto the dock. "She wans what I got."

"No! No, I don't!" I was getting shrill.

"Julian?" A voice from beneath the launch's canopy. "Everything all right out there?"

Dark Boy tossed his head in irritation. "Yeah. Everything's fine." He glared at me to shut up, like we were in this together.

Really?

"Time we were getting back." A woman's voice, older. Or maybe just more sober.

"Yeah, yeah." He pulled a face and leveled a finger at me. "Get back where you belong, den rat. You got lucky this time. Don't try it again. I'll remember you."

"Huh. Not the boss of your life after all. Or mine." The alarms eased, so I could set my jaw and stare at the tip of his finger like I'd any second bite it off. "Who made you the law?"

He snorted. "Law? Ain't no law. Only Darwin."

Oh, I was brave, now he'd been cut down to size, ready show some pluck. Rubio had told me about Darwin. "That so? Come on downtown, and I'll show you who's fit, and what survival really means."

He stared at me like he was ready to go right then, like it might be more interesting than anything else he had planned.

"You wouldn't last a minute." Now I was pushing that luck.

"You'd be surprised."

"Julie? Oh, for godsakes!" A curly-haired redhead all in sequins peered around the side of the canopy. "Leave the trash, asshole. Can we go now? Anyone steady enough to drive?"

"Me!" cheered the pudgy drunk.

"Not a chance," Dark Boy said, still holding my eye.

"Of what?" I murmured. "Driving or downtown?"

His mouth twitched. Almost a smile. "I'll drive," he called over his shoulder.

"Got some sense after all. Mama's boy."

"She's not my . . ." The finger jabbed at me again. "Back where you belong, you hear?"

"Julie, come on," the redhead whined. She swung neatly pointed feet over the gunwale and stood on the dock with her arms folded. Under so much pearly makeup, it was hard to tell her age, but surely younger than she wanted to look.

Dark Boy reached into a pocket, weighed stuff in his hand, dropped some back. "Here. For the lousy fuck we didn't get." Metal rattled on the dock.

I spat on the wood beside them. Who used coins anymore?

"Julian. Now." Movement under the canopy caught my eye—blond hair, blunt-cut, a strong jaw turning toward me into the light, then abruptly away.

Sullen again, Dark Boy folded his leg under him and rose, elbowing his companion to help with the out-cold third.

"Aw, leaf 'im," muttered the drunk. "He falls in, he'll wake up fas' enuff."

"Don't . . ." I blurted.

Dark Boy sneered. "What do you care? He'd been awake, you'd be history."

The girl caught his arm and they all climbed sloppily into the launch, leaving their friend sprawled on the foredeck. Alone on the dock, I craned my neck for another glimpse of the blond woman, but she'd retreated inside. So like the ninja girl, but not.

The boat's engine coughed to life. Shadows moved in the stern. The launch backed, turned, and pulled sharply away, sending up a hard spray that drenched me where I stood. I swore after them and made sure not to swallow, glaring helplessly at their wake. Free to go wherever they wanted. Damn every one of them. But as the water ran away into the spaces between the floorboards, a bright sparkle was left behind. Dripping, I bent to retrieve it.

A woman's bracelet: two rows of small, clear stones set close together, fastened with a broad gold clasp. Could not have been there before. I'd have seen it.

Dark Boy? I was sure it was just coins he'd thrown down.

I waited for the launch to whip around and speed back, but its roar faded between the buildings. The bracelet was mine. The redhead must've dropped it while I was paying Dark Boy too much attention. But what a thing to be careless about! Well, her loss, my gain, and best be out of there. I stowed it in my grab bag. I curled my lip at Dark Boy's scatter of change, then scooped it up anyway and ran, leaving a trail of wet footprints all the way up the gangway.

The ramp emptied through a blown-out window onto a third-floor hallway. Walls and floor stripped to the raw concrete, lit by LEDs spaced too far apart. Probably sucking power from the Causeway—in most pass-thrus, you floundered around in total darkness unless daylight filtered in. I stopped just inside the entry to wring out my sodden tee and dig out my headlamp, then slid down the wall into a damp huddle till I could control my shakes.

Too much input. Fear, envy, outrage, all twisted up like a bundle of string ends. I couldn't pull them straight to see where one began and the other ended. From where I sat, the Causeway was laid out like the background in a video, pulsing with light and music, its glowing pavement all but deserted. Another lesson here, if only I could see it clear.

I glanced down the ill-lit hallway, wishing I didn't have to go there. Spunk warned us about doorways: people might live or just be hiding behind them. Highest danger rating was a door busted in or missing, open to dark and ravaged interiors, handy for an ambush. These doorways were safely sealed with cinderblock, though the blind turn at the end of the hallway gave me some pause. But what choice did I have?

I dragged to my feet and started off. Sure enough. Around the blind corner, a long stretch of black openings yawned back at me. Nothing for it but to go quick and quiet.

At the next turn, light leaked past a solid door, open just a crack. Whatever business went on in there—drugs, sex, the black market—it wasn't mine. Maybe only squatters, living best they could. But a squatter could become a mugger fast enough. Eight blocks more till my assigned sector. The concrete relayed the slightest foot-scrape into an echoing whisper. My foot, or someone's behind me? I held my breath and scooted by the open door.

Corridor after corridor, dark and not so dark. Wavering across footbridges spanning the East 40s, dry down below now but not during a surge. My luck held and the halls stayed empty. Easy beans, so far. I passed the time planning my pick.

In high-rise picking, you hoped that between the third-floor pass-thrus and the high-and-dry sixth, you had two stories of deserted apartments, block after block after block. Above that, the lock you chose to pick might have someone behind it. Still some private houses left as well, along the cross streets, but those were harder to access. Maybe you could drop onto the roof from the window of a neighboring high-rise, but it was risky. If the former owner had been lazy or rushed, some nice stuff might be left behind. Thinking they'd be back, when things calmed down, when the weather got fixed.

At Unca Joe, we had a numbers guy working on a system to predict how long it would be before we'd picked the whole island clean, and our living dried up. Taking things as I did pretty much day by day, I was glad someone had an eye out for our future.

Along Madison between 50th and 51st, the street-facing windows had been knocked out to form a sort of covered balcony overlooking the back end of St. Patrick's Cathedral. Someone with an eye for a view, even if it was of moldy, unkempt gardens and grim stone buttresses. The double spires rising into darkness did lift the heart somehow. I guess that's why they built it that way.

I stopped at the uptown end to gawk at the fabled structure and wave Rubio's regards. No way the tallest building I'd ever seen, but certainly the most elaborate. Pointy arches and crosses and window tracery wherever you looked. Below, the ground was dry, but for the usual puddles in the low spots. A woman trotted by beneath me, a kayak balanced on one shoulder, a full pack weighing down the other. Couldn't make out her den sign. Lucky girl, to have her own transportation.

A boat means freedom. So right. Might be my new mantra.

Flood walls encased the Cathedral's block-long base and outbuildings, topped with razor wire and security lights, the brightest I'd seen anywhere. Rubio said Abel's surge had washed through the crypt but left the main sanctuary untouched. Over the years, storm damage had remained minimal. I was meant to see this as a sign from God, but Rube didn't push his faith on you. As I saw it, just another smart choice of building site.

I leaned out over the sill to peer uptown. Almost to my assigned territory, and ready to do a little poking around before deciding my next move.

A rustle along the corridor jarred me to full alert.

Oh no! Incoming, and I was caught flat and dreaming. No time to run. I hugged my arms around my bag, close to my chest, tucked my head, whirled and flung myself madly at the shadow sliding up behind me.

It let out a strangled yelp and went down, tucking and rolling same as I did, making for a soft landing and a ready getaway. The yelp was familiar, and so was the cackling laugh it wheezed out, back-sprawled on the concrete, arms flung wide in a caricature of surrender.

I sprang up. "Spunk! You creep! You lousy . . ."

"Have sum respect fer yer eldahs!" More helpless cackling.

"What are you . . . ?"

"Whew! Good one, Glimmagirl!" He pulled in one long breath, then quick as a cat was back on his feet, dusting himself off. "Ya learned that lesson right enough!"

Hands on hips, I tried for justifiable outrage. "What are you doing?"

He mimicked my pose. "What*chu* doin', just standin' dere lika lox?"

"I wasn't . . ."

"That's twice ya nearly got bagged tonight."

"Twice?" Ah. Dark Boy. "You been following me?"

He cocked his head, which to me always seemed too big for his body—long and horse-like, with his reddish hair sticking out from under the stained ball cap he always wore, even indoors. "How else I gonna see ya in action?"

"You're still testing me?" My shoulders sagged.

"Looks like I betta." Spunk sidestepped to the window wall and peered out. His half-toothed grin flashed in the glare of the security lights. "Whacha doin' up heah? Prayin'?"

"Not me." I shrugged, flicked a hand toward the cathedral. "Only I told Rubio . . ."

"Ah, fer him."

"Just being neighborly."

"Yeah, yeah. Da boy could use a prayer or two. Not sure he deserves it." He turned to face me. "So whatchu got in yer bag?"

"Huh?"

"Whatchu picked up on da dock."

"Oh. Right."

"Fergot it already, didya?"

"No, I . . ." I snatched up my still-damp grab bag, so relieved that my fingers fumbled at the laces. I fished out the bracelet and coins and presented them on my palm. "Probably plastic. Or maybe glass."

Spunk took the glitter, turned it this way and that in the light, then passed it back, draped on the overgrown hook of his thumbnail. "Goes direct to Rousseau when ya git in."

"Really? Come on . . . you're saying it's real?"

"Mebbe. 'Course I'm no expert. But da tellers ain't neither. You take it straight to da boss. He'll know." He poked at it while I stood holding it, a coil of sparkle in my half-clenched fist. "Funny t'ing ta leave behine."

"Probably fell off her wrist. Must be that girl's so rich, she didn't miss it."

"Mebbe. Whadya say ta pretty boy?"

"Pretty?" I could only sputter. But of course, he was.

He turned away with another cackle, then let it die into silence, gazing up at the misted spires like he'd never seen them before. "Worried I was gonna glom it, right?"

"That'd be okay." I held it out to him again. "You want to take it in?"

Spunk sucked his teeth. "Tem'ting me, are ya?"

"What? Why would I?"

"Good question."

"I wouldn't!" He was moving way too fast for me. After all the months of dark nights and close calls on the street with this man, I should be feeling way more comfortable than I was right then. "Like, you could see it as pay-back, for the extra work you put in on me."

"Dat's my job."

"Yeah, but . . ."

"Nah, it's yer pick."

"What's up, Spunk?" I hated that I could never quite tell what he was thinking. Had he been talking to Peeto?

"Nuttin'." He glanced back at me, then shook his head and shoved off from the windowsill. "Nuttin' at all."

I didn't believe him. I waited for him to ask what else was in my bag. "You saw it all go down. Did I play it wrong?"

"Not so far." He retreated backward along the corridor. "On about yer bizness, Glimmagirl." He pointed at the bracelet, still lighting up my palm. "Keep dat tight, now."

"Of course." I dropped it back in my bag.

"Catch ya back at Joe."

"You bet." I let him get down the hall till I could barely see him. "Spunk?"

"Yeah?"

"I got scared back there."

"Sure ya did."

"No, really scared. Crazy scared. Almost lost it. Like I used to."

Silence, while both of us recalled the time he'd had to slug me quiet to save our skins on the street. "But ya din't."

"No, but . . ."

"Ya snarled 'im down."

"Well, no, it was . . ." Maybe he hadn't heard the summons from inside the boat.

"Sure ya did. Or ya guiled 'im. Whatevah. It worked. Ya walked away."
He was moving again, his voice fading, melting back into the night.

"It was like . . . an almost memory. Something I . . ."

He shook his head, backing through a random shaft of light. I got the
message, had heard it often enough: Don't tell me. I don't want to know.
Save it for the shrink. "Jes' keep doin' whatcher doin'."

And he was gone.

A deep breath, no, several, did little to steady my nerves. Weird about
Spunk lately. Every encounter left me shaken and wary. Just my guilty conscience, or some new level of testing? Had he been checking up on me the
night of the ninja girl? If so, part of my secret was in his hands. Was he
waiting to see what came of it?

Amazing it was only yesterday. I replayed leaving the den . . . could
Spunk have followed? Was he really gone now? I squinted down the night-
black hallway. I hoped this was just his way of proving that easing up on the
streets could be fatal.

And now, less stealthy noises approached along the uptown corridor. I
slipped behind a broad pillar. Four Asian men in silk suits the colors of the
dawn, laughing, talking, confident that they belonged wherever they happened to be. Like the girls on the Causeway. Likely headed there. How
could I not feel a touch of envy?

Once they'd passed by, I moved up to 52nd and put in a dull hour prospecting sad, littered rooms already way picked over before me. In case Spunk
was still on my tail, meanwhile doing everything possible to lose him if he
was. And thinking.

Finally, I neatened up best I could: doffed my headlamp and street cap,
finger-combed up my hat hair. At least my clothes had dried. I stowed the
bracelet in my gut wallet, folded cap and grab bag into a back pocket, then
took the next set of stairs down to street level to nose on west toward the
Souk.

TEN

H ere's what I knew about the Souk, all secondhand from Jake's running tales in the Mess, or Rubio's history lessons.

It was a no-man's-land between Uptown and Down, perched on the rocky outcroppings along the western edge of Central Park, between 59th and 79th Streets, below the first checkpoints in the 86th Street Divide, open to all comers with something to barter or sell, or credit enough to buy. It ran 24/7.

The old park was a series of shallow lakes surrounded by farm plots and muddy pasture for sheep, cows, and goats. North of the wall, a heliport and a police station to patrol the uptown sectors and man the checkpoints.

The wall? Supposedly a flood barrier, but even the strongest surges never reached that high. In reality, a border control. You needed proper ID to travel uptown of the Divide. I'd never been this close to it before.

Trotting west along 59th, past the ranks of shattered glass towers, I felt a difference in the air—the greenhouse reek of dirt and living vegetation. The uptown side of the street was dense with leafy darkness. A throat-tingling hum stirred the quiet and roused my street caution as surely as it drew me toward its pulsing light. From a distance, it was thrilling.

At Sixth Avenue, the first working streetlamp revealed I was no longer alone.

A whole den's worth of people were camped out along the sidewalk. Lumpish shapes sagging beneath the trees, others upright against the trunks. A hundred eyes following me. Spasms of deep coughing, an occasional moan. A shadow detached from the base of the streetlight and shuffled into my path, skeletal hands outstretched. Diseased or just hungry? I swerved away, glaring a warning, then saw his hands were full of stuff too bent or degraded to be identified.

Not begging. Trying to sell me something.

At the next streetlight, more hands, more shapeless merchandise. A voice rasped, "Whatever you can pay!" as I hurried by.

Were these people too far gone to find a den? Were they the rejects, the truly homeless? I hadn't fully considered the implications of 'no-man's-land.'

I wasn't even there yet but already I knew the lessons from the Souk wouldn't all be positive.

The buzzy hum soon resolved into voices, music, the calls of vendors, arguments, electronic beeps and bells. Even a dog barking: alive? Never seen a live one in my den life, but I dreamed of dogs now and then. Maybe one particular dog. Hard to tell. Many dens kept cats to control the vermin, but dogs cost too much to feed. Plus, with plague reports resurfacing, no one wanted a flea magnet around.

The old stone gates at Central Park West were the Souk's official entrance. My stomach tingled as I approached. The Souk! At last!

Outside, next to the toppled statue of Columbus, five uniforms sat on beat-up battery-powered trikes, playing games on their phone cuffs and hoping for some live action. Big, buff guys and gals, looking like they owned the place. Jake called them 'Soukies' and said they wore the old NYPD blue in honor of the officers gone down in the waves, but the Merchants' Association, not the city, now wrote their pay chits. The rule was, they stayed outside the gates unless a vendor called them in. Inside, they made the customers nervous, and I could see why.

As I neared, a quartet of youngsters moved off, pouting and scowling. From Macy's, most likely, the kid den. These were really young, even for Macys.

"Bring your parents next time," an officer called. As if they had any.

The Souk had an age limit? Maybe just a Macys limit. The kids were genius at picking pockets, but why send them packing? They'd just get in at the side, past the end of the wall.

The Soukies eyed me close. One stood up to block the entry. I mimicked the lift of Dark Boy's chin and made like I knew where I was going.

It worked. The guy stood back and let me pass.

"If ya don't find whacha need," one of the others leered, "be happy to give it to ya."

Guess I'd cleaned up well enough. I was getting high on my new confidence.

Inside the gates, vendors' booths pressed tight along the old roadway. Noise, light, and color hit me in a rush. Hard not to stop and stare, with so much to take in and process, but that would give me away as a newbie. Dry weather still, so the crowd was close-packed, spooky for me but easy to blend with. I could seem to go with the flow, like any uptown girl down-dressed for safety and out for a night's shopping.

Getting my bearings and my heart rate down, I fingered spangled dresses and embroidered scarves, peered into armored jewelry cases. New stuff, or only lightly used. Not scavenged. Such plenty! The glamor goods on the Causeway seemed as remote as the glossy photos in old magazines the pickers still brought in. This stuff I could touch and feel.

"For that special date!"

"That color's perfect for you!"

"Rare gemstones from the highlands of New Guinea!"

The other side of life, and I was finally getting a taste of it. Rubbing shoulders with uptowners who came down for lower prices than the stores above the Divide. And nobody chasing me away. I ran a finger across a rack of bamboo cages housing small furry animals I couldn't put names to.

"Looking for something in particular?"

A young woman in a cook's apron, her hair tied back uncomfortably tight.

I had to ask. "For food or cuddling?"

She stared at me for a moment, then pursed her lips. "Whatever."

Further on, a big screen lit up with a video about methane eruptions in the Bering Sea increasing the greenhouse gas levels. Seemed to be new news. Maybe even true. Rube might know, or Jenn. Between two stalls selling tacos made right there, I discovered a use for Dark Boy's spite gift and filled my water bottle at an old coin-op dispenser. Just filtered, of course. Spring water was four times more. I took a long swig by a screen spooling a weather crawl. Heavy rain for later, plus tracking a hurricane out in the Atlantic, already a three and on course to run up the East Coast later in the week.

My body—and the Stormies—had told it straight. Was this an extra-heavy crowd, stocking up for the blow, or was it always like this? Barely controlled chaos.

The place made me floaty with overwhelm. Best to focus and be on with my errand. I snaked through the media sector, where every surface was lit up or moving or making noise. Sound zones overlapped, two or three songs playing at once, one dominating, then fading as I moved from kiosk to kiosk. It was never really quiet at Unca Joe, but this was an all-out ear assault.

Trays of disks and cubes and sticks, plus the rechargeables to run them, all of it second- or third-hand, no better than a picker's haul. Here, the new stuff was under locks and still in packaging, behind barricading counters.

I cruised stall after stall, looking for a bookseller. No sign of print or paper. Even the ads, price lists, and sale signs were digital. Total waste of power!

In the end, I had to ask. I picked an older vendor listing 'classic' e-books. Her booth was deserted, maybe because her signs were handwritten and she wasn't blaring music and video all over the place. Elbows propped on the greasy counter, chin sunk in her hands, she looked like her last friend in the world was the screen she was glued to.

I cleared my throat. No response. You'd think a customer would be more interesting than some forty-year-old soap opera. "Excuse me?"

She turned on her stool. "Yeah?"

I made sure to use complete, uptown sentences. "Do you have books for sale?"

She waved at her grimy stacks of e-books and readers. "All the best, all the best prices."

"No, I mean *real* books. Like, in print. On paper."

She blinked. "You mean, hard copy? Wrong sector. Try Antiques."

"Right. Thanks." I hoped she might offer directions. But she'd already turned back to her screen. No wonder her business was slack.

On I went. I spotted some denfolk in the food sector, trading for meat and veggies or other staples. Ladysmiths, from their sculpted beards, and two clean-cut women from Empire State, den sign worn on their shoulders like military rank. With Florida part of the Caribbean and the Mississippi regularly backing up across the plains, citrus, sugar, and flour were the hardest to come by, never mind afford. At Joe, we sweetened with our own honey. We'd had success with Meyer lemons on our roof, but the crop was small. So far, oranges were a stretch. I slid in closer to listen.

"Buy it now," a grinning vendor advised, weighing a sack of Canadian corn for one of the Empire women. "Gonna be harder getting it."

She had a close eye on his scale. "Why's that? Tariffs again?"

"Nah. Who'd enforce 'em?" The vendor handed over the sack. "What I hear is, they think it's time to start keeping it for themselves."

The woman nodded, pressing her thumb to a tiny screen he wore on one wrist. Was that all she had to do? I knew Jake paid with chits printed out after he'd traded stuff. Well, Rubio often said: all dens are equal, but some are more equal than others.

"That's a quote," he'd add, knowing I wouldn't get it. "More or less."

Now I got it. The other Empire caught me staring and frowned. I turned away to inspect the greens, gratified to see we grew better in Joe's roof gardens.

But the Canada thing was bad news. Unca Joe bartered for corn meal, soy, and rice, all from Canada. Add that to the scarcity of flour due to the global plague of wheat rust.

"What about that co-op trying to raise coffee in the Appalachians?"

The vendor shrugged. "Might have some, if they can get it here. Now it's just what little comes, y'know, round-about from Mexico."

'Round-about' meant the black market. Business as usual at the Souk, though Jake said the distinction between black and legit was blurring fast. You took what you could get, however you could get it. Watching the Lady-smiths haggle and cajole, then fork over more than they ought for too little food, I saw how they stood out. Even the Empire women, who could almost pass for uptowners. Even they were stringier, their eyes more desperate and wary. As if their bodies, never mind their clothes, were stained from too little soap and hot water. Like all denfolk. Like me.

A vision of deep tubs and sweet-scented suds flashed by me. Memory quake? Nah, probably just those old mag photos again. I didn't complain about my quality of life—still too grateful to be alive. But at some point before, I must have been clean and comfortable, 'cause I knew how it would feel.

I moved on, past acres of used clothing, chipped crockery, battered metal, and plastic anything. Sidestepped at least three bitter battles over who'd got to an item first. Maybe this vision of plenty was shakier than I'd thought. I was almost to 72nd Street before I saw signs advertising antiques, like, plac-ing the good stuff closest to the folks most able to afford it. The trees were taller here. There was even some grass. Actual grass. I walked little circles on it, just for the spongy feel beneath my feet. It gave me a boost to keep going, cruise the antique stalls, maybe learn something about old furniture to impress Rubio with.

The booths here were almost stores, wide and platformed, with built sides and solid roofs, and the objects displayed in artful groupings. In the dens, 'old' pretty much meant unusable or the fancy stuff we left alone.

What would we do with these delicate wooden chairs likely to collapse under any real weight, or those inlaid tables with their waxy sheen, the slim desks, the tall bookshelves overflowing with silver and glassware and gold-rimmed dishes? Anything fragile didn't last long in a den. Besides, it took a major operation to swoop in, clean out a townhouse, and be gone by morning. We left that to the pirate crews, and the Merchants' Association looking the other way.

That stuff ended up here, looking elegant and useless in the twinkle of tiny lights strung in the trees. Orphans of the storm, like me. Not that I was elegant. But I sighed over a gilt candelabra. That would sure bring cheer to my bunk space. With so many arms, I'd be trading half my nightly take for candles and end up burning the whole tier down.

Ha, ha, girl. Hot baths and chandeliers? Let's keep those fantasies in check!

The crowd had thinned out, less noise, dimmer light. Classier turf. Still, very few books, and mostly tattered paperbacks, so water-damaged you could hardly read the titles. The occasional hardbacks were warped and torn.

About ready to pack it in, I rounded a corner and right in front of me was a whole row of books shelved neatly above a flatscreen showing an old video. This seemed like a good sign. A spot lit the shiny dark-red bindings, picking out gold lettering. Looked new and like they belonged together.

I nosed up to the counter for a better look. A tall guy with a sparse gray beard lunged over with a stick in one hand and a flashlight in the other. He cracked me hard across the knuckles as I reached for a book, and flared the light into my eyes.

"Hands to yourself!"

I bit back a curse and put on my best air of abused innocence. "I'd like to see one of those books, please."

"You can see it well enough from there."

"Not if you're blinding me."

He lowered the beam a fraction. "Looking or buying?"

I went for the lifted chin again. "I'm interested in the quality of your stock, as I have a book to sell."

The beam dropped to my empty hands.

"But I see now that these are bound in cheap plastic and the lettering is flaking off." I backed away. "My book is of superior quality, so it's likely not your area of expertise."

This time, I knew Jake would be proud.

The snark set his weapons on the counter, folding his arms across his pit-stained suit jacket. "I see. Superior quality, is it? Might be worth a look if you stole the provenance along with the book."

Provenance. A word I didn't know. "I didn't steal anything. The book is mine. My . . . mother gave it to me."

He nodded, then stuck out a hand, waggling his long fingers like some kind of sucker fish. "Let me see this marvelous book. I'll tell you if I'm interested."

Sure, fella, and have you snatch it? "I don't carry it with me."

Suddenly, the idea of even one of his sticky fingers touching the book—*my* book—made my stomach churn. Wait. *My* book? When had I got so possessive?

He pocketed his squid of a hand. "Come back when you do."

"I doubt it."

He'd decided there wasn't any book at all, and that was fine by me. Surely this heat-plastered, too-black-haired dude wasn't the only book dealer in the Souk?

I sauntered away. But once out of his sight, I slumped in a heap on some plastic crates stacked against a tree. Out of steam. Totally done. Even the rustle of real leaves in a grass-scented breeze did not perk me.

I'd failed. First time out on my own, and I'd failed. Not ready to run my life after all. Time to slink back to the den and ponder tonight's humiliating lessons.

I stared up into the dark tree canopy, contemplating the long, hot trek home. But when I dropped my sorry gaze, I saw the most amazing thing.

Large white letters. How had I missed them before?

The crates lined a recess in the row of kiosks, like a storage alcove. At the back, a dark-colored tent was near invisible in the brighter riot. One flap, folded and clipped open, spilled warm light from inside. On the closed flap, the stenciled lettering: BOOKS.

I got a little chill, because really, this was a bit weird. Like some tall tale of magical appearances you'd hear in the Mess, or read about . . . in a book. I went over and peered in.

Racks and racks of books! Real books, everywhere, up and down, piled and stacked and shelved, enthusiastically but not without purpose. Talk about plenty, and no illusion here! Two oil lanterns hung from the ridge pole, throwing light to left and right, but leaving much of the interior in shadow.

So many books.

I shivered, my chest tight. My head felt hollow, a gale rushing through it. A true memory quake this time, brief but a humdinger, unless I was just too played out from a long night's work.

I looked around cautiously. The place seemed deserted. What was so familiar? Not the tent or the angle of the light—a scent or a fleeting sound could often snag me. The interior hush was a relief and the smell of drowned paper one I was used to. The books themselves, then, the sheer, overwhelming number of them? Maybe I'd been brought up in a library? That made me laugh. Wait till I shared that one with Rubio.

"Can I help you?"

I shrank against a bookcase, then grabbed it to keep both of us from toppling.

"Whoa. Sorry. Didn't mean to startle you."

A youngish guy peered up from behind a desk stacked with old magazines and hard-copy comic books, very prized these days since they weren't making any more of them. He had a round and pleasant face framed by cropped brown hair. An easy smile. "Hi. I'm Daniel. Looking for anything in particular?"

I reached for a neutral reply. "I . . ."

He stood up. "You okay? You look . . ."

"Yes. It's . . . um. I'm okay."

He came out from behind the desk, dragging his chair on squeaky wheels. Sitting, he'd seemed languid. On his feet, he was readiness contained. He rolled the chair toward me. "The heat, huh? It's bad tonight. You'd better sit down."

I'd broken out in a sweat. More overwhelm. Embarrassed, I glanced around. His chair was the only empty surface in the entire tent. But total strangers didn't tend to be kind to me. If I sat, I might just burst into tears. "Thanks, it's okay . . . I'm fine."

"If you say so." He seemed to be waiting for proof I wouldn't faint or die on him.

"Really. I'm fine." An enthralled gaze at his overflowing shelves might satisfy him. I needed more distance. "It's just . . . I didn't know there were so many books left."

He smiled, like it had been said before, but he liked hearing it anyway. He had a nice smile, the kind where an ordinary face suddenly beams forth comfort and trust—so right away, I was on my guard.

Seeing me steadier on my feet, he reclaimed his chair and sank into it. I liked that he hadn't pushed it on me too hard. He stretched his legs with a sigh. "I've sort of cornered the market, I guess—on the Island, at least. Not much interest in actual books these days. Even the digital kind."

"Really?" True enough in the den, where reading wasn't cool. Even so, I liked to imagine all those Joes squinting at ruined paperbacks in the secrecy of their bunks.

"Folks are too busy surviving."

"So right." Anyone this friendly had to be out for something. A sale, most likely.

He found his smile again. "You like to read?"

Probably safe to admit it to a guy who sold books. "Sure . . . um . . . well, yeah, I do."

"What do you like?"

"Anything. I mean, y'know, everything." Words on a page, any words. More promising than the life we're all living.

He pursed his lips. "Hmmm. An omnivore. That makes it harder."

"Makes what harder?"

"Recommending the right book."

Okay, here comes the sales pitch. Still, this was my longest reasonable conversation with a stranger since I woke up in the Ward. Had to watch out. His easy manner was catching. "But if I like everything, it won't matter what you recommend."

"Good point. Let's try random access." He reached blindly over his shoulder, grabbed whatever his fingers landed on, and handed it across the desk. "How about that one?"

"Ten Easy Steps to a Thinner You?"

"Oh, gad!" He snatched it back and lobbed it into the shadows behind him. "I'd gladly weed out the self-helps, but believe it or not, they sell now and then. You pick one."

"I . . . um . . . wasn't thinking of buying . . ."

"That's okay. Pick one anyway."

"But . . ."

"Read it and bring it back." He threw both arms in the air like they might fly right off his shoulders. "Ta-ta! Daniel Nathan's Portable Lending Library."

"You'd lend me a book? You don't even know me."

"So? Libraries used to do it all the time. Yeah, okay, you needed a library card. I could write one out if it'd make you feel better. You got a tab or phone that works?"

"Um . . . no."

"Then borrow a hard copy. Help yourself."

Really, what was he up to? "Any book? In the whole tent?"

"Sure! Can't afford books? You should still get to read them. Not so easy since the book sites went down and the public libraries moved out of town." Now he whirled his arms in circles and stamped his feet. "Readers of the Dying World, unite! We have nothing to lose but our minds!"

Perhaps he already had.

I mean, he looked sane enough, well fed and clean shaven, with good color to his cheeks, but he had to be a little nuts. Or trying out a very weird sales pitch. He wore jeans, baggy but in decent shape, and a black T-shirt with the logo of some long-dead rock group. Like, y'know . . . normal.

"How do you know I'll bring it back?"

"Well, I don't, do I." He dropped his arms to his knees and leaned forward until his chair creaked ominously. His eyes were a warm hazel but his gaze intense. Clearly on a mission, whatever it was. Or maybe on drugs? "That's the fun of it. If you do bring it back, I get to lend you another one, and then another, and think of all the books you can look forward to."

Such riches. I wanted to believe him.

"Doesn't it cut into your profit?"

He gave a careless wave. "Ecch."

"Well, it's a good deal, Daniel." Saying his name, even dubiously, felt like a pact of some sort, and it got my nerve up again. The night was wearing on and he was the best—no, the only—prospect so far. "But . . . say I have a book to sell . . . ?"

"To sell." He sat back, his intensity fading, then looked me over more carefully. "That's okay, too. What sort of book?"

"Old. In good shape. With a leather cover."

"Leather?"

"Yeah. The real kind."

He glanced away, then back again. "Is it yours?"

Here we go, and so quickly. "I didn't steal it."

"I didn't say you did."

I stared back at him.

He folded his chin to his chest. "Okay, implication granted. Sorry. Something you . . . found?"

"No. It was . . . given to me. That's the truth."

"I'm glad."

"It really is old, over two hundred years." His chin edged up, so I'd played the right card. "Date's on the first page. It's about this hombre's trip on the ocean, in a sailing ship. It's handwritten."

"Really? So, it's a personal diary? Like, a shipboard journal?"

"I guess." I mean, it was a sea story, yes, and some guy had written it. But Daniel's description gave it a sudden, salt-sprayed reality: a young man in 1849, clinging to a rolling deck, struggling with ink, then when he ran out, pencil, to lay down the very words I could read in the book hidden away in my gut pack. A *true-life* story. It had really happened.

"And someone gave it to you? A relative?"

"A . . . friend."

His brow creased gently, but he decided to let it go. "Is it any good?"

I blinked at him.

"I mean, is it interesting? Could he write? Did he write about interesting things?"

"Does that matter?"

"Well, to me, it does. Doesn't it to you?"

"I . . . haven't read it all."

He laughed, amazed. "Why not?"

I fumbled for excuses. "It's . . . um . . . long. And the writing is hard to read. I don't have enough light in . . . um . . ."

"In your den," he finished quietly.

I gathered myself to duck out of there, quick as I could.

"Hey, wait! Don't leave! Don't run." He raised both palms. "Please. It's okay. Been there myself." I eyed him, rabbit-tense, but he nodded, his whole torso swaying for emphasis. "Truth. Just after Misha, before I got a place of my own. I joined up with some friends who were scraping a den together in Alphabetland."

"Avenue C?"

"No." He knew I was testing him. Avenue C was my quick invention, since Alphabetland was deep under water. "Riverhome. Sometime after Hasan, they commandeered a big old barge and built dome shelters on it. Only every time a storm came, it'd wipe the barge clean." He laughed, like recalling good times. "They're still around. Got a fancy glass building over west now, at the end of the High Line. They raise hens and goats out on the elevated, drive 'em into the second-floor lobby when it blows. I go down and visit when I can."

"Risky. I mean, all that glass by the river?"

"Feet in the river, now," he grinned. "But the glass is hurricane-safe. Supposedly."

Riverhome was a cooperative den, no real leader. It had the rep of being a transitional place: they wanted you to get back out into the world, such as it was, to fend for yourself. I could see how this guy might be telling the truth. We looked each other over again, in silence.

Finally, he asked, "You got a name?"

Not much to lose, and maybe something good to gain. "Glimmer."

"Nice. Suits you. Den tag?"

I noticed how he'd slipped into den shorthand, leaving out the extra words. But it could still be a ploy. "Yeah."

"And before?"

I shrugged.

"Don't know or ain't sayin'?"

I shrugged again.

"Okay." He sat back, like grilling me had worn him out. "Now, about this book."

"I . . ."

"No, listen. You go home and read it first. Or if it's too hard, come back and we'll decipher it together. Then we can talk about selling it."

"I need the credit."

"Turn it in to your tellers." So he did know the system. His open gaze had turned faintly challenging.

"They'd just add it to the cook stove."

"Not if you told them it was worth something."

"You know why I can't."

He dipped his head. "Probably I do."

"Besides, what do you care if I read it or not?"

"It's a thing with me." Then, quick as it had come, the challenge eased off. He let his mad grin rebloom. "I'm the last champion of the printed word, doncha know? Oops." He stood up, looking past me and gone all business. "Give me a minute, will you?"

A customer had come into the tent. I moved aside to study the shelves, slipping from view as Daniel went to greet a slight man in a brimmed hat and a long raincoat, buttoned and with the collar turned up past his ears, like he was chilled, even in the sodden heat.

". . . ephemera . . . old . . . legal documents?"

I caught only a few muttered words, but the last made my skin prickle. I watched past the edge of a bookcase as Daniel led the guy to a row of boxes beside the open tent flap.

"You might find something here." His smile had lost its warmth, his back stiffened.

The man picked up this and that, shaking his small, close-cropped head. Even had gloves on, not the work kind.

"You have nothing else?" His mutter rose to an impatient whine. "Perhaps in back?"

Daniel spread his hands. "There's no back here. What you see is what you get."

Whatever the guy was looking for, it was probably illegal. I was curious to see how Daniel handled it, the legendary Souk black market. Then, through the open doorway, I caught a familiar face, moving by with the bright-lit crowd outside.

Jake.

He slowed like he might turn in to Daniel's tent, thought better of it and passed on. By then, I was flattened into the shadows behind the bookcase. What was Jake doing here? Way too early for his shift to begin. Were he and Spunk tag-teaming me or something?

Time to be out of here.

Waiting till the coast was clear, I read titles on the shelves across the aisle to calm my jitters. Wow. A whole shelf of books about Mars. *The Martian Chronicles, Prelude to Mars, The Sands of Mars, Moving Mars, Martian Time Slip, Red Mars, Green Mars, Blue Mars, The Martian.* So many! Wouldn't old Ellie Mae love that! Too bad I wouldn't be back. I could've borrowed one of those, and she could read it, too.

At last, the creepy guy drew Daniel away from the door. "Let's see what's down here."

When they disappeared behind a tall rack of books, I eased to the front of the tent and peered outside. Still busy, lots of people coming and going. No sign of Jake. I clamped my street cap down low on my head, turned away from where he'd gone, and melted into the crowd.

Didn't stop moving till I got back to the den. So ready for the peace of my bunk. So much to ponder. But there was no peace at Unca Joe that night.

The canoes were back in the Lagoon. A crowd filled the walkway again, oddly hushed, a murmur, not a roar, while the big bell over the entryway clanged like the world was ending.

"What is it? What's happening?" I nudged the girl in front of me, a recent newbie. Her eyes were wild. "Is there a tsunami?"

"They attacked the crews!"

"Attacked? Who did? Was anyone hurt?"

Nodding frantically, she pointed along the walkway like I was a moron. "Four, five, maybe more!"

Now I saw the rope-and-pulley pallets used as cargo lifts were both over the front rail. "But it was just a drill . . ."

"Snipers! On a roof!"

Snipers?

The girl had zero hard info. I shoved through the rubberneckers, looking for someone who might. A row of enforcers blocked the entrance, making room for the lift haulers and the medics to work. Between muscled-up elbows and arms, I saw a scary number of stretchers go by, and way too much blood, red and gleaming.

"How many?" I asked one of the guys holding me back.

"Seven wounded, two dead."

"Dead? No . . ."

"You heard me."

He looked as stunned as I was. We hadn't had a fatality since Rube's friend Vanya.

"What happened?"

"Unclear."

And there was Rousseau, his brow rumpled, bellowing for a clear path, hurrying the stretchers indoors, vanishing after them. The enforcers followed, as a rear guard, and we all piled in behind.

Inside, Main was a babble of misinformation. Names of the dead circulated until there were four, six, seven, eight. More than one returning crew member found himself prematurely mourned, then welcomed with hugs and cheers.

But the celebrations were brief. Rousseau stayed up with the medics, so the harbormaster, Tito, climbed the ladder at the duty board with a hunk of chalk. He was a dour, sturdy little man with a rolling sailor's gait. He took his work very seriously and felt most of us did not. But as he wrote 'Injured,' an uneasy silence settled in the hall.

As I stood waiting for the bad news, an arm curled around my elbow.

Jenn whispered, "C'mon! I've got the best news!"

"Not now!" Tito's hand was poised to start a second list.

"We can see from upstairs. C'mon!"

I tried to ease free, but she had me fast. "Tell me here."

"Can't."

"Didn't you hear? Some guys were shot!" I turned on her, but the scold died in my throat. Her face was flushed, her eyes as bright as beacons. She was hauling on me like a child who won't take no, knocking us into people right and left. Not good. Maybe she'd located her Midwest relatives? More likely she was off the edge again. I let her drag me along, snatching looks over my shoulder as Tito wrote 'Confirmed dead.'

The crowd thinned some by the stairwell door.

"Far enough," I insisted, swiveling so I could read past her head. "So, tell me!"

She let me go, but only so she could fold both arms across her chest and bounce girlishly on her toes. "Guess what?"

Anyone else, I'd have snarled, "People are dead! Don't you care?" But she'd have no clue what I was talking about. In a manic phase, it was all about her, and chewing her out only made it worse. Normally, I'd strong-arm her to the medics, but right now they'd have their hands full with shot-up denfolk. Best I could do was let her play it out.

Tito had written two names in the second column, then backed down the ladder. Two of Rousseau's canoe crew lads. Knew neither of them well.

"You're not guessing!" Jenn's lips were puffy, like she'd been kissed too hard, or had been gnawing on them.

"Can't possibly." So sad feeling relieved that it was only two. "Tell me."

"I got a promotion!"

"Yeah? To what?"

"I'm off picker duty! Rousseau's assigned me to Media."

"That's great, Jenn." I stood tiptoe to reread the list of the injured. Lads again and so not my sort of friends. But still, six Joes down for the count. No info how bad any of them were. Probably still finding that out.

"No more nights on the street!" Jenn did an arm-flung pirouette, missing an older man's cheek by inches. "No more awful work clothes!"

Almost like the girls on the Causeway, the real glimmer girls, oblivious to the broken city around them. But I couldn't be angry at her. "You should've been in Media all along."

"Rousseau used to say I was too old. But the Wiz kids stood up for me. They saw what I can do."

"Good for them."

Now that name and number were known, muttered speculation in the hall had moved on to why. Other dens had lost people to weather or street attacks, but never to random shootings. Like, what do you get from a sniping? It made no sense.

"What say we find something to eat?"

"Now?" Jenn looked puzzled. Her flush was cooling a bit. "Can't. I'm headed right up there! I'll have my own station and everything! I can watch for my news gal all the time!"

"Ought to get to it, then." Most of the Wizzers were down in the hall with everyone else, so she'd be on her own in the loft. If her mania persisted, she'd keep at it, forget to sleep or eat, but at least she'd be focused on work. "I'm really happy for you!"

"I knew you would be!" She lunged, hugged me too hard, then raced off up the stairs.

I let out a deep breath. I'd check on her later, maybe bring her a snack.

It'd be a while before the kitchen settled down enough to produce a meal for everyone who was up, which by now was most of us, regardless of shift. I went looking for Rubio, worried he might have Vanya deep on his mind. No sign, but I found Spunk pacing, his outrage radiating like heat, clearing a space around him. Anxious freshman pickers eyed him from the sidelines.

I fell into step beside him. "Any idea what went down?"

He flicked a scowl, then saw it was me. "Eh, yer back. Had me worried."

"Took a while tonight. But what . . . ?"

"Rousseau's talkin' wit da injad. Den we'll know."

"No idea who?"

"Snipers don' ushally announce demselves."

Scary to see how shaken he was. "Now what?"

Spunk nodded toward the mudroom. "Doubled da sentries, jus' in case."

That gave me a chill. "In case the snipers followed them home?"

"Doubt dey would. But gotta be 'pared fer da worse."

Danger on the streets we took for granted, but den homes were supposed to be off-limits. Part of the downtown agreement.

"What should I do?"

"'Bout what?"

"Um, y'know." Hated sounding like Jenn, buried to the neck in my own concerns. "My . . . take tonight?"

"Oh. Yeah. Dat." Like a maybe-diamond bracelet was nothing. He patted my shoulder distractedly. "Wait till da shit die down some, den take it ta 'im."

"You got it. Thanks."

I made for the Mess. If there was beer tonight, for once I'd be claiming my share.

ELEVEN

I drank beer at the wake. I shared righteous outrage with my denmates and cheered their fist-shaking schemes of vengeance for our dead and wounded, even if we all went down in a barrage of sniper fire. Jake and Spunk had their hands full keeping the lads from racing right out with whatever sorry arsenal they could scare up—garden tools and kitchen knives? But they weren't the only ones questioning our no-weapons policy.

Eventually, Rousseau came down from the Ward to announce that the injured would all pull through. He called off the day shift and ordered us to our bunks. When the lads raised a ruckus, he closeted with them in the Mess for a talk down. You could hear them roaring through the doors. In a windowless mess hall surrounded by a big stone building, how could you feel anything but heroic and invincible?

Alone in my bunk, it was a different story.

Rubio's curtains were pulled tight, but I heard him tossing and coughing as I climbed by. Should've knocked to see if he needed anything, but if he went on about tonight's disaster being Rousseau's fault, I'd have to yell at him.

It was hotter than ever in the tier. Closing the drapes was like sealing your coffin lid. But I lay there shivering. My precious window on the Lagoon could now be a sniper's target. The life I'd pieced together since Abel's Wave was fraying in too many places. Had to hold myself together, not retreat like Jenn had, into monomania or worse.

Reviewing the day: The Causeway and Dark Boy. Spunk. Daniel, whose face was already fading from memory, except for his smile. What sort of life allows you to be so open and trusting? Maybe it was all a front. Even the cheeriest guy might have hidden tragedies.

Go home, he said. Read the book.

Why not? Tired, surely, but too jangled to sleep. Even beer hadn't softened the edges. So I plucked the cloth-wrapped rectangle from my gut wallet, and took up where I'd left off.

10th March, 1849

On the evening of the 9th, we were prepared for a storm as it lightened and thundered very severely all about us but we came out easy from this. This morning, we find a fair wind and are moving on our course at the rate of 6 knots, which I hope will continue.

11 O.C. This day, a sail seen but too far to the windward to speak her. I now feel with the rest of the company in the forward cabin as independent as possible through the exertions of our sail maker who has made a bag which covers the forward hatch and will protect us against the inconvenience of water dripping through upon us.

4 O.C.—we have just now come out of the squall with the loss of the hook to the square sail jack stay. We were going 15 knots during some part of this squall. We also carried away the pin to the main sheet block . . . the Capt. says he never for 15 years experienced so long and continued heavy weather.

Just as obsessed with the weather as we were. There was one point of connection at least. A few pages later, he recorded a 'bill of fare.'

On Sunday
Morning—Indian Meal Cakes & Cornish Hash & Coffee
Dinner—Boiled Ham—Plum Pudding—Tea—Soft Tack & Scouse

Monday
Morning—Mush, Fried Ham & Chocolate—Tea
Dinner—Beef Pork & Boiled Rice—Scouse & Hash—Tea

Tuesday
Morning—Indian Cakes—Coffee—Fried Pork
Dinner—Pork & Beans & Pancakes—Tea—Soft Tack—Tea

Wednesday
Morning—Beans warmed—Mush, Chocolate
Dinner—Codfish & Apple Dumplings—Tea—Hash & Scones

On Thursday
Morning—Codfish Hash—Hard Bread & Coffee
Dinner—Beef Pork & Plum Pudding—Tea—Soft Tack—Black Tea

Friday
Morning—*Indian Meal Cakes*—*Coffee & Fried Pork*
Dinner—*Pork & Beans*—*Pancakes*
Supper—*Tea*—*Soft Tack*

Saturday
Morning—*Warmed Beans*—*Mash & Chocolate*
Dinner—*Codfish & Apple Dumplings*
Supper—*Tea & Scones*

Soft tack? Couldn't bring an image to mind. Mush or beans I could easily identify with. Odd that just reading about food could be soothing. This two-hundred-year-old menu was little better than what we got in the Mess, though there was plenty of chocolate and coffee, rare treats at Unca Joe. And his fish would have been ocean-fresh. Some of the dens tried fish-farming, but we'd had little success with it. Too hard to find really clean water. I read on.

"I had a misunderstanding with Heyden which, if his disposition is good & his word is worth the breath that gave it life, will be as good as a friend as before. I find it is worth something to know the disposition of men, to know how far to depend upon them in future emergencies."

Well, there you go. Some things don't ever change. Like, who could I depend on when it mattered? Crazy Jenn? Sick Rubio? Since the Wave, I'd depended on Rousseau, but was the boss man right about not fighting back?

Downstairs, he seemed to have got the lads under control. The roaring faded, doors closed, debate lingered on the stairs, sullen voices whispered through the tier. The racks shuddered and creaked as people clambered to their bunks. My journal writer went to bed in a three-masted, storm-tossed boat adrift in an endless ocean. Considering that, the stone walls of Unca Joe felt a whole lot more secure.

I put the book away. Face each day as it comes. With luck, Rousseau would cancel the night shift as well, and we could all stay safe at home for a change.

TWELVE

The light was all wrong when I woke, like I'd slept through the whole afternoon. Snores all around me, so I wasn't the only one. No wake-up call. But I knew it wasn't Sunday. Ah, right. The attack.

I stuck my head out. My cross-aisle neighbor, a slight, dreadlocked girl named Kari, was scaling the rack with a steaming mug in her free hand and a hunk of bread between her teeth.

"No call tonight, Kari? What time is it?"

She kept climbing till she could stash the mug in her bunk and free up her mouth. "Eighteen hundred. Rousseau pulled both shifts off the streets for now."

Just what I'd hoped. "Good move."

"Yeah! Guys gettin' shot an' all! Friggin' scary!" She tore off a gob of bread. "Be chores instead, of course."

"I can live with that." The warm scent from her mug made my stomach tingle. I reached for my jeans and tee.

Out on the balcony, I peered down at Main. Freaky to see the big space so still and deserted. A lone teller processed some last-minute turn-ins while two of the older women rearranged stuff on the barter shelves, busying themselves with make-work. Tension hung in the air like an invisible mist. When someone banged through the mess hall doors, they both started, then shared an uncomfortable laugh.

My flip-flops clattered on the empty stairs. At the turn, a pair of strangers nearly ran me down, bright blue messenger vests flapping. On their way to Rousseau's office, probably to take news of the attack around to the other dens. Past me too fast to catch their sign. Didn't matter. Vests on, they belonged to all of us. Rousseau never used the CB for sensitive stuff, in case he'd be overheard. By who? Be interesting to know who the boss was worried about.

That reminded me of the bracelet, and I felt around in my belly pack to make sure it was still there. It'd be a while before Rousseau was wanting to bother about a picker's take, even a maybe-diamond bracelet. Besides . . . sure, Rousseau was my hero, but the privacy of his office always encouraged him to update your report card and offer some stiff advice. I had enough to think about already.

At the doors to the Mess, I couldn't help a glance up at the duty board. There was one name less on the list of confirmed dead. I asked the ladies at the barter shelves what was up.

The younger one dropped her head to hide a smile.

The older woman shrugged. "He wasn't dead after all."

"What?"

"Just out cold. Not a scratch on him. Might have . . . well, just fainted."

Now I was smiling, too. The older woman frowned. "It's hardly funny!"

The younger one pressed both palms to her cheeks. "But it's so embarrassing."

"Better than dead," I said. But that lad would be a long time living it down.

The few Joes awake had gathered in the Mess, sharing rumor, speculation, and the comfort of company. No sign of Rubio or Jenn, but Gracie had commandeered a corner table where she could still see the doors. And beside her . . . Rivera! I waved and headed over.

The poor girl looked dazed, barely upright. I slid onto the stool opposite. "Di! They let you out! How do you . . . ?"

"Threw her out's more like it," Gracie snapped.

Rivera's gaze was wide-angled. One cheek was purpled with bruise and her dark hair looked sticky, like no one had thought to wash the blood off. Her T-shirt was oversized and shapeless, but at least she wasn't wearing what she got sliced up in.

"They needed the cot," she murmured. "Many worse off."

I reached to touch her shoulder. "Shouldn't you be in your bunk?"

"How's she gonna make a three-tier climb, shape she's in?" Gracie flung her long braid around like a whip. "And she needs to eat."

"Get someone to switch till she's better."

"And who'd that be?"

"I don't know. It's your tier!" I wished she'd back off and let me talk to Rivera. "You in much pain?"

A flicker of a smile. "They gave me some stuff."

"Did it help?" I'd always thought Rivera was beautiful, despite the shadow lurking in her eyes. Now she was limp and frail, maybe still in shock.

"It made me dream."

"Pleasant dreams, I hope."

"No." She looked up. "About all the people I worked with . . . before. About my . . ."

Grace slid a tea mug between Rivera's bandaged hands. "Don't, Di—no point stirring all that up again."

"About my baby," Rivera finished doggedly.

"Don't," Grace insisted. "It'll just make you feel worse."

"Let her. If she wants." I'd never heard Rivera's story. "Some things need to be talked about."

Grace was puffing up like a mother hen. "What're you, her shrink now?"

"No, it's okay." Rivera pressed the mug between swathed palms and took a sip. "The one I lost. A little girl. They couldn't save her."

I waited for tears, but she was calm, almost a blank. "Who couldn't?"

"The medics." Grace wanted the topic done with. "She was pregnant when we hauled her out of the water."

"Five months," Rivera said. "They wouldn't let me see her."

"You were there?" I asked Grace.

"Yeah. I worked boat rescues during Abel. Scary friggin' shit. Never want to get near a boat again, 'less I have to."

"Pretty sure you will. We live on an island." I turned to Rivera. "Can't begin to imagine how awful that must have been for you."

"Awful is bringing it up over and over again," Grace muttered.

"Awful would be forgetting," Rivera said quietly. "You'll understand that."

"You're right there, sure enough." I swiveled on my stool. "I'm going for food. You want anything?"

"No, thanks."

"You gotta eat, Di." Gracie leveled a finger at me. "Get her some scrambled."

"You got it." Eggs would cost more than my usual one-chit breakfast, but the girl deserved it.

In the line, I heard the name BlackAdder snarled more than once and brought it back to the table with my rice bowl and Rivera's scrambled.

"BlackAdder. Sure." Gracie set a fork into Rivera's tight-wrapped hand. "I mean, it had to be."

"How do you know?"

"Someone got a look."

"One of the crew?" Like Spunk said, the whole point of snipers was not seeing them.

"Yeah. Or something."

Or something. The rumor mill churning again, and Gracie always willing to put her weight to the wheel. Rubio said if we didn't have BlackAdder, we'd have to invent them. Blame magnets, he called them.

"I mean, that's the sort of lawless, vicious den they are!"

"Mine was solo." Rivera studied her eggs thoughtfully. "Don't Adders usually mob up?"

"More than one sniper," said Grace. "Five or six, I hear."

"I'd have noticed an Adder." Rivera's gaze wandered, as she poked at a memory she'd rather avoid. "I'd have heard bones and skulls and leather. I'd have felt them."

My idea of BlackAdder was like what you get flicking a light around a once-flooded room: a flash of mayhem here, a slice of horror there, no full picture and all the scarier for leaving so much unknown. Adders wore body paint, it was said, or smeared themselves with rotten flesh and blood. They killed for fun and wore their victims' teeth as trophies. When pressed for actual fact, Jake kept it simple: BlackAdder was a gang remnant that attracted every bad habit, imposed no discipline, and had gone off the deep end.

Rivera shook her head. "No, it was somebody really angry. I remember he yelled a lot."

Gracie shoved the egg plate closer. "Let the girl eat!"

We were talking cross-purposes, and what was I doing, playing the rumor game? I hated where it took me. "What does Rousseau say?"

Rivera scraped her fork back and forth, failing to pick up any egg. "What can he say?"

"Talk, talk, talk," scoffed Gracie. "What he does best. Where's the action when we need it? Di, eat your eggs."

Spooning in rice, I said, "Spunk says he's doubled the watch."

Across the room, a posse of the lads stuffing their faces before reporting for sentry duty raised a cheer as the once-dead member of their crew slinked through the doors. Beet-faced, he edged in among them and tried to disappear.

Eyeing them, Gracie said a bit too loudly, "And you'd trust that lot to keep us safe, with nothing but their bare hands and a couple of paddles?"

"They're what we've got." I patted Rivera's back, cleared my dishes, and left, before I walked into trouble defending Rousseau to two people I counted as friends.

Maybe by this time, Rousseau would have a moment free.

His office was a long, narrow room around the corner from the media loft, windowless but for a wall of glass overlooking Main. When there wasn't a line out in the hallway, you'd knock on the half-open door, wait for his signal like at the gate of a sanctuary. He'd found enough deep-red paint to cover the walls, so walking in was like the room swallowing you whole. He'd be hunched over his screen in the thin light leaking in from Main's skylight, or at night, in the warm pool from his desk lamp, the room in shadow but for the gleam of the locked glass case on the wall behind him, protecting the den's small weapons cache. That is, the ones we knew about.

Today, a noisy crowd milled around outside, not the usual orderly line, and the door was closed. As I neared, Jake stuck his head through the door and barked at everyone to keep it down.

"What's the word?" I asked an older guy with sawdust in his hair, one of the handies who built stuff for the den.

"One dead, rest out of danger."

"Heard that. Anything else? Like, who did it?"

He scratched his jaw. "Might never know that for sure."

No chance I'd get to Rousseau now, not with this mob. Fine by me. Eager as I was to unload the sparkly thing, I didn't mind avoiding his scrutiny a while longer. I went back to the media loft for a weather check. A crowd was gathered around the old CB sets used for short-range contact, probably leaking word of the attack to other dens despite Rousseau's cautions. Some of the older denfolk played long-distance signal-bouncing games when the weather was right, scrounging up news of the rest of the world, stuff you didn't get from local sources. Another gang filled the long table of tablets hooked to our rooftop weather station or fiddled with the emergency-band weather radios. We had AM, too, but if you moved off the official frequencies, there was less and less to be found within range.

Amazingly, my favorite machine was free. On my way there, I met one of the Wiz kids I knew slightly, a gangly brown-skinned girl with big teeth and a problem keeping still.

"See Jenn around? I hear she's joining you up here."

"Betcha! Yeah, she come up. Run 'round a bit. Next I look, she's gone."

"Ah. To her bunk, most likely." When Jenn's mania cooled, she crashed hard. "Be good for her, being up here."

The girl's nod was extra-floppy, like I might need convincing. "She best with the crankies. Got 'em in her mind."

The 'crankies' were older machines with outdated software that Jenn recalled how to work with.

I put out a hand to keep her from dancing away. "Maybe you all could help her find her family in Minnesota? You must be doing that sort of thing a lot up here."

The girl pursed her lips. "Not so much."

"No? Isn't everyone wanting to get in touch with friends or relatives on the Mainland?"

"Olders, most."

Jenn was only twenty-seven. This girl was eleven, twelve at most. Me, right in between, though who knew for sure, but suddenly feeling like an ancient grown-up.

"So, you're not looking?"

She shrugged cheerfully. "No reason."

"No reason to look?" Meaning, she had no relatives to search for?

"No reason to leave."

My brow creased automatically. "You mean, you like it here?"

Another shrug, like, what's not to like, or, it is what it is.

"Do the other Wizzers feel that way?" This was new info. Far as I knew, only a few eccentrics like Rubio and Jake were happy to stay on in Manhattan. The rest would hightail it as soon as a chance came up. But den life was all this child had ever known.

"I guess." She looked worried I was probing for disloyal thoughts.

"Okay." I smoothed my frown. "Well, you all take good care of Jenn."

"Will do!" Relieved, she flickered off toward a clutch of her age-mates, grouped around a table heaped with bits of hardware and wiring.

I moved in to claim my machine while I could.

Hurricane warnings popped up everywhere, but so far, the weather held so the internet was up and not cutting out too often—my chance to do a bit of research. Older databases were still sitting somewhere if, like Jenn, you knew where to look. Could I nose around about the documents without calling attention to myself? Did these computers keep records? Meaning to key in 'Arkadia,' my fingers shied away. Something more neutral? Safer if I spelled it differently? To my astonishment, using a 'c' in place of the 'k' brought up a list of files about Mars, stored right there on the computer. Mars again? Curious, I opened a few at random.

Old stuff mostly, history sites, mission logs and news stories from the first and second expeditions. One rare, clear night, Rubio had pointed out the red planet in the sky, told me there'd once been people up there, and how a spacer would breathe cleaner air on Mars than we were right then. The water was pure, too—melted from subsurface ice. Now my screen filled with gorgeous pics of vermilion rocks, towering cliffs, and ruddy skies backgrounding shiny clusters of domes. Rubio called it a huge waste, trying to colonize a frigid desert where you had to live under cover, mine for water, and manufacture air. Better to use those resources to fix our own failing planet.

Apparently, the world agreed. So there was no third expedition. But it made little difference here at home.

Still, it was hard to stop clicking through these beautiful old images. Like a fantasy game. So huge, so . . . unmanaged, like the wild, clean ocean in my old book. Nothing that wild left on Earth except the weather.

"Whacha lookin' at?" Peeto poked his rat's nose over my shoulder. Made me jump a foot. His scruffy ponytail was damp, like he'd just come from the showers. For once, he didn't smell like the streets.

Too late to blank the screen. Plus, I had no urge for dissing anyone today, not even Peeto. "Nothing much. Passing the time."

"Dark days, huh?" he offered.

I nodded.

"I do that a lot."

"What?"

"Come up here an' look at stuff."

"You do?"

Peeto dragged a chair noisily across the tiles. "When I can't sleep, y'know? Give these old machines a tussle."

Interesting, that something might bother Peter Sweeney enough to keep him awake nights—well, days. But I didn't ask what his problem was. I wasn't *that* interested.

He poked at the screen. "That's Mars, ain't it?"

"I guess. Just looking at the pretty pictures." I closed down the Mars pics. "Listen, any chance you've seen my new pack around in all the noise and upset, maybe on some pal of yours' back?"

His mouth drooped. "Still fingerin' me, huh?"

"Just want what's mine back."

"Wasn't me. Honest." He hiked his chair up close. "But ya might ask the boss about it."

"What?" I peered at him sideways. Jenn once called him Rousseau's spymaster, but I took that as one of her odder delusions. Even cleaned up, Peeto didn't come off as anyone's master. "You're saying Rousseau steals people's stuff?"

"Course not!" He reached past my hands to two-pick the keypad. "Just like a heads up. Listen, ya wanna know about Mars, ask Ellie Mae. She'll tell ya a thing or two."

"Are these her files?"

"Pro'bly. Mars is like her thing, if ya can get her to talk."

"And you can?" Hard to believe.

But Peeto was refusing offense today. "Sure. When we hang in the garden together. More private, y'know? She's been warned."

"About what?"

"'Bout keeping her ideas to herself. It's no secret."

Had Peeto flagged me as someone interested in radical ideas? This made me nervous. What if Jenn was right about him? Time for some misdirect. "Does she know sun signs?"

"What?"

"You know, astrology. It matters where the planets were when you were born, so I thought maybe if I learn about planets, I can backtrack to my birth date."

"You believe that stuff?" Never seen Peeto look like he pitied someone more than himself. "Well, ya could always ask. She's got, y'know, an open mind." He leaned into the keypad again. "Like, here's something she showed me. So I got all the sides."

The file came up on the screen. Lots of print and bold-faced exclamations. "See what it says? No dudes ever walked on Mars, there's no Arcadia base, and never was one."

"No what? What did you call it?"

"Arcadia One. The international base. See it right there?"

Arcadia with a C. Did it matter?

"Yep. All a giant media hoax."

I had a mad urge to pull the documents out of my gut wallet and check the spelling. Had to be a silly coincidence.

"Here, take a look." Peeto linked to a site where the Mars story became a government program to distract a restless public from the warming Earth, the rising waters, the wheat famine, the increasingly unstable and noxious atmosphere, whatever. More conspiracies.

He sat back, smiling at the screen. "Everyone's got a theory, right?"

"But what's the truth?"

"Depends on who's talking, don't it?" His head bobbed like he'd laid down a nugget of wisdom. "Just think it's cool."

"Cool why?"

"'Cause it would be awesome to fool the whole world like that. Besides, don't matter if it's true or not. Ain't no one going back to Mars anytime soon, things as they are."

But what if they were? No, that was too crazy.

"You don't think it would be nice to know? Like, if we got to Mars before, maybe we can pull ourselves together again and do something to fix the world."

"Dream on." Peeto buzzed air through his lips, typing in a new address. "But you gotta love the balls of it, right? Goofing on the whole freakin' world."

I started hating him again.

By then, he'd taken over the keypad, and the skylight over the main hall was losing daylight. I'd try Rousseau's office again, even more uneasy than before.

As I turned away, Peeto said, "That hurricane's turned north, sure 'nuff, an' guess what they're gonna call it."

I ticked my fingers. What letter were we at by now? "Lost track."

"J, so they're calling it Joseph!"

Hurricane Joe.

If you believed in omens—almost as silly as astrology—this could hardly be a good one.

THIRTEEN

The line outside the office was shorter now, mostly since it hadn't moved at all, and the smart ones had given up and left. With the crowd thinned, I saw that a lot of who's left were strangers, way too many for comfort. I eased back up the hall, putting space between us. But they were mostly standing around, in loose groups that seemed as suspicious of each other as I was of them. New recruits? Not unless they were transfers. Most were already wearing den sign. One group had it tattooed right on their cheek or bicep. Kind of cool looking, really, but Rousseau didn't hold with tats, unless you had them from before. One of his quirks. Maybe Rubio was right about him being a priest back when.

Just as I'd decided to try again later, Gracie rolled up beside me, her big face lit with expectation. "Come to watch the show?"

"What show's that?"

"The den leader dog-and-pony show."

She knew something I didn't. I leaned closer. "You mean, all these guys?"

"Nah, they're security, most like."

"Not ours."

"So you didn't hear?" She was talking loud, swinging that thick braid of hers, like she meant to be noticed. "Rousseau's got in some other den leaders. Big confab."

"Here?" I studied the strangers more carefully. "Said nothing in the Mess."

"Just heard."

Me, always the last to find out. "From who?"

"The watch dude."

"You talk to the watch dude? Like, a conversation?"

"Sure. Where do we all go to talk private? Out on the walkway. He hears all kinds of shit out there."

I hadn't had much call to talk private, plus the watch dude scared me. "Rube's always saying the dens need to talk more. So, the boss is taking action after all."

Grace shrugged. "Still just talk. And only the dens we trust enough to allow inside."

"How many is that?"

"No count till we see who showed."

Just as she said it, the door swung open. The hallway crowd stirred out of their clustering. Other curious Joes had wandered up to join us. The corridor seemed tight again.

Grace edged along the wall for a better view. "Wish I had my phone."

She was always saying that, but I had to admit, photos would be nice, to show the others. I ghosted in behind her shoulder. "Will we know who's who?"

"Only by rep. Never seen 'em in person."

The first out was a very tall dude, straight as a stick and dressed in shiny, close-fitting black that showed off every perfect muscle. The crowd hushed and drew aside to make a path. Multicolored tats covered every exposed inch of him, even his face, so you couldn't tell what his original skin tone had been. Images of fantastic animals moved as he moved.

I leaned over Grace's arm. "Got to be Tall Tom."

She cracked a grin. "Gotta be. Wow. I'd heard he was totally hot."

He was certainly stunning, but like a work of art. Nothing you'd want to get close to. But Grace was smitten. "Still thinking one of his guys did Rivera?" I teased.

"More like an Adder pretending to be a Tommy."

"Why pretend?"

"Stir up trouble. Maybe why Tall Tom's lookin' so touchy."

He was at that. His thin, handsome profile was pinched, like he'd tasted something bad but couldn't spit it out. He stepped aside to share his grouch with his quartet of equally tall and toned bodyguards, two of them women. The four showed more skin, but it was less colorfully decorated.

A woman came out next, leaning back to deliver a final word to Jake just inside. She was medium height, medium build, medium everything, even her clothing. Tall Tom's total opposite. As she passed behind him, she brushed fingertips across his back, ending with a coy little wave of farewell.

He turned. "Max—you're alone? Take some of my guys with you."

"Thanks. I'm good." The woman patted her hip and kept going. She nodded at us pleasantly as she strode by, but her don't-fuck-with-me look could've stopped a tidal wave.

"That's Maxine, Ladysmith's boss," supplied Grace. "And she's packing. Wonder how she got it past the door. Rousseau must be fit to be tied!"

"That's Maxine?" Rubio had been very taken with this woman. Yet, once she'd rounded the corner, I could hardly recall a thing about her, even what color she was wearing. Jenn would be so disappointed. "I expected a lot more . . . style."

"Style's wasted on the streets."

"Good thing for me," I laughed. "But doesn't a leader need to set an example?"

"You mean, like Rousseau?"

"Rousseau has a style. It's . . ." I groped for the right word. "Funky."

"Yeah, well, Maxine left her guards out on the walkway so they wouldn't have to check their weapons, but she managed to smuggle in her own. I call that an example."

"Outside's where they belong." I saw Grace prepping a comeback and jogged her arm. "Check this one out."

This guy with a shaved head and a downcast scowl had to be from Revelations, who claimed their only true leader was God. His hooded security fell into lockstep behind him and they left quickly, like they couldn't wait to be out of there. All three wore identical, scratchy-looking robes and tucked their hands inside like old-time monks in videos. Didn't mean they were peaceable. Neo-crusaders, Rubio called them, explaining that Revelations kept weapons but only the edged kind—blades of all descriptions, nothing mechanized, like technology had stopped five hundred years ago. So I had to wonder what they had up those long, loose sleeves. At least Ladysmith's let you know they were carrying.

If Rousseau had been a priest before, how did he feel about these guys?

A brighter trio now clogged up the door, getting in each other's way about who should go first. Two men and a woman, middle thirties, decked out in well-fitting suits of honeyed colors, soft shirts, dressy shoes. Their skin had a healthy glow.

"Uptowners?" I breathed. "What're they doing here?"

"They wish," Grace chuckled. "That'll be Empire State. They're only up in the East 20s."

"How d'you know all this?" Hard to smooth all the resentment from my tone.

"Jus' been around longer."

Looking closer, I saw their clothes weren't new so much as clean and cared-for. The woman's jacket was a glowing red. One of the men was dark-skinned, and his open-necked shirt matched his even darker eyes. The other, a shortish blond, was wearing a tie. Like they'd walked right out of those old fashion mags. Rubio admired what he called Empire State's 'corporate structure,' run by a board of trustees. Maybe the blond was their chairman or whatever they called it.

"They sure care how they dress," I noted.

"Keeping up appearances." Gracie allowed just a hint of regret. "Like we all used to."

As the Empires passed Tall Tom, still muttering with his bodyguards, the blond guy made a remark I didn't catch. Tall Tom snapped a reply over his shoulder.

Seconds later, the two were nose to nose, snarling like dogs, Tall Tom looming over the blond, whose head topped out below his opponent's chin. His two companions just watched, the woman looking faintly amused. But Jake quickly wedged himself between, a palm pressed to each heaving chest.

"Tom. Will. Easy now. We'll not be solving this by squabbling among ourselves."

"We're not paying for his frigging army!" the blond guy spat.

Tall Tom shoved Jake's hand aside. "So when you talk about share and share alike, just how do you define that?"

"Gentlemen, please!" rumbled Rousseau from the doorway.

To my surprise, they both hesitated, then stood back a step, still glaring as if ready to launch into it again at any moment. Jake held position between them.

"Those two really don't like each other," I murmured to Grace.

"Probably a guy thing. Y'know, tall and gorgeous versus short and tight-ass."

"Got to be more than that." I thought the blond was okay looking, though better if he'd let his hair grow some, not shear it down to a stubble.

"Maybe so. You'd have to go further back than me for that one."

Jake backed off as Rousseau came up to lay a companionable hand on each tensed-up shoulder. I expected at least Tall Tom to shrug him off, but both gave in to the older man's authority in his own den.

"It's time to put differences aside." Rousseau clearly had a lot more to say, but glancing from one man to the other, den leaders and his equals, he seemed to think better of it. "Please, go in peace. Take the message to your dens. Think about what's been said, and what we should do about it. If anything at all."

He squeezed Tall Tom's shoulder, then slid an arm across the shorter man's back to lead him off to join his companions. The red-jacket woman took him in tow with a cool hand on his arm. They'd brought no extra security, unless like Maxine's it awaited them out on the walkway. After polite thanks and goodbyes to Jake and Rousseau, off they went.

Rousseau turned back to smile up at Tall Tom. A terse little smile with a lot of history, one that said they'd been here before. "Okay, now?"

Tom didn't exactly smile back, but he let go of the glower that had roiled his tattoos into a ferocious mask of fury and was simply handsome again. He offered Rousseau a brief nod, then gestured his entourage ahead and stalked off after them.

Rousseau shook his head pensively and retreated to his office.

A collective sigh whispered among the remaining Joes.

Grace watched Tall Tom till he turned the corner. "That was interesting."

"So who didn't make it?" I was counting dens.

"No sign of the Macys, but that's no surprise. Probably still arguing about who to send. No one from Riverhome, but they could be storm-prepping, out there in the river. And I heard some Gimme Shelter ladies might come, but a baby was due and they might have to stick around."

"Still, it's major, right? Five dens together in one place?"

"Shouldn't take bad news to make it happen. But I've witnessed the miracle and must hereby go forth to tell the tale."

More fodder for the rumor mill. "Too bad about your phone."

"Yah." She grinned. "Words just won't do him justice."

"You're too hard on the Empire dude."

"Who, Mr. Bland?" She was sure I was kidding.

"I mean, at least he looked, y'know . . ." I felt my cheeks heating up. "Nice?"

Her guffaw broke out in a gust. "Who cares about nice?"

"Well, I . . ."

She saw me at a loss. "Hey, don't mind me. It's good you noticed anyone at all, right?"

What did she mean? "I guess."

Spunk appeared in the doorway and scanned the hallway like a guard dog making sure no one snuck back in. Then he gave Jake a reassuring nudge and sauntered off, jiggling his eyebrows at me as he went by, his limp nearly invisible. At least someone had enjoyed themselves this afternoon. Most of the Joes drifted after him.

Jake took in the remains: two older lads, Grace, and me. "Waiting to see the boss?"

"I was just hanging." Grace nudged my arm and sloped off. "See ya later."

Jake eyed the two lads, who wore solemn faces and hands clasped in front of them.

"We'd . . . uh . . . like to discuss . . . um . . . the funeral arrangements?"

"Yes. Good. We'll go to the loft, bring him a plan once we've worked out the details." Once they'd nodded and left, Jake turned to me. "Is it important?"

I shrugged, then reached into my belly pack and dangled the bracelet briefly in front of him. "Only, Spunk said I should . . ."

His eyes widened. "Huh. Let me check."

I expected to be sent away so Rousseau could grab a breather. But Jake was soon back.

"Boss'll be with you in a moment. He's got some notes to get down."

"I bet he does, after all that." But if I was hoping for some info tidbits or special insights from my tier-mate, I was disappointed. He only smiled at me wearily.

"Don't keep him too long."

"In and out," I promised, hoping that would be the case.

"Good." Jake turned to mope away up the corridor, leaving the door open behind him.

The second he left me alone in the long, echoing hallway, my nerves flared up again. I shoved the sparkler back in my wallet, fingers brushing the plastic edges of other, more secret contents. No one, ever, asked you to turn out the insides of your gut wallet. It was the last private place—as Rubio called it, the *sanctum sanctorum,* the key to keeping one's sanity in an oh-so-public environment. But what if Rousseau decided to make an exception?

Rousseau. I wanted always and never to be where he was. Inside his circle of safety, outside his rule of law, which often seemed arbitrary, no doubt due to me missing the bigger picture. Rubio nagged me about making Rousseau a father figure, but why was that such a bad idea? My real father was a total unknown, at least for now. It did make me want to be the good daughter, so there was all that guilt when I hadn't been. Like now.

After what seemed a proper wait, I smoothed my hair back, tugged my tank top straight, then rapped gently on the open door.

"Come!"

I put on my most humble face and stepped inside. "Got a minute?"

Rousseau looked up from his computer, pale screen light caught in the sweat beading on his ebony skin, in the hollows under his eyes. "Hey, Glim."

"Hey, boss. Don't you look all done in."

"Thanks."

"No, I meant . . ." Failed at sympathy. "Listen, if you're too busy . . ."

"Nah, c'mon in. Sit. Give me a break from an afternoon of heavy-duty turf-wrestling."

I felt petty and irrelevant after the high-power that just left. "Don't they want to help?"

"Sure, sure. As long as it doesn't require sacrifice on anyone's part." He shut the lid of his laptop. "Well, I can't blame them. You don't keep a den alive by going soft at the first sign of trouble. It's a beginning. We'll see where it ends up."

It was stuffy hot inside, but Rousseau wore his signature leather vest, over a T-shirt that faded into the blood-colored walls. A mug of herbal steamed at his elbow. Extra chairs were pulled up to the desk or scattered about at random angles. His assistant, Song-yi, slippered about collecting used mugs and cups, then retreated, closing the door behind her.

I gathered myself in front of his desk, too antsy to sit. "Too bad about . . . all the trouble."

He nodded heavily. "A nasty turn of events. Should have seen they'd go off the rez, all revved up like they were."

So like Rousseau to take the blame. "But snipers! You couldn't have known . . ."

"There have been . . . signs."

"You mean it could happen again?"

"No question something's changed out there." His shrug was more a flexing of muscle. Then he folded his big hands on the computer like it might try to escape. "So, what's up?"

"Something good, for a change." I laid the sparkler down on the desk like a prize.

He gave a surprised grunt. "What's this now?"

I ran the story, from the events on the dock up to my turn with Spunk in the pass-thru, every detail. Didn't want to sound like I was withholding. "He said bring it right to you."

Rousseau picked up the bracelet, stretched it between two fingers, then reached into a drawer and pulled out a loupe. He didn't offer victory right off. He studied the even rows of glitter at close range. Impatient, I looked away, at the shapely metal inside the weapons case and the half-dozen police flashlights in their heavy-duty chargers—objects of envy in the den for their really bright light and potential as hand weapons.

"So, what do you think?" Embarrassing if it turned out to be glass.

He sucked his cheek, peered a little longer till I was fairly dancing in place. His broad mouth toyed with a grin and I finally got he was playing me. "Nice find, I'd say."

"You mean it's real?"

He nodded. "Not the best-quality stones, but they rarely are with pieces like this where you're using a lot of them." He set the loupe down on a little tray and put the bracelet beside it. "This'll raise your credit a good bit."

I let myself feel the thrill. "Will it buy me a few nights off?"

"More than a few, if that's what you want." He rocked back in his chair and looked up at me again. He wasn't smiling now. "I thought it might be something else."

"How's that?"

He swiveled the chair and rose. Rousseau standing up was always an event, as he morphed from a benign god behind a desk to a tower of well-padded muscle dominating the room. He turned into the shadows behind him to grab a stack of clothing, clean jeans and patterned T-shirts. He dropped it onto the desk in the pool of lamplight.

I shook off a chill. "Looks like my last night's take . . ."

"Straight from the tellers." He reached behind to add another layer to the pile.

Double or nothing. Just brave it out. "My new pack! Awesome! Where'd you find it?"

"You'd lost it?"

"Betcha! I claimed it legit, and right off, someone swiped it from my bunk."

"So far, so good." One more backward reach, and Rousseau tossed the baggie of blister packs down on top of the stack.

Shit.

My mind blanked, unable to conceive how much trouble I was in.

"Uhhhh . . ."

He waited, his dark face impassive.

I was that bit of storm trash again, lost, mute, hauled from the wreckage.

Finally, he said, more sad than angry, "You turned in the other stuff. Why not these?"

"Um. I . . ." I fluttered my hands like that might get the words flowing again. "I thought . . . uh . . ."

"Thought they might be a good high? What the hell, give 'em a try?"

"What? Me? No! I don't do . . . !"

Rousseau never yelled, never used those meaty fists of his. His voice just got lower, deep and quiet, and he'd fix pitiless eyes on you like you were prey. "Half my pickers would like to eat the food or take the drugs they find, but where would the den be if they did?"

"I'd never hold back food!"

"You don't get to choose what you turn in and what you don't."

"It's just . . . oh, you know . . ."

"No, I don't."

"I thought . . . it's just . . . I kept them for Rubio."

"What, so he could get high?" He flattened both hands on the desktop. "You're his dealer now?"

"No! No!" His outrage pounded at me like a storm wave. I slumped into the chair furthest from the desk. "Like what if they could help him? 'Cause he's getting so much worse!"

After a moment Rousseau said, "Ah." He puffed out a tired little laugh, touched his forehead. "Of course. The wrong gesture for the right reason." He dropped into his own chair, leaning over the desk on folded arms and flicking the ziplock with a forefinger. "But since when are you a medic? You have any idea what these are? You can read, as I recall."

"It was dark. I . . ." I was an idiot. "I meant to look, but then they were gone."

He zipped open the bag to spill out the blister packs in a clatter across the desktop. "This is warfarin. Know what that is?"

I felt the sear of his gaze without looking. "No."

"It's a blood thinner. Also used as rat poison. Rubio would likely have read the label. But if not, you could've killed him."

I shut my eyes, then buried them in my hands. "Stupid, stupid."

"Indeed. No less than the canoe lads bulling off into risky territory. Putting your own needs before the safety of the den. It can be fatal." He gathered the pill packs and shoved them back in the bag. "Spunk's right to keep an eye on you."

I nodded deep into my chest, scary close to weeping. I'd screwed up, in so many ways. Couldn't even steal something right. Like, what if Rubio hadn't read the label? Time to give up, empty the whole wallet onto the desk, bare my greater guilt and fling myself on the boss man's mercy, begging him not to throw me out into the streets. I was so close to doing it. But two details nagged, enough to stiffen my back: why was the ninja girl carrying around rat poison, and how did it end up in Rousseau's hands?

"It was Peeto, wasn't it?"

"What was?"

"Peeto who tossed my bunk. The little creep!"

Did I hear a faint rumbling chuckle?

"No, in fact, it wasn't."

"Who, then?" Humiliation had rubbed me raw. Dignity be damned.

"Not exactly a need-to-know, but . . . I did."

I looked up open-mouthed.

"That is, I had it done." He lifted his chin to regard me over the wide bridge of his nose. "Standard practice with newbies. You didn't notice before because you were always clean." He saw me roiling in disbelief. "Now, before you talk yourself into being the victim here, sit up and listen."

He'd read me clear. Right off, I let his betrayal loom way larger than my own. He was supposed to be the righteous one. I shifted in the chair, the merest sullen concession.

"You made a wrong choice, an ignorant choice, but out of loyalty to a friend. I have to respect that." He caught the pile between his palms and evened it up like a deck of cards, then lifted the blister packs off the top. "So here's the deal. The backpack's a valid claim. It's yours. The rest is forfeit, no credits earned. But we'll keep your . . . misstep between us for now." He patted the bagged pill packs. "These go to the folks who know how to use them." He slid the clothing across the desk. "This goes back to the swap shelf ASAP, the moment you leave here."

The deal was fair, even generous, though it made him feel better than it did me. But even driven by my need to whine and fuss and show how much he'd hurt me, I blessed whatever gods there were that I wouldn't be thrown out of the den.

"Thanks," I grumbled.

"You're welcome." Seeing no show of gratitude, he was done indulging me. "And by the way, it wouldn't hurt to claim a decent pair of jeans next time you find one."

A low blow. So I did have a bit of vanity squirreled away someplace. "What d'you care what I look like?"

"I care what any of us look like, when there's a choice." A stock response. His mind was already moving on to more pressing matters. More pressing than one misbehaving newbie, but it was like worrying a sore tooth—I couldn't let it go just yet.

"What about the bracelet?"

"Glim, Glim. A childish pout is not a useful negotiating tool." Rousseau wagged his head wearily. "Okay. The usual cut is twenty percent. You'll get ten this time, as a reminder. It'll still be a tidy stack of credits."

"Will it buy drugs for Rubio?"

His eyes narrowed. "We don't buy or sell our medical care at Unca Joe, or hadn't you noticed? Did I ask for your insurance card when I dragged you half-dead out of the rubbish?"

I'd normally have heard the ice clipping his words, but I'd gone tone deaf, batting my head against a dead end of resentment I couldn't have named the cause of. I told myself diamonds should bring me glory, not guilt and humiliation. I stuffed the pack and the pile of clothing into my grab bag, making a rat's nest of it, and turned to sulk off.

His fist shot out and pinned my wrist. He half-rose in his chair. "We're not done here!"

I flinched hard.

Whatever he saw in my face made him ease back into his seat and quiet his voice. But he held me firm. "Listen to me. We've no room for self-indulgence around here! Really, I expected better. There's enough bad shit coming down without you sensible ones going off on me. And that includes your buddy Rubio."

"He's only trying to help!" I leaned toward the door, but no way Rousseau would let me decide how this argument ended.

"Saying every other den is better than the one that saved his life, that's his idea of help? He feels that way, he can leave anytime. See if anyone else will take him, sick as he is!" He shoved my arm away like it was my fault he'd got so worked up. Which it totally was. "Now get out of here. Be ready for a morning work call. No night shift till we get this shooting looked into."

I heaved myself through the door and nearly slammed into Song-yi, carrying mugs of fresh tea, a cloud of mint steam traveling with her. The hot flash of rebuke in her glance told me she'd been listening. She guarded Rousseau's peace of mind like a mother hen.

I mumbled an instinctive 'sorry!' and escaped up the corridor, wondering which of so many things I was apologizing for. My tantrum lasted me just past the turn of the hall, where I halted, panting, and leaned against the wall. Only some really deep breaths kept me from throwing up.

What was going on?

In all my months at Unca Joe, I'd never talked back to Rousseau like that, not even at my craziest. It was like some restraint had broken, the lid flying off a jar of rotted food. I'd pushed him to the edge of rage—and meant to. Knowing he'd had the worst of days, I'd kept pushing. It just wasn't like me.

The stash in my gut wallet weighed a ton right then. But the looting of my bunk struck deep. Standard procedure, he'd said, so why should I be the exception? Did I think I was somehow special?

Best to leave it alone, at least till I was calmer. Best to count what I hadn't lost, along with Rousseau's trust and respect. Stuff could be consoling. Like, I had the fancy pack again, and had toted up some solid credits. Most important, the book, the documents, were still my private treasures.

Down in Main, itchy and irritable, I tossed the jeans and tees onto the swap shelf. They'd have fit me, being the ninja girl's. If Rousseau wanted me dressing better, he should've let me have one of those!

Fuck it, I thought, and went looking for Rubio. I could share some of my peeve with him, maybe work the worst of it out. The skylight was a timeless gray and Main was buzzing again. The continuing storm alert had day-shifters crowding the weather board, checking on their next day's call. Night-shifters milled about by habit, not quite believing they were off the hook till morning. Sorting out a double morning shift had the job clerks backed up and more irritable than ever. On my way to search for Rube in the Mess, I found Jenn observing the chaos with the bemused grin of one who didn't have to deal with it anymore.

"Hanging out down here just to make us pickers feel bad?"

"Just done eating." Jenn was cheerful and her shiny bowl of hair looked freshly washed. "But was it breakfast or dinner?"

"Everything's upside down. The picking might be easier, but what makes them think it's any safer out there in daylight?" I noticed Jenn's duds were less fluttery, more trim than her usual. Working on a new look, now she was posted to Media? "Rube in the Mess?"

"Didn't see him. Check his bunk?"

"Good point."

"But . . ." Jenn's half shrug said Rubio was not usually her concern. "When you find him, tell him to keep an extra-low profile."

I sighed. "Now what?"

She jutted her chin toward a loud huddle over by the stairs. Canoe crew and enforcers, the raised-fist boys, in deep discussion. "Someone got the idea that Rubio tipped them off."

"Tipped who off?"

"The snipers."

"WHAT?" I could hardly catch my breath. "No way! Why would they ever think . . . ?"

"They aren't looking for logic, they're looking for blame. Because . . ." She beckoned me closer. "When they got carried away, they went charging off where they shouldn't."

"Yeah, Rousseau just told me that."

"Well, it was BlackAdder's turf."

Inevitable, though he hadn't mentioned it. "He should ground them."

"Can you see that happening?" Jenn's mouth twisted. "Like, how much control does he really have over them? People are wondering."

"But, Rubio? That's just crazy! Who'd believe he'd have anything to do with BlackAdder? How would he talk to them? How would he even find them?"

She shrugged. "Like I said, logic is not the rule of the day."

Not of my day, either, I mused. My attention drifted. "Listen, did you know Rousseau has our bunks searched on the sly?"

"I've heard it happens." Jenn unrolled long sleeves, then rolled them up again, more artfully. "Why?"

"That doesn't bother you?"

"Sure, but . . ." She looked pensive. "As long as we keep letting new people in, I guess I'd call it necessary for good security."

"But . . . our bunks?"

She weighed her hands. "Privacy or safety? Not a choice I'd want to make. Okay, I'm off to the laundry room."

"Your idea of a night off, scrubbing your fingers raw?"

"Better than no clean clothes."

I glanced down at my own, patchy with old stains. Was it only yesterday I gave so little thought to what I wore? "Maybe I should join you."

"Might better rest up for the morning. Big storm on the way. And when you find Rubio . . ."

"I'll tell him."

The warnings I had to pass along were piling up like hurricane wreckage at his door.

FOURTEEN

J enn was more-than-usual stern about sending me off to bed. Maybe she read the floaty distress that hit me after my session with Rousseau. A familiar bunk's the best retreat when the ground turns unsteady. I took her advice.

It was a known fact how there used to be spy cameras everywhere in the city. You still found them tucked away here or there, dead of course, and even if still storing solar, where would they send their video?

Denfolk made jokes about an in-house system, mostly raunchy ones. No one took the idea too seriously. But now I was searching every corner, every crumbling plaster leaf on a column capital, for a hidden lens. Even up in my bunk with the drapes pulled close, I prodded every single inch for signs of a bug. Nothing. But I still felt . . . watched.

I wanted a closer look at the sheath of documents, but didn't dare take it out of my wallet. What about the old book? Did Rousseau keep tabs on every book in the den? I decided to risk it, slid it stealthily out of hiding and opened to my page marker:

> "We have today been divided into watches & are to be on deck and on duty night & day as follows: 4 hours on and 8 hours off for sleep or rest as the time may be. In this night or day, we are divided into starboard, middle & larboard watches, consisting of 7 in middle & larboard & 8 in the starboard and for instance, the starboard watch commences at 8 O.C. at night, then continues until 12 O.C., then the middle at from 12 to 4 O.C., then call the larboard to stay from 4 until 8 in morning & so on throughout the day. I was chosen by the Capt. for the middle watch & I have to be on deck tonight from 12 O.C. to 4 and then go to sleep again if I please."

Not long till I was yawning. Enough of that sort of regimen right here in the den, with everyone's schedule set 24/7 for the good of the community, with Rousseau as the captain of our urban ship, and myself a lowly crew member. Some things never change.

My morning draw was in the West 50s, between Eighth and the river. Which meant mostly Eighth blocks, since everything west of Ninth was more or less *in* the river. Did the job clerks insist on the old riverbanks as boundary markers out of denial or did they have a darker sense of humor than we gave them credit for?

On the streets, a greenish light hung between the buildings, glaring to my night-adapted eyes but heavy with the sweat of the coming storm and the stink of the slime edging the tidal zone. Even once I moved to dry pavement, the whole town seemed under water. I was way off my game, from the heat, the strangeness of working in daylight, plus still smarting from my run-in with Rousseau. I wasn't half concentrating.

The avenues felt busy, the side streets almost crowded. A lot of the dens must have gone on day shift due to the weather alert. I usually avoided other pickers or made sure they avoided me, but today that took real effort. I kept turning a corner to find someone speeding my way. The women from Revelations in their long skirts and face-shrouding bonnets stared through me like I wasn't there. A Tommy might give me a warning snarl, Empires and Ladysmiths a neutral nod. But most were hurrying about their business, eager to be home before the weather turned. All of us kept a close eye on rooftops and open windows, so word was out about the snipers.

The crowd thinned as I moved uptown, which only made me feel more exposed. I imagined armed Adders in every doorway and Stormies at each intersection. Even told myself I heard chanting, closer than I'd like. Instead, as I left a wrecked and long-ago-plundered Eighth Avenue storefront near midday, I got three Macys lined up on the sidewalk, two little girls and an older boy, their grab bags as empty as mine.

We called Macy's the kid den, but it was more a loose bunch of gangs, like BlackAdder started out, only way younger. They'd divvied up a huge old building on West 34th. They were storm-rescues or runaways from other dens like Revelations, which lost a lot of its young ones to Macy 'tribes,' as they called them. Mostly they were kids in love with a lack of adult supervision. These three were the youngest I'd yet seen working the streets.

I halted in the doorway. "Looking for someone?"

The boy curled his lip. "Only yer bag there."

"Dude, I'm a working stiff, just like you."

A shrug. "Too bad. Home empty tonight."

"Already empty."

"Yeah? Give it over."

"No way." The kid had scabs all over his half-shaved scalp. Couldn't be more than seven or eight. "Your chiefs were no-show at the confab yesterday. What's that about?"

"Chief of me!" He gave his chest three hard raps, then glared at the others. "Ri?"

"Ri!" they chorused.

"Don' need no olders tellin' us whatever!"

"No telling, just talking," I said. "Safer if you join in. What tribe, you?" All three wore too-big green T-shirts painted with grinning, nasty-looking elves. Was that how they saw themselves? I pointed to the den sign on my cap. "Macys don't steal from Unca Joes."

"That was then," the kid said, and pulled a blade.

It was small, but sharp and shiny. The girl beside him squeaked deep in her throat, then showed her teeth as cover. My "regulation" jackknife was stowed away in my gut wallet, but I wasn't buying any of this. Mugged by Macys? I'd never live it down. I calculated the distances between the three of them. Spunk always said speed was my best asset.

"So, Macys run in knife packs now? Won't go down well with the other dens."

"Shut up and give us yer shit so we all get outa here!"

I turned my empty bag upside down and shook it, but the leader took a step toward me. I didn't like how the tip of his knife jigged around. Tired or nervous. Either was dangerous.

The smallest glanced to the others, then at me. "Biggest storm comin' . . ."

Like I didn't know.

"Big one? You think so?" I scanned the sky like some doofus, and they fell for it.

As they lunged, I feinted, tucked, and rolled beneath their flailing arms, the patented Spunk maneuver, knocked the middle girl flat and was up and racing off before they'd figured out where I'd gone. Just dumb, frightened babies. Good thing there were three of them. Might give 'em a chance to make it home alive.

Noon, and the light already losing strength to the deepening cloud cover. I sprinted toward Ninth Avenue and the river, dodging a clot of rusting car hulks. The Macys pounded after me, but I'd headed away from their den and that cooled them quick enough. Lost them long before I ran out of breath. I slowed, ducked into a doorway, and waited, to be sure.

A squirrely bunch, the Macys, but I had to credit their nerve. Probably had no clue what a disadvantage they were at, too young to have any real training or practical skills. What else could they fall back on besides picking, conniving, and thieving? Partly why Macys tended to age out. Once the thrill of anarchy wore off, older Macys went looking for a better deal. We had several 'graduates' at Unca Joe, so we knew how it went there. Lots went to the Tommys or Ladysmiths. The girls were too often pregnant by then, would end up birthing at Gimme Shelter, then staying to raise their child and work the farm. The worst kids likely got swept up by BlackAdder. Maybe my would-be mugger would be one of them.

Once sure they'd given up, I walked west to Ninth, checking my mental map. New territory for me. Straight downtown, the water gleamed like wet metal. I'd crossed 57th in my run, so this could be the high ground behind the old hospital and the pale and stately ruins of Lincoln Center. Not many street signs left, even here above the flood zone.

Across the avenue, a big gap left by a building collapse opened up a vista of glass towers rising out of dark silver, the river in the failing light. Boats jockeyed busily at their feet, dusk-time running lights reflected in the water. Uptowners must still have jobs, even offices to go to, but things had to be a lot different than when these towers were built. My notion of uptown life was a patchwork of rumor and speculation, stitched up by my denmates' memories, with zero direct experience to go on. Hard not to give in to yearning and fantasies.

From this raised bit of ground, life behind those few lit windows looked serene and protected, away from the filth and danger of the streets. Rubio had hoped for a Venice on the Hudson, implying that he wouldn't mind so much if sea levels never went down, as long as the climate got stabilized, since Manhattan would make a fabulous canal town. Listening to him, I would dream of a clean bedroom all my own, in a secure tower high above the swollen river. I knew that bedroom's every detail, like I'd seen it in a video. Memory? Invention? Too perfect to be a place I'd ever have lived in. Rubio was right: I'd never really know which bits that came back to me were fact, and which were romantic fiction. But the boats were central. They meant being able to come and go wherever you wanted to.

New gusts tugged at my hair. A long way from home and here I was with an empty grab bag, lingering like an idiot, wishing for a boat. Time to give it one more go.

Uptown a ways, a squat black block cut off the view. A parking structure, hunched all alone in a field of wreckage like a concrete toad. I crossed over, my eyes tracing the upward curve of its ramps until they vanished into shadow. Once it had been filled with shiny cars. I could almost hear their engines humming. Now their twisted remnants spilled down the exit ramp like they'd been puked onto the sidewalk.

The wind was up, sooner than forecast, but the hum was no longer in my head. As I went on alert, listening, it morphed into a low whine. Not the rising gusts, not a boat out on the river. A motor groaning in complaint. Louder now, echoing off the buildings, coming from uptown and fast. Coming my way.

Instinctively, I bolted for cover—into the dark parking structure, past the stove-in cashier's booth, not stopping till halfway up the first ramp. From there, I peered over a knee wall. The worn street reflected shards of moving light. Tires squealed. Music blared.

Not some late-staying tourists or staid uptowners on a twilight spin. Did Adders drive? Wasn't this way off their turf? I ran for deeper cover. The machine roar sped down the avenue toward my hiding place. I rounded the curve to the second level and clung to the street-side railing to watch it pass.

Instead, it slowed and turned in with a screech, disappearing right under me. A bright red car, long and low, built for speed, headlamps blue-white and blinding, blasting out the most pounding bass that ever shuddered my chest. Not your common-sense solar sedan. Who still owned such things? Big feet and muscled arms waved out the open windows. A blue swirl of old-fashioned exhaust rose up around me, tugging at my . . . no! Gritting my teeth, I shoved the blossoming memory aside. No time for that now.

I needed a bolt-hole. The car screamed up the curve and past me just as I whipped behind a pillar. Music thumped, male voices whooped. They made a rowdy circuit of the second level, scraping along the retaining walls, slaloming through the maze of junked vehicles, then up the third-level ramp. A series of sharp cracks rang out, each followed by a shattering of glass. Gunfire. And what a soft target I would make.

I plunged into the shadows among the pillars, praying for an exit stair. My outstretched arms found two metal doors, one locked, one chained.

Only a moaning updraft saved me from pitching into an empty elevator shaft.

The car crested the third level and began a joyride overhead.

Bam! Bam! Bam!!

How long did I have? I backed into a wedge of dark between the up-ramp's curve and the outer wall. The floor dropped away . . . no, just a step. One down, then another. A dank odor rose, the all-too-familiar scent of death. But old death, which I'd pretty much learned to live with. No time to find another hiding place. Testing ahead, my foot nudged a rattling softness. I recoiled, then kicked it away. Bones, from the sound, in a twist of old fabric. When you work at night in the flooded city, smells and sounds you never dreamed you'd know about become old friends. At least the rats had already done their cleanup job.

Thunder overhead, and a sudden revving as the car roared toward the down-ramp. I stumbled, hands flung out. Instead of hard concrete, they met a smooth, cool surface that instantly gave way ahead of me.

Walls in motion, I'm falling, the raw roar overhead. Was the structure collapsing?

The wall came to rest with a mild jolt, pressing my arms into my chest. A draft stirred my hair. A rectangle of faintest light in front of me. A door. I'd fallen against an unlatched door, with space beyond, tucked beneath the third-level ramp. A hidden room? Tires screeched on the curve above. I ducked in and shut the door behind me.

Insane, you'll say, to wall yourself up in unexplored darkness. Who or what else might be in here? But the shooters in the car were certain death if they found me. Behind a closed door, any door, I stood a chance.

Bam! Bam! Bam!

The car roared past, revved into a turn, and sped back up the ramp for another round. I was stuck in this bolt-hole until the boys got bored and left. Boys? Could as well be grown men. But boys was where my mind went. That memory quake was pressing hard to surface.

I scrabbled at the door for a locking device. Nothing. I sniffed and strained to listen past the pandemonium upstairs. The side walls felt close. Was there another way out? I heard no scuttling in the corners or scratching in the walls, smelled nothing dead, at least not recently. The faint glow came from a small blue light on a box high up on the right-hand wall. Was power still feeding this long-abandoned building? Never seen that yet, in my weeks on the streets. Maybe still functioning solars on the roof? On a far wall, strips of gray light seeped around a gust-blown blackout drape. A window. Once my eyes adjusted, it gave just enough light to survey the room.

The ceiling dropped low by the door but rose with the ramp above it, ribbed with metal trusses. The right-hand wall followed the curl of the ramp. The left was the outer wall of the structure. I was in a narrow triangle of leftover space put to some sort of use.

I went to the window and eased the drape aside. A big square of frosted glass swung loose on oddly silent hinges, barred with a sturdy external grate. Inside that, a fine-mesh metal screen explained the unbroken glass and apparently rodent-and-pigeon-free interior. Outside, the wind was doing its on-and-off swirly thing as it prepped for a gale.

I shut and latched the glass pane. It held. I could barely believe my luck.

I'd stumbled on someone's living space, squirreled away where no one would expect. Someone clean and tidy but not been here in a while. I could smell the emptiness. But for a thin layer of soot, concrete dust, and some dampness by the window, it felt untouched since that person had left it.

A long couch nestled against one wall, neatly made up as a bed. On the other side, lockers and a table with two battered metal chairs. A sink. A useless microwave. A lamp that might work if the power source was strong enough, but I wasn't going to test it with the boys still rampaging around. Shelves stacked with pots and dishes and piles of old magazines whose covers suggested the occupant had been older and male. Well above the storm surge, this hidden room was certainly in use pre-Abel, maybe after as well. Whoever'd lived here had laid his tattered copy of *Travel and Leisure* aside one day, put his mug in the sink, and gone out, never to return. I thought of the pile outside the door, shoved aside in my frenzy. His remains? So sad, if he'd died just steps from his own door.

Opening a cabinet tucked into a recess, I found a treasure trove: candles, matches, several flashlights, batteries with chargers, bottles of various liquids, canned goods, packets of freeze-dried food, a row of canisters labeled in block lettering: coffee, sugar, tea, rice, beans. Sugar. Coffee! A whole unbroken can.

I shuddered as another volley of gunshots rang out uplevel. How long would they be at this? Didn't they care that a hurricane was coming? Maybe not. With that car, they could be home in minutes.

To calm myself, I focused on my inventory. Not enough light to read the small print, but the place was a picker's paradise. The sort you hightailed it home to report so a whole gang could race back to clean it out before anyone else discovered it. That is, you would if you hadn't already been infected by . . . what? Maybe call it the freedom virus. In its early stages, no fever yet, but already taking hold in my system. Likely caught it from Rubio. Exactly what Rousseau was worried about.

While a carnivorous car raced up and down above my head, I pondered the promise I'd so recently sworn to him: *I'd never hold back food!*

The window drape was a thick rag of blanket clearly meant to block light from getting out as well as in. I pulled it close and tucked the edges tight. I tested the flashlights, then the lamp. None worked. Too much to hope for. But the blue glow picked out two sets of L-shaped metal hooks, one above the other on either side of the door. Leaning in the corner were two metal rods or pipes. Okay, got it. I dropped them into the hooks, neatly barring the door from the inside.

A quiet settled into the room, distancing the noise upstairs. It was like a good night's sleep. My breath eased, my heart rate slowed. The moment the rods locked into their brackets, I began to feel safe, the kind of safe I felt only at Unca Joe. Maybe safer.

This could be my private den.

A secret hideout, where no one could toss my bunk behind my back. If I found stuff I really wanted, I could stash it here. This room had gone untouched because no one bothered with this kind of building in this part of town, having long ago salvaged every useful scrap from the car wrecks. I could have my freedom *and* Unca Joe.

"Mine," I whispered to the room, taking possession.

As if to seal the deal, the demon car screeched down two levels of ramp, roared past my door and out onto the avenue. It sped back uptown, trailing catcalls, gunshots, and a lingering drumbeat.

I perched on the edge of the couch-bed, testing my welcome.

The engine clamor died into distance, leaving the underscoring of wind at the latched window, knocking to come in. A slow patter of rain. Already? The forecasts had been way off this time, or I should've paid more attention to the updates. But I'd figured to be home too quick for it to matter. Another reason I'd been so out of sorts—my internal weather radar had been beeping away and I didn't listen.

I unbarred the door. The street was slick, water already running in the gutters. Well past time to head home. But I couldn't just walk away from this amazing windfall. Had to secure it somehow. The only lock was an old manual kind. A good thing, with the power down, but where were the keys? A guy this tidy must have kept an extra set at home.

I checked the seal of the blackout drape and lit the smallest candle. Details of the room sprang into view, then faded as I moved around. The walls were painted cinderblock, maybe green. Hard to tell for sure. I searched every nook and drawer and container, dug under the cushions of the couch, shook out the magazines. I uncovered many new treasures, but no keys. In a small metal box with the odd word 'Altoids' just legible on the lid, I found a stash of old paper money, useless now except as an antique. The band holding it snapped as I poked at it, unfolding the coil in my palm. My hands recalled the greasy feel of bills like these—not a full memory quake, more like a minor tremor. Meanwhile, a very long hour back to the den and a hurricane screaming up the coast. Hurricane Joseph.

I was losing daylight as well as time. I considered staying put. Be sensible. Ride out the storm safe and dry. But since waking up in the Ward, I'd never slept or eaten a meal away from the den, never sat through a storm alone. Just the idea stirred up jitters, deep inside where the secret terrors still ruled. Plus, if I didn't show, Rubio would fret.

Where were the damned keys anyway? Then, a grim thought.

I blew out the candle. With one of the door bars in hand, I stepped outside and poked around in the shadows for that tangle of bones and clothing. Wind gusts spat rain through the open sides of the building. The rod clanged against a drainage grate in the floor. Good. Water wouldn't be running into the room. Then, there was the pile. I eased the end of the rod into the tangle, straining over the noise of the wind to listen.

Rattle, thud, rattle . . . there! Clinkety-clink. Harsher than the clatter of bones.

Now I had to go into that blackness, feel about with my bare hands. Gloves would be nice, but no time to get squeamish. Two fingers slipped in among the damp layers of rotting cloth, brushing against bone and dried sinew, finally bumped against a heavy metal ring, a carabiner studded with keys, probably for every door in the building. Unbelievable, the luck I was having! Stomach fluttering, I hooked in a finger, snatched the ring free of the mess, and jingled it hard, as if I could shake off the awful smell. At the door, I tried seven keys before one fit. With rain blowing sideways through the structure and washing down the ramps, I'd leave the others for later.

A last-minute brainstorm made this grim effort more than worth it. I could leave the documents here—be free of them without having to give them up. Not the book, though. I was growing fond of it. And I'd promised the book dude I'd read it before I sold it, so at least I should try. I took out the plastic sheath, left the book stowed in my belly pack.

All the keys but the crucial one stayed behind in the Altoids tin. Hiding the documents was harder. Anyone finding the door and breaking in would search the place up and down. I settled on a narrow space where one of the ceiling trusses poked through the concrete of the inner wall. You could see it only if you stood by the window and craned your neck at a difficult angle. I had to clamber up on a chair to reach it. The plastic folder with its cargo of treasure slid into the slot as if it'd been made for it.

Like losing ten pounds! Keeping them, without carrying them on me.

One thing more: something neutral to bring home as my night's take, to explain why I'd been out so long. I considered the can of coffee—seal unbroken. What a prize! But a vision of sitting here at my own little table with a mug of coffee I'd made myself—wasn't even sure how I'd do that—but it put the idea right out of my head. Instead, I pulled a yellow rain poncho out of one of the lockers, man-sized but workable. I'd need it on the way home. I dragged it over my head and locked the door behind me. The key went into my gut wallet.

Not too bad outside yet. The rain was taking a breather, but the wind rolled over me like a breaking wave and water roared in the storm drains, clogged and already backing up. I laced the poncho's too-big hood over my street cap and started off at a trot.

The early storm music had started up with the rattle and clang of debris caught in the gusts: old signs torn from their final scrap of hinge, the last bits of metal cornice ripped from a façade. Lethal edges on the fly, metal tumbleweeds bouncing along the dusky streets. I balled up the front of the poncho to keep from tripping. The back bloomed out behind like a sail. Twice I was nearly airborne.

I jogged across 59th, sticking to the lee of the buildings, aiming for the shelter of the East Side pass-thrus. Soon I was racing by the entrance to the Souk. When I glanced up and saw where I was, I stopped short. Couldn't help myself.

The gates gaped open in invitation. The Soukies had deserted, scooter trikes and all. Beyond the stone walls, a few lanterns glowed through plastic sheeting, but most stalls were shuttered and dark, or dismantled entirely. The premature storm must have taken the Souk by surprise as well. A few frantic lag-behinds chased wind-whipped flaps or loose merchandise, bellowing at each other to hurry, hurry. Just watching them made me anxious, but my picker's instincts held me to the spot. Might be interesting stuff blowing around in there, and all I had to show for a long day's picking was the poncho on my back.

I wondered about the Book Dude's tent: stuffed with paper and old cardboard, so vulnerable to wind and water. He seemed like a sensible guy. He'd have heeded the alerts and packed up in time. Maybe he'd even left some behind.

But what if he'd been caught short, like these others? All those lovely books?

It was like ten blocks to his stall. If the rain held off and without a crowd, I could make short work of it, give him a hand if he needed it. Better still, pick up the leavings.

A crazy idea, why even consider it? I danced in place, arguing with myself, this new self who kept urging me to follow my impulse. Then, like someone had cut my tether, I launched myself through the gates and ran the whole way, slowing only to scoop up a few choice items—a blue ball cap on the fly, a floral scarf grabbed in midair, a noisily tumbling steel drink bottle—to toss in my grab bag.

The rain had swept by here, too, and everything was spattered. The book dude was there outside his tent, shifting books and boxes inside. I slowed to catch my breath. No point in startling the guy, who likely wouldn't remember me. Or he'd think me a nutcase for showing up now. And maybe he'd be right. I almost turned to leave.

But he'd heard my panting approach. He glanced up, squinted through the failing light, trying to place me. Then he threw me that open smile I'd liked most about him.

"Hey! You're back!" He brushed sweat and rain from his eyes. "What's up?"

"Passing by on my way home." Lame, but not entirely a lie.

"Best be on it, then! Weather's coming up fast!" If his arms hadn't been full, I could tell he'd be waving them wildly. He had on the same T-shirt and old jeans. Maybe his wardrobe was as scant as mine. He nodded at the damp scatter of crates. "I got behind helping pack up the old folks next door. Their stuff is all glass. This one took us all by surprise."

"Maybe I could help . . . ?"

"No, no. You'd best be quick on your way. They're saying it's a monster!"

I was still heaving a bit from my run. "Five minutes?"

He dropped a stack of books into a crate and sealed the lid. "Of course. Jeez. Sorry. Come in and catch your breath."

"So it's a monster now? I've been out all day."

"That's the latest." He dragged the crate inside the tent, which I'd assumed was a flimsy shelter. But with the canvas flaps rolled and tied, I saw what darkness and the crowded racks of books had hidden that first night: the broken edges of a stone-walled building topped by a sturdy metal roof. Two metal doors stood ready to secure the front.

"This is cool," I said.

"Sure is." Daniel looked around, as if rediscovering a bit of luck. "It was an old Park Service maintenance shed. From maybe the 1930s, or even before! Someone blew out the door wall before I got to it, but I made the place tight again and it's served me well. Nothing like an old building for strength."

"So you don't have to haul everything away."

"All these books? Not a chance. Just drag it all inside and lock the doors. Easy beans. Really, Glimmer, why are you here? Thinking about borrowing a book?"

He remembered my name.

"Like I said—racing home from pick duty, west on 57th. A vision of books in the rain blew me off course. Didn't know about . . ." I did an arms-wide turn in the narrow aisle. "All this."

Daniel regarded me like, really? Then the metal roof rattled as the rain took up again. We both glanced out at the piles of stock yet to be rescued.

"Ah, hell. Maybe a little help wouldn't hurt."

"I'm on it."

I shed the trippy poncho. Trash and loose stuff from other booths danced around our legs as we piled up armloads. The rain was gathering itself for total assault, but we were quick about it and the books hardly got any wetter than they'd been, though we were dripping by the time Daniel closed the metal doors to shut the storm out.

"Okay, that's the lot. Thanks."

I edged around a crate stacked with magazines, putting it between us and tugging my wet T-shirt away from my skin. I was not so easy about the two of us alone in a tight space.

He lit one of the hanging oil lamps, stilling it when it began to sway in the draft. He did a muttered final inventory, then took on that problem-to-be-solved look I remembered from last time. "Now let's see about getting you home ASAP."

"You ride the storm out in here?"

"Gad, no. Got a nice high-and-dry crosstown. Long hike for you, though, to Unca Joe."

"Where?"

"C'mon . . ." He laughed at my narrowed eye and shot a forefinger at the brim of my street cap. "I read den sign, y'know. Good choice, Unca Joe."

Creepy that he knew stuff about me, without hardly knowing me at all. "Didn't have much at the time. Choice, I mean."

"Lucky break, then. Rousseau's a good man."

He knew how to talk like you'd been friends for ages. A skill that could catch you off guard. I sure didn't have it, but at least I knew what to watch for. "You know Rousseau?"

"By rep. Not to speak to. Sometimes his buyer Jake stops by for a chat."

I looked up sharp. "Yeah? What do you talk about?"

"Books. Politics. Why? You got a problem with Jake?"

"Nah. He's my tier-mate. But don't tell him I was . . ."

"Here? Don't worry. I know better than that."

I scrambled for a redirect. "Didn't know Jake's a reader."

"Plays, mostly. Don't get many, but I save them for him when I do. Still haven't found him a Complete Works."

"You mean, everything . . . like an encyclopedia?"

"Everything Shakespeare," Daniel chortled. "I could fill the stall six times over with Bibles and Qurans and sutras, but the collected plays of W. S.? Can't be found. Used to be one in every household, not that anyone actually read it."

"Must be the book they all took with them when they left."

He grinned. "I'll use that on Jake next time he asks for one."

"Jake quotes Shakespeare a lot. Least I think that's who he's quoting."

"It is." Daniel swept the magazines off the crate and handed them to me.

"Stow these on that shelf over there, will you?" He hauled several of the boxes further away from the door, then stood looking at me. "So how'd you settle on Glimmer?"

"'Cause when I woke up in the Ward, I didn't have one." My standard joke answer.

"Okay. Got that. A glimmer about what?"

"Anything . . . before."

"Nothing?"

"Not even my name." I shrugged. "It comes back in bits. Sort of."

"Oof. That's rough, losing your whole history. I mean, that's who we are." He nodded like he'd heard it before but never got used to it. "Well, the name suits, since you're all shiny and new. Nothing wrong with starting over. Some would envy the chance." His smile turned crooked. "My den handle was Danny Boy. I hated it."

The wind rapped hard at the metal doors. Daniel stirred purposefully.

"Time to be going. I'll race you to the pass-thrus."

"On your way?"

"Close enough." He tossed the big poncho at me. "Saddle up."

Outside, darkness and the storm were closing in. Got later than I'd reckoned.

Bolting the doors, Daniel yelled over the wind roar. "Forgot to check the tide calendar. Did you?"

I shook my head. He was worried about the storm surge—how big, how soon—and I'd thought to be home by now.

After that, we put our minds to beating through the gale and avoiding unidentified flying objects. Just past the gates, Daniel grabbed my arm and yanked me aside. A scream of wet air past my ear spiraled into a rolling crash on the sidewalk behind us. Whatever had nearly crushed us was already a shadow scudding end over end half a block away. We both broke into a run. Never so glad to see Fifth swim up out of the watery dusk. We splashed across the avenue to the 59th Street access and tumbled up the three flights as if riding the storm itself.

The stripped-down corridors of the pass-thru were a maze of howling wind tunnels.

Daniel was laughing, like he'd enjoyed the run. He grabbed my poncho before I got airlift and veered us toward a darker hallway. "This way!"

I hardly had time to protest before he'd halted at a sheltered alcove housing a bank of boarded-up elevators. From somewhere he produced a small flashlight to shine into all the nooks and corners, making sure nothing lurked. The cinderblock here was in place all the way to the ceiling and the floor was dry, least till we got there. We stood panting and dripping, palming rain from our faces and hair.

I knew this sort of lobby. On other levels, there might still be a fake marble table too heavy to steal, each with a bolted-on metal vase that once held plastic flowers. Daniel set the flashlight end-up on the floor. Its translucent base glowed softly, a portable lantern.

I eyed it enviously. "That's a handy little thing."

"Never without it."

"So bright. How d'you keep it charged?"

"My home solars are pretty reliable." Daniel let his tongue loll and slumped against the wall. Rain shivered in droplets on his short-cropped hair. "Whew. I'm out of shape."

He didn't look that way to me, his drenched tee showing every hard line of his body. And I was breathing a lot harder than he was. Not what you'd expect from a bookish sort.

I recalled what Grace had said about me finally noticing, and glanced away, rearranging the folds of my giant poncho. Rather be more hidden than less. "I got delayed, too. Tagged by a bunch of Macys."

He laughed. "You'll need a better story than that."

"No, seriously. They didn't get anything, but the whole thing put me off my game."

"You're saying some kids tried to mug you?"

I nodded. "Three of them. Babies, almost. What's with that?"

"Wish I could say." He settled more comfortably against the rough block and crossed his arms, like he meant to linger a bit. I could live with that. I'd already scouted out three separate escape routes if I had to scoot, plus I needed to rest up for the long haul home.

"So, did you read your book?"

Figured he'd ask. "Started to. Read a bit whenever there's time. Like I said, it's . . ."

"Hard. Old script. Like you said. Practice should make it easier." He put out a hand. "Let me take a look."

"Ain't got it with me."

"Sure, you do. Like you did last time. Can't leave a thing like that lying around a den."

I put on a scowl. "Do you freakin' know everything?"

He grinned. "Just a good guesser, is all. Remember, I been there."

Why not? After all, he'd given me zero reason not to trust him, at least a little. Plus, he'd know what the book was worth. Before I could think again, it was out of my gut wallet, and I was thrusting it at him. Oddly, letting it go brought the same relief as stashing the documents. I didn't think he'd steal it or anything, but I watched closely as he put his back to the wind and turned into the glow of his flashlight to unfold the wrappings. He let the linen drape around his palm and studied the book without touching its cover, a precaution I hadn't thought to take.

"Nice." He raised it to his nose for a detailed sniff. "Too bad. I hoped it might still smell like shipboard."

My turn to laugh. "After two hundred years?"

"Never know. Vellum, leather, cardboard, glue. All very porous and absorbent."

"Whatever you say. You're the book dude."

"Is that what I am?" He posed with the book held out the length of his arm. "The Book Dude. I like it. A lot better than Danny Boy." He lifted the cover with a careful finger to peer at the crabbed scrawl as if secrets might slip out between the pages. "Really need better light." He closed it with a sigh, rewrapped it, and handed it back. "Can't tell you much now. Bring it to me when the weather's not trying to beat the shit out of us."

I stared at the small thing in my hands. "Is it . . . um . . . real?"

"Real? You mean, a genuine artifact? Oh, yes, I'd say so. Not much value in faking something like this. Now, if the writer was famous or something . . . is there a name on it?"

"Haven't found one. Yet."

"'Cause if what you're asking is, how much is it worth, just in itself, that would require a proper analysis. What's it about?"

I eyed the book like I could see through the wrapping. "In the part I've read, the guy goes off on a boat . . . a ship . . . some kind of business venture halfway round the world, and he leaves everyone behind. His friends, his wife and child. Everyone. Except this one friend who goes with him."

"Are they on the run?"

"No. Everyone comes to see them off, like it's a great adventure. Good-bye party and everything. But . . ." My voice caught. This part touched me deeper than it should.

"But what?" Daniel prodded.

"What about his family? He can't, like, just fly home. He'll be gone for years."

"So he really needed the money. Probably to support his family."

I chewed my lip. "I guess."

"Didn't you take off? From home, I mean, to end up in a den."

"Not on purpose!" But okay, why had I been out during Abel in the first place?

"Except you don't remember, right?" He managed to look mischievous and serious at the same time. "Maybe you were on the run."

"From what? You mean, like a criminal?" Not even Rubio had offered this explanation so far.

"Not necessarily." The mischief faded and his eyes went suddenly bleak. "A lot of things to run from in this world."

Wherever his mind had shot off to, it unsettled me. Hoping to haul it back, I ruffled my poncho noisily. "I don't think I was on the run. More like I was abandoned."

As quick as he'd drifted, he was back again. "Ah. By your parents?"

This was getting personal. "Maybe. If I had any."

"We all had parents. Mine did exactly that."

"Left you behind?"

I expected he'd turn grim again. Instead, he gave an off-hand shrug. "They took off to Europe while we—my sibs and I—were in school. Never came back."

"That's terrible! What happened to them?"

"A better life, apparently. Kid-free. Checking off some end-of-the-world bucket list. We'd catch the occasional exotic internet post."

His too-casual tone made me frown. "You didn't hate being abandoned?"

He shook his head. "More like being liberated. Or it felt that way at the time. We had each other, the house, and were mostly old enough to fend for ourselves."

Happy to shed his parents. I couldn't imagine such a thing. "So . . . they were like, really strict or something?"

Daniel's smile took on a cooler distance. "Let's just say they weren't much good at being parents. Or much interested."

House? Europe? Had to mean uptown. I got wary again. "So you live in a house?"

"Not me. My sibs still do. Eventually we . . . um . . . parted ways." He pushed off from the wall and peered around the corner of the alcove. The gale tore at his cheeks. He ducked back in, blinking away rain. "Definitely getting nasty out there. Listen, why not just come up to my squat, ride out the storm. It'd be way safer."

I didn't think so. "Uh. No. That's okay."

"I could take a real look at the book. We could read some. I'll make us dinner."

So eager. Pushing too hard. "Thanks. I gotta get home."

"How 'bout just till the eye goes over, and we see what the surge is going to do."

"No. Really. I can't."

"C'mon! I feel you're not giving this book a serious try. Or maybe I have something you'd like better." At last he picked up on the dread widening my eyes. "Hey. What's up?"

My legs had me backing away before I knew how freaked I was.

"Oh, hold on, hold on!" He slapped his forehead. "Jeez, I'm an idiot. I'm going on and on, motormouth Daniel, and you're thinking I meant . . . y'know, something other than reading." He stilled, arms awkward at his sides. "Is that it?"

"Sorry." I waited for anger or mockery, like I got even from guys who meant no harm.

"No, my fault. Wasn't paying attention. I get carried away trying to get people to read. Can't seem to help it. It's a character flaw."

"Not yours. Mine. I can't . . . ever since Abel. Something . . ." I shook my head.

He waited, like he knew there was more, had to be, because what I'd said made no sense. A bunch of dots without the connections. But I couldn't take him any further. I stared at my feet.

"Something . . . ?"

"Bad." I choked it out. "Something bad. That I can't remember."

"Ah."

I searched his face. For what? Pity? Compassion? Why should he have any to spare? He'd heard all the stories, too. Bad things happened to everyone in the new normal. Anyhow, what the hell was I doing, bleating my private anguish to a more-or-less stranger, just because he was easy to talk to? Where was all my hard-won protective covering?

But Daniel's gaze had turned dark again. "Well. That sucks."

"Yeah."

"Still . . ." He chewed his lip. "You oughtn't go out in that storm."

"Got to. They'll be expecting me home."

"How 'bout this? Hold out the book. Yeah, like that. Don't laugh, now." He flattened his left palm on the wrapping, raised the other beside his ear. "I, Daniel Nathan, a.k.a. the Book Dude, do solemnly swear never to take unwelcome advantage of or cause harm to Glimmer of Den Unca Joe, or to any other female of my acquaintance." He dropped his hands and stood back, like he might take a little bow. "That make you feel any better?"

He looked so silly, so totally undignified, I had to admire his willingness to go there. "If anything could."

"Now, if only you'll believe me . . ."

"I'll work on it." I slid the book into my gut wallet and zipped it up tight.

"I really wish . . ."

"And I really am. Working on it."

"Okay. But if you get hurt, I'll feel responsible. You'd have been home by now."

"My choice to show up when I did. Okay, I'm outa here."

"If you must." He shrugged uneasily. "Safe home."

"You, too."

"No dawdling, okay?"

I was already on my way.

FIFTEEN

The moment I turned the corner, I knew how dumb I'd been, refusing the chance of shelter. Not just dumb—out of control. What the shrink called my 'male contact phobia' was turning lethal on me. Crazy. Any sane person would've gone racing after Daniel to say yes, please. I didn't. I couldn't. Even though this storm was a monster.

I had nothing against guys. Really. As long as they stayed at arm's length. Look how close I was with Rubio.

No walls here to break the gale. The wind screamed among the stripped-down piers, trying to knock me flat. Rain hosed across the slick concrete. I sprinted from pillar to pillar, clung to any leftover bit of wall to keep from being swept off into the street below. Only upside: the roof over my head.

Best to head down along Fifth far as I could, then across, avoiding the Causeway. The footbridges were terrifying: slim, swaying passages over dark streets where the rush of water sounded nearer than it should have been. A few had already blown away or hung by a shred of cable while the gusts thrashed the wreckage against the building. Backtrack, change of route. Where a bridge looked vaguely solid, I dashed across as if momentum and the ballooning of my poncho could keep me aloft if it gave way beneath me.

I met no one, and for once, this worried me. The whole city had retreated to high ground, even the worst of the worst. Or so it seemed, until somewhere in the 30s, where isolated stretches of wall screened a passageway alongside the avenue. The rest of the building was wide open, so I hugged the partitions, grateful for even a momentary stall in the wind force. Then, ahead, an ominous bright flickering along the edge of a wall. I backed up to the previous partition and peeked around.

A giant bonfire burned mid-block, big as one of the rooms might have been, silhouetting a crowd milling around it. Shreds of wind-borne chant reached me, and the crackle of the blaze. A dark forest of pillars stood between us, but I felt the heat on my cheeks, glimpsed the firelight reflecting off wet skin and writhing, intertwined bodies. I was glad for Jenn's mystery video gal. She'd let me know what I was looking at.

Storm Worshippers. This time, at least a hundred of them. And not just dancing. Who knew they gathered and . . . did their thing . . . in such numbers?

Should I sneak past, or run like hell? Can't claim I had anything like a clear thought just then. Part of me wanted to watch, long enough to bring firsthand info back to the den. Like Spunk always said, observe first, to inform your move. Then move, and make it fast.

The Stormies seemed deep into their ritual, most likely too distracted and fire-blind to notice me slipping by in the dark. What slowed me down further was the sense I got of a happy occasion, a frantic but joyous celebration. Cries of ecstasy, moans of pleasure among the chanting. An orgy, not an immolation. What about those rumors of human sacrifice?

So, I sneaked first, catching an eyeful here and there. Slipping along the wall sections, oozing across the openings between, counting on the cover of darkness, forgetting I wore glaring yellow, until a naked man rose up beside me with a shout.

"Sister! Join hands for the Goddess!"

Hands, and a whole lot more, I thought. Then I ran.

Maybe a hundred yards to the next footbridge. The guy pounding behind me was fast. I felt him snatch at the folds of my poncho and lose his hold. Did I really hear him laughing? Lucky for me, he was barefoot on wet concrete. He lunged too far, slipped and fell. I had on my grippy street shoes. I was going to make it. Then there was another naked guy beside the first, catching up fast. These Stormies were in good shape.

"Accept Her coming and be saved!"

Not on your life. I made it to the bridge and scrambled across.

Thwack! Thwack!

The sound was scary and alien. It jetted right over my head. I slowed to locate this new threat. A stumbling glance over my shoulder sent me whipping behind the closest pillar.

The bridge rocked wildly, lit by the distant, dancing firelight. One man lay face-down on its slats, grappling for dear life to keep from being flung to the street. The second bellowed and rolled about on the concrete of the far edge. The rain stung my eyes, making them play tricks as I squinted and stared, desperate to know what had dropped two fast runners so suddenly. I'd swear each wore a hot splash of blood and a long, thin shaft piercing one limb or another.

My fractured memory spat up a word to match the visual.

Like, *arrows*?

But arrows needed an archer. I scanned the buildings to right, left, above. Maybe a telltale open window, or a flash-motion as . . . whoever . . . ducked out of sight?

Nothing. Driving rain and flying trash. A ringing in my ears from the wind screech and low barometric pressure. And two naked men bleeding at the end of the footbridge.

A third ran out of the flicker of blaze and shadow to squat beside the second man. He searched the same dark rows of windows, yelling behind him for help.

Had to shake off my befuddlement. Get out while I had the chance.

A crowd gathered. The first man was dragged off the swinging bridge and carried into cover as I slipped away. No more arrows came, but the Stormies got the message. No one ventured across the footbridge.

Who? What? Never mind why? My brain wrestled with shock and confusion while my legs sped me instinctively downtown.

Below Fifth and 25th, no more pass-thrus, but I thought the worst was behind me. Just twelve blocks at street level, then the raised walkways at 13th. And I knew the territory.

I heard the boom and roil of water as I loped toward the exit stair. Already? I swerved toward a window gap and peered down. Sheeting rain and falling darkness, but between the blinding gusts, glimpses of foaming ripples where the street should be, where there should have been open ground. The mystery of the arrows faded as I faced this new crisis.

Tide must be coming in, with the surge behind it, pushing the levels higher. I was cut off from the downtown walkways, from any dry route home to my den.

Now what? First, beat back those early tendrils of panic. On my own with no Spunk to slap me back to reason, I had to cling tight to his training. Run through the crisis mantra: First, grab hold of yourself. Second, consider the possible.

Possibility A: shelter in the pass-thru till the storm blew over? Not a chance.

Possibility B: get swept up by Storm Worshippers if I stuck around? Next idea.

Possibility C: swim the twelve blocks. Flood water should still be shallow.

Then I remembered a new walkway at 23rd and Park Avenue South, built for high tides. Only two blocks to swim. Possibility D.

I'd never been there, but it was the best chance left. I ran the two long blocks cross town, hardly slowing to test the footbridges before I was across them. At Park and 25th, the exit stairwell roared. I closed my mind to anything but making the best move for the moment, and lowered myself into the inky void. Down, down, step by step, palms slick on the slimy railing, shoulders roughed by the mossy concrete.

Near the bottom, water swirled around my ankles, ocean chill, tang of salt, but also rot and mold. I sprang back a few steps. How deep? Had to go in to find out. Had to be now, while there was still a chance to wade the two blocks. Before the full surge rolled in.

Down, and down again. Water to my knees. Dirty with refuse. Worry about that later. The air was blood-warm, but my jaw chattered. Amazing what the body does all on its own when you're terrified. The dark stairwell framed a faintly lighter rectangle: the exit door. Only two blocks. I hiked my grab bag up around my neck and waded into the open water.

The gale shattered the rain into a brackish, driving mist. Two blocks down, behind the grimy dusk, my goal was visible only in my mind's eye. The water rose steadily, from shin to knee to hip. Too fast, too fast! Unseen debris slammed against my thighs. I fought for balance and breath, gritted my jaw against the filthy, invading water.

At 24th Street, my flailing arm smacked against something tall and hard. I recoiled with a squeal so the current nearly snatched me, then got some sense and grabbed hold. The faintly swaying lamppost held me up till my sides stopped heaving.

A shift in the current. The furious uptown thrust eased, like taking its own little breather. Even the wind backed off. Slack water! That would give me a minute or two. I lunged forward, pushing easily through the stilled tide, crossing the street, gaining the next sidewalk, only a block, now half a block further. So close to something like safety.

Then the tide turned. But not just a gentle pressing against the backs of my thighs. It grew stronger and stronger, like all the island's water had been ordered back to the sea, and meant to take me with it.

A moment of confusion, the torrent sucking at my knees, then my ankles. My body rebelling. Muscle, nerve, and bone calling up the past, massive memory quake, and then I knew what else was coming. Knew I had to beat it, scrambling, leaping, willing myself through the long half-block of water to the gangway.

Been here. Done this.

Reality shift. Like a kick in the stomach. The plate tectonics of past and present slipping, sliding into double vision: the wave then, the wave now, coexisting. Its grinding growl through the downtown streets, nearing, nearing. My sodden grab bag weighed me down, but it also was, no, wait . . . a woman? Older. Our arms were linked . . . her grasp weak. She kept stumbling in the current, dragging us backward until I caught my footing and hauled her upright. Who? Face behind a tangle of hair, a glint of old-style glasses. A striped, long-sleeved shirt, torn and muddied. Whoever she was, I had to hold on, find that upward stair.

In a building? No. Ahead, the faint tracery of the gangway, slightly off to the left.

I veered to meet it, saw overlapped a battered spiral stair, a shining curve of rail. The remembered flood had gained a soundtrack, the shatter of plate glass, the groan and scream of metal torn by the incoming wave.

Almost there.

The woman staggered, just as I snatched at . . . the slick pipe curl of the spiral stair, the weathered wood rail of the gangway. Which, dammit, which? Time-blind, my hand fell between them, corrected, reached for wood, for the now. I wrapped a leg around a support post and gave in to the curve of steel, to my arm around a woman's thin torso, so thin, was she sick? I clung to the rail until my muscles screamed, straining to pull her up with me step by step as the water rose in thunder like a subway racing by.

The wave engulfed us.

Its force tore the woman from my grip. Under water, I grappled, caught one hand, palm to palm, arms and shoulders tortured with effort. Her nails were shaped and clean. A single silver bangle wrapped her narrow wrist. She held on bravely, head thrown back as if for air, glasses washed away. Her face, revealed, was somehow familiar, but no one I could name. She looked at me fondly, then let her hand go slack. I lunged to catch her, as far as I dared, but she slipped from my grasp. Horror and resignation welled up in her eyes as she tumbled away into darkness. My fingers closed over empty water. I called after her, but only sucked in ocean.

Lungs bursting, I hauled myself hand over hand up the wave-battered gangway, broke the surface with a gasp, and threw myself flat on the top slats, barely a yard above the surging flood.

I lay retching up seawater, lost in a battleground of then and now. But the crazy shuddering of the walkway roused me. The angry surge was tearing at the understructure. I crawled to the supporting brick façade and curled up in a window recess. Hardly shelter at all, but I couldn't see to go any farther. The woman's last glance was tattooed on the inside of my eyelids.

It was a while before I heard anything but my own sobbing. Then, voices, raised above the storm roar. Real, this time. A voice I knew.

I leaped to my feet as if I'd been kicked, backhanding rain and salt from my eyes. More than wind and torrent shook the walkway. Half a block down, a blur of shadows pitched from railing to building and back again. Fists swung and landed.

Dumb, dumb, dumb to pick a fight in the middle of a hurricane. But the voice I'd heard was Rubio's, bellowing in pain and outrage.

I scrambled toward them. The walkway swayed like the deck of a ship. Behind me, the gangway groaned and ripped free. Ahead, three guys and Rubio, roaring and pummeling. Too man-angry to notice the boards and cross-bracing collapsing beneath them. Rube's only advantage was his long legs and arms, but in a close fight, that hardly mattered. No question who was getting the worst of it.

"Stop it! Leave him alone!" I launched myself at the heaving pile, snatching at arms and legs. "The walkway's going! Move it! Move it!"

A screeching banshee dropping out of nowhere, even a middling one, got their attention. The pile staggered apart. Rubio sank to his knees on the quaking deck. The three, Unca Joes each one but just teener boys, not even full lads, regrouped and turned animal glowers on me.

"Three on one? What kind of crap is that?" I tore a loose brace off the railing and raked it wildly back and forth. So what if they could toss me over the rail in less than a heartbeat? "Wait till the boss hears! Now, get the fuck out of here, all of you!"

Cracks rang out like pistol shots. The walkway dropped a foot. The three lads-in-training chose survival and took off for solid ground.

I hauled Rubio up and got him moving, grabbing at the building façade for support.

He leaned on me, like a tall crane with a broken wing. "Stupid motherfuckers!"

"Save your breath," I advised.

Foam licked up between the floorboards and washed away red. He was bleeding from somewhere. The new walkway was narrower, more fragile than the mainline Broadway one. The whole thing could break away and float out to sea in big chunks. I didn't want us to be on board.

"Sixteenth," Rubio hissed through a swollen jaw.

"Right."

A long seven blocks of bad footing and shivery support. Where the surge had ripped gaps in the walkway, window ledges were the only crossover. The wind had blown its worst, so less debris was flying around, but then the rain piled in again, a stinging downpour hard as hail.

At 16th, we stumbled through a blown-out window into a cleared third-floor corner, a public waystation where the new walkway joined the Broadway line. Dark, breezy, and wet inside, but it got us out of the worst of it, and this sturdy old building wasn't going anywhere. Exactly the point.

Other caught-short storm-waifs had taken shelter, scattered about in wet huddles. Complaints and groans, some sobs. People comforting each other. Too dark to read den sign, but this was neutral turf. I didn't expect trouble except what I'd brought with me. I found an open stretch of floor, eased Rubio down, and dropped beside him, our backs to bare brick. When I could breathe steady again, I did a quick self-inventory: no broken skin or bones, likely a serious bruise or two. My grab bag and I had parted ways in the surge, but my gut wallet hung tight at my waist. Check later for water damage. I looked over at Rubio.

"You there?"

"I'm . . . here."

"You're bleeding." It was internals that really worried me. He'd taken some mean kicks and punches.

"I'll make it." Forehead to his knees, his ribs heaving. "Glad you came along."

"Yeah. What was it all about?"

"Don't ask."

"I'm asking."

In a far corner, someone lit an oil lantern. The glow was thin but comforting.

Rubio lifted his head to cough, then slumped back against the wall. Even in dim light, I could see bruises coloring up on his pale skin. "Seems it was my fault the raid went wrong."

I groaned.

He rolled his head my way. "You don't sound surprised."

"It's all over the den. I went looking to warn you before I went out."

"But why would I do that?"

"That's what I said. But it's . . . some of the stuff you say? People take it wrong."

Rubio sniffed. "What, only Rousseau can have ideas?"

"I'm only saying."

He shook his head. "So fucking stupid, all of them."

"What should we do about it?"

"Do?"

"I mean, that's twice. What if they come after you again?"

"Then you'll just have to rescue me again." He grinned weakly. "By my count, you still owe me."

Our friendship had grown out of his scaring off some bully girls in the tier, my first weeks out of the Ward. Didn't take much. A serious scowl usually sent them packing. But I was grateful that anyone would stand up for me.

"It's time to tell Rousseau."

He ran a hand across his forehead. Fresh blood gleamed on his fingertips. He looked old. "Maybe it was his idea."

"No way. He has a beef, he tells you straight." Like he had with me.

"Maybe. But his boyos are dead sure they're doing him a favor."

We sat for a while, breathing deep. Now I could do more than react to whatever immediate crisis, my brain was filling up like a mob had moved in, fighting for space and attention: papers, old book, hide-hole, Storm Worshippers, *arrows*? And Daniel, in my thoughts more than I cared to admit. Ghosting huge above it all, like a faded wall mural: the woman behind my eyelids.

"Hey, Rube?"

He was fighting off a coughing fit. "What?"

"Where's Arkadia?"

"Where's what?"

"Arkadia. Did I say it right?"

"Sure, but it isn't anywhere. It's a myth."

"It's not a place?"

"Well, it was a place, in Ancient Greece, out in the boonies. Later it got to be a symbol of the ideal simple life, the rural utopia. *Et in Arcadia ego.* Why?"

"So it's not a real place now?"

"Plenty places named after it. Towns and such. But the symbolic meaning's what's important."

Only to you, I thought. "Does it matter how it's spelled?"

"It's spelled a bunch of ways, depending on whether you're using the Latin source or some later corruption."

"Did you know there was a Mars base named after it?"

"Where'd you hear that?"

"Peeto was looking at it online."

"Peeto. Figures. Any more off-the-wall inquiries?"

"Just one."

"Ummm?"

"You think I could have been a criminal . . . you know, like a thief on the run . . . before?"

"A criminal?" His eyes drifted shut. "That Peeto's idea, too?"

"No, no. Just exploring all options."

"Well, leave that one where you found it, okay?"

"Why?"

"'Cause you're the straightest, most trustworthy person I know."

A sure sign he was down and desperate, if he was giving out compliments. "Really?"

"Don't let it go to your head."

After that, I'd never be able to tell him what I'd done.

Around the dim-lit room, huddles were stirring. Sodden pickers struggling to their feet, testing stiff or injured limbs, peering out at the waning storm. Reluctant to go back out in it, eager to be home.

I roused Rubio from his daze. The sooner I got him to the medics, the better. "The worst has passed. Can you make it home?"

"Do I have a choice?"

SIXTEEN

The walkways mercifully held for our struggle home, the raw sea fountaining up between the floor slats and the wind several times knocking us flat. I was desperate for a quick meal and a retreat to my bunk for a long, slow think. But it was not to be.

Unca Joe was in an uproar.

Our boats were upside down on the front walk, lashed to the railings. An old windmill had toppled off the far side of Third Avenue, crushing our downtown approach. A crew was braving the tail of the storm to scavenge useful metal parts, scrambling over the huge trusses while waves broke around them and the long vanes rocked in the gusts. Entertaining on another sort of day, and Rubio, the rain still washing red down his cheeks and ribs, would've stayed to watch.

I tugged on his arm. "C'mon. Let's get you stitched up."

"It's mostly surface."

"But what if it isn't?" I gripped him harder. "Besides, no way you're hiding out in your bunk, getting all infected 'cause some dumb kids got the drop on you."

He didn't have the piss left to argue.

The mudroom was a foot deep in churning water, boiling up through the open shaft from the flooded water gate. In Main, the furniture was up on the counters. Shadows shoved past in the pale glow of emergency lights, ferrying goods up to the next floor. Rousseau's voice boomed orders and encouragement.

I hadn't expected chaos at home. As I stood taking it in, some guy rushed up and pushed a large box at me.

"Take this up!" He'd gone back for more before I could tell who it was.

I staggered under the sudden weight, finally on the road to total overwhelm. Seemed to be happening a lot lately.

Rubio grabbed one end of the box. "I'll get it."

"No . . ."

"Hey, you look worse than I do."

"Thanks a lot." But I let him take it. If I got him upstairs, he'd be half-way to the medics.

A bucket line passed stuff up the stairs, hand to hand. Two of the lads went by, lugging a big crate of vegetables, and I drew Rubio in behind to let them break a path. We edged up the crowded stair in a near darkness thick with urgency and heavy breathing. A maze of crates and boxes filled three sides of the balcony, spilling onto the media loft at one end and the bunk tiers at the other. Small furniture and equipment, salvage from the swap counter, food from the Mess, everything that could be carried was piled up wherever space could be found. Oil lamps burned atop the highest piles. Rube swayed under the weight of his load as we stood dripping filthy water on the old marble tiles.

"Stick it over here." Rivera appeared from behind a tower of crates, one arm still in a sling. "Watch out nothing tips!"

Rubio set the box where she pointed, then stood there watching it. Definitely out of it.

With her long hair tied out of the way, I could see Rivera's cheek and jaw had gone purple-yellow, the healing tinge. In the wan lantern light, she looked tense and spectral. "You two get caught out there?"

"In more ways than one." She'd hear about the beating soon enough. "Got to get him stitched up." I nudged Rubio toward the Ward.

Rivera saw he needed an extra push. "Best get in line. It's wall to wall up there. A shit-eating fuck fest all evening."

"And they talk about Gracie's mouth," growled Jake behind me, arriving with an armload of towels.

Rivera managed a grin. "Sorry. Must be catching. What's the water doing?"

"Crested." Jake dumped his load onto a dish crate, then watched Rubio shamble off toward the stair hall. "What happened to him?"

"Long story." I'd let Rubio tell the tale in his own time. Jake would understand.

"And you look like you swam home."

"Partly did."

Jake took a step back. "Then go get a wash up! Before the bad crap soaks in."

"So prissy, Jake!" Rivera slid me a sympathetic look. "But you should.

They're setting up a cold meal in the Loft. Everyone together for some grub, and Rousseau will fill us in on how things stand."

"Jake!" A woman yelled from below. "Next load's ready!"

"On my way!"

"Everyone get in okay?" I asked Rivera.

She glanced away to wave several racks of baked goods into an empty corner. "Haven't stopped for a roll call yet."

"Grace?"

"She's out on windmill salvage."

"Brave woman! Be back soon as I detox."

At the women's, a girl coming out warned, "Showers ain't working."

I stripped anyway, slathering every inch with the waterless antibacterial that Rousseau paid the best sort of trade for at the Souk. He bought in bulk and never stinted with it, since any illness risked the health of all.

On a whim, I tried the showers, found one that gave up a slim trickle, enough for a rinse. I left my clothes in a wet, stinking pile under my hook, then snatched the biggest scrap of towel on the public-use shelf, wrapped it around me, and made for my tier.

The bunk hall was packed. Everyone up and working, stowing small or fragile goods on the lower bunks, leaving the larger stuff on the floor. The already narrow passage was an obstacle course. I had to climb over stuff to get to my bunk. Stripped to a wet towel, a prime target for the grabbers and cat-callers, but nobody bothered me this time.

I'd fully intended to go back to work. But when I spidered up to my bunk and shed the towel, I barely had the strength to dig out my sweats and struggle into them. The wind had blown away my bit of window screen, beading my blanket with rain. I mopped up best I could, then checked inside my gut wallet: dry as a bone. Amazing. Worth every credit I'd saved up for it.

Toweling my hair, I couldn't help listing toward my pillow, which was the last thing I knew until someone nudged me awake.

"Glim?" Jenn peered anxiously over the horizon of my mattress.

I jerked up, then fell back. "Yow!"

"You okay?"

It hurt even to nod. "Everything aches."

She leaned away to the full length of her arms. "You sick? Got a fever?"

"No, no. Just real stiff. Got caught out there and tossed around a bit."

"Oh. No wonder." She eased up the ladder to perch on the far end of the bunk. She was in heavy work duds with her hair an unusual mess. "Jake said you got back, then no one could find you."

"How long . . . ?"

"It's midnight. Rousseau's rallying the troops in the loft. Cold meal and a pep talk."

I tried for a look out my window, but my back and shoulders locked. "Is it over yet?"

"Still raining, but the surge has dropped a bit. Main floor's draining off. The mop squad's already at work." She peered at me hard. Maybe feeling a bit guilty for being inside safe and dry while her picker pals braved the elements. "You need anything? Water?"

"Had enough of that for a while." I sat up with a groan. "What's the count?"

"Serious walkway damage. Lost some solars. Roof garden's a disaster. And, oh, the Loft is such a mob scene! Stuff just dumped everywhere. How will we get the com up again if I can't even get to my workstation?"

"Jenn . . . what's the people count?"

"I'm not really . . ." She looked at her hands, wringing them low in her lap.

"C'mon . . ." I touched her wrist to still her. "How many?"

"We're down four."

"Oof. Who?"

"Zane and little Mikka. But Rousseau says one of the other dens probably took them in." She fiddled with the raveled edge of my blanket, still avoiding my gaze. "I could fix this for you. Make it pretty."

"C'mon, Jenn. We're down four and . . . ?"

Her hands sprang apart. "No one's seen Spunk in a while."

My stomach clenched. "Shit."

"Uh-huh."

I shook my head. "No, no, he'll be fine. It's Spunk, after all. Mr. Streets. He'll have found a hide somewhere and hunkered down, you'll see."

"I'm sure you're right." She didn't look sure.

"No, really. Like I should've. Could've walked home dry after. Like Spunk will."

She was picking at the blanket again. "You think he's invincible."

"No, I . . ." But truthfully, I did. Didn't we all? "Got faith in him, that's all. Nobody walks the streets like Spunk. It's an art form."

Her hands were fussing each other so hard it must hurt. "But maybe he's dead. You know he could be! You could've been, too! If we could just get off this damn island, we wouldn't have to deal with this all the time!"

"There's weather on the Mainland, too," I said.

"It's not just the weather, it's . . . all of it! I hate it! I hate it!"

"Easy there." I laid my hands over hers to still them. Likely the storm stirred up Jenn's Abel nightmares like it did mine. I sidelined worrying about Spunk. "Hey, d'you eat yet?"

"Yeah, a while ago." She'd been looking for an easy exit. "But if you hurry, there might be some left."

"Come with and we can clear a path to your workstation."

That cheered her, for the moment at least.

But I'd missed both the cold meal and the pep talk. The oil lamps burned low. Trays and serving bowls, mostly empty, scattered on whatever crate or piece of furniture came to table height. I scavenged enough leftover rice 'n' beans to fuel me up short-term. At least the herbal was still warm.

The loft was quiet for having most of the den crammed in up there. We were running on batteries, so the computers were shut down but for one in a corner, where a Wizzer worked hard to scare up a weather report. A pair of the older guys hunched around the CB. Rousseau perched on a desk nearby, while people came and went with inventories or damage reports. Song-yi logged them into her personal tablet, the only one in the den. A small crowd pelted the boss with questions, and he answered as best he could. He was good at this sort of crisis, where the solutions were obvious and calming: you do this, you fix that. The not-so-busy had sacked out anywhere a body could fit. But a lot of folks just stared into space or murmured in tired groups. The den had taken this one hard.

Jenn and I moved dirty dishes off a crate and sat. I tried not to wolf my food.

"Look who comes," she noted. "The walking wounded."

Rubio had rounded the corner from the stairs, moving slow but a lot steadier.

"You heard what happened to him?" I murmured while he was still out of earshot.

"Who hasn't? Those stupid boys had to tell all their stupid little buddies. See the glares? No one asks, hey dude, did you really do it? He's convicted already."

"But you know he didn't."

She rolled her shoulders in a complicated shrug.

"No, I mean, you do. Don't you?"

"Doesn't matter what I think. He's marked, and that's that."

How many of Rube's so-called friends were thinking the same thing? I gnawed my lip. "How are the guys who got shot?"

"That's the thing. One more died this afternoon."

Rube slouched over with a plate of pan-scrapings. We made room on our crate. He was bandaged and stitched, but able to shove food in his mouth and still make rude noises about green kids who couldn't deliver a serious beating even though there were three of them and were vanquished by a girl.

Jenn shot him a warning glance and for once he got the message.

"How come you were out so late?" he asked me.

"You mean, other than saving your butt, and the numbnuts boys as well?"

"You were already late by the time you got to me."

I quickly reviewed my storm tale for what to tell and what to edit out. The Macys, yes, and that got a good laugh. Nothing about the hide or the Souk, and especially not Daniel. The Stormies, without the arrows; the surge, yes, even my vision of the lost woman. None of this would be suspect, but I hesitated with the last. Did I sound like a crazy person? Hard not to. Retelling was reliving, and I got all worked up about it again.

Much as he loved to talk, Rubio did know when to shut up and listen. But when I finally wound down, he set his leftovers aside. "It's like some kind of drug trip. Time fractured, parallel events, recalled trauma." His nose twitched, like he'd scented something interesting. "You're sure you didn't know this woman?"

"Only like I'd maybe met her sometime? But not like I knew her."

"What did she look like?"

"Umm . . ." Already her image was fading, except for that final mask of despair. "Not tall. Slim-ish. Delicate face. Sort of . . . blond. I think."

"Delicate? Sort of blond? You mean, like you?"

"No way." I did not see myself as delicate. I fluffed my drying hair. "Hers was long."

Jenn sipped her herbal. "What was she wearing?"

"You would ask. Something with stripes. The water was murky. I re-member glasses."

Rubio nodded. "Okay, so post-Hasan, pre-Abel. Once you couldn't get lenses or surgery on the island, out came the old specs. How old was she?"

"Oldish. Maybe forty-five?"

He swayed gently on the crate like he was praying. "So, who do you *think* she was?"

"How should I know?"

"Don't get riled. What if you had to guess?"

I knew this doggish mode of his. "You're getting at something."

He turned away to bury a rattling cough. "I could make the obvious suggestion . . ."

"Obvious?" I folded my arms across my chest. "Okay, who?"

"Are you being dumb about this on purpose?"

Jenn clucked her tongue. "Rubio . . ."

"Well, look at her!" He jabbed a finger. "Classic defensive posture."

Jenn rose, smoothing out folds, raking back her hair. "Let's not do this now. We're tired and stressed, and . . ." She tugged at her ear, like, see all these people listening?

"No." Rubio put out a blocking arm. "This is important. She needs to remember."

"You think it's important. I think you should leave her alone!"

He glanced up at her, surprised. "This could be a major breakthrough!"

"And maybe it could wait!"

"It's okay." I dragged his arm away so she wouldn't feel trapped.

"Always raking up the past!" Jenn made waving-away motions. She'd had enough reminders for one day. "It's gone, so what's the point?"

"To help her know who she is." When Rubio was sure he was right, he couldn't imagine any other opinion.

"Let him get it said, whatever it is," I soothed. "Or we'll never hear the end of it."

"But I don't have to listen! It's past time for bed." She waited for me to join her retreat.

"You go on. See you tomorrow."

Her raised eyebrow said, you'll be sorry. But she shrugged and went on her way.

I turned back to Rubio. "How can I remember someone I didn't know?"

"I think you did know her." His earnest frown twisted his stiches and bruises into a tragic mask. "Glim, listen. This was not some random vision, okay? You saw this woman in memory."

"How do you know that?"

"Has to be! You were afraid for your life, some trigger got set off, and there she was."

"So?" I wound my arms tighter around my chest. "I still don't see . . ."

"Don't reject the idea before you hear it through!"

"Keep it down, will you?" After the day I'd had, last thing I needed was a public grilling.

"Okay," he said more quietly. "Are you going to listen?"

I nodded sullenly.

"Then here it is: I think that woman was your mother."

"My mother?" Denial swept over me like the surge. "Oh, come on."

"The evidence is there."

"What evidence?"

"You got a mirror? Describing that woman, you could have been describing yourself."

"Or a dozen others, right here at Unca Joe!"

I must have shouted it. Others were looking at us. Even Rousseau glanced up. I ducked my head. He'd think we were arguing about him.

Rubio leaned toward me. "Who else would you have risked your life to save?"

"Anyone. A friend, a stranger, anyone! C'mon, you all say you helped whoever you could during Abel!"

"It didn't have to be Abel. Maybe some earlier storm."

My mother? Oh god. What if he was right? He so often was.

My mother had been a total blank so far. Not a scrap of her remained in my memory. But not knowing what had happened to her let me believe she was still alive, somewhere on the Mainland. I'd taken some comfort from that thought, even planning how I would go about finding her, once I remembered her name.

The tears came before I could stop them. "You're saying my mother is . . . dead."

"Well, yes. I am." He'd been sure of it all along. "So's mine."

"And you're saying it's my fault! You're saying I killed my mother!"

"What? No!" He grabbed my wrists. "I never meant that!"

"Then what did you mean?" How could he plant such horror to fester in my brain?

"Only that it happened. That you did everything you could, everything! Letting go was her decision. She knew you'd both drown if she didn't. She gave her life to save her child."

This was supposed to make me feel better?

I turned my teary face away. He didn't intend to be cruel. Only to welcome me to the fraternity of orphans, to help me come to terms with reality. But he wasn't inside my head, and empathy was never Rube's strong point. I wanted to run, anywhere away, but there was nowhere to go. I felt flayed, my skin inside-out again like those first weeks in the Ward, my bones shattered glass. But I'd lost the numb-button, the psychic-morphine drip I could call on before. If this was full recovery, I wasn't sure I liked it.

"Is there a problem here?"

We jerked around, a matched pair of guilt and upset. I failed to get hold of myself. Rubio stared at his feet.

"Well?" Rousseau was in daddy-peacemaker mode. Only the tightness around his eyes suggested his exhaustion.

"Just a minor meltdown," Rubio murmured. "About the storm."

"Understandable." Rousseau regarded me as I wiped my face with my shirt. He knew avoidance when he saw it. He leveled a thick finger at Rubio. "You are grounded till further notice. You'd be in the Ward if we had the room. But I want you in my office first thing tomorrow."

I wondered when the man had seen his own bunk last.

"I didn't . . ." Rubio said. "I never would . . ."

"I know that. Problem is, they don't. And you do nothing to advance your case." He gave the loft a final survey. "In the morning."

We watched him disappear down the stairs.

"Guess he'll be reading you the riot act," I murmured.

"Don't sound so happy about it." Rubio studied me. "You okay?"

"Fine," I lied. "Just got some processing to do."

He nodded, satisfied. "Now we can move on to remembering your father."

SEVENTEEN

I went after Jenn in her tier to beg a downer. Not my thing at all, but I was totally blown out. No way I wanted to lie awake all night wracked with survivor guilt or tormented by nightmares.

I eased down on her floor-level bunk. "Sorry to be a mooch . . ."

She was busy with her hair. "S'okay, kiddo. I got you covered."

But I saw how her hand shook as she tipped the tiny blue dot into my palm. One less for her. I popped it dry into my mouth 'case she changed her mind, then watched her torture her hair for a while. Not with a comb but an actual hairbrush. I never saw the point, except hers did always look so neat and shiny.

"Any more posts from your mystery video pal?"

"You mean Aitch?"

"She has a name now?"

"I backtracked her tag."

"Just H?"

"A-I-T-C-H. Like a last name, maybe?"

"Or a den name."

"Mmmm. Hadn't thought of that. A brave den girl with a cell phone. Possible. She popped up once this morning before the storm took everything down. Short clips of guys shooting high-tech guns, like military practice, only no uniforms."

I grinned.

"What?"

"I love how you always notice what anyone's wearing."

Jenn frowned. "Don't laugh. These guys were serious. And you could tell she didn't want them seeing her recording them."

"Could you tell where it was?"

She gave a worried shrug. "Uptown. Pretty sure this time. Like, Fort Tryon Park? There were some trees, and you could see the river in the background."

Even uptown felt too close to home for heavy-duty weapons training. "Did you share this with Rousseau?"

"No. You think I should?"

"Well, yeah. I think it's why he put you up there. The Wizzers don't remember real news reporting. They'd likely see it as an adventure vid or a game, like those dickbrain lads watching old riot clips. But you can sort out the real from the fake."

"Sometimes."

But she seemed cheered by the idea of having a serious assignment. She set her brush aside. "Speaking of dickbrains, you went way too easy on Rubio earlier. Are you okay?"

"Still smarting a bit," I admitted.

"Don't know why you let him be such an asshole!"

Smarting aside, I didn't see it that way. "Because Rube is a problem solver. It's like when he criticizes the den. It hurts, but he's trying to help, to make things better."

Jenn rolled her eyes, then yawned. "And look where that's got him."

She had me yawning too. I patted her knee. "Thanks for the meds."

B ack in my bunk, I hauled the drapes tight to say: Do Not Disturb. A long breath later, Rubio came knocking, soft and apologetic.

"I'm sleeping," I said.

"Clearly, you are not."

"But I need to be. Now."

He was quiet a minute, to see if I'd relent. Then he said, "I need to know if we're okay."

"We're fine. Or we will be, once I figure out how to forgive you for dropping a bomb on me without a bit of warning, especially when you have no proof."

"Momentum of the moment."

I yawned noisily. "Jenn's right. You are entirely full of shit."

"Did she say that?"

"In so many words."

"Sounds like forgiveness to me. We'll talk about it tomorrow."

And the next day, and the next, I was sure. "Not if I have anything to say about it."

"Glim, you can't avoid . . ." Another pause. "Okay. Never mind. Later."
I was asleep before the tier stopped vibrating with his descent.

B y morning, the main floor was dry and the kitchen almost up to speed
again. I was grateful to whoever'd stayed up late to schlepp all the equipment and supplies downstairs again. I drifted around a bit, still coasting on
Jenn's downer. Kind of like wearing body armor on your brain. Made the
day a whole lot easier. The scouts brought in the bad news from outside, and
the job clerks posted updates on the duty board. Like what we'd been
through with lesser storms, only a whole lot worse.

"East side, teens to forties, deep water to Third Ave. Scattered flooding
to Park. Extensive walkway damage."

And people were still missing.

We checked the board regularly while we worked on cleanup. After four
shifts, round the clock, we had Unca Joe pretty much back in order. But not
like it was before. More stuff was left upstairs on Three, where moving
about was already claustrophobic, or taken up to Four, out of the way of easy
daily use. I began to see Rubio's point about the den needing more above-
surge living space.

"West side, teens, under water. Twenties to forties, deep water to Seventh."

A lot of my old picking venues could no longer be reached dry-foot.

Rousseau's insistent focus on food production paid off, though. Even
with the pickers on cleanup and repair and the roof garden ravaged, the den
survived off our stores, for the time being, at least.

"Stuy Square Marina, extensive damage to boats and infrastructure."

I was humming away, swabbing stinky mud out of the swap cabinets,
when glad shouts broke out in the mudroom. One of the scouts bounded
into the Hall with Zane and Mikka, our two lost youngsters. Good news at
last. The kids ran about hugging everyone in sight. "Not too much the
worse for wear," commented the guy working next to me.

"Where'd you find them?" someone else called.

The scout—stringy, crag-faced Magda—took up a storytelling posture.
"Revelations took 'em in, thanks be. An' then couldn't wait to get rid of
'em. Those cranky monks welcomed me with open arms!"

"Awesome strict over there." Zane's preteen rasp seemed to have dropped
an octave.

"Sure is!" Mikka was already struggling to release her long brown hair from its too-tight plait. "Men and women can't even eat together."

"And the food was really gross."

"Be glad they fed you at all," Magda scolded. "But good thinking to seek shelter at the nearest den."

Mikka plucked at the coarse fabric of her oversized robe. "They took my tee and jeans. Said they weren't nice—like I should be 'shamed. Made me wear this old rag!"

I crossed Revelations off my list of other dens to consider when I was upset with Unca Joe. It didn't happen often. Not like with Rubio.

Which reminded me about his meeting with Rousseau. He'd gone into hiding after, which was fine with me. I needed a break from his good intentions. I was still holding his mother idea at arm's length, not quite ready to try it on for size. If only I could suss out who else it could have been. Too old for a sister. Maybe a favorite neighbor, or some other relative? Either way, she must have been someone I'd cared about. The loss came back fresh each time I thought about her.

And what he'd said about looking in a mirror . . .

Didn't have many in Unca Joe, unless like Jake or Jenn you'd traded for some little shard, say, from a woman's compact. But why waste credits you could eat or drink instead? There was one decent-sized chunk propped up in the women's, a half-rectangle broken off a larger piece. If you stood back a bit, you got almost a full-body view.

I mostly gave it a pass, a habit from my early days out of the Ward, when staring at a bruised, lop-haired, empty-eyed skeleton didn't exactly speed my recovery. Lately, with my hair grown out curly and near to my shoulders, and a few pounds on in the right places, the occasional glimpse no longer brought the black clouds rolling in. Even liked what I saw, which was a relief, but not like the absolute making of my world, y'know?

So you'd think I'd have been better prepared.

Mid-afternoon, the sun came out, fired up the solars and put the showers back online. Everyone queued up for an overdue scrubbing. I came out into the impatient crowd, dripping and toweling, then glanced up and saw the memory woman standing not three feet away.

Right there, staring back at me.

I shoved my towel into my mouth to smother a scream. Only the other bodies shoving past me brought me to my senses.

It wasn't her, of course. It was me in the mirror, with the same wet blond hair draped like seaweed down the same oval face, the same brown eyes, as horrified now as hers at the moment she slipped from my grasp.

I turned and ran for my bunk.

Soon as I was dressed, I dropped down to Jake's bunk, borrowed scissors from his precious shelf of personal hygiene, and before I could think better of it—or even why—I snipped my hair nearly to my scalp. I stared at the pile in my lap, then gathered up every strand and pitched it out of my bit of window, to be scattered by the sunny afternoon wind.

When I returned the scissors, Jake was just back from checking up on storm damage at the Souk. He gave me a long look, then shook his head. "Back to square one again? What happened this time?"

"You wouldn't understand!" I wailed, then sped back to my bunk to bury my confusion and misery in the old book.

March 14th, 1848

We had a lazy sluggish day on account of a calm until about 11 O.C., when a dark angry looking cloud hove in sight. We lowered down the mainsail so as to catch some fresh water and it was refreshing to get washed and get some drink. We caught about a hogshead and I felt natural again.

While we were all lounging about the deck, the word went out about a man overboard and we all rushed & found Albert Lyman hanging over the side by a rope. After a moment, we had him on board and soon all hands were lounging about as before, laughing and joking as usual. We have had only 24 hours of fair weather in 19 days when we could work at anything. I took out my needles and mended my suspenders & coat. The others with Capt. & all hands commenced fixing their fishing rods & harpoons, preparatory to taking dolphin or porpoise, which they say will eat well.

Thursday, 15th—We have been becalmed all day and busier day was never seen. The sun was very hot and every man that could find a place on deck was spreading out his clothing & beds to get them dry and stop the mildewing of them. Some have nearly ruined their clothing. By being so long *wet, they have mildewed, my own with the rest, but I have less loss than others. The crew were busy repairing rigging and the sail makers mending the sails and we find that Old Boreus has handled us rather harshly.*

Amazing, how someone else's problems can take your mind off your own.

E ventually I missed Rubio enough to go looking to mend fences. I found him in the media loft, taking his irritation out on a defenseless computer. "So, was it bad?"

"Um." He bent his long back closer to the screen. "Still can't get a signal."

"With Rousseau, I mean."

"I know." Rubio jabbed at the touchpad a few times. His jaw was dark with scab and stubble. Without his daily shave, he looked like a derelict. "Damn useless piece of junk."

"You went to see him like that?"

"Like what?"

"You know how he feels about clean cheeks."

"Hurts too much and I need a new blade." He patted his cheek delicately, then looked up at me. His bruised eyes widened. "Jeez, speaking of hair . . . !"

"Huh?"

"What happened to yours?"

You did, I almost said. At least he'd noticed. I smoothed the short ends, already mourning the curls. One impulse I shouldn't have listened to. "Needed a change. Rousseau?"

"Umm. Yeah, well, he piled on the usual tough love and all that, making lame excuses for his boyos, but the gist of it is—and I'm still replaying this to make sure I heard him right . . ." He paused to fuss at the keypad.

"Yes?" I prompted, like he clearly wanted me to.

"Well, he said if I'm so convinced we need a new den home, I should get out there and find us one. Basically, it was put up or shut up."

"Seriously?"

"Seems so." Rubio wagged his head in disbelief. "He said I'm off picker duty, which I'm no good at anyway. That I ought to put my architectural training to better use—get out and evaluate possible sites. What I can't figure is if this is just the easiest way to muzzle me, or if he really wants me to look. I mean, like, what took him so long?"

"Of course he does! After we had the river washing through the main floor again? We can't be going through this every time a storm blows in. This is great!" I pummeled him gently on the shoulder. Good for Rousseau: stamping out a pesky brush fire and moving forward at the same time. "So, what's the deal? Where will you start?"

"Here, I hoped." Rubio closed the unresponsive search program. "I was looking for a high-rez map of the city, a building-by-building view, so I can work out a plan of attack. We had good ones at the firm, but it looks like I'll have to trust my memory for now."

Lucky guy, I mused. You've got one to trust.

The second day of cleanup, while Rousseau worked the main hall with praise for hard work and resiliency, I found Rubio down on his bony knees with a big sheet of brown paper spread out on the floor. He had the curly ends weighted down with coffee mugs.

I peered over his bent back. "What now?"

"Making a map," he mumbled through the stubby shop pencil clamped between his teeth. He spat it into his palm. "Couldn't talk the Mess out of a table yet."

He was copying the large-scale city map mounted next to the duty board, ripped out of some midtown subway station before the water rose that far, the biggest map anyone had been able to come up with. It was the picker's Bible. Rube's version left out all the bus and subway lines but included the latest water levels. He was laying in the street grid, using a thin strip of wood to guide his pencil.

I knelt beside him for a closer look. "Why so big?"

"For the detail." He sat back on his heels. He looked intent and very pleased with himself. "Been a long time since I've done this sort of thing by hand. I'll put in the other dens, like on the duty map, and a few other major landmarks, then those buildings I remember or discover when I go out that might make good new den sites."

On the wall, in addition to recording current water levels, the duty map marked each known den with a big black square, then a dotted line around each one, delineating the five-block radius of that den's local territory. Accepted practice was to steer clear unless invited.

"Very systematic. But already time for an update."

Two of our scouts had trotted in, returning from a survey trip in our little outboard. A small crowd gathered to see how the clerk translated their report onto the duty map. The scouts wouldn't have gone as far as the Souk, so I'd get no hint of when Daniel might reopen his stall. Anyhow, why should that matter to me?

I tapped Rubio's knee. "Look. Chelsea's under water now—Ladysmith's turf, and it's creeping up on Macy's. Maybe there'll be westside walkways soon."

"More boats is a better idea." He rubbed at a healing chin scrape and buried a cough in his palm. "We need to get into serious boat-building if we're going to live like Venetians."

"With serious boats, we'd have a chance to get out of here."

He nodded. "To our new den."

"No. To the Mainland."

He snorted, then drew a series of parallel lines along his ruler. "With the com down, we don't even know if there is a Mainland."

"Of course there's a Mainland! Where would it go?"

He gave me one of his less-flattering looks. "Under water?"

"All of it?"

"Well, no. But at least another good chunk of coast and estuaries. The surge might mostly recede, but the damage will have been done. Another thirty million homeless looking for a perch on higher ground, of which there is less and less. At some point, we'll be the American Archipelago."

"Jeez! Aren't you cheery this morning!"

"Just realistic. Like every morning."

There was a den tendency to think of the Mainland as impervious to the woes visited on the Island. But what had Superstorm Joseph done to Fort Lee or Nyack, up high on the Palisades, and how far did it rage up the Hudson? Until we had a signal again, no way to know, and maybe not even then.

Rubio bent back to his drawing. "Time to move uptown."

Rivera slid up beside us as the clerk redrew the East Side shoreline several blocks further west. The hall buzzed with dismay.

"You look better," I told her. Her dark braid was glossy again, her injuries fading.

Her smile bloomed, tentative but lovely. "Nothing like a day at home."

Grace came motoring over, slapping her thighs like she was ready to take someone on full bore. "Didja hear, the boss is sending out care packages to the dens who got hit worse than we did? The lads are pissed."

"What else is new?" I muttered.

Rivera pursed her lips. "Not sure how I feel about it either."

"Good diplomacy," said Rubio.

"But I can starve just as fast as the next guy . . ."

"I'm sure we can afford a few donations." But I was less than sure myself.

"So, if we feed 'em, they'll stop shooting at us?" Grace crossed her arms defiantly.

"*Somebody* shot at us. We still don't know who. Could've been a loner." Rubio waved her aside. "You're blocking my view."

"Now you're defending them?"

"I'm not defending anyone. I'm only stating what we know." Rubio settled back on his butt and crossed his long legs, warming to the debate. "I'm pretty sure there'll be no handouts to BlackAdder, if that's what you're on about. Helping out Ladysmith's or Tall Tommy—that's called building alliances."

Rivera crouched to study the map. "Probably how Rousseau sees it, too."

"It's not like we don't have our favorites already," Rubio went on. "You saw who showed up at the meeting. The rhetoric may be all about den independence, the rugged commune surviving on its own and all that, but sides are being drawn. We're not getting out of here anytime soon, so we're going to need rules about how we should operate as a society. We can't just keep making it up as we go along. We're going to need all the help we can get when the shit really hits the fan."

I was glad none of the lads were listening in. "Hurricane Joe wasn't shit enough?"

"But that's just weather. I'm talking about when the dens decide to take what they need, instead of trading for it. For now, we'll have the usual post-storm surplus of free salvage, but that's coming to an end." Rube spread his hands. "I mean, sure, we have food, but we're unarmed, undefended, and practically at water level. We need to consider the longer term. We need to . . ."

Speak of the devil, and lo . . .

"Shhh." Rivera jogged Rubio's arm as a scowling pack of Rousseau's lads shouldered out of the Mess, laden with sacks of rice and beans, crates of eggs and vegetables, and stomped past us into the mudroom.

"Man, I don't know how you've lived this long," muttered Grace.

Rubio set his jaw. "Someone has to advocate for change."

Bored with a debate she wasn't going to win, Grace moved on to me. "By the way, nice hair. What the hell happened?"

"Cut it."

"Maybe you could've used scissors instead of a battle axe?"

A stir by the mudroom door exploded into whoops and applause. We all scrambled to our feet.

Grace stretched to peer over the crowd. "Awright!"

A path opened as Spunk limped gamely into the hall, hatless and grinning, looking like he'd survived a war. Everyone mobbed him, the men pounding him on the back, the women cuffing his ears. The tears starting in my eyes caught me by surprise. I'd been more worried about him than I realized.

Rousseau appeared out of nowhere, his smile broad and relieved. He curled an arm around Spunk's back. "Okay, folks, okay. Let the man breathe."

Rubio bent to roll up his map, clutching it to his chest. We all backed off a step, expectant and eager, waiting for the boss to supply the traditional den welcome.

Rousseau delivered it like a quiet roll of thunder: "What took you so long?"

Spunk hooted, shoving matted hair off his forehead. He was scabbed and bruised, but the blood crusting his clothes had dried long ago. His left arm hung loose at his side. His pale eyes danced with cheery malice. "Got caught up wit' soma dem Storm Worshippas."

Murmurs and shivers all around. A jug was passed through the ranks and shoved into Spunk's good hand. He drained it, splashing water down his chest. "Got anyt'in' stronga?"

Rousseau gestured and someone ran for beer. "So how come you're still walking? They couldn't get the bonfire started?"

"Oh, dey was gonna crisp me ta holy cindas, alri'. But I tole 'em I wanna join up." Beer replaced the water and he took a long swig. "Den dey all love me!"

Given my brush with Stormies, I caught Spunk's implication if no one else did. Did Rousseau, this man who might once have been a priest? His skin was too dark to show a blush, and his laugh boomed as if at a joke.

Recalling that firelit tangle of naked limbs, I knew Spunk's full account would be hair-raising and raunchy. But we'd have to wait for it. He was burning his last wisp of adrenaline and the beer didn't help. He sagged against Rousseau's side.

"Okay, let's get that arm seen to." Rousseau signaled two of his lads. "Jorge, Tang, kindly give the man a hand up the stairs."

As he eased Spunk into their grasp, the scout Magda nosed through the crowd to tap his arm. "Update, Boss."

"Say it."

"Tall Tommy lost their lower floor. Gimme Shelter's barn got flooded out, washed away some of their feed stores, but they'd brought the animals over to Empire before the storm."

"Good thinking," nodded Rousseau. Gimme's cow and goats were our backup source of fresh milk and cheese.

"And Ladysmith's wondering if they want to stay put with no land access," the scout finished. "Long and short of it, they're all talking about searching out new digs."

Rousseau couldn't suppress a quick glance in Rubio's direction. "Well, that's something to think about. Lucky for us, we're good for now. Even better if we all get back to work."

Rubio bent his head to my ear. "Great. Now there's competition."

Later that day, a sadder duty faced us. With everyone accounted for, there were still two canoe crew members dead from sniper fire.

Jenn, Rube, and I joined the others watching from the hastily repaired Third Avenue walkway as the crews rigged tow lines to a raft loaded with the shrouded bodies. Rousseau waited in the stern of the outboard, while Jorge and Tang loaded in two jerrycans of precious flammables.

"Viking funeral," Rubio observed. "Precious fuel instead of gold and jewels."

"They deserve it," I said.

"For what? Getting in the way of a bullet?"

Jenn elbowed him sharply.

He shrugged and looked away.

Lines secured, the canoes glided down Third, gathering speed in the outgoing tide. One in the lead, two towing the raft, the outboard in rear escort. As the last motored by quietly below, I saw Rousseau settle a serious firearm by his side. The ante had risen.

"I hate being left behind," murmured Jenn. "What if they just keep going, all the way to the Jersey Shore?"

"Why would they?" Rubio seemed genuinely perplexed.

"Wouldn't mind being able to watch." This was my first den funeral, and I liked how fire seemed both clean and final.

"Like I said," Rubio said, "we need more boats."

"How far out will they go?"

"Open water, down past the Battery Towers. Maybe out by Lady Liberty."

"So far? BlackAdder's down there. And the patrols."

Small cargo ships used the Hudson to supply Uptown, guarded by armed cutters. I'd seen one of those churn by from the window of a westside warehouse I was picking, all lit up and predatory-looking. Even from a distance, it scared me.

"They'll leave a funeral burning alone, long as it's headed out to sea. No one wants more rot floating upriver than there is already." Rubio took a breath, as if what he'd said was too ugly even for him. "As for BlackAdder . . . that's what the rifle's for."

When the solemn caravan slid out of sight, the three of us slouched back to work.

Jenn let Rubio get a bit ahead and leaned in to whisper. "I could trim that scare hair for you. Just give it a little shape, y'know? What do you say?"

I smiled, rueful but half-serious. "Would I have to look in a mirror?"

EIGHTEEN

S punk made Rousseau keep me off the streets even after he'd sent the other pickers back to work, at least till my flood bruises healed. The day after the funeral, I was assigned to the ongoing cleanup of the roof gardens.

Unca Joe produced most of our fresh food in a series of wrap-around terraces rising floor by floor around the central tower of the skylight well. The fifth floor was the barn floor, with sties and coops and stalls on the inside, leading to heavily fortified terrace runs for our pigs, goats, and chickens. The sixth-floor terraces were planted with fruit-bearing shrubs and vines, plus one of our greatest treasures—the apple, plum, cherry, peach, and pear trees espaliered along the walls, for protection from the winds. The sixth-floor roof held the six long hoop houses of our vegetable garden, each with three rows of raised beds and two aisles between. Sounds like a lot of growing space, but it was just as crowded as our living areas. No inch went unused. A sheltered corner was stuffed with compost bins. Solar panels and stubby windmills were fastened wherever there was opportunity.

I had zero gardening chops, which I took as further proof I'd always been a city girl, and probably not raised in one of the urban farm cooperatives that took over the parks when supply lines from the Mainland became less reliable. Gimme Shelter and a few other dens grew out of these. Much of that land was flooded now, at least downtown, where food production had retreated to rooftops and terraces like ours.

Because basic garden maintenance was considered therapeutic, I'd been posted up there my first few weeks out of the Ward. I'd learned how to dig and weed, and I'd got pretty good at the finicky but brain-dead task of thinning young veggie shoots. The day was hot when I arrived on Six, despite a misty drizzle, and busy with storm repair teams coming and going. The place was still a mess.

Picking was vital, but the gardens were our most valuable asset. Like most pickers, I knew this but still tended to take for granted the steady stream of edibles to the Mess. But the shock of coming face to face with the wreckage left on Six by Storm Joseph sure made me reconsider the vulnerability of our food supply.

We weren't the tallest building around by any stretch. Nearby later-built glass towers offered some wind-shelter and sun-reflection, a sense of protection. But they also tended to shed debris during a big storm, their windows blowing out and whatever might be left inside lifting into the gale to rain down on our terraces, puncturing the precious plastic sheeting covering our hoop houses, crashing onto the raised beds, crushing the plants. The sheeting on one house was nearly shredded, now being replaced with a meticulous patchwork of the larger strips salvaged from previous damage.

The disorder was unsettling. Repairs meant change, since we never had enough of anything to fix things exactly as they had been. Always a bit of make-do involved. Rubio could endlessly explain how change was inevitable and necessary, but he hadn't convinced me to welcome it. After Abel, I'd relied on the dull predictability of den life to restore my balance. Now I felt change coming, as inevitable as the next hurricane, as sure as the warm rain on my back.

I joined a team clearing shards of broken furniture and mending tears in the hoop coverings that were small enough for plastic tape to hold the edges together. The tape itself was as precious as the heavy sheeting. We'd been allotted one roll from the materials storeroom. Each piece must be cut to the exact size needed for the repair. No waste to be tolerated. And as this was a team of lads, their idea of me helping was mostly 'hold this' and 'hand me that' while they went on with their loud replay of the sniping and what who should do about what.

Finally, I slipped away into one of the undamaged hoops on the other side, to get out of the wet and find more useful employment. The place was empty, the young vegetables stretching in green rows from end to end. The palaver of goats and muttering hens in their runs on the lower terraces softened the clang of hammers and the rhythmic rasp of hand saws from across the roof. It was almost peaceful. I decided to thin the rows of collards, gathering the thins into a small tub for soup greens.

Stretching my back at the turn of a row, I noticed a woman bent over the carrot beds at the far end. A brimmed straw hat hid her face. Each time I glanced her way, her back was to me. After a while, this weirded me out. Usually, you'd at least offer a greeting when joining someone at work. I picked up my tub of baby greens and wandered over.

"Excuse me . . ."

"Yes?" The woman spoke into the fluffy carrot tops without lifting her head.

"Can you tell me, am I pulling the right ones?" I held out my tub like a total newbie.

She straightened and peered into the tub. "Oh, yes. Very well done. The kitchen will be delighted." She bent back to her work.

It was dotty Ellie Mae.

Now, I'd have said the kitchen was full of cranks, snarks, and grouches, but maybe she knew them better. In the Mess, with the tables crowded with the young and active, this woman seemed frail and gray. Up here, she looked at home and quietly in charge.

I searched for an opener. "Nice to be dry, huh? That third house over is a wreck, but this one made it through all right."

The sides were rolled up now to let the air in. The storm preppers would have unrolled them to the ground and clipped the bottom edges to the sides of the outer raised beds.

She nodded vaguely into her row. "Newer covering, more flexible. It can balloon and flutter without tearing. I don't know where we'll get more when we need it."

Another thing I'd taken for granted: the infinity of supplies in the upstairs storage rooms. But large rolls of plastic sheeting weren't on the pickers' list of stuff easily shoved into a grab bag. "Where did we get it?"

"Oh, a while ago. Rousseau saw the need and stocked up when it was still available."

I felt bad that I might have passed such a valuable item by without thinking to tell anyone back at the den. Time to widen my focus. "I'm pretty much done over there. You need any help?"

"Certainly." She straightened again to blot her temples with the long hem of her white shirt, held as delicately as a lace hanky. She was a head shorter than me and square, her legs set apart like sturdy posts. Her feet were bare and her crooked old-lady toes dug into the soil like they meant to take root. Her big hat threw her eyes into shadow but for a spark of reflected gleam. "There's no such thing as too much help in a garden."

Her tone was cheery but her smile was distracted, her voice low and rough, like she'd been yelling, which was hard to imagine. She gestured at the shreds of plastic scattered across the carrot rows. "Perhaps a bit of cleanup?"

I recognized her double message: *Sure, you can help. Just don't get too close.* The same message I'd been sending out since I woke up in the Ward. But I was curious about Ellie Mae, and this was my best chance so far to get to know her. I moved a long step away and gathered up debris in silence, like I'd read in some book about taming wild animals: let them come to you.

After we'd worked a while, she began to hum softly, a long, complicated tune I didn't know. I was sure she'd forgotten me when she said, "It's young Glimmer, isn't it?"

"Yes, ma'am." Her old-fashioned talk was catching.

"You're on the mend, I see."

"Yes, thanks, I am." I folded a larger sheet of plastic into a bundle to be reused. Ellie Mae worked her way down to the end of the carrot block and started up the kale row across the aisle. Maybe ten minutes later, she was opposite me again. "Was there something else you wanted?"

"No, um . . . well, yes. I've been watching how you work so fast, like, without even looking. How do you decide which ones to pull?"

"My fingers tell me." She tossed a handful of thins into her basket and dusted soil from her hands. "After so many years, it's automatic."

"You had a garden before?"

"I did. Quite a large one. On the roof of my office. So many of us did."

"Us?"

"In the sciences. We knew what was coming and filled every space we could find." She bent over her row again. "My soil was a lot better than what we have here, but we're working on it. You know what they say about beggars and choosers."

"You did science before? What kind?" I knew, but probably she could explain it better than Rubio.

"Astrophysics. I study . . . studied . . . the planets of our solar system."

I recalled her hunched over that screen full of exotic images. "You mean, like Mars?"

"Indeed." She turned her head and smiled across the rows, like to a bright student. "Particularly Mars. Specifically, its climate. Well, I used to."

"You don't anymore?"

"No, dear. Hardly anyone can."

"Why not?"

"Too busy surviving. Did Rousseau send you up here to report on me?"

"What? No!" Her blunt accusation startled me. "I'm just . . . curious. I don't know much about science."

From the shadow of her hat brim, her eyes drilled into me. "I'm not allowed to talk about it, you know. I can't afford to get turned out on the streets, not at my age."

I raised both palms. "I wouldn't . . ."

"Not any of it. He says it's bad for morale."

Bad. Not loony or wrong. "Why would talking about Mars be bad for morale?"

"Oh, not Mars the planet. Mars the colony." She slapped her palm over her mouth as if she'd let fly a belch. "Damn. There I go."

"You mean the expedition base?"

"No, the settlement. And what happened to it." Again, the hand clamped over the mouth, as if both had minds of their own. She gave the softest of moans. "It's wrong to deny it . . ."

What happened to it. A new mystery. Was her hint-dropping a way of talking about it while pretending not to? Peeto had showed me that site about the Mars expedition being a hoax, but he hadn't mentioned a colony, a *settlement*. Here was the crazy part, I decided. Her job had been everything. Losing it sent her over the edge into believing what she wished for? I mean, if there were people actually living on Mars, we'd all know about it, wouldn't we? So, wasn't it overbearing, even silly of Rousseau to worry about some old woman's delusional fantasy? He seemed hardly concerned with what went on off the Island, so what was his problem with Mars?

"Would you talk about it if I promise mum's the word?"

She bowed over the kale again. "No, no. It's not a good idea. For either of us."

"But I can see it's very painful for you. Everyone talks about their life before—why can't you? It's totes unfair! Why did you stay when Rousseau was so unreasonable?"

"Why stay?" She straightened to study me a moment, then let her alarm ease into rueful envy. "Oh, my dear girl. Be glad you don't remember what we're all in hiding from."

Now she'd lost me. "You mean, the weather?"

"That's only the half of it! No, you can't imagine what it was like." Her gaze lifted away, toward the surrounding glass towers and some dark recall of her own. "All the years of disintegration. The paranoia. The raw hatred. The political repression. The rule of tyrants. The death of democracy." Her low voice hardened to a near growl. She grabbed my arm, her stubby fingers digging into my wrist with a gardener's strength. "The scramble for high ground. The hoarding of resources. When you've lived as long as I have, my dear—after all, I'm the eldest here at Unca Joe—you've had the misfortune to have watched too many lovely things be destroyed: relatives, friends, a once-admirable political system, the moral fabric of human society, and finally, our planet!"

"But it's better now, right? Or it will be!"

She shook my arm as if I wasn't listening hard enough. The wide brim of her hat knocked my nose. "At least at Unca Joe, I am still a person!"

I stared at her, like she'd slapped my face. Maybe I even looked scared.

She glanced down, saw how tightly she was holding me, and pushed my arm away. "Sorry. I . . . get carried away. It's still . . ."

I waited, but she didn't finish. And I couldn't think of what to say.

She looked away down the rows of vegetables for a long while, then sighed and said softly, "Is this a new idea for you, then? That as bad as things are for us here, we're better off, that we have more freedom here than we would elsewhere?"

Freedom? Morality? Democracy? My head was spinning. It was one thing to claim, like Jake and Rubio, that the Island was the only place they wanted to be. Another entirely to suggest that it was some sort of last refuge, not from storms or plagues but from the rest of humanity. The old woman was definitely off the rails, but not with some generic madness. She had a cause. Not even Rubio harangued in such broad and grandiose terms. I could see why Rousseau had made her tone it down some, but . . .

"Wouldn't Rousseau be in favor of that idea?" I ventured. "It speaks well for the dens."

She shook her head, calmer, even resigned. "Not if it makes his people lose hope in a better future. A future elsewhere. Hope's what will get us through, he always says. And I understand that. I guess. It's just that . . ."

A clatter at the top of the stairwell announced young Zane, back in training since losing himself and little Mikka in the storm. He waved, rattling an empty pail, and headed for us with the quick step of one quite happy to have been reassigned to the roof. "Got potatoes? The kitchen needs 'em!"

Fantasy or no, I wanted to hear more about Mars.

"Can we talk about your work sometime?" I murmured. "About whatever you're allowed to say?"

"You don't know what you're asking." Ellie Mae dropped her cultivator into the sagged-out pocket of her shirt, spilling damp soil down her front, then moved down the rows as if afraid to be seen talking to me. "Over here, Zany. Bring that big fork. I'll dig you some."

But she hadn't said no.

NINETEEN

I f we told each other things were finally getting back to normal, now that the den was sorted out and the gardens cleaned up, we couldn't have got it wronger. Only the calm before the storm, and this time it wasn't weather.

Two long days stooping and digging didn't mean an early bedtime. Like most of the night pickers, my sleep schedule hadn't caught up yet. Nighttime was our wake time and we all expected to be back there ASAP.

So there was raucous late-hour poker in the Mess, noisy sparring and gymnastics in Main, and percussive video games in the media loft. Wasn't till well after midnight that a person could have a conversation up there, never mind think. I tried reading in my bunk but even the old book didn't help me lie still.

By the early morning hours, I was back in the loft. The crowd had thinned to mostly the Wizzers, the CB obsessives, and me. I could settle at 'my' computer without a line behind me waiting for a turn. Right off, I called up those Mars files Peeto said were Ellie Mae's for closer study. Disappointing. Aside from the spectacular photos, I found mostly official press releases and journal articles from thirty years ago, colorless and brief. Yes, there had been a series of manned expeditions to Mars. And yes, an Arcadia Base had been established and maintained for over a decade, and a lot of science had been done there. But then the stuff just petered out. Fewer reports, fewer articles, then none. No final this or that, no joyous welcome home to the explorers, no horrific report of a disaster at the base. Had I missed the crucial files? Had Ellie Mae misplaced them somewhere? Or hid them on purpose? Had they been . . . suppressed?

As I pondered ways to dig further, the quiet buzz in the Wizzers' corner rose to a distraction. I glanced up to see them thronging urgently around one screen.

"What's up, guys?" I called.

Multiple hands waved me over.

The screen was dark but undulating, like the tide at night when there's rubble just beneath the surface. The camera was in motion, jerky and fast, picking up indistinct forms racing by in blackness broken by sudden flares of fire that lit up an arm here, a face there, but nothing you could read or recognize. A chaos of bright and dark. No audio. Flames and people? I thought of the Storm Worshippers.

"She movin' fast," one of the boys murmured.

"On the run."

"Think she followin'."

She? Then I noticed the time readout in the right-hand corner.

"Is it Aitch?" I asked.

A chorus of preoccupied nods.

"What are we looking at?" I still couldn't make sense of it.

"Think we wake Jenn?" a girl asked.

"Nah. Too late. Record it."

"See that? Timer's off." A boy pointed at the screen. "This an hour ago."

"What's that?" The oldest boy turned abruptly away from the screen. "Hear that?"

The others were too gripped by the video, but I heard it, in real time.

Shrill whistles, faint with distance but nearing, like a relay.

The eldest backslapped his nearest neighbors. "Listen up, dudes!"

"Outside," I said. "Sentry signals."

The den's front entry was guarded but never locked, in case some night picker came home early. We heard feet pounding across the mudroom, then slapping up the stairs.

"Goin' up to Rousseau," noted the eldest.

"Or the medics," I said. "Something's up."

Voices in the mudroom, shouts and cries, brimming into the main hall. Aitch forgotten, Eldest and I ran to the balcony railing. A shadowy tsunami spilled across the dim-lit floor. Men, women, children. I was sure we were under attack by a bloodthirsty mob, until someone flicked on the emergency lights to reveal them staggering and bloodied, half of them holding up the other half. The cries were the wails of children or howls of pain. More sprinting upstairs, and soon, our groggy medics hurrying down, kits in hand.

Rousseau appeared like a ghost beside me, a wrinkled white shirt hauled hastily over his dark chest. He stared down at the milling, moaning mass. "Jesu! It's Ladysmith's."

His hand fell heavy on my shoulder. "Go rouse Jake. And Spunk, if you can find him. After that, everyone with a strong stomach and a steady touch. This'll be all hands on deck."

"Yessir." I lunged for the tiers. Nearly slammed into Grace as she sped by, headed upstairs. "Hey! What's happened?"

"Sonsabitches!" Tough-girl Grace looked like the roof had fallen in. Her unbraided hair flowed like an angry cloud around her shoulders.

"Who? What?"

"Ladysmith's got raided! Big firefight, least a dozen dead, the den on fire!"

"Was it . . . ?"

"BlackAdder! Got to be! Motherfuckers burned them out, grabbed all their provisions."

What Rubio said would happen. Good if he held back the told-you-sos.

Grace gestured upward. "I gotta go get . . ."

"Yah, sorry, go!"

I rousted everyone I could find, then went back down for further orders. The carnage in Main was horrifying, fresh blood and soot mixing in an odorous smog. The bullet wounds, knife slashes, broken limbs, dislocations, and worst of all, the burns, raw and oozing. Our medics were doing their best, but they needed ice-baths and anesthetics, and mostly we had herbal balms and seawater. Rousseau sent runners to Gimme Shelter and Empire to beg for help. The whole den was in shock. Everyone who could was pitching in.

"It's like the triage station in a refugee camp," breathed Rubio, joining me as I tore up T-shirts from the swap shelf to bandage knife wounds.

"You seen Spunk? His bunk isn't slept in."

"Probably off with one of his women." He sighted over the crowd. "There's Maxine. Glad she made it."

Rousseau came in from the mudroom, stunned and grim, supporting the Ladysmith's den boss, followed by several of her crew, like maybe they'd had to drag her out of the burning building to get her to retreat. Her hair was singed nearly to her scalp, her clothing sodden—water or blood, or both. Smaller than I recalled from the meeting in Rousseau's office, vulnerable but hardly diminished as she showered Rousseau top-volume with righteous outrage, and he tried to talk her down to reason. Someone found her a towel, then draped another across her shoulders. When she wiped her eyes, she left pale tracks under layers of oily soot. She looked ready to chew up the first mouth that backtalked her.

Rousseau left off his calming and hollered for a medic and a stretcher.

"I can fucking walk!" Maxine bellowed, clutching one arm close to her belly. "They don't put me down that easy!"

Some of the Smiths started up a wan cheer. The rest of us joined in to make it ring big, as Rousseau and the medic helped her up the stairs to the Ward.

"And so it begins," Rubio said quietly.

So much blood and pain, so many strange faces crowding in—men with beards, women with toddlers at the hip, kids looking lost. And weapons everywhere, out and ready: belt knives, rifles back-slung, sheathed machetes, cudgels, whatever else I couldn't see that had made it into the den before Rousseau could say otherwise.

"Jake! Here!" I grabbed him as he rushed by with a basket of bandages and piled my T-shirt strips on top. "What do we know?"

"Poor Max! Christ Almighty!" He looked wrecked, like caught off guard by a sidelong blow. "BlackAdder, for sure this time! Stole everything they could fit in their boats, big fucking inboards, like a half-dozen of them! A fucking fleet!"

"Since when does BlackAdder have inboards?" demanded Rubio.

"Or the juice to run them?" Jake seconded. "A question everyone's asking. And why burn the building down? Pure, wanton destruction. Makes no sense!"

"It's BlackAdder. What d'you expect?"

Jake shifted his load. "One of you go make a count of empty bunks. We'll be taking in the survivors."

"I'll go," I said.

"Forever?" asked Rubio.

"As long as necessary." Jake's eyes narrowed. "You got a problem with that?"

"Just asking." But when Jake had left, he muttered, "Reduced rations, coming up."

"And a bigger den," I added.

That actually cheered him up. "Right! A whole higher level of capacity to look for."

The Ward filled up fast and we went through the extra bunks in no time, assigning them to the lesser injuries. By dawn, we'd bedded down the rest in sofas and chairs or whatever was left of the floor in the media loft. Jake came through, seeing if everyone had dry clothing, food, and drink. He spotted Rivera, sitting in her nightclothes with two small, frantic girls, trying to get them to lie down on a blanket.

"Maybe this'll help." He passed her a ceramic jug. "Just came down from the roof."

"Thanks." As she took it, a warm, milky smell wafted around us.

Jake leaned in beside me as I sliced bread and cheese to pass out to anyone who was well enough to have an appetite. "Can't find their mom," he murmured, watching as the girls sipped at the jug. "Their dad's out searching the ashes."

I could only nod. The kids were so little, so shell-shocked. Their quiet weeping broke my heart. "Any further news?"

"Definitely a provisioning run," he confirmed. "Caught Ladysmith mostly sleeping, and just . . . overwhelmed them."

"Why didn't they ask first, if they were hungry?"

Jake shrugged. I knew he disliked making gross generalizations, but what could you say about such obvious and oblivious malice?

Rivera said it for him. "Adders don't ask, they take. Hope they took some damage, too."

"Oh, they did." Jake's square shoulders slumped. "Max says it was a war zone for a while. Then the whole place blew up in flames and everyone— Smith and Adder—took a dive for the water. By then, some Tommys had showed up, shooting from the opposite roof, so a few more Adders never made it to their boats. But plenty still breathing. The Smiths lost everything they had."

"Good thing Maxine lets her folks arm up." Rivera's hair veiled her face in shadow as she leaned over the girls. "Gave 'em a chance, at least."

One we wouldn't have had, her tone implied.

Jake's blue gaze was troubled. "And they've brought them all with them."

I cut mini-slices for the kids, but they were too done in, even for goat cheese, so Rivera set the milk jug aside and ate it herself, in jaw-clenched bites. The calm she showed the children barely masked her private outrage.

"Okay, sweeties," she crooned. "Let's get some sleep till your daddy's back, okay?"

I was offering Jake the leftovers when Spunk sloped up beside him. "There you are!"

Jake snatched the plate away just as Spunk grabbed for it. "Where you been?"

"Heard a ruckus on da way home las' night, went ta see. Two Empiahs gettin' sacked by a buncha Macys. Gimme soma dat!"

I mopped up soft cheese crumbs with a crust of bread and handed it over. "What's with the Macys? Three of them tried to rip me off before the storm. Real young 'uns. Couldn't run worth shit."

Spunk's laugh was hollow. "Deese was big kids, but all dey had was numbas an' knives. One a da scouts heard da noise. He chimed in an' we sent 'em packin' quick enuff. But he tole 'bout Ladysmit's, so we all went round ta help." He gazed at me hopefully. "Got any moah? I ain't eaten in . . ."

"Here." Jake passed him the plate. "And then . . . ?"

"Well, da Tommys was already on it an' by da time I got dere, da Adders was long gone an' da den too hot ta go neah. We bin boatin' out da survivahs an' searchin' for moah."

Rivera unfolded a second blanket to lay over the Smith kids, then sat smoothing their hair. I had little interest in children. Hard enough taking care of myself. But Rivera really wanted to be a mom. She reminded me of the old church paintings in Rubio's art books. "What if they come here?" Her voice was low but steely. "They will, you know."

"We've got every pair of sharp eyes out on the perimeter right now," soothed Jake. "Even some of the Smiths volunteered. Those who could still walk."

"So we'll know when Adders are coming with their power boats and their guns and their flamethrowers. Then what'll we do?"

"Dey're vicious but dey're lazy. Dey'll sit tight till dey run outa food agin." Spunk swallowed a hunk of cheese and reached for the milk jug. "We got time."

"Why can't Adders grow their own food?" I asked. "Everyone else does."

"Mos' ev'ryone. Addahs nevah got it goin'. Lotta dem start out as rad preppahs. Got a big stash put away but tired of runnin' on dere own. An' when dey join, dey gotta give ovah all dere stuff. Dat's da deal."

Jake nodded. "And that keeps the den going for a while until the next evil moron signs on. They trade a little at the Souk, but half the stalls close shop when Adders show up. They're takers, not makers."

"Plenty guns at da Souk, but ain't nevah seen flame t'rowers." Spunk glanced over at Jake. "Wheah da hell did dey get dose babies?"

"A lucky salvage? Hardly matters. Could've done as much with a bunch of dry matches." Jake saw my look. "Well, maybe not. Least, not so fast."

"Be good ta know da source," noted Spunk.

"Someone'll know. Rousseau's calling for another den caucus."

"More talk, talk, talk," muttered Rivera.

"Okay, sure, we're sitting ducks. All the dens are. But talk is the start of action, right?"

One of the kids was snuffling again, and Rivera drew the child gently onto her lap. "Damn well better be."

Back in my bunk again, I lay awake wondering what had brought Aitch and her lens to the Ladysmith's raid. That had to be what the Wizzers and I had seen in the video. She went where trouble was and recorded it. But why? And for who?

TWENTY

L ike Spunk predicted, the Adders did not show right up on our walkway, and the sense of doom and crisis eased off a bit. We got the Smiths settled in over the next day or so, filling empty bunks, adding seats to the Mess, giving up feed storage space on Five to new sleeping quarters. The swap shelves emptied as clothing, bedding, and basic supplies were passed out among the newcomers.

At first, everyone wanted a Smith or two at their table, for a show of sympathy and to hear the war stories, how the raid went down. But with our number swelled by a quarter, the same Joes who'd moved heaven and earth to make room for the refugees started asking among themselves when all these strangers we hadn't chosen to live with were going to leave. With the blood and soot washed off and the wounds stitched up, those pitiable victims became forty-seven more bodies eating down our provisions and taking up our personal space.

"Why'd they have to come here?" I heard muttered in the Mess. "The Tommys were closer."

"Is this the new normal, then? Why's he letting her do this to us?"

"Are they even looking for a new den?"

Longer lines at the meal stations, smaller portions, shorter beer rations. Crammed-up sleep tiers. Not everyone who'd willingly switched bunks to allow a Smith family to hang together was happy with their new assignment. They missed their old tier-mates. But the Smiths had a lot more family units than we did, and you couldn't just split them up. Plus, kids are noisy and active, and don't always get the idea of bedtime or sharing, so it took way longer to claim a free shower spigot or computer in the media loft.

I wasn't friendly with all my denmates, but at least their faces were familiar. It could freak me out to round a corner and smack into some guy with a full beard, or to see some stranger cleaning a weapon at breakfast.

The Smiths were not ungrateful, and they did their best. But they were in a bad way. Every one of them had lost family, friends, lovers, and their grief and anger couldn't just be set aside. A week of rain, and we were stuck inside with each other. Tempers frayed. Some dumb lad thinking it helpful to ask, "But why didn't you just . . ." might end up in a scuffle.

And then there were the funerals, so many of them, with quick-built rafts struggling to burn in the rain, often for dead whose remains were never identified or even found. Ashes to ashes. Too wet for dust. The weather stayed grim, and so did our mood.

But it could've been worse. Easy to point out that Tall Tommy was the nearest den, but only by city blocks. Each den had its own style, what Rubio called its 'culture,' partly due to the flavor of its leadership and its founding cadre, but also to how communities tend to encourage the values and behavior they agree on. That is, if they want to stay together.

Jake always said Tall Tommy was run like a military fashion show, and Empire State like a bank. Us Joes might complain about Rousseau's rules, but compared to many dens, we were pretty loose, and so was Ladysmith's. I couldn't see some of Ladysmith's portly family men and women hanging at ease with one of Tommy's over-decorated bodybuilders. Maxine, faced with a desperate choice of where to direct her retreat, showed a good instinct for which den would be most compatible with her own. Still recovering from her injuries, she fell in step with Rousseau's leadership. The two of them went about together, snuffing arguments and handing out patience lectures.

It was Rousseau's idea to start mixing up the work parties: one Smith for every Joe, so we'd get to know each other. Of course, this meant one *armed* Smith. And that's how I teamed up with Breakers and Poppy.

First morning I was cleared for the streets, I was up before the wake-up. Climbing down to wake Rubio, I found his bunk empty. A rumpled mess, so I knew he'd been in it, but unlike him to be up so early. First thought was he'd taken sick. I scrammed downstairs, and there he was in the hall, a breakfast wrap in one hand, a mug in the other. He waved the half-eaten sandwich at two lads dragging over a heavy table.

"Over there, along the wall. No, couple feet farther. Better pull it out some."

"Can we get on with this? I got a long day ahead of me." Jake hovered nearby with an armload of paper and plastic. "And keep it out of the travel lanes, will ya?"

"Back that way a foot, then." Rubio gestured the table closer to the wall, then set down his mug, smoothing the tabletop. "And we'll need some chairs."

The lads stretched their backs, making much of how hard they'd been working.

"Don't push your luck," muttered one.

Jake sighed. "Just find the man a chair, will ya?"

"What's all this?" I asked.

"Ta-ta!" Rubio's grin mixed irony and guilty delight with a mouthful of egg and tortilla. "Den Search Central! All I need is a sign!"

"Yeah. Now the guy's legit, you can't even speak to him." Jake spread his armload across the table. Water-stained street maps, torn bus and subway charts, old real-estate brochures, magazines, even a few yellowed floor plans of buildings. From where? Some private architectural library Rubio had stashed in his bunk? Amazing, the crap that survived, when the stuff you really needed was nowhere to be found.

Finally, one rickety folding chair arrived from the Mess.

"Fine for now." Rubio lowered himself into it and started sorting big piles into smaller piles. The lads slouched off, aggrieved that their habitual target had taken on a project they couldn't rag him about.

"We need to bring the Smiths in on this," Jake said.

"You don't trust me to do it?"

"Sure I do, but they need a new den, too. Let's share the effort."

"Can we spare another chair?"

"In a hurry to see them go, Jake?" I teased. "Thought you'd like having a bunch of new women around."

"I like them fine, but things are getting tight. As it is, Rousseau's sending me to the Souk with a boat and two crew, to talk people into selling more than they're usually willing and haul back as much as we can carry." Jake swept new-washed hair back from his forehead. "You want me to talk to Max about who should work with you?"

I swished my hips. "Oh, Max, is it? No longer Maxine?"

"Hey." The great ladies' man looked flustered, which made me grin. Now I'd be watching how he was with the Ladysmith's boss, who he'd had so little good to say about before.

"Way ahead of ya." Rubio was smug. "Been talking to this guy Irv. He got a little scorched in the raid, but he'll be joining me soon."

Jake didn't mind being bested for a just cause. "Get on it, then."

Great to see Rube so eager and engaged. I cuffed his shoulder and left him to it.

After breakfast, I was hanging over the walkway rail, waiting to meet my new picking partner and meanwhile reckoning the sea-level rise since Joseph. I worried about heading out into a city where one den burned another to the waterline. The rain had finally left off. It was a bright day, despite the cloud. I felt Gracie's shadow cross my back before she leaned over beside me.

"Gonna be tricky getting the canoes in under the window arches now."

I nodded. "Our new den needs a real boathouse. Rube says Empire has one."

"New den," Grace scoffed, adjusting her street cap. Her thick braid was wound tight at the back of her neck and her T-shirt tucked in smooth. She looked battle-ready. "You think Rousseau's serious about that?"

"He is now. Has to be."

"We'll see . . ."

As we stood there, the sun nosed out from behind the cloud cover, sculpting the cornices and steep pediments of Unca Joe with crisp light and shadow. The Lagoon was a still, bright mirror. Looking down, I could see myself gazing back at us.

"Smells so different after a big rain. Almost fresh."

Grace sucked her teeth. "Wouldn't go that far."

We watched some of our guys head out, with their newly assigned Ladysmith buddies. Not a picker in two dens staying home this morning, with fair weather and Rousseau on a mission to rebuild our supplies. Spunk had finally been convinced against solos, so we were all in groups, for safety's sake, with an armed Smith escort.

"Guys with guys, gals with gals?" Gracie noted. "What's with that?"

I shrugged. "Rousseau. Fewer distractions on the streets."

Gracie guffawed. "As if! These Smith guys got hair everywhere. I like 'em smooooth!" Then she slid a step closer, squinting into the glare off the water. "So, listen. What would you say to a really big score? Since it's just us girls?"

I laughed.

"Seriously."

"Now what is it?" Grace was a great one for wild schemes and riskier plans.

"Can't see if you're not there . . ."

Rivera came down along the rail, chatting with a frizz-haired Smith chick in a yellow tee.

Grace murmured, "That's Poppy. Me and Di are sharing her."

"What's her story?"

"Still finding out."

Poppy was freckly-tawny, maybe mid-twenties, and a match for Grace in stature. She looked fresh and strong rather than tough, but carried a lethal-looking machete. Despite some scabbed-over burns and a bandaged knee, there was bounce in her step and she smiled like all was well with the world. I gave her points for that, given what she'd just been through. Later, I'd realize she was mostly glad to have survived.

"I got one to myself," I said. "Waiting for her to show."

"Good. We'll need the help."

"What about our assigned draws? You know the boss when we go off on our own . . ."

"Trust me. With what we'll bring back, no one will give a fuck where we went."

While intros were traded and Poppy and I took each other's measure, I saw Jenn come out of the den with a slight, fierce-looking Asian woman in tow.

"Hey, Glim. This is Breakers. She's with us."

"Us?" I saw Jenn was carrying a wide-brimmed hat. She was always careful about keeping the sun off her skin. "You're picking again?"

"Rousseau said all hands on deck . . ." She gave a mock salute. "So here I am."

"Sorry. I mean, you must . . ."

"Just for a while, he said." She shrugged. "It'll do me good to get out in the air. 'Least I don't have to do it alone now."

But her anxious gaze raked the gaping windows and overhanging roofs, then the bare drowned branch tops at the end of the Lagoon. She'd stay home if she could.

Breakers had a smooth brown face with an old gaze that didn't mind its manners. I put her near forty. Loops of dark hair spiked out from under her den cap. She wore a loose black tee and a rifle slung over one narrow shoulder. Not a big one—she seemed comfy with it. More than I'd have been, but things were so in flux around Unca Joe, it was hard to tell what change was making me nervous the most.

I eased closer to Jenn. "Seems Gracie has an idea."

"How to steer clear of BlackAdder?"

"No worry. Those creeps sleep all day," Breakers said. Her grin was crooked, and died quick, like a light going out.

"We're all together?" Jenn asked. "Is it a party?"

"Might be," Grace laughed. "When we get back."

We refreshed intros all around, just to make sure. No good yelling at someone to duck if you couldn't come up with their name. Then Gracie made sure we all topped off our water bottles and stowed a snack. "Like to be a long day."

Breakers eyed her denmate's sun-colored shirt. "Sure you should wear that?"

Poppy smiled. "In daylight, I'll be less visible than you."

"I've always wanted to wear yellow," Jenn put in. "So where're we headed?"

Gracie raised a brow, gave us a follow-me grin, and soon we six were trouping off on her solemn promise that we wouldn't be sorry. Weird enough picking in daylight, never mind in a group. So noisy and slow, awkward with strangers, but Rousseau and Maxine figured it gave us the best fighting chance.

Gracie in the lead, we went uptown along what Hurricane Joe had left of the Second Ave walkway. The rare sun and clear sky got us giddy, even a little high. Where the planks had washed away or the supports been torn from the buildings, we swung from window ledge to cornice to balcony railing, laughing and hooting like monkeys. Grace and Poppy were both strong and steady climbers, but Rivera was most agile, flowing from perch to perch like an alley cat. Made me feel clumsy, but it was inspiring to watch.

"Best not to stick too close together," Poppy spoke up, like a shadow had crossed her path. With the sun at her back, her springy hair made a fiery halo around her head. Her tone was casual, but we all glanced around. Easy target.

Grace didn't get huffy like with most unasked-for advice. "Right. Let's string out a bit."

Sobered, we spaced for safety, like mountaineers without a rope. The city glowed around us. When you work at night, you forget the mad games the sun plays with all that glass, cracked and shattered like most of it was. And the shimmering water, always in motion with the tide. Shards of light like a shower of sparks. Reflections of reflections of reflections, dazzling our eyes. All that, plus the slow, steady press of the heat, and we were soon glare-blind and glistening with sweat.

Ahead of me, Poppy hitched her blade to her belt to free up her hands. Her cheerful shirt and the light glinting off that big slice of steel might have lent me confidence but for the soft running grumble from Breakers, bringing up the rear.

"Sure, that'll help," she muttered, rifle like a brace across her straight back. "Give 'em time to reload between shots."

I made like I hadn't heard her. Not sure I was meant to.

Next, a grouch about weapons handling. "Lucky she hasn't cut her leg off. She's got a good sheath for that blade. Why not use it?"

I slowed to negotiate a broken-edged gap in the walkway, and Breakers caught up.

"Ain't hard to be both ready and right, y'know." Talking to me direct, she showed me how smoothly she could move her rifle from stowed and safe to set to fire.

"Awesome." Odd to bitch over a denmate so publicly. Where was her solidarity?

Close up, the gun was a handsome thing, well-crafted and gleaming darkly in the sun like a rare antique. But if she'd offered it to hold, I'd have shied away. Like a dog with a snake, as Rubio said when something creeped him out but he couldn't tell why.

"How long you been with Ladysmith's?" Maybe get her talking about herself for a change.

"Only since Abel." She motioned me forward. We could talk and walk at the same time.

"I'd have thought longer."

She gave that lopsided grin. "Why? 'Cause I'm so old?"

"You're not . . ."

"Twice you, I'm guessing." She laughed, like she enjoyed catching you off guard. "Lady's only been going five, six years itself. I stayed solo long as I could. Had this fab studio over on West 88th, but got priced out after

Hasan, when that got to be high ground. Found a squat I could work in on West 53rd. Then one of those upstart militias decided they didn't approve of me and wrecked my equipment. So then I . . ."

"Your equipment?"

"I'm a video artist. Was. I did okay, but how many superstorms can you pick up after? Without my stuff and the internet gone so patchy . . ." She shrugged, palms spread.

Poppy leaned back to give me a hand over a wider-than-usual tear in the walkway. "You'll get the story day by day if you listen long enough. Minute by minute, maybe."

Fine by me. I loved stories. "A militia rousted you? Thought they stayed uptown."

Breakers' grin turned predatory. "I'd catch them at their worst and post it online."

Like Aitch. Maybe Breakers could tell me about her.

"By then, the global art market had tanked anyhow, and I'm not into starving."

"You never tried to leave?"

"Those last posts got my transit documents canceled. Not much left but to join up, and Ladysmith's had room."

We paused for breath on the far side of the gap.

"Break time." Gracie ducked into the shade of a caved-in window wall, wiping her face on her arm.

Jenn zoned in on Breakers. "I did graphics. Web and virtuals. I'd just started, in that hiatus between Hasan and Felix, when there seemed a chance of getting back to normal."

"Whatever that is," Breakers replied.

Once we moved on, Jenn slipped in behind me, and she and Breakers dropped into dueling chitchat. No squawk from me. Denfolk love sharing their stories, but if you don't remember yours, it's hard to join in.

We met no one along the way. A few boats slid by along the avenue, their selfies stuttering across the crazed-mirror grids of the high-rises like an arty video. Each time, we dropped below the railings and watched them out of sight, just in case. But except for one blue-vest racing past us to deliver her message, we had the walkway to ourselves.

"Why's it so empty?" Gracie swiped a damp wrist across her brow. "You'd think everyone would be out on a day like this."

"Must be the other dens went to ground after the raid and stayed there," Jenn said, like she wished we had, too.

"Or they're not as hungry as we are," Rivera said.

"At least the weather's too good for Stormies," I added.

"Except for all those neat piles of driftwood and burnable debris up on the terraces." Grace pointed overhead. "See that? Just waiting for the next bonfire."

I palmed salt sweat from my eyes, but my little hairs rose in a chill anyhow.

Where the walkway ended at 27th, the old high-water mark, there were still long, flooded blocks between us and dry land. Gracie had it all figured out. Up a fire escape, in a busted window, across a burned-out third floor, up and across a low-rise rooftop to a fourth-floor plank bridge over the cross street, that sort of thing. A winding path, but it got us dry at Third and 32nd, between two flat-faced tower blocks.

Jenn gazed at the old Chrysler Building, just breaking the skyline. "Wonder who's living there now?"

"No one," said Poppy. "It's locked up tight. Take a bomb to get yourself in there."

Jenn looked wistful. "You see? Someone plans on coming back someday."

"You wanting that for our new den?" I asked. "No way! Think of all the stairs."

Taking in the spire's pointy, crescent-studded glint, I stored away another major requirement for a good den home: lots of flat rooftop or terraces for livestock and garden space. Rubio'd better be keeping that in mind.

Clouds were scudding in as we hoofed it street-wise to 45th. By then, we were all glad for a dip in the heat. Up ahead, Gracie signaled a right turn.

Rivera slowed till I caught up. "She takes us east, we'll run into water again."

But a block before we did, Gracie halted. Standing chest puffed out, hands on hips like she'd won the den lottery, she faced an empty lot. A wall of glass and metal on the west, brick on north and east, open to the street for a good fifty meters. A big collapse, long before Abel, so a magnet for rubbish and cast-offs, collecting any and all that floated by since.

We pulled up beside Grace's proud grin.

"Damn." For a small woman, Breakers' voice was low, almost like a man's, and she spoke as if every word mattered. "That's a score, all right."

First positive thing I'd heard her say. And with good reason.

Boats. We were looking at boats. A lot of them. Marooned on the heaps of ancient junk and flood debris that filled in between the buildings and spilled out onto the sidewalk. Boats tilted this way and that, balanced, not buried and no tidal muck—recent arrivals on Joseph's surge. Small boats, mostly, canoes and dinghies, a few party boats, their pontoons crushed, a scattering of kayaks. But high on a mound toward the back, like a kid's toy tossed in a corner, perched a long, slim sailboat, its keel and partly snapped-off mast tracing a perfect diamond shape with the two ends of its once-white hull.

I stared at it, struggling with a rush of feeling I couldn't put a name to.

Shining like a promise in the almost-sun, and so beautiful. Made you lean toward it, want to bask against its sleek, bright curve. Wait. Keel? Hull? Mast? Words I didn't expect to know were just there, waiting on the tip of my tongue. Except I was too stunned to talk.

"Someone's whole marina," breathed Rivera.

"Amazing they're still here," Jenn said. "Like, no one else has found them yet."

"Why I was so eager!" Grace was beaming.

"Musta washed up in Joseph," Poppy said. "Look how clean they are."

"How we gonna get 'em back?" asked Breakers. No question of if we should try.

Grace pumped both fists. "We're gonna ride 'em, of course!"

"Really?" Jenn's voice was shivery. "Are you sure it's safe? I don't know how to row."

"Me neither. But with a haul like this, I can learn. We all can. You really want to go running back to the guys for help?"

"No way!" I blurted. The river's edge was a short half-block east. "We can do this."

At Unca Joe, women didn't spend much time on the water, only slogging through it on foot. Jenn might scare at the idea, but I couldn't wait.

Rivera studied the giant boat tumble. "If any of them still hold water."

"Let's find out," Gracie said. "You Smiths stay here, keep an eye out. Just in case."

Don't you just love being boss, I thought. But Poppy swung her machete in an arc over her head and did a little stomp-dance. "That's what we're along for."

Breakers turned away. "Silly twat."

Jenn and I traded looks. Being denmates didn't mean they had to be buddies.

The Smiths took up separate watch points at street level, where they could scan the crosstown approaches as well as the decrepit four-story brownstones across the way. The rest of us clambered up over the junk piles to the nearest small boat, a dented aluminum rowboat, a dinghy really, with a serious bash along one side and no oars.

I hefted it. No visible holes. "I'll get this one. Look for stuff to paddle with."

Rivera dragged on the bow of a scarred fiberglass canoe. She was stronger than she looked. "This one seems okay. We'll need rope, too."

"Next you'll be asking for a trailer with wheels."

"In this heap, we might find one."

A lot of the boats weren't so okay: crushed, stove in, or torn apart. But at the end of an hour, working up some serious sweat and soil, we had five possibles hauled out onto the open pavement: my dinghy, two canoes, a kayak, and a big inflatable raft that by some miracle had ridden the surge more or less intact. No motor, of course, but three paddles were lashed to its tubular sides, one longer than the others.

We looked them over as proud as if we'd made them ourselves.

"Rousseau will love the Zodiac," I said.

"The what?" asked Gracie.

I pointed at the inflatable. "Zodiac. That's what it's called."

"How do you know?"

"Just came back to me. It happens like that."

"Yeah? So, what's that called?" She sent a longing glance at the white sailboat.

"I'd call it a sloop."

She drew the word out slowly, like an incantation, then sighed. "Guess we'll send the guys back for that one."

I didn't point out how we could've brought a whole crew to begin with. Hard not to prefer her idea of 'us girls.'

"Might be good stuff inside," Jenn noted.

"It has an inside?" Poppy asked.

"Sure. See the little windows?"

"Ports," I said.

"Whatever."

Breakers was studying a fire escape across the street. "Make it quick, yeah?"

Grace held back. "What's up?"

"Nothing. Just thought I saw . . ."

"Let's go, Joes," said Grace.

We scurried back onto the junk piles. The big boat wanted to shift on its wobbly perch, so Grace and Jenn, carrying the most weight, steadied it while Rivera and I climbed aboard. As I slid over the stern, I automatically checked the name painted on the . . . what? . . . the transom. She was the *Venezia,* out of Menemsha, MA, wherever that was. A boat called Venice. Wouldn't Rubio love that?

More words spilled from my brain as I balanced on the uncertain deck: Brightwork. Tiller. Cockpit. Sheets. Lanyards. Boom.

Rivera eyed me. "You okay?"

"Bit of a dizzy spell, is all."

"Stay put, then. I'll check the . . . um . . ."

"Cabin."

"Yeah." She faced the hatch with a frown.

I eased her aside, unlatched it, slid it open a crack. Stiff but workable. "Someone's been taking care of this girl."

"Probably just washed up from the Stuy Marina. Half the boats there are gone." Rivera watched as I stowed the hatch cover in its slot. "You know your way around a boat."

"Yeah. But don't ask me how. It's like . . . I look at something, and the name just comes to me. And I know how it works."

"Awesome."

"Awesome weird." I sniffed the air rising from the open hatch. "Salt, mold, heat. Nothing worse."

"Going in, then." Rivera backed down the companionway, her gaze reaching over her shoulder into the shadows below. "Okay so far."

Good she was so willing. I didn't want to go into that cramped, damp, streamlined space I could so easily picture, without knowing why. I cased the cockpit while she was down. Inboard motor, so there might still be an engine belowdecks, good for parts if it couldn't be convinced to work or run on biodiesel. Best find was a solid pair of full-tilt oars clamped to the cockpit's sides. Those would go home with the rowboat.

"Don't take all day," Gracie urged, playing ballast on the bow.

Rivera poked her head up through the hatch. "Looks like someone was living down here. All sorts of stuff, neat and tied down."

"Living now, or before the storm?"

She scrunched her mouth in speculation. "Well, there's no food, but there are some empty freeze-dry packs."

I readied my grab bag. "Send up what we should take now."

"Not a bad place to live," Jenn mused from the stern. "On a boat. Riding the flood."

I almost said, I know a guy who . . . but I'd have to admit how I'd snuck off to the Souk. "I heard Riverhome used to do that, den up on a barge. But they kept getting washed away."

"Chatting or picking, you guys?" Gracie rocked impatiently against the foredeck, her eyes raking the cliffs of glass and brick walling in the open lot. The boat shuddered.

"Hold still!" I complained. "She's not that stable."

"Here you go," called Rivera.

Through the hatch came the stuff pickers always snatch first: flashlights, lanterns, batteries, chargers, med bottles and packs, tarps, extra coils of rope. I filled my grab bag, then passed the rest along to Jenn. The rope was a good find. We wouldn't have to strip the boom sheets and halyards to make tow lines for our homebound fleet.

"What about these?" She handed up a stack of laminated printout. "Looks like maps."

"Coastline, probably. Channel charts. Out of date now." Then I remembered Den Search Central. Any info might help. I found room in my bulging bag.

Rivera came up the ladder with her own, full to bursting. We held the bags side by side, and laughed.

"Plenty credits here!" she crowed.

I hefted mine and groaned. "Good thing we don't have to lug these home on foot!"

"We're fat cats now," said Gracie.

Jenn was giddy. "We'll all get new outfits! I insist!"

"DOWN! Everyone! DOWN!"

The shout rang from down on the street, one of the Smiths, followed by a loud crack. And another. We dropped like stones. Jenn and Gracie took cover behind the hull. Rivera ducked into the hatch. I curled against the side of the cockpit. Water smelling of salt and old diesel sloshed beneath the duckboard. I made myself small. Might be the last sound I ever heard.

"Where?" Gracie yelled.

"Roof! South side!"

I switched sides, nearly braining myself on the boom. Just in time, as a shot whined past my ear and buried itself in the starboard seat. I hauled the boom over as cover for a glance at the street. Poppy, a flash of yellow, had flattened herself behind the belly of the dinghy we'd left upside-down on the pavement. Breakers was sighting over the hull, taking her time.

CRACK!

A fourth shot pinged against the brick wall to their right. The next shattered glass.

"What's she waiting for?" Grace rasped from behind the hull.

Then Breakers fired, one shot. Across the street, a dark shape plummeted off the top of a brownstone. It hit the wet pavement with a sad, soft thud.

"*Madre de Dios!*" Rivera hissed.

"Good one!" Gracie whooped. "Is that it?"

"Think so," Breakers called. "But stick tight. Everyone okay?"

We did a quick roll call, then waited, for a while and longer, mostly for our hearts to slow down. The Smiths stayed down in cover. Nothing moved but the hot breeze rattling the *Venezia*'s rigging.

Uneasy with sitting still, Grace poked her head up to yell down to the street. "Are we clear?"

"Still checking . . ."

"Our fault for hanging out so long," mourned Rivera from inside the hatch.

"We get all this stuff home," I said, "it'll be worth it." But it was mostly bravado, to cover my shock. Our chatty little Smith had just shot someone. Right in front of us.

Finally, Poppy rose from behind the dinghy, slow at first, ready to duck. Then, as Breakers covered her, she sprinted across the street. She wasn't all that fast and a bright target, so I gave her more points for nerve. She came back with another rifle, pocketing its ammo.

"Gone," she called out.

Us Joes eased out around the sailboat, scanning rooftops and window holes that had looked so innocent a moment ago.

"Okay. Abandon ship," said Gracie.

Dragging the heavy oars and our clutch of spoils, we scrambled down to join the Smiths by the salvaged boats, trying not to look entirely freaked.

"Looks like a solo," Poppy said, her voice flat. Sweat beaded on her afro curls.

"Hell of a shot!" Gracie clapped Breakers on the shoulder. Breakers gave a dismissive jut of her chin and moved off to reload her rifle.

"What was he?" asked Rivera.

"She." Poppy was casing out the recovered rifle. "Young. No den sign. Rogue, or squatter maybe."

"Girls are going rogue now?" I asked.

"If they're hungry enough."

"Shit," said Rivera. "We'd have fed her."

"Right." Jenn's head wagged sadly. "But how'd she have known that?"

"She was protecting her home." Rivera hefted her stuffed pack with a moan of regret.

Poppy nodded, her mouth tight.

Then we all had to go over and stare down at the dead girl. She was just brown skin and bones under her camo tee and ripped sweats, hair so dull you couldn't tell its real color from the dark blood pooling behind her wrong-angled neck. If the shot hadn't finished her, the fall sure did. My throat caught when Breakers reached down and gently closed her eyes.

"Jeez. Really young," said Jenn.

The Smiths were coolly matter-of-fact, and considering the horror done to their den a few days back, you could see why. One dead squatter was child's play by comparison, and after all, she had fired first. But I couldn't take it so easy. A knot of outrage swelled up in my chest. I hated that we'd been forced to do this terrible thing. But who could I yell at? Where could I lay the blame?

"Still a child." Rivera wiped away tears. "I wish . . . we could've . . ."

Grace nudged her. "We couldn't. C'mon. There's work to do."

Jenn had gone silent, her arms wrapped tight around her chest.

"There's getting home to do," I said.

We dragged the boats to the river's edge and stood considering the wade ahead to water deep enough to float them. The river was smooth and dark despite the day, as if it sucked down every ray of brightness that came its way.

Jenn stared at the water. "We're really going in?"

"Got to," I said. "Didn't tox me too bad getting caught in the surge."

She nodded dubiously. But the water looked surprisingly clean, storm-fresh, and the tide was heading out. If we were going to get our feet wet, now was the time for it.

"We'll go down Second, stick close to the buildings." Grace was business brisk, testing her leadership skills. "Who's handled a boat before?"

Poppy and Breakers raised their hands. At Ladysmith's, I saw, women got to *do* things.

"No, I need you two to ride shotgun. That means hands free."

Rivera said, "Kayak. When I was a kid."

Breakers smirked. "Aren't you still?"

I'd already gone to work on the dinghy, my fingers knowing how to swivel the salt-crusted oar locks into place, how to set the oars and lay the long ends back on the center seat. Better to get on with it than mope about, feeling sorry for a stranger who tried to kill me. "I can row."

Gracie's brow arched. "Since when?"

"Don't know that, but I do know how."

Rivera pointed at my neatly shipped oars. "Best believe her."

Gracie gave me a look like I'd claimed superpowers. "Wonders never cease."

Ended up me and Breakers in the dinghy, Rivera in the kayak making do with one of the short paddles from the raft, Gracie, Jenn, and Poppy in the raft, with the canoes in tow. Not enough paddles to go around.

I was tying the lightest canoe to the dinghy's port stern cleat when Rivera said, "What're we gonna do with . . . her?"

"Who?"

She tilted her head back up the street.

"Oh. Ah . . . yeah, maybe we oughta . . ." I hadn't a clue what we oughta.

"We oughta just leave her," Gracie said.

Rivera's mouth thinned.

I had zero urge to go back and deal with a bloody corpse, but I got Rivera's point. "We could set her afloat. Den burial."

Rivera nodded. "It's the least we can do."

"Forget it!" Grace snapped.

"Float her on what?" Jenn asked.

"On nothing!" Grace planted hands on hips.

"No, she's right," said Breakers. "My shot. I'll find something."

"It's my find. My call."

"And how good would you have done, carrying all this back by your lonesome?"

"Did y'all forget she tried to kill us?"

"Have some respect, Grace," Rivera murmured. "It won't take long."

"You finish up." Breakers thrust her rifle at me and sprinted back up the block. Rivera hesitated, then raced after.

Gracie watched them go, jumpy now and irritated. She wanted out of there. "Softies. We're a bunch of friggin' softies."

"Long as we can be." Jenn reached to relieve me of the gun. "Hold it like this, kiddo. It's not going to bite you."

"This one's lighter." Poppy offered me the dead girl's weapon.

"No, thanks." I was grateful to be alive and all. But I wanted nothing to do with that dark-smelling piece of steel.

Breakers and Rivera were back by the time we'd packed everything into the raft and dinghy. They'd found a wooden pallet, half-crushed but good enough to hold the small body. They'd even wrapped her in a scrap of tarp.

"That will be so much better," said Jenn. We ran to help drag it to the water. It eased in like it was meant for the task, but then just sat there refusing the tide, as if waiting on us.

"We should tow her out farther." I had the rope ready in hand.

"We should get the fuck going," growled Gracie.

Poppy pointed east between the buildings. "We'll lose light if we don't hurry."

"So we'll hurry." Breakers sounded like gravel in the pull of a wave. "Don't want her washing right back to shore, do we?"

And that settled it.

I was glad for the tow weight on the dinghy's other stern cleat. Balanced the load, and maybe, a little of my guilt. We'd give the girl's sad death some dignity, at least.

We walked the boats to knee-high water and clambered aboard with varying degrees of ease. Rivera was drenched by the time she got the kayak steady and her paddle balanced across the gunwales. But soon she sprouted a relieved look of recognition, like when you meet an old friend. From there, it went along. She took the lead.

The inflatable was sturdy and stable, easy to get into. Poppy knew the basics of using the tall paddle as a rudder. Jenn and Gracie would switch off between the remaining paddle and the dead girl's rifle. Once they were afloat, Jenn brought their tow canoe alongside to clear the stern wash for steering. Despite her earlier shakes, she was settling right in. I had a feeling the dead girl's gun might be going home with her. How could Rousseau object now, with Smith weapons all over the den? Of all of us, Gracie looked the least comfortable out on the open water, even with buildings rising tall on all sides. Well, Rubio'd never said if the Amazons were sailors.

I swiveled my butt over the dinghy's transom and stepped to the center seat. Breakers waited till I'd set the oars, then shoved us off and hopped in, neatly wrangling the two tow lines as I dipped my oars and made my first pull.

Again, my muscles knew what to do. It was strength I'd be lacking for the long run, so I was glad to feel the boat catch in the current and make its own way downtown.

"Tide's strong today." Rattled nerves made me talkative.

Breakers nodded. "Less work for you." Hunched in the stern, rifle balanced on thin knees, she watched me steer with little twists of the oar blades. The faint sun made a dusky curtain of the hair escaping her den cap, faded black like the rest of her clothing. No wonder she got on Poppy for wearing bright yellow. But the Smiths didn't seem to care about blending into the mud-washed colors of the city, like us Joes were taught. Was it 'cause they carried weapons?

"You grew up on boats?" Breakers watched the rooftops while she talked.

"Don't know. Can't remember."

"Can't remember what?"

"Anything, before Abel."

"Ah. One of those."

"I know most words and things, but the events are all gone. And my place in them."

"Weird."

I laughed. "That's one way to look at it."

People usually got all sad and sympathetic about my memory loss. Breakers' response was, like, shit happens. Kind of a relief. Maybe it was time to see my predicament in a different way. Especially if entire vocabularies were going to flood my brain like today, given the right trigger.

"How's Rivera doing?" Facing sternward, I couldn't see.

"Kayak?"

"Right."

"Getting the hang of it." She swept off her den cap to let a surprise fall of black hair fan out around her shoulders, turning her face to the breeze to dry the sweat.

"Heard you have a lot of boats at Ladysmith's."

"Did. Lucky for us, they didn't burn 'em all."

"Every one of them will help. We've just three war canoes and one small motor. Unca Joe's low on transport."

"You're a picker, right? You come across many boats free for the taking?"

"Um . . . no. And not because I ain't looking."

"Because storm after storm, there're less of them, and no new ones being added. Your Grace is gonna be a hero."

I rowed for a bit, thinking about boats, how many shapes and sizes they came in, how they made travel faster and easier in our watery world. "I got a buddy says we should remake Manhattan like Venice, where everybody gets around by gondola."

Breakers snorted. "Make that past tense. Venice is under water. Long abandoned."

"Oh." Did Rubio ever mention that part? "But we do need more boats. We should be building them."

"With what materials? You know anyone still handles fiberglass?"

I shrugged, not even sure what that was.

"The only boat I want to build is the one that'll take me out of here."

"To the Mainland?"

"Sure. Who'd want to stick around if they didn't have to? I heard the Canada Rockies aren't too overcrowded."

I laughed. "You're not getting there by boat."

"Could if I had a good river map. The Great Lakes are a big inland sea now."

Such idle chat was welcome. Almost let me forget the sad load we were towing. We floated along for a while, making good time on the tide. Up ahead, Rivera started singing as she paddled, until Poppy shushed her with a warning that others might be listening. Breakers stretched out her legs and leaned back on the transom, darkly graceful, one hand resting on her rifle.

"So. Glim, is it? You're cute. Got a girlfriend?"

"Me? No."

Again, the lopsided smile. "I'd take you in. Keep you safe." She patted the rifle's stock.

Was she joking? "That how it works at Ladysmith's?"

"Sometimes."

I was sort of flattered. "Thanks, but . . . y'know . . . not my line?"

"Sure about that?"

I had doubts about many things, but that was not one of them. "I'm sure."

She shrugged. "No problem."

And I could tell it wouldn't be. "That mean you're solo?"

"Umm. Lost mine in the firefight."

My arms jerked in sympathy, breaking my rowing rhythm. "What? You mean . . . ?"

She nodded. "Got up to raise the alarm. Sniper took her out. One of the first to go."

"Breakers, I am so, so sorry."

"Yeah." Another nod, slower. "Me, too."

I looked away, let out a long breath. This woman was either stone cold or a total stoic. Or so bruised, she was numb. I wondered if Ladysmith's had counselors. Maybe ours could help. "Guess that's why you stood firm to do right by . . ."

"Would've anyway." Breakers gave that same chin jut she'd used to shut down Gracie. "How far you reckon till deep water?"

Weren't we there already? Only not the kind she meant?

I'd said enough. "East of Gramercy there's a low point."

"Sounds good."

We fell into silence. Peaceful, like we both agreed to back off getting too personal and just let the tide carry us down the long-deserted blocks of pale brick and shattered glass. The late light bleached the details from the east side of the street and dropped the west into deep, corrugated shadow. Plenty threat could be lurking there, but this sure beat walking. Or chatting with a minefield that still needed time and space to mourn.

Gave me a chance to consider: was that the story of my memory? Not lost, just too beat up to function? Like a limb gone numb, but at some point waking up—again, those triggers—with each remembered bit another brain cell stirring, firing at random until it recalled what its particular job was. Sometimes it was images. Today it was vocabulary. A full meal, a feast of boat words. And they kept coming.

Halyard, gunwale, companionway, spinnaker, jib . . . a litany of awakening. I treasured every rescued syllable.

Ears aimed sternward, I heard the sound before Breakers. "Motor behind."

She turned, listened. "Yep. Fast one. West a block, but heading down." She cupped her hands around her mouth. "Pop! Take the next turn east! Look for cover."

Ahead a half-block, Poppy waved assent. Good to see they could work together when necessary. Gracie bent to her paddling while Jenn passed the order forward to Rivera, who made a neat dogleg left into 24th Street. I pulled hard as I had strength for.

He must have seen our wakes or something, ripples along the brick in an otherwise total calm, and got curious. By the time I swerved the dinghy onto 24th, the motorboat had made the cross from Third to Second, running up our tail. Rivera and the Zodiac had ducked into an opening between two yellow-brick low-rises, but as I made the turn, our tow canoe tangled with a light pole poking up through the water. Breakers was still tugging to free it when the motorboat cut its engines and pulled up in mid-channel, watching us.

Then it turned and grumbled our way.

A small blue speedster, needle-nosed, its open cockpit set well back. More deck than seating. Racing stripes. Two people inside, windblown, a shock of dark hair over mirror shades, a frizzle of red beside. Exactly as I remembered him, sleek and beautiful. The redhead was already complaining.

"I can't fucking believe it," I murmured.

He brought his boat to idle about twenty feet off our starboard, grinning like a shark. "Hello there, den rat."

I hoped he'd have forgotten me. "Hey, Dark Boy."

"What's that?"

"Never mind."

"Friend of yours?" growled Breakers, ready to defend me but suspicious that I might know anyone so obviously un-den as these two.

"Not exactly."

Dark Boy aimed his sculpted chin at Breakers' weapon, then caught the second glint of metal down the block. "See you got some rat teeth since last we met."

Given the company I was keeping, I wasn't scared. But his slickness, his lizard ease got me both riled and anxious, stirring up dust in part of my brain that had nothing to do with rational. "Kinda off your turf, aren't ya? Taking me up on my invite?"

"Nah." He brushed glossy hair back and adjusted his mirrored glasses. "Just slumming, y'know? See if there's anything left downtown after the last big blow."

I wished I could see his eyes. "Least you're sober this time."

"Yeah." He cackled, like he relished the memory of being vile and half-crocked.

"The light," Breakers said. "We should be moving along."

"Us, too," echoed the redhead. She'd slunk down in her leatherette bucket seat as far as she could without lying flat. "Ju-li-an, can we just . . . ?"

"When I'm done visiting." He leaned back, one arm draped languidly over the wheel like he was planning to stay a while. "So, what you got on the raft? You poaching some other den's livestock?"

I looked. Blood had seeped through the tarp onto the pallet slats. "It's . . . a friend. We're taking her home."

"Yeah?" He took a longer look, losing some of his ease. "Bummer. What happened?"

"None of your biz, but . . . sniper's bullet."

"Whose?"

"What do you care?"

"Good to know where to watch out for it. Like, bam!" He revved his big engine, but stayed in idle. "That'd really suck. Hear there's a den war brewing."

Breakers tuned in again. "Where'd you hear that?"

Dark Boy studied her, but only briefly. "Around."

"Up or down?"

"Guess I don't remember." He wriggled his shoulders, not quite a shrug, then turned his mirror lenses back to me. "Well, it's been real, den rat."

No way he was going to leap out of his posh boat and come after me, so maybe I could risk a question or two, like who was the blond inside the launch that night? I'd make it sound casual. But would he tell me?

"If you're headed downtown," I said instead, "steer clear of the China-town high-rises. There's a bad bunch in there."

"Ooo-ooh, BlackAdder!" He hooted, but something changed behind those lenses. Couldn't read it, could only sense a difference: a hint of bit-terness? A twinge of fear? "You think I don't know about them?"

"I'm only saying . . ."

"Nothing I can't deal with."

"You'd be surprised."

"No, I don't think so." His shades reflected double portraits of my face, all bright with false bravado. Below them, his mouth had tightened. He shoved the joystick forward and sped off east, slamming the redhead against her padded backrest. We heard her screeching at him till they rounded the next corner. Why was she with him, when he treated her like so much river trash? Was Dark Boy better than no boy at all? I had to wonder.

"What the hell was that?" Breakers demanded.

"Rich kid I ran into on a pick. He decided not to rape me."

Only part of that made sense to her. "So you warn him about BlackAdder?"

"Like I said, he didn't." I spread my palms. "I don't get it either."

Breakers chuckled. "All kinds of gratitude in this world."

We moved on faster after that. Up front, Rivera was flagging, and I was shaky at my oars, my palms and thumbs already red and tender. At East 19th, we shifted east to where the water was deep and the tide ran strong toward the sea. Gathering the boats, we hauled in the pallet, untied the tow rope, and set the dead girl adrift. The current took her like a friend.

Watching her go, the kayak steadied against our gunwale, Rivera mur-mured, "Why did she fire on us? We weren't any threat."

Breakers said, "We were stealing her stuff."

There it was: we were thieves as well as murderers. So depressing. When we got back, how many of us would want to tell this story the way it really happened?

The sentries were ranging farther out than usual since Ladysmith's disas-ter, so they pegged us by East 16th. A good thing. One of the Zodiac's pon-toons was losing air and the dinghy was taking on water. So was my tow canoe, getting heavier by the stroke. With the sentries to take over surveillance, Breakers could bail. The Zodiac tucked in close to the buildings so that Gracie could pull them along while Jenn paddled and Poppy steered.

Then, of course, the tide crested. We lost our free momentum, and the real work began. My shoulders were screaming, my palms raising huge blisters, but Breakers talked new strength into me and we made it the last hard blocks. As we limped up in front of Unca Joe, most of two dens were ranged along the walkway, cheering and applauding, heads and shoulders dusted by failing light. The Smiths were all making this weird, high whooping sound in the back of their throats. Could have been challenge or welcome, but whatever it was, it bucked us up. We shipped oars and paddles to let ourselves drift while Gracie raised-fisted the gathering, pretending we weren't all gasping for our last breath.

Rivera found a third or fourth wind and did a few speed circles by the entry. The Smiths whooped louder. Then she turned the kayak in under one of the ground floor arches leading to the boat landing, the top of its curve mere inches above her head. The rest of us would have to duck. It was a squeeze sideways for the Zodiac, and as I did figure-eights with my oars to hold the dinghy from crashing into them, I saw a strange boat tied up across the Lagoon.

It was sunk in western shadow, but a torch burned in the bow where a sentry had been posted. Painted along its side in block letters: *The Mid-Manhattan Floating Library.*

Daniel. It had to be.

After a day of terror and wonder, I was too beat for coincidence to stun me again. But really, who else would come up with a wild-eyed idea like that?

TWENTY-ONE

W e had all sorts of eager help docking the boats and making them fast, and more after, as we were hoisted onto the shoulders of our denmates, too tired to protest. Our heavy packs were raised behind us like a raiding party's spoils—which I guess they were. Our very wet feet weren't allowed to touch down until all six of us had been carried up the ladder, through Main into the Mess, buoyed by cheers and chants and that odd whooping sound the Smiths made to celebrate.

We were deposited facing a table packed with den authority—Rousseau, Maxine, Jake, and Spunk, plus a few senior Smiths I didn't know. The throng pulled up behind us expectantly. Left to stand on my own, my legs nearly failed me. Next to me, Jenn swayed and grabbed my shoulder for balance. So shaky, and unsure if we'd be praised or punished.

Rousseau turned in his chair, frowning. We'd disturbed a deep discussion. "There better be a reason . . ."

Harbormaster Tito jostled to the front, unable to smooth the glee from his usually sober face. "You'll want to hear it, boss."

Grace had landed with her arms aloft in victory vees. She didn't miss a beat. Her braid loosed and flying, she launched into a vivid blow by blow of our trek, especially her part in it. Fine by me. I'd just seen who was sitting next to Jake, resting back in his chair so his face was blocked till he leaned forward to listen. I'd guessed right. It was his boat.

Daniel caught my eye so briefly, I thought I'd imagined it. The corners of his mouth lifted just as briefly. Somehow, he got that we weren't supposed to know each other. I ducked my head to hide a give-away grin, taken aback by how glad I was to see him.

Around the main table, the lads were falling over themselves to repeat Gracie's story, only louder, filling in details of each boat and the treasures in our packs, like they'd wrangled them in themselves.

With Grace grabbing center stage, I aimed to slip past the big table and join the food line, until Rubio latched onto me.

"What kept you so late?"

"I was with Grace. Was everyone worried about us?"

"Doubt they even noticed, but I was."

I eased out of his grasp. With so many Smiths to feed, the kitchen had been running out of food before the end of the meal period. "I'm starved. Got to eat."

"Get it and come listen in." He jerked a thumb at Daniel. "There's real news!"

By the time my plate was filled, Jenn and Breakers had joined Rubio at a table near the bosses. I'd look unhinged slinking off to eat on my own. Besides, my blisters were weeping into my fists and Jenn had raided the emergency first-aid kit to clean and wrap our battered hands. Breakers, who hadn't touched a paddle, played scrub nurse, way more gently than expected. Rivera had vanished, probably gone upstairs to collapse. I cradled my food and dragged a stool up next to Rubio.

"So what's the big news?"

Rubio dropped to a murmur, like sharing state secrets. "Jake brought in this guy he knows from the Souk."

Okay, it wasn't me he'd come to see. What was I thinking?

"That's his big boat out there. He's sharing a report from a black-marketer he deals with about the Mainland getting seriously ripped up by Hurricane Joe."

"So?" I was only half-listening, focused on my food. "Can't be worse than us."

"But it was! He says Joe was huge, in terms of area, and it barreled onshore without losing strength after landfall like storms usually do." Rubio tensed forward. He relished bad news—it confirmed his dark view of the world. But this had rattled him more than usual. "When you came in, he was telling us about all these *camps* over there."

"Camps?"

"For the surge refugees. Set up along the coast because . . . get this: no one's allowed inland anymore."

"No one? Not even with papers?" Storm damage was old news. But more doors closing? Suddenly my food didn't taste so good. "Since when?"

He flopped back. He'd played his trump card. "Didn't know or didn't say."

"All right, then!" Rousseau's voice crested at the next table. Like flowers to the sun, we all tuned in. "Let's go see these wondrous boats."

Grace stood arms slack, spent but triumphant. Rousseau rose, suppressing a groan. I guessed he'd been too busy or too worried since Ladysmith's burning to get much sleep. But he found new strength and turned his big presence on Daniel. "Delegates from some of the dens are gathering here tomorrow. A strategy session, given what's gone down lately."

Daniel nodded, like he wasn't sure why he was being told. "Good idea."

"You seem to have a more current grasp of the big picture than most, friend. I'd see it as a favor if you hang around to share your views and information with the group."

I noticed Daniel sat up straighter when talking to Rousseau. Maybe we all did.

"I'd consider it an honor."

"Till tomorrow, then." Rousseau waved Grace and Tito ahead of him, then followed. The lads milled in his wake. Maxine struggled in her chair, and Poppy ran to help her up. The human tide bustled and receded, leaving us in a big empty room echoing with the last footsteps, and Jenn and Breakers raking over some guy they'd both known in the downtown art scene and agreed was a dick and a tightwad.

"He'd take art for rent and stash it in a bank," Breakers said. "But he never moved it uptown and Misha's surge flooded the vaults. Last I heard, he was still squatting upstairs, waiting for the water to go down."

Spunk turned back by the doors. "Y'all comin'?"

Daniel pointed a fork at his untouched plate. "Food first, if you don't mind."

"Da leas' we kin do, bro."

Jake hadn't moved. "I hate boats."

"You won't hate mine." Daniel worked on a mouthful. "It's full of books."

"I hate all boats. They never sit still."

Spunk looked to me.

"Seen 'em already," I said.

"Das ri', ain't it!" Spunk shot me his raw grin and pranced a bit, his injured arm flapping in its sling. "Later!"

Jake watched the doors swing closed. "'Uneasy lies the head that wears the crown.' Hard news, but he had to hear it. They all did. The boss needs a rest he ain't gonna get."

Daniel nodded thoughtfully. "A bit more than he signed on for, you think?"

Jake pushed back his chair, now there was room enough. "Well, he was always about preserving community. And living, as best as we could, a moral and responsible life. Suddenly it's about armed defense? Just not his skill set. Or mine, for that matter."

They looked so companionable, their dark heads bent in talk: smiling, easygoing Daniel and earnest Jake, the sharp planes of his handsome face creased with doubt. It came to me that they were really friends. Made me feel like a kid eavesdropping on the adults, but I wouldn't have left for a handful of credits.

Daniel said, "I hear he was a good man with his fists."

I expected a quick denial. Instead, Jake nodded ruefully. "In the alleys, in the bars, breaking up fights. Finding the quiet drunks a cot for the night."

"You?"

"Way too often. What else was there to do but drink, with all the theatres closing, not even anything to go see? Why even bother to get up in the morning?"

Daniel's gaze wandered off into the mess hall's shadowed corners. "That's the thing, isn't it—finding a new reason when your old one is gone."

"Yep. Took a while, but Rousseau talked me dry. So I guess I made him my reason, him and the den."

"Good choice."

Jake laughed. "My liver thanks him every day."

The chat across the table had turned intimate. I looked to see if Breakers was putting the moves on Jenn now, but no, they'd found another friend in common, lost in Misha, and were mourning her demise. Surprising this sort of thing didn't turn up more often. Or maybe it did, but people got too tired of revisiting the names of the dead. Had to wonder: if I met someone I'd known before, would I even recognize them?

Rubio gathered up his dish and mug. "C'mon. I got questions for this dude."

Hated to interrupt Jake's trip down Memory Lane, all interesting news, but Rubio was on a mission. He slid up beside Daniel like they'd been buddies for life.

Jake made the introductions. Daniel nodded politely and tucked into his meal. His bright, rose-colored T-shirt was freshly hand-stenciled. It said: The Book Dude.

"So, these refugee camps? You got any details?"

Daniel looked to Jake, who nodded. "He'll find out soon enough. Every-one will."

A light went on in my brain about what else Jake did at the Souk besides trading for food and supplies. Rousseau's eyes and ears. His spy. Who didn't always share what he learned with the rest of us.

Daniel swallowed a forkful of tofu and rice. "Okay, yeah . . . it's deten-tion, really. Remember all the hype about processing centers, supposed to funnel the refugees off to where there were still jobs and housing, into com-munities that would accept them? Well, forget it. They've stopped process-ing anyone."

Jake settled back, looking depressed. He'd heard it already.

Rubio took it in slowly. "And that would be because . . . ?"

"Officially? They're overwhelmed. Can't catch up with the paperwork."

"Fuck the paperwork!"

"Euphemism."

"For . . . ?"

"Locking the gates."

"To the camps?"

"To the country."

Rubio stared at him. "Wait. No. The whole country? Is that legal?"

Daniel's shoulders slid up and down in opposite directions. "Who's to say these days?"

"But where are people supposed to go, if they get flooded out or . . . ?"

"They're not," Jake put in. "You heard it here. Mainland's pulling up the ladder."

Rubio shook his head, like he might hear different afterward. "What, it's not enough they already control the flow since Hasan and the quarantines—checkpoints, documents, bridge closings? Why make it harder now?"

"Bigger storms, more refugees, pressing further inland," Jake said. "The usual."

"Ten years since Hasan." Daniel wasn't smiling now. "There's less inland to share. With everyone running for the hills, the reasonable people aren't in charge anymore. My source didn't want to go into it."

"He could at least say who's running things!"

"Depends on where you are—local control winning out over national. Governors, even mayors, declaring sovereignty." Daniel set down his fork, eased his plate away. "Besides, my guy lives there. Under pressures we can only guess at, the situation changing daily. He needs to . . . get along. I don't push him, in case he clams up on me."

I dearly hoped Jenn was in deep enough with Breakers not to hear any of this.

Head in hands, Rubio was practically vibrating. "How could we not have known . . . ?"

"Too busy surviving," said Jake. "Our heads in the sand."

Daniel nodded. "It snuck up on us—quiet hirings and firings, resignations, assassinations, executive orders. Machinations under the surface while the big news has been floods, storms, crop failures—the stuff you can see and are affected by directly."

"We got way too reliant on the internet being always up and running," Rubio added.

I was still processing the idea of camps. "Risky housing refugees along the coast . . ."

Their silence told me I was one big step behind.

"Exactly the point," Rubio said finally.

"But . . ." Once the token dropped, I fell mute before visions of Hurricane Joe scouring the crowded coastline. Joe's Wave, they'd be calling it, if anyone was left to remember it.

Daniel saw it, too. "Locked in, no escape, the so-called shelters too flimsy to protect them! No attempts to rescue, even warn them." His fists worked, open and closed. "Too many mouths to feed? If the pandemics aren't doing enough, let the weather take over your population control."

"Maybe being isolated down here has its advantages," murmured Jake.

Daniel shook his head. "Don't get feeling too safe. Now there're guys going around selling 'security' to the Souk vendors."

"Is that a bad idea?"

"Read the small print. Next time, it won't be voluntary."

"Protection rackets!" Rubio was grimly delighted. "A fine old New York tradition."

"You going to pay?" Jake asked.

"Not a chance." Daniel showed his teeth, a sudden morphing from easygoing to hard as nails. I sat back a bit. "Where would it end? The Merchants' Association, once your basic coffee klatch, is busy writing bylaws and vendors' contracts. Talking about charging rent."

"They don't own the park."

"But who's there to stop them?"

Jake sighed. "The end of the Souk as we know it."

"And there's talk of going on a total cash economy."

"Wait . . . you mean, no barter?" Jake was finally roused. "That'll cut ninety percent of their trade! Who can come up with hard currency on a regular basis?"

"How can *denfolk* come up with it," corrected Rubio. "They're looking to change their buyer base."

Jake said, "It would mean starvation for anyone not producing their own food."

"Of course. But the Association is all puffed up, going on about 'running this place like a business!' For whose benefit? The old survivors' camaraderie is out the window."

Rubio asked, "And so, the boat?"

"Thought I'd give it a try, before they raid my shed in the name of security." Daniel dug a scrap of fabric from his jeans to wipe his face and hands. "They don't own the waterways."

"Not yet." Jake sat back, drumming fingers against his knees. "Not allowed off the Island but can't go anywhere else. Squeezed from both sides. What's the point?"

"Starve us out," said Rubio. "It's a grab for diminishing resources. Same as the Mainland. With more people crammed into a smaller landmass, it's inevitable."

"Thanks for the long view." Jake heaved himself out of his chair with a heavy hand on Daniel's shoulder. "Enough. Get some sleep, dude. I'll pass it all on to Rousseau."

"There's a solution. We just have to find it." This declaration restored Daniel's cheer. He pounded a soft dance rhythm on the table and smiled around. "Which reminds me . . . after dinner's the perfect time to settle down with a good book! I was heading over to Riverhome for the night, but I think I'll move the boat to the walkway and open up for business. Want to come browse?"

Jake reminded us how he felt about boats and took himself off to find Rousseau.

I nudged Rubio. "What do you say?"

Rube shook himself out of a dark study. "Got any art books?"

Daniel laughed and scrubbed his palms. "Sure do. Lots left behind after every evac. Too heavy to carry with all that ocean coming at you."

Rubio brightened. "You ever think about museums? Like, being able to go look at a Rembrandt or a Manet, even a Dos Santos, the real thing, whenever you want? I miss that."

"Me, too. But a book's the next best thing."

We scooped up Breakers and Jenn on our way out. They'd moved on to galleries and gallery owners they'd like or hated.

Breakers said she'd look for exhibit catalogues. "Remember those two guys uptown that stayed in business through the evacs selling work about the destruction downtown? Wonder if they're still around."

"Why not?" returned Jenn. "Their clients were mostly rich Mainlanders, who still make their gawking-tourist visits."

"Maybe not much longer," said Rubio.

"Oh, think positive! People will like you better!" Jenn slapped him playfully on the arm. "So what did that cute guy have to say to you all?"

Cute guy? Is that what she saw? I felt a vague stirring of unease.

"You mean the Book Dude?" Rubio squinted after Daniel assessingly. "He was sharing news of the Mainland."

"What news? He has news? What did he say?"

"Rube, don't . . ." I began.

Too late. Jenn was already slipping among the boat admirers backed up in the mudroom, Daniel hard in her sights. I was glad the crowd had thinned by the time we climbed down the ladder to the underbelly. The float wasn't large, planks laid across plastic water barrels, maybe twenty by twenty. Once a vast cavern under here, now Rubio's head near brushed the ceiling when the float rocked on a swell. The three war canoes, ganged in parallel along one side to save dock space, were being readied for the nightly patrol. Rousseau stood by with Tito, discussing moorings and repairs for the new arrivals.

Daniel hollered that the Floating Library would be opening. Several people charged up the ladder to be first in line. He grinned after them, then hopped into his own dinghy, a tidy little wood shell fitted with a small solar outboard. The storage batteries took up most of the cargo space. "One passenger for the Book Boat. Any takers?"

Rubio raised a hand, but Jenn beat him to it. "Me!"

She was an old hand at boats now, also at putting her own needs first.

Daniel saw an eager, pretty woman and helped her in. I watched them motor off, confused by wanting it to be me in that boat instead of Jenn.

Rubio leaned in like he'd read my thoughts. "You gonna show me your big score?"

"Right." I pointed out the Zodiac, the battered canoes, Rivera's kayak, and finally, my shabby rowboat. "Not much, but it got me home."

"Got us both home." Breakers nosed in beside us. "Needs bailing already. I'll go find something."

Rube studied the shipped oars and the slosh of dirty water in the bottom. "Gracie said you got right in and started to row like you were born to it. That true?"

"I guess."

"And you could name every obscure part of a sailboat."

"Don't know about obscure . . ."

"It's a big clue, you know."

"But it doesn't lead me anywhere."

"Well, it does." Rubio gazed out through the arches as Daniel moored his dinghy to the big boat across the Lagoon. "It closes off some possibilities. Like, only folks with some means know their way around a sailboat."

"Means. You mean, money?"

He nodded. "Usually. So you weren't living on the streets. But I knew folks who lived on their boats. Their only home. Tied up at a marina, or later, just anywhere sort of safe. More and more of them, as the waters rose."

"I could've read about boats in a book."

"You don't learn to row from a book."

Breakers dropped down the ladder with a plastic bowl from the Mess. She knelt by the rowboat to scoop out water.

I laughed. "It'll take all night with that."

"All the kitchen'd give me, stingy bastards! But if I don't, she'll swamp by morning."

The low rumble of the Book Boat's engine rolled across the open water as Daniel eased it into the current and back toward Unca Joe. It was low to the water and chunky, with a long, raised cabin taking up most of the hull. He brought it alongside the window arches, tied up, and tossed a rope ladder up to the walkway where the line was forming. Jenn clung to the forward rail, looking helpless. I thought, who is she kidding? I saw her paddling that Zodiac like a pro. Oh well. Why was I letting it bother me, anyway?

Rousseau finished with Tito and came over to congratulate me personally.

"She's the one who saved our lives." I nodded toward Breakers, still bailing. She stood to take his offered hand.

"The sharpshooter," he noted gravely.

Breakers' chin lifted. "Maybe not your idea of the right solution, Joe boss."

"Call me Rousseau. Please. And perhaps it was the only solution, at the time."

"I thought so."

He sighed, began a reply, reconsidered it. "Well, you have our thanks."

I'd never seen Rousseau at a loss for words, or even holding back the ones he'd rather say. But Breakers was a Smith and, as he saw it, not his to manage.

"No need to bail," he added. "The boat crew will haul out the leaky ones for repair before we lose them."

Breakers flicked a little salute but knelt again to bail anyway. "Just in case."

Rousseau shrugged, but I could see he approved.

Rube and I followed him back up the ladder like a line of ducks. Jake was loitering at the top, determined to lure Rousseau toward a power nap, if not a full night's sleep. Breakers had said she'd be turning in when the bailing was done, so it was Rubio and me as the line thinned at the walkway rail, waiting while old Ellie Mae struggled down the ladder to the big boat's rear cockpit, near glowing with anticipation.

"Books!" she breathed up at me, as I leaned over the side to be sure she made it.

Rubio's gaze measured the boat's length and breadth. "Clumsy-looking thing."

"Oh, come on!" But I had to admit it: Daniel's boat was built for calm water and slow travel. The cabin walls were slanted and studded with rectangular windows, like a house with skylights. The roof rose in a shallow peak, paved with solar panels. There was just enough deck along the sides to give access from the stubby bow to the broad, open stern. Badly needed a coat of paint.

"A river barge. Or a canal boat." I prodded his ribs. "You should like that."

"Not my type of canal boat."

"You want all boats to look like a gondola."

He sniffed and elbowed me forward as the ladder cleared. He set a worried eye on the knotted rope and wood slats. "After you."

"Just like climbing the tiers," I called from halfway down. Easy, even with my hands done up in gauze. I dropped into the stern and held the base of the ladder taut for him. Another thing I knew to do without thinking. His grip on the side ropes was white-knuckled, but his tight face suggested pain and weakness more than fear. I caught his elbow as he found the last rung and felt him sway and shudder. Illness was sapping his strength.

The stern pit was wide and deep, so the doorway into the lighted cabin was tall enough for even Rubio's comfort. The woody interior was fitted with two long rows of tables with raised rims to keep the books from sliding off. Strings of LEDs swagged cheerfully among the rafters. Right off, I saw why Jenn had pushed herself into the dinghy so eagerly. It wasn't to flirt with Daniel. It was to pick his brain about the Mainland. Should've guessed.

Maybe a dozen other denfolk jostled up and down the center aisle, picking up a book, setting it back down, squeezing past each other in the tight space. Stocky Ellie Mae leaned up on tiptoes to riffle through a stack of thin pamphlets shoved way to the back. Daniel eased through the crowd, offering help and suggestions. Jenn shadowed him, dropping a question into every gap in his sales pitch.

"But there's a thousand miles of coastline," she pressed him, as Rubio and I came up. "If the military is fracturing like you say, there's no way they could monitor all of it!"

"True." Daniel leaned past her to return a book to its proper stack. "In a small boat at night, you could probably slip ashore somewhere. But then what? You'd need someone to pick you up, or who's willing to take you in once you get there."

Jenn chewed her lip. As far as she knew, her relatives were far off in the Midwest.

"It's not just about avoiding what's left of the police or the Navy," Daniel said patiently. "They're mostly gate-keeping along the coasts. The danger inland is civilian patrols protecting their turf. Outsiders and refugees are not at all welcome. Say you do locate your cousins. How will you get to them?"

"The usual way, I guess. Trains? A bus? I could hitch a ride."

"No, no, you don't want to do that!" Daniel's look seemed to ask what century she was living in. "Even if a ride did come along, it'd likely be your last. As for trains and buses, maybe you'd get lucky, but you'll need the right tickets and transit permits, and even then, I'm told they're running far and few between, the schedule shared only with insiders."

"Wait, wait!" Jenn flattened her palms at her temples. "I know it's bad along the coast, but it has to be better someplace!"

"Why?" Rubio muttered. "No one's doing anything to make it better . . ."

I saw Jenn headed for a meltdown and kicked his shin.

He coughed lightly into his fist. "Listen, Dan, about those art books?"

"Over this way."

"Wait . . ." Jenn made to follow.

I linked an arm with her elbow. "Give the guy some space. He's trying to do business."

"But you hear what he's saying?" She gazed after Daniel like her exit tix were hidden in his pocket. "I can't . . . I won't believe . . ."

I couldn't blame her. Hard to be told it was bad everywhere, hard to let go of the hope for an escape hatch. Hadn't quite absorbed it myself. "Hey, he's just saying what he's heard, not what he knows for sure. Could all change tomorrow. You'll find those cousins, and they'll figure how to get you there. The search'll go better once the internet's up to speed again."

"If it ever is!" She flicked away frustrated tears and threw a last look at Daniel's receding back. "Where does he get his info?"

"All sorts pass through the Souk." Not my place to mention Daniel's source.

The close crowd was getting to me, so I elbow-walked Jenn back to the stern, offering whatever silly encouragement I could invent. She'd miss it if I didn't. When she'd retreated up the ladder, I settled on a storage seat for a breather. The night was unusually dry, and very dark. No moonglow spreading behind the overcast. The dance of the cabin lights across the water was broken by colliding ripples from the war canoes now silently patrolling the Lagoon and the gentle rocking of the Book Boat as people moved around inside.

I flexed my bandaged hands. The blisters were shrinking, cooling off from the medics' herbal salve. A long, hard day on the water hadn't totally wrecked me, and there I was again, feeling most at home on the back of a boat. Rubio had it right. There was a connection here, if only I could follow it out.

Daniel came out of the cabin with an older Smith I hadn't met yet, a pudgy dark-skinned guy cradling a stack of water-stained paperbacks.

He patted the top cover. "I saved one of hers from Abel, but it burned with the den."

"Might be more in storage," Daniel said. "I'll take a look."

"Thanks! I'll bring these back in good shape." The Smith turned back from the ladder. "In fact, if there's any way I could buy them . . ."

"Currency, chits, or barter." Daniel offered his most winning smile. "I'm open to anything that buys my next meal."

The Smith beamed, suddenly boyish. "I'll come up with something."

"Meanwhile, enjoy them for free, um . . . ?"

"Irv." The Smith juggled books and stuck out an eager hand.

Daniel shook it. "Later, then, Irv."

"So glad you came!"

Rubio's new friend, I realized, who'd be joining Den Search Central. Geeky, but seemed nice enough. I watched him labor his armload up the ladder, all too aware of Daniel looking me over like he hadn't seen me just moments ago.

"So. There you are. Home in one piece the other night?"

I struggled to sound offhand. "More or less. But getting back was pretty hairy."

"Did you have to swim?"

"Worse. Halfway down the pass-thrus, I nearly got napped by Storm Worshippers and thrown onto their bonfire."

Daniel snorted. "I'm guessing they had other ideas in mind."

I felt heat in my cheeks and was glad the spill from the cabin lights was dim. But a wild thought grabbed at me. "Don't suppose you're a whiz with a bow and arrow?"

"A what?"

"You know . . ." I mimed shooting, but Daniel looked mystified. Of course. Couldn't have been him. "Never mind. As my buddy Rubio says, all in a day's work."

He sat on the bench opposite, still scrutinizing me. "You cut your hair."

"Umm." My hands went to it before I could stop them. Good thing I'd let Jenn do that trim. "Easier when it's short."

Daniel brushed his own close crop. "Absolutely. So, say. You like my floating library?"

"Amazing! You threw all this together since Joseph?"

"No way. This is my picking barge. I live on it, when I'm away from my squat. I low-throttle around the flood zones, tie up at a likely windowsill and see what's inside. No one coming back for their books anytime soon."

"Our tellers think books are something to light fires with."

"So do squatters and rogues, for the most part. Sometimes I'll get into a beautiful, dry room lined with bookshelves, and all there'll be left is a pile of ashes in the middle of the floor. Maybe a readable spine or two, so the loss cuts even deeper."

"Boats are the best way to get at stuff." I recalled the den girl shouldering a kayak outside St. Pat's. "But as long as a picker's got two feet, she's expected to use 'em, least till there're more boats to go around. Where'd you get this one?"

Daniel stretched his legs out, taking in the quiet of the night and the patrolling canoes. "That's a long story."

"I got time."

The arched brow and smirk hinted at secrets. "Maybe when I know you better."

"What, like, you stole it?"

"Hey, no. But it *is* a long story. Like with your old book." He looked relaxed, but his eyes swept the surrounding building tops, the dark yawn of windows, on a regular circuit.

"Then how about this source of yours? Are you sure he's saying true?"

"Just full of questions. And I figured you a hard woman to get a word out of."

"My friend was pretty upset, and I'm not big on guessing games." I wriggled my shoes, still damp from the day's row. "I'd never say anything that'd put your guy in danger."

"Promise?"

I set my lips tight. "Now you're making fun . . ."

"Not at all. Swear on the old book? Like I did, remember?"

Silly as it felt, my hand went to my gut wallet. "I . . . um . . . okay, sure. I swear."

"Good." He slid around the stern bench to settle in beside me. "It's a two-source relay. I have a friend with a working landline, who has a contact with same on the Mainland."

Huh. "What's a landline?"

Daniel chuckled. "Forgot who I was talking to. It's a phone tied to a physical cable. Runs under the river. Not many left, and even fewer work-ing, but my friend . . . well, he lives in a bygone era. Never believed in cell phones, and turns out, he was right. Managed to turn up some working numbers over there."

Sounded like magic. But I had to wonder how sensitive this information really was if he'd told me so easily. Unless he wanted it out there for some reason, and thought me a likely leaker, despite my promise. Didn't much like how that felt.

"So I check in with him now and then. Lately, even he can't believe what he's hearing. He's concerned for the folks he's in touch with."

"Where are they?"

"He doesn't say. What I don't know, I can't tell." He turned away to smile at the denfolk milling about inside the cabin, discussing possible pur-chases or stalled with an open book in hand, reading intently. "Look at that. That's why I do what I do."

"Are you changing the subject?"

"What? No, not really. Not much more I can tell you. Why does it matter?"

"Like I said. Wondering how true it all is."

"I don't think he's lying to me."

"It kind of cuts off a lot of possibilities. But you don't seem too worried about it."

"I don't?" It was like his mind went blank for a moment. Then he said, "I am. Of course I am! But jeez, it's too nice a night to be talking grim, whatever the news. Speaking of which, congrats on the boat find."

Definitely changing the subject. "I guess."

"What? There's a downside?"

"A squatter girl had to die for it."

"Ah." He turned to look at me. "Better her than you. Or one of your denmates."

"That's what everyone says. But that's just letting it go by."

"Accepting a necessity isn't the same as letting it go by. Didn't that Grace say you gave her a proper funeral?"

"You think that's enough?"

"It shows regret and respect. The best that can be expected, given the circumstance."

I shrugged. Something itched between my shoulders. My overactive conscience? I tried to mirror the water's dark calm, reflecting only what I wanted him to see.

"Hey." Daniel reached across to touch my bandaged hand with one finger.

It was kindly meant, but I jerked away. "She was so young."

"So are you."

"I'm not a baby! I see where the world is going."

His voice hardened. "I meant, now you have your life ahead of you, instead of losing it to a sniper's bullet."

His sternness stung like a rebuke. I preferred the smiling, madcap Daniel to this old scold. But something distant in his eyes backed me off a full-tilt pout. "Rousseau calls me resistant."

"It's good to hold tight to your values. So few do."

"But sometimes it's just plain dumb, right?" I eased away from him on the seat. I needed to keep him at arm's length.

"I didn't mean . . ." He rubbed his brow fitfully. "Okay, redirect. How's the reading?"

But he did, didn't he? "Reading? Storms and death raids and the breakdown of order on the Mainland, and all you can talk about is reading?" I zipped open my gut wallet, yanked out the old book in its linen wrapping, and thrust it at him. "Here. You keep it."

"What?" He drew back like I'd offered hot coals.

"I don't want it anymore."

"Why not?" His stricken look said I'd thrown him off balance at last. "Aren't we going to try reading it together?" He unwrapped the book, letting the linen lie soft in his hand, then opened it and held it out to me.

"It's too dark out here."

"We can go inside."

"I don't want . . ."

"Glimmer, what on earth is the . . . ?"

"Outstanding!" Rubio burst through the open door as if spat out by the crowd, waving a large black rectangle. "I can't believe you have a copy of this!"

"Really?" Daniel glided back to the stern bench, looking both troubled and relieved. "What is it?"

"*Lost New York!*" Rube fanned it open to show black and white photos of old buildings. "It's a rare collector's item, did you know? Even before the superstorms!" He dropped beside me and plunked the big book in my lap, flipping pages. "Look! This one, and this one?" It was too dark to see any detail. He must have had them memorized. "Remember I told you about the 1964 World's Fair and the first Madison Square Garden? And Coney Island?" His delight shamed my pout. But who even thought about such ancient history?

Daniel laughed. "I should've sold direct to the dens long ago. Don't get this kind of appreciation uptown."

"What'll it cost me?" Rubio asked.

"What are you offering?"

I knew Rubio was counting up his meager possessions, sure he was falling short.

"What I mean is," Daniel added, "the price is negotiable. And the currency flexible."

Rubio brightened. "Okay . . . need anything done around the boat? Painting? Caulking?"

"Take it with you. I'll be around a few days. We'll work it out later."

Rube held out his hand, then gripped Daniel's with both of his own. "I can't thank you enough, Dan." He snatched the picture book from my lap and nearly scurried up the ladder.

I watched until he gained the top. "Wow. Haven't seen him that charged up in ages."

Daniel eyed me. "It's nice, making people happy."

"Oh, you'll never make Rubio *happy*. Excited, thrilled, but happy's not his thing."

"Looks like he's had a bit of a dust-up, your friend."

I'd stopped noticing Rubio's healing cuts and bruises. His deepening cough was a greater worry. But he'd broken my sullen mood. People had worse problems than me. "Bullies in the den. Didn't like his ideas. Except, since Joseph and all that happened to the Smiths, they're everyone's ideas."

"Lucky for him." He let the quiet linger for a bit. "Are you okay?"

I couldn't look at him. "Sorry. Sometimes I just get . . ."

"I get it. I think." He leaned closer, holding up the old book again. "What do you say?"

Too close. I inched away again. But one problem had just been solved. Rubio had seen Daniel holding the old book, which made it okay for me to have it now, out in the open. No more contraband burdening my gut wallet. I'd just say I'd borrowed it from the Book Dude.

"What?" he asked, as relief spread across my face.

"Nothing." I was tons lighter. And with the book no longer a liability, I wasn't so eager to be rid of it. I scraped at tired eyes with both hands. "I'm . . . could we do this later? It's been . . ."

"A long and trying day." He held out the book, nodded when I took it. I carefully rewound its wrapping and tucked it away. "That's better. Go get some sleep."

"And you'll be here . . . ?"

"Tomorrow. I will."

When I glanced back from the top of the ladder, he was still sitting there, watching me leave.

TWENTY-TWO

Tired as I was, I was restless in my bunk, so settled in a long think.

At first, about Daniel and my increasingly schitzy reaction to him. I'd hoped he'd be a friend, but was that all? And if I wanted more, why did I back away so fast when he seemed to be offering it? Was I reading him wrong? He wasn't suggestive or threatening, like Ace or Dark Boy, but in a way, that was more unnerving, like he was sizing me up, the whole person, and how could I stand up to that? Until I got my past back, if I ever did, I'd always feel incomplete.

This confusion wasn't easily resolved. I got anxious just pondering it, so I moved on to a comment of Jake's that had stuck like a burr in my mind, about how the dens had our heads in the sand.

I'd try this thought cascade out on Rubio next time I saw him, but my brain was already working it overtime. What Jake seemed to be saying was that all our complaints about den life and the endless talk of leaving was so much hot air. Empty talk. A trope we'd got used to, when in fact we—that is, the dens—weren't truly dissatisfied with our situation. As long as things remained fairly stable downtown, we got on with it and didn't care much what went on in the rest of the world. Like, 'survival' was really about maintaining the status quo.

But raiding and burning a den? That was a different story.

Clearly Jake and Daniel had known each other for a while. Daniel had access to the sort of info we claimed to need but couldn't get. So why did Jake wait so long to bring him downtown? And was his news really a surprise? I'd accepted the Mainland as a common goal, but really, it was the younger denfolk who fantasized about escape. Rubio or Jake might talk about changing dens, but never about leaving the Island.

Maybe Rousseau, Maxine, Tall Tommy, and the rest preferred being den leaders, controlling their own bit of turf. If denfolk all took off to the Mainland, where would their power base be? And if society and government really was crashing and burning on the Mainland, best we learn about it now so we'll forget about going there and focus on preserving the den system and everyone's place in it.

Seriously dark and disloyal thinking. It roiled my stomach worse than bad milk in the Mess. Holding back a few items from the tellers paled by comparison. Was I totally off base?

There was an inner room in a high-rise across the Lagoon that the lads had cleared of debris to play a noisy game they called handball. My brain felt like that room right then, my careening, colliding thoughts racketing off the walls in unpredictable directions. As a wet dawn brought me light enough to read, I reached for the old book, hoping it would soothe me toward a few hours of sleep.

Later, if I got up the nerve, I'd confront Daniel directly with some of these questions. If I got up the nerve . . .

March 16th

We today saw a pretty bottle floating close to us and corked tight. We could see that there was a rool of paper in it—the bottle was not a common one but figured & stained very prettily. We did all we could to get it but could not—we could not get out our boat as it was full of Leigh coal and we dare not jump in and swim for fear of sharks. I am very curious about it as it might contain the loss of the steamer Hartford or some other vessel, but we can only speculate upon it. We all feel much anxiety but hope it was only thrown over by someone just to make talk and news for the papers.

When I went down to breakfast, Daniel wasn't there.

Not my business, but still, I was bothered. I shook out my salvaged poncho and climbed up to the walkway to grab a look before I ate. Hard rain chewed the rising water into chop, one of those hot rains we hated, the far side of the Lagoon blurring in the steamy downpour. At the rail, I peered across at a shuttered book boat, returned to its earlier mooring, its boarding ladder rolled and neatly stowed in the stern pit. The dinghy, tied up alongside, was covered with a tarp.

"Trusting sort, ain't he."

"Huh?"

Breakers was folded into the watch shelter, rifle held close to keep it dry. "Leaving it all like that, I mean."

I glanced back at the boat. "Probably just trying to get some sleep."

"Nah. The guy I relieved said he took off." She moved over to make room for me under the canopy.

I stayed where I was. "Took off? When?"

"Middle of the night. Shifted mooring, then somebody showed up in a small, fast motor and whisked him away. Our guy said it sounded like a woman."

"He was sure?"

She shrugged. "It was dark. Looks like the dude's got friends all over town."

She didn't need to add: friends with a fast boat and fuel. *Rich* friends.

"Yeah, well, he would. From the Souk, y'know?" I fiddled with the hood of my poncho. Rain was dripping down my front. "Weird, though, to take off in the middle of the night."

"Depends on where you're going."

"You mean, something . . ." What, wrong? Illegal? Criminal? Meaning-less words in a lawless town. "Against the den? He wouldn't do that!"

"Not what I had in mind."

"Oh." Breaker's ironic grin implied a romantic tryst, but my brain shot off in another direction. "You mean, something happened uptown?"

"Something." She was still smiling.

But having said it aloud, I was sure it was true. Daniel, the bearer of news. From a friend with a landline. Hints about risk. And there was that creepy guy in the raincoat, my first night at the Souk. Someone should go check. But today was the next big caucus. The den would have other priorities.

I pulled my hood tight. "I'm for the Mess. You need anything?"

"Not a thing, thanks for asking. 'Cept maybe a drier job."

"That's what you get for being so good with that gun of yours."

"Rifle."

"Right. Later, then." I shot another look at Daniel's boat, then retreated. In the close heat of the mudroom, I dripped puddles onto the floor and wrestled with anxiety. Why so worried? Daniel could take care of himself. He had his own life. It was, like I said, none of my business.

But I couldn't put it to rest.

I snatched at my poncho to haul it off. My head and hands tangled in its oversized wetness, made me grapple more frantically. When I'd thrown it off and onto a hook, I snarled at it, breathing hard. But I couldn't make it my true frustration. It was just a poncho.

Across the floor of Main, Smiths and Joes clustered over breakfast bowls and mugs, driven from the Mess by the ear-piercing screech and bang of furniture being dragged around as the lads set up for the caucus. Rousseau and Maxine had agreed to open this meeting up to any den member wishing to attend. A big crowd was expected.

Rubio was in his corner, Den Search Central, circling the table and stabbing a bony finger at a big map of the Island spread out on top. His other hand hid his cough rag down by his side, but I didn't miss the faint blood stains, or the fevered light in his eyes. The hall was airless and stank of tension and sweat. Jake stood nearby, stripped to his shorts and an old towel draped around his neck, talking with a pair of Smiths, all three of them holding their chins and nodding like den elders, while Rube did his dance. I noticed a long, heavy knife sheathed at the older Smith's waist. The other seemed unarmed. The map was plastic, water-worn and brittle, parting along its folds. It crackled whenever Rube's stiletto finger made dive-bomb contact.

"Easy, now," Jake complained. "We paid hard coin for that map. Actual cash money."

The map gave me an idea. I needed Rubio's attention, but if I wanted him to go along with my brilliant, spur-of-the-moment plan, I'd better not interrupt.

"So, we know the big museums are locked, boarded, wired, and remote-sensed every which way," Rube was saying. His hair stood up in a thicket, like he'd been yanking on it, and I was pretty sure he'd slept in his clothes. "Even though the collections were shipped to high ground long ago. But a big, solid block like that is what we need."

"As if they're ever going back to those buildings again," grumped one of the Smiths. "They should open them up for public use."

I recognized pudgy Irv who'd been so jazzed about his book find the night before. Intent on the map, he seemed edgier, more purposeful, but still soft-contoured and soft-spoken. The rain drumming way up on the skylight nearly drowned him out.

"The Guggenheim is leaking like a sieve," Jake noted. "Big chunks crumble off with each new blow."

Rubio waved a hand. "Too small. Besides, would you want to live life on a slant?"

"Riverhome's already in the Whitney."

"Too much glass."

"Hurricane-proof, so they say. Now, there's the old Armory on Park, but . . ." Irv glanced at his senior denmate while hovering a palm over the map.

"Third on my list. Is there a problem?" Rubio folded his arms, waiting.

Irv stood back, studied his hands.

The older guy shrugged. "It's share and share alike, I guess. Word is that Storm Worshippers have moved in there."

"No shit?" Jake wiped his brow, then his whole damp chest, with the end of his towel. "You sure?"

"We heard it from Empire."

"Really? I was just over there, and they didn't tell me."

The Smiths looked uncomfortable.

"Okay, okay. You got a different deal with them. No problem." Den politics. Jake let it pass, and primed the pump instead. "But the Stormies have stuck to small groups scattered about town. Irreconcilable differences about dogma and ritual, we always heard. Is that changing?"

The older Smith scratched his peppery beard. "It's about the worst you could imagine. Instead of staying splintered and relatively powerless, the Stormies seem to have found a leader to cluster around."

"C'mon!"

"No, really. Some woman. One of their preachers."

"Since when do they have preachers? They're anarchists. They worship chaos."

"They got 'em now. One, at least. Young, beautiful, charismatic. Or so Empire had it. They've got someone embedded."

Embedded? Empire planned ahead. Again I asked myself how come everyone was better informed than us at Unca Joe?

"It's her mission to unite the factions," Irv explained. "To spread storm worship throughout the Island and beyond. 'A new faith for a new world.'"

Jake groaned. "Just what we need."

"Well, she thinks we do."

One of the lads muscled up to snatch the two chairs drawn up to the map table. Jake waved him off with a quick jerk of his thumb.

Irv gently flattened his palm on the map. "In the Armory, they can build their bonfires on the drill floor without burning the joint down. And they've got room to grow. Empire says there's a couple hundred of 'em there now, maybe more."

Jake asked, "How is this preacher girl planning to spread the faith?"

"As yet unknown."

"Scratch the Armory." Rubio gestured cross-wise. "Moving on . . ."

Since he was between candidates, I tugged on his elbow. "Got a minute?"

"Not really."

"Please?"

With a sigh, he turned aside. "What's up?"

No way he'd give me the time to try out my new theory on him. Best to cut to the chase. "Think you're heading out anytime soon, like, to look at possible den sites?" Up close, his breath sounded wheezy.

"Rather wait for a longer list. So far, we're snagged at zero. Why?"

I fidgeted. How to make this sound reasonable? "The Book Dude's gone, and left his boat behind."

"So?"

"That doesn't seem strange?"

"What are you, his keeper? He's running an errand or something."

"A boat came by and picked him up in the middle of the night. Sentries saw it."

"Okay, a *private* errand."

"But he promised Rousseau he'd stick around for the den caucus."

"So, he'll be back. What's the big deal?"

"Something might've happened."

Rubio scrubbed his cheek. "Like what?"

"Like, at the Souk. Remember what he said about those guys coming around?"

"Look, Glim. He's a grownup. He'll deal with it."

"But what if . . ."

"I'm in the middle of something here. I can't . . ."

"Rube, I want to go up there."

"You do? Why you?"

"Because no one else will right now, with the caucus and all."

"It's pouring out."

"What else is new?"

"So, go."

"Alone?"

"When has that stopped you?" He shrugged. "It's how we work out on the streets, in case you've forgotten."

"It's different now."

"And you're looking to *me* for protection?" He flapped his bony arms. "That's a laugh."

"Rousseau might let you take a boat, y'know, to do research. We'd get there faster."

"I get it. And you don't think I should be here for the den caucus?"

He had a point. "If we left now, maybe we'd be back in time."

"I don't see what's so . . . I mean, jeez, we just met the guy." His chin lifted and his gaze slid away. "Oh, wait. Must be you took a liking to him, huh? That was quick."

Not quite an eye roll, but close.

"He's . . . a friend."

"Well, so am I, but would you go chasing uptown after me in the middle of a monsoon?"

I glared at him. "Who threw themselves into the friggin' hornet's nest out on the walkway to save your butt?"

"Okay, okay. What say we wait to see if he shows up for the caucus? If not, then we'll see about a boat, okay?"

Not okay. But a tantrum was beyond me. I stood hip-slung, pondering my next move.

Rubio turned to drift back to his map, then stopped, listening. "Hear that?"

"No." So like him to end an argument with a distraction.

But I did hear it. Less a sound than a bass vibration, a deep thrumming under the din of rain on the roof and the screechy furniture movers in the Mess.

At the table, Jake said, "What is that?"

As if by magic, the rain drum slackened, leaving behind the heavy throb of an engine. A big one, right outside our door. Around the hall, the scattered groups of breakfasters sat up from their snoozing and chat.

"Some den showing up early for the caucus?" Rubio said into the silence.

"Way too early. Besides, what den has engines that big?" Jake tossed his towel aside and reached for his T-shirt.

Amazing how quickly casual wariness can balloon into full-tilt alarm. Bowls and mugs clattered aside as the room rose to its feet. Rubio scooped up his map, folding it reverently into a portable package.

Then, a rumble of footsteps in the mudroom, and in strode a clutch of the older lads, our enforcers, escorting a smaller posse of unknowns. A guy in a pale gray suit and open-collar black shirt, giving out a big, horsey smile. Hardly a raindrop darkened his shoulders. Behind him, four drenched muscle boys, his own security. One of them was closing up a giant red umbrella. Plenty jostling in the crowd, but so far, our guys were keeping it formal.

Our squad's senior glanced around for the nearest authority, settled on Jake, and nudged the suit toward him. "Wants to see the boss."

"Double inboard," supplied his second. "Burnin' gas."

Jake turned to me. "Go get Rousseau."

"Me?" I wanted to stick around.

Jake's eyes went flat. "I said . . ."

"On my way." Okay, I was the fastest Joe nearby, but I didn't have to like it.

I found Rousseau in his hotbox office, bare-chested and sweating, his chin propped on steepled fingers. The door was open and I didn't take time to knock. He blinked at me, powering back from whatever deep ponder he'd been having.

"Problem?"

"There's this guy just showed up," I panted.

"What guy?"

"A suit. A lot of teeth. Jake says you better come."

He didn't rush. He rarely did. Part of Rousseau's hold was keeping in check all those impulses most others gave into so easily. He took a moment, stood, took another moment, then unhooked his leather vest from the back of his chair. He rolled into it like it was a full suit of body armor. His broad mouth pursed, then relaxed into a grin. "Ready for anything."

Back in the hall, the enforcers had the intruders corralled in open space. Trailing the boss man down the stairs, I saw the crowd had drawn up a perimeter around them, staring and whispering. The suit was trying for small talk with Jake, who was having none of it. The muscle boys stood close and alert. They wore a bright mishmash of color, like they'd looted someone else's hamper. The suit just kept throwing out that smile, like he loved being the center of attention so much that he was deaf to the buzz of suspicion circling him.

Rousseau pulled up several paces inside the circling crowd. A night's sleep later, he looked dark and dangerous, his open vest a challenge to the shorter man's slink uptown tailoring.

The suit knew Rousseau by sight. He stepped forward, thrusting out his hand until he ran into an enforcer arm slapped hard against his chest.

"Let him," Rousseau said.

Jake moved from the table to just behind Rousseau's shoulder. Spunk materialized out of the crowd on his other side. Just in case.

Released, the man lurched forward, grabbing Rousseau's hand before it was offered. "Name's Bright. How are you, sir?" He was so clean-shaven, he was shiny, with neat, colorless hair and all those teeth. An uneasy glance not quite in sync with the smile. "A pleasure to meet a legend in person."

Rousseau extricated his fingers from the man's two-handed grip. "Welcome to Unca Joe, Mr. Bright. What can we do for you?"

"Well, it's an old cliché, sir, but a true one. The real question is, what can I do for you?"

I wondered how anyone could stretch a smile that wide without splitting a lip.

Rousseau cocked his head. "I'm guessing you're going to tell me."

"T'ought dis sort washed out wit' da first big surge," muttered Spunk.

Behind Bright, the least patient of his posse shook off a Joe enforcer's over-eager grip and a tussle ensued. The crowd roused like a pack of hounds until the dude was face-down on the tiles in his own puddle of rainwater, a pair of Joe boots pressed into his back.

"Boys, boys. Mind your manners." Bright's jumpy eyes swung a complicit glance toward Rousseau. "We're all friends here."

Rousseau circled a forefinger, and the boots lifted away.

The downed guy leaped to his feet, glowering and brushing off his rainbow wear like our floor might give him a disease.

"Feckless youth." Bright grinned and slid a palm beneath Rousseau's elbow to walk him away from Jake and Spunk. "I'm here on a matter of business. Shall we talk in your office?"

Rousseau wasn't going anywhere. His still mass swung Bright around and back toward his men like a planet in orbit. "We share our business here at Unca Joe. Speak your piece."

Not exactly true, but it put the man off his stride.

"Excellent. Democracy in action. I'd heard otherwise, but every den has its style."

Jake decided to join in. "What den do you call home, Mr. Wright?"

"Bright. It's Bright. But call me Mike." He pulled out the cleanest

snot-rag I'd ever seen to blot his shiny brow. He refolded it carefully, focus-
ing on it instead of Jake. "No den, actually. I'm independent, in business for
myself. I like to think I serve all the dens. Or hope to."

Spunk leaned in. "Wha' kinda service mi' dat be, nah?"

Bright's tongue flicked across his lips as he debated his target. He chose
to stick with Rousseau. "It's come to our attention that . . ."

"Our?" said Spunk. "Thought ya wuz independent."

"My *associates* and I—other independents—have heard there's been an
uptick of random violence down here among the dens."

Spunk folded his arms. "Who'd ya heah dat from?"

A listening quiet in the hall. Even the rain's roof drum had ceased.

Bright recharged his smile. "Can't say as I recall."

Rousseau returned only mild curiosity. "Presuming this rumor to be
true, Mr. Bright, what's your interest in it?"

"My interest is your interest, Mr. Rousseau, and your den's, seeing as you
might be in need of my services."

"You haven't said what that is yet," Jake noted.

"Your safety, Mr. Reilly. Unca Joe's safety."

Jake frowned at this use of his last name, rarely shared in the den, and
Bright's grin spread. "I'm in the security business. Times are changing. The
city is changing. Not like it was in the latest aftermath, with the survivors
still in shock and the playing field more or less level. For a den such as your
own, with a peaceable reputation and resources to preserve, it makes sense
to job out your protection needs."

Rubio stirred beside me. "Sound familiar . . . ?"

But Daniel had described roughneck thugs. This uptowner was hardly
that.

"For instance, in an earlier day, these fine young men of yours . . ." Bright
gestured broadly behind him without turning. ". . . would be more than ad-
equate to keep a den safe and secure. But today . . ." He gestured again, small
and quick. His four guys freed themselves with sudden, noiseless ease, pulling
compact semi-automatic pistols from . . . wherever. Too fast for me to see,
enough to take my breath away. I snatched at Rubio's arm, thinking to drag
him to cover beneath the table. The foursome dropped into box formation
around Bright, their bland faces slick with rain, weapons leveled at the four
corners of the room. Shrieks from the crowd, people ducking, running. The
Joe enforcers falling back open-mouthed, then regrouping to charge.

"Settle!" Rousseau's short bark froze everyone in place.

Bright nodded from inside his fortified square. "Advanced martial arts training is also among the services we offer. Stand down, boys. Demonstration over."

At a jerk of his chin, the automatics vanished into pockets or boots.

A few people laughed. Others applauded, like they'd recognized a sales pitch all along.

"Neat trick," said Rousseau.

Bright offered a tiny bow. "Thank you."

My jumbled thoughts about the downtown status quo shifted yet again.

"Don't just stand there!" a voice shrieked from above. "Take him!"

A rustle of clicks and snaps, the clang of steel against steel. Suddenly Bright and his posse faced an array of Smith weaponry, poking out of the crowd like fangs. The muscle boys had no chance to pull their fancy handguns.

Maxine stood at the stair hall door, in borrowed overalls, her singed hair bound in a bright green turban. Up on the balcony, Breakers sighted her rifle down Bright's throat.

His smile faltered, then flared. "Madame Maxine! An unexpected pleasure!"

"You blood-sucking sonofabitch! You snake! You insect!" Maxine raged through the crowd as fast as she could manage, bandaged hands flailing, staring at Bright all the way. Jake offered his arm as a path opened, but she shoved past him till she was right up in Bright's face. "You killed my den!"

"I . . . what?"

Rousseau, a dark rock holding down the center of the room, eased toward Maxine, signaling Jake around to her other side. "What are you saying?"

"Don't you give me that innocent face, you slime, you murdering bastard!" Jake's offer of support became a grapple of restraint as Maxine lunged for Bright's face. The room erupted with outraged shouts and the clatter of wood and steel, Smith and Joe alike.

Spunk loosed his knife in its sheath. "Jus' say da word."

Maxine bucked against the prison of Jake's grip. "Do it! Tear out his fucking throat!"

"A slice for each one we lost!" Breakers yelled from above.

"NO!" Rousseau bellowed. "This stops right now!" He turned his back on Bright to lay one hand on Spunk's shoulder and the other on Maxine's. "Not here. Not at Unca Joe."

Bright said nothing. He looked panicky and stunned.

When the room was quiet and it seemed no one was going to die right off, Rousseau faced Maxine. "What is this all about?"

Maxine drew into herself, got some control, then nodded for Jake to let her go. She jabbed a gauze-wrapped finger at Bright. "This trail of slime showed up at my den with the very same offer, not two days before the raid. Some vast price we could never afford. When I declined his services, he said he hoped I wouldn't regret it."

"Now, that's a nasty coincidence," said Jake.

"Raid?" asked Bright. "You can't think I . . ."

"Who wouldn't?" snapped Jake.

"My business is defense, not offense." Bright's boys were muttering among themselves. He hushed them. "What happened?"

"Don't give me that!" Maxine's body spasmed with outrage, her eyes wild. "You didn't watch all our stores carried away? You didn't see my entire den fired to the ground? You didn't smell the bodies burned to char, the children made orphans?"

"I didn't know . . ." Bright turned to Rousseau, hands spread. "I did make an offer. If accepted, my men would have been there to protect my clients. But I never . . ."

"You fucking creep! You sent those Adders in!"

Whistles and harsh whoops of fury echoed around the hall, rousing, hard to resist. I surged forward, but Rubio yanked me back by the wrist. "What are you *doing*?"

A good question. Was I ready to see blood spatter the tiles, eager to turn our den into a killing field, Rousseau's worst nightmare? Maxine's folk awaited only her signal. Even the mild-mannered Irv, hunkered with us at the table, quivered with rage and readiness.

"NO!" Rousseau roared, and in this hall, he was still the boss, if only by a hair.

He waited until the shouting died to angry murmurs. He met Maxine's glare squarely, pushed past mediation and ready to say his piece. "Den Ladysmith. We have taken you in and mourned with you. We've fed and clothed you and soothed your wounds. While you are here, you will honor our values, and I tell you now: killing is not our way."

"You'd see it different if it was your den destroyed," Maxine snarled.

"Not how it is," Jake chided.

"Maybe I would," Rousseau allowed. "But first we're going to figure how to protect ourselves without turning into madmen. Otherwise we become our enemy. I know there's a better way, and as long as you're under our roof, we'll work on finding it *together*. Is that agreed?"

Maxine glanced away, thin-lipped and fuming, but she nodded.

"A noble goal, brother," said Bright. "But don't look to it happening anytime soon."

Rousseau's big shoulders sagged. He took a breath, then rounded on the man. "You. Walk your evil out of here now. Don't make me say it twice."

Bright dipped his head toward Maxine, like he couldn't look her in the eye. "Madame, I . . . your loss is tragic. It is . . . the world we live in. But I am not the enemy. I believe . . ." He turned back to Rousseau. ". . . that the problem is bigger than you imagine. And I hope to be part of the solution." He eased two fingers into his breast pocket, cautious in a room full of hair triggers and ready blades, and slid out a thin black rectangle. He thrust it at Rousseau like a gift. "If you decide to reconsider my offer, activate this. I'll get the signal."

"You need help leaving?" Rousseau crossed his arms so tight, his leather vest creaked. "We'll be happy to provide it."

Bright shrugged, like he'd done the best he could, and pocketed his device. "We'll be on our way, then."

The crowd jeered as he walked to the mudroom door. I thought he looked relieved to be getting out of Unca Joe with a whole skin. His posse fell eagerly in around him, and soon we heard the thunder-rumble of their motors firing up and veering off.

As the engine racket faded up the flooded avenue and the crowd fell into heated declaration and debate, Maxine stalked up to Rousseau and slapped him hard across the jaw.

He hardly budged. "Do it again, if it'll make you feel any better."

"You fucking do-gooder!" she seethed. "Always turning the other cheek! Letting him just walk out of here! Don't you know he'll be back? Or he'll send BlackAdder in for the kill!"

"We're not going to let that happen."

"How the hell are you going to stop it?"

Rousseau's mouth worked, like he was keeping back a yell. "By calm thinking and planning ahead."

"Fuck that shit," she spat, and stalked toward the stair hall.

Jake looked tempted to follow, but a glance at Rousseau stayed him. The crowd drew away to regroup in murmuring clumps, leaving the two of them worn and conflicted.

Jake said, "She'll cool down. Too rough, having that guy show up again."

"We need her for the caucus."

"She'll be there."

"Do you think he's the Adders' man?"

"Well, that's the question, isn't it?"

"Where'd he get his boat and gas?" wondered Irv from across the table. "Not from the Adders, if they wanted our stuff so bad."

Rousseau nodded pensively. "Or anything else they're carrying. The Adder's never been a tight operation. Not good at marshaling their resources." He moved toward our group at the table as if relieved to find a rational corner of the room. "Something about this doesn't fit right. What do we know?"

Jake said, "We can assume he's lying."

"But about what?" Rousseau mused. "He seemed genuinely surprised by the details of the raid."

"I know a performance when I see one."

"Perhaps. But all this about his so-called associates. And a trained escort, not some Adder thugs. Too organized. I'd say BlackAdder's the tool, not the planner, and there's a new player in the mix. Might be Bright. Might be somebody else entirely."

I thought about the newly fortified building over on Seventh Ave, news I'd forgotten to convey. I asked Jake, "You told him about the guys selling protection at the Souk?"

"Never got that far."

The watch bell clanging out on the walkway put us all on high alert again, until one of the scouts popped in, surprised to find all heads turned in her direction.

"Um, boss . . . there's a boat from Empire just pulled up, asking for docking permission. Looks like the Tommys right behind them."

Rousseau's eyes lidded briefly, like things were heating up too fast for him. "Good, good. Signal them in. Get the mooring sorted out. Okay, folks. Let's make room for our guests. Seating's been set up in the Mess. Remember: be friendly, stay orderly, but suck up as much information as you can. Maybe Bright has paid others a visit." He glanced around. "Where is the bookseller? We could use him at this meeting."

I cleared my throat. "He took off."

"When?"

"Middle of the night."

"Huh. Not sure how to interpret that."

"But he left his boat behind. I mean, like he'll be back? Or he . . ."

"Or he what?"

"Or something's happened." I gave it a shot. "We could send someone up to check. Like, to the Souk?"

Rousseau shook his head. "Can't spare anyone right now. But be sure to send him in if he shows up." He turned away to greet the delegation from Empire State as they trooped into the hall. More of them than last time, spruced up and looking determined to be heard.

"Told ya." Rubio was back at the map table, tethered to his latest obsession.

"Told me what?"

"No boat. We got bigger fish to fry."

"Right. Never mind." Didn't need Rubio bringing his smug along. In fact, now that I thought about it, I didn't need him along at all. I'd manage on my own.

It was a perfect chance to get lost, with the crowd busily debating the Bright incident and ogling the arriving den reps. Decision made, I moseyed toward the mudroom as everyone else pushed toward the Mess. I'd miss breakfast, lunch, and the meeting, and that was too bad, but they could do without me. *Someone* should find out if Daniel was okay, right? Kept telling myself, like I told Rube: I'd feel the same if it was him suddenly gone AWOL. It almost worked.

I bought a stale granola bar at the swap counter, then filled my water bottle at the mudroom tank, hitched it to a shoulder strap borrowed from a stray cubby. Soon I was down at the deserted boat launch, looking over the possibilities. I chose Rivera's kayak, for speed and portability. Didn't know if I could handle a kayak, but I'd watched her do it, and the kayak hadn't been taking on water like the rowboat or the canoes. Plus, it was hull-up on the float with its paddle tucked underneath, like it was waiting to be stolen . . . or just borrowed for a time. I set it in the water, climbed in gingerly, and didn't capsize.

"So far, so good," I murmured, pushing off from the dock.

TWENTY-THREE

I glided into the open water of the Lagoon. The only sentry left topside shot me a friendly wave. Had to worry about Unca Joe's security, unless my rep as one of the 'boat girls' gave me some sort of special permission. But I was glad she'd seen me. If I didn't make it back, she'd have some clue where I'd gone.

I was way out of line, stealing a boat and going AWOL, but I couldn't not. Like someone else was hijacking my decision-making. Some Glimmer I didn't quite recognize.

The rain had let up, leaving behind a dull wet gleam. I circled the kayak till I had the knack of it, then turned my nose uptown. If I stayed east and went up Second, I'd have water most of the way to 59th, the faster choice even with the long walk crosstown.

With the tide heading in, the kayak moved along with little effort. Way faster than walking but twice as vulnerable, so I snugged in alongside the buildings for cover, scanning the rooftops and broken windows for the glint of a gun barrel. Not much traffic, just a few small boats headed downtown, played-out motors straining against the current, but nobody gave me the eye. When I ran out of paddle depth, I slung my water bottle across my back and stashed the kayak inside a burned-out storefront. It needed to be there long enough for me to return it to Unca Joe.

High tide and dirty run-off sluiced across the pavement at 59th, but I could jog the sidewalks without splashing. Should've been more scared all along, but being so hard on mission had dulled my anxiety. On foot again, I pondered my giving in to crazy impulse. Like Rube said, I barely knew the guy. And what help could I really be if he was in trouble?

But it wasn't just about Daniel. Some big truth was being ignored, or even withheld from us downtown, and I wanted to get up to speed. Besides, too late for cold feet now. I was nearly there. I drank deep from my water bottle and pressed on.

The wind was up, raking my nose with the bite of smoke. Not a good sign. Denfolk tell of the infernos that raged across the Island after the first big superstorms—due to ruptured gas lines, lightning strikes, or just plain arson, the fire-fighting gear already damaged or destroyed. I missed all that. But the fire-bombing of Ladysmith's was horror enough.

From Fifth and 59th, I plotted a straight diagonal across the park to where I thought Daniel's stall would be. But this was unfamiliar ground. I kept plowing into deep water or choosing paths that abruptly snaked away from my goal. I skirted several blue-tarped squatter camps, tangling in the ragtag fencing they'd thrown up to hold livestock in the bug-infested swampland. Hard to believe Rube's tales of playing on grassy lawns as a boy.

The smoke thickened as I trotted uptown, hanging low among the battered trees. A rumble of voices drifted with it, like a distant argument. In the market outskirts, where the stalls were often just tarps on the ground, vendors were hurtling about in the haze, packing up their goods. After the morning's drenching, what could be dry enough to burn?

I hit the Souk's central lane somewhere in the antiques sector. Too far north. Doubling back, I had to dodge dealers racing to pile furniture and crates into handcarts, bundling their tents haphazardly on top, bellowing at each other to hurry. Like the full-scale emergency evacuation we drilled for in the den. Had I missed a major storm warning?

Except here and there, a merchant stood calmly by, dusting or rearranging the stock, looking smug. Not a storm, then. Something else. I'd find out soon enough.

I nearly overshot Daniel's spot, hardly recognizing it—or him. Stunned, I pulled up sharp and ducked behind the tent next door to take it in.

His stall was a wreck—books and papers scattered, shelving all tipped sideways, crates overturned. He was in one piece, but mud- and soot-stained, the lettering on his rosy Book Dude T-shirt barely readable. I had no plan beyond making sure he was okay and reminding him about the caucus, and no excuse for showing up uninvited—again.

But what was he up to?

Not packing, or even cleaning up. Just burrowing through the toppled, sodden piles. He'd reach for a book, shake it, and toss it down again. Finally, he upended one book and paper fluttered to the ground. He snatched it up and dropped it in an old pail beside his foot. The book went into a plastic crate behind him.

Must be looking for something. Well, I could help with that, whatever it was.

I called three times before he heard me. He straightened and turned, pail in hand. His eyes were red-rimmed, his jaw stubbly, smeared with black. He looked . . . older, harder. And not particularly welcoming.

"Glimmer. What are you doing here?"

Seemed I kept making my entrance off-cue, at least where he was concerned. "Wondering if you're okay."

He frowned, like so much smoke and wreckage was normal. "Why wouldn't I be?"

"You took off. Left everything behind. People were worried."

"People?"

"Like Rousseau . . . and Jake. You said you'd talk at the big den meeting."

"Ah. Right. And you're their appointed messenger?"

"Something like that." Not on solid ground here.

"Huh." He relaxed into a weary bemusement and regarded me across the jumble of damp paperbacks and broken shelving like he could see right into me.

I had to look away and gesture around the stall. Humiliating to be so transparent. "So we were right to worry. What happened here? Why's everyone in a panic?"

Daniel stretched his back, stealing a long, wary look down the line of booths toward the heaviest smoke. "You really shouldn't be here."

I crossed my arms. "I guess you won't make it to the caucus. Unless there's stuff I can help you with."

He swung the pail fitfully in one hand. Whatever he'd been doing, I was keeping him from it. "There's not much time."

"For what?"

"Till they get here."

"Who?"

"The reason you should leave. Now."

"Not till I know why."

"Then you will?"

I shrugged.

He sighed and rubbed his eyes. "Okay. I talked about the guys selling security . . . ?"

At last I was one up on him. "Was it a guy named Bright?"

The pail stopped swinging. "How'd you know?"

"He wrecked your stall?"

"Not hands on. He'd muss up his suit. He delegates."

"You have proof?"

"Does it matter? He came 'round with his offer, and then . . ." Daniel glanced around, hands spread, then down toward the smoke again and back at me. "How'd you know?"

"He showed up at Unca Joe this morning, with his muscle-boy escort." I stepped over the cascade of shredded hardbacks so we wouldn't have to yell at each other.

"They're going after the dens? Anyone hurt?"

I shook my head. "Rousseau ran him off."

"Not likely. Or, not for long."

"Maxine nearly ate his face. Accused him of . . ."

A sudden whoosh of heat and crackle drowned me out. Damp grit and paper shards swirled around us as flickers of orange lit up a darker, swelling smoke cloud. Down the line, people were bellowing.

The pail clattered aside. Daniel grabbed my shoulders, spun me around with a shove. "Go! Get downtown and warn your den! Now! These guys don't wait."

I dug in my heels. If I left now, I'd be none the wiser, not even enough to excuse my going AWOL. "Rousseau knows. Bright was at Ladysmith's just two days before BlackAdder torched them. Daniel, I'm here. Let me help!"

"Go home!"

I scooped up the pail. "Wasting time. Just tell me what to do!"

His growl of exasperation wasn't quite a curse. "Desperate measures . . ." he muttered, and paced away, turning his back and pulling something from his pocket. Something like a mini cell phone. As I strained to see around him, he had a short argument with it, scowled at its tiny screen, then slid it back into his jeans.

I blinked as a gust blew hot ash into my eyes. "That works here?"

"Sometimes." He looked caught. Did he think I wouldn't know what a cell phone was? "Look, Glim, the mess down there is headed this way. I'm going to have to deal with it and I don't need you getting in the way."

A cell phone working as far south as the Souk. News to bring home, but maybe not to Rousseau. "You gonna pay up this time?"

"Hell, no. So it's going to get nasty."

"Then we gotta pack! Save your stuff!" I peered about for a cart, wagon, even a hand-truck hidden in the chaos.

"Glim, this is not your problem! Besides, the good stuff's on the boat already."

"But there's still *something* you need or you'd be on the boat, too."

Daniel rolled his eyes. "You are really . . ."

A few stalls down, another shouting match erupted. Several deep voices, one higher. Glass shattered. Shots were fired and a woman screamed.

Guns? Now I was scared.

"You need to go." Daniel reached for his phone again, not bothering to conceal it this time. He tapped a brief message and put it away, staring down the line. "That'll be the old couple with the oil lamps. Frail and unarmed, of course. Damn. Damn!"

"Should we go help?"

He hooked my elbow as I turned that way. "I tried already. Ran around to recruit resistance, get a group to stand up to them. Everyone looked the other way, and those old folks were sure I meant to steal their stuff. It's every man for himself up here!"

"So put me to work. Whatever it is you're doing . . ."

"Do you ever listen to reason?"

"If the situation is reasonable . . ." Carried away with my own bravery.

"Okay, okay!" Pushed past his patience, Daniel pointed me at a tumble of paperbacks. "Flip through them, see if anything's inside."

"What sort of anything?"

"Papers, page markers, scraps, anything not part of the book. Find something, toss it in here." He plopped the bucket down between us. "The books go in that crate."

I heard 'papers' in capital letters, but what kind he meant would have wait till I found some. I slid my water bottle behind me and bent over my assigned heap. Daniel dropped to his knees to paw through a neighboring scatter. He seemed to pick up books at random, but those already in the crate had the word 'Mars' on most of the spines. Coincidence? Rubio swore there's no such thing. Like, I doubt I'd had a single thought about Mars before this week. Now it was turning up everywhere. If it's not coincidence, what is it? A plan?

Down the line, the woman's screams dulled to weeping and faded behind the crackle of flame. I prayed the old couple hadn't lost more than their inventory. Then, as I shook open a water-stained copy of something called *Swords of Mars,* a thin fold of paper fell out.

"Good." Daniel snatched it up before me, and dropped it in the pail.

"What are they?"

"Later. Keep looking!"

Another searing whoosh. Flames sprouted over the lamp dealer's stall, leaping into the trees. Oily smoke roiled through the branches in a wave that made me cough and hold my breath. The already gray afternoon darkened.

"Hurry!" Daniel snatched at books so fast his fingers blurred.

"Can't hardly see . . ."

"Just grab. Work by touch."

We bent to it until I was truly smoke-blinded. I stood up to wipe my eyes on my wrist, then froze with a book in each hand as a half-dozen masked and armored figures stepped out of the fog like intruders from another dimension, futuristic weapons in hand, gleaming tanks strapped to their backs.

Brand new, shiny black. Weirdly out of place in the rough-hewn Souk, but I'd seen that kit-out before, minus the tanks and the guns with nozzles. Was I still in my bunk, writhing in a cartoon nightmare, the sort where you feel reality spinning out of control?

"Daniel . . ."

"Stay calm," he murmured. "Say nothing."

"That's not Bright. Who . . . what are they?"

"For once, do what I say!"

I shut my mouth.

He straightened, his back to them, slowly dusting ash off his knees, grasping the rim of the waste pail as if to empty it. Turning, he seemed to discover the high-tech posse, strung out in an arc of threat and posturing. Suited up like the cloned infantry in a video game. Almost comical. Except this was no game.

"Ah. Visitors." Like it was some minor interruption, Daniel handed the pail off to me. "Slip away," he whispered. "Quick and quiet." He stepped forward to meet them. One man in a hand-stenciled T-shirt against all that flash hardware? Was he out of his mind?

My slumbering survival instincts finally kicked in. Clutching the pail, I scorched through my options: *duck and run, hide, get invisible!* Hammered into me over and over in the den. Making a stand? Never part of the lesson plan. Let the other guy take care of himself. So why wasn't I gone already?

Behind me, a keening wail rose above the flame crackle and the dealer woman's sobs. Not human, not animal. Couldn't place it. More of my comic-book nightmare? The day slid further toward the surreal.

Like such apparitions showed up often at the Souk, Daniel raised a hand in greeting. "Can I help you gentlemen?" He shoved the book crate behind him with a sideways kick.

The shortest of the posse cradled his complicated weapon and drew his mask down to his chest. He was ruddy-cheeked and confident, a baby version of Bright. "You know what we're here about, book man."

"I do?"

The guy just smirked.

"I hope it's not to buy books. I seem to be fresh out of anything readable."

The pail weighed heavy in my hand as I struggled to put two and two together. Was I meant to hide it? Spook it out of there, along with myself? Like the Ninja Girl tossing me her pack? Had to be it. These dudes wouldn't notice some den rat taking a fade while they focused on Daniel.

It would be nice to be the hero for once, but now was not the time. I had my marching orders. I let the pail drift behind my butt and slide-stepped backward, a special Spunk maneuver to put distance between you and an attacker without seeming to move at all. But behind me, that shrill whine was closing in, dropping in pitch till I pegged it as a vehicle. The posse's reinforcements? Was I trapped already? I looked for a clue from Daniel, but he seemed to have forgotten me. New fear gripped me as he faced the thugs with nothing but a few books and a smile. If he refused to pay again, they might just shoot him, like they'd maybe done to the lamp seller. And I was helpless to stop them.

Daniel tossed his handful aside. "Hate to keep wasting your time."

Short Guy shrugged. "You heard the deal. You want your goods safe, you gotta pay up."

"Yeah, well, so little left to protect. I'll take a pass."

"Still got your space. That'll cost you now."

"I pay my dues to the Merchants' Association."

"That's them. This is us."

At my back, the engine mutter deepened to a growl. Tires crunched on gravel and the vehicle pulled up right at my back. Before I could duck or turn, the pail was snatched from my grip. The momentum dragged me around.

My hiss of protest guttered in a squawk.

It wasn't a platoon of new muscle. Nothing so logical. Only a lone figure on a three-wheeled solar-cycle, dark hoodie and skintight jeans, mirror shades reflecting tongues of flame and gray sky.

Dark Boy.

Glowering at me, hair matted like he'd just got out of bed. The waste pail swung from his handlebar. Okay, a nightmare for sure.

"Get on, den rat. We're going for a ride."

Nothing left to do but run.

On the fly, Dark Boy grabbed my arm. "No, you don't."

"Lemme go!" I writhed in his hard, one-handed grip. "Lemme go, lemme GO!"

"Keep it down!"

This couldn't be happening. I bared my teeth, aiming for his wrist, but they were both cuffed with leather. "Figures you'd be on their side!"

"Shut it!" he hissed. "You *trying* to get him killed?"

Was I shouting? "Who?"

"For whatever reason, he wants you out of here! Get on!" He buried his nails in my arm to haul me backward. I struggled wildly, falling against him, knocking his shades askew.

For a second, a curtain parted, and I stared into the panicky eyes of a boy forced to deal with a crazy woman. Vague understanding dawned. Then one of the thugs noticed my fuss and pointed. Two pulled handguns from their belts. A third unholstered a grip attached to his tank and adjusted the nozzle.

"Aw, fuck," said Dark Boy, grappling with his sunglasses.

Then all hell broke loose.

One! Two! Three! Sudden splats in the mud at the posse's booted feet. Three bright, feathered shafts vibrating in the hazy air. The thugs stumbled backward, swinging their pistols up, firing at random into the smoke-hung treetops, one deafening burst after another.

Arrows. Again. Could this dream get any weirder?

Dark Boy twisted me at the passenger pad. "Get the fuck on or you're left behind!"

In the wreckage of his stall, Daniel turned circles, as if searching the branches overhead, but his gaze locked on me long enough to mouth one word: GO!

Took the fight right out of me.

Gun barrels rotated back in our direction. Flames advanced up the line of booths. Flying ash burned in my throat and eyes. It was one sullen young-ster versus a pack of trigger-happy goons, and Daniel's look had been insistent.

"What about . . . ?" I wheezed, my head lolling in a backward glance.

"Old Dan'll take care of himself. Better if we're outa the way!"

Old Dan? I gave up trying to force reality into a shape I recognized. I let Dark Boy bundle me onto the cycle.

I was barely on when he slipped the clutch and surged forward. Just in time. The roar of acceleration drowned out the first volley, the pistols mutely puffing out smoke and empty casings. My ears rang and I tasted blood. I'd bitten my tongue.

Normally, I'd have sat back as far as possible. Now, I could only turn my brain off, clamp both arms around Dark Boy's waist, and tuck in to make a smaller target as the bullets screamed by. Lucky for us, their aim was crap.

Dark Boy swerved away into the curtain of smoke, running a crazy zig-zag among the tents and stalls along the fringe, then out through the squat-ter camps. Startled residents leaped from our path or flung themselves headlong to duck the gunfire. Through every squealing near–crack up, each heart-stopping, two-wheel turn, Dark Boy kept us upright and racing for-ward. The eager set of his shoulders beneath my shuddering jaw said he relished this sort of mad race. I held on for dear life.

And fought off visions of Daniel laid down by a hail of gunfire, no one to help him. Bleeding. Dying. Already dead.

If this was really happening, it would end at some point and I'd deal with it then.

The park perimeter road was rutted but empty. The smoke thinned. Only a scattering of vendors fleeing the Souk with their goods in tow. The aura of dreamscape faded some as the wind battered my eyelids, but expla-nation danced out of reach.

Daniel and Dark Boy. What was the connection? Had Daniel taken him on as a project, aiming to reform a wayward rich kid? Like Rousseau with Jake and others, back in the day?

In the desperate clutch of my arms, through the silky drape of his upscale hoodie, Dark Boy felt slim and rangy, truly a boy. Not starved-skinny like most denfolk, but hardly filled out yet. I'd been too frightened to see it at the dock, or behind his glitzy shades and matching speedboat. Maybe four-teen, fifteen? Younger than the medics said I was, by four, five years at least. Only playing the role of hardened adult.

'Course, being young didn't make him harmless. Something about the look of him still put me on extra-high alert. I shivered as memory stirred behind one very closed door. But he had to be safer than bullets.

Now they'd stopped flying, I needed some distance. I eased my grip and sat back far as I could and still stay on the bike. When we had 59th in sight, he slowed to keep the wind from tearing the words from his mouth.

"Need to ditch you, den rat. Got a safe hide nearby?"

"I can hide anywhere." Least he wasn't planning to drag me off to some dark corner.

"Time to lighten my load. I got . . . people waiting."

"What about Daniel?"

"Told you. Not to worry."

"You and Daniel are . . . friends?"

"On occasion." He raked windblown hair from his eyes. His wrist cuffs wrapped halfway up his forearms, like the ones from the ninja girl's pack—real leather that bent when he did, studded with real silver along the seams. The latest uptown fashion? They were worn but well-cared for, and I coveted them for their beauty. "Where're you getting off? Make it close."

He'd got me out. Now I was extra baggage.

The rain started up again as we left the park, its brooding blanket of cloud ready to give us a pounding. Dark Boy turned west on 59th, along the ranks of newer towers. Glittery, tire-slicing rubble choked the gutters. When we cruised past the Columbus Circle entrance to the Souk, four security trikes fired up to roar after us.

Dark Boy whooped, flipped them the finger, then hunched into the rain and gunned the engine, his leather-clad wrists pressed to the handlebars.

"Soukies!" I yelled. "What's their problem?"

He was gleeful. "I'm their problem! They hate me!"

Easy to imagine Dark Boy misbehaving at the Souk. And now if I didn't think fast, he'd dump me in the open, a handy decoy to distract the pursuit, and I'd be in trouble all my own.

"65th and 11th!" I hissed in his ear.

"Fuck! Nothing closer?"

"Best I can do."

"What's there?"

"Old car park. You could lose them in the upper levels."

I could almost hear him thinking it over. Unbelievable. I'd just revealed my brand-new hide to the likes of Dark Boy. So desperate, my mouth was working faster than my brain. But it might give us a chance.

"Still see 'em?"

I twisted in my seat to look behind. "Only on the long blocks."

Dark Boy brushed at his eyes again. "Visibility is crap!"

"So is theirs!"

He laughed, a harsh rat-tat-tat. Enjoying himself again. United in speed and danger, we'd reached a tentative détente. He laid down another zigzag, alternating street and avenue, cutting across empty lots, scooting between piles of rubble. Rain was building up on the pavement, making the cycle sideslip menacingly.

Finally, I dared it. "Maybe slow down a bit?"

"Ain't no joyride, den rat. You get that we're dead if they catch us, right?"

Like it really didn't matter if we were? "No point doing the job for them."

His back stiffened. "Another fucking sensible woman."

Me? Hardly. But some woman in his life had been giving him grief. The redhead? I couldn't see it. "Why're they so eager? Isn't it Daniel they're after?"

Again, his raucous cackle, like the tale was too long to tell. As we screamed up the final stretch of 11th, the blocky garage loomed ahead, the entrance a gaping black hole.

"Turn in here." I gripped his shoulders like a wheel.

"Who's fucking driving?"

"Sorry!"

He kept on straight, then at the very last chance, wrenched the cycle into the turn, skidding crazily on the flooded pavement, nearly spilling us. Just because he could. But then we were inside, out of the punishing rain, into the concealing darkness, cruising up the ramp. The rain would cover our engine noise until the Soukies caught up. At the rear of Level Two, Dark Boy braked, backed up, then nudged me roughly off.

"Hold this."

The pail, and its now sodden contents. I swayed, dizzy with speed and fright.

Dark Boy eyed me. "Not gonna crap out on me, are you?"

I snatched the pail from him. "I'm fine."

My chance to run. Now, while he struggled to hide the heavy three-wheeler between the outer concrete wall and a tall tangle of discarded car parts. I could slip off to the room. If he came after, I could lock him out. But I didn't. For all his threats, he hadn't dumped me in the street. He'd groused about my destination but had taken it on. And so far, not the slightest hint of sexual aggression.

If he was Daniel's project, I had to honor that. And keep in mind that he was not whoever he reminded me of.

I frowned at the pail. "What d'you think happened after we left?"

"Hellfire and brimstone."

Not funny. "We deserted him."

He put his shoulder to a bumper, heaving it aside to widen the slot. "He'll be fine."

"What makes you so sure?"

"'Cause I am."

Whatever their history, Dark Boy wasn't ready to share it. When he'd shoved the bike as far in as he could, he dragged over a rusted car door to close the gap. He came away, dusting his palms, then turned back, reluctant to abandon his means of quick escape. Outside, the downpour eased. We heard the saw-buzz of electric motors coming up fast.

Dark Boy faced me. His hair drew inky streaks across his forehead. His cheeks were smooth and wind-blushed. Maybe even younger than I'd thought. "You better be leading me straight, den rat."

I felt I had his number now. "Why wouldn't I?"

"Are we chatting or finding cover?"

I jerked my head. "This way."

The stairs were easier in daylight. We scurried down while I scrabbled in my gut wallet for the key. The Soukie trikes pulled up outside just as we rounded the curve of the upward ramp and dropped into its deepest shadow. No help from the rain now, so we moved like mice, down the steps into the little triangle of darkness at the door to my hide-hole. Dark Boy was good. Moved quiet as a picker.

Muttered debate drifted in from the street. "In there? Whaddya think?"

"Waste of time."

"Maybe not."

"We'll lose him, waiting around here."

"Take a quick look. Might flush him out."

"You stay out front, nail him if he takes a runner."

No mention of me. I'd been invisible on the back of the bike?

Then it was déjà vu. Engines revving up the ramps, echoing crazily off the concrete. Noise enough to cover the clink of the key in the lock. It turned, and the door gave silently. Thanking the poor dead dude who'd kept his lock clean and his hinges well oiled, I nudged Dark Boy inside and eased the door shut.

A flash of light behind me, a narrow beam on the door. Dark Boy with an LED penlight. Something else to covet. But I swatted it down. "What are you doing?"

"Looking."

"How 'bout them seeing?" Still bright enough out there so light wouldn't show under the door. But this was my hide and I was calling the shots for a change.

The light vanished. An obedient cuss, when he saw the sense of it.

I felt for the rods and barred the door. We stood in the dark, catching our breath, listening as the trikes rumbled up the ramps, around the second level, third, then down again, regrouping in the street.

"Nothing up there but old wrecks."

"Told ya. Lost him again."

"Slippery mothafucka."

"Kid's got speed. Trade mine for his any day."

"It's mine when we nab him."

"Who says?"

Dark Boy shook with silent guffaws. Soon we heard them splitting up the search party and motoring off in different directions.

"Idiots," he sneered.

"Shh! Might've left one behind."

"I counted the start-ups."

"Better be right."

"I am!" Pride-stung I'd doubted his call.

"Okay, then." I felt past him in the darkness to slide the blackout drape aside a few inches. Fading daylight revealed the room in shades of gray and lavender. "Why're they so fired up after you?"

"'Cause I give 'em trouble every chance I get."

He nosed around, taking in every detail: the couch with its bedding, the table and chairs, the useless microwave, the neatly shelved provisions. He opened the lockers, ran a finger along the shelves.

"Make yourself at home," I muttered. His poking about made the space feel smaller. ˈ

He tried the dry faucets in the sink, riffled the old magazines, then crossed his arms like it hurt to say it. "Fine hide, den rat."

"Name's Glimmer." My water bottle had battered me all through the ride. I unslung it and set it beside the hot plate. Silence from the other end. "And yours is . . . Julian, right?"

He was not pleased that I remembered. Like having an actual, human name might tarnish his cool. He made a big deal of peering out the window, leaning over, arms wrapped around his chest.

"You got some other handle you go by?"

"Like you den rats, you mean? What the fuck kind of name is Glimmer, anyway?"

I nearly crossed my arms too, but saw I'd look as dumb as he did, all trussed up in his own surly limbs. "I always say it's all I had left when I rolled out of Abel's Wave."

He snorted. "Here comes the sob story."

"I only share stories with my friends."

A feral grin flitted across his face. "Glad we got that settled."

I wondered what friendship meant to a kid like this one. Was that redhead he carried around a friend or an accessory?

He slid his palms down his jaw, flicking water off his fingers. "Anything like a towel around?"

I pointed to one hanging in a locker. It puffed off dust when he snatched it, but he shrugged and wiped himself down. His sleek hoodie seemed to shed the rain. He threw the towel in the sink, like someone else might hang it up for him, and returned to the window. He unlatched the sash and swung it out just enough to fit a hand through the opening. In his palm, a little phone like Daniel's. He worked it with an agile thumb, then pocketed it and closed the window. He dropped into a chair, stretched out his legs, failing to look relaxed. So young to have lost all his softness and ease. "So, how'd you hook up with old Dan?"

Didn't want to think about Daniel and what might have happened to him, but he was all we had in common. "I could ask you the same."

He smirked. "I didn't have much choice in the matter."

Damned if I'd ask for more, just so he could blow me off again. I plopped down on the couch. "I met him at the Souk. Tried to sell him a book. Now his boat's tied up at my den."

"Oh yeah. Unca Joe." His attention drifted off into the shadows.

I felt on the defensive. "What do you know about it?"

"All I need to know."

Jeez, he was irritating! But maybe useful? Like, could I needle info out of him? A long shot, but . . . "So, you're a know-it-all. Maybe you know about the arrows?"

His gaze slid my way under lowered brows. "What arrows?"

"The ones plunked down back there? When those goons were shooting at us?"

"Didn't see any arrows."

"C'mon . . . you didn't?"

He gave a slow shrug, like, *she's off the rails.* "Plenty bullets. No arrows."

I was not, was NOT, imagining things. "Are you sure?"

"I was too busy doing big brother's bidding, saving your ass."

"Right. Wait . . ." I sat up like a stick. "What did you say?"

"About saving your ass?"

"About Daniel."

"About doing his dirty work?"

"No. You said . . . you're Daniel's *brother*?"

"Oh. Yeah. To my eternal pain and misfortune. Yep."

"His brother." I dropped back heavily against the couch, arms spread. "Wow."

"What's the big deal?"

"You're not . . . a lot alike." I'd been probing for info, but this was a surprise bonus.

"Yeah, well." Dark Boy—still couldn't call him Julian—retrieved the waste pail and took it to the window. Pushing aside the drape to let in more light, he picked through the contents, held up a paper or two, shaking each gently.

"So why aren't you concerned?"

"About what?"

"Daniel! Your so-called brother!"

"Are you deaf? I said he'll be fine."

"Don't you care about anything?"

"What's the point? They'll only take it away from you."

Hard to deny. I sighed. "I'd give anything for family."

"Take mine. I got more than I need."

"How can that be?"

"Try being the youngest. Dan freakin' woke me out of a sound sleep to save your ass."

"But you came."

He sucked in like he'd tasted something sour. "Not doing it ain't worth the nag."

The notion of mild, smiley Daniel ordering this snarky wildling around made my brain itch. Never mind how he could go up against the posse from the future. Well, either he could, or he was dead. Pretty simple. The law of the streets.

But I felt lied to. No, misled. My wrong assumptions encouraged so that I misjudged them both. Couldn't blame Dark Boy. His wildling persona was his armor and camouflage in the streets. That he actually answered to someone made him less of a threat. But if Dark Boy was uptown, wouldn't his brother be uptown, too?

I'd let Daniel become a kind of hero-saint in my mind: the Book Dude, standing up for peace and decency in a violent, amoral world. Saints aren't supposed to get down and dirty with the villains. It put me off-balance, like a trusted walkway had gone wobbly beneath me.

The room felt overcrowded now. "If the Soukies are really gone . . . I'm due at my den."

"Give it ten, just to be sure. And I ain't riding you home, so don't get any ideas."

Like I might actually want to ride with him again? "I stashed a kayak over east . . ."

"I got you here. You're on your own."

"Do you have anything but a totally aggravating tone of voice?"

"You're no stroll in the grass yourself, den rat."

Whatever was left of the churlish adolescent in me, Dark Boy brought it out in spades. So we both sulked for a while, he at the table by the window sorting through the damp contents of the bucket as if nothing could be more interesting, me cross-legged on the couch, rearranging the even damper contents of my mind, with an eye to making sense of the last several hours. There had to be a through-line, if only I could grab onto it.

Must have drifted off. Next I knew, a series of rhythmic raps on the door made me start and leap up, disoriented and flailing. "They're back!"

Dark Boy looked up from his stacks of paper. "Relax. It's Dan. That's his knock."

"Daniel? Here? He's alive?"

"He better have dinner with him or he won't be."

I was at sea again. "How did he find us?"

He patted his jeans pocket as he crossed to unbar the door. "GPS, stupid."

It really was Daniel, leaning breathless against the doorframe in the pale creep of light from outside. He was drenched and sooty, wearing new cuts and bruises and a fired-up wariness more like a warrior than a bookseller. He slipped in with a furtive backward glance, shutting the door quietly. "Everyone okay in here?"

I didn't realize how tense I'd been until my joints all went liquid. I stayed where I was.

"Danny boy!" crowed Dark Boy. "About time! I'm fucking famished!"

"Hello to you, too, Jules." Daniel slung a weighty backpack off one shoulder and tossed it to him. "Your order, sir. Save some for us."

"You'll have to kill me first."

The backpack delivered, Daniel sagged against the closed door, chest heaving. "Whew. Break time. Haven't slowed down in twenty-four hours." He looked my way. "You okay, Glim? Julie behaving himself?" He registered my stare and cocked his head sternly. "What's he done?"

"No, no, it's . . ." I looked from one to the other, and back again. "He really is your brother."

Side by side, even in the dim light, the resemblance was obvious, once you had the idea of it: Daniel, the rounder, more restrained version of Dark Boy's lean and scowling good looks. With Daniel gone all filthy and feral, they made a pair. I reckoned eight to ten years between them.

"Sorry." But his smile was unapologetic. "Couldn't stop for introductions."

"He'd rather no one knew." Dark Boy dug eagerly into the backpack. "I'm the Nathans' best-kept secret."

I noted the plural. Were there more of them?

"Actually, he washed in with the tide."

"You wish." Out came bread, cheese, apples. Dark Boy set them along-side a sleek thermos. No mention of us having met before. I didn't bring it up either.

"You're a mess." I pulled the towel from the sink and passed it to Daniel.

"Thanks." He blotted bloodied mud from his face and hands, watching me. "Sure everything's okay?"

I reached for my battered water bottle. My throat had gone dry. "Sure."

I had a head crammed with questions and no idea where to start. Food was a safe beginning and I hadn't eaten since breakfast. "Apples! They even look fresh!"

Daniel put the towel aside. "Toss one over, will ya?"

"There's only two."

"Give her mine, creep."

A shiny red-gold apple sailed into Daniel's beaten-up palm. He passed it to me, then took a moment to gaze around, taking the room's measure, just as Dark Boy had done. "Nice find, Jules."

"Not mine. Hers."

Daniel offered a thumbs-up.

"Accident," I mumbled, through a crisp, sweet chaw of apple, like noth-ing I'd tasted in ever so long.

"A lucky one. And just when I needed a new hole to hide in." He did a slow collapse onto the couch beside me. He smelled of smoke and sweat and, yes, gunpowder. "Ouh, that's better."

I swallowed, savoring the juice. "Where can they still grow apples like this?"

"Way north in Canada."

"You get these at the Souk?"

"I get them."

Which meant, don't ask. One more unanswered question.

Dark Boy flicked him a grin. "Den rat was sure you were a goner, Dan."

"O ye of little faith!" Daniel poked me, looking smug.

I eased away slightly. "All that hardware, what else could I think?"

"Yeah!" He bent to look past me. "You see 'em, Jules? Way more flash than last time."

"I caught that. Someone's put in for a major upgrade. Any idea who?"

"Not yet."

I was feeling sidelined. "What happened after we left?"

"I ducked out pretty quick. Too much lead in the air. You and Jules were the perfect distraction."

"You must've moved pretty fast."

"He does," Dark Boy sniggered. "When he puts his mind to it."

"But did they torch the tent?"

Daniel nodded wearily.

"What, *everything*?" If he was too done in to be outraged, I was ready to do it for him.

Daniel spread his hands in a way that was becoming familiar: his gesture of worldly acceptance. "New beginnings. On to the next phase of my career. Safety in mobility. Plus it saves me a trip to the dump."

"The what?"

"Dump. Great word. Onomatopoetic. There actually is one now, beneath one of the bridges over the 81st Street transverse. Officially designated by the Merchants' Association. Can you believe it? Even with the artifacts of daily life gone rare and precious, we still have stuff to throw away. You sharing any of that cheese, Jules?"

A hunk of cheese came flying, then a chunk of bread. Daniel tore both in half and handed me one of each.

Food was fine, but information was higher on my list, and not about dumps. I tried to keep it casual. "Still a miracle you aren't dead."

"Nah, they weren't trying to kill me. Twist my arm more." He bit into his cheese. "Dead men don't pay."

"I felt those bullets whizzing past . . ."

"All for Jules. Everyone wants him for target practice. It's the look."

"It's my criminal skill and daring!"

"With me, it's money they're after."

"The family silver . . ." Dark Boy waved an airy hand.

"Gone with the wind . . ."

"Our inheritance squandered . . ."

I took this as an old joke between them. If I'd been more on the ball, I'd have let it play out and learned something useful about the Nathans. But I was fixed on course.

"What about the arrows?"

Daniel's mouth was full. "The what?"

"The arrows."

"What arrows?"

Not again. I set my apple down. "No, really." I jerked a thumb at Dark Boy. "Maybe he didn't see them, but you must have! They landed right in front of you! Out of the trees!"

Offering more cheese and bread like it might soothe my overheated imagination, Daniel shrugged. "Hell of a lot going down right then. Must've missed them."

My hands were fisted so tight, even my nubs of nails cut into my palms. "I should've ripped one out of the ground and brought it with me!"

"Some kids playing around?"

"I didn't see any kids."

Behind the dam of rational thinking, the flood of my doubt and frustration was rising. I was sure I was being stonewalled. Like, if I asked about the diamond bracelet, would Dark Boy say, what bracelet? All this snappy chit-chat and brotherly banter suddenly struck me as a smokescreen. Sure, a family has a right to their secrets, and yes, I had intruded into their business. But with the three of us hiding out together, wasn't I in as deep as they were?

I popped up, ready to make a scene, but the space was too narrow for a real fit of umbrage. I pinwheeled my arms, fighting the whine I knew would get me nowhere. "I am not delusional, no matter what you're trying to make me think!"

"Why would I do . . ." Daniel began.

"I know what I saw! Okay, you won't talk about the arrows? How about the papers? A hair-raising rescue of a bucket of wet scraps? What's all it about?"

"Whoa, whoa," placated Daniel, but he glanced sideways down the room.

"Wet but legible," Dark Boy said.

"Glim, listen . . ." Daniel gathered up scattered bread and cheese and set it on the arm of the couch. "It's just family business. Some stuff my sister needs got left in the books . . ."

"Got hid, you mean!"

"Okay, but I needed to recover it before the goons torched the place. I knew they were going to. I'm sorry you got mixed up in it."

"Way I heard it, you barged in on your own," Dark Boy reminded me.

"That's so helpful, Jules."

"Fuck you, too."

I glanced from one to the other. I needed to slow my brain down, get a grip. Spunk always said everyone's got an angle. To really know them, you had to find out what it was. "Solar bikes, cell phones, apples from Canada! Old pails full of paper scraps? Is it some sort of black-market scheme you two are running?"

Daniel was rueful. "A black market in books?"

"In whatever you're hiding in them!"

"Our stuff's not all that great," mused Dark Boy through a mouthful of cheese. "One of those flamethrowers might come in handy."

If he'd been close by, I'd have wacked him. "Forget it! I don't care what you're up to. Better if I don't know!"

"Boy, Dan, so right about this crazy den girl you needed off your hands."

"I never said . . . !"

"Shut up shut up shut up!" Just like that, my brain did a perceptual reversal, like when you see in for out, or front for back. One moment, Daniel and Dark Boy; the next, two uptown guys united against me. My little room was growing smaller by the second. "I'm going home!"

"Glim, listen . . ."

"I need to be out of here!" I was losing it and for once I didn't give a shit. I snatched the door key from my pocket and threw it at him. It bounced off his bruised cheek and fell to the floor. "Lock up when you're done with all your . . . family business!"

Somehow, Daniel made it to the door before me. "Not yet. Wait a bit, then I'll get you home safe."

"I don't need your help!"

He backed against the door. "You don't want to go out there."

"Don't tell me what I want!"

"Alright, let me rephrase it. There's a dead guy out there."

"Since when?" Dark Boy demanded.

"Since I clocked him so he wouldn't find the door."

Dark Boy clucked his tongue. "Ah, Danny. I can't take you anywhere."

It took a moment to find my voice. "You . . . killed someone?"

"Well, he might not be quite dead." Daniel watched me coolly. "But he will be, if his pals don't show up in time. Must've stayed to snoop around."

"But . . ." I didn't understand the challenge in his gaze. "You don't carry a weapon."

"Scrounged up half a cinderblock."

"Euw, messy!" Dark Boy pumped a fist. "So let's finish him and split. I got a date later."

"Can't. I activated his alarm."

"What the fuck for?"

"So someone else has to clean up the mess for a change!" Daniel threw his head back, the words spilling out like rough water. "Because my stock just went up in flames! Because I hate being shot at! Because I'm sore and hungry and filthy and just too fucking tired to solve one more problem I didn't create!"

"Whoa, bro. Like you always tell me, go home and cool off."

"His friends'll be here any minute."

Moaning, I buried my face in my hands. "You really killed someone? Just now?"

"Are we back with the poor little sniper on the rooftop?" Daniel slumped against the door. "You'd rather I let the guy in?"

Of course not. Then we'd all be dead. More shaky ground. Like, what was I really defending? Didn't all that Smith weaponry at Unca Joe make us feel safer? Hadn't Rousseau himself carried a rifle out to the funerals? But Daniel? Ready to crack a man's head open without a sign of remorse? Somehow, this was unbearable.

I sensed the familiar early signs: the sped-up heartbeat, the tightness in my chest, the circular thinking. Not a good time for a panic attack, but then, it never is. Pacing each breath, I turned away and wedged myself into the corner of the couch, longing for the walls of my den, not these walls that seemed to be closing in.

Daniel pushed off from the door. "He'll probably survive."

"That's not the point!"

"Then what is?"

"Quiet!" Dark Boy quick-stepped to the window to draw the drape shut tight. The last trace of light abandoned the room. The air grew thick and stale. Outside, vehicles approached.

"That'll be them," Daniel murmured.

A draft stirred as Dark Boy powered past me to ease the bars into place.

Trapped. In total darkness. With a man I no longer trusted, and one I never had. I curled tighter into the corner of the sofa. Calm down. Disappear. But the usual techniques were not doing the job. Deep breaths only made my head spin. The heat and darkness pressed in, like an arm heavy against my chest.

Like many arms, pulling at me, holding me down . . .

Gasping, I bolted for the door. I knew where the bars were. I could get them open before they could stop me. I ran smack into Dark Boy.

"What the . . . !"

A flailing of hands and fists, his, mine. Then he caught my wrists, twisting them behind me, pinning me tight against his side as I bucked and twisted in his grip.

From nearby, a hissed "Quiet!"

"Here! You take her!"

Even in darkness, they kept hold of me. Except my feet.

"Ow! Stop, Glim! What are you doing?"

Fighting for my life. Far from here, yet not so. In a room like this one, only not. Salt spray in the air. Fear like acid on my tongue. I've sensed this place a thousand times in nightmare, invisible, only imminent. All I know of it is that I am not alone there. Now its image blooms behind my eyes in every terrifying detail. The row of ripped-out sinks, the shattered mirrors, the flickering overheads. The baying whoops echoing along the tiles. I am running, ducking. I am prey.

Hide! Here inside the stalls! Get small. Disappear. They'll ignore you and go away.

Someone is moaning. Loud. Louder.

"What the fuck? Jesus, Dan, shut her up!"

Get away! Get away! Don't touch me!

Harsh breath in my ear. Arms cinching my chest. Hand pressed to my mouth.

"Shh! Glim! Shh! They'll hear you!"

Air! No air!

The room is murky, tinged in blue. Pale, moldy tile, cold beneath me. An ocean is pouring in. The stink of terror and lust. My head goes under. I cough up salt and blood and oily harbor water. A smooth-faced, dark-haired boy is tearing at my shirt, shredding my pants. Another like him holds me down. A third yanks at his drawstring while a fourth looks on, eager . . . so eager.

"Glim? Hey!"

I'm hauled upright, shaken, then bent, shoved over hard, head forced between knees.

"Breathe, dammit! What are you doing? Breathe!"

A pounding on my back. So hard, it hurts.

But the pain is real. It yanks me forward to the here and now. At the edge of consciousness, I breathe.

Vast haling gasps. Air rushes into my lungs like a rip tide, a typhoon, a tsunami. The images coursing through my brain—the sinks, the tile, the dark-haired boys, the roaring, inundating wave—crystallize into meaning. The door to my past flies open.

And stays open.

The force of it slams me against the inside of my head. And it keeps coming, rushing like the surge.

Can one small skull contain so much memory? Yet I am hungry for it. Ravenous.

I hold myself still. The slightest move might jog the door, swing it shut again.

When it does, my brain is full to bursting and I am grateful for the reprieve.

The pounding has stopped. The pushing, pulling hands are gone. Voices remain, but only in whispers, querulous and urgent. They also are here, not there. Now, not then.

I hover in between.

Lizzy?

A woman is calling.

Lizzy, have you done your homework?

I am a long-ago child, stretched out on deck, staring up at a rare blue sky.

Lizzy!

The voice is my mother's.

"Coming, Mom!"

Then, very quietly, so not to disturb the whisperers, I let myself weep.

TWENTY-FOUR

" **W**hat'd she say? Something about her mother?"

Lizzy!

With the name came so much history. Not a straight through-line. More like islands of recall in an ocean of days and months, of past years lost to me since Abel's Wave. I could've floated a long, long time on those waters, in between then and now, the calm after the storm, island-hopping from one memory to another. I wanted to.

But with the name came a doubled self, not yet fully merged, containing both past and present, both Lizzy and Glimmer, like conjoined twins. Like being poised between the dock and the boat in a swell, unsure where to put your weight next.

With the now demanding my attention.

"Glim? Are you with us?"

I needed time. To absorb. To draw my two selves closer together. Wasn't going to get it. Not yet. The whispered summons became a hand on my shoulder, shaking me gently. It was dark. Unclear where I was, or why. Something about danger. Survival might depend on being functional. Or at least, pretending to be.

"Glim? Can you hear me?"

The fog thinned. The room took dim shape around me. The man and the boy. The need for a place of safety. Unca Joe. I was finding a balance.

I had to act normal, for long enough to get back to my den, to a private space where I could tackle this flood of data on my own terms. Best to lean toward the Glimmer half: talk and walk like the person I'd been moments before. The man looming anxiously over me would expect that. He'd also expect an explanation, would keep after me till he got one.

Sitting up would be a start. At least that effort was just mechanical. I unwound from my twisted retreat in the corner cushion and waited for the time-travel vertigo to pass. Would my voice sound different? Would Lizzy shine out through my eyes?

The man was . . . yes, called Daniel. How could I have forgotten?

He crouched in front of me, caught in a faint drift of light from above. "What's going on with you?"

So earnest, so sympathetic. Of course, it was nothing personal. Just the face he presented to the world. I understood that now. When I raised my eyes to his, I felt her in there, Lizzy looking him over, judging. For Daniel, it must have been like peering through a window at a face inside. His head jerked, an almost invisible recoil.

"What?" he whispered.

Sure that I'd already said it, I tried again. "Sorry."

"Okay, but what happened? You were . . ."

"I was . . ." So very far away.

The boy shushed us from the door. Who? Ah yes . . . Julian.

Daniel rose to sit beside me on the couch. I didn't mind. Such distance between us now. Even an inch felt like a mile. "One moment you were pissed as hell, the next you were . . . well, really scaring me."

"Sorry." But that wouldn't satisfy him. "I . . . had a . . . I remembered stuff."

"What stuff?"

"Before. Memory quake."

"That's good, right? But . . . is it always that . . . rough?"

"This was . . . a big one."

"Shut the fuck up!" Julian hissed.

Something going on outside. Even in my distraction, I registered the racket echoing off the concrete. Vehicles pulling up, big ones with motors that growled instead of whined, screeching tires, curses and exclamations.

"They've found him," whispered Julian.

"Later, okay?" Daniel laid a finger on my knee, like he'd pin me to the spot if I tried to move. "It's dark and the door's well hidden. But for now, sit quiet. You good with that?"

Quiet suited me just fine. I nodded, so he'd be done and leave me alone. If acting like you're in control is the same as being in control, even while your mind is slipping sideways, I was there. Probably I was in shock, seeing how my responses were so tamped down. I'd seen it enough in newbies rescued into the den to recognize the symptoms.

Julian rechecked the security of the door bars, then slouched over to the window, sliding the curtain open a crack to let in a slice of dusk. Not much, but the room expanded in my mind and I breathed a bit easier. Daniel rose to grab one of the silvery water bottles. He set it in my lap. When I just sat there, he uncapped it and wrapped my fingers around it.

"Drink."

This seemed a reasonable, non-threatening idea, so I took a long, long swallow. The water was cold and sweet. Spring water, from somewhere I'd never be allowed to go.

Boots pounded around on the other side of the cinderblock. One vehicle took off uptown at a roar. Others charged up and down the ramps.

Julian fretted. "Better friggin' keep away from my wheels."

Daniel went to the door, laid an ear against it. After a while, he straightened. "He's walking."

"You sure?" Julian was disappointed.

"They just told him to look sharper next time. And no talk about a door." Daniel resettled himself at the far end of the couch. "Guess I didn't hit him so hard after all." He let his head loll against the back. When I glanced at him sidelong, he was asleep.

After an endless time, engines revved, drove off. The boots seemed to gather in a pack and clomp off down the street. Voices faded, along with the light from our small window, its curtain half-drawn, until we were sitting, still and silent, in the almost dark.

I put the time to use: shove the emotional baggage aside, like the image of Daniel braining some poor dude with a cinderblock. Start cataloguing the new input. I probed for the memory that went back farthest, then worked forward to Abel. There were huge gaps, but Rubio had guessed right: boats and the water were a big part of it. The rising oceans. Marina life, a blur of sailboats, the striped swell of a spinnaker. And yes, I'd lost my mother to Abel's Wave, but not the way it went in my storm vision, where I took full blame. I'd been securing stuff below when *Haiku*'s boom snapped its tie and swept her into the tempest. Never saw her go. But survivor guilt works overtime, conjuring horrors. I'd have a lot to share with the shrink when I got back to the den.

And now I knew why Julian—his feral gaze, his lawless manner—set off my alarm bells. That first meeting on the dock stirred up blocked memories of Abel. That tiled room—why was I out in the storm? Searching for my mother? That gang of boys . . . but not Julian. He only looked like them.

Daniel stirred, listening, then got up, ghosting to the door. "Time to call in a drive-by."

"More than time." Julian inched open the window. Faint light still shone high on the gridded glass towers downtown. He nosed out his phone, ran a finger over it, then balanced it on the sill. Awaiting a reply, no doubt, from yet another confederate.

Seeing it reminded me of an issue from earlier. "You have working cell phones."

"Sometimes they work." Julian put his away. "Don't yours?"

"Do you see me with a cell phone?"

"Not now, you two." Daniel rubbed his eyes. "Nothing special about our equipment."

"It's special to me."

"What I mean is, it's not so hard to come by as you think."

I laced my arms into the tightest package possible. "Then how come I'm running around the city with nothing more than a pry-bar and a friggin' jackknife?"

He eyed me cautiously, like I might explode on him again. "Not my place to say."

"Consider where you live, den rat," said Julian.

Daniel eased back into the couch. "I don't like talking against the dens. They've helped so many survive. There when no one else was. For me, even."

"We were there for you, Danny. You just didn't want to be there with us."

"You know why, Jules. Choices were made I couldn't get behind."

I'd lost interest in Nathan family squabbles. "What've the dens got to do with it?"

"Everything."

I waited.

Daniel sighed. "Okay, here it is. But you won't like it. Let's say that all the dens have not . . . kept up."

"How you gonna keep 'em down on the farm . . ." Julian sang softly.

"Kept up?" I asked.

Daniel nodded. "Some dens prefer, even enforce, a . . . simpler lifestyle than is necessary, at least these days. Take Revelations: they're not into sacrifice and discipline because it's the only way to survive. They believe machines are evil, along with everything they produce. They're Luddites. They don't want to know what's still out there and available."

"Technophobes," echoed Julian.

"I know that," I said. "Won't even go solar. But that's Revelations."

"Sure. But here's the hard part. Other dens have chosen a more moderate road in terms of food and energy production but keep a lid on media and communications tech in order to control the flow of information from outside. Helps keep things manageable. Of course, when they blame technology for screwing the planet, they're not wrong. But it's done a lot of good, too. Given the current conditions for survival, some of us feel it's better to use the tools available . . . while they're still available."

I considered Rousseau's cell ban, and other tech voids at Unca Joe. "Do your phones work downtown?"

"Sketchy," Julian allowed.

"There are . . . people . . . whose mission is to restore some coverage," said Daniel.

"But sometimes they work there?" Contrary to all we were told. "And Rousseau knows?"

"I'm sure he does," Daniel said.

And no doubt Spunk and Jake.

Daniel was over-explaining, hoping to soften the blow by larding on the detail. "It's always true after a big one. Nothing works. But as a tower here or there gets back online . . . well, some prefer to ignore it."

Huh. A conspiracy of silence at the top. Add my den elders to the list of heroes I felt betrayed by. Not that I'd ever thought of Jake or Spunk as saints. But Rousseau . . . maybe.

"Okay, we're good to go." Julian shut the window and began refilling the backpack, starting with the stacks of paper from the bucket, neat piles into side pockets.

"What'd she say?" asked Daniel.

"Nothing. Just the all-clear."

"You go on. I'll stay here." If I could sit alone in a quiet place, maybe I could clear my head, resolve who I was going to be from here on.

"Not a chance." Daniel found a second wind, capping the water bottle, scooping up food scraps. He slipped the door key from his pocket and handed it to me. "They'll be back to tear the whole place apart, and this time, they'll find the door. Honestly, Glim—have you even the slightest instinct for self-preservation?"

If only he knew . . .

But he went on neatening up. Covering our tracks.

On our way out, just before locking up, I said, "Hold on. I forgot my poncho."

Not a lie, but in case Daniel was right and my hide was no longer secure, I ducked behind the half-closed door, retrieved the cached documents, and slid them into my belly wallet.

Outside again, poncho in hand, I said, "I have a kayak stashed a bit east of here."

Julian's look said I'd been trouble enough already.

"I said I'd get you home safe," Daniel countered. "And that's what we'll do."

Several changes of vehicle later, we were cruising down Second Avenue in Julian's sleek inboard, my kayak slung along the port side and my head spinning with the abrupt turn of events. Like Julian said, Daniel moved fast when he put his mind to it.

The speedster was a tight fit for three, with me in the front, silent beside Julian as he drove, Daniel squeezed crossways into the slot behind, called a rear seat but better used for small cargo. The backpack was balanced on his thighs. The darkness kept our speed to reasonable, and staying alert for threats from the cross streets or the approach of other boats limited talk. Which was good, since Julian was in a monumental sulk, and I was tired of being someone's unwanted responsibility. Daniel was irritable, leaning in between us to comment on Julian's driving or choice of route. His jaw was tight, his eyes squinty from searching the shadows. All patience and ease had gone out of him, like he was wrestling with thoughts he didn't care to share.

Amazingly, after the expected smart-ass debate, Julian did what he was told. No hint of brothers or sisters so far in my big memory quake, so I might've missed out on sibling dynamics. Maybe their constant jabbing at each other was part of being brothers? Still, the hierarchy was clear, the way I'd submit to seniors in the den even if I didn't agree with them.

A water taxi turned out of a side street, heading uptown. Julian slid us into the deeper night along the building face and cut the running lights. The taxi took this as a threat, sped up and passed us by.

This boat was agile and easy in the water, a pleasure to ride in, even if she was a stink pot. I was feeling steadier. Just being out on the water brought me back into focus. I stroked the gleaming teak dashboard.

"Does she have a name?" I asked Julian.

He made a sour face. "Just the one she came with."

"Of course." Bad luck to change a boat's launch name.

"*Sea Sprite*," supplied Daniel, his voice as flat as his mood.

The worst sort of boat cliché. "Bummer."

Julian shot me a sideways glance. A hint of a smile? In the darkness, hard to tell. But I sensed a faint easing of our mutual animosity. I settled back in my seat and retreated into my memory scan: what about my father? Where was he? Right away, like it had been lurking close to the surface, I found the day he lost a final argument about it being our last chance to evacuate, how there was no future along the coasts. My mother saw no future elsewhere. We had to stick it out till things got back to normal. *Normal!* My dad's fists knotted in rage and frustration as he was reduced to incoherence, but he was not a violent man. Soon after, he took the motor launch out for a supply run and never came back. The memory didn't totally kick me in the stomach, so I must've had time to get used to his desertion before Abel rolled in. But when I tried to picture his face close up, he'd be in silhouette, or there'd be a flash of sun off the water, and his features would be lost in a burst of light.

Daniel nudged me out of my reverie, pointing ahead. "Is it always that bright?"

A flickering glow heated the low clouds south of the Stuy Square Marina to a warm gold. "Oh, no! That's Unca Joe!"

Julian eased the stick forward.

"Don't go straight in," Daniel said. "Go to 6th and cross. Around the back."

"That'll take forever!" I was sure we'd find Unca Joe up in flames, the boats burning, denfolk leaping into the water, but passing 7th, we could see west to the sprinkle of bow lanterns on a crowd of watercraft clustered across the Lagoon, and the many torches flaring along the walkway.

Giddy with relief, I stood up in my seat to peer ahead, like all my confusion and upset could be sorted out if I could just get home. "Must be the meeting's still on."

"Down, before you fall in!" Daniel grabbed at my shirt. I sat.

Sentries hailed us on the corner of 6th and Third, passing us on to a checkpoint, two war canoes stretched across the downtown end of the Lagoon, a well-armed Smith in each bow.

"Be good, Jules," warned Daniel.

Julian sighed, dropped to idle, and let us drift. I knew one of the crew vaguely and another recognized Daniel from his visit to the Mess. They waved us on. Julian threaded *Sea Sprite* through the crush of boats to pull up neatly alongside the book barge at the Lagoon's western edge. I was into the stern pit with the bow rope before Daniel could untangle himself from *Sprite*'s rear seat.

"Don't tie up," Julian told me. "I'm gone soon as you get that peapod off my deck."

With *Sprite*'s engines throttled down, we could hear the rumble of voices, the occasional shout or burst of group laughter, even what might have been singing, rolling in a cheery chorus out of Unca Joe. A gathering announcing itself to the night.

Daniel unlashed the kayak while I held *Sprite* alongside the barge. "Sounds like the meeting has morphed into a party."

I frowned. "Rousseau would never let that happen . . ."

"Perfect time to get caught off guard."

"There are sentries out everywhere." But still, I worried.

Drumming his fingers on the wheel, Julian studied the ragtag collection of boats: whalers, canoes, dinghies, even a pontoon boat or two. No mooring buoys. No bottom soft enough to hold an anchor. Tied to the walkway posts, tied to each other. Few of them had motors of any size. Nothing as trim and agile as *Sea Sprite*.

"A whole marina full of rodents," he remarked, then glanced at me slyly.

I laughed. Couldn't help myself. And so what? Arrogant prick that he was, he'd brought me through a lethal sort of day and, though he didn't know it, had sparked my biggest memory quake ever. I owed him. "Thanks for the thrill ride, Dark Boy."

He tossed his head, flashing a tiny, closed-tooth grin. "Any time, den rat."

Daniel hefted the kayak onto the side deck of the book barge. "Done."

"Shove off," Julian called.

I tossed *Sprite*'s bow rope onto her forward deck and gave her nose a push. She floated free. Julian raised his leather-wrapped wrists and crossed them above his head, maybe some private victory gesture, then gunned her into a tight turn and took off.

From the bow, Daniel watched *Sea Sprite* snake a quick retreat among the close-packed hulls, setting them bobbing and knocking against each other. He watched long enough to be sure Julian didn't tangle with any super-alert sentries. I busied myself in the stern, setting the kayak in the water, mating the paddle's two halves and shipping it beside the seat. The torches along the walkway beckoned, their reflection in Julian's wake offering a rippled path toward home. I couldn't wait to be there.

Daniel walked back from the bow, checking his tie lines, the backpack dangling from one hand. He seemed calmer, ready to mend fences. "You and Julie got on okay. Thought I'd find you at each other's throats when I got there. What'd you call him? Dark Boy?"

"It's a long story."

"I'm sure. Do I need to be jealous?"

What? I looked up from my fussing with the kayak, but he'd turned away to throw himself down on the stern bench with an explosive sigh.

"Fuck of a day."

"Yes, it was," I offered neutrally.

"But we survived it." He stowed the backpack in a corner. "So, tell me about what you remembered back there in the hide."

Not what I'd expected. "Now?"

"A quick preview?"

I stood. "Really not ready to talk about it. Still processing."

He regarded me across the few feet between us as if it was a half a mile, then patted the seat beside him. "Come sit for a minute."

"I need . . . *we* need to get over there . . ."

"A minute. Please?"

I didn't sit, but I didn't leave either. Had he really said jealous?

"You're mad at me. Or something."

"I'm . . ." I couldn't say what I was, but it wasn't angry.

"You are, and I don't know why." He leaned forward, forearms on his knees, the torchlight bright on his weary, soot-smudged face. "I thought . . . tell me if I'm wrong . . . I thought we were kind of working on something, you and me. What happened?"

Nothing and everything. The past and present. "My fault for showing up where I'm not wanted."

"Who said not wanted?"

I took a diving-deep sort of breath. "Anytime I come by, you yell at me to leave."

"You mean, at the Souk? With your perfect pitch for arriving just as a crisis boils up?"

I chewed my lip. My timing had not been stellar.

More quietly, he said, "I miss how you look at me."

"How I what?"

He sat back, folded his arms. "Well, if nothing else, with a bit of interest. With . . . hope? Maybe even trust? Now I'm getting the cold shoulder."

"From the crazy den girl who won't leave you be?" I blurted.

He rolled his head back. "Never said that! Just Julie making trouble."

"Why would he?"

"It's his game of choice."

I could see that, actually.

"By my best recall, I said, 'Got a girl here who needs a lift out before she gets herself killed.'" He looked at me. "Do we have that sorted out?"

I shrugged. This was how he'd smooth over a rough afternoon, salvage a friendship. He was a friendly guy, after all—at least, on the surface. I crouched on the gunwale. "I got a bunch of surprises today. It's a lot to deal with."

"Anything to do with me?"

"Some."

"Ah." He considered this. "Okay, name one."

This was confrontation, and I was bad at it. "I don't . . . I really should get . . ."

"What? What is it? How can I fix it if I don't know the problem? Uh-oh, there's that stare again. Like you've never seen me before in your life."

A particularly raucous chain of catcalls and laughter tumbled across the water from Unca Joe as a clot of revelers spilled out onto the walkway. Soon the other dens would be heading home. The dark, lantern-studded marina would churn with boats starting up, with parting jokes and safe-home farewells.

Daniel leaned forward to be heard over the ruckus. "Glim, I could have brought this boat to any other den in the city for its opening gig. Why did I choose Unca Joe?"

"Jake's idea, I figured."

"Hardly." He mimed scribbling on his palm. "Memo to self: make your intentions clear. Next problem?"

When I could only stare at my hands, he said, "It's the guy outside the door, isn't it."

There I was again. Totally transparent. Plus naïve, foolish, uncool. All those things. Still, I couldn't help feeling in the right. "I didn't think you were the sort to kill someone . . ."

"I didn't!"

". . . with your bare hands."

"The weapon makes a difference?" His sincerity took on an edge of pique.

"No, I . . ."

"Well, I am, if the need is there. But this time, I just put the guy down for a while and trussed him up tight. It was Julie wanting to go out and finish him. My bloodthirsty little brother. And he would've. Had to improvise to keep you both inside."

"It scared me. You scared me."

"I had to, to keep you safe. When you get stubborn, nothing else works."

And when he was being so reasonable, it was hard to argue with him. I needed to be elsewhere so I could think, think him and everything else out. "Sorry to be such trouble."

"You're not . . ."

From behind me came the loud slap-creak-slap of an inexpert oarsman.

"Glim! Glim!" Rubio in the old dinghy, splashing up fast though the scrum of boats. In the stern, Breakers warded off near-collisions with the butt of her rifle. "Where you been all day? We missed you at the caucus."

My escape hatch.

I looked back at Daniel. "If only you'd talk to me about the arrows . . ."

Then I could trust him again.

The light was dim, but I thought his eyes turned sad. "What arrows?"

My heart, wanting so much to open, closed tighter than before.

"Rube! Rube!" I whirled to wave wildly. "Over here! I need a ride home!"

TWENTY-FIVE

Rubio ran the dinghy against the docking bumpers, so hard the whole barge shuddered. I jumped into the bow and shoved us off like something was chasing me.

"Bring the kayak, will you?" I called over my shoulder as we drifted away. Daniel's arms were in a 'what the hell?' spread.

"We could make room." Rubio was all elbows and knees with the oars, unsure which way to row.

Breakers gripped the stern sides as the dinghy rocked. "Maybe not."

Rubio frowned. "We need him at the table!"

"He'll get there." I reached to adjust Rube's spidery hands on the oars. "It'll go better if you do it this way. Should've let Breakers row."

"Busy." The Smith patted the rifle laid flat across her knees and waved an arm toward the rooftops. "Besides, I got my good clothes on."

She was still all in black, so who could tell?

As the bow swung round toward the walkway and home, I faced Daniel watching my retreat. Our eyes met across the dark, flame-rippled water. He'd put his memo right into practice: *make your intentions clear.* I had to look away.

Not ready to take on that much. At least, not yet. Like, I hardly knew him . . .

How far would that excuse carry me? I swiveled toward Unca Joe.

"Look who's leaving," Breakers noted.

A brisk but silent hustle on the walkway and the sweaty sheen of torchlight on seven shaved heads announced the delegation from Revelations, long robes snarling in their sandals as they backed down the ladder into a handful of small boats ferried in from mooring.

"Figures," she added acidly.

"Why? Don't we like Revelations anymore?"

"Things got too lively for that bunch of teetotalers." Rubio leaned toward me. "The Tommys brought mead!"

"Friggin' cowards, more like," Breakers growled.

"Yeah, that was bad." Rubio swung a bit too wide avoiding them, then had to scramble to aim the dinghy under the farthest window arch to reach our boat dock. "Revelations thinks we should make a deal."

"What deal?" Past Rube's ear, I glimpsed Daniel settling into my kayak, testing its balance, hefting the paddle.

"With Bright."

"No way! Why?"

Rube shrugged with both oars, scattering water 360. "Guess they'd rather pay to pray."

"So we won't be seeing them again?"

"Hard to say. They hung in longer than expected."

"Reconnaissance." Breakers brushed spray from her rifle stock.

Rubio rolled his eyes. "And I thought I was paranoid . . ."

"More than knives up their woolly sleeves. You'll see."

"Maybe."

"I was sure everyone would be gone by now," I said.

"Just got started!" Rubio laughed. "Mired in protocol! Like, it was noon before détente was reached on the seating pattern. Chairs and tables rearranged for two full hours! Then it was nearly three before the air was cleared of complaints and accusations, and then of course Maxine had to relate every detail of the raid. By four, they'd managed to agree on the facts of the current situation. And then . . ."

"Hard ahead!" warned Breakers, as the float came up too fast in the darkness.

I turned to catch the edge seconds before collision, then held us to the dock while the dinghy settled. Rubio paused for breath, then a cough, his oars drooping into the water.

"Shouldn't talk and row at the same time," I said.

"And then . . . the potluck had to be shared out equitably. Wasn't till after dinner that any real issues got laid on the table. Then Revelations delivers their bomb, which sets everyone off again."

"Waited till *after* we'd fed them," said Breakers. "Ate more than their share."

"And then the mead came out," Rube added.

I grabbed the oars from his slackening grip before they floated away, and stowed them alongside. "Did they bring anything?"

"A half dozen bricks of the driest damn break-your-teeth bread ever baked!"

Rubio coughed again, wiped his mouth. "Of course, in any given group, there's a limited number of functional participants to any discussion. Mercifully, that group is still in the room talking."

"And everyone else . . . ?"

"Eating. Drinking. Gossiping. Arguing. Sleeping. Playing cards. Even had a skins versus shirts game going in the hall until it got too dark to see the nets. Or the ball."

Stepping onto the float, I recalled Daniel's warning: the perfect time for a raid. "I hope Security is on their toes. The only strength we'd have is in numbers."

"Not a bad one to have," noted Breakers, vaulting gracefully onto the float after me, rifle aloft in one hand. "Woulda made a difference back at Ladysmith's."

After what I'd seen at the Souk, I wasn't so sure. But I nodded.

"One thing everyone agreed to: cancel all picking till we figure out how to keep our people safe on the streets." Still talking, Rubio clambered out of the boat while we steadied it. He moved slowly, like it was hard work, like his overactive brain was consuming all his energy, energy that should be fighting his illness. "Tommy says he's had a half dozen of his folks not come home from night shift. Just vanish."

"Oof! That's bad."

"It's all bad," Breakers said.

A quick glance through the window arch showed Daniel speeding the kayak deftly among the jam-up of boats. This felt like pursuit, so I ran.

"Yeah, Empire's lost a few, too," Rubio went on. "Irv thinks it's packs of Stormies vacuuming up whoever they run into. Hey, wait up!"

Leaving Breakers to tie up the dinghy, I was halfway up the ladder. "Missed too much already!"

"I can fill you in!"

I kept on. In the mudroom, a mournful chorus floated in from the stairwell. I peered around the corner. My tier-mate Kari bent over one of the den's salvaged guitars, picking out a maudlin melody for singers crowding at her feet. No one sounded entirely sober. I refilled my water bottle at the potable tank, then drank as I went along. Didn't want Daniel catching up with me here.

The main hall was a tipsy mass of humanity, humming and content, with barely a lantern or candle burning. Denfolk were used to living in the dark.

I eased through, apologizing right and left. Most hardly noticed. Rousseau must be totally distracted, to let all this go on, and so late.

The mess hall, so bright and loud at mealtime, was dim and stuffy as a cavern. The painted walls slumped away into shadow around a central circle of light. Lanterns and hurricane lamps lit a neat square of tables in the middle of the room. Chairs and benches were scattered across the humid darkness, dense partisan groups separated by no-man's-lands masquerading as aisles. Mostly empty now, with a few seats pulled up close by diehard spectators or aides to the official delegates. The rank-and-file audience might have lost interest, but the tension at the tables left a stale taste in the air.

I nosed in quietly and slid into an empty chair a few rows behind the Unca Joe delegation. Set corner to corner, the tables formed equal sides—no head or foot, no one position of authority. Water jugs and cups clustered among the lanterns and crumb-dusted plates. Near-empty baskets tempted me with leftover fruit or scraps of bread. Nothing but a few bites of apple since breakfast. Hardly sustaining. But I restrained myself.

At the table in front of me, Rousseau sat between Jake and Spunk, his dark face somber. He'd pulled his chair back, like he was holding off from the argument, there to listen rather than hold forth. But his fingers played fitfully with the buttons on his leather vest.

Jake was hunched and frowning into the cross of his arms rested on the table. Spunk looked like he'd rather be anywhere else, though he'd spruced up for the event, in a clean tank top and sweats. He was even hatless, his wild hair dampened and combed into a dark red helmet. That, more than anything, said this gathering was unusual.

At the table opposite, a blond guy was droning on with facts and figures. But nobody was yawning, not even Spunk, who rarely sat still for lectures of any kind, even his own. I recognized the Empire dude from the first caucus, who'd had the face-off with Tall Tommy.

Rousseau's assistant Song-yi perched behind him on a bench, slim and erect, dressed in her usual self-effacing gray. She tapped away at her tablet, an ancient device she was allowed to recharge every night, no matter what the power situation was. As my eyes adjusted to the low light, I was amazed to see Peeto and Ellie Mae among the small contingent of Joes still hanging on. Not only there, but sitting next to each other, an odd couple if ever there was one: she leaning eagerly forward, hands folded on her knees like she was watching a tight game, Peeto slouched all over his chair like a rag doll, but both somehow in relation to the other, familiar as old friends. This wanted further exploration.

But not now. Rubio clattered into the chair beside me, still breathing hard. He echoed my stance as I leaned in to catch what the Empire guy was saying.

". . . if the situation is growing critical, as we have determined it is . . ."

Right off, Rube began a murmured commentary into my ear. "Okay . . . that's Will Dubowski, CEO of Empire State. Empire Will. Nice handle for a proto-fascist, doncha think? Which he's not, despite the tight-ass look and affectless delivery. Closer to libertarian, in fact. Next to him is his husband Arjay Gupta, called R period, J period. He's the VP. Supercilious but sharp as a tack."

No suits on the Empires this time. Trim casual instead, like they'd known what sort of day this would be but owned nothing that wasn't somewhat stylish. The men's clean-shaven faces looked well-schooled to conceal inner doubt or concerns. The woman was all nose and cheekbones, pale as the moon, with short waves of salt and pepper hair.

"How do they do it?" I whispered. "All that careful grooming, in a den? Why bother?"

Rubio smirked. "Keeping up appearances in case the media turn up? The fierce lady in power red is their CFO, Katja Ferrar. Red Katja, they call her."

"What are you, my tour guide? I've seen these people already."

"But do you know their facts?"

"Okay, no. What's a CFO? What's libertarian?"

"Haven't I taught you anything? Just listen."

"But check out their tech." Tablets as thin and faceless as gray paper glowed in front of each. The Nathan brothers weren't the only ones with access to the latest.

Rubio nodded. "No way their pickers found those just lying around. Song-yi must be curdled with envy."

So, no need to challenge Rousseau about the tech gap. Empire was doing it for me.

Rube pointed a finger past my nose. "Okay, to the right, with the all-over tats . . ."

"Tall Tommy. The Adonis of the Dens."

A pause in his patter. "Really? You think so?"

"What all the girls call him."

"Well, I don't get that, but anyway, full name, Tom Doyle. With his lady friend Mitsuko. Don't have ID on the other two yet."

His finger picked out the matched pair sitting back, one knee slopped over the other, scanning the room's dark corners.

"Muscle," I said.

"Obviously, but why? Everyone else brought their brain trust."

"Maybe Tommy thinks he's brain enough?"

"More like he thinks muscle is more important."

Tom Doyle, his height exaggerated by bone-sculpting leanness, looked no happier than he did the last time I'd seen him. Watching Empire Will sidelong, even the ink swirling across his face could not conceal his distrust.

At our table, Jake lifted his mug and drank it dry. "So, Will, how long are we saying?"

"Another three, maybe five months at most."

Rousseau gave a quick shudder of negation.

"You could be making that shit up," said Doyle.

In the hush that followed, sad music wafted in from the mudroom, faint as a breeze. The din in the main hall had eased, with an undertone of snoring.

"But I'm not." Empire Will took a clean square of fabric from his pocket and blotted his upper lip. "We've run the numbers, if you'd care to review them."

"Nervous," I noted to Rubio.

"Angry."

"Young for a den leader."

"Unless you're a Macy."

Maybe Will's posh manner was to compensate for looking so boyish.

He laid a finger on his tablet. I hoped he was going to hand it around—I wanted a closer look. Instead, his mate R.J. scooped up a sheaf of printout and offered it across the table like it was proof positive, of what I still didn't know, having come into the middle of the discussion.

"Empire can afford to give away printout?" I murmured to Rubio. We'd heard they were rich, as dens go, but this was a show-off gesture.

"Long as they can keep their copiers working."

A middle-aged woman wedged into the corner between R.J. and the Tommys passed the papers along.

Doyle waved them away. "Only number we need is how many guns we can muster." The woman tilted her braided head in mild reproof. "Can't eat guns, Tommy."

Doyle grinned at her, then curled his lip in satirical disdain.

She clucked softly and slid the papers back to the Empires.

"That's Zuleika, from Riverhome," Rubio murmured. "A Zen powerhouse."

Wasn't sure what that meant, but I could see she was beautiful: dark and elegant, a combo I admired but couldn't imagine achieving, especially the way she did, in a sleeveless tee and faded overalls, even with a few more pounds on her than she needed. Riverhome. Daniel's old den. I studied her more closely.

Across from Doyle, Maxine stretched out a hand, waggling her two un-bandaged fingers impatiently. "We'll look at those."

She wore her bruises proudly, and someone had trimmed her burnt-back hair till it looked almost chic. To either side of her sat the two Smiths who'd been working with Rube at Den Search Central.

The printout went back around the square, stopping in front of Irv. He brushed a fist across his damp forehead, then drew a lantern closer to study the figures.

"Irv's her numbers man," supplied Rubio.

In the corner between the Smiths and the Empire table, two ponytailed young women in pale shirts and jeans had tucked in stools. Their bodies tilted protectively toward each other, like kids eavesdropping on a family quarrel. Gimme Shelter girls, most likely. I hoped the baby who'd kept them away from the first meeting had made a happy entry.

I counted dens. "What happened to Macy's?"

"Never showed."

"Why not? Too busy mugging people?"

"Chickened out, I guess."

Irv cleared his throat, shifting pages. The room waited on his response. Or maybe it was just a good excuse to take a break. Water was poured. Spunk speared a chunk of bread with his long fingernail and gnawed at it with his few teeth. Maxine read over Irv's shoulder, now and then groaning in dismay. Out in the mudroom, Kari's singers were still at their drunken mourning.

I nudged Rubio. "Three to five months of what?"

"Food and potable water."

"In the dens?"

"On the island."

"Come on!"

"If their numbers are right." He shot me his darkest grin, like, isn't apocalypse exciting? "And unless we figure out how to increase production and purify more water."

"What about supply from the Mainland?"

"Didn't say." He frowned. "Jeez, could he mean worldwide?"

"He couldn't! The riots and camps—that's mostly along the coast. What about inland?"

Rubio shrugged. "One question everyone's asking is why the Adders, with no food or necessities production of their own, would think that burning out a den that produces well is a good strategy for long-term survival. It's killing the goose, y'know? They'd be better off encouraging production, especially if they intend to steal it."

"Maybe they don't think. Maybe they just do."

"Rousseau's convinced there's something bigger going on."

Daniel had implied the same.

As if I'd conjured him, air stirred behind me as Daniel brushed past. No one would have noticed the hand he laid on the back of my neck, just long enough for his thumb to sketch a circle around the top of my spine and make every nerve in my body stand on end. He took the chair next to Rubio.

"You're a nice mess." Rubio mimed brushing soot off his arm.

Daniel sighed. "Every time I tried to wash up today, something else happened."

"I've had that kind of day." Rubio swallowed a cough. "Did you lose Breakers?"

"Kayaking back to guard my boat. Said she's got no taste for politics."

Rube's chuckle roused a deeper cough. "Her politics live in the barrel of a gun."

"Rifle," I murmured.

"Good thing she's on our side, then." Daniel stretched into a listening slouch and folded his arms. Given how tired he was, I worried he'd nod off.

I leaned in to Rubio. "Tell him to go say what's happening at the Souk."

"Let the man catch his breath."

"No, really! He has to. Empire can't have figured that into their calculations."

When Daniel started yawning, I got up to pluck at Jake's elbow, pointing behind me.

"Ah. There you are." Jake smoothed the rat's nest he was making of his hair and waved Daniel toward the table. "Got to hear this, Will."

Daniel found his third or fourth wind and rose to scattered nods from around the gathering. Most seemed to know him already. He told his story of mayhem at the Souk, one hand braced on the table like he needed the support. He left me and Julian out of it. All that mattered, all they needed to know, was about burning food stalls and a potentially barterless economy. His description set Red Katja poking at her tablet. The staccato click of her long fingernails on the slick plastic made me glance down at my own, clipped to the quick and not entirely clean. She even wore nail polish.

"My tent is an ash heap," Daniel finished. "I was lucky to get out in one piece. Not sure about everyone else. Those who paid up should be fine, as long as they kept the fire from spreading to their own stuff."

Rousseau shook his head heavily. "You warned us. But that it should happen so soon!"

"The full slash-and-burn," muttered Jake.

"Waste in a time of scarcity," Zuleika mourned.

"Flamethrowers and assault rifles?" Tom Doyle seemed more stirred up about hardware than losing his main source of supplies. "These guys were Adders?"

"Hard to tell under all that armor," Daniel replied. "If they were, someone's put some training into them."

"What are you going to do?"

"Me?" When he wasn't goofing, Daniel could muster a certain authority. "Better to ask, what are *we* going to do?".

Doyle's face tightened. "That's what I meant, of course."

"Charismatic for sure," Rubio whispered, "but not the sharpest knife in the drawer. I'm guessing it's Mitsuko who guides that ship."

The Gimme Shelter ladies, one light, one dark, fixed Daniel with anxious stares. "Our cow lives on grain from the Souk," one said. "What will we do for the children's milk?"

Maxine leaned over to Irv. "How much would we have to increase production to manage without the Souk? How much can we?"

"Max . . ." The papers sagged in his hands. "We've nothing left to produce with."

Maxine dropped her forehead to her bandaged fists. "Oh god, of course we don't."

The older Smith patted her arm in awkward sympathy.

Red Katja stirred, clearing her throat. "It's not the end of the world yet. Most dens have kept this sort of data private, so our prediction is based on estimates. For a truer picture, we need accurate, updated stats from each of you: in-house production versus picking versus volumes of foodstuffs purchased at the Souk." She smoothed her blood-colored tunic, adjusted a matching scarf, then glanced from table to table like she was asking for the time of day instead of carefully guarded secrets. "Can we all agree to provide that?"

Rousseau said, "Whatever's necessary."

Between fisted hands, Maxine muttered, "You're welcome to our old data . . ."

"One question," Irv began. "The numbers certainly aren't good, but they never have been, and the dens have managed so far." He fanned the papers out in front of him. "Maybe I've missed something? Why so short a predicted time frame till crisis?"

Empire Will's glance to Red Katja said: at last, someone who speaks our language.

She nodded. "Exactly why we need real data. Different dens work differently, but some basics are true for all of us." She ticked off points, nails flashing red in the lamplight. "One: we're consuming more than we're producing, some dens more than others, but we averaged it out. Two: our relative comfort so far has been sustained by reserves, especially in dens such as yours, Mr. Rousseau. You saw what was coming and secured substantial stores of basic provisions you wouldn't be able to produce in house."

Tom Doyle stretched in his chair, yawning noisily. Mitsuko nudged him to attention, which made me sit up. I'd been drifting a bit, distracted by the chance to observe Daniel when he wasn't observing back.

"At Empire," Will noted, "we focused on tech and its essential supplies, and socked away extra cash to get us through."

"That was when cash was still worth something and we assumed order would be restored," Katja continued wryly. "At least to the extent it has been after past big blows. But here we are, four months after Abel—

downtown has been totally abandoned, uptown is more than ever a sanctuary for the rich, the climate is still on the downswing, with no global will for a fix. And we in the dens have pretty much run through our food reserves."

"Or had them stolen from us," Maxine added.

"With more of that expected," Katja agreed. "And with this disruption at the Souk . . ."

"Disruption?" Doyle growled. "A fucking all-out, if he's telling us true!"

"It'll happen a lot faster," Rousseau supplied grimly.

"Right." Will looked to Daniel. "Any chance the Souk problem will blow over?"

Daniel spread his hands. "If you want to play by the new rules . . ."

"And submit to the latest tyranny . . ." Zuleika murmured.

Daniel's nod to her was a fond greeting. To Katja, he said, "Hold on to that cash. The Merchants' Association is threatening a return to cash or credit only." The sooty rose of his T-shirt flared as he stepped into the light of a nearby lantern. His gaze circled the room. "But the real concern is, what does it mean? Why this sudden crackdown on indie vendors like me? Because the Association members are scared. They're the wholesalers, the black marketers, the major pipeline for goods from the Mainland—or anywhere. They supply Uptown, and it's made them rich. But word is, the flow is drying up."

Will's frown seemed out of place on his reserved face. "How do you mean, drying up?"

"As in, stopping."

"How can that be?" breathed Maxine. "They're . . . they've . . . got all that land."

"Word from who?" Doyle made it an accusation.

"Plenty of evidence at the Souk," Daniel replied evenly. "For a while now. Prices rising for staples such as flour, oil or sugar, any sort of meat or produce. Daily restocking running out sooner. Even the cheapest factory goods are more expensive and harder to come by."

"It's true about the rising cost," said Jake. "And people are buying in bulk, way past their needs, when they can afford to."

Daniel nodded. "Hoarding."

"You could call it replenishing reserves," put in R.J.

Doyle's glower deepened. "So, what's the why? Mainland's cutting us off on purpose?"

"There've always been cutbacks after a major storm, but now I think Uptown's grabbing a bigger share of what does come in," Daniel said. "The supply drones to the enclaves are less frequent. With so much cropland and factories either burning up or going under water, there's no returning to normal production levels, and why would they send us what they need themselves?"

Katja shoved back the loose sleeves of her tunic to peck at her tablet. "I'll see what our own buyers' records say."

I yawned, then couldn't stop yawning. Maybe some good news would keep me awake?

"Why are we just finding this out?" Maxine complained. "Why weren't we warned?"

Spunk, silent for unusually long, barked a laugh. "Who the fuck's gonna warn us?"

Jake said, "Uptowners don't care what happens to the dens, Max."

"Some of us do," said Daniel.

Uptowner. He was. Kept forgetting that. Did it matter?

Empire Will studied him, rating his credibility on some private graph. "Have the merchants made any effort to locate . . . y'know . . . alternate sources?"

"Pirates?" Daniel laughed, then took in Will's hopeful expression. "Sure, any port in a storm. I deal with a few myself. But you can't steal it if it isn't being shipped. So far, only small quantities to the richest customers who can pay in cash."

"Y'know, Will," snarked Doyle. "People like you."

"Ease up, Tom . . ." said Rousseau.

Rubio murmured to me, "Those two have been sniping at each other all day."

"What's their history?"

"Damned if I know. Jake might. He and Doyle used to hang. Irish mafia, y'know?"

I didn't, but I let it pass.

"Me, I sell books," Daniel went on wearily. "Most of which have been on the Island since publication and are never in huge demand till we figure out how to eat them. So, I'm out of the loop about shipments from Europe or the far east, electronics and the like. But they've got the same problems we do and all the same needs. Even if global productivity wasn't failing, between weather and fuel shortages, it's hard getting anything anywhere."

Doyle glanced at Mitsuko. Her thin, silk-hung shoulders gathered up around her jaw, then abruptly drooped.

"Pirates are . . . chancy, Will." Rousseau sounded like he'd never heard of pirates and wouldn't go near one if he had. "Maybe you had a different source in mind?"

Will copied Mitsuko's big-scale shrug with unconvincing diffidence. "One hears that there are such things."

"Oh, one does, does one?" Doyle parodied Will's high tenor perfectly. "You gonna share some of that with us or not?"

"Rumors, Mr. Doyle. Rumors. Nothing we've been able to substantiate."

"*Mister* Doyle . . ." echoed Doyle softly.

Maxine played with the water rings on the table in front of her. "But if there's anything to these rumors, they'd be worth chasing down."

"Who cares where it comes from?" retorted Doyle. "We all need to eat. If Mr. fucking Empire here would favor us with his private fucking info, we could go right to the source!"

Will leaned across his table so far, I thought he'd pitch over. "We have no private info!"

"Gentlemen! Please." Rousseau held up a staying hand. "Jake, we need to know the full situation at the Souk. First thing tomorrow. But make sure to take backup."

Spunk waved a tired hand. "I'll go."

"And take some of ours," said Maxine.

Rousseau's intervention sent a breath of restraint around the tables. Tom Doyle slumped back in his chair, smiling at Mitsuko like he'd made his point. Will Dubowski sat to consult his tablet. Something had been agreed to, an action set in motion, minor as it was. But something was also being avoided.

The gloomy mudroom chorus had resolved itself. Gone to bed or passed out where they were. Instead, in Main, a rustling like leaves. Folks getting ready to head home.

"But, my friends . . ." Zuleika stirred in her wedge between the tables. I wanted to touch the shining, intricate braiding of her hair. "We must focus our energies on improving our own means of production! Clearly, we can no longer rely on the Mainland. For anything."

And there it was. The elephant in the room. The conclusion no one wanted to face. What were the dens without the Mainland? It had been central to all visions of our future. Weren't we all headed over there, as soon as possible? Mutters floated up from behind the tables. Not all the remaining spectators had fallen asleep.

Doyle roused from his slump. "First we need to focus on our means of defense!"

"Or offense," Maxine said.

"Yes!" Doyle was eager to claim an ally. "What I've been saying! We got to arm up! Be ready for 'em next time! If BlackAdder can access heavy weaponry and powerboats, so can we. Where's it all coming from?" He jerked a thumb at Empire Will. "I'm betting Biz Guy can tell us! You think all their corporate connections washed away with the Wave?"

"I don't think this is . . ." Rousseau began.

Maxine narrowed her eyes at Will. "Is he right? What do you know?"

"Empire State has no contacts with arms dealers!" Will's face was so hard-set at neutral, even I had to wonder if he was lying.

"But could you find out?" Maxine pursued.

"I . . . what is . . . ?" He stared at something past her shoulder.

I stood to see what it was.

Rubio rose beside me. "Oh my god . . ."

A murmur, like a collective groan, pressed into the Mess, agitated den-folk in a protective arc around a group of filthy, sodden children, maybe twenty of them. They clung close, the oldest carrying the smallest, empty-eyed and terrified. Even the dim light couldn't hide the dried blood, the livid bruises, the scabbed-over wounds, the small limbs at wrong angles.

"What . . ." Rousseau echoed hoarsely, ". . . is this?"

The senior scout, Hawkeye, pushed forward. "It's Macys, boss."

For a moment, no one spoke.

"What happened?" Rousseau managed finally.

"Unknown." The scout rubbed her forehead. "Kids aren't talking. Just showed up on the walkway. I sent a recon party crosstown to their den while we wrangled this bunch back here. They'll move faster on their own."

"BlackAdder," Maxine said.

"Fuck," said Doyle. "What'd I tell you?"

Rousseau turned aside like it hurt just looking at them. "No one's talking? Not a one?"

"Traumatized." Hawk's glance roamed, like she couldn't face them either. "We were out on perimeter when we caught 'em trying to steal our rations. Once we offered, they ran at it. Don't think they've eaten in a while."

A bustle outside the Mess.

"Hawk?" A second scout shoved his way in, breathless.

"Here!" She waved him over. "What'd you find out?"

"Adders again!" the scout panted.

Maxine stepped forward. "Burned them out?"

"If only!" Scouts got a hard skin from all they saw on the streets, but this one was young, not hiding his distress. "They're moving in! Taking over the den!"

"The whole building?" Rousseau asked.

I'd seen the Macy den. It took up an entire city block. The Macys rattled around in it.

"There are a lot of them. Bringing their stuff by the boatload from downtown. Plenty sentries, major guns, so I couldn't get close to see what else they're up to. I left a watch."

"What about the other Macys? This isn't all of them."

The scout winced. "Hard to say. Can't imagine it's good, though."

"No. It won't be." Rousseau wagged his head slowly. "Any guess when?"

"Couple days ago, seeing how moved in the Adders are."

Daniel spoke up. "I heard one of those Chinatown high-rises collapsed during Joseph. Others looking chancy. Saltwater corroding the steel faster than expected."

"Even the Adders are looking for a better den," Rubio muttered. "By taking somebody else's, wouldn't you know."

"Did I do right, bringin' 'em?" Hawk asked.

"Totally!" Rousseau exclaimed.

"What do we do with them?" Jake was stunned as helpless as the rest of us.

"Feed them!" Rousseau boomed, his arms waving in all directions. "In the name of Christ, offer them comfort and sustenance!"

Jake eyed him warily. "Right away, boss!"

Getting hold of himself, Rousseau turned to Song-yi. "Tell the medics. And rouse the kitchen staff."

"You got it." Jake shouted for volunteers as he shoved through the crowd around the open doors. On his way, he grabbed Peeto by the scruff. "Time to earn your keep, boyo."

Then everyone was in motion. The two women from Gimme Shelter hurried toward the ragged, wide-eyed kids. Daniel and Zuleika grabbed pitchers of water from the conference tables and followed. When the kids shrank in terror, they set the pitchers on the floor and backed off. Jake got a taskforce working to roll up the metal blinds on the kitchen hatches, to root around in the food bins and drag out whatever could be eaten raw. He sent Peeto upstairs to rouse the morning-duty cooks from their bunks.

"We could all use a bite," remarked Rubio, moving off to help.

All strength had drained out of me. Forget my own hunger, or all the bad news weighing me down. Nothing compared to the Macys'. But I did know how they felt. Those blank-faced little girls . . . right after Abel, that was me.

Food appeared on the counter. The Gimme girls bundled up little care packages and set them beside the water jugs, soothing with soft words and gestures. Some of the kids' eyes began to focus.

"Give them some space," Zuleika said. "They need to know they're safe."

Safe? How could any of us feel safe now? The Adders were right across town!

"Of course." Rousseau cleared the room of idle onlookers. "Over there against the wall, lay in blankets, pillows, whatever can be spared."

Go wake Rivera, I told myself. She'll know what to do. But still I couldn't move.

Once cushions and blankets were piled at the far end of the room, the Gimme Shelter girls urged the kids to sit or lie down, got a few of them drinking water, and the worst injuries sorted to the medics. Daniel and Zuleika brought bowls of fruit and day-old rolls.

Rousseau herded the other den leaders away from the kids. Spunk, with his odd talent for making anyone his student, enlisted the Tommy muscle to move the conference tables. They regrouped at the far end, talking in low, angry tones.

"The party's over," Rousseau muttered, to no one in particular.

So many ways he could've meant that.

Suspended between, I watched Daniel settle cross-legged beside a skinny, dreadlocked kid, no more than six or seven. Daniel began some quiet story, while the boy stared into space. As if she'd heard my thought, Rivera came in with a gaggle of Smith kids, the same ones she'd comforted not so long ago. She scattered them among the Macys, urging them to share what they'd been through. Her competence shamed me but released my paralysis. But I was no use here. Those poor kids had enough good intentions leaning on them already. I drifted away toward the tables.

"Escalating the conflict is not the answer!" Rousseau was insisting as I found a long bench to drag up behind them. "Whatever we find, they'll find bigger."

"I'm thinking a direct connection to the Mainland military," Red Katja mused.

Will sounded less sure of himself now. "Why would the Mainland be arming an Island den? They've got enough problems on their own turf."

"What the fuck does it matter?" Doyle's hands fisted on the tabletop. "We need to take the fight to their doorstep!"

"How're you going to do that if you don't know who they are?" R.J. said.

"We could just . . ." Doyle's girl Mitsuko was speaking, so softly and unexpectedly that everyone shut up to listen. ". . . pick up a few Adders and ask them."

Doyle grinned, while Rousseau stared down at clasped hands and chewed his lip.

"Nah," snorted Spunk. "You woan get nuttin' outa dem. Betcha dey doan even know."

"Might be satisfying to try," said Doyle.

"Probably Bright brings the stuff in," Maxine said.

"Then we ask *him*!" Doyle's voice sharpened. "Say we'll deal, then take him for a little boat ride."

"We could," agreed Jake. "But would anyone who values their profit tell the middleman about the route back to the secret source? He's got some neutral pickup point."

"Then we find that out! You rather sit about moaning while they do us in den by den?"

"No one's suggesting that," snapped Will.

"What are you suggesting, then?" Doyle did his uncanny mimic again. I wondered if he'd been an actor before, like Jake. Maybe why they'd been friends?

Will glanced at R.J. sidelong, his restraint wearing thin. "We're suggesting a more businesslike, long-term solution. One that won't leave half of us slaughtered in our beds."

"Won't happen if we hit 'em hard enough! And soon!"

"Who? Who?" yelled Will. "Who are you going to hit? And where?"

"Whoever! Wherever!" Doyle rose, bracing his arms on the table. His flanking muscle boys slammed their feet to the floor and sat erect. "You can hide behind your fucking numbers all you want! Won't save you when the Adders come knocking!"

"Enough, Tom." Rousseau scraped his chair back. "Not while the children . . ."

"Long-term strategy, my ass!" Doyle's long arms windmilled in the lamplight. He scooped up the papers Empire had offered and tore them to shreds. "More like fucking cowardice!"

Will snatched at the bits. "It's morons like you bringing the world down on top of us!"

Then he was up, too, and the Tommy muscle was standing, and Doyle had flung back his chair so it bounced and clattered across the painted concrete. Next, we were all out of our seats, unsure whether to run or pitch in. So fast no one saw it happen, Spunk's hunting knife glittered at the throat of one Tommy lad while the other gaped and feinted. R.J. ducked between Doyle and Empire Will, arms out stiff like a sports referee.

"You have to stop! Please, stop this now!"

The voices were high and anguished. Everyone stilled. The Gimme Shelter girls had finally taken in what had happened to the Macys.

"We need to leave! Our den . . . !"

"Oh no!" Maxine gasped.

Rousseau said, "With us all here, they're totally unprotected!"

Women and babies. Perfect Adder targets.

"All our dens!" Doyle dropped his battle stance. Will backed away. Spunk let his Tommy go, clapped him on the shoulder, and sheathed his knife. I was prouder of denfolk than I'd been a mere moment before.

Mitsuko gripped Doyle's arm. "C'mon. We'll take them."

Doyle signaled his escort. "Get the boat."

"Take a squad of mine with you," Maxine offered.

Will had a phone out and was talking into it. "Our patrols will circle around your way," he told the girls.

"I'll head out, too," Zuleika told Rousseau. "Your folks have the kids in hand."

"Watch yourself going crosstown," he advised.

"Always." She stretched up to kiss his cheek. "Thanks for all you do."

Mitsuko hurried off with the girls. Doyle and Maxine followed, trading vengeance scenarios. Irv and the older Smith watched her go, sharing an uneasy frown.

Deflated, I went back to my bench and lay flat on my back. Time for a retreat to my bunk. I needed sleep like a drug. But I was too wired, sure that if I left the room, some new disaster would blow up. The Adders would be upon us. Or Bright. And no one had even mentioned the newly unified Storm Worshippers. The dens were in danger for our lives, and still no one could agree. Or would. For the first time in a while, I tasted real despair. Had the whole caucus been for nothing?

The Empires were last at the table, packing up.

Rousseau touched Will's sleeve. "Please. Stay a moment? Just till we know better what's happened."

"We're concerned about . . ." R.J. gestured vaguely uptown.

"Of course. But we still need a plan." He spread his palms. "Just . . . something."

Will looked to Katja.

"We do," she conceded. "At least a short-term one."

"Yes." Rousseau's bunched shoulders relaxed a fraction. "So that we live long enough to make good on the long-term one. We've got away with our ad-hoc system for so long because no one wanted downtown but us. But now . . ."

"Now," agreed Will, "the shit is really hitting the fan."

"They may be doing this just to divide the dens. Individually, we're no threat. Together, we might have a chance."

"We still don't know who 'they' is," said R.J.

"Or why they see the dens as a problem."

Irv collected Rubio from somewhere and sidled over. "Can we say something?"

Rousseau seemed ready to consider any input. "Please do."

Irv glanced at Rubio, then cleared his throat. "This won't be the answer you've been aiming at, but . . . it might be a solution."

TWENTY-SIX

"**A** solution to what?" Rousseau frowned. He hadn't expected serious input.

Cowed, Irv sucked in his cheeks. "Everything?"

R.J. chuckled. "Bring it on, dude."

Rousseau looked embarrassed. "Now's not the time for . . ."

"No, really. If you look at the numbers . . ." Irv was a diffident guy. Under his neat beard, his cheeks flushed, but figures were his territory. "Your scout said there were lots of Adders, but how many? We need to know."

"Our man on recon should give us a closer count."

"Whatever, it's too many," said Will, moving toward the door.

Irv plowed on. "Maybe not. You'll notice that, except for Gimme Shelter, the dens the Adders have left alone are the biggest ones. Not necessarily the best armed."

Rousseau gave him a closer look. "You're saying, what? Safety in numbers?"

Irv nodded. "At Ladysmith's, we were armed to the teeth. Small arms mostly, but lethal in a close fight. Thing is, there were only thirty-four of us. Not enough to fight off a surprise attack from more guys with bigger weapons. So now we're only twenty-six."

"But counting you, Unca Joe's over a hundred."

"A hundred and twelve." Irv glanced toward the Empires. "And you're what, well over ninety?"

"One hundred eighteen." Will turned back, his interest caught. "We've picked up a few lately, independents who can't hack it solo anymore, or move-ons from other dens. Even a few uptowners who aren't comfy with the power politics being played up there."

Irv bobbed his head again, a nervous tic. "And Tall Tommy's at sixty-five or seventy?"

"Yes, but they're all so intimidating, it's like twice that." Will offered a rueful grin, the first I'd seen on him. I saw kindness behind his corporate sleek. "What about Riverhome?"

Red Katja fired up her tablet, like any question was worth an answer. "Various, since they're so transient, but currently, seventy-three."

"So . . ." Irv heaved in a long breath. "If we all got together . . ."

"Like we just tried to do?" Rousseau said wearily. "And failed."

"If we did . . ." Rubio nosed into the circle. "They'd think twice before they took us on."

Rousseau rubbed his eyes. "Where would we put everybody?"

Irv and Rubio traded a glance.

"It was your find," Rubio prodded.

Irv's flush deepened. "Okay. Here it is. We think we've found the place to do it."

"Do what?"

"Live together. One den home."

"All of us in the same den?" Will shook his head, like he'd misheard. "All the time?"

Rousseau's chin tucked uneasily. "Who thinks that's a good idea?"

"We'd kill each other before sunrise," R.J. muttered.

"Wait. Think it out," Rubio urged. "Give it a chance. After all, it's worked out here, taking in Ladysmith's."

"But we're each looking for a new den of our own," said Rousseau. "Aren't we?"

"That was before Macy's. Now we really need the strength of numbers. But we're already jam-packed, and if we keep taking in survivors . . ."

"Gimme Shelter won't last long on their own," Irv said. "They're sitting ducks and sure to be next." He glanced down the room at the gathering of children and caretakers, noise and motion quieting as the kids found courage to drink, eat, lie down, even to sleep. "And they have a cow! We could share our resources and build on them, instead of keeping everything secret."

"Easy for you to say," said R.J. "Since you have nothing left to share."

I lifted my head from my bench. Hadn't paid the third Empire much mind till I heard that edge in his voice. He was slight and brisk, all business, wasting little on diplomacy.

Irv drew back, stung, but Rubio dug his feet in. "They have their weapons. Don't reject an idea just because it isn't yours."

Glancing down the room, I saw Daniel had switched to listening mode.

Now the terrorized boy couldn't stop talking. I wanted to hear his story, but getting up now would call attention to myself, and I might be asked to leave. I really didn't belong in this company.

Rousseau turned away, then back again, stood a moment in indecision, then dropped into a chair beside the tables. "Okay. Let's give this some thought."

To my surprise, Will settled opposite him, leaning forward on his elbows. "Really? You think it could work? We'd need a lot of space."

"No way," growled R.J. "I'm not shacking up with the likes of Doyle, having to prove my manhood every five minutes!"

"That's why it'll work!" Rubio drew up a chair, sketching curves and ovals in the air above the table. "The place we've got in mind is big enough for each den to run its own sector. Before, we'd rejected it as too big for two dens to handle, but . . ."

"One and a half," muttered Irv.

"But with all of us . . ."

"You're thinking a high-rise?" Red Katja let the idea out for a test run. "Hate those. Shoddy construction, fire traps. Too many stairs. Our old university building is bad enough."

"So right," Rubio agreed. "But what would you say to ramps?"

Empire State's den home was not the building of that name, but a brick-and-glass pile with a central atrium in the East 20s. Not exactly a high-rise, but close enough.

"Not another dead hospital," said Will. Empire had one next door. "Useful for left-behind stuff, but ours gives me the creeps."

"Nope." Rubio looked smug. "This one's solid built, shaped like a fortress, no close neighbors, surrounded by open water. No one could sneak up on you. We'd been pushing too hard for closed-in spaces, for security's sake. But with still-rising temps, you really need a breeze running through the den, to keep from growing mold or dying from heat stress."

It was like playing My Fantasy Den Home. Except now we were playing it for real.

Irv chimed in. "I did the sea rise calculation against the available building stats, and we think there should be a defendable water-level entrance for boats, and a large protected harbor inside the walls."

That won them some real interest.

"You think?" Katja asked. "You mean you haven't been there yet?"

Rubio said, "Not since the Zones A and B evacuation."

Will's laugh died into a puff of breath. "You actually have a serious candidate?"

"You thought we didn't?"

"I thought . . . y'know, mere speculation?"

"Good solid research."

"Out with it," said R.J. "No time for guessing games."

Another conspirators' glance. Irv shrugged and studied his feet.

Rubio folded his arms. "Okay, our number one choice is . . . Yankee Stadium."

Blank looks were traded around the table. A choked laugh or two.

"It's a joke, right?" said Will.

"It's not even on the island," added Rousseau.

R.J.'s brows folded to a thin, straight line. "A ballpark? Like, outdoors? That's insane!"

"Were you ever there?" Rubio was on a roll now, his eyes lit.

"No. I don't . . . didn't . . . do sports."

"Then you don't know how much support space a big open-air stadium requires. First of all, it's friggin' huge. Used to seat fifty thousand. Sure, a lot of it—the locker rooms, gyms, players' lounges, all that ground-level sort of thing—will be under water. But there's practically a whole office building and a couple of malls' worth of service and public spaces scattered through-out the upper complex: cafés and restaurants and bars, shops and restrooms. Miles of fiberoptic cable, which we could turn into a local com system. All those private boxes with walls of window facing the field . . . that is, the harbor, with at least twenty feet of draft, maybe more. Plus, all that tiered seating and surrounding roof space, open to the sun and air, a perfect place for terrace gardening." Winded at last, Rubio paused for breath and a lengthy cough.

"Impressive," said Katja. She seemed on the verge of a giggle.

Rousseau pressed both palms to his temples. "This has to be the most cockamamie idea I've ever heard!"

"I know!" Rube agreed giddily. "Thing is, it might actually work."

"Yankee fucking Stadium?" breathed Will. "Isn't that one of the old ones?"

"Yeah. 2009. But it's limestone and granite. Built to last."

"I was there once." Katja allowed a tinge of nostalgia to soften her face. "Is it empty?"

"Well, that we don't know," admitted Irv. "But the East and Harlem Rivers have flooded deeply into the South Bronx, so the stadium is basically in the middle of a bay . . . another huge advantage. And it's close to the Mainland, but not too close."

"An island fortress," said Will.

"There's no word of a community up there," Rube added. "But to know for sure, we need to reconnoiter."

"This is seriously radical." R.J. eyed his two denmates like they needed hauling back from the edge. "We'd have to bring the idea to our board."

"Needs a deep going-over," agreed Rousseau. "Just among ourselves."

But Will clapped his hands and let wonder carry him. "Yankee fucking Stadium!"

Prone on my bench, I didn't care that the phrase 'Yankee Stadium' brought nothing to mind. Rube would fill me in. Whatever it was, it sounded perfect. I hoped no one had claimed it already. If it was really what we needed, we'd have to take it by force. What would Rousseau say to that?

Katja yawned hugely, then slapped a hand to her mouth, shamed to be caught at it.

"We need to get home. Make sure it's still there." Will reached to shake Rousseau's hand. "I say the idea's worth a follow-up. Sooner rather than later, yes?"

"Sooner it is." Rousseau offered one of the smiles he gave in place of praise. "Thanks for carrying so much of the load today." He reached a hand to R.J., the other toward Katja. "I'll be in touch as soon as we have new info. Your place, next time?"

"Before you go . . . !" Daniel called from behind, striding up fast. "You need to hear this."

I struggled up, set my feet on the floor.

"More bad news?" Katja asked him.

"The worst."

I don't think I'd ever seen a face so transformed by outrage. It tightened the skin around his eyes, sharpening his cheekbones. Like he'd taken in all the terror and anguish his Macy kid had poured out and transformed it into hard, bright purpose.

Spunk loomed out of the shadows and slid onto the other end of my bench. "Alerted da watch," he told Rousseau.

"Good man."

Daniel leaned back against the table, letting the others gather around. "My kid is good. Even while he was being beaten and abused, he kept his eyes open. He says the Adders are doing the expected to all the girls and the prettier boys, even the youngest ones, but keeping the strongest kids for slave labor. The weak, the small, or the ones they're done with, they're selling off to the Storm Worshippers!"

"Selling?"

"Seems they've some kind of . . . agreement."

"But these are children!" Rousseau blurted. "Children!"

"And mostly clueless," added Daniel. "Not a lot of organization. Perfect targets."

"Dey'll be da lucky ones," muttered Spunk.

Will nodded. "The Stormies'll take them in to swell their numbers. BlackAdder probably bought into the rumors of human sacrifice."

Rousseau looked up. "Definitely not true?"

"Threats and talk, but our embed's never actually seen it. You don't gain world dominion by burning up your congregation, after all. This new leader is counting souls."

This is what comes of the dens not talking more, I thought. We've each been living in our own ill-informed bubble.

"They're not all clueless," Daniel went on. "The smart ones ran for it when the attack started. Some, Hawk picked up. Others hid, may still be hiding, in that big building, trapped in their own den. The few old enough to fight back were killed. And now . . ." He paused, as if this was the part that put him close to the edge. "The Adders are partying."

Spunk growled deep in his throat.

"A few more slipped away once they got too drunk on rape and Macys' raw brew to notice. My kid? Says he's seven years old. Stole his jailor's hunting knife and slit his throat, then cut a bunch of his denmates free and took off."

For a long moment, we all stared at the floor. Better than staring at each other and seeing the horror all over again in each other's eyes.

Rousseau, just about swaying on his feet, finally broke the silence. "We need to do a sweep of the area, pick up any stragglers. Will, any chance of that?"

"I'll send a search party, but I'm not ordering anyone inside the building. Not with those maniacs."

R.J. said, "For once, Doyle was right. That den needs taking out."

"Yah," said Spunk. "But we gotta wait on dat. Need time ta musta a defense. Go in dere short, dey'll trow everyting dey got atcha. Cut yer strength in half fer nuttin'."

"Alone might be the best way to do it," Daniel said quietly.

"Suicide mission," R.J. scoffed.

Daniel shrugged. "Probably."

"If Doyle gets wind of this," said Will. "He'll be in there in a heartbeat."

"Let him," said R.J. "One less thing to worry about."

"No, no, no! He'll start a war we can't win, and he won't be there to help us!" Rousseau walked away, pacing in and out of the shadows. "Spunk's right. We need time to plan. Round up the stragglers, Will, but keep it quiet. For now."

"As best we can."

"Let me bring this kid," Daniel said. "He can help call in his denmates."

"Good. And . . ." Rousseau turned back. "We need a bolt hole for when they come after us. Which they will." He shook his head ruefully. "Can't believe I'm saying this, but I'll send an exploratory party upriver tomorrow. See who's playing at Yankee Stadium."

"I'll go," said Rubio.

I stirred in protest. "You shouldn't! You're not . . ."

"I'm going."

I looked to Irv. "He's not well enough. Can't you see . . . ?"

Irv shrugged. "And me."

Spunk nudged me. "Let da man do his t'ing."

Idiots. Macho idiots! But I was fading fast. My clock had tripped toward twenty-four hours without sleep. I'd catch Rube in the morning, talk sense into him then. I lay back on my bench. Hard, narrow, but better than remaining upright.

Just rest a bit, I told myself.

TWENTY-SEVEN

I woke to the scrape of furniture. I was stretched flat out on the bench in near darkness. A few lanterns guttered on the disordered square of tables at one end of the Mess. Vague shapes shuffled through the shadows, cleaning up food debris, resetting tables and chairs for breakfast, rousing others like me who'd fallen asleep where they'd sat or lain down. Gray daylight seeped through the open double doors. I could hear rain pattering on the main hall's central skylight.

I stirred, swung my feet stiffly to the floor, and shook my head like a dog. I could say that because I remembered a dog now, Lizzy's dog Magus. No, *my* dog—I was still schitzy about this past I'd just inherited. My dog, then. A bright-eyed, curly-haired mutt who loved the boat and swam like a seal. What had become of him? I felt loss, but no specifics. Perhaps I wasn't ready to face that memory yet.

"Magus," I whispered, the joy of remembering undercut by a piercing longing.

"What's that?" Daniel shifted his feet off the chair in front of him and sat up. I must have looked startled, even scared. "It's just me. The Book Dude, remember? We used to be friends?"

Having your brain straddle two time periods can be very confusing. Wary of falling into the gap between, I shook my head again.

"No? Really? Not at all? Could've fooled me."

"Don't! Please!" I pressed my palms to my eyes. "I can't think straight!"

"Sorry." He nudged my foot with his own. "Let's start over. Who's Magus?"

I blinked at him. The hard-edged glow of rage from the night before had faded to bleary concern. If possible, he looked dirtier and more banged up than before, but a certain weary satisfaction rounded his shoulders. "Oh! The Macys! How did . . . ?"

"We scooped up a bunch more from here and there, with Jandi's help."

"Jandi?"

"My Macy kid. But he can name a dozen more, likely still inside."

"Can anything be done?"

"Working on it. Right now, a mob of Stormies have the building surrounded with a flotilla of rough-built rafts. For several hours. And they're
singing."

"What?" Maybe I was still dreaming?

"Well, chanting, really. Like they're blessing the place. Or exorcising it."

"Bizarro."

"Truly. They are the wacko wildcard in this mix. Unpredictable as the
weather they worship. Maybe that's the point."

I shifted on my bench, longing for a more comfortable seat. "You look
wrecked."

"Who isn't?"

He stood, stretched painfully, then dragged his chair closer until he was
right opposite me, slouching into it until our knees almost touched. "So
who's Magus?"

And I thought I'd steered him off track. Ha. I stared at my feet a long
while. How much of the past now crowding my head was I ready to share,
with him or anyone? "A dog. That I remembered."

"Back at the hide?"

"Just now."

And that was interesting. New memories were slipping quietly into my
mind without much fanfare. No need for a full-scale memory quake.

"What else did you remember?"

I wet my sleep-parched lips, feeling a pressure from within: *talk to him.*
Like she wanted him to know, even as I hesitated. "My name."

He sat upright, blunt fingers pinning his knees. "Really? That's
fantastic!"

I nodded faintly. Not new news to me. The on-going dilemma was
whether I was going to carry Lizzy around like a stowaway or find a way to
be Lizzy again without losing Glimmer.

"Will you . . . tell me?"

I'd always presumed it would be Rubio or Jenn, maybe Spunk, or even
Rousseau who I'd share this news with when my life finally came back to
me. Daniel was . . . unexpected. But telling it, saying it aloud, might help
me make my peace with it, with her . . . with me.

"It's . . ." I cleared my throat to make it come easier. "It's Lizzy."

"Lizzy."

He made it sound like a revelation, but also a caress, like he was savoring the sound of it, tasting it, so possessively intimate with it that my sleep-dazed instinct was to shove him away immediately.

"That's not all I remembered."

He leaned forward, missing the warning. "Tell me."

So I told him what else, in gruesome detail—about Abel and the tiled room and the boy gang who looked like Julian. All of it, up to Rousseau pulling me out of the wreckage, mute and incapable. I let it tumble out, spill into the dim room like a torrent of wet garbage.

And thought, that should do it. He'll be disgusted. He'll go away and leave me in peace.

But this was Daniel, so of course, he listened. He said nothing, letting me run on like a crazy woman until I had no ugly memories left to reveal till the next ones came back to me. He stayed still and silent while I shuddered and sobbed and brushed away tears of terror and self-loathing.

Only when I was calm again did he stretch his legs and bury his hands deep in the pockets of his jeans. "That's a bad story, all right."

I waited for him to say how sorry he was, how lucky I was to have survived, how he understood. Or some other lame cliché.

Instead, he took a long breath. "Jake told me you had issues."

I winced. "You talk to Jake about me?"

"Just to get a few clues. Is that okay?"

"Not really."

"You don't talk about yourself much, you know. About how you . . . feel. At first, I thought there must be someone else, but Jake said he'd know if there was. He warned me not to press too hard. But looks like I went ahead and did it anyway. Too-eager Dan." He shifted uneasily. "I . . . um . . . I've been alone for a while and I'm ready to change that. But you . . . you're really not . . . are you?"

Unbelievable! I throw my worst at him and he only steps closer! "I don't know what I am! I'm two people in one skin! I'm . . . a mess! Why would you even look at me?"

His smile was quizzical. "Why would I not?"

I shook my head. But a faint glow of hope bloomed. He was so patient, so persistent. I could almost imagine feeling safe with this man. "I need . . . time."

He looked down. "I am pushing too hard, then. It's all that's going on now. I'm ready to restart my life now."

"What, like we might all get Addered before I learn how to be normal about things?" I'd lost control of my tongue. I needed sleep. In an actual bed. Alone.

But his glance darkened far more than one irritable remark deserved. He stretched in his chair, then rose. "Something like that."

He rested a hand on my head, unthreatening but still nudging the boundary. "To be continued." He turned away. Nearly at the door, he muttered, "*Addered*. Didn't know that was a verb."

TWENTY-EIGHT

S omeone was pounding on my cabin door. Or maybe the hull. It was loud, like right by my ear. The rhythm was broken, irregular, like the person was exhausted or desperate. Hoped it wasn't anyone I knew. But then, no one I knew would be wandering around the marina at this hour. No way was I getting up to check.

Where was Magus? He should've been barking up a storm. Then I remembered. Oh, Magus. My dear, sweet boy. The loss was still so fresh.

The pounding stopped, started up again. I shrank into my berth, glad I'd locked the hatch, locked the cabin door, even locked the single port above my berth, and drawn the blackout curtain. The narrow space was hot, airless, and heavy with darkness. I felt for my big police flashlight. I could blind or brain him if he managed to break in.

Then I shuddered and was awake. Not Lizzy in her berth on *Haiku*, but Glim in my bunk at Unca Joe. When I got my bearings, I swung my legs over the edge and sat very still, woozy with time-slip and disassociation. First time dreaming my past. Way more vivid than simple remembering. I'd *been* there.

Haiku. Our fifty-foot catamaran/house boat. Now I could draw a picture of it, a deck plan, a rigging layout. If I'd had paper and pencil, I'd have done it right then, to keep these new memories from slipping away, as dreams so often do.

But the pounding went on, so that was actual, a bridge between dream and reality. And now, raw tearing noises, sudden choruses of shouts, echoing thumps that made the building vibrate. I threw on some sweats and dropped down the tier to see what was up.

I'd slept later than I meant to, but even so, the place was weirdly deserted. Even during fire drills, some laggard or three were always left behind, to be rousted out by the monitors and scolded about how they'd just been asphyxiated or burned to a crisp. Only another major crisis would turn every last soul out of bed.

More murder and mayhem? I hurried to the balcony to peer down into Main.

But the frenzy was an orderly one: what looked like every able-bodied Smith and Joe, carrying loads of materials in from outside—water-sodden wood beams, weathered planking, rusted steel—filling the hall with head-high stacks, only narrow aisles between. Aloft on the tellers' desk like a captain on the poop deck, Rousseau directed traffic, pointing each load to a particular location. A group of lads milled at his feet, calling up to him. Either he was ignoring them, or he couldn't hear with all the racket, but they didn't look happy about it.

Den Search Central's big table had been shoved up against the wall next to the mess hall doors, the only clear space left. Rubio and Irv huddled over some of the nautical charts I'd brought back from the marooned sloop. I flew down the stairs, ducking and weaving to keep from being mowed down by incoming construction materials.

Deep in discussion, Rubio and Irv ignored the chaos flowing around them like whitewater. Two fact geeks stoking each other's excitement.

I had to shout to get their attention. "What's going on?"

"East River." Rubio lifted a chart to squint at it closely. "Oh, Glim. Glad you're here. Do you know what this means?" He laid the chart down and poked at an upper corner.

"I asked, what's all this?" I waved at the piles as a fat coil of rope skimmed past my ear on a beefy shoulder. Somewhere, an argument was brewing, loud enough to be heard.

Irv's sparse beard looked newly trimmed. "It's the walkway. Rousseau's ordered it taken down as a security measure. Now the only entrance will be that shaft up from the boat dock. Easier to defend."

"C'mon!" Rubio tapped the chart. "You're the boat girl. Give us some help here."

"Knowing how to row doesn't mean I can read charts."

"You knew what they were. C'mon, take a look!" His tapping got insistent. He looked feverish, his eyes red-rimmed from the strain of pretending he was fine. "Like, what do these wavy lines mean?"

I bent over the chart, to keep him from breaking a finger. To my surprise, I did know what the symbols meant. "Umm . . . tidal rip, or some other dangerous current thing."

"NO!" Rousseau's bellow rang across the hall. "And I won't hear another word about it!"

We fell silent, along with most everybody in the room. When life resumed, so did the argument, but at a lower pitch.

"What's with the boss?" I murmured.

Rubio's mouth twisted. "Some of the lads have a hard-on to avenge the Macys attack. They want to go in all barrels blazing."

"So does Maxine," noted Irv.

The Macys. Again, I'd totally forgotten. "How are they doing?"

"Winning converts. Rousseau sounds shakier every moment."

"I meant the kids." The mess hall doors were closed, probably to block the noise.

Rubio shrugged. "Rivera took 'em in hand after the other dens left. What's this little number in a circle?"

No getting past this obsession. "Refers to an adjoining chart. Which you might not have."

He leafed through the stack of charts. "This might be it."

"You're planning a route to that sports place?"

"Tito's shifting the outboard to the rubber floaty thing," Rubio said. He and Irv pumped fists at each other like boys.

"The Zodiac." Irv gave me an approving smile. "Rube told me your story. It's cool you knew all this stuff and now you're getting it back again."

"Slowly, yeah. It's coming." And you don't know the half of it. I meant to fill Rube in about my memory quake, but if I tried now, he'd barely pay attention and I'd be devastated. "Can I go with you?"

Rubio gathered up charts and maps, sliding them into a plastic hold-all along with a tattered sketch pad and a bundle of pencils. "No room. Not your area of expertise."

"What isn't?"

"Baseball."

"Maybe I'll remember all about it. And if you get lost, who'll read the chart symbols?"

"Why I've got to pick your brain now. We're taking Hawk and two of the lads. Rousseau insisted we take some muscle."

"Why? They'll just get in the way. Better off if you took Breakers . . . or Spunk."

"He and Jake are already off to the Souk to suss things out up there. Actually, I think he wants us to get these two gumbos out of the den." He waved a careless hand toward the argument. "They're ringleaders of the mutiny."

"Mutiny? It's that serious? But Rousseau's their god . . ."

Irv said, "Pretty sure our guys are encouraging it, with Maxine stirring up the pot."

"Hard to blame her . . . or them," Rubio said. "With the Smiths armed and all, the lads have something better to fight with than their fists."

No wonder Rousseau was yelling. But I had other worries. "Why don't you let me go, and you stay home and rest? You don't look so good."

"I'm fine."

"I don't think so."

"Fuck it. I wouldn't miss this trip for all the world."

"How far is it?"

"About eight miles, if you're walking."

I debated how hard to push. "Could we borrow one of Empire's boats? Bigger, faster, easier on you . . ."

"We already asked. No go. R.J.'s convinced we're on a fool's errand. Doesn't want to pull a crew off their security watch."

Past the piles of damp wood and steel, the argument swelled toward a roar. People dropped their loads to watch or join in.

Rubio clasped his chart-stuffed hold-all to his chest like a shield. "C'mon, Irv. We can help break that up. By the way, Glim . . . you have garden duty today. I checked."

"Thanks a bunch."

"Don't mention it."

Rube at his snotty best. Ever since he'd been given charge of the den search, he had a lot less time for me. I turned away toward the Mess.

"Hey, one more thing . . . what does MLWN mean?"

So unfair, that my lowly status in the den meant always getting left behind. I set my jaw. "You figure it out!"

To darken my mood even more, I'd slept through breakfast, had just missed lunch, and there was no mercy from the kitchen staff. With all the extra mouths to feed, supplies must be running low. The lights were off, but for a few at the far end where the Macy kids still slumbered, wept, and murmured. The cabinets and coolers were locked up tight. Hungry, pissed at the world in general but Rubio in particular, I stormed up to the roof to take my snit out on innocent plants.

The garden beds were busy with pickers and thinners. A team of planters moved seedlings from the greenhouse into a recently harvested row. I glared at them, when I should have been sympathetic. After all, we were all here together, stuck at home, missing the Great Adventure.

I stalked to the notice board to see what needed doing that I would resent the least. Raspberries, ready to pick. Fine. I grabbed a stack of the pint baskets molded in our shops from ground-up paper. Mud-colored and ugly, but they could be chopped up again and, with more binder added, infinitely recycled. A useful tool in the den. Like me.

The raspberries were down on Level Five, trained up the south side of the chain link fence that enclosed the hens, offering them a bit of shade and wind shelter. The flock was pecking away at some imagined treat in the sawdust when I stopped at the first set of canes. A motley crew, rescued from flooded rear courtyards and terrace hen houses. Occasionally, Jake would bring a new bird home from the Souk. As I tossed my baskets down, the rooster came racing over to scream at me. A nasty piece of work, he was the target of constant assassination plots intended to make the chicken run safe for human presence. But we needed to keep the flock growing and roosters were hard to come by. This one seemed to know his own worth. He flung up his crest and flashed his spurs at me.

"Get a life, bird brain!" I snapped.

I started picking hard and fast, until my hands were wet and sticky with crushed fruit. I licked at them, shocking my mouth with the sweet/tart juice and then my conscience, when I glanced into my basket at the damage I'd done, at the waste.

Really, Glim?

It was like Lizzy scolding me from inside. I clamped my eyes shut. Wrong side of the bunk this morning. The dream put me all off-kilter. What about the Macys, wounded and traumatized down below, or the Smiths with no den to go home to? Shame on me for sniveling about being denied a boat ride!

I made myself pick more carefully. We needed every single berry.

With my nose out of my navel, I finally noticed the day—what denfolk call a Before day: mild, sunny, with scudding clouds, and the usual suffocating humidity thinned by a salt-tinged ocean breeze. Good day for a sail, if only I had a boat. No, not going there again. Up here on the roof, even the stink of the Lagoon was faint. The solars would be soaking up the rays. Full batteries for a change. Maybe even hot water. So rare. You had to live the good stuff while you had it. I breathed in the hopeful scents of soil and living vegetation and my grouch finally drained away.

About time, nudged Lizzy.

I settled in to pick at a steady rhythm: one for me, five for the basket, and so on. Hunger problem solved. I tossed the overripe ones to the hens. When my stomach stopped growling and my muscles started to cramp, I stopped for a break. Five pints picked. A decent start. Stretching my back, I looked around to see who else was enjoying the sun and clear air. Up on Level Six, set back to create the terraces on Five, one of our garden gurus was teaching two Smith teeners how to prune storm-damage off the peach trees. A small maintenance crew repaired a section of the perimeter chain link, ripped away in the last big blow. Down at the eastern end of Five, Jenn and Ellie Mae had teamed up to bind the tomato vines to their cages. Of all the garden veggies, the tomatoes were the most pampered, kept down here in a sheltered spot.

Digging, weeding, thinning, cutting, pulling. Soothing and regular. I actually liked roof duty . . . except when it meant being left behind. For now, the sun and air were a fair trade. I shook off my irritation and felt, for a moment, at peace.

But there was always the threat of the empty glass towers to the north and east. Not even squatters lived up there, least not for long. Still in the shadow of last night's grim news, hard not to see every shattered window as a potential sniper perch. Or a source of unguided missiles. The wind would howl in one empty frame and straight out another, stirring up a shit storm of paper and loose junk, dragging office chairs and dining tables till they piled up against the broken glass and blew right out into the street. Or onto our terraces, like during Joseph. Wouldn't we be more secure in a den where nothing loomed over us? Like, on a boat. Out on the water, you're the tallest thing around. Out there, no one's shooting at you. Oh. Except. Except . . . what? I snatched at this latest memory shred, but it was gone with the breeze.

Muttering to myself, I gathered up my filled pint boxes to move them to the shade, turned, and nearly slammed into Daniel, standing in the path before me.

I must have staggered. He reached both hands to steady me. "Hey. Sorry."
I backed away, hands full of berry boxes.

"Didn't mean to startle you. I said hello. You were . . . somewhere else."

"I was . . . yes." I squinted at him. Couldn't shed the glare off the waves.
Daniel's face was like my father's in memory: lost in a flare of light. I fumbled the pint boxes. I'd forgotten a tray to carry them in.

"Need some help with those?"

I thrust them at him. "Over there. In the shade."

He hesitated. "Sure you don't need some shade yourself?"

"No, I'm . . ." My wrist brushing my forehead came away soaking wet.
"I was . . ."

"Hold on a minute." He took the berries to the work table by the stairway door, snatched up a tray, and came back. "You were . . . ?"

"Miles out to sea . . . I think."

"Ah. Another memory quake?"

I shook my head. "I couldn't quite . . . someone was shooting . . . I
think."

"Memory can be unreliable."

"I didn't say I imagined it. It just wasn't clear what was happening." I
turned back to the berries and started filling another pint.

"Let me help." Daniel took up a box and went to work beside me.

For a long time, we said nothing. I was glad he didn't press for details I
didn't have. I did need to talk this out, and with Rubio sunk in his own
obsession and everyone else saying how cool I remembered anything at
all . . . well, why not Daniel?

"The thing is . . ." I set a full pint aside. "They're coming at me—the
memories— so often now, and so real that sometimes I . . . like, lose track
of where I am. Or who I am."

"Let me reassure you." Daniel set his pint beside mine in the tray. "You
are who you always were. Lizzy. You've just added to her, a new dimension.
A bit of glimmer."

"Cute." I was unconvinced.

He took up an empty box. "Can I call you Lizzy? Maybe that would
help?"

"It doesn't feel like my name yet, so I might not answer. I . . . haven't told
anyone else."

"Thanks," he said softly.

"No, it's just that . . ." Didn't want him getting ideas. "I mean, I will, but . . ."

"I know." He shook his head. "No, wait, I don't. Not at all. I'd be celebrating. Why aren't you?"

"It's too confusing. It's like I've been lying about who I am."

"No one will see it that way." He shook his box to settle the berries and went back to work, avoiding the clingy thorns. "I thought about you . . . after. Most of the night, in fact—well, what was left of it. I thought about what it took to tell me what you did. To relive it again. Bad enough recalling it the first time. I wasn't . . . very helpful."

"I wasn't looking for help."

"Sometimes that's when it's needed most."

And when it's the hardest to ask for. "Maybe."

For a while, he kept picking, a careful, mechanical distraction. Then he put his basket down and sat back on his heels. "Can I tell you a story? It's my turn. Not like, my trauma is bigger than your trauma. More like, I've been there, and maybe we can help each other. Go below the safety line. Get some of that trust back."

Will we finally talk about arrows? Did he have any clue that I'd thrown my trauma at him in hope of scaring him away?

"You ready for a core dump?" His hands, resting on his thighs, curled slowly into claws. He laughed, a harsh escape of breath. "Not sure I am."

"You don't need to . . ."

"No. No, I do. Like I think you did." He stared at his hands as if just noticing the berry stains, then shrugged and plunged in. "I was married before Abel. Actually married. Not many bother these days. She was . . . Sara. A wonderful woman. The love of my life, at the time. We were at university here in the city, during the Long Hiatus after Hasan. People were rebuilding. No superstorm for eight hopeful years. A future seemed . . . possible."

He stopped, looked down. I was practically holding my breath. Not the sort of story I'd expected. I'd never given a thought to his life before Abel.

"But I was . . . my parents were . . . on and off. They'd never been happy about the marriage, then Hurricane Felix put the city back to square one. Sara and I retreated to . . . well, my family's place upstate, away from the floods and curfews and rationing, to raise what we hoped would be our kids. The area was already crowding up with refugees, but it was high ground, you know? There was room enough for a garden, animals. I was working on a novel." He laughed, like *can you imagine anything stupider?* "Who would print it? Who would read it?"

I settled myself more comfortably, pointlessly shifting berry boxes on the tray.

"Sara had been pre-law in college. For some extra income, she acted as a negotiator in some of the land disputes that constantly went on. I'd go off on research trips now and then, for my book. One night, I . . ."

He paused for a long while, then scrubbed his chin roughly and sighed, as if there was nothing for it but to leap off the edge. "One night I came home to find the place lit up by police flashers, a SWAT team deep in a standoff with a group of gangbangers who'd invaded the house looking for food and guns, and Sara . . ." He glanced away. "My wife, already zipped up in a body bag at the bottom of the driveway, shot dead as she called 911 and tried to escape."

"Oh, Daniel . . ."

"You could still do that then, 911—upstate at least. We had no guns in the house, and Sara would have fed them, if only they'd asked."

Like Smiths and Adders, I mused fleetingly.

He breathed in sharp, let it out slow, like relieved to be past the really hard part. "Well, I went off the rails. Shut myself up in the house. Stopped answering my phone. Burned my novel page by page. Forgot to eat. The usual sort of thing when you can't understand why you're alive when your loved one isn't.

"Then one day, Julian showed up. My bad-kid brother. He'd stayed in the city with his friends. At least a year since I'd seen him, maybe three. He'd been this truant pre-adolescent. Now here he was, all sleek and tough, telling me to 'get a fuckin' grip.'"

So totally Julian. With the worst revealed, I felt I'd been invited back into the conversation. "Did you?"

"I said, what do you care? Then we yelled at each other for a week or two, threw the occasional punch." His smile was so faint, it was practically invisible. "Yeah, I know. But people show their real stuff, turning up when you least expect it . . . when you don't even know how much you need them." Daniel wet his lips, smiled crookedly. "Julie said, 'The whole fuckin' world's falling apart, Dan. Why not enjoy it while you can?'"

I could picture it. "What did you do?"

"My life upstate was finished. I'd been ready to find a gun, pull the plug.

Curiosity . . . and Julian . . . saved me. Had to see how this screwed-up mess will work out. I let Julie drag me back to the city. That was two years ago, and here I am." He spread his hands, and I saw the gesture as stoic instead of cynical. He turned back and started picking again. "Not so rare a story these days. But I wanted you to know."

I let out a long breath. "Do you still write?"

"What would be the point?"

Any words of comfort I could conjure were way too trite. Plus, I was among the lucky. I'd survived my ordeal, and his Sara had not. I was glad he'd loved someone before, enough to get married. It made him human, wounded like the rest of us, not the all-knowing Book Dude I'd built up in my mind. "Must have been hard to leave, with all you had up there."

"Not really. That life was over." He read the doubt I was struggling to hide. "You're thinking, a house in the hills, a garden, I should have stayed? Don't buy that fantasy. I'd have to weapon up, defend every inch of turf, every goat in the barn, every carrot in the row. I've no problem with guns, but that's not a life. Sooner rather than later, I'd end up as dead as Sara. When someone wants what you have, you can't build walls high enough."

What about the walls of Yankee Stadium? The raspberries crushed in my palm were so alive, so fresh. Bright as new blood. "Things are that bad on the Mainland?"

"Have been for a while now."

"Worse than here?"

"No one wants what I have here . . . at least not until recently. There's four or five families squatting in that house, my sister tells me. She gets around more than I do. Says they're cutting down all the trees again, to build shacks and palisades."

Wanted to ask about the unnamed sister, how she 'got around.' Another hint at his uptown roots. But . . . not the time for it now. "Then why are we all still hoping to go there?"

He relaxed into a slouch. "Everyone needs a dream. Easier to believe the beautiful lie than face the darker truth. But nowhere's going to be good or safe for a long, long while." He set another full box of berries on the tray and wiped juice-stained palms on his pants, dark, close-fitting, and full of pockets. "It's going to be fortress mentality from here on, unless by some miracle, they figure out a climate fix, that is, if anyone's still looking. And even miracles rarely arrive in time."

"You're just full of good news today." I'd reached overload with darkness. "That why you're all in black? You look so . . . serious."

"I'm a serious guy."

"Could've fooled me."

He grinned, then glanced at the sky, the gathering clouds, the sun sinking behind the taller buildings across the Avenue. "Listen, I didn't come to drop doom and gloom all over you. I need to ask a favor."

"Okay . . ."

"I'm heading out for a few days, me and Julian. Figure if I tell you ahead of time, you won't come chasing after me."

He laughed. I didn't.

"In fact, best not to even notice I'm gone. Except I need you to watch my boat." He fished an old metal key ring from a pocket and dangled it in front of me. "You could even open up for sales, if you don't take too big a cut."

His making light suggested this trip would be just the opposite. "More family business?"

"You could call it that."

"When will you be back?"

"When I'm done."

"What if people ask about you?"

"Off on an errand. Book prospecting."

I looked away. "Everyone's leaving but me."

"It's called holding the fort. Just as important." He shook the ring so its two keys swayed and jingled. "Do we have a deal?"

Resigned, I reached for the keys.

He drew them back a little. "You never asked her name."

"Who?"

"My boat."

"Not the Book Boat?"

"That's just for fun. She's the *Melville*." He wrapped his hands around mine, flattening the metal against my palm. "Glim . . . Lizzy. Promise me you'll stay put this time?"

I looked for some smart backtalk, but he cut me off.

"No. Promise. Swear. I need to know you'll be here when I get back."

There it was again, that faint bloom of hope. Lizzy, urging me to give the unexpected a chance. But say it aloud? No way.

All I could do was nod.

TWENTY-NINE

D inner time came and went. Too soon to expect Daniel, and besides, it was only me waiting for him. But Jake and Spunk should have been back and Rubio's scouting party upriver hadn't scheduled an overnight. The den was subdued, feeling the risk of our reduced numbers, worried for our absent denmates. Rousseau and Maxine had holed up in his office. Was he was now regretting his cell phone ban, each time the door watch sent a runner upstairs with a useless update?

I huddled in the Mess with Rivera, Poppy, and Jenn, pushing tepid veggie stew around the sides of my bowl. Poppy had slipped right into our girl group like she'd always been a Joe, and maybe she should have been. Her diffident cheer helped ease us past the occasional tension or disagreement. With Rivera so distracted by the Macy kids, it was good to have a new voice in the mix. She didn't even mind when we called her Machete Girl.

The kids were mostly sleeping, but lanterns glowed late out in Main, folks clustering in the dim pools, speculating quietly. The Mess doors were propped open so we'd hear an alarm from the watch, but also to catch any stray breeze. With all windows and doors boarded or locked tight for extra security, the den was more like an oven than usual. We were all stripped down to the least we could wear without causing a ruckus.

"I can't believe Gracie bulled her way onto the boat!" Rivera's long hair was bound up in a clasp on top of her head. Rogue tendrils escaped as she jabbed her spoon into her bowl. "Telling Rubio she knew all about the Zodiac!"

Poppy's nod was half-admiring. "Bullshit goes a long way."

"You wouldn't have gone," I reminded Rivera. "You'd have to leave the kids."

She shrugged. "True. But it's the principle of the thing."

"At least they took Breakers." I'd had a lesson in useful lies and ruthless confidence, watching Grace work Rubio over. "She'll share the inside chat when she's back."

"They all got so full of themselves," Rivera said. "Even that geeky Irv."

Old habit made me defend Rubio. "They say if this works out, it'll change the whole structure of den life. Move us into the future."

"Such as it is," muttered Rivera.

"I don't want to move. Until it's off the Island for good." Jenn eyed my bowl. "You leaving all that?"

"Not hungry." I slid it her way.

She didn't offer it to Poppy and Rivera. She scooped the remains into her bowl and pushed the empty back at me. "Waste not, want not. You ought to eat better."

"I eat."

"Not like a normal person."

"Eh." I leaned in. "Why don't you want to move?"

"Because here, we know what the problems are. Up there . . . ?" She shuddered.

Poppy mopped her brow. "Bet it'll be cooler. Certainly be more space."

We were filling the air, but even nattering was more soothing than silence. Our heads turned as a runner trotted across the main hall and up the stairs toward the office. Nothing urgent, by the pace of her step. Four shrugs of disappointment. Better if Daniel had left me his phone rather than the key to his boat. But there'd be no number to call.

"I'm heading upstairs." Jenn stood to stack our empty bowls. Her wrist bangles chimed a merrier sound than any of us felt. "See if the com is up, now we have power."

"I'm game." Poppy rose to help. She had her rough edges, but was always ready to lend a hand, sort of like a nice version of Gracie. "No point moping around all night."

I nudged Rivera's elbow. "Weather check, at least? I heard rumors of a cold front."

"I'll check on the children first."

The rest of us trouped after Jenn, sheep following the clink of her bells. But in the loft, the big screen was dark, showing only a 'no signal' message.

"Nothing?" Jenn flattened both palms against her jaw.

A clump of Wizzers crowded around the favorite workstation, batting ideas back and forth like ping-pong balls.

Jenn waded in among them. "There was sun all day. We should have power by now."

"Power we got. But maybe they don't. Mainland's gone dark."

"All of it? Did you try . . ."

"Loss of signal. Like it's been shut down," someone replied.

"Or someone's jamming it," muttered another voice.

Poppy and I stood back. This was Jenn's turf.

"We're getting weather warnings on the CB," said a boy. "Relayed from down the coast. So there's power down there. But no signal."

"Wait! Check this out!" A dreadlocked girl at a nearby laptop flapped her arms as if trying to fly. She snatched up the device and lifted it over her head to show the screen: a glare of flame against a darkening sky.

Jenn tapped the thin shoulder in front of her. "Get that up on Main."

The big wall screen flared with color. Brilliant, pulsing light wrapped in a shroud of smoke. The image swayed and jerked, ducked and swooped. A camera in motion. No sense of scale. Could be a close-up of a match flame, until I spotted the bright voids of blown-out windows.

"That's a burning high-rise."

"Drone vid," the dreadlocked girl declared.

"Is it real?" Poppy asked.

"It's on Captain's Blog."

The teeners shared sober nods.

"What's Captain's Blog?" I whispered to Poppy.

"New to me."

Jenn glanced over. "That's Aitch's site. Used to piggyback on other sites. Lately, she's had her own, and it looks like they're down and she's not." She turned back to the screen. "How's she doing that?"

The dreadlocked girl said, "One day she's Mainland, next day here. Her drones got cosmic range."

"Look!" A boy pointed toward the top of the screen. An angular tracery of trusswork collapsed and folded into the smoke with an explosion of flame. "Ain't that a cell tower?"

"Which one? Can you tell where?" Jenn was dancing on tiptoe.

"Must be why no signal," said the boy.

"Oh, that's bad!"

I moved in beside her. "What's the big deal?"

"More equipment destroyed that we can't replace! Could be transmitters in there. Or servers! Whole banks of them!"

"The Empires use phones, you know."

Jenn's nod was weary. "I know."

Everyone but me, apparently. "You never said . . ."

"Don't get all huffy." She beetled slim brows at me. "You never want to hear anything against Rousseau's rules."

True, once upon a time, as long ago as last week. "If everyone knew, why go along with the ban? Phones would make our lives so much easier, and safer."

"Or maybe they wouldn't." Jenn put her back to the on-screen mayhem. "You don't remember life before, how everyone lived on their phones, re-lied on them for everything."

Recall slid into my head just by thinking about it. I'd lived on mine, too. When it worked.

"No backup systems. Every time a storm took the phones down, the city was crippled. With the signal so unreliable, Rousseau didn't want us depen-dent on it. It makes sense."

Poppy let out a gasp, and we turned back to the fiery screen in time to see the top floors of the building collapse in a shower of pyrotechnics. The blaze dropped into the lower floors, devouring the building from the inside. The drone circled, drew away, and the screen went blank.

"Thing about Aitch," Jenn mused, "You're never sure why she's showing you something. Never any voiceover. Her only commentary is her choice of subject."

"Whatever catches her interest?"

"More like, what she thinks is important."

"Important to who?"

"Well, that's a good question. But she always seems to know when some-thing's happening, in time to get her drones there." She gazed at the dark screen wistfully.

"You're envious."

"Aren't you? She can do things. Make a difference."

Farther along the balcony, the stairwell suddenly filled up with people. Turning, I caught a glimpse of Spunk being carried up the next flight. On his way to the medics, by the broken and bloodied look of him. He couldn't walk without support and his left arm hung limp and twisted. But he was alive and already making a joke of it. The crowd trailed behind, offering help and encouragement. Jake and Rousseau watched up after him from the landing, then came down the hall toward the office.

For a guy claiming not to be a fighter, Jake looked to have put up a damn good one. He had a rag pressed to his head, still soaking up blood. The stocky woman beside him was mostly bruised and scraped. She and her clothing hadn't seen a shower in a while.

"Give me the quick version," said Rousseau.

Jenn and I leaned against the balcony rail, listening in.

"We got to the Souk," Jake began dutifully. "We surveyed the remains, seeing who was still in business, what was still for sale. Answer is, not much. Selling to the dens is now prohibited, but a few of my old vendors were willing to share news. The families that control the Merchants' Association are at each other tooth and nail in the boardroom, but the richest are building their security forces into standing armies." He regarded his bloodied rag with concern. "Got me worse than I thought."

"Head wounds bleed," the woman murmured. "Not as bad as it looks."

"Relieved to hear it."

"The quick version," Rousseau reminded.

"Right." Jake turned the rag inside out and kept blotting. "Like Dan Nathan said, anyone who relied on the Souk is looking elsewhere for food. So Spunk and I were in the tent burbs, checking who had any livestock left. There's a dust-up down the way, and we go to see. A couple of Stormies are trying to drag a live cat out of this kid's arms. He's maybe eight or nine, screaming and hanging on for dear life, and we don't think this is cool, so we pitch in, and suddenly there are Stormies plunging in from everywhere, and we're way outnumbered . . ."

"Seven of them, plus me," the woman put in. "Two scouting parties."

"Well, it felt like a shitload," said Jake. "And Spunk was getting the worst of it. Cassie here blew her cover to help get us out of there."

I studied the woman more closely. She wore a knee-length, loose-fitting tunic. Through layers of oily stains shone the vivid greens and blues favored by the Storm Worshippers.

She offered Rousseau her hand. "Cass Meyer. Empire Security."

He shook it gratefully. "You're Will's undercover with the Stormies?"

"Was. For the last couple months. Scouting the new preacher girl."

"Wish Will had mentioned it sooner."

The woman's shrug was unapologetic. "When you're embedded, the fewer who know, the safer you are."

Rousseau nodded but did not look satisfied.

"Not a real threat while they were scattered about," she went on, "but this girl's got dreams of glory."

"So we hear. What's her plan? Are they . . . armed?"

"Mostly with their faith. Couldn't stand up to the family militias, but there's a lot more of them than we figured."

"And the Armory's too close for comfort to Gimme Shelter," Jake observed.

"And their animals," Cass agreed. "They're near us, too, so our boats patrol regularly."

"The point is," Jake insisted, "without the Souk and with so many more to feed, the Stormies are starving. They could be down on us any minute. Relocating's looking better sooner rather than later. Max'll go along with it. Not sure about the other dens."

"I'm giving it every thought." Rousseau finally noticed Jenn and me eavesdropping. He took Cassie's elbow to steer her down the corridor. "A moment more in my office, then let's get you seen to and fed before you report back to Will and Katja."

"I hear the upriver tour is still out," Jake said as they moved away.

I'd been hoping he knew what was keeping them. I slouched back from the rail. Adders after us, now Stormies, too? News just got worse and worse.

Poppy had stayed by the big screen. "How does a fire start at the top of a building?"

"Not by accident," said Jenn. "They were after the tower."

"But why?"

Jenn sucked in her cheeks. "First thing you'd do in a coup is seize control of the means of communications. Or if you're on the weaker side, destroy them. Maybe it's those uptown families Jake was talking about."

"Gracie mentioned a to-do uptown," I recalled. "The day we brought the boats in."

"It's not like the Island's got a functioning government anymore," said Poppy. "Power pockets in free fall. But isn't the Mainland still in charge?"

"Supposedly," said Jenn. "But I'm beginning to doubt it."

I think we all were. I wished Jake had brought news about Bright or the fire posse. Flames eating an entire high-rise? Like, this could be it. It could all end here. All our efforts, our struggles to survive, to preserve some quality of life, a vaguely sane social structure, all along hoping for rescue? For escape? Who could believe these fantasies anymore? If Daniel was right, no place was any better than anywhere else.

I hated thinking like Rubio. "I'm done. I'm heading in." I waved at the screen. "Someone should tell Rousseau."

"For sure. When I make my nightly report. But I'll watch a bit longer." Jenn was hoping for more from Aitch, whoever she was.

In my bunk, I sweated and tossed about, flames flickering behind my eyelids. I couldn't stop listening. Was that the slosh of a returning Zodiac? The distant hum of Julian's speedboat? Then I was sure I smelled smoke, though no alarm was raised in the den and the depleted tiers around me rumbled with snores. I sat up to peer through my shard of window at the Book Boat, steady at its mooring across the Lagoon, cabin windows dark. Turning over, then back again, like the princess and the pea, I kept feeling the hard knot of Daniel's key ring in my gut wallet.

I'd used up my last candle, so couldn't even turn to the old book to read myself to sleep. Hours later, I gave up, dug out the darkest clothing I owned, got dressed, and slipped downstairs.

I had to talk my way through two security checkpoints just to get within range of the boat dock. Raised voices in the mudroom proved to be Maxine and Rousseau, arguing about how much biodiesel could be spared for Lady-smith's raid-scorched pontoon boat, and who would go with it to check on Irv and Rubio. A patched-up Jake was trying to mediate.

"You are NOT getting on that boat!" Rousseau leveled a finger. "Your people can't afford to lose you!"

"It's MY boat," Maxine yelled. "And who's saying I'll get lost?"

"Max . . ." pleaded Jake.

I ducked over beside the young Smith on sentry at the dock ladder, and we both stared. Two den bosses squabbling in the middle of the night like an old married couple. Hard to watch. Things were falling apart.

I murmured my mission to the sentry. Rousseau, even Jake, would've stopped me had they noticed, but the Smith girl didn't know any better. She nodded me past and down the ladder, where the even less informed dock watch helped me set the battered kayak in the water.

"You sure this is a good idea?" he offered. "Big new storm in the forecast."

"I heard. Do we know when?"

He half-shrugged. "Well, early next week. Maybe sooner."

I smiled. "Only going across the Lagoon."

He stood back, adjusting the pistol on his hip in a kind of shrug, and I pushed off.

With the walkway gone and the watch torches doused, the building at my back loomed dark and blank as a canyon wall. The night was windless and still, the Lagoon a black mirror reflecting only the faint, cloud-shrouded moonlight. Wishing I could silence the splash and drip of my paddle, I made straight for the Book Boat.

THIRTY

The Book Boat swayed gently as I secured the kayak and clambered on board. No, she's the *Melville*, I reminded myself. That would take some getting used to. I gazed around the stern well, checked the security of the mooring lines, scanned the buildings walling the Lagoon. As best I could see, everything looked shipshape. But what next?

I got it that Daniel had given me the keys to tie me down. He read me well enough to know that assigned a task, I'd stick around. Even if only to raise the alarm, come fire or theft, and hope enough sleeping Joes could be roused in time to save his boat.

I perched on the stern locker, getting my bearings. The barge's tall tiller creaked companionably at my back. It was both strange and natural to feel the deck move beneath me, the constant faint roll of a tidal harbor remembering the sea. Like I was. The sea, and so much more. This old boat was keelless, wide-bottomed, stable enough in smooth conditions but poorly fit for rough water. *Haiku*, on the other hand, was a seagoing vessel. My father's idea, I recalled now. He bought it just before his company downsized and relocated to Montana, like so many were doing. *Haiku* was to be our escape hatch, the St. Lawrence Seaway to the Great Lakes, when life in Manhattan was no longer bearable.

Bearable. By whose definition? Like, what would either of my parents have thought of life in a den? From my seat in the quiet stern, their faces still eluded me, but now I could summon up the bellow and wail of their arguments: the job held for him out there, but how long? My mother didn't believe the job promise: Montana was a dust bowl, the whole Midwest was on fire, we could live on her salary. My dad's hands in the air: Your clients are all leaving! Then what do you do? Two problem-solvers facing the unsolvable.

When words finally failed and he took off, emails arrived, smug at first then increasingly tentative: the work was still part-time, he'd find a place to live soon, he'd send money next month, use this train ticket, take this bus, whatever. I cried when my mother deleted them. After a while, they stopped coming. Was he dead or alive? Would I ever know?

Soon after, she made *Haiku* and the marina our permanent home. It was true that her clients were leaving. The apartment was too expensive, even though after Misha, many had stopped bothering to pay or collect rent, at least in our downtown neighborhood. My mother said it was immoral to squat, never mind dangerous. Each time the power went out or the ground floor flooded, the climb to the twelfth floor got harder. The stairwells were no place to venture into alone. Living on *Haiku*, when riots broke out or home invasions threatened, we could cast off to the safety of open water, with only the weather to worry about. A boat made "sticking it out" possible, my mother declared. We non-quitters were "going the long haul," until the climate fix took hold and life returned to normal.

Normal. Like anything could be, with the weather like it was. Or, *fix.* Like it could happen tomorrow or the next day, a magical spell. The maddest sort of delusion. So, why didn't I question it at the time? I was old enough to know better. So were most of the stay-behind kids. But by our definition, what unhinged our parents could have no bearing on our lives. We were the children of the Wave, one wave or another, too busy being cool survivors. I'd be out late roaming the half-empty streets with my stay-behind friends or grinding down on my online high-school courses—a sure way not to face reality. Or later, queueing up for erratic grocery deliveries at the market, and eventually, at the local food pantries. It was like Jenn not wanting to leave Unca Joe unless for the Mainland. A sort of madness. The next time someone called me stubborn, I'd say it was genetic, on the female line.

We should have gone with him when we had the chance.

The more the memories surged through me, the less I understood Rubio's nostalgia for pre-Abel New York. But he'd been old enough during the hiatus to make the best of it, to live something close to a normal urban life. I was in my early teens when Felix came down on us.

I kicked my heels against the doors of *Melville*'s storage locker and bounced to my feet. I could see how, when you had a past, you could waste a whole lot of time stuck in it, chewing it over and over like stale bread. What was the point, when there was squat you could do to change it?

All tight topside. Time to check below. I fished the key ring out of my wallet, fumbling in the deeper shadow by the cabin door until I got it open. Spooky being on a strange boat alone. Stepping down into darkness, I grabbed a flashlight from the solar charging station just inside. The racks and bins of books leaped to life as I played the beam around, along the chest-high rows of double-hung windows, into suspicious corners. Flipping on the overheads, even with the blinds closed, could stir up unwanted attention from outside. And I shouldn't run down the batteries, even after the full day of sun we'd just had.

I edged along the narrow center aisle, picking up stray books and magazines that had tumbled off their stacks. Everything felt thick with damp. I placed the escapees in more secure positions. Making myself useful, at least.

Two-thirds of the way forward, a sliding door separated the bookstore from the living quarters. Beyond was personal territory. I hesitated, then leaned into the handle. Locked. But Daniel had given me two keys. Didn't that amount to permission to enter? An invitation to know him better? I slipped the second key into the lock. Inside, the flashlight reflected off a streamlined galley to one side and a basic shower and head on the other, clearly a retrofit with scavenged equipment, but clean and tight. Past them, a second slider, closed but not locked. I eased it aside, and because the utter darkness inside drained my nerve, I scrabbled around for a light switch. The first of three produced soft light from recessed fixtures on either side of a surprisingly comfy cabin. A desk set into storage lockers to port; to starboard, more lockers and a com station with the usual equipment and mare's nest of manuals and charts. Under a pair of shuttered casement windows facing the bow deck like half-length French doors, a double berth stretched across the cabin's width.

Suspended at the hatchway, I scrutinized the cabin for clues of the man who lived there. Okay, he didn't really. He'd once mentioned a high-rise squat near the Souk, so probably his real life was there. This was more like a work space, compact and organized, with few of the personal touches you'd see in most boat cabins—or in a den bunk. No old family photos taped to the locker doors, no favorite quotes, no lists of daily chores stuck to the com station. But there were books—one crowded shelf above the desk, others stuck into any bit of available space, a pile at one end of the berth tucked up beside a small reading lamp. Good to see Daniel read books as well as sold them.

There was a scatter of clothing on the bed. One of the drawers below the berth was open, half-folded T-shirts hanging off its edge. The bedclothes were wrinkled and the pillows all bunched up, like he'd thrown himself down, slept in his jeans, then changed in a rush and left. Maybe Julian had come for him early. Or that family business was more urgent than he'd let on.

I set the flashlight down on the desk, turned on the bed lamp, and gathered up the bits of clothing. I could fold them at least, so he didn't have a mess to come home to. In the close, hot air of the cabin, their aroma was a sense memory—smoke, sweat, gunpowder, and a hint of diesel—the entire last twenty-four hours, starting with my ill-advised trip to the Souk. I pressed my face to the pile and inhaled. Not sweet or even very clean—after all, by my count, he'd worn this shirt and jeans since yesterday morning—but it was definitively Daniel. For an instant, I imagined holding him instead of a crumble of soiled duds. I'd forgotten what desire felt like, the thrill of bodies coming together, and it shook me that it felt so good. Would it be there the next time I had him in front of me?

The den shrink once said people hold on to phobias because they're more familiar than change, which makes you face the unknown. But though this terror of intimacy was deep in Glimmer's identity, it had never been part of Lizzy's. She'd had lovers . . . I had. Like Tayco, whose parents had taken him away to the mountains of Maine. Or that guy Amir. I remembered them now, but it seemed like ages ago, not just . . . what? Last year? Abel had distorted my sense of time along with so much else.

Not ready yet. But getting there.

Under the cast-offs lay a fat book with a bit of paper tucked in like an oversized bookmark. At the top, it said: *Lizzy*. He even spelled it right. I slid the scrap out and held it nearer the lamp.

In case you get tired of that other book you're reading, this should keep you busy.

Like he'd known what I'd do, in his space, with his clothing . . . or hoped I would.

It was an old book. Heavy, but comfortable in your hand. I turned its spine to the light.

MOBY DICK.

I sighed, dropped the pile on the bed, folded it into a neater stack, and set it on the corner of the berth. I returned the clean scatter to the drawer and closed it. Now my hands felt empty. I'd checked the boat, the ropes, even straightened up a little. I switched off the recessed lights. The tiny bed lamp couldn't be drawing much power. I'd leave it to welcome him home.

So. Nothing more to do here. But I didn't want to leave. It felt good being surrounded by his ambiance, without having to deal with the man himself. I picked up the book, but its weight was intimidating. Besides, I was too tired to read. My feet were leaden, the cozy cabin more welcoming than my claustrophobic bunk. Yawning, I sat on the edge of the berth, the famous tome like a stone in my lap, holding me in place. The bed stretched out invitingly. A few days, Daniel had said. I could catnap, say, till it was light, and be gone before he was due to return.

I'd always slept well on a boat.

I woke listening, sure I'd felt the boat rock, like someone had boarded. Quiet as I could, I raised up on one arm. No pale rays of dawn seeping through the bow shutters. But for the contained glow of the bed lamp beside my head, the cabin was dark as a well.

"Sorry to wake you, den rat."

"What're you . . . !" Somehow, I managed not to shriek.

"Calm down." The intruder was close by. The intonation was oddly Julian's, but the voice was deeper, and a woman's. My own voice deserted me, but my face in the lamplight must've said enough.

"Nervous little thing, aren't you?"

The lamp spread to the edges of the berth, just dusting the knees of the shadow sitting in the desk chair. A stranger, since no local would call me den rat. A deliberate provocation. I grabbed for a snappy comeback but lost my grip. "What do you want?"

"Does Danny know you've moved onto his boat?"

"Haven't!" I squeaked, hugging my knees up tight like a six-year-old. But wait! I was in my rights here. She was the break-in. Still, she called him Danny. I cleared my clumsy throat. "He gave me the keys, to keep an eye on it. Who the fuck are you?"

"Oh, now we get brave." The shadow rose and moved into the light, settling on the far end of the berth, eyebrows raised. "Remember me?"

Blond hair, blunt cut, square jaw. All that, I remembered, but not quite like I remembered. She was . . . older, and with less of a glow. More like a hard shine. But it had to be her.

"Ninja girl!"

The woman snorted. "How's that?"

"What I called you, after." I let the memory bloom: the golden girl dressed in gauze and light, a dream to aspire to. Never quite real, even as I'd watched her that night, holding her own in the sheeting rain. If not for the pack and the documents, it'd be easy to believe I'd dreamed her. But here she was, and for a moment, I forgot to demand what she was doing on Daniel's boat in the middle of the night. My bad for not locking the doors. "'Cause of how you put those guys down!"

"Oh." She rubbed her chin, then smirked. "Right. Guess I did."

"This is sure a . . . um . . ." I gestured at her vaguely. "Y'know . . . a different look?"

She checked herself out, like she'd forgotten what she was wearing, then crossed her legs, neatly sheathed in a close-fitting black overall. Her black tank top exposed strong, sculpted arms. No makeup, but she didn't need it. Her skin was pale and smooth, like I remembered. She must have access to sunblock. "Uptown clothes that night. Bait."

Bait? I didn't dare ask. "What were they after, those goons?"

"Some stuff I had."

At last, the tale would be told. "And so you laid it on me."

She shrugged, an assent. "Needed my hands free, right then."

"Why not just ditch the pack?"

"Because one of them would've scooped it and split, while the other kept me busy."

"I figured that. So now you want it back."

Another shrug. She didn't make for easy chitchat, this woman.

"How'd you find me?"

"Not so hard."

"I mean, it's a big city." I tried a rueful grin. "And we *obviously* don't run in the same social circles . . ."

"Got that right."

Well, fuck you, too, I thought. So much for my imagining us meeting up again and becoming friends. I crossed my arms. "How'd you know who I was?"

She looked quizzical. Then her face smoothed, except for the deeper stress lines at her eye corners. Like, maybe worried I'd already sold her stuff. "Okay. I'm guessing he hasn't told you."

"He?"

"Daniel. I'm Hannah, his sister."

This took me a moment. "Right! The one who gets around a lot!"

Her laugh barely escaped her throat. "Is that what he said?"

She had to be the other side of thirty. I searched her face for the resemblance the brothers so clearly shared. "You don't look like his sister."

"Half-sister. Different mother. Mine died."

"Huh."

Irritation plucked at the corners of her mouth. "Believe what you like. Here I am. And yes, looking to reclaim my stuff." She leaned back on her hands, tossing hair out of her eyes with a jerk of her head. "He didn't say you were sleeping together."

"We're not!" Smack on the defensive where she wanted me, never mind what business it was of hers.

Yet another dismissive shrug. "One sure way to guard my stuff, right? But Danny's always been a trifle overzealous. What did you say your name was?"

I stared at her, inner hackles rising. So much bad news packed into one short remark. What was her beef with me? I'd acted according to program. She should be thanking me. Sure, it was her right to reclaim what she'd put into safekeeping, whatever was left. But the implication that Daniel hung around only to guard her stuff? That was personal, a skilled hit at my wavering self-confidence. Like, here's this poised and well-groomed, obviously powerful woman—what could a brother of hers see in a garden-variety den rat? How could she know just how to swing at me, if Daniel hadn't coached her?

On the other hand, maybe she was full of shit and would say anything to get what she wanted. I jacked myself upright. "Lizzy. My name is Lizzy."

She frowned. Like she'd been told different and wondered what game I was playing. So, a few things brother D hadn't passed along. At least, not yet.

"Well, *Lizzy*, you do agree you have some items belonging to me?"

She let the silence stretch out till it weighed a ton.

"Some."

"The clothing and drugs got traded soon after, I'm guessing. Maybe even the pack. Could've come by earlier, but I needed my hands clean. Too bad. I liked that pack."

"It was a nice one." Emphasis on past tense. If she believed it gone, so be it.

"But since you kept the book, I presume you have the papers as well?"

"Why would you think that?" Daniel had seen the old book, but not the papers. After two weeks of carrying her stuff around 24/7, hard to let it go too easy. Even though she'd get what she wanted in the long run. "They didn't seem like much, so I tossed them."

Ha. Had her for a moment there. Almost.

She shifted, changed the cross of her legs, then smiled like she'd got me on the run. "I'm pretty sure you didn't."

"You're right. Actually, I sold them."

"No record of anyone trying to use them."

My tongue was poking about against my teeth. Spunk or Rousseau always caught me in a lie, so maybe I wasn't much good at it. Anyhow, why was I bothering? She was better at it, and what was I going to do with the stupid papers? "Okay. I got 'em."

She leaned forward over her bent knees like she couldn't quite hide her relief. That same flap of bright hair cascaded over her eyes and she shook it back abruptly. "So now we begin negotiations?"

"No." I zipped open my belly pack, snatched out the string-bound packet and slapped it down on the bed. "Street rules. They're yours."

"Ah, the honor of the dens."

I nudged the papers toward her. "Are they for real?"

"Better be. Paid enough for them."

"You're going to use them, then?" Maybe this was how she did her coming and going. But there'd been no return tix.

"Soon as. You have the other item . . . ?" She opened and closed her palms. Clean and smooth, I noted, but with close-cropped nails.

The book. Oddly, this was harder. Among other things, it had brought me to Daniel. I pulled it out and laid it carefully beside the packet but rested my hand on it. "Is it from some ancestor of yours?"

That throaty laugh, tinged with mockery. "Nah. Dan gave it to me a while back. A metaphor for our lives, he said. At mercy of the winds and waters."

No question Daniel had acted like he'd never seen the book before. Or, I'd presumed, and he'd let me believe. Lying by omission. Now I *was* feeling used. On the other hand, why take what she said at face value, when she was so busy laying out her low opinion of me. If she just wanted her stuff back, she'd do better being nice about it.

I fingered the stained leather binding. "Didn't finish reading it yet."

"So?"

"Like to find out what happens."

A touch of surprise amid the scorn. "What do you care?"

"Stories should have endings."

"But it's not your story."

"Not yours either. You just said."

She brushed at that insistent fall of hair again. She was done with me. "I'm not a lending library. That's Dan's territory."

I left the book where it was and sat back.

She did the same, letting her gaze roam the darker corners of the cabin. "I must say, from his description of you, I expected more of a pitched battle. At least the last one was a fighter. For all the good it did her . . ."

Did she mean Sara? A hard case, this woman. "Yeah, I'm a real pushover. Truth is, I'm tired of carrying it around, worrying about it."

She watched me, considering, then let the spark of contention fade in her eyes. Not worth the effort, now that she had her documents back. She palmed the packet, tucking it away in a tabbed pocket of her overall, taking care that the flap was fastened. She slid the book back in my direction. "Keep it. Pass it to Dan when you're done. But make it quick."

So he can be done with me, too? She wanted me to think so. I took the book anyway. "Where will they take you? The papers."

"Well, that's a bit of a mystery. Far from here."

Meaning she didn't know where 'Arcadia' was, either? "For good?"

She shrugged languidly. "No profit in hanging around here any longer. For any of us."

Us, as in everyone on the Island, or as in Julian and Daniel? I thought of the pail of paper scraps, so arduously rescued. Make it quick, she'd said. Was it a family exodus? I felt that possibility like an unfamiliar hollow in my chest, but no way was I letting this woman see it mattered more to me than I'd understood myself.

Seemed like we didn't have much to say to each other after that. In the lengthening silence, we both came alert to a distant hum.

Boat motor. Approaching with speed.

"Get the light!" Hannah was up and at the cabin door before I saw her move.

"Why?" I switched off the bedside lamp, and the cabin went dark. "What is it?"

"Quiet!"

A faint clink of the blinds out in the bookstore sent me stumbling after her. Predawn glow between lifted slats at the nearest window outlined her taut shape. She'd known I'd do what she said, and why not? Same as I'd have done on my own, only she made me do it faster. Maybe not my golden ninja girl, but certainly a ninja woman. Didn't have to like her to allow her points for skill and daring.

"Your sentries are getting all exercised," she murmured as the hum approached. She pushed up a second slat to peer out sideways. "Wait. Sounds like . . . Crap! I think it's Julie."

Julie. She must really be their sister.

I nosed in beside her. "They're back so soon?"

The perimeter watch, thinned out to one or two voices, whooped their alarm codes to the boat launch guards: *Emergency! Let this one in!* Still night out there, but early light enough to see the oval shape of *Sea Sprite* tossing up wake as it swept into the Lagoon.

"He's got a load on," Hannah noted.

"What? He's drunk?" I pushed closer.

"Julie? Never. Even when he looks it. But he's got . . . looks like a bunch of kids! Fuck! Now what?" She pulled away, cutting through the darkness toward the stern door.

I lingered long enough to see Julian throttle down and head for Unca Joe's dock. Out in the stern, Hannah whistled sharply, a four-note sequence. Julian glanced up in surprise, then turned *Sprite*'s nose toward the sound. He could barely steer for the small bodies pressed around him, crammed into the passenger and cargo spaces, a few flattened on the rear deck, clinging to the rails. No sign of Daniel. I plunged after Hannah.

Julian drew up alongside a dark canoe tied up behind my kayak. Hannah's, no doubt. I counted seven bruised, half-naked children in the boat, some as young as three or four, all of them numb-eyed, confused, too terrified even to cry.

Julian glared at Hannah. "Where've you been?"

"Where've *you* been? Where's Dan?"

He shook his phone at her like a fist. "We've been trying to reach you!"

"Phones are down below 42nd!" She gestured uptown. "Arson at Tower Four. What's all this crap?"

"This is more Macys." Julian looked almost as distraught as the children. For once, he looked his age. "Why are you down here?"

"Gathering up the odds and ends. It's time."

"Now? No, we can't. What's the rush?"

"Big storm on tap in a handful. And things are in motion uptown. There's been . . . an incident."

"Now what'd you do?"

"Not me this time. An inside job. But they'll think otherwise. Best to slip out while we can." She threw me a withholding glance. "Fill you in later."

But I'd seen eagerness override her irritation, like she got off on this sort of thing. Something they had in common, Julian and Hannah. A yen to stir up trouble. And Daniel? Was he just quieter about it?

"Got this biz of Dan's to clear up first," Julian said doggedly.

"We don't . . ."

He ignored her. "Glim, need you to talk me past security. Got to land this load and go back. We got most, but still a few to go."

"Daniel went to Macy's?"

"Where'd you think?"

"He didn't say."

Not a trace of a sneer from him. Must be bad over there, to produce this earnest, urgent Julian. Or maybe it was Hannah's presence. "And he's . . . ?"

"Still there."

Hannah muttered, "Told him not to go in alone!"

"He wasn't alone. I was there. I'm not nothing, you know!"

"Close enough."

Julian tapped his wheel, speared me with a glance, then looked across to Unca Joe.

"I'm on it." No room in *Sea Sprite*. I loosed the kayak's tie-up, got in, and shoved off.

"You're taking me with you," Hannah told Julian.

"You bet I am."

"And after, we're out of here. I mean, *out*."

Julian only jutted his chin, a trace of Dark Boy resurfacing. He powered up to a slow glide across the Lagoon, waving me up alongside. As I maneuvered around his stern, Hannah ducked inside the *Melville*'s cabin. When I was level with *Sea Sprite*'s port bow, Julian leaned over the side.

"Got to keep this quiet." He jerked his head at his passengers.

"But the dock watch is already alerted." I pointed at the signal lantern waving a path to the dock. "Got to rouse the medics at least. These kids need care."

He scowled, but I saw anxiety rather than irritation.

"Why quiet? I thought the Stormies had Macy's surrounded."

"They left, all of a sudden. Like someone rang the dinner bell. The Adders are still partying. Dan's in there stealing kids out from under their tanked-up noses with his bare hands."

"What? He's inside the building? Alone?"

He nodded. "Touchy situation. If a whole flotilla drops in, the stealth move is blown big time. And maybe Dan with it."

No, no, no. Leaving was one thing. If he was. But dying . . . no way. "I'll do what I can."

I peered ahead at Unca Joe's façade, a tower of darkness against a hint of dawn sky, then back at the *Melville*. Hannah came out on deck with a canvas sack in hand and a camo-covered tube slung across her back. One foot up on the gunwale, she stared after us. I remembered Daniel standing just so, not long ago, and I finally saw the resemblance. Not in their features, more a shared body language: the same upright, can-do posture, shoulders open to the world, as if nothing was impossible. How could either of them still believe that?

Then I was fielding sentry challenges as we slid beneath the arch toward the dock, but got a landslide of luck. Finally. The dawn dock watch was Poppy and Rivera. I wondered if they'd been to bed since I'd left them.

I waved to Poppy, squatting like a tawny bear at the foot of the ladder, her machete laid flat across her knees. She yawned, as if disappointed it was only me returning.

Rivera's eyes were sharper, and she had the lantern. She bent at the edge of the float to catch *Sea Sprite*'s bow. "Oh, no! Not more!"

I snugged the kayak at the far side, making space for Julian. "He says more to come!"

Roused by Rivera's hushed concern, Poppy grabbed my bow line. "I'll call the . . ."

"No!" I leaped out. "Rack this for me, will you? We're going back and it needs to be quiet." I couldn't have said when 'he' became 'we.' "A crowd will blow the whole rescue!"

"But . . ."

"Wait till we're gone before you take 'em up."

"You can't go alone!"

"I'm not. Take my word for it, okay? You have to!" I leaned into *Sprite* to lift the closest small body onto the dock.

Rivera was already wrangling kids. I admired her doing it so willingly. She handed a filthy, sobbing toddler to an older child who scarcely looked strong enough but had managed to climb out on her own. Once out of the boat, the others mostly collapsed to the dock, able to weep at last. They recognized a rescue. Their dulled, haunted eyes followed Rivera as she took a last half-conscious boy from Julian and settled him into her own arms. Poppy and I herded the children around her.

"Now, we'll wait for help getting up the ladder," she told them. "But you know who's already up there . . . ?" As I turned away, she was sharing out some of their denmates' names. Leave it to Rivera to have actually learned them.

Poppy planted herself between me and *Sea Sprite*. "You're going back? Where there's Adders?" She threw Julian a hard, dubious glance. "You and what army?"

"Daniel's there. Inside. Please, we . . ."

"And you'll do what when you get there?"

I shrank before the aptness of her challenge. If only I had some idea . . .

"Can she use that show-off blade?" Julian put in from behind the wheel.

"Um . . ."

Poppy about-faced, a fighter warming to the attack. She was bigger than any of us, including Hannah.

Julian nodded.

She slid her machete into its back sheath. "Let's go."

"This is Poppy," I said. And that was that.

Hannah waited on the *Melville*'s forward deck, arms folded, fingers tapping her biceps.

"Do we have to take your sister?" I murmured to Julian as we slow-motored toward her.

He shot me his Dark Boy grin. "Scared you, did she?"

"She . . . comes on strong."

"Well, get used to it. She's the best weapon we got."

The weapon was not happy to see me or Poppy in the boat. "Oh no, you don't. Den rats ashore!"

"Reinforcements," Julian countered. "Armed. And dangerous, I hope."

Hannah scanned Poppy. "Okay." She jerked her chin at me. "What's she along for?"

"Maybe keep Danny from throwing himself onto the fire . . . ?"

"That's ridiculous."

I thought she was right, but Julian's shoulders hunched. "Every Adder looks to him like Sara's killers."

"He told me to stay put," I said quietly.

"All the more reason to go. Give him a reason to be careful."

"Oh, high drama," Hannah mocked. "You think this is one of your game outings?"

"Fuck you, H. I'm the one who's been there all night!"

"We'll be tripping over all this extra fluff!"

"My boat, my choice."

They glowered at each other as *Sea Sprite* nudged against the *Melville*'s squat hull, and I pondered the complex dynamics of the Nathan family. And what he'd called her, was that just H, or maybe, 'Aitch'? Hard not to jump to conclusions . . .

"Wasting time," Hannah muttered finally. She pointed at me. "You. In the back." She swung the tube off her back and lifted her canvas satchel.

Julian tossed me a nod, grabbed his mirror shades from the dashboard and shoved them up high to keep hair out of his eyes. Facing down his big sister seemed to restore his confidence.

I hoisted myself out of the passenger seat to perch on the back deck beside Poppy, feet in the cargo slot, knees clamped around the edge.

Poppy nudged me, eyes all lit. "We'll have some fun now, eh?"

Hannah stowed her baggage under the dashboard and slid in beside her brother. "Don't count on it."

THIRTY-ONE

I signaled the all-clear to the outlying sentries as we sped up Third Avenue. I guess they were getting used to me coming and going by now. Another sunless dawn touched the westside façades with dull silver, the hot air so humid we were practically drinking it. The tide pushed in roughly, like urging us to hurry.

"Up there." Hannah pointed out a column of smoke lifting above the uptown skyline. "The whole building's a loss."

Poppy nudged me. "What we saw earlier, up in the loft."

My chance to ask Hannah if she flew drones, but answering would require her to acknowledge my existence with more than a thumb jerk. Besides, I wanted her knowing less about me, not more.

"Were you there?" I asked instead. "Any idea who did it?"

"The usual suspects," Julian supplied. Hannah just watched the smoke rise.

"But who? Is it, like, random destruction?"

Julian was happy to talk, if only to annoy his sister. "Hardly. BlackAdder ain't the only gang in town. They can call themselves families, they can call themselves the law, but gangs is what they are. Nobody elected them."

Jenn had it right, then. An uptown power struggle, with the dens caught in the middle, pawns on the chessboard. Seeing a burning high-rise on screen was one thing. Being out here, in smoke so acrid even breathing felt risky . . . it brought the reality home. The Adders might be drunk and partying, but what about all those Storm Worshippers? Where were they now? I felt small and vulnerable. I was glad Julian kept to the east side of Third, cloaking us in deep shadow.

For reasons of his own, he turned west on 11th, running us past the burned-out Ladysmith den, avoiding the half-submerged wrecks of several torched boats. Did he know Poppy was a Smith? Must be the machete told him.

She gazed impassively at the blackened ruin as we glided by, but she loosed the guard strap on her blade. "Don't worry. I haven't forgotten."

"Don't," said Julian.

Which reminded me to ask her if Rubio had got back while I was sleeping.

"Not yet. Even the scouts sent after are still out. Hope they didn't run into trouble."

I gnawed at my thumbnail.

"Nah, the place is huge," she soothed. "A full survey will take a while."

Julian was listening in. "If your den's planning a move, better get on it quick. This new storm's said to be massive, and coming up fast."

"Which is why we need to get a move on ourselves," Hannah said.

The Macys had chosen their den home because, like Unca Joe, it was an older building, mountain-solid and big enough to offer separate living areas for their tribal lifestyle. Conveniently, the structures just downtown were stories shorter but for one newer high-rise that had collapsed after the first chained Category 5s. As we went across 30th, I peered uptown from the Broadway intersection at the old pile rising over its nearest neighbors: nine or ten stories of weathered brick and stone. Below a raw blank where a heavy cornice must have been, a row of arched windows was still framed in alternating black and white. What held my eye was the washed-out red wrapping the downtown corner.

When the first kid-gangs moved in after Felix, the streets around Macy's still dried off between storms, even high tides. Now there was water at all tides, shallow but enough so we could motor right up. Julian slowed a long block away, the engine quieting.

"In case someone's finally woke to us . . ."

"Adders are a sloppy bunch." Hannah bent to the canvas at her feet, undid some fastenings, and hauled out a tangle of metal parts, which she began to fit together into some sort of double-layered arc with a thick central shaft, pulleys, and a crisscross of connecting wires, but lightweight, like an enormous insect. I stared at it without a guess.

But Poppy murmured, "Slick! That'll put a few down!"

"More than." Hannah turned the thing our way. Matte black, as if swallowing the rising dawn. "Kill at fifty meters."

"I had one when I was . . . y'know, before. Not that fancy, though. Yours is . . ."

"Douse the chatter," Julian growled. "We're right on top of them. Fuck,

I wish it was darker." At Sixth Avenue, he kept on west. "We'll go around the back. They left a loading door open."

Hannah nodded. "Like I said. Sloppy."

"Over-confident. Gave us a chance. Dan should be waiting."

No time to ask about Hannah's weapon of choice. We came around the corner of Eighth at low speed into a tide of noise rolling down 35th like a flash flood: music so loud you heard only volume, felt its bass like a beating as it mixed with swooping cheers, catcalls, and whistles. Below the bass, an on-off vibration, like the pounding of a hundred feet, one of Rousseau's let-off-steam basketball games on steroids. No question where it was coming from. The Macy's building took up the entire block. Ears ringing, we floated toward the intersection with Seventh.

"No wonder you could sneak up on them," Poppy said.

"How many are there?" The four of us felt mighty puny all of a sudden.

"Wasn't this loud before," noted Julian.

"Reinforcements? Maybe the Stormies went inside."

"Nah. They're just more lit."

"Where's the party?" Hannah peered upward.

"Fifth, sixth floor, mostly. But also scattered about. Y'know . . . private events."

Poppy craned her neck. "What's actually going on in there?"

Julian's glance was a warning. "According to Dan, the worst you can imagine. And a lot you'd rather not."

"You didn't go in?" I left the rest unsaid. He'd let Daniel go in alone.

He shrugged. "Had to secure the escape route."

"All show and no go," said Hannah.

Julian's chin lifted. "That's me, ma'am. Just the driver."

"You drive pretty good, as I recall." Someone should stand up for him. Likely Daniel had made him stay outside.

He tossed me a smirk and cut his engine. Momentum took us across the intersection as we scanned for sentries or other boats. The noise crested suddenly and a ragged ball of flame flew out of a high-up window. It rose in a bright arc, then stalled and plummeted, sending up a plume of steam as it hit the water.

Had I seen arms and legs, flailing as it fell?

A short way up the block, the row of loading doors loomed out of the gloom, a long mural of faded street tags and shredded paper. One was raised

to head-height, a darker rectangle at the near end of the dock. A few battered dinghies were tied up further down. Past them, one bigger, with a
small wheelhouse, maybe an old fishing boat. Hard to tell if she was still
seaworthy.

No sign of sentries, but no Daniel either.

"Where the fuck is he?" Julian fumed. "He was supposed to wait . . ."

"He was supposed to do a lot of things," Hannah retorted. "But did he
ever? Pull up short so we're . . ."

"I know. Out of line of sight." Grumbling, Julian nudged us in sideways
against the remains of a bumper strapped to the concrete edge. Truck tires,
long past their sell-by date.

"Look!" I pointed to the far end of the open door.

"Quiet!" Hannah steadied the boat against the dock. "I see them. You
two, out."

Poppy and I clambered onto the ragged apron. Poppy's blade was un-
sheathed and ready, reflecting the dawn as a dull silver grin.

"Put that away!" I hissed. "You'll terrify them!"

"And lose seconds on the draw? Forget it."

I moved toward the two gray lumps huddled against the door frame: bare,
bruised feet, scrawny arms and legs wrapped in stained tatters of clothing.

Poppy grabbed my arm. "Could be bait."

"Thought they didn't know we were coming . . ."

But Poppy's hold was insistent. A quiet melody of clicks and whirrs
sounded behind me.

"I'll go in." Hannah moved past us to stand, back to the wall, by the near
edge of the door. She held her spidery apparatus in both hands, at the ready.
It was the slim, barbed shaft centered in its stacked arcs that told me, finally,
what it was.

Arrows!

I must have tensed. Poppy doubled up her one-handed grip.

I said it aloud.

"Yeah!" agreed Poppy. "Wish I'd thought of that! Takes some deep skill,
though."

"What do you call that thing?" My brain was on fire. The clicks and
whirrs inside my head were the sounds of things falling into place. Some
things, at least. Most of which I'd have to put off considering till later.

Poppy dropped into her comic know-it-all voice. "Dude! That there's a serious compound crossbow with laser sight and automatic quiver. Weighs maybe five pounds. Custom built. Didn't find 'em in stores, when there were stores. What is she, military?"

"Maybe." That'd account for her getting around and her access to special weaponry.

But arrows? Wouldn't a gun be easier?

I couldn't put it all together. Like, had Hannah been following me all this time?

A second burning object cascaded from far above, trailing sparks and smoke, landing close enough to Julian to rouse a startled curse. From her listening post by the door, Hannah pivoted around the edge and into darkness. I recalled her dancer's grace from that night on the street, not so long ago as it seemed, a few weeks really. Soon she was back, as silently as she'd left. She signaled me toward the lump of kids and Poppy to follow her. I made to object, but Hannah's sharp glare stopped me cold. No question who was in charge. Anyway, I looked the least threatening, carried the least authority. Better if they'd brought Rivera, but I'd have to do. I bit my lip and eased over toward the kids while the roar of whoops and whistles from inside rose to a sustained crescendo and the pounding rhythm built, like an army on the march.

But where was Daniel?

The leaden dawn was as bright as it was going to get, enough for me to make out two, no . . . three pairs of frightened eyes tracking my cautious approach. At least they were alive. One lump turned out to be two small boys clinging so close, you could hardly tell which foot or arm belonged to who. The third, a girl, struggled to stand, failed, then hauled herself on hips and elbows up between me and the boys. One leg dragged limp behind her. Her stare was as hard as Hannah's.

I spread open palms. "No worry. We're here to help."

Her gaze didn't waver, but it softened a little. She was desperate to believe me.

I crouched just out of reach. "Hurt your leg?"

She flicked a glance at it, like it was someone else's. "Must be broke."

I wasn't going to ask how. She was maybe six or seven, too big for me to carry. I made staying motions and ducked inside the door to kick around in the rubble I knew would be there, searching for a broken board or a length of pipe she could use as a crutch. Stumbling over a dented metal folding chair, I pictured some Macy sentry in better days, sitting by the door, keeping a comfortable watch. For all the good it did when the Adders fell down on them like a building collapse. But now the chair would get this kid to safety.

She got the idea right off and let me help her stagger up on her good leg, the chair tucked tight beneath her arm. It was a pretty good fit. She gave a little shiver, like a dog righting its fur, and tried a few steps. Awkward, but it let her stand straight and loosed her tongue. She peered up at me, revealing a fresh bruise from cheek to jaw, and older ones around both eyes. "Gonna eat us, they were. When they run out of food."

I blinked. "What? No, they wouldn't. Bad people say that just to frighten you."

"Nope. They were. Did everything else they said they would."

She couldn't be right, about the eating at least. I mean, really? But I didn't argue. Julian was hissing at us to hurry. "Why don't you help me get these little guys up and moving so we can all be safe?"

At the girl's urgings, the toddler pair untangled and rose on unsteady feet, even let me take their hands to lead them to the boat. As I lifted the second boy into the back seat, a sudden flare shot up above the dark profile of the rooftops across 35th Street, flushing the wall behind us with an orange flicker. For a second, I was sure the sun had broken through the heavy cloud cover.

"Holy fuck! Another one!" Julian twisted in his seat for a better view.

"Another?"

"Cell hub." He pulled out his phone to jab at its tiny screen. "That'll be . . . Tower Two."

Off toward the West Side, a second broad column of smoke smudged the flat gray sky above the rooftops, hot points of light eating it from within.

"Shit! Must be after them all!" He waved his phone like it had betrayed him, then bent to it again. "Bad move. It'll backfire on them."

I settled the lame girl in next to the toddlers. "Sure it's not Adders?" If there were Adders out there still sober enough for targeted arson, they could be back here any minute.

"Nah." Julian kept at his phone. "Like I said. Uptown stuff. Adders couldn't pull off a coordinated take-down. They're basically meat on legs. Ever tried to talk to one?"

"Me? How would I?" I was appalled. "You have?"

His head sagged a bit between his shoulders, then lifted again, defiant. "Used to hang with them."

"You never!" More Dark Boy bravado, surely.

He glanced away, pocketing his phone. "Did."

"But why . . . ?" My jaw must've dropped open as all the bad and scary thoughts I'd first had about him came howling back. "How could you . . . !"

"You really want to know?"

Not sure I did, but he was intent, both hands fisted on the wheel, hovering between pride and shame, like he needed to get it off his chest. "Okay . . ."

"Me and my guys. Whoever was left. After Felix. When everything looked, y'know, finished. It was the cool thing to do. Drugs, booze, nookie, anarchy. Those high-end, off-grid penthouses down in the Battery. Leftover luxury. The Adders had it all. Like they were the fullest expression of the time."

"Maybe for you."

"Yeah? And what were you doing then, Ms. Perfect? Dan says you remembered some stuff finally."

"I wasn't shacking up with Adders!"

"My parents fucking abandoned me! Emptied most of the bank accounts, took off for parts unknown. And not with each other! Hannah was still in Africa. Dan was upstate. The world was ending. Why not break loose? Take what you need. Live in the moment. Have some real fun." He looked at me straight, daring me to contradict. "Like, where was I supposed to go? Some cold-water den, working my butt off day and night for a bowl of slop?"

"We don't eat slop!"

"I ate steak and drank the best left-behind wines! At least till they ran out." He laughed, his Dark Boy bitter cackle. "Adders! Like watching a super-gross horror vid, all around you, 24/7. One thrill after the next."

He was trying for shock, and he had me. "How *old* were you?"

He sucked in air. "It was Dara's year, so I was . . . yeah, I was eleven."

Out in mid-street, a wad of charred debris bobbed to the surface, a remnant of the flying balls of fire. I thought I made out the blackened curve of an arm, but it was so stiff, it might have been a mannequin. Plenty of them around, stripped and abandoned. You'd see them floating out with the tide.

"That's all you did, watch?"

Julian shrugged. "Mostly. They were bad then, but not this bad. It passed the time."

He looked to see what I was squinting at, gave it his attention. But his voice had gone rough. "Then they killed a friend of mine. Just like that. Beat him to death when he wouldn't share his girl around. Won't go into what they did to her. Held the rest of us down to watch. We couldn't do shit to stop them . . ." He spat out the last words as rage, guilt, remembered impotence and grief surged across his face in waves. For a moment, he drifted helpless in the wake. I worried he'd burst into tears and shame himself further. I let my eyes wander, sparing him a witness. But soon enough, he raked both hands through his hair and found his sleek bad-boy mask again. "Yep. Meat on legs."

I pictured the dead friend like the other young drunks at our encounter on the Causeway. Soft-cheeked. Entitled. In way over his head. "So Dark Boy became Julian again?"

He buzzed air through his lips. "Don't make it into a morality tale. The risks outweighed the thrills after, that was all. We got . . . careful. Stuck to ourselves since then." He sang softly, like quoting a lyric. *"Been wild all night, but ain't no jungle animal . . ."* Then his flat gaze scorched past me. "Okay, here's some action now . . ."

I whirled, sure he meant Adders. But it was Daniel, shepherding two more battered children. Poppy followed, helping an older kid limp along. Hannah brought up the rear, backing through the bay door with her bow trained on the dark interior.

Julian stood up in his seat. "Where the fuck we gonna put 'em all?"

Daniel was . . . barely recognizable. Not just the blood and ash as thick as paint smearing his skin and clothing. Or the sweat washing through it in rivulets, leaving him zebra-striped, like a gore-streaked villain in a video game. His predatory stance, every muscle taut, the gleam of the hunt in his eyes. How had such a terrifying creature convinced small children to come away with him?

He took in the scene on the loading dock without visible response: me beside *Sprite*, Julian's nearly full load, the brightening dawn. His gaze swept past us to the old fishing boat at the far end of the dock, like making sure she was still there. But I read it as a suggestion.

Really? She looked a wreck to me, but maybe he'd already checked her out. My brain fired up like a lit match: Is she sound? Is she fueled? Was a key left behind? Will she even start? If she would, problem solved.

No point waiting for answers or permission, or for Daniel to yell at me for always being where I shouldn't. Next thing, I was sprinting toward the old hulk. Finally, something I could do to help.

A faint odor of oil and gas as I got near. Hopeful, as was the rainbow slick hugging the stern. She'd been run within very recent memory. Her transom said she'd been called *Zephyr,* out of Montauk, but her name had been crudely painted over so it read *ZeRO.* Some Adder trying for clever. I wasn't having any of that. Trite as it was, *Zephyr* she would be.

She was high at the prow, long and low at the stern. Her aft cockpit had been cleared of the usual net winches, masts, and icing boxes. Her stubby, stick-built wheelhouse was sunk into her mids. Hardly a lick of paint left on her, but the scum I stepped into as I vaulted over the gunwale was only ankle-deep. If she'd start, she'd get a few more of us out of here.

I waded to the little wheelhouse, a step up and only moldy-damp inside. Not even a shard of glass in the surround of paned windows. I glanced back to see Poppy already herding the stumbling new rescues my way, while Daniel hissed at her to hurry. Hannah grabbed his shoulder, a staying gesture, but he shook her off roughly.

I turned to the control panel. It was battered and greasy, with gaping holes where the radio and other instruments had been. But the lighting and bilge pump switches looked intact, and the wheel and stick moved easily enough when I jiggled them. No key in the slot, but I knew the usual places to hide one. All of it coming back to me in a flood, a data download. I felt around here and there, found a key on the fourth try, a dangle of metal and plastic, hooked beneath the console. Slid right into the slot.

"Any luck?" Poppy called, over the bass beat and cheering from upstairs. The boat rocked as she loaded Macys in one by one, searching out dry spots to perch them.

"We'll see," I muttered, and turned the key.

Nothing. But a few tries later, the engine caught, then died, then caught again with a roar and a chuff-chuff. At last, it settled in pretty good. Poppy pumped a fist and I lifted a victory V, then spotted Daniel and Hannah facing off in the loading bay, in furious argument.

I left the engine complaining to itself and came to the cabin door. The noise from above drowned out their voices. "What's all that?"

Poppy's frown was quizzical. "He wants to go back in. She says enough is enough. Something about getting the hell out of dodge, whatever that means. The new storm's got her all riled, but y'know . . . bad time for a family quarrel."

"There's more needing rescue?"

"He's got something else in mind . . ."

"Like what?" I watched Daniel slash his arms across Hannah's gestures, like clearing a screen. He looked out of control. No, more like totally in control but deaf to any purpose except his own. While Hannah railed at him, he turned away toward *Sea Sprite*, barked a few words at Julian, then went sternward to open a storage locker behind the cargo seat. He lifted out a soft-sided carry-all, its contents shifting inside, and set it on the dock. He looked to Julian with a jerk of his chin toward the darkness of the open bay door. Julian returned a slow not-on-your-life wag and returned to battening down his restive Macys. Every twitch of his slim body said he was way past ready to be out of there.

With a warning shout, Hannah ducked away from the doorway, her bow raised. Daniel threw himself in the other direction, tucking and rolling across the dock till he fetched up against the building wall.

Hannah yelled to Julian, "Go! Go!"

Sea Sprite roared to life and swerved away from the dock, spewing wake, as bullets spattered the concrete and two half-naked men charged out of the bay, blinded by drink and daylight, firing at random. Poppy and I dragged our Macys into *Zephyr*'s wheelhouse and laid everyone low. *Sea Sprite* vanished east on 35th.

"Least someone's awake in there," Poppy murmured.

"Awake, maybe. But sober?"

The pair—one big, one small—were staggering around, as if propelled by the rhythmic kick of their automatic weapons. Lead sprayed right, left, high, low, but not for long. Hannah's bow took them down silently and in seconds. The close-range impact sent both men sprawling on the dock. Behind me, the Macys were whimpering again.

I hushed them, mostly to settle my own rising panic. Where there were two Adders, there were likely a whole lot more. But I eased upward for a better view. I'd never laid eyes on a real Adder before.

Poppy peered over my shoulder. "Don't look like much, do they?"

Had to agree. Other than being well armed and wearing nothing but some sort of decorated loin wrap, these fellows were disappointingly ordinary. No paint, no masks, no puffed-up body armor. No different from Rousseau's lads.

"Maybe they're newbies? Stuck on guard duty and missing the fun upstairs?"

"Short career," Poppy said. "And getting shorter . . ."

Daniel had scrambled to his feet while Hannah covered him from the edge of the bay. To my horror, even before checking for signs of life, he grasped the nearest arrow shaft, jerked it free, and moved on.

"Ow!" hissed Poppy. "No wasting time, your guy."

Mine? No. This was some other Daniel Nathan. Not the one I knew.

Two arrows in the big guy, one through his neck. His legs went into spasm as he bled out, wet ribbons of red coursing from under him. The smaller guy's back arched in agony as Daniel yanked at him roughly. He was still alive.

Daniel tossed the arrows at Hannah's feet, moving at double time. She scooped them up to reload. Grasping the smaller Adder's arm, Daniel dragged him toward the water.

"What is he . . . No!"

Poppy grabbed for me but missed. I was out of *Zephyr,* racing to plant myself between Daniel and the edge of the dock.

"He's alive!" I wailed.

Daniel straightened, his fist tight around the guy's wrist. Took him a moment to identify the obstacle. "Out of the way! Or you'll go in with him."

"*What?*"

"Out of my way!"

"Daniel, he's *alive!*"

"Not for long!"

What I saw in his eyes made me back away with a shiver as he rolled the moaning Adder into the water. The Adder's face flashed upward as he tumbled over: a pimply, terrified kid, not much older than some of the Macys. The splash sloshed red-stained water across my feet, but I was rooted to the spot, sure now that I lacked some basic understanding, some crucial life lesson. Because it made no sense to be killing each other when we all needed every bit of help we could get.

Daniel didn't spare me a glance as he went back for the first guy. This one was bigger, rotund at the middle and, by now, dead weight. Daniel struggled, impatient, eyeing the open doorway and Hannah's rigid back, her raised, bow-bristled arms.

Finally, he snapped, "Give me a fucking hand here, will you?"

Me? I glanced around. Maybe Poppy had come up behind?

"Glim! We're running out of time!"

"No. I can't!" My throat closed. Touch that naked skin, the blood and fecal stench? "I can't!"

"You can!"

"He's dead! Leave him! Why does it matter?"

"It matters. No sign left behind."

"Who cares?"

Another chorus of whistles and roars burst from overhead. And after, that same pulsing pounding, louder and louder.

"They will! Ditch their guns, at least!"

"Adders in motion!" Hannah called from the doorway.

"Where?"

"Over east. Still upstairs. I think."

Daniel bent back to his grunting and hauling, inching the guy toward the edge. What more would a body tell them, with the dock already slick with blood? Did he mean to hide that, too? But the grim weight slid easier on the wet, and soon it was at the edge and tipping over into the water. Like I had all the time in the world, I watched it sink, then watched Daniel kick their rifles in after them, aware I'd ceased functioning but unsure what to do next. Moving was a start. I turned back toward the fishing boat. A task I understood.

"Oh, no. We're not done yet." Daniel's fist closed on the nape of my neck, shoving me toward the bay door. He'd caught up the bulging carry-all and slung it across his back.

At the doorway, Hannah blocked the way. "Leave it, Dan. Be out of here while we can."

"This won't take long."

"Too long."

"Only if we stand here talking."

"I save your butt over and over and do you ever listen to me?" Hannah sucked her teeth, scowling. "At least leave her here."

"She needs to see this."

"What the fuck for?"

"Okay. I need her to see it. Call it a chance for full disclosure."

"Dan, they're onto me. The door is closing."

Daniel stared her down until she set her jaw and shouldered her bow.

"Okay. But make it quick."

I was silent, like a leaf on a branch, dangling loose at the end of Daniel's arm even as I leaned away toward *Zephyr* and escape. His grip was only firm. I could have shrugged it off but lacked the will to try. I let him—determined, implacable—sweep me along. Halfway across the unlit bay, I remembered Julian's remark about Daniel throwing himself on the fire. Maybe now I got what he meant. He'd seen his brother this close to the edge before. If Daniel went into the building without some sort of sea anchor to drag him back, he might not come out again. Even scary as he was right then, I couldn't let that happen.

I jiggled my shoulder inside his grasp. "I'm okay. I'll stick by. I promise."

"Like you promised to stay back at the den?"

"Julian said I better come."

"And you listen to him now?" But he slowed, studying me in the scant light.

Hannah answered for me. "She was holding us up, stubborn git."

"She is that." His grip eased on my neck as the jungle in his eyes retreated some. "Okay, Glim. On your honor. But make yourself useful. Put your picker's eyes to work."

What happened to calling me Lizzy? "What am I looking for?"

"Anything like a Macy that's still breathing."

He stared at me hard, waiting for me to break and run. So of course I couldn't.

Hannah jostled. "Are we doing this?"

"Now."

To the right of a second row of rolled-down doors, Daniel cracked open a smaller door, peered in, then gestured us through. Raucous shouts and pounding tumbled down from upstairs like distant thunder. Daniel gathered us just inside. "We'll do a final sweep, then go lay them in. Take the rear, H."

Aitch? Click, whir. Had to be. But whose side was she on? Anyone's beside her own?

We moved ahead into darkness, through another door, and suddenly, into silvery light.

The ground floor was cavernous and smelled of the mold rising from flooded basement levels. The center was scoured clean, with sodden wads of unidentifiable muck jammed up along the walls, typical of big spaces after a serious storm surge has washed through. Too bad the Macys hadn't tidied up more, but they were kids—and worse, orphans. No one to make them clean up their room. Freed of glass and most of their mullions, the tall windows created an open arcade along the flooded street, bright with watery reflection across the walls, shadowy among the long rows of columns cut by the diagonals of frozen escalators. So much for den security.

Seeing flickers of movement, I recoiled, bringing Hannah up short. But it was only my own image slipping by in mirror shards still clinging to facets of the pillars.

Hannah nudged me with the curve of her bow. "Keep the pace."

I'd had it with her attitude, but this wasn't the time for backtalk. She'd taken against me and that was that. Nothing to do but press on. At least she'd stopped calling me den rat.

Daniel led us up the first escalator we came to, past the pendant remains of giant stained-glass chandeliers. For a moment, I forgot where I was, and what I was likely headed into. I wished Rubio could see this old building, struggling to hold on to some trace of its former glory, like the city he loved. Thinking 'Rubio' and 'building' stirred up a minor brain shudder: of course I knew Yankee Stadium. I'd sailed past it many times, and now could almost remember what it looked like. I hoped Rube's mission was working out better than mine, and that he'd be home before the weather arrived.

Surveyed from mid-escalator, the second floor looked dim and uninhabited. Still too close to surge levels for the Macys to have set up living space. Daniel passed it by. Climbing to the third, he got more cautious. He pointed out a glow behind a stripped-down stud wall at the eastern end. Slow-moving shadows slid along the further wall and I was sure I heard snatches of drunken singing, different from the din upstairs.

"No problem there," Daniel murmured. "They're too busy having each other."

But he avoided the escalator to the fourth floor and took us the long way round to the fire stairs. Here and there, we came across signs of Macy use: small encampments walled off by piled-up display counters, some with the open sides forming kid-sized sleeping compartments, a mini version of the bunk-tiers at Unca Joe. Tossed bedding and scattered clothing spoke of a violent wake-up. I hadn't liked Macys much, but nobody deserved this.

The unlit stairwell stank of piss and vomit but was less exposed. Reconnoitering the fourth floor showed us larger, more evolved encampments along the window walls where the light was strongest, with the Macys' colorful gang tags claiming possession of this sector or that. And now there was a scatter of bodies to creep around. Adder bodies. Big, male, naked or half-clothed, curled up on cushions, overflowing from bed cubicles, spread-eagled on tattered sofas, sprawled on the floor. Sleeping, passed out, nodding out, often in their own puke and piss . . . or just plain dead. Hard to tell. Daniel wouldn't let us get close enough. He satisfied himself that no Macys lay undiscovered in the mess and circled back to the concealing murk of the fire stairs.

Always, the noise surrounded us, invaded every pore, ricocheted along every nerve. It made me jumpy, clouded my mind. How could they stand it? At the fifth-floor landing, Daniel passed the exit by and kept climbing. The moment we'd cleared the halfway turn, the door below burst open. A handful of Adders stumbled through, dragging another by his heels. One held the door open to let in the light. We dropped low and shrank against the stinking upper wall, peering through the railing. The guy on the ground struggled vaguely, raising a chorus of guffaws from the others, who proceeded to toss him down the stairs. He lay groaning on the landing until they staggered after him, still roaring, then hauled him up again and tumbled him down the next flight. After that, he didn't move, and the fourth-floor door slammed shut as the others left him there.

"What could he have done that they . . . ?" I murmured.

"Not enough," said Daniel. "Adders punish restraint."

Hannah rose to gaze over the railing. "Maybe the game is to see how many bones you can break before he actually stops breathing."

"And that's only an appetizer," he added.

We weren't going to help the dude, even if he was dying. I'd learned that lesson already. "Why hurt your own guys?"

"Culling the weak." Daniel slumped against the railing, exhaustion snatching at him. He fought it down, swiping at the muck on his forehead to keep it from his eyes. "You're presuming survival as a primary goal."

Wasn't it everyone's? "What, then?"

"Status. Macho. How many men it takes to hold you down. How long you can go without sobering up. Adders aren't really a den. They're a tidal wash-up of guys sharing nasty appetites and a willingness to do anything to satisfy them."

If I hadn't yet realized that I might die here, I got it now.

Hannah's nails tapped the railing. Letting reason surface long enough for conversation was no advantage right then. Daniel shoved himself off the wall. "Let's go."

We continued upward, just as the stairwell below got busier, shouts and scuffles, doors slamming, feet slapping downstairs. Nothing heading up, but I feared for our escape route.

"Looks like you got all the Macys," I noted. "And Poppy's down there on her own. Shouldn't we head back before it's too late?"

"I'm for that," Hannah seconded.

"And let them off easy?" Daniel threw me a glance, a mix of regret and intransigence. "Or you."

Hannah fussed with her bow. "Dan, our window of . . ."

"Can wait. I've a chance to finish something here, and I'm not missing it."

"You mean, avenge," she murmured.

"Whatever." He adjusted the carry-all strap on his shoulder and mounted the last few steps to the sixth floor. The door was off its hinges. As we neared, all three of us shrank from the odor sifting through the opening: a rancid, swampy reek with a tang of something metallic. My gorge rose, and I buried my nose in my palm.

From the landing we had a clear view of a wide, railed gallery and the open space beyond, broken only by derelict light fixtures. Dawn had become morning. Pallid daylight squeezed in through parallel rows of dirty skylights. The long sides of the gallery widened to make room for walled cubicles, maybe offices, now repurposed as living quarters for Macy higher-ups. Not just den tags but names proudly decorated the doors. Here and there along the railing, sturdy rope ladders dropped to the floor below, the one we'd passed by, where the commotion was coming from.

Daniel set the carry-all down carefully, then dropped to his knees and crept forward, waving at Hannah and me to follow. The railing had a solid base to about shin-height, just enough to conceal us. My ears throbbed. The gallery floor, the railing, the entire building shuddered with the din from below. Couldn't help thinking of the power they were wasting! I sneaked my head up to peer over the edge and ducked right down again.

"No. Look." Daniel's thumb jabbed my ribs. "Take a really good look. See what we're up against!"

I moaned a protest. Adders down there. Masses of them. But Daniel jabbed me again. I lifted my head and looked.

Nothing, not all the den gossip and warnings and scary talk, not even the

Ladysmiths who'd fought them and fled, had got BlackAdder right. This was no pirate fantasy, lethal perhaps but slim and hard and bedecked with glorifying war paint, faintly dashing.

This was mostly skin, pinkish and hairy. A tangle of legs, shoulders rocking, arms waving, shiny heads bobbing, bare feet stomping. A chaos of pale naked flesh: all those monochrome Adders writhing in a pit, just like their namesakes. A game of sorts was underway.

A rough rectangle was framed by seating levels made of stacked office desks, cabinets, and larger hunks of electronic equipment. Sweaty, naked men crowded the tiers. Their one point of fashion was a single long hank of hair sprouting from the top of each otherwise shaved head, braided or beaded or bound at the base and flowing loose like a horse's tail.

They were mostly solid, thick-necked, sliding toward pudge. Like the two who had died on the dock, so ordinary—lounging, sleeping, drinking, nodding out, or sloppily cheering on the players shoving each other around in the open center. Shouldn't evil have a more distinctive face? Despite the oppressive heat, I was shivering.

"How many, do you think?" Daniel murmured to Hannah.

"Sixty, seventy. It's most of them, I'd say. Minus Bright's upgrades."

"Good."

"Sure about this?"

"Never more."

"Where are the women?" I asked.

Hannah laughed low in her throat. Daniel turned away.

Didn't they have any? Or were they locked away somewhere? I could believe that. At least I saw nothing like a left-behind Macy. The game held the Adders' total attention, those who were still conscious. It seemed to be a combo of soccer and basketball. The ball could be kicked or tossed, and metal barrels at either end served as baskets. The beige-tiled floor was a scumble of dark streaks spreading damply underfoot. The players' pale skin shone with sweat and the same dark streaking. Paint? Maybe team colors? But there didn't seem to be teams, or anyone cooperating with anyone else. More like every man for himself, a total free-for-all. As they bobbed and jigged around each other, a bright flash from a player's arm caught my eye, then I saw it everywhere, stared hard, then sucked in breath in disbelief. Each player had a short, curved blade strapped to one wrist, like the spurs on that menace of a rooster back at Unca Joe. Along with owning the ball, it was slash-or-be-slashed, and the dark streaks were a mix of sweat and . . .

Not paint. Blood. Everywhere. I felt Daniel watching me, intense as the Adders at their awful game. How much more of this did he need me to see? And why?

A player found an opening. His arm raked up in an arc as he slung the ball at the nearest basket, right below our hiding place. As the ball tumbled toward us, I got a real look at it. I clamped both hands across my mouth to keep from giving us away.

The ball had eyes. And a mouth. A young girl's mouth. And a ragged, bloody stump where it had been ripped from its body.

I jerked away, backward belly-crawling to the landing. Daniel caught me at the door.

"Hold her," he ordered Hannah.

Hannah shifted her bow to one hand so she could wrap an arm around my waist while I coughed bile onto the floor behind her. Even she looked faintly round-eyed, and she gave him no argument. "Hurry, Dan."

Daniel hefted the carry-all. Hugging the cubicle walls, he slipped around one side of the gallery, disappeared into an open door for a moment, reappeared and moved on around while Hannah held me still. I gave no thought to what he was doing. I could barely catch my breath, fighting the nausea and a burning need to scream and flail and beat my fists, while down below, the nightmare game continued.

"How . . . could . . . they . . . ?"

Hannah leaned into me. "Get a grip, girl. We know they're animals."

"But . . . but . . . why?" I bent over double, heaving.

"You think everything has a reason? Forget it." Her voice poured calm into my ear. "Adders have no why. They just do. If you told them it was wrong, they wouldn't understand the term."

'Animals' didn't half describe such . . . such what? Cruelty? Depravity? Evil? No word seemed extreme enough. My own Abel trauma paled by comparison. And she was right. I had to get a grip or be a hitch to any of us getting out of here alive. I wiped at my mouth and twisted in her grasp, trying to sit upright. When I made it to my knees, she let me go but kept her hand pressed to my back.

"That's better." She sounded almost kind, but it was more likely relief.

Daniel made the circuit of the gallery, ducked into a final doorway, then came toward us, bundling up the empty carry-all. He tossed it into the last cubicle he passed. He looked relieved but still grimly determined.

"Done," he said to Hannah. "Take her down, okay. I need to check a few things."

"No! No, you can't!" I swiped at my mouth again. I must have looked as crazed as I felt, but I knew this was the moment Julian wanted me here for. "I'm not leaving with just her!"

"What? Why?"

"Because she'll . . ." I didn't really think Hannah would hurt me, but if he thought so . . .

"Safety in numbers. We go down together." Hannah caught on quick.

Daniel looked back, scanning the balcony circle. "But if it doesn't . . ."

"It will," she said. "Dan. Now."

His gaze at me was speculative. Then he shook his head. "Okay. Okay. Slow and quiet all the way." He jabbed a finger my way. "No bolting."

We moved into the dark stairway. Shielded from the loud chaos of the game, we could hear tumult on the lower landings. The crowd was breaking up. Daniel pulled up short, listening. There was a broken kind of group rhythm to it: door opening, boisterous entry, descent amid drunken bragging and trash talk, door closing, pause, repeat. If we timed it right, we could slip by in between.

"Forget about slow." Daniel waited out another gang of revelers, then launched himself down the stairs as soon as the door shut, me and Hannah tight on his heels. We passed the fifth-floor door, rounding the halfway to the fourth at full speed. Down on the fourth-floor landing in the light from a half-open door, a single Adder swayed as he pissed into the center well. He looked up as we came at him, his unsteady squint slipping past Daniel to focus on me, then Hannah.

"Pussy!" he bellowed in slurry delight.

Daniel hit him with a body block, knocked him flat on the concrete, and kept going. Terror cleared my head like a breaking wave. With escape my only thought, I hurdled the sprawl of arms and legs—faster than avoiding it. Hannah hesitated, lifting her bow, then decided against and followed. Half a flight downward, the guy we'd mowed over was already yelling his lungs out, down but not out, sober enough to raise the alarm. We took the next three flights full out, as best we could in the dark, snatching at the railing, flinging ourselves around the corners, almost in free fall.

Say what you will, sodden as they were, the Adders responded fast when called to alert. Dropping from second to first floors, we felt the vibration of heavy feet pounding down behind us. The clamor upstairs backed off, shifting toward a more focused aggression. As we gained the ground floor and dashed across its open center toward the loading bay, we heard scattered gunfire from above and thunder on the escalators.

"They're shooting out the windows!" Daniel shouted. No point in quiet now. "Outside, stick to the wall!"

"Poppy's out there!" I had barely breath to yell, and no chance to catch it. Could only hope she'd taken cover in time.

Daniel barely slowed at the loading door, a half-second to judge the thickness of the lead hail from the upper stories, then he was out and scooting sideways along the row of doors with us in his wake. We were out of sight to anyone above and the shooters didn't think to aim straight down. They were venting their fury on the bodies floating in the middle of the street. Maybe thought they'd got us already.

I glanced ahead at *Zephyr*, saw Poppy peering out of the wheelhouse just as she spotted us. Damned if the engine wasn't still running. I nearly cheered. Felt like we'd been inside that hellhole for hours, but probably wasn't more than ten, fifteen minutes.

Daniel pulled up opposite the boat and flattened himself into the recess of the final loading door. Hannah and I tucked in beside him. He signaled Poppy to stay put. The guys above hadn't noticed her yet, and I prayed the thin layer of exhaust gathered around *Zephyr*'s stern wouldn't tip them off. Poppy flashed her machete at us, nodding toward the tie lines, front and back. Stupid me hadn't thought to undo one at least when I'd had the chance. Daniel returned her nod and raised his arm, readying the go-ahead.

"She'll need cover, H."

"We all will."

"Glim, you're driving."

Of course. At least he hadn't asked if I was up to it.

It was a short sprint to *Zephyr*, maybe twenty feet, every inch potential death. Our best bet was speed and surprise, and each of us doing our job. I was so stoked on flight adrenaline, working out my path to the wheelhouse and the controls, counting the steps, I barely noticed the brap-brap of the semi-automatics continuing to spray the water and the other end of the loading dock. But we all heard the sharper crack of the sniper's rifle when it came, like a high note rising above a chorus.

"Shit." Daniel glanced upward, his arm still raised.

"Hope he's as drunk as the rest of them," said Hannah.

"Here comes the infantry!" Daniel dropped his arm. "Run!"

I bolted for *Zephyr*'s mids. Poppy vaulted out of the wheelhouse and onto the dock, slicing the nearby stern tie line in practically the same motion. I heard Hannah's bow thunk behind me as the first wave of Adders boiled out of the loading door, then halted in confusion when a few went down in friendly fire from above. I was over the gunwale and at the wheelhouse door when Poppy flashed by, heading for the bow line.

Crack!

She spun and went down. I started toward her, but Daniel reached from the dock to shove me back. "Drive!"

Crack!

Wood spat at me from the roof of the wheelhouse.

I whirled to the controls, feeling *Zephyr* shiver as Hannah dropped into the stern. Under the console, huddled at my feet, the last of the Macys stared up in terror. Through an empty window frame, I saw Daniel snatch up Poppy's machete and cut through the bow line. He scooped her up by the waist, rolled her onto the bow deck, and dropped down beside her, using the wheelhouse as cover. *Zephyr* was already moving.

Crack!

More wood chips flying.

Crack! Clang! A ricochet off Poppy's machete, lying abandoned on the dock.

I shoved the stick forward hard as I dared, told the old boat she better be up to some serious abuse. The sniper kept at us, but he must have been seeing double, and the confusion on the dock thinned out the threat from the ground.

Zephyr didn't have *Sea Sprite*'s gusto, but she got us out of there.

Soon as we turned the corner, Daniel was up and dragging Poppy into the rear. Her heels left a red trail along the foredeck.

"Is it bad?" I called as they went by.

He gestured to Hannah to help lay Poppy out on a side seat. "What's it look like?"

Hannah bent over Poppy's bloody thigh. "Through muscle. Don't think it hit bone. There's an exit wound. It'll bleed some."

"Got to get her home soon," Daniel called to me. "Head down Broadway and . . ."

"Getting shallow over there. This boat has . . ."

". . . stop at 32nd."

I turned to him. "Stop?"

"Just do it!"

Hannah set her bow aside to haul off Poppy's T-shirt and tear it into strips, handing them to Daniel to bind her up. Poppy's freckled face was pale and her lips pulled in tight, but she insisted she could sit upright once the bandaging was done. To my surprise, Hannah stayed by her, supporting her weight against the boat's motion.

At 32nd and Broadway, though we were surely in the sniper's range if he'd changed position and got lucky, I slowed, eased *Zephyr* into reverse to cut our momentum, and let her drift. I was on autopilot, confused to numbness. Easier just to follow orders. The music still blared uptown, overlaid now by shooting, furious shouting, and battle whoops. I squinted up Broadway, looking for angry Adders piling into their boats to come after us. But what boats? Besides *Zephyr* and some dinghies, I hadn't seen any.

"Where are their boats?"

"Cut loose after the Stormies left." Daniel's mouth curved, but it was hardly a smile. "Rousseau should send someone to round them up."

He moved to the starboard side, wiped his hands on his jeans, and fished out his phone. He tapped in a lengthy sequence, then another. Messaging Julian while he still had signal?

"Better work." He tapped a few more times. "'Cause it's all I got. Glim, get ready to light-speed out of here." He hesitated, shut his eyes briefly, then touched the screen once more, gazing expectantly across town.

The flash reached us an instant before the deafening boom, as the upper stories of Macy's exploded into 35th Street. A second blast was closer to Broadway. A third fractured the grand old 34th Street façade. A fourth collapsed it. The fireball swallowed the block. Black smoke ballooned skyward. The concussion echoed on and on.

My fists drifted up to pin my open mouth. My brain balked.

"Yes! Yes!" Poppy found a secret well of energy. "Take that, you motherfuckers!"

"Go!" Daniel yelled. "Now!"

Good thing my autopilot was working, because I was not. My eyes stung. I couldn't see, even think past the hot debris raining down around us. It was Lizzy's hand on the stick as I shoved it forward. What had he . . . we . . . done?

Fiery missiles pocked the water, hissing into steam. A few landed in the cockpit bilge and died. Acrid smoke billowed along the cross-streets, dragging with it the raw thunder of collapse and a very bad odor.

The Macy kids unfolded themselves from under the console and gathered silently at the wheelhouse door to see their den go up in flames and shower a ten-block radius with ash and wreckage. Never mind the shattered bodies of sixty or so Adders.

No eruption of victory yells and back-slapping in the back of the boat. The devastation was too sobering. Poppy grinned bravely through her pain and Hannah looked darkly satisfied, but Daniel sat still and erect, watching the inferno eat up Herald Square as if only now facing the horror he'd brought about. Finally, Hannah set to breaking down her bow, returning unused arrows to the quiver still slung across her back. She nudged Daniel with a supportive fist, but he turned away, rubbed viciously at his face, then sat elbows on knees, staring into the ashy water washing around the bottom of the boat while I drove us out of there.

He didn't look at me. I guessed it would be a while. He would guess how I was taking this. And what could I say to him? I didn't understand the deal he'd made with himself. If only it had been Tom Doyle or Empire Will, someone I didn't want so much to think well of. But it hadn't been easy. Julian was likely right about Daniel not caring if he walked away from this righteous wrong. His burden of guilt spoke loud in the slump of his shoulders, the crushed stillness of his spine. Well, good. He'd be no better than Adders, otherwise.

"Any more speed in this tub?" Hannah demanded.

"Push her too hard, she'll quit." But I settled *Zephyr* into a steadier run. We were already at risk from the boat's shifty fuel gauge. Better to get home and face our reckoning there than break down halfway.

Hannah eased an arm around Poppy's back. "Fast as you can."

At least we'd done our best to save the Macys. One less thing to feel guilty about.

THIRTY-TWO

O pen water steadied me a bit. The sailor in me shoved the horror aside to focus on tide and wind direction, maybe to avoid the worst of the smoke, and the grim debris still silting down around us. I was glad to be inside the wheelhouse. Nobody told me different when I turned down Fifth for the quickest water route. We motored toward home in silence. Even the little Macys seemed lost in grisly contemplation.

Near 23rd, chugging noisily through the western edge of Empire territory, we were suddenly surrounded by sentinel patrol boats. I counted four making themselves known, each bearing the silvery Empire logo on its side. Super-high alert, but so neat, so precise. So . . . civilized.

Hannah whistled under her breath. "Must have their entire fleet in the water."

Not really. Empire had twice as many.

The lead boat, a trim four-seater almost as sleek as *Sea Sprite*, pulled alongside, matching our slower speed. At the helm, a tough-looking older woman gave us the eye. Her hair was slicked back so smooth, it looked glued down. She wore what Jenn would have called designer fatigues and a side-arm holstered at her hip. The other boats held their distance—for now.

Daniel stood up, smiling a bland welcome. I wondered where he'd found it.

"So it's you, Dan. Just come crosstown?"

"Heading for Unca Joe."

"Big noise off west just a while ago."

"Heard it myself."

"Looks like you might've caught a bit of it."

Daniel brushed at his T-shirt. The blood had mostly dried to black. "Some."

The woman glanced toward our stern. "*ZeRO,* eh? Used to be an Adder boat."

"Not anymore."

She nodded, like her guess had been confirmed.

"Her name is *Zephyr*," I muttered from the wheel. The old scow had saved my life. I wasn't having her disrespected.

"The whole town's going up in smoke. Plus this monster weather on the way." The patrol leader sucked her teeth noisily. "Any idea what happened over there?"

Daniel shrugged. "I'd guess a bit of freelance demolition."

The woman pursed her lips, resisting a sour grin. "I'd say about fucking time."

The Adders weren't going to get much sympathy.

"We've a bit of a medical emergency," Daniel said. "Mind if we move on?"

Her cool gaze raked *Zephyr* dismissively, took in the wet red staining Poppy's shin. "Tell you what. Share your info and I'll speed her downtown myself. I've got some news to lay on Boss Rousseau."

Hannah stirred. Poppy was leaning hard against her. "Soonest might be best, Dan."

Daniel turned to help Poppy to her feet. "If you can fit me in, I'll explain along the way."

"Deal."

Not the way Hannah wanted it to go, but she couldn't very well object, with Poppy looking weaker every minute. "See you on the *Melville* soon as," she told Daniel pointedly.

"Yep." But it sounded like the last thing on his mind. He eased Poppy into the patrol boat's back seat and settled in beside her.

"Dan . . ."

"I'll be there."

A sure way to avoid confrontation. Motor away from it. Maybe not in as big a rush to leave as his sister was?

The patrol leader sent one boat west to reconnoiter, and the others to continue their rounds. As she moved off and built speed, I heard her remark to Daniel, "Big doings down at Unca Joe, eh? You see anyone from Revelations skulking around over west?"

He leaned forward to reply, but their voices were lost in engine roar.

Doings? Revelations? Now what? I put *Zephyr* back in gear.

Hannah stared after them, then turned to me. "Fast as you can, den rat!"

So we were back there again.

The news about the Adders arrived before we did. First Julian, then the Empires must've spread the word. Downtown, Unca Joe's rooftop outliers greeted us with whoops and raised fists as we passed below them. When we limped in, Zephyr's engine basically running on fumes, the Lagoon was as crowded as I'd ever seen it. Had the other dens all rushed over to celebrate?

Hannah came up to the wheelhouse as I searched for space to park. "This can't be just about Adders."

I guessed it could be.

"Tie up by Dan. We'll ferry the kids in from there." She poked her head through a broken-out window. "Something else going on."

No sign of the Empires. They'd come and gone. But out in the center of the Lagoon, a mess of small boats were rigged side by side in an open rectangle. Planks laid across their gunwales made a floating platform for a work crew to access a large, flat object being assembled inside the rectangle. I recognized bits and pieces of the former front walkway being lowered from the den's upper entrance, down to a secondary chain of plank-topped boats that crossed the water to the work area.

I turned back to my driving, just in time to throw *Zephyr* into reverse so I didn't run up *Sea Sprite*'s ass where she was moored to the *Melville*. Julian watched us come in from the book boat's foredeck, arms folded, a quick head count his only sign of concern.

He shot Hannah a dark look as we pulled up. "So I missed the fireworks."

"One less thing to worry about."

"Guess that'll show 'em."

She looked up at him. "You ready?"

"As I'll ever be."

"Where's Dan?"

Julian glanced toward Unca Joe. "Debriefing the chiefs."

"Rousseau's like to be spitting nails," Hannah said quietly. "Dan needs to get his ass back here or they'll be arguing till noon."

Wondering how Hannah knew about Rousseau, I shut down the engine and tossed Julian my bow line. My job was done. Let these Nathans rush about on their mysterious errands. Too hard to keep up with them. "Poppy get to the medics okay?"

Julian drew *Zephyr* farther along the *Melville*'s side and made us secure. "Must've. Dan took her in. I had to steer clear of that Empire woman."

"Why's that?"

Clambering into *Sea Sprite* to reclaim her crossbow, Hannah chuckled.

Julian looked sly. "Used to harass 'em some, now and then. The Empire patrols."

"What for?"

"For fun. They take themselves so fucking seriously."

"Like the Empires in general, you mean?" Had about a half-inch of smile left but I gave it to him. "We got the last of the Macys. Can you run them in?"

Hannah was already making the transfer. No second wasted.

Once Julian was off, I sat in *Melville*'s stern pit just to be still for a while. The work in center Lagoon was soothing to watch—wood and rope and hammers and saws. Simple and real, and I needed that, to stop my head spinning. Everything happening too fast and the pace increasing. Like the whole day rolling downhill toward a crisis I couldn't see the shape of. Running on autopilot left me lost in space, with horror images looping through my brain. A flaming missile of human limbs, a young girl's head tumbling through the air, a pimply Adder face sinking into the water. I pressed my palms to my eyes. It didn't help.

To the denfolk in the Lagoon, we were heroes. We should be celebrating. Feel relieved, at least. And part of me did. A world without BlackAdder would be a better place, no doubt about it. But it was hard to square with the violent life-taking it required. Most denfolk would say the Adders couldn't be fixed, only exterminated. Well, maybe. I wished I'd been there to hear Rousseau's response. Might've helped me see it more clearly. The shrink had warned that another trauma might tip me into shutdown again, but I wasn't letting that happen, no matter how bad things got.

"You look about done," Hannah said. I'd forgotten she was there. "Head home and get some sleep."

Home? Sleep? And let the nightmares flood in?

"Yeah, I need to . . ." Couldn't say what. Instead, I gestured across the bustling lagoon. "Find out what's up."

She was barely curious. "Busy as little bees. You need a hand with your kayak?"

Hannah being helpful and kind? Nah. She was nosing me off the boat. That put my back up, and I was set to wave my keys in her face. But I caught a glimpse of blond braids and big shoulders in the crowd at the front entry: Gracie, for sure. Next, I saw Breakers, above in a window opening, keeping watch on the Lagoon. Rubio's group must be back.

I dropped my kayak in the water. Needed to get home after all.

I lost track of Grace in the milling download of building materials from the den, so I hailed the first familiar face as I stroked by.

"What's up?"

My tier-mate Kari was wielding her hammer like she meant to teach that wood a lesson. "You heard about the Adders? Ain't it the best!"

"Sure." I backpaddled to stay level with her. "But what's this you're doing?"

"Oh. Building a raft."

"What for?"

"For all our stuff! Doncha know? Where you been all night?"

I almost said: *on a mission*. But it wasn't my mission, and I had no heart to claim it. "Out and about. Did Rubio's gang get back?"

"You bet." She straightened, brushing a stream of sweat from her eyes. The floating walkway shifted under her as she retied the bright bandanna holding back her forest of cornrow braids. "And now it's a whole big rush."

She didn't look happy about it. "To do what?"

"Move out."

"Now?" I stared at her. "Just like that?"

"Yep."

"And Rousseau's okay with it?"

"No choice, he says."

Leaving Unca Joe? Wow. My hands tightened on my paddle. As much as we'd talked and debated about it, argued for it, this was like the proverbial tsunami. Had I seen the den search as a mere distraction—to calm mutinous den members? Or had the morning's events stripped off the last of my armor? I fought through a flashback of my mother announcing we were leaving our apartment to move onto *Haiku*.

"But why so . . . now?"

Kari kept swinging, her thin brown arms awhirl, so I could barely hear her over the construction racket. "That monster that's coming. The CB relays call it a super-superstorm now. Need to be in safer quarters before it gets here."

"And that's the stadium?"

"Looks like it. The crew came back raving about the place. Solid . . . perfect . . . defendable. Room to grow. That sort of stuff."

Must also mean empty. No one to evict.

"And everyone's going?" Along with the Joes and Smiths, I'd noticed a few of the older, abler Macys among the builders and carriers. Our numbers were growing. "All the dens?"

"Debate ongoing. Won't know till they show up. Or meet us there."

Huh. Not like Rousseau to dive into a move so radical without a full-out plan. This new storm system must be a real humdinger. "How long till the weather gets here?"

"Three to four days, depending . . ."

Right. We all knew the freaky genius of these storms.

"Jeez." I wasn't quick with surprises. Needed processing time. "You seen Rube around?"

"Not since they got back."

"He'll give me the details." I waved and shoved off. Threading though the jam-up to the underbelly took all my concentration. We could've been a flourishing old-days marina, for all the boats and people and building going on.

Up in Main, the steamy air was electric. Every inch of space cleared of walkway bits and pieces was filled with the slamming together of crates and storage boxes. Through the open doors of the Mess, I saw the kitchen being dismantled. The cook staff ran about with lists amid a constant flare-up of debate about what should go where. I wondered how they'd keep us fed during the pack-up. Say-It-Again Sam hovered empty-handed, dismayed and disoriented. The sudden disruption was going to be really hard on him.

Rousseau stood by the tellers' counter, directing traffic—goods, people, materials—his deep fatigue apparently swept aside by this new emergency. His dark face glowed with purpose and certainty. He looked like a leader again. And the lads were willingly busting ass.

Good on you, boss. Who thought you could move so fast? Who thought *we* could?

Daniel must've done his debriefing and gone back to the boat, where Hannah would be waiting, urging speed. And off they'd go. Well, that was that. Time to get back to my life in the den. Spunk was still in recovery and I didn't see Jake anywhere. Out on new orders? I checked for Rube at Den Search Central, but the table had been removed to make room for stacks of finished crates. I spotted Irv pressed into a far corner with Maxine, talking her through a sheaf of water-stained papers, maybe his notes from the trip upriver. Both were frowning and intent, like Irv was trying to reassure his den leader, or maybe convince her. Any end-of-the-Adders celebrating was already shoved aside, to focus on the newer crisis.

I went up to the media loft, searching for Rubio. The whole teener IT squad was there yanking plugs, winding up cable, settling the cranky laptops and monitors into battered plastic tubs. I had a flash memory of cardboard boxes, how they'd become so precious that you kept each one till it was too shredded to be mended again. If cardboard was still being made these days, we weren't getting any of it. But the plastics had lasted.

"Anyone seen Rubio?" I called over the youngsters' frantic bustle. A chorus of nopes and head shakes, plus several thumb jerks followed by pleading looks toward the other end of the loft.

Not Rubio who concerned them, but Jenn. Penned inside a small thicket of equipment, like she'd hauled it up around herself for protection. She'd tap at one screen, then leave it to squint and tap at another, then move on to the next. In the dim loft, the bright screens lit her chin, nose, and cheekbones, but threw her eyes into deep shadow.

"What's it about?" I asked one of the girls.

"Started with weather, then it was relatives. Can you get her to stop? Got to pack up."

"She wouldn't?"

"She's . . . um . . . y'know . . . not listening."

I took in the erratic speed of Jenn's movement. "Got it. Do what I can."

Jenn gave me a brilliant smile as I came up. Too brilliant. If I could see her pupils, they'd be way dilated.

"Welcome back, kiddo!" she chirped. "Thought maybe you'd run off with the book guy! Sure wouldn't blame you!" Immediately, she was back at her screens. Her bowl haircut, rarely a hair out of place, was a bird's nest, like she'd forgotten to comb it for days. "Listen, can you give me a hand here? I'm tracking the storm, okay? But also, I gotta . . . just sit here."

Words like 'calm down' were useless when she got like this. "Jenn, you know I'm a klutz with e-stuff."

"No, no, no, this is easy!" She drew me inside the circle of machinery. "Just sit here and watch till you see one of these names come up." She pushed a scrap of paper in front of me and nudged me onto a stool. "When you do, press this symbol."

"What for?"

"It's a phone file I found. See if they're listed."

The monitor was scrolling so fast I could hardly make out the letters, never mind read her pencil scrawl of names. "Listen, you seen Rubio?"

Her hands dipped and hovered over one of the old keyboards, like I'd shattered her train of thought. "No. But when I do, I'm slapping him upside for this stadium idea. Crazy, stupid time to be tearing the world apart and moving!"

"Why?"

"The storm, of course! And . . . and . . . you know!" She came up behind me. When I swiveled on the stool, she was way into my personal space, arms waving. "We're sure to get caught out in the open, with all our worldly goods tied to a bunch of slapped-together rafts! Or some rogue wave'll wash us all out to sea! What's the chance we'll ever make it to fucking Yankee Stadium?" She rotated her hands between us, as fast as the scrolling, so I could barely catch them with my own.

"JENN! Stop. Please. We can't do this now. The kids need to pack up this equipment."

Her eyes loomed huge as she fixed them on me. She leaned in, whispering frantically. "No, no, you see, I've told them where to find me! I've left that message so many times, they must have gotten it. I know they have! If we move, they won't know where to look!"

'They' had to be her cousins in Minnesota. "We're only going upriver. You can send a new message when we get there."

"What if they come while we're out on the water?"

"What if they *come*?" She'd talked herself into a drive-by pick-up now? "Jenn, I don't think that's going to happen." I tried to hook her arm under my elbow, to ease her away from her machine corral.

"Don't touch me!" Tears welled up. She wrenched her wrists from my grip and whirled away. "You never did believe me! You just pretended to!"

"I believe you! I do! But how would they get here? Even if they can, they're not going to travel that far with a super-storm on the horizon. They'll wait till it's over."

Jenn bent over a screen to type so rapidly I had to think it was random.

I wasn't helping things. Hopeless to reason with her in one of these moods, especially when my own self-control was stretched near as thin as hers. "Forget it. How 'bout this: you keep your favorite to work on and the kids can wrap up the rest?"

The teeners were already circling at a distance.

Suddenly, Jenn flared up, right in my face. "It's all Rubio's fault!"

"What's his fault?"

"We wouldn't be going if he hadn't stuck his nose into things!"

"Rousseau asked him to . . ."

"To shut him up 'cause all he did was complain!" She swiveled to her keyboard. "Serves him right what happened!"

"What do you mean? What happened?"

She turned back, her eyes mean with triumph. "You didn't hear? He's up in the Ward."

I recoiled a step. "In the Ward?"

"Oh yes, he's very sick! In isolation! He's dying."

"Rubio's always dying." I made light of it, but fear surged in my gut.

"This time it's for real!" Her triumph winked out like a candle flame. She reached to wrap me in a teary bear hug. "But it's okay, because when he dies, it'll be so much better for you, you know it will, because then you'll be free to go off with the book guy with all his money and special access and you won't have to worry about taking care of Rubio who never appreciates anything nice anyone does for him, ever!"

"What are you talking about?" I struggled in her too-tight embrace. Who was she was maddest at: Daniel, Rubio, or me? "Daniel doesn't have special access . . ."

She shoved me to arm's length. "Of course he does! And money. Plenty of it. Who else would have his own boat and a landline and be able to survive in this world selling worthless old books? Or pretending to sell them. Are you freakin' blind?"

Okay, whew. People just kept throwing stuff at me today that left me breathless. Access? Of course. How else could he get his hands on what it took to destroy an entire city block? And sure, the *Melville* could make it to the Jersey shore, even as far inland as it was these days. I wasn't blind. I just hadn't looked at it real close. Maybe I'd even looked away from it, until Hannah showed up, calling me den rat and crudely warning me off her precious brother. Given what I knew now, she might be doing me a favor.

Jenn dropped her chin to sob into her chest. "And you'll be the one who gets out 'cause he'll take you, while the rest of us are stuck here! Forever!"

I eased my wrists from her grip. "I'm not going anywhere. Except to

Yankee Stadium, with everyone else. And you're coming with us. Did you know it's practically on the Mainland? Now tell me really. What's up with Rubio?"

She slumped away, like nothing mattered any more. "He's in the Ward, like I said."

Now it was me grabbing too hard. I even shook her a little. "You're telling me true?"

But I'd heard it in her voice, seen it push through the manic light in her eyes.

Her hands flew to her mouth. "Oh, Glim! I'm so sorry! I'm so bad! I'm . . ."

I was out of there, pounding up the stairs.

THIRTY-THREE

The fourth floor was chaos like the rest of the den, but its medicinal smells made the rush feel more desperate. I near-collided with Poppy as she crutched along the busy upper hallway, her shot leg wrapped and splinted. I was dancing with urgency but owed her at least a moment. "What, you're up already?"

"Had to be." Her face was strained, her body tight with effort, but she tried for a grin. "Taped and stapled, and got a boat to catch. Mobile sick and injured are going up first so the medics can get a dispensary set up there. Spunk's at the dock already."

"He's mobile?"

"More or less. You know how he is. Don't worry. I'll keep an eye on him."

I thought she was looking rather fond. Poppy and Spunk? Now there was a combo. "You got enough painkillers?"

"Some. Short supply."

Like everything else was about to be. "Listen, I'd help you downstairs, but Rube's up here somewhere. I gotta check on him."

Poppy's grin faded. "Yeah, I heard. I'll be fine. You go find him." Gathering herself, she joined a group cutting a slow path through the confusion with their walkers and canes.

Once someone could tell me what room Rube was in, I got stopped at the door. The guy we called the Med Bouncer was on duty, which was really not good. He was Unca Joe's version of quarantine.

"Sorry. Can't go in right now."

"Just want to see Rubio. I won't take long."

"Not right now."

"But he'll want to see me! I know he will!"

"No one's allowed in."

"Then at least tell me how he is . . ."

"The doctor's with him. You'll have to ask when he comes out."

Flat-voiced and blank-faced. Ex-cop or military. Even Unca Joe had a few. Doing his job, but right then, I hated him for it. I turned away to lean against the opposite wall. This was bad. Very bad. I had to get in there somehow.

I knew the Ward. Nothing had changed much in the months since my time in Psych. The medical ward was a large, high-ceilinged room divided by a new-built wall. Big half for injuries, small half for infectious, nurses' station in front. Rousseau, pragmatically prescient, had recruited early and hard among his disaffected medical friends when the shit really started hitting the fan. Once the downtown hospitals went down, only Empire State had better health care than Unca Joe. Of course, success varied with the staff's ability to keep their salvaged and out-of-date equipment functioning, and even more on the rapidly decreasing availability of viable drugs and supplies.

Drugs were what worried me most right now. Did they have what Rubio needed? Sometimes a quick trade at the Souk could solve that problem, but with the Souk up in flames, that was no longer an option.

Meanwhile, the Med Bouncer had his hands full keeping the door shut, with packers coming through with loads, setting them down along the corridor, and heading back for more. Didn't take long to find someone wide enough to cover me. I scooted in behind him.

The nurses' desk was piled high, the tiny space too crowded. The door to Infectious was just closing after a load came through. I slipped right in.

With the beds all filled next door, the first bank of sheet-walled cubicles had been given over to the most critical Macy injuries, small bodies coming dopily awake, wondering where they were and what all the fuss was about. A secondary plastic curtain crossed this space, reserving the rear third for contagious cases. I peered through the split.

Several face-masked figures were gathered around a corner bed. The cubicle curtain was half drawn, concealing the head of the bed. I could see only large, slack feet under the thin cover, but there was no mistaking the irregular, harsh gasping for breath. My alarm bloomed into full-blown dread. I ran for the bed but got only a glimpse—Rubio's stark-white face framed in a dark scrawl of hair, his mouth wide in a grimace—before someone whipped an arm around my waist and hauled me out of there.

"Please! Let me see him!" I screeched. "Let me see him! I have to!"

I was dumped roughly in the corridor. The door shut tight in my face. Made no sense to pound and scream, be another catastrophe in the chaotic hallway. I wasn't getting in. Best I could do was pace, up and down, up and down, knocking heedlessly into people burdened with pack-up, mindlessly apologizing. Finally, one of them planted himself in front of me, arms spread, so I had to stop. I looked up into Irv's round, remorseful face.

"Glimmer? I tried to find you once we got home . . ."

"Irv! What's going on? What happened? Why is he . . . ?"

Irv took my elbow and guided me out of the traffic to a quieter eddy along the corridor wall. "He wouldn't rest. He was so worked up and not taking care of himself, even before we left. I think he was feverish the whole way. We got there and the stadium was amazing and he was so excited. We all were, running around like madmen, and he was coughing and there was . . . blood. But he wouldn't slow down."

"Is it the malaria?"

He nodded. "With complications. They're not saying much yet."

"Complications." I hated the sound of that.

"They're trying to improvise some sort of apparatus to help him breathe." Irv's shoulders drew an arc of dejection. "He wouldn't stay in the boat when we got there. Had to see every inch of the place, prove to himself he'd been right about it. On the way home, he just . . . well, collapsed. We got him back as quick as we could."

"I'm sure you did. It's not your fault. Rube's never had much sense where his health is concerned." I patted his arm distractedly. He was too new a friend to know Rubio's habits well. But while I was grateful for the update, I didn't have time to ease his conscience right now. Had to focus on Rube's recovery. "Irv, thanks for coming to find me, but you must have a lot to do for the move. I'll hang here and keep an ear out, okay?"

He eyed me like I was an alarm set to go off. "Sure you'll be okay?"

I made myself look brave and steely-eyed. "Yeah. I will. Thanks."

He knew a brush-off when he saw one. He nodded, then slouched sadly away through the hubbub in the corridor. I slid down the wall to the floor and, elbows on knees, settled in to wait.

I think I slept. I must have, 'cause I started and glared up stupidly when I felt someone nudge my foot. Doc Lee, the chief medic, regarded me with tired sympathy.

I scrambled up, shaking out my stiffness. "How is he? Can I see him?"

Doc Lee shook his silver head. "I don't think that would be wise." His gaze followed a whimpering Macy passing by on a stretcher. "We sent to Empire to see if they had a ventilator. They do not."

"He'll want to see me," I pleaded. "Really he will."

"I know this is hard to hear, but there's no way around it. It's too late. We've . . . lost him."

"What? You've what?"

"I'm sorry."

"You're saying he's . . ."

He clasped his hands at his waist and nodded. "About fifteen minutes ago."

"No! It can't be! He's been through bad stuff with his malaria before!"

"A new bug this time. And pneumonia. He lacked the strength to fight it and . . ." His chin dropped, the age-old healer's outrage pulsing in his jaw. "We didn't have what we needed to help him. I am so very sorry."

I slid back down the wall. The floor was a lot harder than a moment ago.

"Can I send for a friend? Someone?"

And who could that be? Jenn gone off the wall, Jake out on orders, everyone so busy?

Rubio. Dead? How could he be?

I couldn't wrap my mind around it. I buried my head in my arms. "I'll . . . I'll . . . be fine. I'll just . . . sit here a while, okay?"

"It would be better if . . ."

"Please! Just leave me alone!"

Doc Lee gave a quiet, dubious grunt. Then he turned and went back inside.

THIRTY-FOUR

D on't know how long I sat there. Time wasn't exactly on my mind as I struggled to accept Rubio's death, and learn how to be without my friend, my anchor in the den, my guide in the post-Abel learning curve. Father, brother, and friend, all rolled into one prickly, fractious being. Who was I without him?

Grief so far had to do with the past, with Abel, with the loss of my family, my identity. Felt mostly in retrospect. Never like this. Never so . . . *immediate.*

Of course I'd imagined him dying. Stupid not to, with his bad health and all. I'd imagined the drama: Glimmer, the queen of his funeral at sea, keening and moaning, ranting about how I'd warned him about his crazy mulishness and rogue behavior. But I never took it for a real possibility.

Now here it was, and there'd be no keening and moaning, or throwing myself about. The reality was too stark, too . . . actual. As flat and featureless as a beach at low tide. My fantasy theatrics had been all about me. This emptiness, this paralysis, was about Rubio, and how terribly, completely he was gone.

So much we would never know about each other.

I never got to tell him my real name . . .

Oh, where was that blessed numbness I used to wrap myself in so easily?

Hours or days later, someone lowered themselves against the wall beside me, close enough to feel the warmth.

"Go away, whoever you are. Leave me alone!"

"Nope. Not this time."

Daniel. Had there always been this huskiness in his voice or was he finally showing the toll this day had taken from him?

"Not you," I moaned. "Can't deal with you right now."

He shifted, getting comfortable. "Then I'll just sit here till you can."

Easy enough to lean on him, but so many reasons not to. I buried my head deeper in my arms.

He went quiet for a long time. Then he said, "I'd like to help."

"He's dead!"

"Yes."

"You can't fix that!"

"No, I can't."

"He was my best friend! Like . . . my only family!"

"I know."

If he finished with 'just how you feel,' I'd jump up screaming. Maybe throw myself into the Lagoon. No, that was more dumb theatrics. Besides, Daniel did know how it felt to lose someone you love.

"I made a mess of calls when I heard. Tried to find the right drugs. Nothing out there."

I should be grateful for the effort. Instead, I was furious with him, for being alive when Rubio was not, for his damnable equanimity, and because when Daniel went away, it would be by choice, not a tragic accident. He still got to choose.

"Why are you even here?"

"Support? Comfort? That sort of thing?"

"I mean, why are you . . . still . . . here?"

"To be with you."

"With that big storm coming?" My mouth tasted sour as my words. "Aren't you Nathans rushing to get out of town?"

I felt him shove his head back against the wall, thumping it a few times in frustration. "Ah. Hannah."

"She hates me, and still she tells me more than you do. Least now I know where the arrows came from."

"What'd she say?"

"She took the papers back."

"Papers?"

"You know. ID, permits, passes, tickets. Scraps of fucking paper! Come on, Daniel. Don't play me like a total idiot!"

"I haven't . . . I . . . ."

"Yes, you have! You and Hannah and . . . well, no. Julian's been pretty straight with me."

"Julie has a lot less at stake." For the first time since we'd met, Daniel moved in on me. I stiffened my arms to shove him off, but my strength was spent. He drew me against his chest, wrapped himself around me like a garment, and held me tight. "Lizzy, Lizzy . . . I have so much explaining to do."

That did it. I burst into tears. Then sobs. Then wails.

More hours or weeks later, when I'd drenched his T-shirt and he was still murmuring mindless comfort in my ear, I finally ran dry and struggled up away from him. He smelled of soap and clean fabric. Somewhere between the last of the Macys and now, he'd grabbed a wash and a change of clothing, luxuries I hadn't seen in what felt like days. How could he stand to be near me?

"Tell me how it happened," he said.

Like he must have known, it was oddly calming to tell Rubio's story, what I knew of it, even though I suspected he'd heard most of it from Rousseau already. By the time I was done, I was sitting up on my own, breathing more evenly, hiccupping now and then but talking like a sane person. Daniel's steadiness had helped me find some distance.

"Maybe he knew he was at the end," I mused. "Decided to go out in glory."

"Could be. Wish I'd got to know him better."

"He wasn't always easy to know."

"I get that. After all, I've lived half a lifetime with Hannah Nathan." Daniel straightened his legs along the floor, working out the kinks. "Exceptional minds in a world not up to their standards. It's hard on them. But he did a great thing for the dens."

"You see it that way?"

"Absolutely. Yanked everyone out of their slump. Got them talking for a change."

"I think the raids had something to do with it."

The activity in the corridor had thinned a bit, but loads and people were still coming and going, detouring around us as we sat against the wall, like boulders breaking the flow of a river. I took some comfort that, in the end, Rubio's legacy would be a positive one. But first, we had to get ourselves and all our worldly goods to the stadium in one piece.

I pressed my back against the wall's granite wainscoting, feeling flat-lined and worn to the core. I looked up, studied Daniel's profile. The pensive, downcast brow. The crop of his dark hair. The smooth plane of his jaw. He'd even shaved. All conflicts and disagreements aside, I would really miss him. "And now, you're leaving."

After a moment, he nodded. "That is the plan."

"Hannah's?"

"Hannah's, mine, Julian's. Handwriting's been on the wall for a while now."

Were we finally on the road to truth? A victory of sorts, though I wasn't going to like it much. Pyrrhic, Rubio would've called it. Kind of like exterminating Adders so the rest of us could live. Ah, where was I going to learn pretentious new words with Rubio gone? I crossed my arms and stared at the floor.

Daniel cleared his throat, as if to deny the catch in his voice. "I was hoping you'd go with me."

What? Wow. Hadn't seen that coming. Not at all. What Jenn predicted, and I'd dismissed as nonsense. Every den girl's dream offer. Could he really be serious?

"Sure. Hannah would love that." I was surprised how bitter I sounded. Was the idea tempting after all?

"Hannah's my sister, not my boss."

"'Cept when she sends you off on family business . . ."

"The choice is mine to make."

"She thinks I'm . . ."

The catch was gone. Each word came out clear and hard. "I don't give a rat's ass what Hannah thinks."

"Den rat, she would say. Besides, I don't think that's true." I turned to face him. "Like, why stonewall me about the arrows?"

"Yeah, the arrows . . ." He sighed. "Okay, that was for Hannah. She's obsessed with secrecy. People are . . . after her. For stuff she does. Good stuff. Right stuff. But when you can trust only those you know best, family means a lot."

I kneaded the floor with a heel. "I wouldn't know. Rubio was my friend and my family."

"You were lucky, then. Hannah and I are family, but we're not friends."

I yelped as my knee was jogged hard by a passerby who couldn't see over the boxes he was carrying. Daniel gathered himself and stood, holding out a hand. "C'mon. Not a good place for the talk we need to have."

"Maybe later."

"There is no later."

"I get it. You're leaving . . . now."

"To beat the storm."

A stack of folded bed sheets tumbled off a moving dolly right at my feet. Someone swore a blue streak. Along the corridor, doors opened and shut. Reality closed around me again, with its awful news. Daniel's open hand demanded my attention.

My instinctive thought: *I'll run this by Rubio, see what he thinks.*

Not anymore.

Best would've been to sit there forever, head down, working on keeping my mind a soothing blank. But the noise and bustle got hard to ignore. I really was in the way. I got up on my own steam, straightening my tear-damp T-shirt, then turned away. "I should be helping with the pack-up."

"No, you don't." Daniel set himself in front of me, backing down the hall as I moved to slip past him. "No running away this time. We have a decision to make."

"We? Haven't you made it already?"

"If I had, I wouldn't be here."

As we reached the media loft, I looked for Jenn. The space was empty and most of the equipment gone.

Daniel stayed just ahead, shouldering backward through the movers. "Besides, Rousseau agreed that, after everything, you deserve a break. By my calculation, you haven't slept in a day and a half."

"How would you know?"

"I keep track." He offered a sympathetic grin, so at odds with the guy I'd seen toss a bleeding young Adder in to drown. "Like, when was the last time you ate?"

Between Adders and Rubio, I'd pretty much lost my appetite. "Your point is?"

"No disrespect, but one thing your buddy Rubio wasn't likely to teach was how to take care of yourself."

That rankled, even though it was true. "I'm fine."

He stopped short, so I nearly smacked into him. "No. You're not. And you have every reason not to be." He gripped my elbow and muscled me out of the line of traffic with the same quiet economy I'd noticed at other crisis points, at the Souk with the thug posse or in the Adders' den. "But right now, I need you to put aside Adders and Hannah and Rubio, and spare *me* a thought or two for a change!"

His tone made me hold still and stare, like I worried he might hit me.

"Sorry!" He tossed his head in dismay and let me go. "It's just . . . Lizzy, sweetheart, we're on a deadline here. You can't hold me at arm's length forever. At some point, it has to be yes or no."

"Yes or no what?"

"Yes or no . . . me."

We'd washed up against the balcony railing, overlooking Main—filled with my denmates, busy and intent with purpose. Rousseau's rich baritone rose occasionally over the clatter and clang, doing what he was best at: organizing, inspiring the masses. I recalled Rubio's belief that any life can be divided by its 'defining moments,' the sort after which everything will be different. My returning memory helped me chart a few of my own. My father turning his back on the city to raise his sail at the outward channel marker. My mother abandoning the claustrophobic safety of the high-rise for the flexible uncertainty of boat life that would kill her anyway. Rousseau hauling me out of the flood debris. This was another.

Daniel watched me, waiting at the top of his voice.

I was glad I'd already wept myself dry. "Where is this place you're going?"

"Far from here."

Hannah's words, exactly. "Have you been there?"

"No."

"But what's it like?"

"Defensible high ground. Potable water. For details, ask Hannah. Does it matter?"

"Well, it should. Why don't you care? Will you be safe there?"

"Maybe safer than here. Settlers have made a life on the frontier before."

My father believed a civilized life awaited in Montana, if not exactly a return to normal. But now inland was the frontier, and thanks to Rubio, I had little faith in the happy homesteader ideal. "That was with an abundance of natural resources, clean water, and healthy land, never mind a settled climate." I shook my head. "We'd survive if we're lucky, but for how long?"

"It's not like we'd be at it with our bare hands," Daniel said. "We've prepared for this. Hannah has. We have . . . resources."

"But would we have neighbors? Friends? A community?" I swept an arm out over the hall. "Would we have . . . backup?"

It must have been late afternoon. The low, angled sunlight seemed the bravest thing in the world, straining to push through the grime on the skylight. How was it the decision came to me so clearly now?

"Daniel, you are . . . have been . . ." I lost all the right words. "I can't go with you."

"Why not?" Like he'd expected that answer but was determined to press on anyway.

But saying no, finally landing on one side of the dilemma, cleared my muddled thinking. Or most of it. "Because it wouldn't work, not with Hannah on my case all the time, and Julian calling me den rat. We'd be in the wilderness hating each other."

"Probably not the wilderness . . ."

"Wherever! I wouldn't fit."

"You fit with me. That's what matters."

"How can you say that? Most of the time, we end up in some stupid argument."

"And each time, we come back for more. We're learning each other's limits."

He was getting quieter, in that deliberate way of his, while my heat was rising. "I mean, how have you put up with it all this time, working so hard to keep me in orbit while I carried Hannah's papers around like a good little messenger bunny!"

"That's Hannah's version, not mine. Leave her out of this."

"How can I? You didn't choose me, she did!"

He looked appalled. "That's how she laid it out? Believe me, your first encounter with her was pure chance."

"But then she got you to keep an eye on me."

"Could've done that without you ever knowing." His voice dropped as he reached to run his knuckles down the length of my cheek. "But you kept showing up. Causing me trouble. Snagging my interest."

No, no. Don't try to woo me now. I backed away. "Can you really see it? Me tagging along, a last-minute add-on to a family as tight as you Nathans?"

"Actually, Julie's a total convert. He'd love to have you along."

"I'd be a burden before you got there, wherever it is. I don't want to be some guy's useless appendage, like that poor redhead Julian drags around!"

His hand fell away. "You'd never be . . . !"

"Like, what would I do?"

"Do?" He studied me, distress tightening his jaw. What was obvious to him should be obvious to me. "You would . . . be with me, feed me, take care of me. Let me do the same for you. The things couples do for one another." Then he frowned, like my words had delivered another, hidden message. "Hold on. Don't you want to get off the Island?"

"Not just so you don't have to go out into the wilderness alone!"

A pained moan deep in his throat. "Is that what you think?"

"No! Yes! I don't know!" My tongue was running away with me and a new flood of tears was ready on tap. "It doesn't feel right! It's too much like my father, cutting and running. Leaving behind everything he'd worked for, he and my mother. Sure, I wanted to leave when it was all everyone talked about, all that got you up in the morning, when everything seemed hopeless, when my view of the world stopped about three feet in front of my nose. But now . . ."

"Now . . . ?"

"Now I'm just finding myself . . . finding Lizzy . . . again. What if being here, where she . . . I . . . lived before . . . is the only way those memories can be triggered? Daniel, I can't be a couple until I'm a whole person! Can I?"

To my astonishment, he looked relieved. So relieved, I thought he might collapse. He started to speak, then didn't. Instead, he grinned and shook his head.

Why not? I'd just taken the burden of my expectations off his shoulders. He was free to go. But I'd started my declaration. Might as well finish.

"And then there's all of this!" I gestured wide across the tumult in the hall. "The dens. Our new sense of shared purpose. You said it yourself—all these people working together, so many different personalities and skills and ideas. It's a chance for what Rube believed in and worked for, even when no one would listen and everyone called him a traitor. A chance to remake den life. Create a possible future for all of us, long-term and sustainable. To make it work . . . and last!"

I awaited his rebuttal—the sustainable part was always the risky assumption. But he just kept smiling. I thought I read pride in his gaze. For what? For who?

I felt the need to elaborate, in case he didn't get it. "Rubio called the dens 'blueprints for the new society'—each den working on a different way to live in this fucked-up world we're left with. He'd go on about how we have to face being on our own, because the world isn't going to be fixed any time soon. We need to be flexible and adapt. The move to the stadium is the next phase: taking what's good with each system and melding them into something new. Sure, this move could destroy us, but it could be the key to our long-term survival. Maybe I'm crazy, but I don't want to run away from that challenge. I want to be a part of it, to see what happens. Like you said you felt, even after . . ."

His smile dimmed. "After Sara died."

At least he'd been listening. "Yes."

"Hadn't figured you for such an idealist."

I was surprised myself. "Must be Lizzy's influence."

"You really don't want to go?"

"No. I can't."

"Well, you're not crazy." He turned to rest his arms on the rail beside me like we were two old cronies at the pier watching the fishing boats come in. After a long moment, he said, "I committed a terrible violence against the Adders. I had access and opportunity that others didn't, and I wanted a future for the dens but couldn't see one that had them in it. Figured if I was going, I should at least leave the town safer than I found it. At least for a while."

"I understand."

"It wasn't . . . easy."

"I know." And I thought I did. Now.

"Do you? Really? Can you love a man who's done something like that?"

"What? Oh . . ." This rush of truth had its own momentum. "Pretty sure I already do."

His head went up, like he'd spotted something startling in the distance. "Well, that's it, then."

"I know." Unbearable, really. Losing both Rubio and Daniel in the same day, and just when I felt I'd sort of found him. "At least Hannah will be happy."

"Not exactly."

His hands gripped the railing. His stillness confused me. I guessed he was sorry, too. Best just to wait him out.

Finally, he bent his head to gaze at me past the curve of his shoulder. "Now, don't call me wishy-washy and without convictions. I mean, I'd have gone if you wanted, if you'd have gone with me. But the truth is, I don't want to go. Never did. Just seemed like the best option left. But I like yours a lot better."

"What are you saying?"

"I'm saying let's you and me see what happens together."

"You mean . . . you'll stay? Here with us?"

"With you. If you'll have me."

Then I understood that the earlier point of crisis I'd focused on had been mine, not his. His had been a moment ago, passed through so quietly that I'd missed it. Best I could do was nod, and nod and nod again. Once again, words had quit on me.

He slipped an arm around my back, careful not to crowd, and pressed his lips to my temple, letting go a long slow breath of relief into my ear. "There is one condition."

"What's that?"

"You have to help me explain it to my sister."

We got less than a moment to consider, never mind take in, the sudden possibility of a life together, spreading out before us like the afternoon sun across the hall. Because there was Julian, down on the main floor, scowling and waving at us to hurry the hell up.

THIRTY-FIVE

"**Y**ou were with us all along and suddenly, you're not?" Hannah raged.

In the *Melville*'s narrow center aisle, Daniel and I packed up his display books to make room for more useful cargo—people, plants—during the trip up to the stadium. Julian slouched against the shelves behind his sister. I stuck close to the stern door in case I needed to beat a retreat from all the pain and animosity flying about.

"Don't you get it?" Hannah kept her voice down so no one outside would hear, but she spat each word like they were poison meant to kill. "It's out of control uptown. And that jacked-up Stormie woman is making alliances, even uptown. The Island will be a war zone before you know it! You've lost your fucking mind!"

"I don't think so." Daniel worked briskly, tossing books in the crate too hard as he struggled to seem unruffled. "More like I've found it. You never did get how we differ on notions of sanity."

"Her?" Hannah stabbed a forefinger my way. "That's your reason? Crap, Dan, if you need a woman that bad, we'll pick one up along the way! Someone more your speed."

"More like you, you mean? That's what you're going to make this about? Dan needs to get laid, so he'll take whatever comes along? You have no idea what I need! There's a much bigger picture here, H."

"Damn right there is! Bigger than some pissant den utopia where it's all share and share alike and everyone talks at once and expects to be listened to! I know the bullshit that sanctimonious ex-priest preaches. Never guessed you'd be dumb enough to buy into it!"

"Actually, the move wasn't Rousseau's idea."

"It's still bullshit! You deserve better!"

"Better is what we're aiming for."

Hannah rolled her eyes. "Has it slipped your mind what a rare chance this is? Pine woods, open fields? Space to raise those sheep again? A clean place to make a stand with like-minded people?"

"I am with like-minded people."

"Well, I mean, you know . . . oh, screw it! Bring her along, if you must."

"She doesn't want to go. She has . . . other priorities. Priorities we share."

Julian shifted uneasily. His high-maintenance redhead was outside tapping her shapely fingernails in *Sea Sprite*'s passenger seat. All three of them were dressed to move fast, be prepared for anything, and look like you know where you're going. Kind of like tourists.

Daniel flung in a handful of books. The crate shuddered. "You didn't approve of Sara either, as I recall."

"Ancient history!" Hannah snapped.

"Not to me." Daniel topped off the crate and thrust it at me.

"Easy now . . ." I caught my balance, then stowed it beneath the racks, passing up the next empty.

"Sorry." He set the crate between him and Hannah, then stopped to wipe his face with an old T-shirt. We were all dripping sweat, not just from the heat of the day. "What you refuse to hear is that it's about so much more than who I spend time with. I went along with the Arcadia idea because I was fresh out of viable alternatives. I told you that at the time. Now I have one."

"Yankee Stadium?" Hannah pressed both hands to her temples like she was fighting to keep her brain from bursting. "Viable? Come on! You really believe this hare-brained scheme will survive the next big blow or food shortage?"

"More food riots on the Mainland than there have been here," Daniel pointed out.

"Along the coasts mostly. Instead, you have firebombers raiding your provisions! I track current events, remember."

"I think we put a stop to that for a while," Daniel said quietly.

I pushed forward. "Do your drones have range to see what's going on inland?" I hadn't promised to sit out the confrontation entirely.

"Of course not. But my contacts . . ."

"The dens have emergency reserves . . ."

"Oh, sure. For a week, maybe two?"

"A lot more!" We were talking over each other, hissing really. I was ready to make up a number if pressed.

Daniel eased me behind him, shaking his head. He'd regained his calm. "You've only seen the dens from the outside, H. Most of them are pragmatic and well-organized, and this move means combining their resources. I've eaten well at Unca Joe, and you couldn't get a better business team than

Empire State. Based on the site survey, Yankee Stadium was built like a fortress, has stayed in good condition, has no current occupants, a whole flood plain for a moat, and plenty of room for all. With Arcadia, the refusal to supply confirmable information always bothered me. Truth is, you don't know it'll be any better there!"

Hannah held up her phone. "Look at the video again. Better is what we're paying for!"

I guessed they'd put up most of what the family had left, buying those documents.

"But maybe the video's out of date. Maybe they've sold more slots than they're saying. Maybe it's all a big lie!" Daniel brandished a handful of books. "We're both gambling. Only I've chosen to play a different game."

"Way riskier, I'd say."

"Yours is no fucking luxury cruise!" He threw his fistful into the crate. "You weren't ever told the final destination. Like, where is this secret Eden, specifically? I could never find it on a map!"

They really didn't know? No wonder Hannah had been defensive when I'd asked if the documents were for real. Suddenly, my mother's voice was in my ear, clear as day: *better the devil we know, Lizzy . . .*

This new cascade of memory left me breathless. But not for long.

"He's not going! And you shouldn't either!" I stared at Julian, like begging him to come down from the ledge. "What if it's all burned up with the wildfires? Or too hot and dry to raise crops? Or they've cut down all the trees for shelter? When my dad evacked without us and sent emails saying where we should join him, each time it was someplace different. Like there was no best place, or even if there was, it was already taken!"

But Hannah's faith was firm. "If our guide's the only one who knows, no refugee hordes will be able to follow us there. Can't say the same for Yankee Stadium."

Julian shifted again and glanced toward the door. Was he truly on board with Hannah?

Daniel stood back, folded his arms. "Look. The agreement was that we'd leave if and when the situation on the Island got terminally desperate. Terminally, Hannah! I don't think we're there yet. Tell me this: why didn't we leave before?"

She frowned. "What d'you mean?"

"I mean we had chances, plenty of them. To get away to places we knew something about. Nice places, some of them. Why did we stay? Why are we still here?"

Julian finally spoke up. "Something to do."

"C'mon, Jules. You've been having a high old time."

"So what if I have?"

"So, we stayed because we like it here. This is our city. It raised us and sustained us, but now it needs our help. We shouldn't abandon it just because the fun's not so easy anymore." He put a hand on my shoulder. "She's right. You both should scrap Arcadia and come uptown with us."

Hannah bowed her head. She seemed to be running out of arguments.

Julian eased out of his slouch. "Dan, they're shutting down the exits. This is our last chance to get off Manhattan without doing end runs around a shitload of heavy private security. It's down to two factions uptown, playing a squeeze game with guns. That Bright dude and the syndicate he's working for are moving for takeover. They want the Island to themselves, every inch of it. There's gonna be a whole new set of rules soon."

"We're clear to go now, but the chance is last and final." Hannah waved her documents in front of Daniel like bait he kept refusing to take. "Got to grab it!"

"Then you'd better hurry up."

Hannah flattened her palms against her thighs, blinking at the floor. Her pale hair fell across her face as if as tired as she was. "I can't believe you're doing this to us."

"I'm not doing it to you. I'm just not doing it to myself. You'll do fine without me. You always have."

"Spare me the middle-child pout. We've been there for you when you needed us."

That finally riled him. "Oh really? Like you were when Sara was shot?"

For once, I saw Hannah caught off guard.

"I was in Africa . . ."

"Yeah. Playing gonzo militant. No time for a minor domestic crisis."

"We were hardly playing . . ."

"Tell me, H—do you really begrudge me a second chance?"

"Can we ditch the dirty laundry?" Julian cut in. "The first ticket says 8 p.m. We have to get through the uptown checkpoints, then find a berth at the ferry terminal for *Sprite*."

"Why bother?"

"You don't just walk away from your boat, man!"

"Why not?" Daniel glared at him. "It's not like you'll be back for her anytime soon!"

He wasn't quick tempered, not by a long shot, but when he finally got there, his anger came big. I stepped around to snatch up the half-filled crate and shoot him a warning glance. His face had lost years to remembered rage and resentment. He looked about twelve years old. I wondered what deep hurt Hannah had done to him then, even before he'd had a wife to mourn.

"This isn't useful." I handed him the crate.

He shut his eyes, collected himself, and took the crate. "Absolutely right."

"Okay, we're out of here." Julian shoved past us, steaming for the stern door. Maybe he figured only actual leaving could make Daniel change his mind. Daniel followed, swept up in his wake. I tagged after to watch Julian try to jam three loaded backpacks into *Sprite*'s rear cargo hatch. Clearly, they'd expected to be riding *Melville* to their departure point. When he was done, he stood on *Sprite*'s deck, staring down at us. His handsome face was blank as a board.

"You could stay, Julie," said Daniel. "I wish you would."

"You know better than that."

"She never did you any favors."

"Taught me how to survive . . ."

"There are more ways than Hannah's way."

"It's the way I know."

"Okay, then." Daniel stuck out his hand. "Good luck."

"Fuck you, too."

Hannah came out behind us, shouldering her bow case and quiver. She took a fat plastic sheath of documents from a pocket of her sleek leather jacket, grabbed Daniel's outstretched hand, and counted papers into it like paying out currency. She chose the most water-stained ones, the pail rescues. "In case of a last-minute sanity attack . . ."

Daniel handed them back. "Sell them at the gate. There's sure to be someone with cash, eager to go along."

Her mouth thinned. "These are VIP docs. The world was after them. We busted ass to keep them safe. And we don't want just anybody where we're going."

"Hannah. We're both doing what's right for us. Can't we wish each other the best?"

"Oh, Danny. Stop being so fucking reasonable."

She turned and stepped lightly into Sprite's back slot. Unseating the red-head would have messed up her exit, so she settled for second class.

"Hannah?" Daniel rested a foot on *Melville*'s gunwale.

Hannah stilled, halfway into her seat. I caught her flush of hope, even if Daniel didn't.

"The Stormie woman . . . ? What alliances did you mean?"

She dropped herself into the slot like a hunk of cargo. "Guess you'll have to figure that out for yourself. Drone Girl is outa here."

Julian turned to me. "Take care of him, den rat. Somebody needs to."

He slid behind the wheel, started up, and shoved off roughly. As he swerved away, he sent up his signature curl of spray, dousing boats and raft-builders in his path across the Lagoon. We watched until they turned the corner onto 8th Street. I was afraid to break the silence. When they'd gone, Daniel let out a sound somewhere between a grunt and a moan and disappeared into the cabin.

I found him slumped on the edge of his berth, face in hands. He glanced up, fixed me with a thousand-yard stare, and looked down again.

"My family. My unspeakable, fucking family. In a normal world, we'd have nothing to do with each other."

"There's still time, Daniel. You could catch up with them. One of the Empire boats would be fast enough."

He shook his head, tiny little shakes like a shudder. "Hannah's nuts. You see how crazy she is. I don't approve of her. I don't even like her. But . . ."

"She's your sister."

"Yes."

I crouched at his feet. "I thought maybe Julian would stay."

"No. Hannah's his goddess. He thrives on being yelled at. He thinks it's attention." He took a long, tired breath, then let it out. "I was never the strongman he needed. Or thought he did."

"I'd say you're very strong."

"Resilient, flexible. I try. But Hannah is . . . dramatic. Colorful. A glory-seeker. In the news. I couldn't compete." His voice caught, and he waited till he'd got hold again. "So sobering that I'll never see them again."

"You don't know that."

"Of course I do. How would I find them? With the world closing down like it is? Once upon a time, you could go anywhere you wanted, whenever you wanted. Not anymore."

I cupped my palms on his knees. "It's all my fault. You'd have worked it out with Hannah if I wasn't in the way."

"No, no, and no. I don't think that, and you shouldn't either. This goes back further than you can imagine. But it's so fucked up that it has to be this way!"

"What can I do?"

"Nothing. Unless you can find a middle ground between yes and no options. Too late now, anyway." He flopped back on the bed, arms splayed like a dead man. "You've lost your best friend. I've lost what's left of my family. Orphans of the storm."

I crawled up beside him and laid my head on his chest.

He curled his arms slowly across my back. "Wait a minute. Are you actually here, next to me, on my bed?"

I nodded.

"Then hold me. Hold me, girl. For the rest of whatever."

"Yes." I burrowed into his side and pressed my face to his neck. I could feel his smile. Animal comfort, nothing more. Soon we were both fast asleep.

Later, we woke, with the last of the daylight filtering through the blinds, and found ourselves studying each other with a kind of rapt wonder. Which went on for a long time. Which finally made us laugh.

"Hello, my new life," Daniel murmured. "So worth waiting for."

At long last—for me, at least—it felt safe and right, even necessary, to shuck our few clothes and make love until we fell asleep again.

dreamed I was on *Haiku*, far out at sea, with no idea how I'd got there. Loosed from our mooring, alone and adrift on the slow, steep swells of the deep ocean.

I bolted upright in darkness. Had to get topside, raise a sail, steer for land . . .

But taking in the unfamiliar width of the berth, my unusual nakedness, the even breathing of the man asleep beside me, I recalled where I was.

I considered how I felt about that, surprised by the intensity of my desire, while *Melville* continued to rise and fall just as *Haiku* had, that same deep-sea rhythm of my dream. But that wasn't right. Except in rough weather, our sheltered Lagoon never got more than a tall wake.

Had *Melville* slipped her moorings?

I fumbled to crank open one of the old wooden shutters covering the forward windows. Black night out there. I couldn't see Unca Joe from this angle, but the usual watch torches tossed ruddy light across a flurry of motion: heads, backs, and arms hard at work across the Lagoon. But quietly, like a video with the sound thumbed off. Was I still dreaming?

"Whassit?" Daniel murmured, winding a groggy arm around my waist to draw me down again. "Mmmm . . ."

"No, wait. Daniel, there's something odd . . . the swell . . ."

"Tide . . ."

"No, it's like . . . waves."

He heard the worry in my voice and sat up, yawning but assessing. "The storm."

"Already?" How long had we slept? "We were supposed to have three days!"

He yawned some more, put both feet on the floor. "The really big ones send messages ahead."

"But there's so much to do!"

He sighed and reached to turn on the tiny bed light. "Then we'd better get to it."

Two quick showers later, we went out on the stern deck to see what was up. The air was heavier than ever. Couldn't move without breaking a sweat. And, sure enough, there was my weather itch stirring, a prickle in the back of my brain.

"Well, if it isn't Sleeping Beauty and her Prince . . ." Breakers opened the panel of her dark lantern. She sat cross-legged on the cabin roof, the inevitable rifle resting across her thighs. "Thought I heard you banging around in there."

I scowled up at her. "Ha, ha."

Daniel offered his ready smile. "What're you doing up? What time is it, anyway?"

"Too late." Breakers patted her rifle. "You think incinerating a few Adders makes us safe as houses?"

"It couldn't hurt."

Breakers' long hair was splayed around her shoulders like a dark hood. Her eyes were shadowed but her lopsided grin caught the lantern light. "Nah, you did good. We're all in your debt."

Daniel sketched a satirical bow and changed the subject. "What's up with the storm? Got a swell on already."

Breakers stared into the night like she'd spotted the Big One raging up the avenue. "CB chatter says it's moving way faster than expected and we're dead in its sights. It's got a name now. Leon."

I wondered who was left with the authority to name hurricanes. Was there still some place where the old order prevailed? Maybe where Julian and Hannah were headed? And we were not. Was I having second thoughts? Was Daniel? If so, he gave no sign of it.

"Superstorm Leon," Breakers repeated. "Nice sound to it, yeah? I had a friend once named Leon. Really cool guy."

All of Breakers' friends seemed to exist in past tense.

"So, we're on night shift?"

"24/7. They're talking one hell of a blow. Category 6."

"There's no such thing."

Her husky laugh. "Is now. Anyhow, it's all hands on deck till we're outa here."

I thought of the old book, how a storm at sea in those days really did need every hand they could muster to save the ship. To save their lives. Ropes snapping, masts cracking, sails torn away, sailors scaling the ratlines. Breakers was an artist, not a seaman. I doubted she knew the origin of the phrase. But the book . . . where was it? I ducked back into the cabin, racing past half-packed crates to the forward berth. The book lay on the floor beside our rumpled bed. I snatched it up and stuffed it in my gut wallet. Where it belonged.

"What's the storm's ETA?" Daniel was asking when I resurfaced.

"Got to be deep in shelter by dusk two days from now." Breakers adjusted her weapon like it was an extra limb gone to sleep. "So, if you two are done getting it on at last, we need to start loading this boat. Bought you all the time I could."

Great. I'd been the butt of endless crude jokes for *not* coupling up. Gonna be the same, now I finally had?

Daniel laughed. "Done for now, at least. But there's packing left."

"Do it, then." Breakers shifted her weapon again. She must have been sitting there a long and painful time. "You're listed to go out at the end, but they want to bring the plants down while it's still dark."

"Why's that?"

"Draws the least attention."

"That's why it's so quiet." I gestured across the Lagoon. Surreal, so much work going on with none of the usual trash talk or singing. The raft-building was done. No hammers or saws. Just load it on, make it fast, and keep it down.

"Yeah. Trying to keep the Big Move under the radar. Leaves us so vulnerable. A bunch of boat repair won't raise interest, not with a storm coming. But loading out your entire roof garden says something special is up."

The Big Move. Exactly what Rubio would have called it, if he'd had the chance. Rubio! Not that I'd forgotten. I'd just set him aside for the while. I turned away, breathing hard.

"What about the other dens?" Daniel asked. "Empire? The Tommys?"

Breakers held the line like she felt it her duty. "They've been invited, but we're not broadcasting the hurry-up schedule. Rousseau doesn't want time wasted on procedural disputes and pissing matches."

I could see his point, with what I'd watched go on between Tall Tommy and Empire Will.

Daniel wasn't so sure. "Don't we need their boats? To move all these people?"

"We'll make more trips."

Daniel shook his head. "No way this'll stay secret."

"Long as we can. The medics went up under power just after dark. Sent out the first couple of raft loads when the tide turned at midnight. Say one thing for your Joe boss—once he decides, he gets right on it."

So it was really happening. Yankee Stadium. Rubio's dream den home. Poppy and Spunk should be on their way up with the medics. It was like finding yourself at the back of the parade when you didn't even know you'd joined it. Hannah and Julian could have already left the island.

"You heard about Rubio?" Of course she would've, but I needed to make him part of the conversation. He'd seem a little less dead, somehow.

"Did. And I'm real sorry about it."

"Yeah."

"Meanwhile, good you brought in that Adder clunker. Rousseau's gang got at it, fixed it up right, even found some of that dirty fuel, so it can be like one of those big engines you used to see pushing the heavy stuff up the river."

Adders. Oh god. Another thought I'd shoved aside.

"Tugs," I said thickly. "Tug boats."

"Yeah. Those."

"Glad she could be of use," I murmured, recalling the horror of her diesel exhaust mixing with the thick odor of blood. Daniel eased closer, his palm light on the small of my back.

Breakers gave me one of her deep looks, felt more than seen in the darkness. "Anyway, the tide is helping. Running high and strong. They got it all timed out, who goes when."

Daniel was insistent. "Really no word at all from the others?"

"Just the Gimme girls. They're coming. As for the rest . . ." Breakers shrugged. "Still not convinced, I guess."

But we were leaving, the Joes and Smiths and what was left of the Macys. Some of us already on the water. Poppy and Spunk might even be there by now.

What about Rubio's funeral? Would it get lost in the shuffle?

A stir rolled across the Lagoon like a freshening breeze. We turned and squinted into the night. Hushed cheers, a ripple of motion flicking back torchlight, a path being cleared through the work site. Breakers strained to her feet on *Melville*'s roof for a better look.

"Someone . . . two in a canoe."

"Let me see." I nudged Daniel for a leg up onto the roof. Two paddlers. Jake in the bow. I knew that taut profile. The stern was a woman. "Pretty sure it's Jake. And . . . wait, it's that undercover woman. Cass, I think her name is. They might have news." I watched them glide in. "Poor Jake. He hates boats."

Daniel laughed. "Only when he needs to."

I frowned. "What does that mean?"

"You haven't figured it yet? Jake is whatever he needs to be at a given moment. If he doesn't want to deal with boats, he gets seasick. If he needs to get somewhere quick, he's the old man of the sea. Once an actor, always an actor."

"Huh."

"Likely Rousseau sent him uptown to hang with his high-rise friends for a while, see what he could learn."

"Jake has high-rise friends?"

"Well, they think he's a friend. With money and connections. One of his favorite roles. He's very convincing."

"You've seen him at it?"

"Now and then." Daniel looked uneasy. "I feel like I'm blowing his cover."

"And yours," I said.

He laughed, but he didn't deny it.

"Tell me about it someday. Can I take the dinghy?"

"I'll go with you."

"You finish with the books. I still have to clean out my bunk."

I turned to go, but he held me back. "It's going to be crazy over there."

"I know. I'm used to den craziness."

"This is different. Lizzy, please?"

The name, so new yet not at all, got my attention.

"Don't get distracted, okay? Or sent off on some errand. Things are moving too fast and info isn't always being shared. Get back here ASAP, you promise? No matter what."

"Why wouldn't I?" I hugged him hard, hoping he'd get the message: not everyone will leave you behind.

As I stooped to untie the dinghy, Breakers called down to me. "While you're over there, maybe you can give them a hand with your friend Jenn."

I straightened. "What?"

"She's barricaded herself in her bunk. Won't pack out. Won't let anyone help. Something about relatives coming to pick her up?" Breakers snorted. "As if."

Exactly what I'd worried about.

"Ask Jake what he's heard about the Stormies!" Daniel called as I threw myself into the dinghy.

I nodded and bent to my oars.

THIRTY-SEVEN

F or once, my timing was right.

I monkeyed up the rope ladder to the front entry and snaked between the columns of outbound crates and stacked luggage lining the stair to the mudroom, just as Jake came up the ladder, in deep with Rousseau, both of them talking at once. The noise and bustle in made it hard to listen in without intruding. I made a big deal about filling my water bottle.

Jake looked peculiar, beyond his stitches and bruises from yesterday's attack. Finally, I realized it was his clothing—not his usual baggy jeans and T-shirts, but sleek, pale, and tight. Uptown clothes. More Empire State than Unca Joe.

"How'd you explain that back-alley face to your penthouse pals?" Rousseau was asking.

"These days, not even uptown is surprised if you get beat up on the street. I didn't go into detail." Jake ducked around a dolly piled with duffle bags heading his way. "You're sure going now's the right call? Will we beat the storm? We couldn't ride it out here?"

Rousseau drew him out of the heavy traffic. I slid behind a stack of crates. "If surge predictions are correct, we'd have to haul everything to the third floor and likely still get washed out. Max and I thought . . . no matter. We're committed now. Is that Empire operative still with you?"

Jake shook his head. "I sent her on to Will and Arjay. Let them decide how much to tell Doyle. If they're still speaking."

"For sure she'll let them know we're leaving. Just as well. What'd you hear uptown?"

"Fear. Desperation. A lot of brave chat about the ship finally sinking. Those with a high and defensible perch are hoarding up and barricading the doors. The black market is booming if you can handle three hundred percent inflation and rising. To us, they've had it easy, but these folks see themselves as the last Manhattanites. Leaving is a defeat. With the police and military mostly gone to the riots along the coast, uptown's basically lawless."

"Like downtown, if it weren't for the dens."

"Yeah, except up there, well-armed private security forces are snarling at each other all across Inwood and Washington Heights, even parts of Harlem. Several of them number in the hundreds, small armies. That guy Bright's group is one."

Rousseau tugged fitfully at his vest. "What's the armament level?"

"So far, no one's waving anything really big around. But we should keep an ear out for rockets or mortar fire. Whatever the military had stashed uptown has been deployed back on the Mainland. That's the word. But if you had it, would you admit to it?"

"Any aircraft?"

Aircraft? Couldn't recall the last time I'd seen anything bigger than a cargo drone.

"One or two light copters. Nothing you could really mount an attack with. Fuel's too scarce, even uptown. But turf battles will escalate, then someone's try at total takeover, and next you know, uptown is not high ground but ground zero. Total breakdown of any supply route we might have hoped to maintain."

"Then we're right to cut ourselves loose."

"If we make it in time. But we will be truly on our own."

"With a better chance to hold on to what we do have."

The stocky harbormaster Tito shoved through the crowd toward our corner. "Boss!"

Rousseau turned, ready for one more crisis to spin out of his control. "Here."

"Will Dubowski just pulled up in his fastest boat. Wants a word with you."

Jake and Rousseau traded looks.

"I'll bet he does," Rousseau said. "Send him to my office."

"That was quick," Jake muttered.

"Empire has ship-to-shore. Cass probably radioed him the minute she left the Lagoon."

"Let me just grab a bite. I'll join you upstairs."

"Good luck with that. The kitchen's near packed up." Rousseau shrugged wearily and strode off through the crowd.

I was still fuzzy about the time. When had Jake and Cass gone uptown? He might not know about Rubio. As he pushed toward the Mess, I snatched at his elbow. The moment he saw me, he opened his arms. He knew. I walked into a long, sad hug.

"Glim, Glim, I can't believe we lost our guy! Who am I going to argue with now? Who's going to keep me awake tossing and turning above my head?"

I mumbled agreement into his chest, fighting off a new bout of weeping.

"'One woe doth tread upon another's heels, so fast they follow.'" Jake let me go and draped an arm across my back. "Hardest on you, sweetie. My tier-mate, yeah, but he was your best bud. How are you holding up?"

"Best I can."

"Once we're safe in the new home he found us, we'll throw him one hell of a wake! On my honor!"

I sniffed and fussed at my eyes. "He'd like that."

"Walk with me. Let's see how Spunk is doing."

"Upriver already, with the medics."

"Yeah? He's okay, then."

"Okay enough. But which of his nine lives is he on now?"

Jake laughed. "Only Spunk knows for sure. Eat with me? Or should I say, scrounge?"

"Thanks. I would, but I got to see about Jenn. She's acting up."

"Now what?"

"Doesn't want to leave."

He frowned. "What makes her think she has a choice?"

"She's not thinking. That's the problem."

"Well, get up there and tell her to get her shit together! If anyone can talk sense into her, you can."

"Thanks. Do my best." I started away, then turned back, remembering. "Jake, you hear anything uptown about what the Stormies are up to?"

His eyebrows arched. "Huh. Lot of people asking the same. Seems no one's seen them in a while, not even around that armory they took over. Which is odd, since a big storm usually brings them out. It's like they've dispersed and gone to ground. Like, since Dan, um . . . had his way with the Adders."

Had to think for a minute. How long ago was that? Mere days. And already I'd sectioned it off in the *Do Not Go There* part of my brain. "What does it mean?"

"Damned if I know. Nothing good, you can be sure. Now, go on up and deal with Jenn. And don't forget: one hell of a fucking wake!"

"Right." I squeezed his arm and loped away to the stairs.

Dawn was seeping through the front entry as I raced up, from as sullen a sky as you could imagine. Out on the Lagoon, the work platforms and rough-built rafts creaked in the slow, deepening rhythm of the swell.

When we did evacuation drills, we never took our stuff with us, so it was chilling to see the bunk tiers so stripped and naked. Piles of bulging back-packs, totes, and duffles lined the balcony rail. Best to pack myself up first, then go to Jenn, so she could see me leaving, too.

But in my tier, I found Peeto, hanging one-armed like a scrawny squir-rel, emptying Rubio's level-two bunk, dumping everything onto the floor. I nearly lost it.

"What the hell are you doing?" I screeched.

He swiveled, still grasping the cross-brace, fighting his usual cut-and-run impulse.

"How dare you touch his stuff!" Maybe my teeth were even bared.

Peeto's whole jaw quivered. "Don't get on me! Boss told me to!"

"Sure, he did!"

"You go ask!"

"He was my friend! I should be doing that!"

"You weren't here!"

My default with Peeto was pissed-off, dismissive, or both, but I couldn't deny his point, even pitched as a whine. And his pinched look did slow me down. Anyone else, I'd have said he was teared up, damp cheeks and all. He dropped clumsily to the floor and we both stood there, with Rubio's scant possessions scattered around us, Peeto looking everywhere but at me.

"I was just . . . the boss said . . . forget it. You finish up." He turned away, swiping at his nose with his fist.

An actual apology stuck in my craw, though for once, maybe he deserved one. "Okay. Just hand it all down," I grumbled. "We're on double-time now. It'll go faster with two."

My abrupt capitulation made him suspicious, but he climbed up again to gather the rest. We finished in silence. Other sharp exchanges or angry re-torts echoed through the empty tiers, even the occasional outbreak of weep-ing, as the packing wrapped up. Peeto and I just got the job done. It didn't take long, and not much longer to fold Rube's stuff into the suitcase he claimed he'd arrived with, stored under Jake's bottom bunk. Up-tier, the take-down crews got loudly to work salvaging the planks and posts to be reassembled at the stadium.

When we were done, Peeto stood back, quirking a hand at the open case. "You want anything?"

By tradition, a lost denmate's stuff was first offered among his/her tier-mates. If there'd been any worthy keepsake, a reminder of Rubio and our friendship, I'd have taken it. But there wasn't. I knelt and pulled out the half-dozen books, including the big hardback Daniel had given him. The rest would go to the swap shelves in our new den home.

"These can go to the book boat. The tellers don't value them."

Peeto nodded soberly.

Shame nudged at me. Time for a peace offering. "Anything you could use?"

"Me?" His narrow face got tighter.

"Not trying to catch you out. You were his tier-mate, too."

"But not, y'know, his friend. I mean, Rube was easier on me than most, but . . ."

To say true, Rubio had been as ready to dump on Peeto as the rest of us, but I'd always sensed a hidden sympathy for a fellow social misfit, even if he rarely acted on it.

"Go ahead." My hand hovered over the suitcase lid. "Last call."

Peeto squatted, fumbled among the thin layers of clothing, and snatched out a clean black T-shirt. Rubio's signature color. It would hang on Peeto like a shroud, but it was soft and entirely without stains or holes.

"I'm sure he'd approve." I snapped the case shut. "Can you take it down? Got my own to do, then I have to see about Jenn."

Peeto's eyes widened. A cache of oily gossip waited behind that look.

I held up my hand. "Don't say it. Just don't. I'll get her out of there."

I could maybe sympathize with Peter Sweeney, even feel sorry for him. But I was never going to be his friend.

THIRTY-EIGHT

Packing out my bunk was quicker than Rubio's, even with only me doing it. I knew I wasn't coming back, so I stole a moment to say goodbye. To my cracked window. My peeling plaster wall. My looming cornice, home to my two flood-frazzled books. This cramped but private space that let me feel safe enough to recover, to find myself again. What comforts would I find in a big, clanking stadium? Still, it was clearly time to move on.

Inside the desperate hurry-up swirling through the den, I sensed an undertone of relief at the change of routine, even anticipation of a new adventure. I'd embraced it, not only for the den's sake but in Rubio's memory. But it didn't come easy.

I drew Hannah's soft leather backpack from under my mattress, stowed away for just such a day. Everything I owned would fit inside. Packing brought a sharp memory of leaving stuff behind to move onto *Haiku*. Even so, I'd taken a locker full of clothing, clean sheets and towels, books, cosmetics, a phone. A dog. Perched on my bunk, I wrapped my toothbrush in my threadbare washrag and slid my mostly used toothpaste tube in beside it. Such small nonperishables were still to be found in abandoned apartments or dry-ground drug marts. Like, who'd bother to loot toothpaste? Or soap? Well, maybe. For resale at the Souk. But given recent events, how long till even those items became scarce luxuries?

We'd have to learn to make our own. Our own everything.

Like, how picked-over were the city blocks around our new den? Yankee Stadium might be uninhabited, but it was in the Bronx, which was actually the Mainland. The coastal Bronx was under water, but there'd be dry ground not too far north. Which meant more people, more competition, local posses and militias. In reality, moving to the Stadium was moving to the Mainland. A good argument to give Jenn for leaving. Had to get to it. The take-down crew would be here soon, though Jake had yet to clear his bunk, and he had more gear than most of us.

Footsteps rounded the corner, and there he was. Still in his uptown duds, but the neat row of stitches on his forehead vanishing into newly damp hair.

My eyes widened. "It's raining already?"

"Not yet. Had to wash off the uptown grease. Even better once I get out of costume."

"Are you avoiding Empire Will?"

Jake smirked. "They don't need me listening to Will trying to talk us out of going early."

"Why? 'Cause you might agree with him?"

"It's all shoulders to the wheel right now." Jake tugged at his ear and left it at that.

His loyalty to Rousseau was like a fixed star. I did up the smooth brass buckles on my pack and climbed down with it slung over one shoulder. "You need help packing?"

"Nah. Oughta leave most of it behind. Travel light."

My picker's instincts went into gear. "Not if someone else can use it!"

"Right. Waste not, want not. How'd you make out with Jenn?"

"Just heading her way. Sorted my bunk out first."

He gazed at his own bunk gloomily. "Makes sense."

"Any regrets? I mean, about leaving?"

Jake scanned the tier as I had done, a slow 360 turn like he was dragging a weight behind him. "Two minds. Always. It's a problem I have."

The sawing and hammering in the next tier was broken by a pained bellow, followed by the clatter of wood falling and some serious cursing, then silence.

"Everyone okay over there?" Jake called.

"Yeah. Shit. Yeah, sort of."

"We're fine," another voice chimed in.

Jake sighed. "Better get to it, or they'll be pulling the place down around my ears."

"I can help." I started hauling gear out from under his bed.

"No, really. Go see to Jenn."

"Okay." I got up, picked up my pack. But I wanted more from him. "You have your doubts about this, right? Like, it's so . . . sudden?"

He nodded. "It's a risk, but it had to happen. I tried to think otherwise, hoping for a sure thing. Which you never get. In the end, we got shoved along by Mother Nature."

"And Rubio."

"And Rubio." Jake paused, like he wanted to say it right. "He gave us the push we needed, and just in time. One angry guy who expected to be listened to, or maybe he was angry because we didn't listen. Either way, he understood that our small, self-sustaining communities won't work for the long run, that we need to adapt to whatever gets thrown at us. To be truly sustainable, to find a way through this mess that's ahead of us, we need a certain critical mass and a deeper diversity of skills."

"Definition of a community . . ."

"Sure, but a hard future to believe in when you watch Tom Doyle and Empire Will go at each other all the time. And hard to hear when you're busy keeping your own den fed and safe, on a day-to-day basis, all white knuckled and hanging off a fucking cliff!"

"I know." Easy to think the guys in charge are having all the fun. I'd envied Jake because I'd never seen his job clearly. I wondered if Rubio had. "Rube rarely shared his opinions politely. Or saw why he should."

He nodded slowly. "His own worst enemy. So often, the good ideas never made it through the smokescreen of criticism and contempt."

I sighed. "Well, he was good to me."

"He was. And I honor him for it."

We both glanced at the empty space above Jake's bunk.

"Will there be time for a funeral?"

"Let me look into it."

"You heard about the Adders?"

"Did. A major break. Bright'll be short on street muscle now."

"For sure it was him arming them?"

"That's the word uptown."

I fitted the pack straps around my arms. When I looked up, Jake was gazing at me like I was an egg he'd hatched.

"Speaking of which, I hear you and Dan Nathan are spending time together."

Knowing I was blushing made me blush all the more. "A quaint way to put it."

"Quaint, schmaint. A good choice, Glim." He chuckled and threw me a wink. "Even better than me."

"Er . . . ?" Peeto had materialized behind Jake. "Hey, Glim. You still here?"

"Just leaving."

Peeto sidled in on Jake's far side. "Need any help?"

"Help?" Jake turned on him, slow and grandiose, like a king in one of those old plays he was always quoting from. "Do my ears deceive me?"

I nudged him. "Just let the guy help. He's making up for past sins."

I left them to work it out. The short way to Jenn's tier was blocked with stacks of old plywood, battered 4x4s and stacks of 2x8s studded with rusting hardware. I had to trot around the long way to the uptown entrance. Jenn's bunk was level three. When I pulled up below, a posse of Wizzers was crowded around, trying to lure Jenn down with their geekiest idea of bait.

"Your own dedicated terminal . . ."

"Like, your own room! There's plenty up there."

"Maybe better signal from the Mainland!"

I shooed them away, dropped my pack on the bottom bunk, and scaled the tier to settle on the edge of Jenn's bunk. "Hey. What's all the fuss?"

Jenn was pressed into a back corner, her pillow clamped to her chest and her belongings tucked up tight around her like a defending army. She looked rational enough, except that her hair was a worse rat's nest than before and her eyes were so huge and luminous in the shade of the upper bunk, I thought she'd put on heavy makeup.

"Glim! You came to wait with me!"

Wasn't going to say no right off. "For a while. Whacha waiting for?"

"Not what. Who. C'mon, you know."

I swung my legs over the edge like it was any old day in the den. "You heard a big storm on the way? Superstorm Leon?"

"Oh, they'll be here before that."

"Coming up faster than predicted."

"They'll be keeping an eye on it."

I made to notice her stuff pulled up around her. "So why aren't you packed? They won't want to hang around with a storm coming."

"Oh. My. Of course I should!" Like she hadn't considered it. She let the pillow fall in her lap, grabbed up a packet of soap, put it down, reached for her sewing kit, put it down.

"Where's your bag? I'll help." I jittered a bit, like I was ready to climb down. "And then, in case they get held up by the weather, you can come with us and they'll pick you up at the Stadium after it's passed. Be easier all around. And a lot safer."

"But how would I let them know where to find me?" She wrinkled up, on the verge of tears. "Those wretched children stole all my equipment!"

"Not stole. Put it in safekeeping. So you'll have it uptown." Was it time to start lying through my teeth? "Daniel could probably contact them for you."

"Daniel?" Her yard-wide gaze drew in a bit. "You mean, before he leaves?"

I played my next card, worried my hand was already growing thin. "He's not leaving."

"Why not?"

"He's coming with us. With me."

"You said he couldn't go?"

"We agreed we didn't want to."

"You both gave up a chance to get off the Island?" She sent me a long, disbelieving look, then turned away. "What a waste."

"You know the Stadium's only a few water blocks from the Mainland, right? Officially, it is the Mainland."

She hadn't factored this in. She said slowly, "I was never at Yankee Stadium."

"Me, neither. But now I recall sailing past it on occasion, once the river covered the parking lot." I wished that memory had returned in time to share with Rubio. "So I know it's huge and solid, with all these tall, arched windows, lots of roof area for the gardens and solar, and the playing field can be a sheltered harbor for all our boats. It'll be like a real marina."

Below us, one of the demolition crews had arrived, tools in hand, jostling about impatiently, giving us the eye.

"They're going to pull this tier right out from under us," I noted. "What say we pack up later, go talk to Daniel now, see what he can do?"

Jenn nibbled at her lip. "You know, they'll probably send a drone. Should have thought of that before! Yankee Stadium would be easier to find."

I nodded vigorously, shamed to be encouraging new heights of fantasizing. "A cinch. From the air or the water. And a safer place to land."

"They'll need coordinates."

"Easily done." I was setting Daniel up for trouble, but if it got Jenn moving, it was worth it. He'd understand.

"Okay." She uncrossed her legs, straightening them in front of her, and spent some time staring at her toes. Then she glanced around in surprise. "Jeez, this place is a total mess! I'm a terrible hostess! Make sure I tidy up when we get back, okay?"

"Sure thing." I poked among her things, handed over her comb. "Your public awaits."

She touched her hair. "Is it that bad?"

"Maybe just a touch-up."

She ran the comb through several times, knowing exactly how to restore her usual shining cap. I'd need a mirror for that level of repair. "Better?"

"Perfect."

I watched close as Jenn levered herself out of the bunk and started the climb down. Every change of hand-grip, I worried she'd reconsider. But she made it to the floor, flashing a vaguely flirtatious look at the demo crew.

"What are you all in such a hurry about?"

The crew chief rolled her eyes, but I made covert bag-packing gestures, and she nodded. I collected my own pack, linked elbows with Jenn, and urged her on ahead, like she was leading me. In the outer hall, she pressed my arm tight against her side.

"You are a good friend to me, Glim!"

Nice. Would she feel the same once she realized I'd shanghaied her to Yankee Stadium?

THIRTY-NINE

The tide had turned while I was inside the den. Not with its usual downtown rush, but eddying and sluggish, like something southward was pushing it back.

Jenn's gear was piled in Daniel's dinghy by the time I got her into it, along with a load of tomato seedlings and precious seed stock stored in metal canisters. Breakers hailed us as we approached, rifle raised in salute. Daniel met us in *Melville*'s stern, smiling with relief. I hadn't had time to warn him of my promise.

I grabbed the hand he offered. "You were right about the chaos over there. And I caught up with Jake. He says the Stormies have gone to ground. Then we needed a moment about Rubio."

"Of course."

Jenn's smile was tentative as Daniel helped her onto the *Melville*. She spent a moment rearranging her colorful layers, then got right down to it. "Glim says you might be able to help me."

He seemed to guess what was coming. "How so?"

I made myself busy unshipping tomato plants.

"You see, I have these cousins in . . ." Turning to plead with him, she got a full view of the Lagoon. She paused, her gaze flicking frantically across the hectic crowd of boats, from Unca Joe shorn of its lattice of walkways to her denmates and so many others madly building, carrying, and loading. Her ingratiating smile faded until her mouth formed a silent O. She dropped her eyes and began to weep.

I brushed compost from my palms and went to put my arms around her, even knowing she'd dreaded close contact as much as I, since the Wave. It seemed the only comfort left to offer. Jenn didn't pull away.

"It'll all be fine," I said, without any real reason to believe it would. Like Jake said, it was a huge risk, but necessary.

Jenn eased me to arm's length and took another, more considered look around the Lagoon. "Oh, my. That was a deep one, wasn't it."

I nodded, always stunned by how fast her realities shifted.

She brushed tears away. "What you must think of me."

I patted her, smoothed her hair. "I don't think anything at all."

"Ahoy, the Book Boat!" The battered rowboat I'd brought home not so long ago pulled alongside, a tow-headed young Smith at the oars and Ellie Mae perched in the stern with a small, root-balled tree on her lap, its leaves pressing against her face. Every other inch of space bristled with potted or burlapped vegetable plants. Ellie Mae's sturdy, old-woman's body was erect and purposeful. Even before Daniel had them tied up, she was handing him the tree with care and ceremony.

"Our newest Meyer lemon. It'll want a special placement."

"I know just the spot." To me, he said, "Take Jenn forward. We'll get all this stowed."

"Thanks." As I bundled Jenn inside, she stumbled on the steps, then gripped the edges of the book racks as we went along the aisle. Exiting a manic phase, she was always spent. In Daniel's cabin, the berth was still mussed from our lovemaking. I quickly smoothed it, but Jenn didn't seem to notice. She went right to it and sat, limp as a rag.

She eyed me beneath heavy lids. "I really do have cousins in Minneapolis."

"I know. You've told me . . ."

"No, really." She flopped over on her side, grasping for a pillow. "But they wouldn't care if I lived or died."

The truth, at last. I hoped it was a good sign.

I settled beside her. "Well, we care. The den's your family now."

I sat with her till she was asleep, then went up top to hug Daniel, mostly to feel his ready response, his body tight to mine. This new miracle of twoness filled me with gratitude. Then we got back to work, toting plants, stowing them tightly on the emptied book racks until the main cabin was green as a jungle.

"That's all for this load." Ellie Mae poked her white head in the door. "It's good they'll be under cover when the storm comes."

Daniel brushed past a rosemary, releasing its scent. "We'll have them to the Stadium before it does."

"Better still." But a twist of her mouth betrayed her doubt.

"Will you ride up with us?" I wasn't sure where we'd put her.

"No, dear. I have to head out sooner with a full load of young trees to chaperone on one of Maxine's pontoon boats. It has a canopy, but the sides are open, so I feel they'll need some extra care. Peter's coming to help."

"Peter? Oh, you mean Peeto?"

"Yes, of course. He's a great hand with the plants."

"He is?"

"My right arm in the garden."

Live and learn. No wonder his hands were always dirty. "Safe sailing to both of you."

She was stiff getting into the rowboat but settled herself briskly as the young Smith pushed off with one oar. She'd worked steadily, pacing herself so that she seemed no wearier at the end of the job than she had at the beginning. Daniel and I watched them glide away, rolling gently in the building swell.

"Crazy Ellie . . ." I mused.

Daniel laughed. "Crazy like a fox."

"You know her?"

"She used to wander up to the Souk now and then. Until Pete Sweeney started running her errands for her."

Amazing. About both of them. I'd assumed Ellie Mae to be pretty much confined to the den, due to old age or Rousseau's constraints. "What sort of errands?"

"Ellie's my best customer for books about Mars, fiction or non. Her field of study, when you could still have such a thing. I'd look for books, old journals, save them for her. Sometimes we'd get to talking."

"That's why all the Mars books? Oh, jeez! I thought . . ." I pressed both hands to my face. "Well, you can't imagine what I thought, like, when all the transit papers turned up in them."

"No, but I'd like to."

I groaned between my palms. "Don't make fun, okay? You know what the international base on Mars was called, when there was one?"

"Can't say I do."

"Ellie Mae never talked about it?"

"She's . . . careful, talking about her past. Her work."

I was sure he was holding back but couldn't really fault him for discretion. "Arcadia. It was called Arcadia."

"Arka . . . oh." He started to laugh. And kept laughing, until he was breathless and wiping moisture from his eyes. "Arcadia Base! That sure qualifies as a final destination!"

I thought it more embarrassing than funny, but better he laugh than be brought down by the reminder of Hannah and Julian's departure.

He caught his breath, still chuckling. "It was . . . the Mars books . . . just a way to remember where I'd hidden the documents, after people started snooping around for them."

"Rubio said there's lots of Arcadias out there. At least one in every state."

"We never did find Hannah's on a map. Likely a code name. Hannah . . . on . . . Mars!" Daniel intoned. And started laughing again.

Sentry whoops rang across the Lagoon.

Breakers roused herself from her nap on the cabin roof. "Got a boat returning!"

A relief to see *Zephyr* chug into the Lagoon with her empty raft in tow and head scout Hawkeye at the wheel. She'd brought her downriver with a single deckhand. Across our makeshift marina, tired workers stood up to holler and cheer.

Maxine and Rousseau were soon out front to get a report. Empire Will trailed behind them, hands thrust deep into the pockets of a yellow slicker, bright over a clean white polo. Didn't look like he'd been winning many arguments.

Hawk took a kayak in from Zephyr's mooring, already debriefing as she scaled the entryway ladder, the den leaders leaning eagerly over the rail to hear. The human noise in the Lagoon fell silent as we all listened in. Sound carries well over water.

". . . rafts are heading back with the tide," Hawk was saying. "About an hour behind me."

"If they arrive in time . . ." Rousseau spoke up for all ears, more instruction than observation. ". . . we can reload and start back up when the tide turns."

Will nosed in more quietly. "Any problems? Anybody see you along the way?"

"If they did, they were quiet about it," Hawk replied. "It was smooth sailing all the way."

Maxine lifted her face to the rising south wind, letting it worry her short-cropped hair. "Let's hope it stays that way."

"If the first batch is there safely," offered Will, "The rest could wait out the storm here."

"And haul all that's left back inside?" Rousseau scolded. "There's no time for that, Will!"

"What about your people? Where're you going to put them all? Surely not on open rafts?"

"We'll make as many motor trips as we have to."

"That's what you don't have time for! This storm is . . ."

"Will! If Empire State is staying put, that's your call. But stop trying to manage Unca Joe!"

"I'm only thinking of . . ." Will paused as the sentries started hallooing again. I saw him squint across the Lagoon, then grimace and shake his head as Tom Doyle turned the corner from Fourth Ave at high speed, cutting a wake that Julian would have envied. No mistaking that ink-dark face. He slowed just enough to twist a showy course through the scrum of floats and passenger craft. To my surprise, he was driving an old wooden four-seater, gleamingly cared-for. As it glided past the *Melville*, I read 'Chris-Craft' on its side.

Daniel whistled softly. "That's a two hundred-year-old boat. Where'd he find it?"

"He's brought one of the Gimme Girls," I noted.

Doyle stood up at the wheel as he reversed engines to approach the access ladder. His boat swaying in the swell didn't bother him, but a gust caught his open, knee-length vest—the same iridescent green-blue-black as his tattooed arms and chest. For an instant, he nearly went overboard. "What the hell's going on?"

"The Prince of Darkness," Daniel muttered.

I thought he looked magnificent, obviously the point of such a get-up. But who was he trying to impress? Himself?

"Just getting a jump on the storm," Rousseau yelled back.

"Were you planning to tell anybody?"

More sentry cries as the Zodiac clattered into the Lagoon on a cranky, half-burnt motor salvaged from the Ladysmith raid. Empty raft in tow, its crew of two grinned and waved like they'd won the free meal lottery. By this time, Jake had joined the cluster at the entryway, and Will took advantage of the building confusion to slip down the ladder into his own boat and start it up. He slowed alongside Doyle's boat and called to the passenger.

"Arla? Everything all right?"

"Why wouldn't it be?" growled Doyle.

"I'm asking her."

The girl looked anything but all right, her face tight and her bare arms wrapped defensively around her chest. She was thin and blond and looked about twelve. "So sorry, Will! We heard Empire wasn't going, so we tried to come by the walkways, but there are gaps now and the cow wouldn't . . ."

"We said we'd get you there," insisted Will. "But after the storm."

"We need to go now," the girl wailed. "The surge . . . !"

"Yep," Daniel said to me. "This one could wash over Madison Square like a tsunami."

"Planned this one well, didya, William?" Doyle grinned, his dark coat wrapping him like beetle's wings.

"Okay." Empire Will, moon-pale in yellow and white, struggled to keep his temper. "You stay here with the Joes, Arla, and I'll get to moving the rest over as soon as possible."

"Once he knows what it'll cost him." Doyle loomed over the girl. "Do the math first!"

Now Will was up on his feet, one hand on his wheel for balance. "At least I'd know how!"

"If I were you, girl," Doyle advised, "I'd watch they don't try corporatizing your cow."

"Please! Please!" Arla moaned. "Stop it, both of you! We don't have time!"

Beside me, Daniel stirred restlessly. "Doyle's itching for a fight. Must be the weather. Ah, good. Someone's got some sense."

Will had resettled in his seat with an air of purpose. He keyed his boat and, without further word, took off out of the Lagoon. Doyle stared after him, his jaw working in frustration. Then he sat and eased his boat forward to join the group in the entryway for a private conference.

I nudged Daniel. "I could take the kayak. Go listen in."

"You'll want to keep an eye on Jenn."

"She's crashed. Out like a light."

"You're staying put. If there's news, we'll hear about it."

Getting bossy with me again. Surprising how quick my back got up. I felt my mouth thin to a line. Like, hadn't I survived the streets every night, thank you very much?

He saw me tense up. "You think I'm bullying you."

"You think I can't take care of myself."

"Not true. But I do know your gift for walking into trouble." He jostled me gently. "Humor me. I won't make a habit of it."

Always listen to second thoughts, even if you don't act on them. This had to be about losing Sara, then Hannah and Julian. He was going to be needy, this man, and who could blame him? He'd been patient with my rough edges. Time to give space to some of his. But I could see this two-ness was going to take some work.

I gave in and leaned into him. "Okay. I'm here. What's left to do?"

He wrapped me tight, then eased away reluctantly. "Not much till the tide turns again."

"You seem busy enough."

"Just checking on things."

"Huh." I jerked a thumb up at Breakers, who'd slid back into her upright doze. "Maybe she's got the right idea."

So, while Daniel clambered all over *Melville*, tightening latches and neatening coils, I stretched out on the stern bench and tried to relax enough to nap. Not easy, even rocked by the early swell. Eventually, the Smith launch puttered in, slow and steady, with her empty raft bobbing behind. This good news finally let me sleep.

Next I knew, there was a wet wind gusting up my nose and Daniel shaking me awake.

"What's up?"

"Not sure yet. Some of Doyle's core muscle just hammered in, armed to the teeth. The watch went in to get him."

It was noonish, judging by the angle of light, which was already greenish and storm-heavy. *Zephyr* and the Zodiac bobbed beside loaded tow rafts at the uptown end of the Lagoon, ready for their next trip. No sign of the Smith launch. Several other rafts were being stocked, but the Lagoon looked emptied and the work frenzy had slowed. Denfolk were sacked out on every horizontal surface.

I sat up, shaking off my drowse. "Where are all the boats?"

"Upriver," Daniel said. "Since the first group returned safely, Rousseau stepped up the pace. The power boats have made a second round trip. Wind's with us and the tide just turned, so the guys from Riverhome rigged sails and rudders for the rafts without a tow."

"Riverhome's here now?"

"A bunch showed up while you were asleep. They've sent their own boats up already, filled with cargo. They're hoping we'll have room for passengers."

"Will we?"

"Better have. Some will crew the rafts."

A shriek of whistles overlaid sudden shouting from inside Unca Joe.

"I don't care if he's sleeping! Get him up! Get him out here! Get them all out here!" Tom Doyle stormed out of the den and dropped down the ladder into his waiting Chris-Craft. But he wasn't leaving. He pulled alongside the most central float in the Lagoon, carpeted with napping workers, and bounded out, his long vest flapping in the wind.

"Up! Everyone up! We've got a situation!" He stalked around, nudging the nappers with his booted foot, then took up a waiting pose. He could shout from there. His recently arrived patrol crews stationed their boats around the perimeter of the Lagoon and sat in idle. Act II of his performance, perhaps?

On the roof, Breakers stirred. "What's he on about now?"

"Are they keeping others out or us in?" I asked.

Daniel grunted. "Looks like there's news."

"Maybe it's a coup," Breakers offered snidely.

"Be careful what you wish for."

"Nah. Tommy doesn't want to run things. He just wants to make the biggest noise."

"I wouldn't be too sure."

Doyle began to pace. "Listen up, everyone! This is not a test!" He sent broad ripples around the Lagoon as the float shifted with him. "The Stormies are rallying!"

The wakened nappers caught his urgency and gathered around him, squatting, kneeling, so not to block anyone's view.

"There are hundreds of them . . . and they're headed here!"

Consternation exploded across the Lagoon. Daniel slid an arm around my back.

Tito came out of _Zephyr_'s wheelhouse wiping his hands, and the crowd hushed. "How'll they get here? They got no boats."

"They do now," Doyle called back. "Because Revelations has joined up with them."

"Did I hear that right?" Rousseau was at the den entrance, tugging on his leather vest while the wind tried to turn it into a sail. "Revelations?"

"Yah," said Doyle. "The motherfuckers!"

"Why would they?"

"It's that new girl the Stormies raised up. She's preaching about how, between them, they can turn Manhattan into God's Island."

"*God's Island?*" Rousseau made it sound like an insult.

"Something like that. Where everyone obeys their fundamentalist rule and no one has any fun. No surprise, Revelations took to the idea. Then they got wind of your move and saw an opportunity. Now they're massing along Park, hyped on sermons, ready to invade!"

Massing. I didn't like the sound of that one bit.

Daniel muttered, "Great. Someone else who wants to own Manhattan."

"But the Stormies worship hurricanes. Where does God come into it?"

"Got me. Why is it the people you least expect turn out to be the most trouble?"

I recalled Rubio saying we hadn't heard the last of Revelations after they'd walked out of the den caucus. "Maybe you should go blow them up, too."

He stared at me. "Hey."

I ducked my head. "Sorry." Just the sort of thing Rube would've said, so I had to say it for him. "It's my weather itch. Makes me jumpy."

"Your what?"

My turn to change the subject. "I feel weather coming. Like, physically. Some kind of nerve twinge. Probably the pressure change, y'know, like a barometer? Rubio always gives me . . . gave . . ." The change of tense caught in my throat.

"Okay there?"

"Yeah." My shoulders drooped. "It's just . . . you forget, and then you remember and then . . . he dies all over again."

"I know."

Of course he did. "Anyhow, Rube gave my itch the benefit of the doubt. Knowing now that I spent most of before on the water, it makes better sense. Like those old sea dogs who hung around the marinas. They always knew when weather was coming."

"Also called a weather eye." Daniel snorted softly. "Hard to see you as an old sea dog."

"Can it, willya?" Breakers complained. "I'm trying to listen."

"Is she preaching any sort of battle plan?" Rousseau was asking, as Maxine joined him at the rail. Jake hovered in her shadow.

"Roll like a wave," Doyle replied. "It's all storm rhetoric, in her speeches."

Tito, who really was an old sea dog, wanted the facts. "How many boats?"

"Maybe a dozen. And they're already worrying the edges of the rally, like raiding parties. That's how I know. They jumped some of my guys running patrols."

Maxine's hands fisted. "What are they carrying?"

"Any sort of blade, you name it. No firearms. But they say those fucking monks are mean hand to hand. My guys beat 'em off but they took some hurt."

"And the Stormies?" demanded Rousseau.

"Walking downtown!" Doyle stood arms spread, like he was thrilled to be bringing this news. "Or will be, once the priest girl is done with her sermonizing. Like army ants, devouring everything in their path! When the monks' boats are filled, they'll use the pass-thrus! When they run out of those, they'll take to the walkways!"

All eyes turned to the storm-wrecked end of the Third Avenue walkway.

Rousseau raised his arms. "Then we'll make sure to be gone when they get here!"

"Not a chance!" Doyle whirled to face him. "You don't have the boats or the speed to get everyone out of here in time! Our only hope is meeting 'em face to face! I say we clear the harbor and set up an ambush!"

After that, everyone was shouting. And snarling and shaking their fists. Once more, the outer sentries signaled an intruder, and the entire Lagoon reached for the nearest thing you could call a weapon. But it was only the Ladysmith launch, returning late by hours.

Daniel pointed. "She's missing her raft."

Doyle's escort boats closed around the open-canopied boat like Stormies might be hiding in the bilge. One of his men boarded for a quick search, then waved the all-clear. The crew brought the launch in beside the rope ladder to report to Maxine, unaware that their breathless news was already old. Surprise attack by knife-wielding monks. Sliced the tow rope. Stole the empty raft. Would've taken the boat, scrammed when shot at.

"Why steal an empty raft?" I asked.

"Transportation." Breakers shifted in her seat and checked the load in her rifle.

Rousseau turned his back to lean heavily against the railing, clearly wracking his brain for his next move while Maxine yakked away at him. Everything about his stance said he wished she'd just shut up and let him think. Jake stood by with his stitched-up face, failing to talk her down.

"Rousseau could so easily lose control of this," Daniel murmured.

"No way he'll go for an ambush," I said.

"Might have no choice. The tide's with us only another three or four hours, and Doyle's right: not enough boats and rafts to ferry everything that's left in just one trip."

"When are we meant to leave? *Melville*, I mean."

"With the final push. Being covered and under power, we can stand a bit of weather if the storm gets here early."

I shuddered, like a dog shaking off rain. "We shouldn't wait that long."

He studied me. "Why's that?"

"Been bugging me since I woke up. We're looking south for the storm, right? Superstorm Leon moving up the coast. But my itch says there's something brewing out there." I nodded due east, out to sea.

"You're saying, a second storm?"

"Just . . . something."

"Better give Rousseau a heads up."

"They'd never believe me."

Doyle moved into planning mode. "How many men do we have? How many weapons?"

"Hold on," said Rousseau.

Doyle beckoned Tito to join him on his floating podium. "Can't let 'em catch us here in the Lagoon. What's the best spot for an ambush?"

Tito stayed where he was, glancing to Rousseau.

"Tommy!" Rousseau bellowed, leaning over the rail. "I'm not letting you risk everyone's life just because you're hot for confrontation!"

And there we were again, in that same bad place: half the den ready to race into battle, the rest even readier to speed away and avoid bloodshed. The gathering around Doyle shifted as those not up for a fight crept off the float while the willing shoved their way on with waving fists and roars of support.

Rousseau called to Tito for an updated count: how many boats, how much people and cargo? But anyone could do the math: three power boats strong enough to pull a loaded raft, two of them already overladen and fully crewed. Five other rafts, each rigged with sail and rudder, already loaded, already crewed. The remaining small craft—canoes, kayaks, dinghies— could take about another dozen people between them. I ticked off available spaces versus the thirty or forty . . . no, make it exact . . . forty-two people needing transport.

"What about our war canoes?" I hoped this was a new idea.

"Went out with the second shift," Breakers said. "Crammed to the gills with Macys."

Save the children first. Well, why not? They'd been through so much already.

"What if those who want to fight just stayed behind?"

Breakers sucked her teeth. "Suicide mission, if Tommy's got the numbers right."

Massing, Doyle had said. Like army ants. I turned to Daniel. "What would you do?"

"Me? I'm for splitting soon as everyone has a ride uptown."

"Really?" Silly to be so relieved, since enough rides was exactly the problem. But I did.

He gave me a wan smile. "I'm not as bloodthirsty as you think."

"I don't . . ."

"You do. But whenever I opt for the extreme course, I like the odds to be on my side. Doyle's setting us up for a massacre. And tell me true: in a court of law, would you honestly be able to plead a mercy case for BlackAdder?"

I had no answer for that, and Jake saved the need for one, whistling for silence.

Rousseau planted both fists on the railing and surveyed the crowd. "Here's the reality. Even a hundred Stormies are too many for us to fight off in open combat. If we retreat inside, they'll lay siege, and we've sent too much of our food and water upriver, along with most of our able-bodied men and women. We couldn't hold out for long. We don't have enough boat space left for both people and cargo, and then there's . . ." He glanced up, raising an open palm.

Like a sign from above, it had started to rain.

"So here it is: we're going to off-load cargo till we make room enough to get everyone out of here. Stuff can be replaced. People, never. We need to go! Now!"

Maxine stepped up beside him to signal agreement, though she didn't look happy about it. "The trip up takes an hour and some for a power boat hauling with the tide—which turns in three hours. We don't want to be working against it. Let's move!"

"The coward's choice!" Doyle yelled. "Go on, turn tail! And while you're sneaking off, Tall Tommy will be up along the rooftops, picking off fuckin' Stormies one by one! Join us, if you've got the nerve!"

He roused his dozen or so hangers-on and waved in his escort boats to pick them up. But the two out past us at the Lagoon's far end were raising a new alert.

"Intruders to the south! Possible enemy advance!"

Seconds later, Unca Joe's downtown sentries added to the clamor. Again, everyone grabbed for a weapon. Doyle stood tall on his float, his face alight. Perfect timing.

The rain was blowing up a fine mist, fogging the distance. Vague shapes approached up Third Avenue, but it was hard to ID them. A low humming like a busy hive mingled with the wind noise, rising as it neared.

Old fears die hard. I shrank against Daniel. "Is it the surge? Already?"

"Can't be. Sounds more like . . ."

Breakers swayed on tippy-toe, like she was dancing. "Holy crap! Holy fuck!"

"What? What?" demanded Daniel.

"I don't believe it!" She fought for footing on the wet, windblown roof. "It's boats!"

"But whose?"

On the roof, she had a better vantage point, but once I wiped the mist from my eyes, I could just make them out, a long convoy of low, dark boats. Maybe six or eight of them.

Daniel unlatched the starboard stern locker and fumbled for a pair of binoculars. As he stared through them, his alarm eased into puzzlement.

"Is it Revelations?"

"No . . . it's . . . a fleet of water taxis?"

"Yes, yes, yes!" crooned Breakers. "It's . . ."

"Wait! Don't say it!" Grinning, he handed me the binocs. "Have a look."

My hands shook, half-expecting scowling monks with pointy teeth. I steadied the glasses on *Melville*'s tiller. Yep . . . water taxis. The bigger kind that carry groups. And . . . oh! In the lead boat, a figure in safety-yellow foul-weather gear, somehow familiar. As the boat approached, the man brushed back his rain hood. Still blond and smooth-faced but looking a bit shaggy now I saw him up close, like he hadn't shaved in a while. I whooped for joy.

When he drew within everyone's view, a collective sigh stuttered across the Lagoon. Weapons clattered to the deck, and Empire Will Dubowski motored in to a wild round of cheers and applause.

He slowed when he came level with *Melville*, waving the other boats ahead. I could see he liked things to look easy, but stress was getting the better of him, especially around the eyes. "Hey, Dan. Best welcome I ever got."

"Just in time. Doyle was getting ready to lead the charge of the Light Brigade."

"Sorry. Took a while to round these up. Had to get Gimme on their way first."

"Yeah." Daniel offered a mock-frown. "Can't ever find a cab when it's raining. Who'd you lift 'em from?"

"Oh, these are ours. Empire owns the medallion. Not that it matters anymore."

"What about the rest of your clan?"

"Gone upriver with Gimme, except for the patrols. You'll see them along the way."

"You're coming with us, then? That's the best of news."

Will shrugged deep inside his shiny slicker. "Yeah. I don't know. Yankee Stadium. Just sounded too good to miss." He pulled his hood into place. "Well, got some fares to pick up. See you uptown?"

"You bet. And, Will . . . ?"

Dubowski cocked his head.

"Tom Doyle will try to eat you for breakfast. You've totally spoiled his fun."

Will glided away, laughing.

"How 'bout that? A chance we might actually make it." Daniel brushed mist from his hair. "Let's roll out the rain canopy. Breakers, get down and lend a hand, willya?"

We were all soaked already, and the wind swept the fine rain under the stern canopy anyway, but it felt like protection, a roof over our heads while we waited for the last of Unca Joe's worldly goods to be loaded onto the rafts, and a seat found in the water taxis for every Joe, Smith, Macy, River-homer, or other stray. Breakers went below to scrounge up tea and something to eat. I asked her to check on Jenn, then pressed myself into Daniel's side, like Magus used to do.

"Well, that was fucking amazing."

"Don't get cocky." He stroked my back. "We're not there yet."

"In so many ways." Across the Lagoon, Tom Doyle was haranguing his dwindling cohort to arm up and follow him to the rooftops. "Y'know, I asked Rubio once: if he hated Unca Joe so much, why didn't he move to some den he approved of? He said that wasn't the point of criticism. He wanted people to listen, then make it better where they lived. But sometimes you need outside help. We'd have been cooked if Will hadn't showed up. Probably we'd all be dead."

"Maybe. Well, probably. Now, maybe not. And that's about sharing resources and working together." He bent for a long kiss damp with rainwater, then stood away. "Which reminds me: we'll be picking up a tow on the way out."

He pointed to two small rafts being loaded at the front of the den. Resting on piles of scrap lumber and other burnable trash were the sheet-wrapped forms of the two Macy kids who didn't make it, and the long, narrow shape of my friend.

"When we get to open water, we'll give him a light and set him free."

ide turning in three hours, and there was still the weather to deal with.

By the time we got everyone and everything loaded up, the wind was tearing whitecaps off the swells rolling through the Lagoon. The rain was heavier, but I convinced Daniel to take down the stern canopy before it got blown away.

"Ahoy, Book Boat!"

This time it was Rivera, pulling up in a water taxi full of Macys. They clustered around her, chicks with a mother hen. Her dark hair was in messy braids, like some stiff-fingered little Macy had done them for her. The sadness that had shadowed her beauty was fading behind a satisfied glow.

"She looks so . . . happy," I marveled. "Despite all this mess."

"I'd say she's found her niche," agreed Daniel.

"Got a favor to ask," she called over the gusts.

I tossed the bumpers over the side and waved the driver alongside. "What's up?"

Rivera urged one of the Macy boys forward. I recognized the kid Daniel had spent time soothing the night of their horrific rescue. "Alejandro would like to come aboard."

"Sure, but . . ."

She gestured vaguely behind us. "You're taking Rubio out, right? And the others?"

"Oh. Yes . . . ?" I was still puzzled.

Rivera straightened, her delicate face gone formal. "Jandi would like to do the honors for his denmates."

Daniel eased up beside me. "*Jandi! Qué tal?*"

Even scrubbed and fed, his cuts and bruises healing, the boy seemed to be just barely managing. His teeth worried his lower lip and his gaze jumped about. But seeing Daniel steadied him. His tense brown face brightened. "It's okay? I can come with you?"

Daniel offered him a hand, and the kid danced from gunwale to gunwale like a leaf blown into our stern. Safely landed, he glanced back at Rivera for approval.

She pumped a fist, encouraging the other Macys to do likewise. *"Vamos al estadio!"* She held Jandi's gaze as the taxi veered away.

Daniel offered the boy a corner of the canopy. *"Bienvenido a bordo, chico. Vas a ayudar a mi hoy?"*

"Sí!" The boy moved to help, shy but certain. I admired his poise.

Rousseau climbed down the ladder to hurry the loading and convene a last-minute planning session in *Zephyr's* stern. We would convoy, all craft staying as close as safety would allow, but the route was still under debate.

Tito advised open water. "Sure, more wind, but it's with us, and a lot less chance of a wave smacking you into a building."

Will agreed. "The others did fine going right up the river."

Jake kept shaking his head. "Weather's worse now. We're safer with some wind shelter. Less worry of being blown out to sea."

"And buildings offer something to swim to if anyone gets swamped," Maxine added, "or cover if attacked."

First Avenue won in the end, at least until it dead-ended in the Bay of South Bronx.

Tom Doyle avoided the conference until he'd come up with a way to save at least some degree of face. After a bout of grumbling and stalking about, letting the wind whip his long coat flaps aside to expose his double shoulder holsters, he motored over to *Zephyr.* "Here's the deal. I got a few olders who aren't up to a hand-to-hand, so if you'll find room for them, me and my patrol crews will ride security as far up as 96th. Then we'll head home to brave the Big One."

"That'll be good," Rousseau said mildly. "Thanks."

The others let him do the talking. As it turned out, nearly a third of Tall Tommy had no stomach for an ambush or for riding out the storm in their glass-sided East Chelsea den. Some had been helping with the raft-building. Others arrived in small craft as the convoy was lining up, and seating adjustments in the taxis had to be made.

"Y'know," I told Daniel as we watched boats and rafts jockeying for position, "there are good reasons ships put out to sea when a hurricane's due. But a canal boat like Melville . . . best in calm water, right?"

"Wait till you see how she handles in the open." Daniel had a genius for looking smug without making you feel stupid. "She's had a few . . . modifications."

I tilted my head up at him. "Anything in your life that hasn't?"

"Like you said: criticize and improve."

"So, open water's where we're heading?"

He nodded at Jandi, who'd settled himself by the tiller. "Got our good-byes to make. We'll catch up afterward."

I hated abandoning our home, our Unca Joe, without ceremony. That great hulk of old brick and glass and stone had kept us safe through crises and bad weather. We should've thrown it a party. Instead, Rousseau closed and locked the empty den and climbed down to his ride like we planned to return. The tide would turn soon. The sail-rigged rafts would struggle for headway, even with the wind in their favor. We had to be going.

Maxine stayed on *Zephyr* to lead the convoy, agreeing so long as Jake came with her. She seemed to be getting attached. Empire Will took up a middle slot. Rousseau moved into rear guard in one of the Empire taxis. We'd follow till First, then head for the river.

As I heard *Zephyr* get the go-ahead and rev her engine, Breakers reappeared topside with a steaming bowl and a sly look.

"Guess you're riding with us . . ." Daniel grinned.

"Don't see why not. Someone's got to keep an eye on you two."

"Know how to swim?"

"As if." She settled in the lee of the cabin to slurp her noodles. "Instant ramen, by god! Ain't had that in a while! You got some fine provisions in your hold, book man."

I saw Jandi list toward her like he hoped she might share.

"Restocking won't be so easy next time, with the Souk up in smoke." Daniel rummaged in one of the lockers and plopped a life jacket at Breakers' feet, then hauled out two more.

I buckled mine right on. Force of old habit. It was too big and stank of mildew, but I was glad for it. Not a lot of them around, and we were heading into rough waters.

Jandi held his up with two fingers. "I swim good!"

"Put it on. Both of you. Captain's orders."

"Yessir." Breakers corralled the jacket with a foot and waved her spoon. "The Souk'll rebuild, doncha think?"

"Doubt it." Daniel squinted into the distance, like he could see the future from the Book Boat. "If it does, it'll be a whole different thing. The dens won't be shopping there."

"In that case, *carpe diem!*" Breakers set her spoon aside and raised the bowl to her lips.

"And we're off." I looked to Daniel. "Still no regrets?"

"Not so far."

Breakers sighed. "He could've said how he'd miss you more than he'll miss ramen."

He laughed. "Behind that rifle sight lurks the soul of a romantic."

"Found me out."

The cargo rafts untied and raised canvas, one after another like a flock taking wing. Sailing a raft is tricky even for a tight helmsman, and these weren't even square-rigged. A mast and a boom for a standard triangular sail was all there'd been materials for, plus the crudely pointed prow added to each raft to help cut through the waves. The rudder-and-tiller assemblies were so makeshift, I was ready to take bets on how many would survive the trip. Good thing the rafts were crew-only now. They'd need some serious sailing.

As the ersatz fleet lumbered around the corner onto 8th Street, Rousseau's taxi dropped alongside *Melville* with the two funeral rafts in tow. Jandi scurried to help Daniel retie them to our stern.

"Your job to wrangle them," Daniel told him. "Till it's time."

I didn't know whether to stare or look away. That long, shrouded form, once my living friend and protector, now stretched out on a ragged pile of scrap wood and stinking of flammables. The closest I'd been to him since he died. The fabric was well-soaked, to make sure it would burn in the rain. It pressed against the outline of his face, his elbows, his knees. If I hauled on the tow rope, I could give him a goodbye hug. But we'd never been huggers.

He was . . . so still. Like the two much smaller mummy-wraps on the raft next door.

And so silent. Which in life, he never was.

The wind dropped suddenly, as if waiting. Rousseau handed over two swathed torches, like we used for signal flares. Never one to miss an opportunity, he cleared his throat.

"My greatest regret, among many, is that I will never be able to thank him for . . ."

All stiff and formal. I shifted my non-gaze. Begging my patience, Rousseau offered a look as sympathetic and remorseful as any we'd ever shared.

". . . for all he was and did for us." Then he just had to add, "Despite our differences."

I looked away, like I'd got rain in my eyes.

"Come see me when we're settled upriver. I hear you're remembering now. I hope you'll share what you've learned."

His earnest interest caught me off guard. I nearly teared up. "Soon as you have time."

"One thing more . . ." He slid two fingers into the pocket of his vest and drew out the flattened cylinder of a plastic lighter, the sort where you could dial up the flame. A rare item, always high on the picker list, though the ones you found were usually empty. You'd think with the gazillions made, there'd be more of them about. "Might come in handy."

I gave him a nod of thanks. Sometimes the smallest gestures mean the most.

"See you uptown." As the wind picked up again, Rousseau stepped back from the gunwale, gesturing the taxi driver onward. Behind me, Jandi was naming his dead denmates for Breakers, saying what had been special about each. She bent close, listening. She understood about loss.

Daniel coiled an arm around my shoulders. "Let's get her started."

I turned toward the stern. But the tall tiller had been lifted from its housing and locked into a pair of storage cleats on the transom. Freed up, the rudder wobbled loosely. "Huh?"

"This way." That smug little smile again. He waved to Breakers as he led me into the cabin. "Cast us off when you hear the engine rev."

"Aye, aye, sir!" She parodied a salute.

So, *Melville* still had secrets to reveal. In the forward cabin, we found Jenn awake and struggling to decode the workings of the ship-to-shore.

"Won't get much response in this neighborhood," Daniel explained. "All the on-shore stations are down. Maybe when we're farther north, close to the Mainland."

Jenn's clever hands see-sawed in mid-air. No screen, no keypad. Just a bank of toggles and dials. But for all her gestures of confusion, she was clearly in control of herself again. "This is, like, the dark ages!"

Daniel laughed. "All the more reliable for its simplicity. But you need a living presence at both ends and line-of-sight transmission. Marine band. Heard of it? It's like CB, only VHF." He showed her how to send. "It'd be good to set up our own station at the Stadium, to keep track of our boats out on the water."

Jenn wagged her head, like he was talking about unicorns. "What's the range?"

"About five nautical miles. With the internet collapsing and the satellites crapping out, it'll be our best bet for near-distance com."

"Collapsing? Not everywhere . . ."

Daniel's brow creased. "Pretty much. As a global system. According to my intel."

Her eyes went startle-round. "But how can that be?"

"Well, maybe not across Europe yet."

She stared at him a moment, then swiveled back to the com as if seeing it in a new light. "You have the equipment for a station?"

"Not on me. But I'll find it somewhere. When I do, you'll be in charge of it."

He drew me to the far side of the cabin and unlatched a door. What I'd taken for a floor-to-ceiling storage closet revealed a narrow set of steps leading to a tiny cockpit hiding under the forward section of roof. You'd never have thought to look for it. A smoked-glass window, shaped to fit the starboard half of the roof, looked over the bow. There was a single pilot's swivel chair, a full control panel, and just enough room for me to tuck in beside him, life jacket and all. Cramped, stuffy, but dry and out of the ripping wind.

He reached past me to flick a toggle, then draw a slider from zero to six.

Click. Whirr. Clunk. The hull shuddered faintly.

"Centerboard. Of sorts," Daniel explained.

Sure enough. The *Melville* suddenly felt more stable. Then a turn of the key, a rev in neutral while Breakers cast off, a twist of the wheel, a light push on the control lever, and we were on our way to our new home.

The convoy gathered momentum as we tacked east on 8th Street, following Rousseau's taxi as she chugged ahead. The other taxis had placed themselves between the rafts, close enough to haul people up out of the water if needed but keeping a safe distance. The going was slow and rough while we ran parallel to the swell. Daniel kept our nose into the roll by tacking as much as he could as the wind fought to slam us into the buildings. A few times, we had to hold position while one of the rafts got itself unhooked from a window ledge or rusting fire escape. We hauled our little tows in tight to keep them from tangling.

At First Avenue, the convoy turned north, picking up speed as they ran with both wind and tide. *Melville* continued east on 8th, across the Tompkins Square Lake, braided with whitecaps. The buildings were shorter this far east, just the top stories showing above water, in some places nothing at all. With our wind cover shrinking, Daniel worked hard to keep us from drifting sideways. At Avenue D, the grid opened out into the stretch of water broken by the many x-shaped stubs of the Riis development. Flooded and abandoned for years, crumbling long before Abel. Now I recalled sailing *Haiku* among them during a rare outing with my father when he snatched a morsel of time off from work. Rubio had declared Riis an example of what urban revamp should never be: block after block of cookie-cutter designs built on the cheap. But for now, they would do him a final service.

Daniel pulled into the lee of a more or less intact structure, three levels of blown-out windows and weathered brick looming above us, and slid out of the chair. "Hold her steady while I tie up."

I nodded, reaching for a feel of the controls. So glad he trusted me to handle his boat. When I felt her tug steadily at her mooring, I cut the engine and went up. I passed Jenn at the com desk, still jousting with the ship-to-shore.

"You coming? It's Rube's send-off."

She shook her head without raising it. "Funerals aren't my thing. He'd understand."

"Yeah. He would." He'd probably hate that we were doing anything at all.

Topside, the wind nearly knocked me flat. Jandi was tucked into a corner like he'd been told to go there and stay put till told otherwise. Daniel and Breakers were playing out lengths of the oldest rope in the lockers, lengthening the tow of the funeral rafts, then tying the free end to whatever they could find on the building wall. I sussed it out pretty quick: with the tide heading in, the rafts bobbed against the brick. When it turned, they'd be drawn downstream into the open water between the buildings. The rope would burn with the raft, releasing the debris into the current, hopefully to carry it out to sea. At least, that was the idea.

Easy to say, not so easy to do in rough weather.

With the tow lines finally secured, we drew the rafts alongside. The rain alternately spat and pummeled. *Melville* rocked on the deepening swell.

"Got the torches?" Daniel was impatient to get on with this.

I signaled Jandi to the cabin door. Inside, we unwrapped the oiled paper protecting the torch heads, filling the cabin with the cool reek of paint thinner. I pulled Rousseau's parting gift from my gut wallet, weighing it in my palm. I meant to keep it as a gift, not a loan. Like, when would the river of cheap, mass-produced goods flow by us again? Ever?

In the drafty open doorway, the lighter failed to hold a flame. Fearful of setting the cabin and its precious plant cargo alight, I backed in a short step and got a tiny tongue of fire. It did the trick. The torch half-exploded.

"Hold it high!" I thrust it into Jandi's willing fist and sent him racing toward the stern, then followed with my own. Then we both stood staring down at the rafts, blazes in hand, unable to make the final gesture. Should we say a prayer? I never prayed. Nor had I understood how one as dark-minded as Rubio could find a reason to, but he claimed he did, now and then. Jandi's lips were moving, so maybe that's what he was doing. Or maybe just saying a last goodbye.

We were using up precious time. Breakers never showed much emotion, but Daniel was beginning to radiate urgency. He had a boat hook handy to guide the rafts away, once caught. Still, no one said, hurry up so we can cut and run.

Finally, I lowered my torch to the near corner of Rubio's raft. *Think of it this way, dear friend. I am finally lighting that candle for you.*

Even in the rain, the flame grabbed hold, racing along the raft's rough planking. Jandi let go a gasp and flung his torch at the center of his raft. It landed between the two small wrapped bodies.

Fire erupted. The guttural whoosh carried over the wind.

"Nice one!" Breakers crowed.

Daniel shoved both rafts away hard, tossed the boat hook to Breakers, and plunged into the cabin to get *Melville* moving again.

The rafts drifted off, hissing and crackling. The flames rushed up and around Rubio's body, a final purifying embrace. I approved of this ritual, both horrifying and beautiful, but begged the wind to keep the odor of my friend's burning flesh as its own grim secret.

Melville vibrated beneath us, and we veered away from the sheltering brick and headed uptown. Breakers leaned against the boat hook, like a gardener on her rake, musing over her handiwork. I drew Jandi into a sympathy hug as we watched the twin fires recede behind us, bright against the gray water, then fading, then lost in a mist of rain.

Suddenly Breakers jerked upright. "Hear that?"

"What?" All I heard was wind, rain, and engine.

She laid the boat hook down and snatched up her rifle. "Shots!"

"Where? C'mon. That's just the fires snapping."

"I know fuckin' gunshots when I hear 'em!" She brushed her loose hair back, winding it into a tight bun. "You just don't wanna hear 'em!"

She had that right.

Then Jandi caught it. He swiveled and pointed inland. "¡Sí! ¡Por ahí!"

Breakers punched my arm. "Go tell him! Now!"

Now even I could hear it: a pop-pop-pop, rolling across the water.

I darted forward to the little wheelhouse. "Shots heard on shore!"

Daniel swore and beat a fist softly on the console. He peered past the slow arc of a window wiper. "Can't see shit out there. Take the helm. Same course till I reconnoiter."

He was back in five, drenched to the skin. He had Jandi with him. "Stay below, chico, no matter what, less I say different. This is Jenn. She'll help you find something to eat while there's a chance." He nosed in beside me. "We have to go see what's up."

"Of course."

We steered toward the gunfire, somewhere above 14th. As we neared, a line of water taxis streamed out of the cross-streets, pushing their motors as hard as they dared. Built for comfort, not speed.

"There's people up on the canopies!" I gasped. "Fighting!"

One boat trailed smoke, while a frantic trio in its stern scooped pails of water to douse the flames. Visibility was crap, but one of them looked like Gracie.

"Heads down!" Breaker's rifle cracked above us, once, twice, and a dark figure tumbled off the top of one of the taxis.

"Hope she's sure who she's shooting at," Daniel muttered.

He moved in closer till we could see faces. Grace's taxi ran past us, its fire under control. On the next boat's canopy, two Smith women grappled with a big guy in a robe, trying to wrestle a machete away from him. Bloody water drained over the roof edge.

Breakers' shout was as sharp as her rifle. "Nina! Rox! Down!"

They heard, ducked. Another shot. The robe jerked and fell back into the water, struggled a moment, then sank.

"That one's clean." Daniel pulled alongside the taxi and slid open a side window to yell across at the driver. "What's happened?"

"Friggin' ambush!" An older man from Empire, cheeks flushed with outrage.

"Who?"

"Everyone who isn't us! Will said get to open water!"

"He's right! Keep going!"

The man glanced inland. "The rafts are taking it bad!"

"We'll do what we can! Go!"

The driver nodded and swerved off. As they passed, I saw Rivera in the passenger seats, white-faced and clutching her flock of Macys.

Daniel shut the window. For a moment, he let us drift, staring into the rain-swept distance. "Okay, here's what we'll do." But he left it at that, shoved the stick forward, and headed inland.

At 16th and Avenue A, two more water taxis fled past us, the first charred but no longer burning, the second with Will Dubowski at the helm and a pair of Tommys tossing bodies off the roof. He flung us a tight-jawed look as he sped by.

"That's all of them, free and clear." Daniel had been counting taxis.

So had I. "But for one."

"But that'll be Rousseau's, in there mopping up."

"Only if it's over . . ."

But it wasn't. We could see through to the intersection of First and 16th: a collision of boats and rafts and bodies moving through wind-whipped smoke and rain.

"That's how it went." Daniel pointed. "Bastards strung rope bridges over the streets, window to window. Just dropped down on any boat passing under."

It would have been a total surprise. You're sailing up First, clear water ahead, and suddenly the air is full of fire-wielding Revs and Stormies.

"No point just barreling in there. We'll go round the back. Go put out the bumpers."

He meant to land us. The idea terrified me, but I did what he said. We slipped west on 15th, just shy of First, and tied up in a sheltered alley, under an ancient fire escape. Back in the cabin, Daniel got brusque and edgy. He pressed his thumb to a sensor on a bottom drawer. It slid open silently.

"Ever fired a gun?"

I put up both palms. "You know I haven't!"

"Take this, then." He dug in the drawer, then handed over a sheathed knife, like the one Spunk carried, that I'd coveted for slinking around the streets at night. Now the chill weight of it in my hands was less than welcome.

"What'll I do with it?"

"Use it," he growled. "If you have to. Where's my fucking sister when I need her!"

"Daniel, I can't . . ."

"You might have to." He loomed over me. "I'm not leaving you here unarmed!"

"Leaving me?"

"I can fire a gun," said Jenn from the com station.

We both turned in to her steady stare.

"Carried one in my purse. City life, y'know?"

"Good." Daniel chose quickly from his secret arsenal, passing Jenn a small pistol and extra magazine. "You and Jandi are on boat guard. Check the load."

She didn't need to ask how. "Ready to go."

As usual, everyone around me was moving faster than I was. I buckled on the knife. It lay flat along one hip. "I'm coming with you."

"Really?" Daniel turned back to his drawer. I waited for some exotic mystery of a weapon, like Hannah's crossbow. Instead, he found the match to Jenn's pistol, shoved it casually in his waistband, then bent again for a pair of bolt cutters and kneed the drawer shut. He hooked the cutters over one shoulder. "Then come on, if you're coming. Got no time to argue."

Daniel at his coldest. Good thing I'd seen it before, so I could roll with it.

Breakers was already on the fire escape, a coil of rope in one hand, rifle slung across her back. We clambered up beside her, Daniel signaling her toward the roof, three stories above. She climbed, agile as a monkey, until just hidden by the parapet. Even before we got to the top, she'd nosed over the edge and started firing. Now we were the surprise ambush.

Three shots. I guessed three new bodies.

She waved an all-clear and hunkered down, then turned to mouth at us. "Adders."

"Ah, shit. Guess there's no way I could've got them all." Daniel kicked out the remaining panes in the fire-escape access window and dropped inside.

Stomach clenched like a fist, I followed him into a maze of gaping doorways and dark, ruined rooms. "Where did Adders come from?"

"Does it matter?" He paused, orienting himself. Then he nodded, eased the pistol from his waistband, and moved ahead, out a central door, down a hall, toward the source of light and noise. The first room we passed was empty, the plaster shredded from the studs and strewn across the floor, puffed up from rain blown in the open window. The second was also empty, but Daniel breathed a quiet cheer and slipped in. Here, a divider between a pair of wrecked windows supported one end of a rope bridge. Cable, actually, when I looked closer, and vibrating. Someone out there on it. Daniel waved me to cover along one wall, stowed his pistol, and flexed the bolt cutters. Snap, snap, and it was done. The cut ends snaked to either side of the divider and the bridge collapsed. Daniel peered around the window frame, then held up two fingers, then three, then four.

"Next . . . ?" he mouthed, grimly alight.

What do guys find to love in all this? Then I thought: no, Hannah would be loving it, too.

Two rooms closer to the Avenue, a monk-robed figure balanced in a window opening, bellowing what might have been a prayer into the street. A second bridge, rope this time, stretched away from the sill.

Daniel pointed to my knife, adding a sawing motion. Then he plunged through the doorway and shoved the teetering Rev off the ledge. The ropes went taut as the monk fell against the bridge, then slacked again as his hold failed and he toppled free.

My big knife sliced through the first two ropes with only moderate effort. By then, Daniel had the bolt cutters on the other two. When the bridge dropped into the water, a few glad cheers echoed along the buildings. Daniel stood back, grinning and dusting his palms. Someone down there— maybe Tom Doyle?—was barking battle instructions, broken by an occasional war yell. The voice kept shifting position, like from boat to raft to window ledge to boat again, a moving target. Doyle in his element, if it was him. I listened for Rousseau's deeper bass but didn't hear it. I drifted toward the opening for a peek.

Shots sang through the window and ploughed into the opposite wall.

"Stay the fuck DOWN!" Daniel hissed.

We ducked out into the hall, searching for bridge number three. Only a matter of time before the Revs and Stormies figured us out. One bridge failure could be an accident, but two? Definite sabotage. Daniel signaled me to hurry.

The third bridge was at the front of the building, spanning the Avenue. Cable again, for the wider reach. Another empty room. Part of the street wall had collapsed, exposing the empty bridge and giving a sidelong view of the intersection. The boats and most of the rafts were lined up along the window ledges where their occupants had taken shelter or were battling hand to hand inside.

Gunfire was sporadic now, and more than one sniper hung limp from an upper windowsill. Breakers claiming her toll from the roof.

A roar from behind, and a top-knotted Adder loomed in the doorway, huge and furious. He held a length of wood poised as a club. He was dripping wet from his loincloth to the ammo belt strung across his bare chest. I guessed he'd been on one of the first two bridges and lost his weapon in the drink.

Daniel flung the bolt cutters at him, shoved me in one direction, and dove in the other. The Adder rushed him, swinging hard. Daniel ducked, backing away, grabbing for his pistol just as the end of the timber caught his shoulder. The gun went flying, tumbling across the warped floorboards. The Adder didn't seem to notice. Scrabbling on my knees along one wall, freaked and terrified, I fixed on the loose gun like a lifeline. It dampened the shrieks and wing-flaps in my head that were blocking all thought. It was an opening. A solution.

The Adder put his back to me to go in for another swing at Daniel. Just a girl. I didn't worry him much. Daniel launched himself straight at him to avoid another wallop from the timber. I skittered in behind and snatched up the gun. But now what? The two of them were grappling madly, swinging this way and that, and what did I know about guns? If I fired from there, I might hit Daniel. To be sure of my target, I'd have to get in too close, and then the Adder might . . . flashback panic toppled me like a wave. I crabbed backward on my butt till I was scrunched in a corner, trying for invisible.

The Adder shook Daniel off, sent him careening against the wall. He'd lost his club in the grapple, so he put his fists to work. Daniel was no match for a berserker giant. He took a pair of deep gut punches and slumped, heaving for breath. Then the Adder backhanded him across the face. His head slammed against the wall. He dropped like a stone. A few unnecessary body kicks, and the Adder turned toward me.

"Now for the fun part," he said.

I'd seen Adders only when they were drunk and stupid. This guy was sober, with a smart, mean gaze, and he was pumped on fight adrenaline. He'd left Daniel behind so casually, I was sure he'd killed him. The gun was buried in my fists, cupped against my belly, barrel out. The room was dim. Either he didn't see it, or he figured I was too freaked to fire.

He took a long step forward. "Just what I need."

No. Not again. No way was I letting this happen a second time.

A yell rang out from the hallway. "Pike? You there? Need you down here, man! Two loads of Tommys just pulled up!"

"Give me five." The one called Pike untied his loincloth and let it drop, brandishing his erection. "Or c'mon in. You can have her after."

Should or shouldn't never crossed my mind.

The rush of water, gale winds roaring. Lizzy screaming.

No . . . fucking . . . way!

I shot him in the chest. The little gun bucked against my belly. He stumbled, and I shot him again, lower down. He collapsed, howling, then lay still.

"Pike?"

A second Adder appeared in the doorway. This time, it was Rubio's voice I heard: *In for a penny, in for a pound.* An antique saying he loved—like, when you're already over the cliff, why worry about falling?

I shot the second one and watched the shock bloom on his face along with the hole in his throat. He stepped through the door, then toppled next to his pal.

I waited.

With every nerve and muscle in my body, I waited for the whole friggin' army of arsonist, decapitating, child-murdering, rapist sons of bitches to burst right in, so I could shoot every last fucking one of them.

But it was still in the room after that. The Adders ceased gasping and gurgling. I heard nothing but my own tight breathing. As my blind fury ebbed, I slid toward the comfort of shutdown. Hunched in my corner, cradling the cooling little death-dealer, unable to move for what felt like forever. Be so easy just to go off again. From horror to denial to . . . simply forgetting. To sweet oblivion, my dear old friend. As I curled up to welcome it, the gun butt poked me hard in the belly.

And then . . . thought is astonishing, how it light-speeds into your head. Nothing there one moment, then suddenly . . . a thing my shrink hinted I'd figure out when I was ready. About the lie I'd been living. Memory loss wasn't something that had happened *to* me. I'd let it happen. I'd *chosen* it. Because it was easier.

All that heroic Wave survivor stuff? Total bullshit. Truth is, when Rousseau found me, I'd already given up and gone down for the last time. My survival had been pure chance, nothing more.

Was I back there again, ready to let go and drown?

Had Rousseau, Spunk, Jake, even Jenn, and especially Rubio taught me nothing?

Was victimhood more precious than knowing if Daniel was living or dead?

Noise from outside penetrated my fog, a rush of whooping and cheering. I'd clamped my eyes shut, avoiding the grim evidence of what anyone can and will do if hard enough pressed. I made myself look, scanning the dim room for the two lumpish, half-naked bodies sprawled in the gleam of their own blood, and against the wall, the darker form of Daniel, face down. Was he even breathing?

His faint groan got me moving, on my feet, then on my knees beside him. Every place I touched was sticky with blood. I struggled to turn him over, as if he weighed a ton. *Dead* weight, I feared, until he groaned again, louder. Once I got him on his back, he coughed and gasped, sucking in air like it was life itself. I pressed his shoulders down, urging him to lie still, but he shoved my hands away and fought to prop himself up on one elbow.

"What . . . ?"

I sat back on my heels, watching him get his senses back, then take in the half-lit, rain-drenched room, the scattered Adder dead.

"Who . . . when did I do . . . ?"

I shook my head and set the pistol down in front of him.

"You? Really?" The realization seemed to stun him more than the Adder's blows. "Are you okay?"

Wasn't ready to answer that question. Or say anything at all, not yet.

"Are you?" He peered at me like he wasn't quite sure who I was. I wasn't either.

I rose and went to the window. Something—other than me—was . . . different.

"Lizzy!" He was hoarse as an old man. I heard the scrape of the pistol as he dragged it to him, then his struggle to get up, wheezing in pain. "Away from the window!"

I waved him quiet so he could hear the cheering.

"What?" He made it to his feet, balancing against the wall. "Is it over?"

I ignored him. I needed to stand full in the opening to be sure. And . . . yes. Now my voice could work again, because it had to. I drew to one side, only to calm him. "It's over, pretty much. But . . ."

"But what?"

"The wind's changed."

"So?" Hand over hand, he edged along the wall, ready to be stern with me about taking cover. When the light touched his face, I couldn't help but wince. One eye swollen, jaw raw and bruised, blood staining the front of his shirt. He'd taken a bad beating. He squinted around the edge, saw Revs and Stormies swimming, climbing for their lives, and Tom Doyle directing the mop-up from the remaining rope bridge as it rocked madly in the wind.

The wind.

He watched me inhale it, nostrils flared like an animal, drinking it in, then turned his own face to it. "Oh."

Coming from the northeast now. "When have you felt air that cold?"

"Not for years," Daniel breathed. "It's just like you said."

I nodded.

I saw it in my mind's eye, like the old satellite weather videos. The counterclockwise swirl of two mammoth storms hurtling toward each other, Leon from the south, the unnamed newcomer rolling in from farther east, out to sea, in the first steps of a vicious tandem dance that would bring them to an apocalyptic merger.

Category 6.

reakers came looking, found us wet and windblown at the open window
frame. "Aces with the bridges, book guy! But stay back, will ya? Still some
live ones out there!"

"I know." Daniel was hovering. Had the storm image become visible,
swirling in my eyes? No, my hands were shaking, my whole body, a deep,
internal shudder that went on and on, like a volcano building pressure. He
seemed to know the last thing he should do was lay a hand on me, even in
comfort.

"Well, don't listen to me." Oblivious, Breakers roamed the room, nudging bodies with a toe. "Adders! Coming out of the woodwork! You got a
few, I see."

"Not me," said Daniel.

"Not . . . ?" Breakers scanned the dim corners for other possible shooters,
then squinted at me. "Really? Atta girl!" She scrounged a bullet out of the
first Adder's cartridge belt, sniffed it, tossed it down. "Too wet. Thought
you'd done 'em in already."

"Only the party animals. These must be the elite troops."

"I'll say. Wait till you see the weapons I got off them."

"Bright," I muttered. My brain seemed to be working again. Almost.

"Probably." Daniel slid a hand under my elbow, tentative, like I might
recoil and run. "Breakers, need you to go tell the others, if they haven't
noticed already: wind's changed direction. There's . . . something like a
nor'easter coming, and we're heading into it."

"Instead of Leon?" She was disappointed.

Daniel looked to me.

"In addition to." I was as hoarse as he was.

"Oh." Breakers slowed her wanderings. She'd finally caught on to the
tension in the room. "Okay, that's not good. I'll let them know." She stepped
away, then back. "But you'll come along quick now, right? Let me clean up
that face of yours some."

"We will."

I turned to follow, but Daniel held me back. "Hold a moment."

I didn't resist. I was thinking about weather.

When Breakers had gone down the hall, he said, "I just need to know if you're okay. We've some hard sailing ahead. You've got to hold it together till we're somewhere safe."

"I'm fine."

He looked unconvinced.

Okay, sort of a lie. I was hardly in full control. In between conjured images of Category 6, I kept flashing back to the big Adder's hungry gaze dropping on me like a net, to the gun's hot recoil, but all with an odd sort of disconnect, like only my quaking body was reacting to what I'd done. I'd killed a man. Two men. Bad. But it really had been them or me. I wasn't letting terror win out again and drag me back into the void I'd been working so hard to climb out of. A beacon to lead me forward.

I eased out of his grip. "I'm okay."

"You sure?"

"I'm sure." Needing to sail for my life should provide a potent distraction.

Daniel prodded me back to *Melville*, loading both of us for the climb down with Breakers' collection of state-of-the-art sniper's rifles, stacked at the top of the fire escape. Seeing Jenn and Jandi emerge scared and hopeful from the cabin shored up my resolve: we had to get everyone through this in one piece.

"Is it over?" Jenn called.

"Pretty near." A definite lie this time.

We didn't mention the weather, which seemed to be taking a breather— the rain slackened and the wind gusted restlessly, like gathering itself up for the next onslaught.

As Breakers got out the first-aid kit to patch up Daniel, I handed Jenn my high-tech armload. "Can you find a safe place for these below?"

She looked them over. "Wow."

Jandi saw me glance sidelong at the billowing sky and followed my gaze with a worried frown. His threadbare tank top was stuck to his ribs like a second skin, and his skinny arms were puckered with goose bumps, even with the temp not much below 80 yet. As Daniel motored us around the block to rejoin the convoy, I dug one of my smallest tees out of my backpack and made the boy put it on under his life jacket, then found one for myself.

Couldn't recall the last time I'd actually felt cold.

The intersection was trashed. Raft debris and loose cargo washed up along the building walls and caught in the trailing ends of the rope bridges. We heard sporadic fighting inside the buildings and on the rooftops, but the gunfire had stopped. As we cleared the corner, two howling Smith women overwhelmed a wounded Rev and shoved him from a third-story window. The swell slammed him against the bricks until he sank.

The raft crews had suffered the worst. They were being taken in tow by the late-show Tommy patrols who were dragging our floating wounded into their boats. I counted at least a dozen casualties being lashed to the biggest raft. No guilt about leaving Adders or Revs to drift out with the tide, but we'd bring our own dead home for the pyres.

"Where's *Zephyr*?" I asked Daniel.

"Don't see her. They were right up front, so with luck, they scrammed uptown when the shooting started."

Maxine wouldn't want that, I was sure, but hopefully Jake had over-ruled her.

At least Rousseau and Doyle were both upright, but deep into a shouting match in the stern of a rocking water taxi. Daniel pulled up to idle nearby.

"They caught us here, they could catch us again, anywhere along the way!" Rousseau argued, his voice and shoulders tight. The ambush had dealt him a heavy blow.

"Were you dreaming we'd get through this unscathed?" Doyle was as bloodied as any Adder, all waving arms and battle-hyped grimaces. "No way! But we got those fuckers on the run now! Got the advantage! Taking the avenue'll let us pick off the rest as we go. If there are any. Make life easier down the line."

"In open water, we've only weather to battle, with two hours yet of favorable tide."

"Less," the taxi's grizzled skipper muttered.

I waited for Daniel to put in a word, bring up the wind change, but he kept *Melville* steady in the rolling water, just listening in.

"Tom, I can't put my people through that again! Too many dead and I . . ."

"It's not about you!" Doyle roared. "I lost men, too, and that shouldn't be wasted! If you're so on about working together, you got to do more than talk about it! You got to listen to other ideas, maybe go with them. You're not always gonna be right!"

"I . . ." Rousseau stopped, glanced around. Looking for Jake or Spunk? Without their routine loyal support, he seemed less certain. Vulnerable. I saw he'd taken in Doyle's accusation and was grappling with it. Like, sharing leadership meant . . . actual sharing.

"Not sure he deserves all that," Daniel said to me. "Not like Tommy's so democratic . . ."

"Rousseau identifies with all of us," I said. "He sees himself as our voice."

But Doyle saw an opening. "Lose a lot more out there in the friggin' storm than to a few Adders and Revs camped along the way!"

"My guess is, they blew their wad here," said the skipper, though no one had asked him.

One of Rousseau's lads stepped into the taxi to mutter the names of two more dead Joes, and one who wasn't going to make it.

Rousseau said, "I need to go to him."

He turned away, following the messenger out of the taxi.

"Nice way to lose an argument," noted Daniel. "Walk away with the moral high ground."

Doyle fumed in frustration as his win went unacknowledged. In the end, he bartered with his boats. The Tommy reinforcements would walk back to their den, leaving their powered craft to take on the raft crews and tow the laden rafts uptown. But only if they took the avenue.

So for the next hour, the convoy battled erratic winds and intermittent drenchings to slog up First Avenue, with *Melville* back in the rear. While Daniel piloted from his forward wheelhouse, I harnessed up in the stern, ready with the boat hook to clear the rudder or shove us off buildings when we got washed too close. I was glad of the foul weather gear he'd hauled out of yet another well-stocked storage locker. Jenn and Jandi stayed below, with the boy running occasional messages to and from the wheelhouse. In the cabin lee, Breakers watched for snipers, sending me the occasional are-we-there-yet glance. The front of the convoy was too far ahead to see if we'd caught up with *Zephyr*, leaving me to worry about Maxine and Jake.

The wind was in convulsions, like practicing changing its mind. The sea swell built steadily. I started counting blocks, so I had some idea of our progress, so much slower than we'd hoped for. Somewhere in the 90s, a roll of thunder echoed along the buildings, a bass vibration almost felt more than heard. *Melville* thrummed in sympathy.

Though the implications were dire, I found the dropping temperature refreshing. The thunder spoke of the collision of cool and warm and was soon joined by lightning that whitened the grim slices of watery horizon visible down the side streets. Like Tom Doyle and Empire Will, a meeting of opposites would never create calm weather.

When waves started breaking over our bow, I thought again of the old book, of its long-ago adventurer, writing with enviable calm of his first storm at sea. Either he was as nerveless as Breakers, too pride-bound to show his fear, or he took it as a matter of course that a sail might be lost in a gale, or a mast shattered. If danger or chaos was expected, wouldn't be such a big deal when it happened. It'd be . . . how life went. Didn't I already see things that way? Maybe not as much as I thought.

The river was visible several blocks ahead in the 100s when a burst of sound blared over the wind noise, like a boat horn. Sniper fire sprayed from above. The first shots near-missed Tom Doyle, in the open passenger seat of his personal speedster. His driver took quick evasive action, all but spilling Doyle before he hunkered down, gazing upward in astonishment as bands of attackers erupted from the window openings along both sides of the street, throwing themselves onto any boats close to the walls, swinging on ropes to drop down on those farther out in the water.

"Stormies!" Breakers yelled, swinging her rifle to aim.

The Stormies were naked and poorly armed, but there seemed to be hundreds of them and they were . . . stoked. Howling, leaping, lashing out with whatever tool, plank, or rod they had as a weapon. Behind the first wave, a second filled the windows and roof lines to rain down a barrage of bricks and sharp bits of old metal and wood, a deluge of lethal junk barely aimed but thick and steady. It kept people ducking and covering instead of firing or beating off the invaders. Denfolk tumbled into the water as the Stormies shoved right and left, vaulting from boat to boat until ganging up in the stern of any power boat towing a raft. And over it all, the horn continued to blare, like a call to battle.

Melville was back far enough to be out of range of both jumpers and junk. Daniel reversed and rushed out of the cabin. "They're after the supplies!"

Breakers growled in frustration, unable to fire into the tight pack of bodies without risk of hitting one of ours.

"Get the sniper!" I'd spotted him, a surviving Adder, still dropping random fire on the convoy from a rooftop.

Breakers drove his top-knotted head below the parapet and kept it there.

But I'd also seen something else. "Look up there!"

Across the street from the sniper's roof, a lone figure stood out in the open, wind whipping the trailing sleeves and full skirt of her dazzlingly white robe. She held up a long golden horn, like an angel's trumpet, the source of the blaring alarm.

"Like something out of an old painting!" I exclaimed.

"That's gotta be her!" Breakers whirled on this new target.

"No!" ordered Daniel, pushing the rifle down and aside.

"What? Why?"

"Listen!"

Ahead of us, from his boat mid-convoy, Rousseau was ducking falling debris and shouting, "Go! Go! Let them have it! They're hungry! Let them have it!"

Packs of Stormies had two small rafts cut loose and rolling in the swell. Others leaped into the water to swim the rafts away to be pillaged. But new boats had joined the fray, muscling in from the side streets, their crews sweeping attackers off the decks of the Tommy power boats and the larger rafts, urging the cleared boats upriver, away from the rain of junk and bodies.

I recognized the hard-faced woman at the lead boat's helm. "The Empire patrols! They found us!"

Seconds later, a matching boat pulled even with her on the far side of the convoy, and I caught the bright yellow of Will Dubowski's slicker. In tandem, and another pair behind, they worked along the length of the convoy, evicting yowling Stormies and hauling wounded or spilled Joes, Smiths, and Tommys on board. But they honored Rousseau's directive and didn't chase after the two small rafts. The angel on the roof blew her horn, and the junk rain stopped. The Stormies converged on their plunder, a tangle of naked bodies tearing at the ropes and protective covering.

"Whatever's on those rafts," Daniel remarked. "I hope it's edible."

"So much for God's Island," I said.

"Oh, they'll regroup. But by then, we'll be ready for them. And maybe they'll remember that we gave them a bit of a break." He glanced up at the white-robed priestess as we drifted by underneath. "But ain't she something?"

The four Empire boats powered past us, turned around, and started back up along the convoy in a last sweep of survivors. Will sent us a quick thumbs up as he glided by.

"Have you seen *Zephyr*?" I yelled across to him.

He glanced back with a nod and gestured upriver. I waved my relief and thanks.

But when he drew level with Tom Doyle, several boats ahead of us, the two of them just stared at each other. Doyle's back was rigid, his face blank. Will kept pace for a moment, then shook his head and moved on.

Daniel laughed softly. "Be a while before Tom can admit to himself that Empire Will just saved his butt."

"And ours, most likely."

"Most likely." He headed for the cabin to get *Melville* going again.

By the high 120s, the tide was slowing, ready to turn, and there were wider stretches of water between buildings—empty blocks or old parking lots. Low-slung warehouses and derelict factories hid just beneath the surface, as treacherous as reefs to anyone straying from the deeper water of the avenue. The dropping temp had raised a dense fog that hugged the water. Visibility? Maybe twenty feet ahead. Down the side streets to our left, the higher, dry ground of West Harlem hovered like a thickening of the mist. More than one of us peered up those streets in exhaustion and envy. But no refuge for denfolk where people like Bright's bosses held sway. It was Yankee Stadium or bust.

Soon, the last buildings vanished below a huge, storm-tossed estuary. Between us and open water remained a wilderness of broken concrete piers and collapsed trusswork, looming out of the fog like a forest shredded by a cyclone, only the sturdiest trunks left sticking out of the water. A faint line of gray stood darker against the sky—the distant shore, the South Bronx.

Progress slowed again as the convoy worked through the obstacle course, fighting wind and wave to keep from being smashed against a piling. The tide had ceased its northward pull. Slack water. Daniel eased back the engine and came topside fastening his foul-weather gear to re-engage the hand tiller, so he could steer with a 360 view.

"Go on below," he told Breakers. "You've done your part."

She cradled her rifle and didn't complain.

He clicked into a safety harness, then rechecked mine. "Welcome to the Harlem River."

I stared at the charred and shattered block, the twisted steel. Out in the misted bay, if you squinted hard, you could see a single squared-off span of trusswork remaining upright. "What happened here?" It couldn't just be storm damage.

"This was a while ago." Daniel circled one arm. "Used to be a whole complex of bridges up here: the Willis Avenue over the Harlem River, the Triborough over to Queens and Long Island, then all the upper Harlem ones . . ."

I recalled Rubio going on about the uptown bridges, heard their names in his voice, and got beat up again by crushing loss. Had to clear my throat to get a word out. "I remember now. Some idiots blew them up, Rube said. He loved bridges."

"Mmm. Well, bridges are cool. But in this case, a North Shore citizens' committee got worried about low-class Manhattan refugees overrunning their valuable real estate. Hired a couple of ex-Army Corps to do the deed just as a Cat 5 was on the way, I forget which one." He huffed out an ironic laugh. "So the bridges were destroyed, but within the next few days, most of their land was under water and their fancy homes washed out to sea." He zigged *Melville* around a jagged islet of concrete that had been invisible till the swell dropped around it. "This was the Willis."

I hadn't thought much about bridges when boats were a part of my daily life, except for making sure whatever I was sailing would fit under them.

The tide was fully turned by now, heading out, but the north-riding swell made for directional agitation. Threading *Melville's* forty-two feet through the bridge wreckage slowed us down. We were barely free of it when the wind stepped up its pace and the rain came on again full force, chill and biting. Waves splitting over our bow sent spray slashing into our faces. And the storm was only getting started.

"You going back up front?" I yelled over a sudden return crack of thunder.

Daniel shook his head. "See better from here."

But better was practically nothing. The rain and the spray were a thick curtain, and his battered eye made it worse. We lost sight of the end of the convoy every time we dropped into a trough. Worse, the light was fading. The trip was taking way too long.

"How much further?"

Daniel squinted toward the uplands off to port. If he saw anything identifiable, I congratulated him. "Twenty minutes, maybe."

Twenty minutes of bleary, salt-stung eyes and muscles cramping from holding on too hard. "Whoa! Look out ahead!"

A dark hulk crested over the top of the swell just ahead. It hung there, caught in a flash of lightning, then zoomed toward us.

"Loose raft!" Daniel slammed the tiller away, swinging our bow sharply to starboard. The engine whined as the screws were lifted out of the water. I careened against the gunwale, arms outstretched. *Melville* wallowed broadside for a beat, then Daniel pulled us straight again, nose into the wave, as the raft grazed alongside us with a rending squeal. Then it was past, trailing its broken tow rope and dropping into the trough behind.

"Nice sailing! Did you get a look?" I was shuddering again, this time from pure relief.

Daniel stared after it till it rose again on another swell. "Cargo raft. No one aboard."

At least, not by the time we met up with it. But one more batch of supplies less than we started with.

I was still getting my breath back when a strange clatter started up around us. Little white balls bouncing about everywhere, pinging on my head and shoulders. What was . . . oh. Hail. Took me a minute. Like, when had I ever seen hail? At first it was a novelty. I caught a few in my palm and popped them into my mouth, caught a few more, offered Daniel some. He couldn't suppress a grin, but soon the steady beating became annoying, and pretty quick, started to hurt. Daniel signaled me to shelter below.

"No way!"

He shrugged, raising the hood of his sou'wester. I did the same, and we hunkered down as best we could.

The pounding softened, but now the air was full of soft, wind-driven white stuff. Damn, it must be snowing! Was that even possible? Didn't seem cold enough, but what else could it be? Friggin' snow! Coating the tiller, the gunwales, the cabin roof, mixing with the melting hail to fill the stern pit with an inch of cold slime. We both struggled to keep our footing. My hands had gone stiff. Temp maybe 50 degrees and dropping? My body wasn't used to this. And up above, it had to be a whole lot colder.

"Gonna freeze before we get there!" I yelled.

But suddenly, there it was. *Melville* climbed the face of a foam-edged wave and the stadium ghosted into view through a veil of frozen rain: a broad, stubby oval standing amidst the waves of the Great Bronx Bay like a fortress set on a lonely rock. Our fortress.

Daniel and I exploded with whoops of joy, loud enough to bring Breakers to the cabin door, gripping both jambs to keep her balance.

"What?"

"We're there!"

By then, we were back in the trough, and Breakers saw nothing but a looming wall of water. She glanced around at the clingy white stuff, swore, and ducked back inside. The next broken swell lifted us in view of the cluster of boats backed up along the stadium's curving wall of tall arched windows. The arches in one section were wider and glassless, with the water high enough above sill level to provide a water entrance into a covered atrium. The openings would be easy in calm weather, but the skippers were taking their time squeezing through, to keep from being crushed against the arch supports.

Daniel pointed out one set of arches where a central divider had broken away at sill level, leaving a much wider opening. "We'll make for that one."

We were too far off to pick out faces, but several of the water taxis, lightweight and overloaded with rescues from the lost rafts, were riding dangerously low, probably shipping a ton of water. At least one raft still in tow was upside down, its cargo ruined or lost to the depths. The smaller boats, like the Tommy patrol boats, were being roughly tossed about. Every boat had bailers hard at work.

The waiting was worse than the travel. I wished the skippers would be braver about the entry and hurry the hell up. No real idea when the two storms would combine and reach their peak, but if the convoy wasn't inside the stadium soon, we'd have disaster on our hands. The snow had turned to wind-whipped pellets that bit our cheeks and coated every surface with a rime of ice. My muscles were screaming from the work of simply staying upright and being jerked to the full extent of my harness whenever a wave came at us from an unexpected angle, driving *Melville* sideways toward the southern shore until Daniel could force our head up again. If we rode broadside up a steep enough swell, we could capsize.

I'd been listening for a while without realizing it, picking up a slight change in the storm din rushing past my ears. A distant, high-pitched buzz, like cicadas used to make, coming at us from the northwest.

I nudged Daniel. "Hear that?"

He was fighting the tiller, playing *Melville*'s engine like a fine instrument. But he threw a glance around—like, had I heard shooters, though it made no sense, out here in the middle of the bay?

The buzz rose and fell with the swell. I pointed upriver. "Sounds like a boat. A fast one."

Which could be shooters. Daniel's eyes lidded in exhaustion. "Not more. Not now. We're so close!"

He raised our speed to avoid the tangle of boats slipping into the stadium two, three at a time, putting us between the convoy and the incoming.

The intruder was being pushed to the limit, like a mad animal screaming, fit to burn out its engines. And just the one. A suicide mission?

"What if it's a bomb? Should I get Breakers up here?"

"No." Daniel's head went up. "Wait. That sounds like . . . no. How could it . . . ?"

The incoming crested a wave, a splash of white and blue against the sullen water, then dropped from sight.

"Get the binocs! Hurry!"

I had to snap out of my harness and crawl hand over hand to reach the right storage locker. Balanced on spread legs like a circus act, I waited for the intruder to rise on the next swell. He was much closer this time.

"Oh, my god! Daniel, it's *Sea Sprite*!"

He nodded once. "Sounded like."

"They changed their minds!" So why didn't he look more relieved? He was getting his family back.

"Keep watching!"

On the next wave, *Sprite* was there, rolling within thirty yards of us. I had the binocs glued to my eyes. "She's all shot up! And . . . oh, no!"

Julian clung to the wheel, pale and bleeding. His engines sputtered as he throttled back. An oil slick spread wide where *Sprite*'s fuel tanks had been punctured. The passenger side was empty.

"Where's Hannah?" Daniel bellowed across the churning water. "Julie! Where . . . is . . . Hannah?"

Julian's eyes rolled back. He slumped over in his seat.

Daniel grabbed me by the scruff and shoved the tiller into my hands. "Bring her in!"

"Daniel! No!"

But he'd already shucked his harness and his foul-weather gear and bounded up on the gunwale. He caught his balance as *Melville* rolled, then dove into the water.

The next swell hid them both, boat and swimmer.

Time stops. No, slows, like it's making every second last to hold off disaster.

I take a step toward the gunwale. Julian might be dying, even dead. The tiller swings free and *Melville* veers broadside to the swell, heeling precipitously. Go after them and likely drown, or save the ship and crew—my ship now, and Breakers, Jenn, and Jandi—never mind the plant wealth on which the new den's survival surely depends? *Melville* carries our hope for the future.

It isn't a choice. I'd already made it when I told Daniel I wouldn't desert Unca Joe. Daniel chose in a nanosecond, not for me or the den but for family. He's on his own.

Is it grief or fury, this fever that boils up in me like magma? Or simply a sense of purpose?

I fall on the tiller to wrench *Melville* around, nose to the wave. It breaks over us, but the good craft plows through. I scan ahead for *Sea Sprite*, for a glimpse of Daniel in the water. Bobbing and rolling, I see Julian rouse himself enough to toss a lifeline. Another dip and rise, and there's Daniel grappling for *Sea Sprite*'s side rail as she slides past him down the face of the trough. Using the wave as a boost, he manages to fling himself onto her stern deck. He lies there, panting, gripping with every part of his body to stay on board.

Suddenly I see my father. That sun-struck vision, all I'd kept of him, faceless and godlike. How I felt when he abandoned me. But now, as if that long-ago sun has dropped behind a cloud, I see him clearly: tight-mouthed, slightly pouty, anxiety hiding under a tinge of bravado. More show than go. My mother was the steady one. As I must be, now.

The fever drains away to ice. *Sprite* is rushing toward me, lifted on a froth of breaking wave. I must get *Melville* out of the way or kill us all.

I throw my whole weight against the resisting tiller and jam the stick down. *Melville* coughs and growls but surges forward. Glancing back, I see Daniel roll Julian into the passenger seat and drop himself in front of the wheel. My shout of joy is lost in the gale. After that, I have all I can do to keep my own ship upright.

Which I can do. I must do, on my own. My eyes and muscles know the drill. In the stadium's mammoth lee, where the pale limestone arches seem to rise out of sight, I fight the swell to line us up on the bigger opening. Waves are crashing against the wall and rebounding in a second, drenching cross-assault. The wind is kicking up the spray, wrapping boats and stadium in a concealing mist. *Sea Sprite* vanishes behind me. I holler Breakers up from below once we pull in close. I'll need her ready with the boat hook to guide us past the catchy parts. I can just make out the two boats in line ahead of us, a water taxi full of exhausted Smiths and an Empire patrol boat. The taxi fits tight, and so will we. I toss Breakers Daniel's rain gear.

Blinking into the driving wind, her eyes flit around the stern. "Where's the book guy?"

I'm calm now. Laser-focused on my sailing. I've granted Daniel's mad choice because unlike my father, he kept the big picture in mind. He took on the present emergency and left the future in my hands, trusting me to take care of it. I jerk a thumb over my shoulder.

"Fuck! No! He's . . . ?" Then she spots him through the mist, wave-tossed, angling *Sprite* up behind us, engine sputtering, spent of fuel, Julian folded over against the dashboard.

"Had a pickup to make."

She glares at me.

My grin is fierce. I feel it stretch the sides of my mouth till they might rip wide open. Breakers narrows her gaze to a slit. Her hair is a dark, wind-torn swirl around her face and shoulders. She's worried for my sanity. Then she shakes her head and grins back. She turns away to arm herself with the boat hook.

FORTY-TWO

Melville slipped through the archway, tight as childbirth, the swell rising behind us for an extra push. Breakers hollered and jabbed with her boat hook. I stole a quick look over my shoulder for *Sea Sprite*, but she was lost behind a wave.

Inside the arch, a tall atrium curved to either side, vibrating with surf boom and wind howl, plus a bellowing scramble of denfolk racing to make everything fast. The inner wall loomed ahead, wave-splashed, maybe forty feet away. A former balcony, now a sort of boat landing, ran across it at water level, crammed with people and off-loaded goods, all of it inches from being swept back into the water.

A vast ceiling of skylights crisscrossed high above, mostly intact, so the blinding sleet was reduced to surprise cascades of ice dropping through scattered empty panes. Where the outer arches held their sturdy glass, the inner curve was more sheltered, busy with boats and too many people yelling over the wind as they struggled to rope the boats into a giant raft, able to rise and fall together without wrecking each other. Outside, the storm was ramping toward maximum. The sky had melded with the sea in a canvas of total white. My hands on *Melville*'s tiller ached with cold. We'd made it just in time.

Rousseau stood spread-legged at one end of the balcony, ignoring a constant drenching as waves broke along the inner wall, counting the boats and passengers wrestling through the arches. Even his big voice was lost in the din and wind screech. He'd fallen back on hand signals—where to land and unload—urging each boat on around the curve to tie up, making room for the next in line. I looked again for *Sea Sprite*. A glimpse of blue in the shredded mist? Maybe. Could only pray she was still working her way in behind me.

Below *Melville*'s hull, I made out the dark bulk of an escalator, its top rail just below her extended keel. Had to rock at idle till there was a slot to pull in parallel to the landing. Breakers put out the bumpers and leaped off to tie up. Jandi and Jenn piled out of the cabin the minute we bumped alongside, eager to regain solid ground.

"Hola!" Rivera elbowed her way to the edge, waving joyfully and trailing a bunch of Macys. "We've been waiting!"

Jandi yodeled a greeting and charged into their arms. A hero's welcome.

Jenn came to hug me. "We made it!" She took in the gathering of boats and rafts, the faraway skylights, the curving march of the arches. "This place is . . . wow! Awesome!"

"Yeah!" I caught her arm as a swell rocked *Melville* against the landing and nearly spilled her. "Can you help unload?"

"But . . . where's Daniel?"

"On his way. He had to . . ." Too much to explain.

"There he is!" Breakers called, as *Sea Sprite* shuddered through the arch wall.

Sprite had had rough handling since she'd left the Lagoon. A dozen or so bullet holes pocked her hull, along with broad dents and oily blotches along her water line. Ice coated her deck and Daniel's hair.

"That's the last!" Rousseau crowed. "We're home!"

Those few who could hear him raised a cheer.

"Now! Everyone inside to the upper levels! Take shelter!"

Already the water rolling through the atrium was breaking over the docking ledge. People snatched at crates and luggage to haul them back from the edge. We still had a Cat 6 to live through.

Halfway to the landing, Daniel was on his feet in *Sprite*'s cockpit, shouting for a medic. I didn't see how the docs could be that organized, but a serious-eyed woman pushed through the crowd, searching out the source of the call. Not one of Unca Joe's. Her blue scrubs were already darkened with the day's injuries. She had a brisk, Empire State look to her. Leave it to Empire to be on the ball already. Like, could they have saved Rubio, if he'd got to them in time?

I must have been shaking my head.

"What?" Jenn asked.

"Just thinking about Rubio. I hate that he's missing all this." I shooed her toward the landing. "Grab a plant and get uplevel!"

"Grab two!" Peeto nosed through the crowd, one fist around Ellie Mae's arm to keep her from the edge. "As many as you can carry! This whole tier is going to flood."

"Quickly!" Elsie Mae was as agitated as I'd ever seen her. "Get these plants upstairs before they freeze!"

I glanced over at *Sea Sprite*, then to Breakers, wet and wind-buffeted on the dock. "Can you manage *Melville*? I need to . . ."

"Go take care of him. I'll figure it out."

"We can help!" Rivera was already directing her throng of Macys into *Melville*'s stern. Jandi ran to open the cabin door. Small bodies ducked around me as I vaulted onto the dock.

Daniel pulled in near Rousseau and shut down his sputtering engine. The water level along the inner wall dropped abruptly as a huge wave sucked back and crashed against the arches, flinging arcs of spray across the atrium like a round of punches. *Sprite* knocked hard against the edging. Pushing through the crowd in the medic's wake, I staggered and spat salt water. My ears rang.

"Everyone inside! Upper levels! Now!" Rousseau herded people away from the landing.

I darted against the crowd to grab up *Sprite*'s rope, then found nowhere to tie it. The medic volunteered two nearby Smiths to bundle Julian's limp body out of the passenger seat. "Upstairs," she ordered. "Sick bay."

Daniel clambered out, dripping rain and seawater, his bruised face livid with chill and salt. "I can carry him."

"No, you can't," the medic barked, waving the Smiths into the crowd. "This way."

Daniel staggered past me, dogging her heels. I watched after helplessly, *Sprite* yanking on my arm like a leashed dog, till an older Tommy, a stranger, took the rope from me.

"You go on. I'll see to this."

I flashed the guy a grateful smile and plunged after Daniel, staying a pace behind in case he collapsed but also out of his way. No room in his mind right then for anything but Julian. I couldn't even ask: where is Hannah?

The storm slammed against the building, shaking it like prey till the floor shuddered. We climbed a ramp into dimmer light, switchbacked and climbed another, jostled by the upward-fleeing throng. We shoved past a trio from Gimme Shelter, coaxing their freaked-out goats up to safety. Up ahead, their cow lowed anxiously. Some of the Joe lads loped by, shouldering crates of squawking ducks and chickens.

"Noah's friggin' ark," a man complained beside me, avoiding a soft pile of animal leave-behind.

"Gonna need some cats," said his friend.

Above the sea of bobbing heads, thin, leafy stalks waved back and forth. Anyone with a free hand had been given a baby tree or young tomato plant to carry uplevel.

The stadium stretched out vastly around us, the wind screaming through the overhead beams and trusses. No one was sure where to go. Anywhere safe. For now, just up, up, up, away from the pounding, invading sea. In, in, find shelter from the tearing, icy blasts.

When the faded wall signs read 'Tier 3,' our medic turned right. The Smiths carrying Julian were panting. We hurried along a debris-littered inner concourse lined with derelict shops. Fancy signage, glass partitions, empty ransacked shelving, scattered mannequin parts. A wreck and still windswept, but dry. Busy Smiths and Joes were clearing space and hauling in the sea-soaked cargo from the rafts. Small clots of denfolk drifted like fall leaves into sheltered corners, too tired to go another step, digging in wherever to ride out the storm.

The Empire medic took a left. "In here."

The thrown-together medical ward filled a large former store with double glass doors still on their hinges. Here at last the wind was kept at bay. Swept clean, it made a roughshod ER with a multi-bed recovery space, using display counters and the few cots and gurneys that had come upriver. The room smelled of blood and salt, and every one of a dozen working surfaces was occupied. Less critical patients waited in folding chairs or slumped against the walls. Four or five docs, all Joes and Empires, and twice as many helpers raced back and forth, unpacking, washing and stitching up gun wounds and blade cuts hastily staunched during and after the ambush. The occasional agonized cry suggested bone breaks being set. The docs lacked proper anesthesia and decent light and enough skilled hands for the work but were making do as fast as they could. A steady stream of supplies and equipment kept arriving from the boats, adding to the noise and bustle. A biodiesel generator chugged away in a corner, powering a sterilizer.

As we brought Julian in, I noticed a glass-fronted room next door that had also been cleared. It was lit by a single lantern and was empty but for a half-dozen shrouded forms laid out on the floor in a respectful row. A scattering of stooped figures moved or knelt among them. Shoulders shook, but the weeping was drowned out by the wind.

With some relief, I recognized Jake, crouched by the lantern, watching as a new casualty was set down at one end of the row. He questioned the bearers, then bent his head to tap a note into a small tablet.

The ER doors closed behind us just as the storm hurled a particularly convulsive burst against the walls. All work paused. The wind shriek crescendoed. The very air seemed to vibrate. My ears popped. The whole building shook as if in an earthquake, but then stood firm and settled. Everyone heaved in a strangled breath and went back to what they'd been doing. The next shuddering assault roused less concern. The stadium was proving its worth.

Our medic directed Julian's carriers to set him down on a sturdy crate, his back against a wall. His head lolled. She grabbed a basin and rags and went to work swabbing him down. Daniel dropped to his knees, holding Julian upright.

"Most of the blood isn't his. Been there a while." She scissored off Julian's stained tee. "Surface gun wounds. A graze on the right shoulder. One over there." She pointed out a dark tear across his ribs. "He's been shot at, but mostly missed. Nothing needs stitching."

"How long ago, you think?" Daniel asked.

"Hours. Dried before the rain, or more would've washed off."

"So he's not in danger?" Daniel eased back on his heels, his whole body going slack.

"Shock, exhaustion, dehydration, trauma. They take a toll. He'll come around when he's ready." She flicked a glance at Daniel. "He's your . . . ?"

"Brother."

"Good. Then you can take it from here." She handed over the basin and swabs, slapped a spritzer of antiseptic and some bandages on the crate, then passed me a half-full mug. "Try to get some liquid into him. Infrastructure's a bit thin yet. We're crisis-low on drinking water, so don't waste it."

"Yes, ma'am," I said.

Daniel seemed to notice me for the first time. He smiled wanly.

"Keep those cuts clean." The medic tipped Daniel's chin up with a gloved knuckle. "Yours, too, by the way. Check back when things calm down if there's any sign of infection."

And then she was up and moving on to more serious cases.

"Thanks for taking time with him," Daniel called after her.

I slipped a towel off a nearby stack and eased in to drape it across his wet shoulders.

Daniel shrugged it off. "I'm okay."

I wanted to pat him, stroke him, towel the sea from his hair, anything to lay hands on him in relief for having him back in one piece. Instead, I asked, "Has he said anything at all?"

Gently probing Julian's rib wound, Daniel shook his head.

"What do you think's happened? Maybe he chickened out, or . . . could she have left without him?"

"She wouldn't. Ever."

"Then . . . what?"

"Only he can say."

In other words, I can't think right now. Stop trying to make me.

"Hey! You made it!" Jake gripped my shoulder and hunkered down between us, the sleek, Empire-style tablet in his free hand. His drying sweats were salt-stained but cleaner than anything I'd seen since landing. "Well done! How was the trip?"

"How was anyone's?" I looked him over. Not a scratch on him. "Except yours, I guess."

He glanced away. "Yeah, I got off easy."

"You missed the ambush."

"Got the tail end. Max wanged off a few good ones, then ran out of ammo. We were up front with a boatload of Smith kids and elders, and I'm . . ."

"I know. A lover, not a fighter."

"'To thine own self be true.' So I made our skipper scoot. We were here before the storm really cut loose." Jake let go of my shoulder so he could tap at the tablet's screen. "I'm counting heads. Two more live ones accounted for."

I nodded toward the makeshift morgue. "Have we lost many?"

"A few. Any is too many. But between Revs and Stormies and the friggin' weather, it could've been a whole lot worse."

"Weather's not done yet," murmured Daniel.

"Neither are the Stormies, according to Doyle. He thinks that girl will have learned a lesson or two about attacking before her people are ready. And that Rousseau giving up those provisions will only encourage her to try again."

Daniel shrugged, rinsing his bloodied rag in the basin. "But it might put the notion of trade into her head instead."

"Always the bright side, Dan." Jake peered at Julian's slack face. "Is this a Macy I missed?"

As if. Julian would be horrified.

"My brother," Daniel said. "Julian."

"Didn't know you had one. Is he gonna make it?"

"Doc says he'll be fine."

"Good to hear." Jake stood up briskly. "I'll add him to our list."

"Max came through okay?" His familiar face had cheered me, like things were getting vaguely back to normal. Whatever that would be now.

"Oh yeah. She's upstairs claiming prime turf for Ladysmith." He grinned. "I think she wants her own sky box."

"I could go for that," Daniel said. "Are there a lot of them?"

"I heard, fifty or more."

"Mmm. Could get nasty." Daniel rinsed the swab again and started on Julian's face.

"Rousseau's pushing for a lottery." Jake nudged Daniel's arm. "Take care of your bro."

I watched him go off. He was actually whistling. "Never seen Jake so . . . cheerful."

"Relief can hit you that way."

Finally, Daniel let me in to help, and together, we cleaned Julian up, got his wounds salved and bandaged. I was taping a square of gauze over a nick on his cheekbone when his eyes fluttered, then lazed open.

"NO!" He flailed at my wrist. "Leave me a- . . . !"

"Sorry. Almost done," I murmured.

He winced away from my hand and slumped back, eyeing me like I was the last person he expected. "Oh. Den rat."

"Right the first time."

"Where . . . ?" His gaze swept back and forth. "Fuck . . . you mean I made it?"

"You did. Welcome to Yankee Stadium." I held the mug to his lips. "Drink."

He took barely a sip. "I need . . . where's Dan? . . . is Dan okay?"

"He's fine."

Daniel had stepped away to dump the wash water. "Right here, Jules."

Julian squeezed his eyes shut. "Oh, man! It was so . . . I didn't . . . I couldn't . . . !"

"Easy, Jules. You're in shock. You need to rest."

I offered the mug again, but he turned away from it, his bruised face twisting. "You should've been there, Dan! If you'd been there, it would've gone down different!"

Daniel hesitated. "How did it go down?"

"You would've have talked it right!"

"Probably not."

"No, no, with you there, she wouldn't have . . . oh, man!"

Out in the corridor, sharp cracks rang out as the floor shook and a sudden updraft hurled loose objects against a wall. Glass shattered somewhere. A thundering of waves echoed through the tier. Julian recoiled, searching about wildly, like for the nearest escape hatch.

"Easy, easy. You're safe now." Daniel rested a hand on his brother's knee. "What happened, Julie? Where's Hannah?"

"I can't . . . you'll think . . ."

"Can't think anything till you tell me."

"I know, I know . . . I . . ." Julian pressed blood-caked palms to his eyes. Whatever it was, it was bad, and he was seeing it all over again. I knew how hard it was to talk about terror. When his hands came away, I urged the water on him again. This time, he drank most of it down, dripping onto his bandaged ribs.

"Was there trouble at the ferry terminal?" Daniel prompted.

"Shit, Dan, we never got that far!" Fear and outrage surged across his face, loosened his tongue. "We got to the marina to tie up *Sprite* and the whole waterfront was swarming with uniforms! Not even military. Nothing you'd recognize!"

"Private security?"

"Militia, patrolling the wharf."

"Mainland militias?"

"Who the fuck knows! Big guys with big guns! And they're looking at us like we're trash under their feet. 'Marina's full,' one says. 'Ferry's closed,' another yells. 'For good. Go back where you came from!'" Julian grabbed at a deep breath, stopped when it hurt. I held up the mug. He drained it and looked for more. I spread empty palms regretfully.

"And then . . . ?" Daniel asked.

"And then H says, 'Let me deal with this.' She gets out, she's in her up-town clothes, and she goes up to the biggest one, saying he must be mistaken, we live just around the corner. We have all the required documents and permissions, and he needs to let us through. We have biz on the

Mainland and we need to be there before the storm, so we don't miss our connections. And she shows him the papers."

"And he . . . ?"

"Rips them out of her hands. 'These again,' he says. He passes them along to the others. 'We've seen a few of these today, right, guys?' His guys pass them back and they're all laughing, like how stupid do you think we are?"

Julian's hands tightened to fists on his thighs. The words came faster now, like a flood he could no longer hold back. "So H throws a few names around, people she says won't be happy if we don't show up across the river. Big guy just shrugs. H goes: 'So what are you saying?' He goes, 'I'm saying you got scammed, lady.' And he ticks off papers, tossing them on the ground one by one: 'There ain't no ferry. Airport's shut down. Heliport's closed to the public. You ain't goin' nowhere.' And H goes, 'But I'm not the public, and who the hell are you?'"

Daniel hissed softly, an intake of breath.

"Yep, she starts giving him lip, and they're both waving papers and yelling at each other, and I'm leaping to the dock, thinking to calm her down, then . . ." Julian's fists flew to cover his face again. "Oh, fuck! Oh, fuck! I can't . . . !"

"Say it, Jules. You have to."

"One of the other guys, like from the back, he's messing with his phone. Suddenly he moves to Big Guy to show him the screen. Well, well, says Big Guy, and he steps up with his pistol drawn and puts it to her head. 'Yeah, we know who you are.' And H . . . she grins, like she's daring him. The rest are still laughing and she's making to slap the gun aside, and I'm, no! no! and he . . . and he pulls the fucking trigger. Right there, Dan! Just like that! He blows her away right in front of me, and I couldn't stop him!" His hands wove frantic patterns of denial in the air. "She drops and her brains are on me and blood everywhere and there was nothing . . . ! I couldn't do shit!"

He doubled over like a rag doll, seized by raw, childlike sobs. My eyes welled in stunned sympathy. I turned away, trying not to see what he'd so wrenchingly described, moment by moment. Daniel laid a hand across the back of Julian's neck, his gaze distant, weary, infinitely sad.

When Julian could breathe again, Daniel said, "Not your fault, Jules."

"Useless piece of shit! I ran! Jumped in *Sprite* and floored her. They shot after me, but they were laughing so hard, their aim was crap. I left her! I left her there on the dock! I . . . ! Did she know, Dan? Did she know he'd do that?"

"She was gone, Jules. Nothing you could've done. Right to have come here."

"I . . . drove in circles for a while, but I was bleeding and *Sprite* was . . . so I came looking for you. All I could think of." Julian lifted his gaze to meet Daniel's at last. "What do we do now, Dan? What do we do now?"

Daniel combed wet tangles of hair back from Julian's brow. "We ride out the storm, bro. It's all we can ever do."

Which storm did he mean? The one raging outside, or the storm of rage and guilt inside the Nathan brothers? The first would pass on. The second might lessen, but never go away. And I guessed, or maybe hoped, on some future day, those militia guys—if they live so long and Julian can ID them—will be hanging out, eating their lunch or hassling some other citizen, and the world around them will explode and them with it. And I will agree that they deserved it.

Meanwhile, the storm outside shook the stadium until the walls seemed to tilt and the floors roll like a boat deck. I felt more than heard ocean rampaging through the lower tiers. We found Julian a dry corner out of the wind tunnel, a couple of blankets to soften the dank chill of the tiles and a towel for a pillow. Telling his trauma had drained him flat. He swallowed a painkiller, another mug of precious water, and was out almost before Daniel laid him down.

Daniel sat with him for a while, watching him sleep, processing his own dark thoughts. I let him be and busied myself by clearing the mess we'd made tending Julian's wounds. Hollow, deafening booms echoed along the corridors as the sea pummeled the stadium. The floor shuddered and groaned. Walking steady was a challenge. Dumping the bloodied rags in a hastily labeled waste bin, I glanced into the recovery ward on the far side of the surgery and spotted Spunk, trussed up on a gurney but gleefully harassing a terrified Gimme Shelter girl who'd shown up to help nurse. Poppy stood by, swaying on her crutches like tossed in a gale, glancing at the ceiling like it might collapse with the next wave assault. But there at last, in a dim corner, was Gracie, stretched out on a low cot, her bruised face so frighteningly still that I hurried in to make sure she was breathing.

Poppy clumped over. "She's out of it, lost a lot of blood. They say she'll be okay."

"So much hurt," I murmured. "So much pain."

"Better be worth it."

I let Poppy spin out the tale of her trip upriver until Daniel came to get me.

"He'll sleep for a while now. Walk with me. Let's see this new home of ours." He headed away from the crowd, walking too brusquely and too fast, away from Julian's grim news, into the wind-swept, unlit depths of the stadium.

There was no quiet place, no corner where the storm yowl, the boom-boom of the waves, the bone-jarring shudder of the floor didn't penetrate and overwhelm thought and conversation. In the open concourses, the cold was shivering. I was glad to still have my foul-weather gear.

"How are you?" I asked. I almost had to yell.

"Ask me later."

We slowed to thread a path through a scrum of kitchen staff clearing debris from the husk of a restaurant, one of many we'd passed but with its glass front still intact. Battered crates and boxes were piled up outside, dripping seawater on the concrete. Inside, old beer signs and a vast and faded mural of a baseball game in progress. Vinyl-covered booths stacked in the corners. Through double doors in the back, a scatter of kitchen equipment shrouded in darkness—sinks and shelving and metal prep stations. Amazing to see so much useful stuff left lying about. If the solars had made it upriver in one piece, there wasn't going to be any problem with food service in this new den.

The food itself . . . well, not so easy.

Daniel pressed on, like someone was chasing him. Climbing, turning corners, trying doors, we discovered a curving row of shallow rooms, each with a long, rain-spattered window wall overlooking the enclosed lake that had once been the playing field. A few café tables and some broken chairs lay about on their sides. I pressed a palm to the glass, felt it bow and contract with the gale. But it muffled the wind roar. After the din of the concourse, this narrow space felt hushed and private.

"Skybox," Daniel said. "With luck, Max hasn't claimed this one yet."

He righted a chair to face the window and dropped into it. Nothing to see out there but storm-shredded mist and the rain sheeting against the pane. The gray daylight was gathering gloom. The lake surface was invisible. He spent a long time staring at it anyway.

Finally, the silence got to me. "You knew, didn't you. Before he told us."

"I knew my sister."

"When did you know?"

Daniel traced sleety raindrops down the glass with a finger. "When the guy said the papers weren't real. No way H would accept she'd been scammed. She'd push it to the limit. And she did."

Not much I could say to that. "He'll never forgive himself."

"He will. Unlike H, he's flexible. He'll find a way."

But will you? I knew better than to ask out loud.

Daniel scrubbed a hand through the dark brush of his hair. "I'd kill for a hot shower."

Normal conversation? "Be a while till they get that going. You didn't answer his question."

"Which one?"

"Did she know how pushing it was going to end."

He stretched his legs out, arms folded across his chest. Another long, storm-chased silence. Then: "Thing about H, she was always willing to take the risk. Maybe she needed the acknowledgment. Like, have I mentioned her delusions of grandeur? Not so much a class thing, though she had that, too. More like she was a superior being, more evolved than the rest of us." He watched the storm for a while, squinting into the fading light. Seeing Hannah, I guessed. As she was in life. "A confirmed Darwinist, my sister. The only problem being her jungle definition of 'fittest.' She and the Adders had that in common."

I peered over at him. "You sound angry with her."

"I am! Angry that she mouthed off and got herself killed. Even if she wanted to, it was for nothing. For a fantasy. She bought into the biggest lie of all—that there's an easy escape, that you are special and can buy your way out of a mess instead of fixing it. A mess that everyone is in. It's like your friend Jenn and her dreams of flowers and porch rockers in Minnesota. But Hannah was cannier than that. She should've known better."

"But you were going with her . . ."

He shrugged. "Like I said: if both of them were leaving, nothing to keep me here—until you came along. And . . . maybe I never really believed they'd leave without me."

"At least she didn't take Julian down with her."

"Almost did. Would have, but for his deep survival instinct."

"Maybe it was real when she bought into it. The documents, I mean. The whole itinerary. Then it all fell apart with everything else."

"Now you're defending her? She treated you like dirt."

I shrugged. "She did save my life a couple times."

Daniel sniffed, impassive as the darkening gray on the far side of the glass. "Part of her game."

"Game?"

"Puppet master stuff. Power and invisibility. She liked messing with people's lives. She liked messing with mine."

"I kind of got that."

"But I never fell into her orbit like Julie did, like she expected, no, demanded." He looked away. "You're going to think I'm the coldest heart in the universe, but . . . it's almost a relief. I can live my own life now, a life I determine. Maybe help Julie find a better one, too."

Yes, he was angry. Easier for him than grief, at least for now.

"What about the redhead?"

"Who?"

"Julian's girl. He didn't mention her."

"Oh, her." Daniel made a wry face. "Darcy. Probably dropped her off uptown. No way H would start a new life with that hanging around, not without you and me along to water her down. She's a rich girl. She'll manage. As well as anyone will."

"If rich is all it takes, Hannah'd still be alive."

Daniel shook his head. "I mean, rich enough to buy *in*, not out. And willing to be what others want her to be. She'll find some militia boss to take care of her."

Maybe, maybe not. Such deals only hold within a working social structure, and Uptown was sliding toward full-out war. Street rules would be history.

"Rubio called it so right," I mused. "He'd have said it's three storms really. The one inside us, the one outside the walls, and the one tearing civilization apart. He used to go on about how the old structures are collapsing, and we need to build new ones, so there'll be a future of any kind. For the longest time, I assumed he was talking about architecture."

Daniel smiled wanly. "Smart guy, your friend."

A concussion of air jarred the room, a sharp crack followed by a vast, rolling rumbling. The window quaked beneath my palms, and out over the storm-shrouded lake, light exploded and died, exploded and died.

"Jeez! Stand back!" Daniel sprang up to haul me away from the glass. We fled to a back corner of the room, huddling against cold cinderblock while the crack and roar went on and on, shaking me till my teeth chattered. The window wall turned white.

"Thundersnow!" I breathed. "There's warm air coming from some-where!"

Assaulted by the gale, the pounding seas, and this new offensive of sound and light, the entire stadium writhed like a creature in agony. Its beams and trusses groaned. Its acres of tempered glass trembled and rang. We were inside a giant drum while the storm gods beat out the call to a final battle. Whose front line was right where we stood.

We were about to learn what Category 6 looked like.

Like a long day in Hell. How long did we cower, desperate for the scant warmth of each other's arms? Minutes? Hours? There was nothing to be done. We could barely talk, or even think. We could only wait out every basso concrete moan, every rending wail of rivet and bolt, could only pray that the next attack would not bring down the roof, flatten the walls, let the vengeful tempest and the furious sea invade, destroying all our efforts, all our hopes. Everything.

But at some unmarked moment, I felt Daniel's insistent grip on me soften, his body ease back from crisis. The gusts screaming under the door dropped in pitch and were faintly warmer. Slight changes but promising. Most promising of all, the thunder died away and it stopped snowing. Wind and rain still beat at the window wall, but the mist was thinning, the glow-ering sky faintly lightening. The wave-torn lake took on a darker gray and separated from the roiling clouds. Like scared kids emerging from a bomb shelter, filled with wonder at a world still intact, we moved cautiously, hand in hand, and approached the glass.

Daniel pointed. "You can see the far side now. Used to be seating on those tiers." Above the distant curving wall leaped the ragged foam of waves breaking against the outside. "Either we're through the worst of it, or this is just the eye and there's more to come. What says your weather itch?"

I considered. "I'd say, the eye. But if we got through it once . . ."

I felt the stadium settling around us, the creature released from agonies of torture with a groaning sigh as stretched seams and joints came together again, even if only till the next assault. The sense of animal presence was so vivid, I reached to stroke the nearest surface in gratitude. My own relief nearly buckled my knees. Relief and pride, that this place we had come to, this new home that Rubio had chosen for us, had taken everything the weather could throw at it, kept us safe, and would again.

"Hey!" Lights flashing out on the lake made Daniel lean into the glass. "Look at that."

Down below us, some of the water taxis were venturing out from under the second-level seating tier, buffeted by the wind but stable enough in the flatter swell. From where we stood, the level below us looked to be completely under water. But to either side, I could see steps rising above the lake level. The boats were moving down along the seating curl, then turning back under the overhang. One of the taxis had pulled alongside a sleeker power boat. Two men face to face, arms in motion, fingers pointing this way and that, while their pilots struggled to keep the two boats from colliding.

"Uh-oh!" I squinted through the wind-shredded rain. "Is that Tom and Will?"

"Yeah. Looks like."

Tom Doyle was armed with a chunky flashlight, waving it here and there. "Is this the chance they get to kill each other, with no one there to stop them?"

"No-o-o." Daniel drew out the word thoughtfully. "I don't think so."

I wished I could see their faces better. "What's up, then?"

"I do believe Tommy's taking his own advice."

"Which is . . . ?"

"He's listening."

I stared harder. "How can you tell?"

"Read the body language."

I cupped my palms to the glass as Will thrust both hands forward in parallel, then shot one of them off at an angle and held it there. Doyle looked behind them, flashlight searching the shadows, then reluctantly nodded. Will's hands went to work again.

"It's like, if we do this, and put that there, then this will happen," Daniel said. "Semaphore. Tech talk. Fantastic! They're working something out down there."

"More than where to put stuff, I'm guessing."

Daniel grinned, a real grin, the first one in ages. "Exactly."

A tumultuous, sodden, green-gray dusk was dropping over the lake. At the far end of the oval, the storm tore whitecaps off the water to hurl along the seating tiers. When the eye passed over, it would be dark, and the stadium would be sunk in night. But I was pretty sure dawn would bring a better day. Rocking madly, the taxi powered up its running lights. The stadium shuddered, a reminder that the storm had punches yet to deliver. Will and Tom were still not yelling at each other.

"I think one of them found a water route to the field—maybe floating the boats in through the vomitories. The back of that first tier must be above water." Daniel rubbed impatiently at an obscuring layer of condensation. "There's our sheltered harbor! And if we haul the smaller boats up under there before the eye passes, they won't crush each other tossing around in the atrium. Dry storage, like a beach with a roof." He chewed his lip, peering along the darkening tiers. "I wonder if *Melville* will fit through the voms."

"Those two . . . of all people . . . working together?" Watching them, I felt the future-possible stretch out before us like a road. A highway, even, paved and marked. "It's like a miracle."

"For now, at least. Maybe only so long as it takes Tom to work off his debt to Will for routing the Stormies. But it's new, and it's what we'll need to move forward from here." A bit of light was back in his eyes. "But it'll need all the encouragement it can get. Shall we go offer some?"

Out into the storm again, now that I was finally dry and warm? Shouldn't we be finding a safe crib to crash in while the second half wreaks its havoc? "What about Julian?"

"He'll be fine. He'll have a girlfriend by the time we're done. Maybe two." Daniel held out a hand. "C'mon. While the eye gives us a break. Let's go help."

How could I say no?

ACKNOWLEDGMENTS

Endless gratitude to all my first readers, busy people so generous with their time and wisdom:

Amy Pratt	Christie Kellogg	Joy Johannessen
Antonia Bryan	Jan Tiura	Nancy Callahan
Barbara Newman	Jarvis Kellogg	Stacy Wakefield Forte
Brian Brock	John Kellogg	Vicki Davis
Charlotte Walker	John O'Connor	William Rossow

Thanks to DAW's Joshua Starr for shepherding me through the time-scant final processes.

Special thanks to the West Kortright Centre's Fiction Writing Workshop, led by Mermer Blakeslee, for listening to excerpts of this book over the course of several summers and for their cheerful and invaluable critiques.

And I humbly acknowledge the free use of verbatim excerpts from the sea journal kept by my great-great-grandfather Henry Kellogg (1819-1894) during his trip around Cape Horn to San Francisco in 1849. He returned to Connecticut two years later.

Last, but never the least, perennial thanks to my life-long editor extraordinaire, Sheila Gilbert.